D0093308

BOOKS BY PETER FORBATH

The Last Hero
Honorable Men (*with William Colby*)
The River Congo
Seven Seasons

A NOVEL BY

Peter Forbath

SIMON AND SCHUSTER

NEW YORK · LONDON · TORONTO · SYDNEY · TOKYO

THE LAST HERO

SIMON AND SCHUSTER
Simon & Schuster Building
Rockefeller Center
1230 Avenue of the Americas
New York, New York 10020

This book is a work of fiction. Names, characters, places and incidents are either the product of the author's imagination or are used fictitiously. Any resemblance to actual events or locales or persons, living or dead, is entirely coincidental.

Designed by Edith Fowler
Manufactured in the United States of America

10 9 8 7 6 5 4 3 2 1

Library of Congress Cataloging in Publication data
Forbath, Peter.
The last hero : a novel / by Peter Forbath.
p. cm.
1. Stanley, Henry M. (Henry Morton), 1841–1904—Fiction. I. Title.
PS3556.O65L37 1988
813'.54—dc 19 88–15086
CIP
ISBN 0–671–24285–7

To Absent Friends

Contents

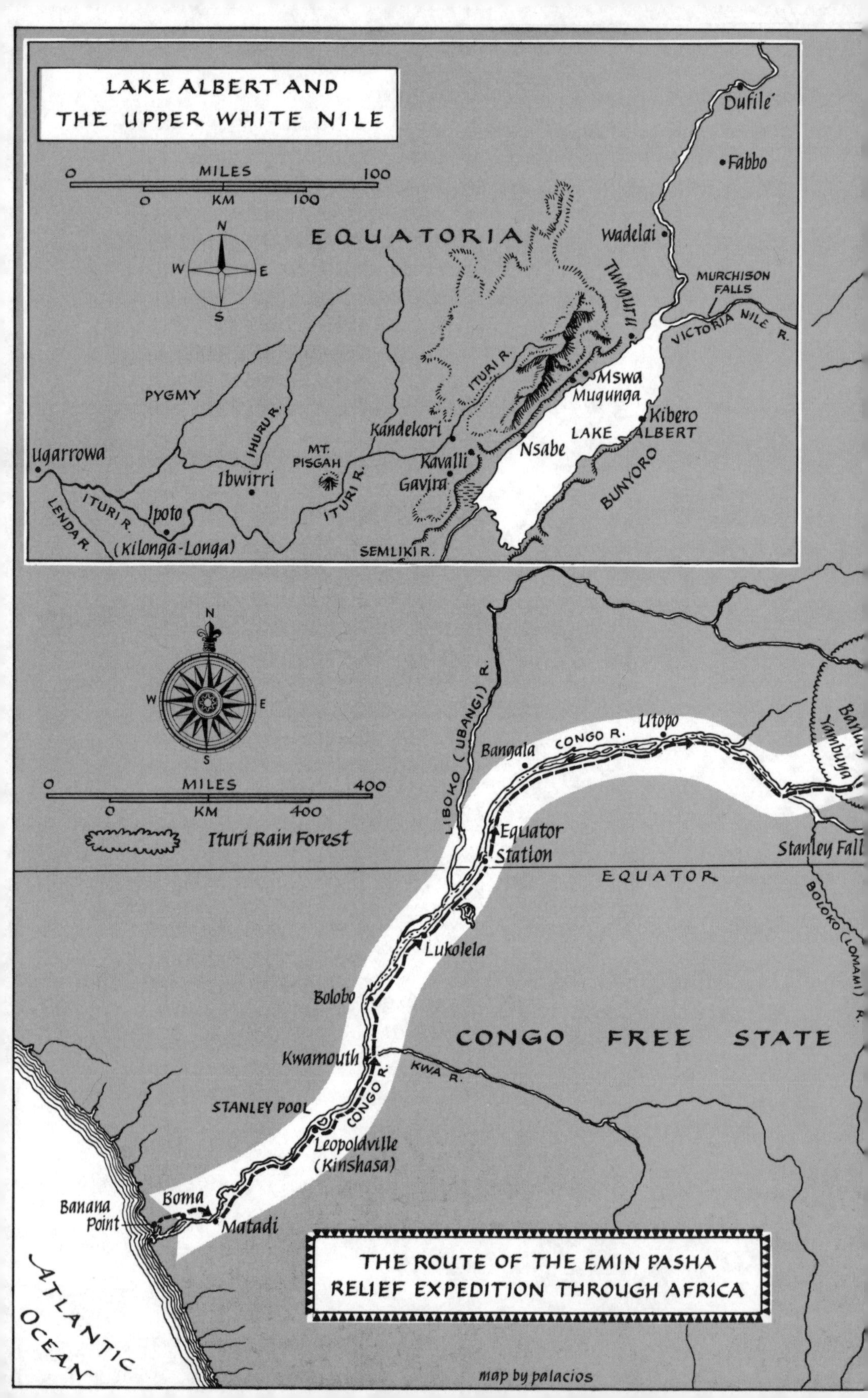

LAKE ALBERT AND THE UPPER WHITE NILE
0 MILES 100
0 KM 100
N
W
E
S
EQUATORIA
Dufilé
Fabbo
Wadelai
Tunguru
MURCHISON FALLS
VICTORIA NILE R.
ITURI R.
Mswa
Mugunga
Kibero
LAKE ALBERT
PYGMY
IHURU R.
Kandekori
Nsabe
Ugarrowa
MT. PISGAH
Kavalli
Gavira
Ibwirri
ITURI R.
BUNYORO
LENDA R.
Ipoto
(Kilonga-Longa)
SEMLIKI R.
N
W
E
S
0 MILES 400
0 KM 400
Ituri Rain Forest
LIBOKO (UBANGI) R.
Bangala
CONGO R.
Utopo
Yambuya
Equator Station
Stanley Fall
EQUATOR
BOLOKO (LOMAMI) R.
Lukolela
Bolobo
CONGO FREE STATE
Kwamouth
KWA R.
CONGO R.
STANLEY POOL
Leopoldville (Kinshasa)
Boma
Banana Point
Matadi
ATLANTIC OCEAN
THE ROUTE OF THE EMIN PASHA RELIEF EXPEDITION THROUGH AFRICA
map by palacios

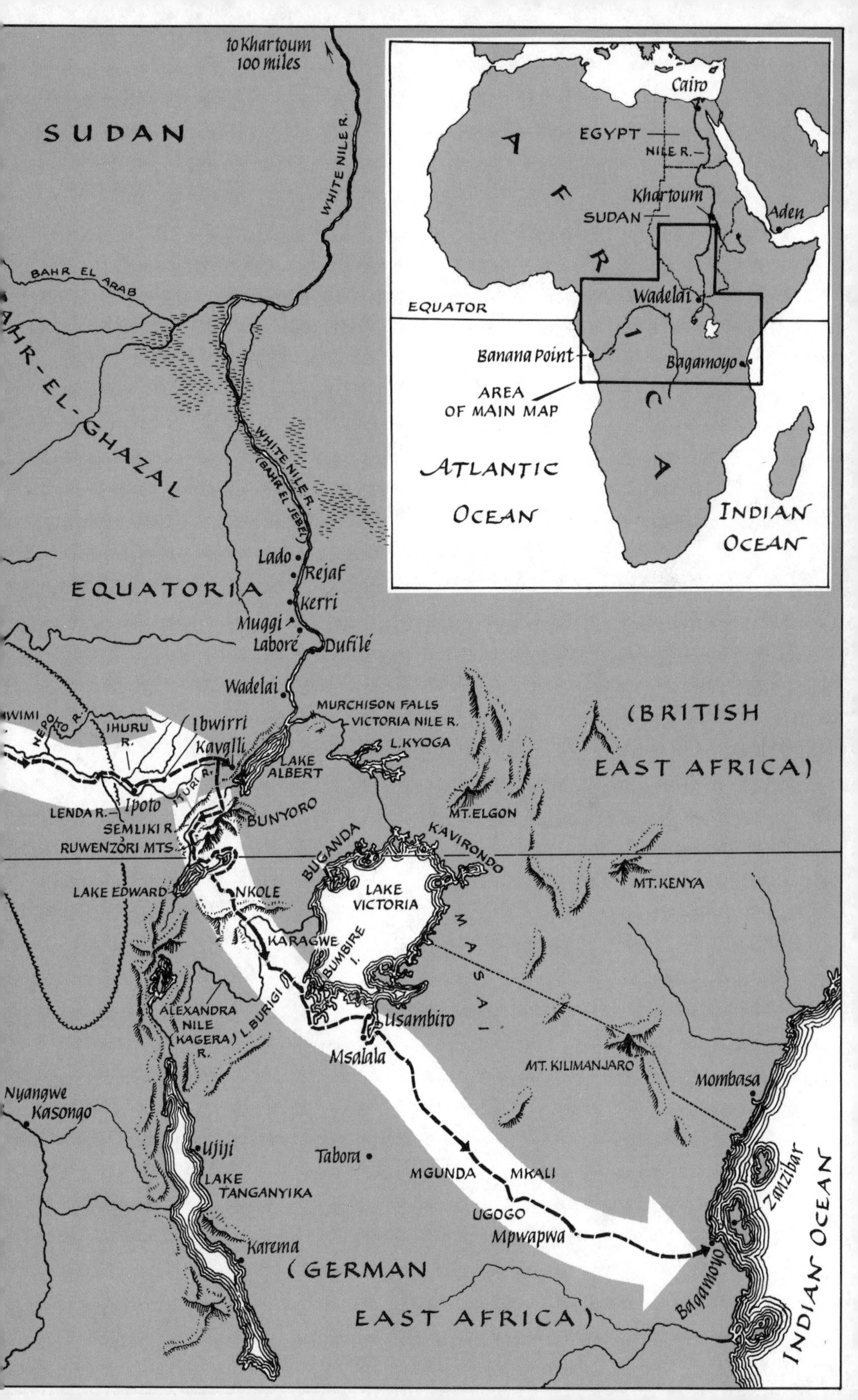

to Khartoum
100 miles
SUDAN
WHITE NILE R.
BAHR EL ARAB
BAHR-EL-GHAZAL
WHITE NILE R.
(BAHR EL JEBEL)
Lado
Rejaf
Kerri
EQUATORIA
Muggi
Laboré
Dufilé
Wadelai
MURCHISON FALLS
VICTORIA NILE R.
L. KYOGA
(BRITISH
EAST AFRICA)
WIMI
NEPOKO R.
IHURU
R.
Ibwirri
Kavalli
ITURI R.
LAKE
ALBERT
Ipoto
LENDA R.
SEMLIKI R.
BUNYORO
RUWENZORI MTS.
MT. ELGON
BUGANDA
KAVIRONDO
LAKE
VICTORIA
MT. KENYA
LAKE EDWARD
NKOLE
KARAGWE
BUMBIRE
I.
MASAI
ALEXANDRA
NILE
(KAGERA)
R.
L. BURIGI
Usambiro
Msalala
MT. KILIMANJARO
Mombasa
Nyangwe
Kasongo
Ujiji
Tabora
LAKE
TANGANYIKA
MGUNDA
MKALI
UGOGO
Mpwapwa
Zanzibar
Karema
(GERMAN
EAST AFRICA)
Bagamoyo
INDIAN OCEAN

Cairo
EGYPT
NILE R.
AFRICA
Khartoum
SUDAN
Aden
EQUATOR
Wadelai
Banana Point
Bagamoyo
AREA
OF MAIN MAP
ATLANTIC
OCEAN
INDIAN
OCEAN

Prologue

THE NILE was falling.

For five months, the Mahdi and his fanatical army of 100,000 ansars had laid siege to Khartoum, awaiting the day the Nile would fall low enough to ford. For five months General Charles Gordon, his 8,000 soldiers, and the 34,000 civilians trapped in Khartoum with them, had known that if the rescue force making its way up the Nile from Cairo under Sir Garnet Wolseley's command did not reach them before that day, that day would be their last.

And so it was; the 26th of January 1885.

The moon had set early the night before, and by the chill ghostly light of the desert stars, fully half the ansars, more than 50,000 warriors, armed with rifles and muskets, axes and knives, spears and shields, their jubbahe billowing, dashed across the mud flats and sandspits exposed by the fallen river. Gordon watched them from the roof of his palace. He wore his white dress uniform, his ceremonial sword, a holstered Webley revolver, and the tasseled maroon fez of his rank as Pasha, the Governor. Every male above the age of eight was in the lines, also watching. There was little they could do but watch. They were starving, having lived on rats and roaches and palm bark since the previous autumn. They were in a trance of fever, suffering from malaria, cholera, and sleeping sickness. They were out of ammunition, having emptied the arsenal in countless skirmishes since the siege began. They were demoralized and utterly without hope. They might as well have been wooden soldiers. And Wolseley's force was still fifty miles to the north, bogged down in battle at the oasis of Abu Klea.

At 3 A.M., the hour before dawn, the Mahdi's mortars and mountain guns began the bombardment, and the ansars, raising a blood-curdling cry, sure in their faith that to die fighting the infidel would obtain them paradise, stormed the walls and gates of the city. Although the orgy of killing and pillage and rape that followed went on for days, in fact Khartoum was captured before first light that morning. Within minutes of the assault, the city's defenses were breached and the streets filled with hordes of screaming fanatics. Gordon fired into them until his revolver was empty, then came to the head of the stairs that led down from the palace roof. His presence there, "standing in a calm and dignified manner, his left hand resting on the hilt of his sword," as a Khartoum merchant who survived the massacre was later to recall, created a momentary uncanny hush. The ansars hung back, looking up at him in awe: Gordon, the legendary Chinese Gordon, hero of the Crimean War, leader of the Ever Victorious Army, Governor-General of the Sudan, adventurer on camel back, Bible warrior, mystic, whom even the Mahdi described as the Perfect Man. But then an ansar bolder than the rest rushed forward and hurled his spear. It skewered Gordon through the breastbone, bringing him tumbling down the stairs. Moments later he was decapitated. His body was flung down a well and his head was taken to the Mahdi in his encampment in Omdurman.

It was the Mahdi's ultimate victory. In less than four years, in a series of battles and sieges as bloody and brutal as the final one at Khartoum, this charismatic, cruel, tyrannical Moslem holy man from Abba Island in the White Nile—who proclaimed himself the Messenger of God, Messiah of Islam, and who had gathered to himself an army of ferocious desert horsemen in a jihad against the foreign rulers of the Sudan—had conquered very nearly two million square miles of Africa, a territory greater than all of Germany and France and Italy combined.

The Sudan belonged to Egypt, annexed sixty years before by the Khedive Mohammed Ali. But, at the time, Egypt itself—and by extension its Sudanese possession—was effectively under the control of the British, having been taken by them after the opening of the Suez Canal in order to protect their investment in that crucial passageway to the Indies. So the Mahdi's insurrection was something more than merely a holy war. Its appeal to the khalifas and emirs of the Upper Nile Valley was as much political as religious, and its aim as much the expulsion of the hated Anglo-Egyptian occupation as the purification of the One True Faith in Allah's name.

Given the terrible swiftness with which the Mahdi succeeded in this aim, it is remarkable, looking back now, to see with what fatal nonchalance he was regarded at the onset of his career. When word first reached Khartoum of his seditious preaching, the Anglo-Egyptian authorities there dismissed him as just another of the many wild-eyed fakirs and snake charmers with delusions of glory who in those days regularly sprang up like dust devils in the souks and bazaars of the Sudan. They sent a handful of Egyptian soldiers to Abba Island to arrest him, but clearly this was no ordinary dust devil of a fakir. According to contemporary accounts, he had from the very beginning a reputation for incredible sanctity, approaching the divine, and when in 1881 he declared himself the Mahdi, the Promised One, a strange splendor, we are told, radiated from his person. His name was Mohammed Ahmed ibn-Seyyid Abdullah. He was in his late thirties, a tall, powerfully built man with broad shoulders, a large handsome head, a thick black beard, three tribal tattoos slashed high on his cheekbones, piercing brown eyes, and singularly glistening white teeth, with a V-shaped gap between the two front ones, which in the Sudan was considered a mark of good fortune. And that mark was much in evidence, because he seemed always to smile, a magnetic, captivating smile, as magnetic and captivating as the rich, resonant timbre of his voice; and when he preached, smiling, forever smiling, he inflamed his listeners with an awful passion. And so when the Egyptian soldiers came to Abba Island to take him prisoner, his followers rose up in fury and butchered them to the last man.

With this first ritualistic spilling of blood, the jihad was launched in earnest; and seeking greater freedom of action than Abba Island allowed, the Mahdi led his ansars into the deserts of Kordofan, west of the Nile. The authorities in Khartoum, however, still refused to believe he was anything more than a provincial nuisance, and the column of 1,500 soldiers they ordered out of the garrison at Fashoda in his pursuit was confident it could put an end to this nuisance with dispatch. On the third day of its march into the desert the column was ambushed, and 1,400 of its number were cut to pieces before they could fire a shot in their own defense. This stunning victory enormously enhanced the Mahdi's prestige; it seemed in truth that his destiny was guided by Allah's will, and tribesmen throughout Kordofan and also Sennar, farther to the west, first in the thousands, then in the tens of thousands, rallied to his green banner. And Khartoum at last realized that it had to take this man seriously. An army of 6,000 was assembled and put into the field against him. It was too little, too late. One flaming desert dawn, hordes of howling Arab horsemen—whom English history books for generations afterward would refer to in horror as dervishes as if they had been the legions of Satan himself—swept down on this army and utterly annihilated it. Leaving behind as a monument to the victory a pyramid of heads, the Mahdi went on the offensive, marching his ever-growing army against El Obeid, the principal city of Kordofan. It had a population of over 100,000 and was defended by a sizable garrison of Egyptian soldiers, who, although Moslems themselves, knew that the dervishes regarded them as no better than infidels because they served the British and therefore would grant them no mercy in the event of defeat. And so they made a gallant stand. They held out for half a year but were finally starved into submission; and when the gates were battered down, all within—every last man, woman, and child—were either murdered or enslaved. It was January 1883.

Until this time, the dervishes were an extremely primitive fighting force. Although brave and merciless and animated by a fierce religious and political zeal, they were armed only with spears and shields, bows and arrows, making their victories so much the more astonishing. But with the fall of El Obeid, they came into possession of a large store of modern weapons; and so, as fearsome as they had been, they now constituted a dreadful threat. The authorities in Khartoum appealed to their overlords in Cairo for help in meeting it. William Hicks, a general seconded from the British Indian Army, along with a staff of veteran European officers, took command of a formidable force of 10,000 troops and 5,000 camels, equipped with the latest in repeating rifles and field artillery. They sailed from Cairo up the Nile to Khartoum and in March of 1883 struck off westward into the Kordofan desert, bent on the recapture of El Obeid. It was a beastly trek through a waterless, sunbeaten waste, and on November 5 the massive caravan was still thirty miles from its objective. But that was as far as it would ever get. On that day, 200,000 dervishes fell on the caravan. The battle lasted three days. Perhaps, at most, 300 of Hicks's soldiers survived; but neither Hicks nor any of his European officers was among them.

With that, the Mahdi's insurrection appeared everywhere, and everywhere it appeared invincible, sweeping the deserts of the Sudan like a murderous sandstorm. In the east, from the right bank of the Nile to the Red Sea, tribe after tribe rose up and went on the rampage. The vital port city of Suakin, the link between Suez and Khartoum, was threatened. Another British Indian Army officer, General Valentine Baker, marched an army out of Cairo in an attempt to save Suakin. At El Teb, north of the city, in February 1884, Baker met the dervish horde. After the first howling charge of the Mahdi's horsemen, Baker's soldiers laid down their arms and gave themselves up to the slaughter. Meanwhile in Darfur, the Sudan's most westerly province, Rudolf Slatin, its Pasha, fought a series of desperate losing battles against the tribesmen who had gone over to the Mahdi there; then to save his life he professed his conversion to Islam, only to be taken away in chains. Bahr-al-Ghazal, the province south of Darfur, was next to fall. The dervishes overran it with horrible ease, and its Pasha, Frank Lupton, after watching the last of his garrisons razed and the population massacred, surrendered and also was enslaved.

And now it was Khartoum's turn.

In England—indeed, throughout much of the world—the catastrophic events in the Sudan, the humiliating spectacle of British armies defeated and British officials taken into slavery had been followed with feverish concern and mounting disbelief, and now all anxiety focused on Gordon and his people in Khartoum. Reliable news as to how they were faring ceased on March 13, 1884, when the telegraph line between Cairo and Khartoum was cut, but what news Gordon managed to send out by native runners in subsequent months was all bad. Khartoum was utterly isolated. Omdurman, on the Nile's west bank facing the city, had been captured. A hundred thousand dervishes had moved up for the siege. Food and ammunition were running low. Disease was rampant. Troops were deserting to the Mahdi, and those who remained were growing mutinous. In September, Garnet Wolseley, the Commander-in-Chief of the British Army, sailed for Cairo and, with an expeditionary force of 7,000 crack British soldiers, began the grueling 1,500-mile campaign up the valley of the Nile. They crossed into the Sudan at Wadi Halfa at the end of September, but mindful of the appalling disasters that had befallen Hicks and Baker, Wolseley proceeded with the utmost caution and it wasn't until January 28, 1885, that he at last reached Khartoum. He was, as we've seen, two days too late.

It would not be too much to say that Britain's defeat at the hands of the Mahdi's dervish legions ranks among the most shocking and shaming in her imperial history, and on learning of it a mood of near hysteria, of outrage and mortification, gripped the nation. Crowds gathered outside the Prime Minister's residence at Ten Downing Street to hoot and jeer and weep. Queen Victoria fell ill of, as she put it, "grief inexpressible" and in a letter of condolence to Gordon's sister wrote of "this stain left upon England's honor" by the failure to "rescue your dear, noble, heroic Brother." In the press, in the Parliament, among the general public, the calamity and disgrace were debated with such relentless passion that William Gladstone's government ultimately was turned out of office because of it. But after all had been said and done, after all the recriminations had been exchanged and all the blame assigned and all the excuses made, the hard, painful truth remained: Britain had been expelled from the Sudan, and a silence descended on that distant savage desert land, the eerie silence that comes after a sandstorm has passed and swept everything before it away.

And then startlingly in the autumn of 1886, nearly two years after the fall of Khartoum, that silence was broken. Out of the heart of Africa, making his way almost 2,000 miles across the continent down to the Indian Ocean coast, a lone courier reached Zanzibar with astonishing news: Not all of the Sudan was lost. One province, the most southerly, called Equatoria, which stretched upriver from the edge of the White Nile's great swamp, the Sudd, to its source in Lake Albert under the Mountains of the Moon, the province whose Pasha was a certain Mohammed Emin Effendi, the Faithful One—that province was still holding out against the Mahdi.

The news electrified England.

Now it is true that at this time virtually no one had any idea who this Emin Pasha was, where he had come from, or how he had accomplished his incredible feat; indeed, at this time virtually no one had even heard his name before. Nonetheless, in that startling moment when his brave and defiant message reached the outside world—"We shall hold out until we obtain help," he had written, "or until we perish"—this mysterious Emin Pasha became England's hero. Here was the last of Gordon's lieutenants doing what even Gordon had been unable to do. Here was the faithful soldier standing alone, surrounded on every side by savage enemies but refusing to surrender, gallantly defending against unimaginable odds the last vestige of Anglo-Egyptian rule in the Sudan. But above all here was England's chance to avenge her humiliating defeat at the hands of the dervishes and efface that inglorious stain on her honor. The press seized on him. The public took up the cry. He must not be left to perish. He must receive the help he called for. A relief expedition must be mounted. Weapons, ammunition, and supplies must be gotten through to his heroic beleaguered garrisons on the Nile, and gotten through to them in time. In that startling moment, all the emotions that had died in the two years since the fall of Khartoum revived, and the rescue of Emin Pasha became Britain's most wildly urgent, most passionately felt popular cause.

• •

"Over here, Percy." The burly red-faced Scotsman with bushy white muttonchops got up from the sofa in the lounge of his London club, the Athenaeum, and signaled with a folded-up copy of *The Times*. "Over here, old boy."

Sir Percy Anderson looked around. In contrast to the Scotsman, he was a skinny little chap with a pinched clean-shaven face and an air of perpetual irritation about him. This was on a sunny Saturday morning in late November of 1886, just a fortnight after Emin Pasha's electrifying message had reached England. The club lounge was fairly well deserted because most of the members had already gone off to their country estates for the weekend. Indeed, Anderson himself had planned to be out of London by this time, enjoying a partridge shoot in Surrey, and much of his irritation just now was due to his having had to stay in town for this meeting at the Athenaeum.

"Awfully good of you to come, Perce, old boy," the Scotsman said and, taking Anderson by the arm, steered him into a billiards room off the club lounge. It was empty; a marquetted chess table stood between two leather brass-studded chairs there, set with a silver coffeepot, fine Chinaware, starched linen, jars of butter and jams, and a basket of scones. "I really do appreciate it. I'm sure you had far more amusing plans for the day than this. Do sit down."

Anderson sat down rather stiffly on one side of the chess table, folding his hands over the head of his walking stick; the Scotsman sat down on the other side. Although it would be impossible to tell from Anderson's cool manner, the two actually were not only good friends but political allies as well. Anderson was director of the Department for African Affairs in the Foreign Office. The Scotsman was Sir William Mackinnon, proprietor of the British India Steamship Company, whose vessels, despite the firm's name, called regularly at Suez, Aden, along the East African coast and at Zanzibar and Cape Town. Their friendship and alliance was born of a shared view of the future of Africa and Britain's role in it.

"Will you have coffee? Or perhaps you'd prefer port."

"No, no. Too damn early for port. Coffee'll do."

Mackinnon placed his copy of *The Times* on the table and proceeded to pour coffee for both of them.

"What, my dear fellow, could not wait until Monday?" Anderson suddenly asked testily, setting his walking stick aside. "All you said in your note was that it was urgent that we meet. What, I should like to know, can be so bloody urgent that it couldn't wait until Monday? You owe me a very sharp explanation. You've made a hash of my weekend. My wife is furious. And on top of everything else we have the Wolseleys for house guests, and you know what a problem they can be."

"I'm sorry, Perce. Truly I am." Mackinnon, having finished pouring the coffee and not sounding sorry at all, sat back in his chair. "But you see how quiet it is in here on the weekend."

"Like a bloody tomb."

"Yes, but you will admit it affords us a good deal more privacy than we could hope to have had on Monday."

"Privacy, my dear fellow? What in God's name do we need privacy for? Are we up to some sort of hugger-mugger?"

Mackinnon smiled. "Have you seen this?" He picked up *The Times*.

"I looked through it in the cab on my way over."

"No, I mean this. Quite specifically this." The newspaper was folded open to the Letters to the Editor page and Mackinnon pointed to a particularly lengthy correspondence there about Emin Pasha.

Anderson looked at it and burst out in exasperation, "Good Lord, Mac, don't tell me you've brought me here and spoiled my weekend in order to talk about Emin Pasha. That's all I have been talking about for the last fortnight. The poor bugger. A second Gordon. Mustn't let him perish. All that rot. My dear fellow, all I wanted of this weekend was a bit of partridge shooting and two days without hearing another word about what we're going to do about that poor bloody Turk or whatever in blazes he is."

"And? What are you going to do about him, Perce?"

"Pardon?"

"I said, what has Her Majesty's Government decided to do about that poor bloody Turk?"

"Come now, Mac. You know better than to ask that. Nothing. Not a blessed thing."

"Not a blessed thing?"

"That's right. Not a blessed thing."

Mackinnon shook his head mournfully.

"Now see here, Mac. You don't suppose Salisbury is so stupid as to let himself get stampeded into sticking England's nose back into the Sudan, do you? Oh no, no, no. He learned the lesson well enough from Gladstone. It would be the same sorry business as with Gordon all over again. I mean, good Lord, man, just look at the map. Just look at where Equatoria *is*. Smack, square in the middle of the continent, cut off on the east and west and south by thousands of miles of the worst sort of wilderness, most of it never traversed by any white man, and on the north by these blood-sucking dervishes. How in God's name can anyone in his right mind imagine a relief expedition could get through to him, let alone get through to him in time? No, no, no, it would be the height of folly. It would be the Gordon business all over again. Yet another calamity, hot on the heels of Hicks and Baker and Wolseley. And besides, do you realize the cost? But why am I telling you this? I don't have to tell you any of this. You know all the arguments as well as I do."

Mackinnon stood up and went over to a billiard table and idly picked up an ivory cue ball.

"I'll be damned," Anderson said after a moment. "So it really is about the Turk that you had me meet you here."

"Yes," Mackinnon replied.

"Well, what about him then? Surely you didn't need me to tell you that Salisbury doesn't propose to try and rescue him."

"No."

"What then?"

"I propose to try and rescue him."

Anderson stared at his friend for a moment, then rolled his eyes in an exaggerated expression of vexation and picked up his coffee cup.

"Listen to me, Percy." Mackinnon came back from the billiard table with the cue ball clutched in his fist. "Salisbury and the rest of you chaps in Whitehall, no matter how ardently you might like to convince yourselves otherwise, cannot in fact simply do nothing about Emin Pasha. The country won't allow it. All England wants that Turk saved, Perce. If Salisbury simply sits on his hands and lets the poor bugger get his head chopped off like Gordon, the country will go up in arms. All right, that's putting it too strongly. But it will cause one deuce of a row. Just read the papers." Mackinnon snatched up *The Times* and rattled it at Anderson. "Save Emin Pasha. Save this second Gordon. Redeem England's honor. Give those blood-sucking dervishes what for. Everybody's screaming for it, Perce. Salisbury can't just let this fellow go the way of Gordon. He'd never survive it. His Government would fall. Surely you realize that."

Anderson didn't reply. He sipped his coffee.

"Of course you realize it. In fact, that's precisely what you chaps in Whitehall have been talking about and racking your brains about this past fortnight. Ain't I right? If Salisbury and the rest of you didn't realize you have a mighty sticky problem on your hands here, there'd be nothing for you to talk about. You'd forget the whole thing and get on about your business and let this damn Turk go to the devil. But you know you can't. You know the papers and the societies and the whole damn country will keep hammering at you until you do something. And there will be hell to pay if you don't."

Anderson set his coffee cup down and took a cigar out of his waistcoat pocket.

"But the trouble is, you don't know what to do," Mackinnon went on. "Send a relief expedition? Good God, no. That would embroil us in the Sudan all over again. War with the dervishes. Millions in sterling. The lives of British lads. Not to mention the furor that would be raised if the expedition failed into the bargain. So best stay out of it in the first place. Best not get involved and hope it will go away. But it won't go away. The country won't let it. Something has to be done. Oh, Percy, dear boy, I can hear your arguments, back and forth, all day long. What's to be done? All of you wringing your hands and chasing your tails. What's to be done?"

"Well, what *is* to be done?" Anderson snapped, throwing down the unlit cigar. "Can you tell me that?"

"I just did."

"What?"

"I will rescue Emin Pasha for you. I will get up a private relief expedition and take you chaps off the hook."

"I'm afraid I don't quite see—"

"Look, Perce." Mackinnon pulled his chair around the chess table closer to Anderson's and sat down. "Something must be done about Emin Pasha. We can all agree on that. But Salisbury feels—and with good reason, I suspect—that the government cannot afford to be drawn into the affair. Too costly. Too fraught with political complications. Very well. Still something must be done. There's no getting away from that. So why not dispatch a private expedition, one that has no connection to the government, one for which the government takes no official responsibility, a strictly private humanitarian undertaking in response to the public outcry to save this gallant Turk, this last of the beloved Gordon's lieutenants? Surely that would satisfy the country, wouldn't you think? That would fulfill the requirement that something be done. And at the same time the government would have kept well out of it."

"And if it failed? As, I may add, I'm perfectly satisfied it would."

"It wouldn't matter. The main thing is that the effort had been made, that England hadn't cold-heartedly abandoned this gallant fellow to his terrible fate. You chaps would be off the hook. You couldn't be blamed one way or the other."

Anderson picked up his coffee cup again. It was empty; he stared into it a moment, absently swirling the dregs in the bottom. Then he said, "You realize that what you are talking about here is an expenditure of fifty or sixty thousand pounds sterling. We've made the calculation at the Foreign Office. Forty thousand at an absolute minimum."

"I know."

"Why in God's name would you do it then? What would you expect to get out of it?"

"Equatoria."

"Oh?" Anderson looked up from his cup.

"I want Equatoria, Perce."

"I see. Now we come to the hugger-mugger part."

"Tell me, dear boy, how long is it now that you and I and Kirk and Hutton and Grant and de Winton and heaven knows who else have been saying that the time is long overdue for British private enterprise to peg out a claim to the trade in the African interior and stop leaving it to the Arabs? How long is it since we first said we must push beyond our piddling depots and forts on the coast and start expanding the British Empire into the rich virgin heart of the continent itself? Eight years? Ten?"

Anderson nodded.

"But we've also always said no British entrepreneur could be expected to undertake such a venture on his own. He'd have to have some very solid government backing. At the very least, he'd have to have a royal charter from the Crown."

"And the Crown has always refused," Anderson interjected. "You know bloody well how hard Kirk and I and the rest of us have pressed the idea, first on Gladstone and then on Salisbury, and how they have always turned us down."

"But they can't turn us down now, Perce."

"And why not, pray tell?"

"Because of Emin Pasha. Because of this gallant Turk I propose to rescue for them." Mackinnon sank back in his club chair still clutching the ivory cue ball.

"That smacks a bit of blackmail, Mac."

"No need to put it so rudely. Why not just look at it this way? I will organize a syndicate, or a committee if you prefer—yes, let's call it the Emin Pasha Relief Committee—subscribed to by a number of our like-minded friends and business associates. We'll raise the financing required to dispatch an expedition to Emin Pasha with whatever relief supplies he requires to go on holding Equatoria against the dervishes. If it succeeds, that is to say if the expedition manages to get through in time to secure Equatoria, then the syndicate or committee which put up all the monies and ran all the risks would be granted a trading monopoly in the province, under a royal charter from the Crown. If it fails, well that's the committee's lookout. Either way, it's no skin off the government's back. That seems fair, wouldn't you say?"

Anderson didn't say.

Mackinnon sat forward in his chair and placed the ivory ball on the chess table. "It's a golden opportunity, Percy. It's everything we've been talking about all these years. It could be the beginnings of the first British colony in the African interior. And we wouldn't have to start from scratch. That's the best part. There are forts and trading stations already there. There's a functioning administration, clerks, craftsmen, native soldiers. And there's this Emin Pasha. Let's face it, Perce, whoever he is, he must be an extraordinary chap, holding on like that against all odds. We could take it all over. We'd make him Governor. We'd have our Imperial British East Africa Company at last."

Anderson still remained silent.

"What do you say, Percy? Good God, man, say something."

"It's all rather breathtaking, is what I say."

"I know it is. Of course it is. But we'll never have a better chance. Equatoria is there for the taking. The government wrote it off long ago. Until a fortnight ago we thought it was in the hands of the dervishes. Well, it ain't. So let's take it for ourselves, Perce."

Anderson looked around the billiards room. On Monday, on any weekday, it would be crowded with gentlemen at their games, curious as to what the director of the Foreign Office's Department for African Affairs could be talking about with the proprietor of the British India Steamship Company. Now, however, it was still empty. Not even a club steward had looked in. Doubtless Mackinnon had arranged it that way.

Anderson looked back at him. "All right, Mac," he said. "All right, let's take it for ourselves."

"Good chap. I knew you'd see it my way. But we've got to move quickly. Who knows how long that Turk can hold on."

"I'll speak to Salisbury Monday and arrange for you to see him at his earliest convenience. Probably Wednesday or Thursday. There's a Cabinet meeting on Friday, and I think it best you lay all this out for him before then."

"Right."

"But tell me one thing, Mac."

"Yes?"

"You're damn certain this expedition will succeed, aren't you?"

"Yes, of course I am."

"You wouldn't be willing to undertake it otherwise. There'd be no point. A great deal of expense and bother and no Imperial British East Africa Company, no royal charter, nothing, if it failed."

"Quite so."

"Well, how can you be so sure it won't fail?"

"Because of the man I will engage to lead it."

"And who is that?"

"The Rock Breaker, Perce. Bula Matari, the Rock Breaker."

PART ONE
The Expedition

· ONE ·

IT HAD STARTED to snow; flurries swirled in the light of the gas lamps along the cobbled avenue outside and the tall, slender young Englishman, on stepping into the foyer of Delmonico's, paused to brush the quickly melting flakes from the velvet lapels of his topcoat. Immediately the girl from the cloakroom hurried over. He peeled off his pearl-gray gloves and popped them into his bowler and, bending backwards a bit so that the girl could reach up to help him, wriggled out of the coat. Then, absently fingering his stylish black mustache, he looked around what was New York's most fashionable restaurant. The Christmas decorations were up—a full fortnight before the holiday and, as such, rather too early by London standards—and from behind a yew tree hung with ornaments a little maitre d' appeared.

"Can I be of service, sir?" With a practiced eye, the maitre d' had sized up the young man—the elegant tailoring of his clothes, the refinement of his handsome profile, the delicacy of his long fingers—and was prepared to be deferential, which was hardly ever the case when an unknown person walked into the famous restaurant.

"I am looking for Mr. Stanley," the young man said. "I was round to his hotel, and they tell me he is dining here this evening."

"Are you with his party, sir?"

"No, but I should like to have a word with him nevertheless. He is here then?"

"Yes he is. May I tell him who's calling?"

The young man took an engraved visiting card from his waistcoat pocket and handed it to the maitre d'. "Please say that I am awfully sorry to intrude in this way but the matter is urgent."

"Certainly, sir. Would you care to wait in the bar?"

"And perhaps you had best also say that I've come from Sir William Mackinnon in London."

"Mackinnon, sir?"

"Yes. Sir William Mackinnon of the British India Steamship Company. Shall I write it down?"

"That won't be necessary. If you will, sir, the bar is just over there, behind those curtains." The maitre d' hurried off on his errand, refraining with splendid tact from looking at the young man's visiting card, at least until he had carried it off far enough into the dining room to believe that he wouldn't be seen doing so. Then he glanced at it. It was inscribed simply: A. J. Mounteney Jephson. And although the name meant nothing to him, it had a smart enough ring to allow the maitre d' to feel confirmed in his evaluation of the English youth. A. J. Mounteney Jephson indeed; very likely the son of an aristocrat, perhaps heir to a minor title.

Jephson smiled; he had observed the maitre d's surreptitious check of his credentials because he had not retired to wait in the bar as had been suggested. On the contrary, he had followed the maitre d' a step or two into the dining room to see where he would go, whom he would approach. For the young man, despite his elegantly cool outward manner, was in fact boyishly excited by the prospect of meeting the fabled Henry Morton Stanley.

And then he saw him. He was caught unawares. He hadn't expected the maître d' to reach his destination quite so quickly. He had rather imagined that Mr. Stanley and his party would be dining in one of the private rooms, discreetly out of sight. But the maitre d' stopped at one of the most prominently located tables, and the party seated around it—four men, five or six women—seemed almost ostentatiously on display. They were colorfully, if not to say garishly, dressed—a great many pink and purple and orange boas and feathered hats blossomed around the women—and they were carrying on raucously, explosions of shrill laughter punctuating their noisy chatter, as if deliberately calling attention to themselves. It was not at all what the young aristocrat had anticipated, and his heart sank with disappointment as he watched the maitre d' bend over the man at the head of the table, whose back was to Jephson, and deliver his card.

But then the man turned.

His face was square, perfectly square as if hewn from a block of granite; square across the forehead beneath close-cropped iron-gray hair; square in the jaw, which seemed tensed by some private fury; and roughened overall, very much like a rock, by the pits and cuts of smallpox and other scars. Under the broad, often broken nose was a mustache as unstylishly short-clipped as the hair but grayer in color, barely concealing the hard, thin line of the mouth. The cheekbones were unusually high; and the eyes, deeply set in their shadow, were narrow and slanted, almost Oriental, and of a strange color, flickering in the flare of the restaurant's gas lamps somewhere between gray and green. These eyes stared at Jephson piercingly, trying to make him out, fix him among the other figures lounging in the foyer, as a hunter might stare at his prey or a killer at his enemy.

He stood up. Surprisingly, he was only of medium height—Jephson had thought he would tower over the little maitre d', yet he was the taller by barely half a head—but he was as square in his body as in his face and as rock hard, the muscles of his arms and shoulders visibly straining the cloth of his jacket. He came toward Jephson with fast, long strides, appearing to grow larger, more powerful, angrier as he approached; and reflexively the slender youth stepped back to get out of his way.

"Mister," he said in a low, hoarse voice; then he looked down at the visiting card in his hand. "Mr. Mounteney Jephson?"

"Good evening, Mr. Stanley. I'm terribly sorry to have intruded on your dinner."

"Never mind. It isn't the first time it has happened and I don't suppose it will be the last," Stanley said; and although his words were civil enough, his expression remained one of apparently implacable anger. A restless physical strength seemed to radiate from him, almost tangibly disturbing the air around them and most definitely to be felt in the bone-crushing handshake he gave Jephson. "You've come from Mac Mackinnon, Maurice tells me."

"Yes, sir."

"How is the old pirate?"

"He's very well, sir."

"Glad to hear it." Stanley studied Jephson with those piercing gray-green eyes. "You're not any kind of kin of his, are you?"

"Oh, no, sir."

"I didn't think so. You're far too pretty a looking lad to have any of that old pirate's blood in you."

Jephson smiled weakly; he didn't think that was meant exactly as a compliment, and so he said hastily, "He and my father are great friends though, and I am presently in his employ, through that connection."

"Oh, has Mac sent you to see me on business?"

"Yes, sir. And it is rather urgent business. Otherwise I wouldn't have dreamed of bothering you at dinner."

Stanley shifted his penetrating gaze from the young man's face.

"Come along then," he said. "Let's step into the bar over there and see what sort of urgent business that bloody pirate has for me."

The bar was crowded, but Stanley had no trouble getting a table. The chief barman, spotting him immediately, came over quickly and showed him and his companion to a comfortable corner banquette where they could sit facing each other.

"Let me have a brandy and soda, Sam," Stanley said to the barman. "And what will yours be, lad?"

"The same, thank you."

"All right now," Stanley said when the barman left. "Tell me. What sort of business does that pirate have in mind?"

"He is getting up an expedition for the relief of Emin Pasha, sir," Jephson replied.

"What? An expedition for the relief of Emin Pasha? You must be joking, lad."

"No, sir. Not at all. And he wants you to lead it, sir."

"Emin Pasha," Stanley said again. "Well, I'll be damned." He pursed his lips, giving to his face an expression finally of something other than implacable hardness—perhaps it was one of bemusement—and sat back against the banquette.

"You may not as yet have heard it here in New York, sir, but Her Majesty's Government, after an awful lot of heated argument, have decided not to undertake an attempt to rescue Emin. Lord Salisbury is convinced that Emin's position is utterly hopeless, as hopeless as Gordon's was, and that an official expedition to his relief could only result in the same sort of disaster for the government as that caused by Wolseley's failure to reach Gordon in Khartoum in time. But beyond that, sir, Lord Salisbury believes that such an expedition, whether successful or not, would be bound to draw England back into war with the dervishes and that is something he is extremely anxious to avoid just now. It is his government's policy to leave well enough alone in the Sudan. Its loss hasn't materially damaged England's imperial interests, Egypt remains firmly in our control, the dervishes do not threaten the Suez Canal, and so on. He feels, therefore, that it would be the height of folly to embroil England in that part of the world once again."

Jephson paused, expecting that Stanley might want to say something at this point. But he didn't; he simply rested against the banquette and watched the youth with narrowed eyes.

"Well, as you might imagine, sir," Jephson continued, "this wasn't exactly a wildly popular decision at home. In fact, it has stirred up quite a furor. The country has rather taken Emin to its heart, you know—the gallant soldier, a second Gordon, defending England's honor and all that—and it's fairly up in arms over the idea that he's to be left to go the way of Gordon. A number of people, including members of Lord Salisbury's own party, are saying the government could very well fall on the issue."

Stanley nodded. "I see," he said and sat forward again. "And here's where our friend Mackinnon steps into the picture, is it? He has offered to get Salisbury off the hook by dispatching a private expedition, one for which the government have no official responsibility, a strictly private venture by humanitarian-minded chaps like himself in response to the public outcry to save Emin Pasha. Very neat. How could Salisbury resist? The country calms down, Parliament is satisfied. The noble Turk, or whatever he is, isn't to be abandoned to his bloody fate after all. Englishmen are making an effort to rescue this defender of their honor. And at the same time Salisbury and his chums remain happily well out of it and avoid all political consequences if the expedition fails. Yes, very neat indeed. But what's the quid pro quo?"

"Sir?"

"The quid pro quo, lad. Didn't that pirate tell you what he expects in return for getting Salisbury out of the soup?"

"No, sir, he didn't say anything about that but . . ." Jephson reached into the inner pocket of his suit jacket and brought out a long white envelope. "But he asked me to deliver this to you personally, sir, and to say that he and his associates feel most strongly that you are the only man who can make a success of this venture and that, as you will see, it is a venture very much worth making a success of."

Stanley took the envelope, turned it over and examined its unbroken red wax seal; it was that of the British India Steamship Company. "Are you with Mac's shipping line, lad?" he asked, opening the envelope and extracting two closely written pages.

"No, sir. Sir William has taken me on as secretary to the Emin Pasha Relief Committee."

"Ah, there's an Emin Pasha Relief Committee already, is there?"

"Yes, sir. It is raising the financing for the expedition. Sir William is chairman."

"Who else is on it?"

"I'm not entirely certain, sir. I know that Mr. James Hutton of Manchester is and Colonel Francis de Winton and also Colonel James Grant, I believe."

"Ah, yes, that same old gang, hankering after a piece of Africa to call their own," Stanley muttered, but he had started reading the letter and no longer was paying any attention to Jephson.

The brandies and sodas arrived. Stanley, absorbed in the letter, did not touch his. Jephson hesitated for a moment, then decided to go ahead without waiting for the older man.

How old was he actually? Jephson wondered, peering over the rim of his snifter and taking this first unguarded moment to study the fabled Henry Morton Stanley a bit more closely. One couldn't tell just from his face. From that battered, scarred face alone, one might guess him to be well over fifty. But Jephson knew that couldn't be the case. After all, he himself remembered—although he was a child of five at the time, such a fuss had been made about it that he could never forget—when Stanley found Livingstone. That was in 1871, fifteen years ago, and Stanley then was not yet thirty, more likely twenty-eight or twenty-nine, so he would be only forty-three or forty-four now. But after that had come all those stupendous journeys of African exploration—the sources of the Nile, the course of the Congo, the building of the Congo Free State for King Leopold of Belgium—fifteen murderous years of it, crossing the most terrible jungles and mountains and deserts and swamps and rivers and savannas, where no white man had ever been before and very few had dared go since, those stupendous journeys that had made of Stanley the most heroic, awesome adventurer of the age. And all of it showed in his scarred, battered killer's face. Jesus, that was what Africa did to a man, Jephson thought with a sudden shiver; it battered you into this image of a killer—or it killed you.

But, he supposed, still watching Stanley with irresistible fascination, that probably had been the only way for a man of Stanley's wretched background to have ever raised himself to his present position of fame and fortune. After all, what was it that was always whispered about him? That he was the bastard child of a Welsh whore, who had abandoned him to a workhouse at the age of six and from which he had escaped at fifteen by murdering the headmaster and fleeing to America aboard a cotton clipper. Something of the sort or something equally sordid, in any case something that would have guaranteed his never gaining access to anything remotely resembling polite society had he not performed those impossible feats in Africa—something indeed, if the truth be told, that had prevented him from ever being truly accepted by that society despite those feats. No, Jephson mused, sipping his brandy, Henry Morton Stanley had never been truly accepted by polite society.

Acclaimed, admired, respected, made use of, yes, even a bit feared but never finally accepted, despite his feats, or perhaps just because of them. For who but a most desperate, dangerous, unacceptable man could have ever performed them?

Stanley looked up abruptly, as if he had overheard Jephson's unflattering thoughts. But no, he had merely finished reading Mackinnon's letter. He replaced it in the envelope slowly and stared off into the distance, lost in his own thoughts; the muscles in his jaw were working furiously, as if chewing on a private rage. But then, with a brisk motion, he tucked the envelope away in his jacket pocket, picked up the brandy and soda in front of him, drank it off in a single swallow, and again turned his burning gaze on young Jephson.

"Now, lad, let's get to matters closer at hand," he said. "Tell me, when did you arrive? Do you have lodgings? And, above all, have you had any supper yet?"

"Yes I have, sir, thank you. I dined earlier with the British consul. I am staying at his residence. He is a friend of my cousin, Dorothy Tennant, and I went there directly after the steamer docked this afternoon. It was he who put me on to your hotel."

"Did you say Dorothy Tennant?"

"Yes."

"Is that Dolly Tennant?"

"Yes, sir, it is. Why? Do you know her?"

"We have met."

"I say, how jolly. She is my cousin, you know."

"You said."

"Yes, I did." Jephson would have liked to pursue the coincidence of Stanley's knowing his cousin, exploit it a bit in order to put himself on a more familiar footing with this formidable man. But Stanley's cold reaction to Dolly Tennant's name warned him off.

"So, you are well settled and I need make no arrangements for you," Stanley went on briskly. "Splendid. I like that. And now tell me, how long were you planning to stay?"

"In New York?"

"Yes."

"But, sir, that depends entirely on you. Sir William instructed me to put myself at your service and to accompany you on your return to England. The next steamer bound for London, the *Eider*, departs on the fifteenth, Wednesday, in four days' time. I took the liberty of booking passage aboard her for both of us. However, if that doesn't suit your schedule, I can arrange our passage aboard an

Australian merchantman that departs on the twentieth. But, as I am sure Sir William indicated in his letter, time is very much of the essence in this matter. There's no way of knowing how long Emin Pasha can hang on out there, so I felt that the earlier ship would be the one you would prefer."

Stanley smiled. "You are quite the up-to-the-mark lad, aren't you? I can see why Mac fixed on you for this job."

Jephson was delighted; but it wasn't so much because of Stanley's praise, although that pleased him immensely—it was also because of his smile. It was such a handsome, disarming smile, suddenly transforming that rock-hard face into something very human, that Jephson, grinning back, was suddenly swept by a warm filial affection for the man; and he realized that in that smile some of Stanley's awesome power must also reside.

"But, my boy," Stanley went on, "I'm afraid you have jumped to an unwarranted conclusion."

"Sir?"

"You have assumed that I will accept Mac's commission and hurry back to London to take the leadership of his relief expedition."

"But I say, won't you? Sir William and his associates are awfully keen that you do."

"Oh, I'm sure they are. I've no doubt they are. They must be, my boy. Because they are right, you know. I am the only one who stands even half a chance of getting a relief party through to that Turk. Does that sound immodest? I am sure it does. But it's the truth. Who else is there? Look at the mess they made with Chinese Gordon. I knew him, you know. I wanted him to come out and work with me in the Congo Free State. We were going to split the river between us. I was to take it from the Falls to the Pool and he from the Pool to the sea. But then he got the call to go back to Khartoum and he couldn't resist it. He was a strange chap, no doubt about it. Maybe, as some folk like to speculate, he was seeking a martyrdom in the desert. But he didn't deserve what he got. He deserved a better fate than that." Stanley broke off for an instant and looked away. Then he said, "Wolseley should have got through to him in time. I would have. And I could get through to Emin Pasha now. It would be a hell of a thing, a hell of a killing thing. But I could do it like no other man could." He paused again, now staring intently at Jephson. Then he said in his low, husky voice, "But why in hell should I?"

Jephson didn't reply. He was spellbound by Stanley's manner of speaking, the curious mixture of boastful arrogance and genuine toughness along with an almost feminine tenderness when he mentioned Gordon. And besides, he didn't think Stanley expected a reply. It was a rhetorical question surely, to which Stanley would supply his own answer. Or at least Jephson hoped so, because he didn't have the faintest idea how to answer it himself. He knew far too little not only about Stanley, of course, but also, if the truth be told, about the whole Emin Pasha affair itself. For this elegant young Englishman had come down from Oxford only just the previous spring and had been living the conventionally frivolous life of a rich man's son in London ever since.

To be sure, he had glanced through the newspapers from time to time on his way to and from his club in St. James's, for example, or on his way to and from the gaming tables in Mayfair or the theater in the West End or the house parties and weekend shoots in the country. But all he had bothered to learn about Emin Pasha was that here was some gallant, mysterious chap—a Turk or something—stuck off in the middle of Africa somewhere, who was in desperate need of saving. Not only didn't he know who Emin Pasha was—admittedly very few people seemed to know that—but he hadn't quite sorted out how Emin Pasha had gotten to where he was or what predicament exactly he found himself in now that he was there or what would be involved in trying to get him out of it. Jephson simply had been too preoccupied with his own lively activities to inquire into the matter in any great detail. And that very likely was how it would have remained hadn't his father become thoroughly fed up with his useless life and spoken to William Mackinnon about him.

Now, when it came right down to it, young Jephson had had very little choice, but in fairness to him it must be said he rather liked the idea of taking a position with the Emin Pasha Relief Committee. In the first place, it didn't require him to turn up at an office at regular hours, as would have been the case in a bank or ministry. Moreover, there wasn't a terribly great deal of work to do—merely looking after the committee accounts and correspondence and running errands for Sir William and now, presumably, also for Mr. Stanley—and once the expedition was actually under way there wouldn't even be that much. But really the best thing about the position, in Jephson's mind, was that it would put him smack in the center of what rapidly was becoming the most talked of event of the London season, and surely some of its glamour would rub off on him as a result. And he rather fancied that. He could imagine how the young gentlemen and ladies of his social set would gather about him as he made the rounds of parties and balls and theaters and casinos and weekends in the country and eagerly ask him for the latest news of Henry Morton Stanley's heroic race through darkest Africa to save Emin Pasha. Oh, yes, he did fancy being privy to special information, the admiring attention, the reflected glory. And so when Sir William had summoned him to the offices of the British India Steamship Company in Pall Mall and put the proposition to him, he had leaped at it. And before he had had a chance to do anything about his shocking lack of knowledge about the affair, he had been sent off to New York to fetch Mr. Stanley.

And so here he sat opposite this imposing rock of a man in this noisy, smoky bar, hoping fervently that he wouldn't be forced to reveal the depth of his ignorance by being pressed to come up with an answer to Stanley's perfectly straightforward question. Why, indeed, should Stanley accept the command of the Emin Pasha relief expedition? What could there be in it for him? Tremendous hardship certainly and tremendous risk, the risk of death, of course, but also the risk of harming his legendary reputation if he failed. And for what? Fame and fortune? But could a man like Stanley, who had had nothing but fame and fortune heaped on him in the last fifteen years, be tempted by that? Could he be expected to gamble his life and his reputation especially now in the twilight years of his remarkable career, for that? Surely he had had more than his full share and need not risk ignominy or death for more. No, there must be something else, another reason, a reason beyond fame and fortune, a reason, however, that Jephson, in his callow ignorance, had no way of knowing.

Stanley apparently was aware of that and no sooner had he asked the question than he turned away and signaled the barman for two more brandies and sodas. This time he drank his slowly, reflectively. He leaned against the maroon velvet plush of the banquette and, swirling his snifter absently, looked past Jephson with narrowed, distant eyes. He seemed to have forgotten about his presence, and as Jephson couldn't think of anything to say, a not altogether unpleasant silence fell between them.

A short, fat man in a loud tweed suit interrupted the reverie. "Damnit, Bula Matari, what the devil are you doing?" he asked in a booming American accent. "The ladies were sure you'd run out on them."

"Ah, Pond," Stanley said and sat up. "Major Pond. Mr. Mounteney Jephson."

"How do you do," Pond said, shaking Jephson's hand.

"Major," Jephson replied, rising from his place. "Pleased to meet you, sir."

"Pull up a chair, Pond," Stanley said. "This will interest you."

"What could interest me more than our ladies," Pond said, but he turned to find a vacant chair and dragged it over to the banquette.

"Major Pond is my lecture agent," Stanley said to Jephson.

"Oh?" Jephson had assumed when he heard the military rank that Pond must be an old Africa hand who had participated in one of Stanley's adventures and was moderately disappointed to discover otherwise.

"And a bloody good lecture agent he is too. He has me booked on tour all over the United States. Tomorrow it's Boston, isn't it, Pond?"

"Yes," Pond said, waving for the barman.

"Then it is somewhere in Vermont."

"Saint Johnsbury," Pond said and, having placed his order for a whiskey, joined the conversation with enthusiasm. "And then I have the old boy booked into the Town Hall in Hartford. That's in Connecticut. After that we're off to St. Louis, where I've arranged for Mr. Samuel Clemens–that's Mark Twain, you know–to make the introductions. And then onward across the Mississippi and up and down the length and breadth of this great land. We finish in San Francisco."

"Sixty thousand dollars, lad," Stanley said. "What do you think of that?"

"Sir?"

"I shall earn sixty thousand dollars for this nonsense."

"It ain't nonsense," Pond said. "Why is it nonsense? Do you know how wild people are to hear this man, to see him in the flesh? This here is Henry Morton Stanley. Do you have any idea what that means to these people? Do you know how much they admire him for what he has done? It's more than admiration. It's worship."

"It's nonsense," Stanley said. "Standing on a stage in front of a gaggle of old ladies and young boys and titillating them with nasty tales about the dark continent–Christ, it's worse than nonsense." His narrowed eyes shifted off again into the smoky distance where, apparently, his private thoughts were to be found.

Pond shrugged and took a generous swallow of his whiskey. Then he asked, "What was it that was going to interest me, Bula Matari?"

"Eh?"

"A minute ago you said that this conversation you were having with Mr. Jephson was going to interest me."

"Oh, yes, Pond, that's right, I did. It would interest you."

"Well?"

"Mr. Jephson wants me to cancel the tour."

"He wants you to do what?"

"Yes. He has just come over from London with a proposition from an old friend of mine which, if I accept it, would mean we would have to cancel the tour."

"Don't make jokes like that. I don't want to hear rotten jokes like that." Pond's pudgy face flushed a sweaty apoplectic crimson and he pushed himself away from the table in such agitation that he spilled his whiskey. "They ain't funny. They ain't funny one bit. Cancel the tour? Do you know what that would cost me?" He scrambled to his feet and dabbed at his waistcoat with a napkin where the whiskey had spilled. "I wouldn't care if this lad had come from Queen Victoria herself, there ain't no way this tour can be canceled. No, sir. We're taking the afternoon train to Boston tomorrow just like we planned. And now I think we ought to get back to the ladies before *they* run out on *us*. You will have to excuse us, Mr. Jephson. It was nice meeting you."

"Sit down, Pond." Stanley's voice was like a pistol shot.

And Pond sat down.

Stanley waved the barman over to the table again. "Sam, get Major Pond another whiskey. He's had a little accident. And bring me some writing things, will you?"

"You were joking, Bula Matari, weren't you?" Pond ventured after a few moments, and when Stanley didn't reply he looked at Jephson.

Jephson didn't look back. He looked at Stanley instead, at the closed hard face, at the muscles working in the square jaw, at the eyes narrowed now to the point where they had virtually vanished in the deep shadows of the rugged cheekbones. Stanley seemed filled with that secret fury again.

The barman returned with the whiskey for Pond and paper, envelope, pen, and ink for Stanley.

"Wait a minute, Sam." Stanley pushed his brandy snifter aside and adjusted the nib of the pen. "This won't take but a minute." He made no effort to conceal what he wrote, but neither Pond nor Jephson tried to see what it was. And indeed it did not take but a minute—a few scrawled lines. Stanley blotted them carefully, folded the sheet, and slipped it into the envelope. Then he removed Mackinnon's letter from his breast pocket and copied out Mackinnon's London address on the envelope. This too he blotted carefully and handed it to the barman. "Have this run round to the telegraph office, Sam. I want it cabled off the very first thing." He dropped a silver coin in the barman's hand and watched him carry off the note. Then he turned to Pond and Jephson. "Well, gentlemen," he said, "shall we join the ladies now?"

As he was an unexpected guest, a great deal of fuss was made about fetching Jephson a chair and finding him a place at the table. Then there was a rather confused round of introductions, with everyone interrupting everyone else, making silly jokes and bursting into gales of laughter. This had mainly to do with the ladies. Oddly, they were introduced only by their given names, names like Lola and Fanny and Flossie and Flo and Zizi and Carmen and Fifi and so on. But as there were only five of them, these all obviously couldn't be their names, and of course that was what the hilarity was about, that no one really knew their names. They were whores. And the other two men in the party were hardly of a much higher social station: loud, foul-mouthed penny-a-line reporters from Stanley's old newspaper, the *New York Herald*, the one that had sent Stanley out to find Livingstone in the first place. But the fellow next to whom Jephson was finally seated (with Leila or Gigi or Rosie or whoever it was on his right), with a name something like Noe or Nye, claimed to have been a colleague and friend of Stanley's long before that famous event. And in fact no sooner had Jephson sat down beside him than he proceeded to regale the young Englishman with slightly drunken but immensely colorful accounts of his adventures with Stanley—in the Indian wars of the American west, on assignment in Constantinople, covering the Carlist uprising in Spain, with Robert Napier's campaign against Emperor Theodore in Abyssinia. It was such marvelously hair-raising stuff that Jephson wasn't sure what if any of it he should believe; and anyway, as he was keeping a sharp eye out for a chance to have a private word with Stanley to learn what reply he had made to Mackinnon, he didn't listen too carefully.

"His name ain't really Stanley, you know," this chap Noe or Nye said, refilling Jephson's champagne glass. "Not many people know it, but actually he was born John Rowlands. He took the moniker Stanley after he came to America. He once told me that it was the name of a rich cotton broker in New Orleans who adopted him after he jumped ship there as a fugitive from some limey workhouse and who took care of him until he went off to fight with the Dixie Greys in the Civil War, but I never believed that. There's never been any sign of that father or any other father. I think he just made it up, liked the sound of it. Hell, any name was bound to be better than his real one, considering he was on the run at the time. As a matter of fact, when I first met up with him, he was giving out that his name was Henry *Morelake* Stanley, not Henry *Morton* Stanley."

"When was it that you first did meet up with him?" Jephson asked. He saw that it would be some time before he'd manage to get a moment alone with Stanley—Pond had engrossed Stanley in an agitated conversation on the opposite side of the table—and he was intrigued by the stuff this chap Noe or Nye was prattling on about so knowingly.

"When? Let me see . . . 1864 or 1865. It was toward the end of the Civil War anyway. We were in the Federal Fleet together."

"The Federal Fleet? Excuse me, but I understood you to say that Mr. Stanley fought with the Confederacy in the war. With the Dixie Greys, wasn't it?"

"That was at the start. But he was captured at Shiloh and in order to get out of the prison camp he agreed to come over to the Union side."

"Are you saying he turned coat, sir?"

"Oh, you don't have to use hard words like that, lad. He wasn't American. He didn't have any particular loyalties to one side or the other. He didn't even have to be in the war on either side. He went into it just for the fun of it. Anyway he came aboard the *Minnesota* when I was on her, and we saw the last major battle of the war together, the assault on Fort Fisher in North Carolina. After that he talked me into going out west with him to seek our fortunes in the Colorado silver mines. We didn't have much luck at that though, and so Stanley hit on the idea of our writing for the newspapers. You see, Colonel Custer was mustering the Seventh Cavalry at Fort Wallace for the campaign against the Cheyenne, and Stanley reckoned that—"

But the chap never had a chance to say what Stanley had reckoned, because just then Pond leaped to his feet and pitched face forward across the table in a dead faint. A terrific commotion ensued. The ladies shrieked; waiters and busboys rushed over; diners throughout the restaurant jumped up to see what was going on;

there was much shouting of advice about loosening the poor fellow's cravat and giving him space to breathe.

Jephson himself jumped up in astonishment. Then he realized what must have happened. In the midst of all the hubbub, he suddenly caught Stanley's eye. Stanley had not gotten up; he had leaned back in his chair, and when he saw Jephson looking at him he smiled. Jephson sat down, and a thrilling shiver ran through him. He knew then that Stanley had decided to go after Emin Pasha. But he still had no idea why.

When he looked at Stanley again, Stanley had taken hold of the collar of Pond's jacket and, hauling him off the table, reseated him in his chair. Then he gave him a brisk slap across his pudgy cheeks and whispered something in his ear. Pond opened his eyes. One of the ladies offered him a glass of champagne, clucking at him sympathetically, but he waved it aside. With a series of elaborate gestures–tugging down his waistcoat, smoothing his hair, mopping his forehead with a silk handkerchief, and so on–he pulled himself together, stood up, and with a curt bow to the company but without a word to anyone marched stiffly out of the restaurant.

Instantly, of course, everyone at the table wanted to know what *that* had been all about and began buzzing at Stanley from all directions. For a while it seemed as if Stanley wasn't going to say, but Jephson, watching him closely, suspected that he was rather enjoying the little drama he had created and was drawing it out only for effect. He called for more champagne and had everyone's glass refilled while parrying the questions with a shrug, a wave of the hand, a tug on his mustache, but always with that wonderfully captivating smile on his battered face. And then, with exquisite timing, just when the ladies' interest might have begun to wane, he relented.

"I will be returning to Africa," he said in his rough, low voice. "Major Pond, not unnaturally, was upset by the news, since it means that he has to cancel the rest of my tour."

"Returning to Africa?"

"What for?"

"Where?"

"To do what?"

"Is it for Leopold?"

The questions came thick and fast from the two men. The ladies found the whole thing divinely exciting and terribly adventurous, and they twittered and sighed and swooned and vied with each other in expressing their admiration for Stanley's daring. But the two men, journalists both, realized that they were onto a splendid story for their Sunday editions—Stanley to Return to Dark Continent; Famous Explorer Undertaking Expedition to Scene of His Greatest Triumphs—and they were eager to ferret out the details. But, to Jephson's surprise, their line of questioning was far off the mark. For some reason they assumed that any return to Africa by Stanley must be on behalf of Leopold II, King of the Belgians.

Now, to be sure, Stanley's most recent activity in Africa had been the pioneering of outposts and trading stations on the Congo River for the Belgian King's Congo Free State. But he had terminated that work and returned to Europe more than eighteen months before, around the time when rumors had started circulating about the repugnant methods Leopold's agents were using to harvest rubber and ivory in the Free State; and it was generally believed that Stanley had quit the Belgian King's service because of that. Yet the two journalists behaved as if this wasn't the case. They seemed to think that Stanley was still in Leopold's employ, that the Belgian King had first call on his services in any new African venture. Jephson, knowing what mission in fact was taking Stanley back to Africa, could not understand how this could be. But Stanley didn't explain. He let the mystery remain.

· TWO ·

"Bula Matari."

"You're looking fit, you old pirate."

Henry Stanley and Sir William Mackinnon shook hands, and with his free hand Mackinnon also grasped Stanley's forearm in a special gesture of affection. "I can't tell you how pleased I am you've accepted this commission, Henry," he said.

"You don't have to, Mac. I can guess it easily enough." Stanley grinned at the Scotsman, then disengaged his hand. "And here's the rest of your thieving crew," he said, turning to the three other men waiting in the billiards room of the Athenaeum.

"You know everybody," Mackinnon said.

"I know them." Stanley shook hands with each of the three: James Hutton, the Manchester industrialist with trading interests in Zanzibar and the Gold Coast; James Grant, the retired British Indian Army colonel who had accompanied John Speke in 1861 in the search for the White Nile's source in Lake Victoria; Francis de Winton, a British Army colonel with a distinguished record of pioneering and colonization in other parts of Africa. "But don't tell me this is all there is to your Emin Pasha Relief Committee."

"Not formally." Mackinnon led Stanley to a table set with a silver service for high tea. "We have over a dozen subscribers financing the enterprise who *formally* are members of the committee as well. But this is . . . What shall I call it? The inner circle. The four of us and you, Henry. And of course our young secretary over there. Come and join us, lad."

Jephson had hung back on entering the club, allowing the old friends to renew acquaintance, but now he hurried forward eagerly, carrying a battered leather valise of Stanley's.

"Sit here, Arthur," Mackinnon said, indicating a chair at the tea table between himself and Stanley. "I expect it's proper that you attend this meeting. But I don't see any need for you to keep minutes. Don't you agree, gentlemen? No, no minutes, Arthur. For the moment we had best regard this as a matter just among ourselves."

It was Christmas Day, less than twenty-four hours since the SS *Eider* had docked at Southampton, and ordinarily these men would have been off with friends and relations celebrating the holiday. That they weren't was, of course, a measure of the urgency they attached to the task that lay before them. As it was, over a month had elapsed since Emin Pasha's electrifying message had reached England. Weeks had been wasted in debate over how Her Majesty's Government should respond to the astonishing news and whether Mackinnon's offer to send a private relief expedition should be accepted. And then more weeks had been lost waiting for Henry Morton Stanley to be fetched back from America. During this time no further word had been received from Equatoria; the curtain of silence had once again fallen over the beleaguered province. Indirectly though—from a missionary in the vicinity of Lake Victoria, from an Egyptian spy passing himself off as an ivory trader in the souks and bazaars of the Upper Nile—word had come that Emin Pasha was still holding out. But clearly no more time could be wasted or lost. Every day was precious. Even Christmas Day could not be set aside.

Stanley was to meet with Lord Salisbury later that afternoon. The Prime Minister had told Sir William it was imperative that he see Stanley as soon as he returned to London in order to make certain he understood that Her Majesty's Government would be playing no official role whatsoever in the expedition, that it was strictly a private venture, that the committee sponsoring it assumed all costs and risks, and that if it got into trouble it could not expect the government to come to its assistance. Mackinnon had touched on this in the letter he had sent to Stanley with Jephson, but he was anxious to explain and somewhat soften these rather worrisome conditions before Stanley was subjected to the discouraging way Salisbury was bound to present them. And so, once the men were seated and helping themselves to tea and sandwiches, this was the first topic he brought up.

But Stanley cut him off. "I'm not counting on the British Army, Mac," he said sharply. "Don't worry yourself. Salisbury won't scare me off with that. I'm not going into this with the idea that if I get into hot water the lads in scarlet will bail me out. Fat lot of good they would do me anyway. Gordon counted on them and a fat lot of good they did him, the poor devil."

The two colonels, Grant and de Winton, took offense at this

remark, felt duty bound to put in a good word for the Army and justify Wolseley's failure to save Gordon in Khartoum.

But Stanley cut them off as rudely. "Don't dish out hogwash to me, chaps," he said. "Wolseley made a thorough mess of the operation, and that's all there's to it. Good Lord, man, he had seven thousand hand-picked British troopers. If I had had command of a force like that, Gordon would be alive today. And you chaps know it. And that's why you sent for me for this job." He turned to Mackinnon. "I'll tell Salisbury he doesn't have to lose another night's sleep worrying that I'll draw him back into a war with the dervishes. I won't. I'll do this on my own, like I've always done. So let's not waste any more time with it and get on with the serious business."

Grant and de Winton shook their heads in exasperation, but Mackinnon smiled. Stanley's bravado pleased him. It was going to take just that sort of bullheaded arrogance to make a success of the expedition. "By all means, Henry," he said. "Let's get on with the serious business."

"First off then, what do we actually know about Emin's situation?"

"Not a great deal, I'm afraid." Mackinnon unbuckled his briefcase and extracted a few sheets of paper. "He's lost all his outlying garrisons to the north and west. That much we do know. The dervishes, coming out of Bahr al-Ghazal, overran them in the first assault. But he managed to pull back most of his forces to a chain of forts and trading posts along the Nile itself." He read from the papers in his hand. "There seem to be seven or eight of them, as best we can make out. Lado is the most northerly, the one most directly under siege, on the edge of the Sudd. Then Rejaf, Chor Ayu, Duffile and so on southwards upriver, maybe two hundred and fifty miles, to Wadelai, about thirty-five miles from the shore of Lake Albert. Apparently he's moved his headquarters to Wadelai, as far away as he can get from the dervish lines, but most of his troops are still concentrated at Lado." He looked up.

Stanley had taken out a cigar and was busily preparing it, but there was no doubt he was paying close attention.

"Obviously," Mackinnon went on, "his idea is to fight a series of rearguard spoiling actions when and if the dervishes make a full-scale assault, retreating upriver from each of these forts to the next until he's forced to make a final stand at Wadelai. I suppose he reckons that in this way he not only can gain time and make the dervishes pay dearly for every inch of ground they take but that he also can draw them out of the desert and into the grasslands and forests of the Lake Albert region, where they are bound to feel less at home and fight less effectively. My guess is that the dervishes must see it that way too and that's why they haven't launched a major assault. They probably figure they can save themselves a lot of bloodshed by simply starving the garrisons out."

Stanley nodded, lighting his cigar. "Do we know how many soldiers he's got?"

"About four thousand." Mackinnon consulted his papers again. "Egyptian officers, Sudanese troops. The Sudanese are mostly niggers, Dinkas, Nuers, Baris, and the like, not Moslems, that's why they've not gone over to the dervishes. He must have trained them pretty well too. They've certainly put up a good show so far. Besides that though, he's got two or three hundred clerks and tax collectors looking after the province's administration, plus their families, sundry traders, camp followers, and other civilians. There are probably ten thousand people hanging on out there with him."

"Let me have a look at that," Stanley said and, taking the papers from Mackinnon, leaned back in his chair puffing on the cigar.

Mackinnon and the others waited, giving Stanley all the time he needed to study the papers. A liveried servant looked into the billiards room to see if the gentlemen might be wanting something, was intimidated by the silence that had descended, and left without a word. Hutton and Grant lit cigars; after a bit so did Mackinnon, then de Winton filled and lit a meerschaum pipe. The room soon was thick with the pungent blue haze. Only Jephson didn't smoke; he sat rather stiffly on the edge of his chair, following everything with interest.

"Well, gentlemen," Stanley said, lowering the papers, "as I see it, I've got two jobs to do here." He dropped the papers on the table and reached for his teacup. "One is what all England is expecting me to do: get to Emin and get to him soon enough and with enough supplies and arms so that he doesn't go the way of Gordon. But that's only the half of it." He popped a small sandwich into his mouth. "If I've understood you chaps correctly," he said, then paused until he had swallowed what was in his mouth. "If I've understood the proposition you outlined in your letter, Mac," he began again, "our aim here is not so much simply to save Equatoria from the dervishes as it is to take it for ourselves. That's the deal you struck with Salisbury, isn't it? That's the quid pro quo. We put up all the money and run all the risks and get Salisbury off the hook in this ruckus, and in return Her Majesty's Government grants our committee a royal charter under which we take over Equatoria as our own private trading monopoly. Isn't that it, Mac?"

"That's it exactly," Mackinnon replied. "And it's a smashing deal, too, you must agree. Look what we'd get if we can bring it off. Those seven or eight forts and trading stations on the Nile. Those four thousand troops. A functioning administration of a couple hundred clerks and tax collectors and trading agents. And above all this remarkable Turk or whoever he is, this Emin Effendi, to run the whole bloody show. It's perfect, Henry. Everything we need is there. We wouldn't have to start from scratch. Under a royal charter from the Crown we can have an Imperial British East Africa Company in Equatoria to rival Goldie's Royal Niger Company, or Rhodes's British South Africa Company.

"Yes," Stanley said. "And that's why I say that my making a bold dash in there to rescue Emin from his present predicament isn't good enough. Oh, it would make the press and the public and Lord Salisbury happy as kittens in a punch bowl, I'm sure. But from our point of view, it's still only half the job. If we mean to develop and exploit Equatoria, we've got to be able to *keep* a flow of arms and supplies going in there so we can sustain and protect the province over the long haul. And that means I've got to open a permanent and secure route to the province over which we can keep sending in those supplies, a route that connects Equatoria to the outside world."

Mackinnon nodded.

"Which brings us to the question of the route."

"Henry, dear chap," Mackinnon said, "as you must know, we are all agreed that as regards the planning and execution of this expedition you are in sole command. Whatever you decide, we stand behind you. We are completely in your hands."

"I'm flattered," Stanley said dryly. "Nonetheless, I've no doubt that you have your own ideas on the matter. You have, Jem, don't you?" he said to Colonel Grant. "And so have you, Frank. I can see it in your eyes, old boy. How could you resist?"

Colonel de Winton smiled. "I suppose I have, Bula Matari. As a matter of fact, Jem and I have been having something of a lark going over our old charts."

"I'd be interested to know what you've come up with." Stanley turned to Jephson. "Let me have the valise, lad," he said and, taking it from the youth, undid its brass buckles and pulled out a large map of Africa. "Perhaps we had best use one of those billiard tables for this."

Suddenly there was a thrilling change in the atmosphere, a palpable ripple of excitement. Jephson felt it as the men pushed away from the tea things and gathered around the billiard table on which Stanley unfolded the map. It was the excitement of an adventure getting under way. Only one of the six men standing around the billiard table, Stanley himself, of course, would actually make the journey. But all of them now watching as Stanley spread the map out on the green baize surface and anchored its corners with ivory billiard balls, all of them could imagine for a moment making the trek with him into the heart of the continent that this sheet of parchment pictured.

The map was old and soiled, stained by some kind of oil or grease, much handled and beginning to tear and fray in the folds, a map that Jephson was sure Stanley had carried with him on his other journeys into Africa. There were all sorts of cryptic notations on it, in different color inks and lead, lines and circles and dashes and arrows, pyramids and squares and stars and crosses, words and phrases and numbers, notations clearly marked on it after the map had been printed, marked almost certainly by Stanley's own hand and marked by him, Jephson fancied, on the scene itself to indicate the routes he had taken and the discoveries he had made. It was a marvelous map, a living thing, as alive as memory, the memory of adventure transformed into an object that could be possessed forever.

"Go ahead, Frank," Stanley said, stepping back from the billiard table. "Show me how the matter appears to you and Jem."

"Well, let's see." Colonel de Winton picked up a cue stick to use as a pointer. "Here's our objective." He placed the felt tip of the cue stick on the southernmost portion of the Sudan, just a bit to the right or east of the virtual center of the map. "Lado," he said. "The stations along the river." He ran the cue stick down the map along the blue line tracing the Nile back to its source. "Wadelai, Lake Albert. As Mac says, we understand Emin has transferred his headquarters from Lado to Wadelai. Doubtless he gets up to Lado frequently and makes regular tours of inspection of all the river stations, but he probably spends most of his time in Wadelai these days, so we figure the expedition ought to make straight for it. It's where you'd have the best chance of catching up with him, and besides you'd be a safe two hundred or two hundred fifty miles south of the dervish lines there."

De Winton lifted the cue stick from the map and, leaning on it, turned to Stanley. "Jem and I reckon there are two feasible routes to Wadelai. There's no point wasting our time with the nonsense that's been flying around London since Emin's message arrived: fighting one's way up the Nile from Cairo or coming down out of the southwest from the Abyssinian highlands. That's just stuff for armchair geographers. The two routes Jem and I looked over are, we think, the only possible ones."

He turned back to the map and pointed at an island in the Indian Ocean just off the east coast of Africa at about six degrees latitude south of the equator. "And both begin here, in Zanzibar. You do the final outfitting of the caravan there, then cross over to the mainland here, at Bagamoyo." The cue stick flicked to a point on the coast opposite Zanzibar. "From Bagamoyo, the first leg of both routes is the same. West by northwest across this grassland plateau to Msalala, here, at the southern end of Lake Victoria. That's a fairly easy trek. The Arab trading caravans from Zanzibar make it regularly. You yourself made it when you went up to the Kabaka's kingdom in '77, and it's pretty much the same route Jem followed with Speke in '61. It shouldn't present any serious problems. Open country, friendly niggers by and large. Now, once at Msalala, there are two possibilities. One is to cut due north, straight across Lake Victoria like this, to the Kabaka's kingdom, and then keep on going through Buganda, through the forests of Bunyoro and come up on Lake Albert and Wadelai from the south."

Again de Winton lifted the cue stick from the map and turned to Stanley. "This is unquestionably the most direct, the shortest route," he said. "But it does pose a logistical problem: Where do you get the boats with which to cross Lake Victoria? You might reckon on acquiring them on the spot, from the tribesmen at Msalala. But that leaves a crucial element out of your control. Everything finally would stand or fall on whether the Msalala niggers have enough boats and whether and how quickly you could get hold of them. A way around that, of course, would be to bring the boats with you. But the number required would be considerable, and their portage from Bagamoyo to Msalala could so slow your progress on the first leg of the journey as to wipe out the advantage of the shorter distance of the second leg across the lake."

"Not to mention the hell you'd catch from the Buganda and Bunyoro," Grant put in. "Those buggers aren't exactly friendly you know. Speke and I had a beastly time with them. So did Baker. Without meaning to detract from Emin's bravery in hanging on in Equatoria, I'd wager one of the chief reasons he doesn't withdraw any farther south than Wadelai is because of the hostility of the

Buganda and Bunyoro at his back. You'd have a bloody time of it hacking your way through their country. I reckon the Kabaka alone could put two hundred thousand spears in the field against you."

"So Jem and I have sketched out this alternative," de Winton went on, turning back to the map. "You don't go north across the lake from Msalala but west, along the southern shore of Victoria, then keep going west until you reach the Karagwe country here. Only then do you turn north, when you're well west of the lake and well west of the Buganda and Bunyoro, then on up through the Nkole and Nkori country here and approach Lake Albert and Wadelai from the west. That way you circumvent both the problem of boats and the hostility of the Buganda and Bunyoro."

"That's clearly the best way, Henry," Colonel Grant put in again. "We're all pretty much agreed on it. The Nkole and Nkori ought not prove much trouble. You've dealt with worse. A few brisk skirmishes and they'll stay out of your way. They're nothing like the Buganda or Bunyoro. They've no experience with firearms. A few rounds from a repeating rifle and they'll clear off like rabbits."

"What's more, it's perfect for the second half of the job you were talking about a moment ago, Henry." This was James Hutton, the Manchester industrialist. "It's a route you could open up for us for the long haul. The first leg of it, up to Msalala, is open already. The Zanzibari Arabs have beaten a good track from village to village with trading stations and supply depots all along the way. All we'd need is a firman from the Sultan in Zanzibar to use them for ourselves and that wouldn't be hard to come by. As for the last leg, around Victoria, that's virgin territory, ours for the taking. As Jem says, a few sharp skirmishes and a display of firearms, and the chiefs in the region would come round to our way of thinking in a hurry. You could sign a few treaties establishing a right of way and whatever supply depots we might need in there, and we'd have a route connecting Equatoria to Bagamoyo and the outside world."

Stanley nodded. "I see you've not been wasting your time, gentlemen. You seem to have settled the matter of the route most satisfactorily."

"Hold on, Henry," Mackinnon said. "This isn't a matter for us to settle. I said before, we are all agreed that you're in command. Frank and Jem have put forward a suggestion, that's all, nothing more. This isn't settled until you settle it."

"It's a good route, Mac. It's the obvious one."

Mackinnon studied Stanley with searching eyes. "But it isn't the one you had in mind."

"I didn't say that. As a matter of fact, it was the first one that occurred to me when I received your letter."

"But?"

Stanley suddenly gave out a bark of laughter. "Christ, Mac, what's troubling you?" He turned to the other men, whose eyes were also fixed on him with a searching expression. "What's troubling the lot of you? I'm not quarreling with you, am I? You've done your work splendidly. You've selected the most obvious route, the very one that immediately sprang to *my* mind." He turned back to the billiard table as if about to begin folding up the map, but he hesitated. Leaning over the large soiled sheet, he stared at it as if something he saw there stayed his hand. And then he said softly, more to himself than to the others, "But there is another possibility."

"What is it?" Mackinnon asked, moving up behind Stanley to look at the map over his shoulder.

Stanley shook his head; now he did in fact begin folding the map.

"No, show it to us, Bula Matari." De Winton stopped him as he and the others again clustered around the billiard table. "Is it one that Jem and I didn't consider?"

"Not only is it one you and Jem didn't consider, Frank, I don't suppose even the most harebrained armchair geographer has considered it." Stanley smiled but not at anyone; he remained bent over the map. "Because in this one, you wouldn't start from Bagamoyo or anywhere on the Indian Ocean coast at all," he said. "You would start from the other side of Africa entirely." He placed his finger on the continent's Atlantic Ocean coast, less than an inch below the equator. "You would start from here."

Mackinnon was the first to recognize where Stanley's finger pointed. "The Congo?"

"Why would you ever want to start from the Congo?" de Winton asked in complete astonishment. "I don't see that at all."

"Don't you, Frank?" Stanley still did not turn around. "Then just follow me for a moment. Just imagine this for a moment." And slowly he began moving his finger along the thick blue line that marked the Congo River—the river he himself had discovered barely ten years before and had relentlessly explored ever since—tracing it from its mouth on the Atlantic, northeastward upstream across the equator into the heart of the continent to the point where it veered around, beginning a great arc back to the south. He stopped his finger at that point. "Just imagine, Frank, we would travel up the river to here, here just below Stanley Falls, here where the Aruwimi flows into the Congo, here at the village of Yambuya. Now where are we?"

"That's what I'd like to know," Grant interjected. "Where in blazes are we?"

"I'll tell you, Jem," Stanley replied. "We are only about three hundred miles west of Lake Albert. Look. Follow the Aruwimi River back toward its source, through the Ituri forest." And he proceeded to do that, tracing a line eastward from Yambuya practically straight across the center of the map through a large area shaded dark green, marking out a vast equatorial rain forest. "And we come out at the southern end of Lake Albert. Now, up the lake's western shore and, gentlemen, Wadelai."

"You can't be serious," de Winton said.

"Why not? I admit it's an unorthodox approach but it's not without merit, Frank. After all, very nearly two-thirds of the journey would be accomplished by waterway, on the Congo." Stanley retraced that portion of the route, from the Atlantic Ocean coast to Yambuya. "And that would represent a tremendous saving not only in wear and tear on the caravan but also, more importantly, in what will be the most precious commodity to me on this expedition: time. This is going to be a race, Frank. Time is everything in this. Once the dervishes get wind that a relief expedition is on the way, they're not going to be able to just lie back the way they've been doing and wait for Emin's garrisons to be starved out. They're going to have to attack then. They're going to have to attack with all they've got and try to take the place before the relief gets there. And Christ knows my chances of getting there with the relief before they do that would be a hell of a lot better traveling two-thirds of the way on the river than by marching the whole of it overland. On this route I'd only have to march the last three hundred miles or so overland." He ran his finger through the green-shaded area at the center of the map again. "I'd only have to march through the Ituri."

"And you'd lose everything marching through the Ituri that you might gain traveling on the river," Grant said. "Everything and then some. Because you'd never make it through the Ituri."

Stanley looked around at Grant. His square scarred face had taken on a stony expression; the muscles in his jaw bulged like steel ropes, and his slanted eyes were narrowed down to two burning points.

"For God's sake, Henry, how can you even suggest going through the Ituri. Nobody can make it through the Ituri," Grant went on, but he looked away from Stanley's piercing glare and over to de Winton for support. "Nobody ever has. Not even the Arab slavers dare venture into the Ituri. Not even Tippoo-Tib would dream of taking his raiders into that green hell. It would be madness, suicide to take this expedition in there."

"Jem's right, Henry," de Winton said more quietly but with no less grim certainty. "You know it yourself. You've seen that forest. You've stood at Stanley Falls and looked into it. There's only death in there."

"That's not the point," Hutton interjected. "Listen to me, Henry."

But Stanley didn't listen to him. He looked from Grant to de Winton and back again. His eyes still burned, but his voice was very soft. "You are mistaken, gentlemen," he said. "I could make it through the Ituri. Perhaps no one else could; but if I set myself the task, I would make it through."

"That's not the point," Hutton said again. "It doesn't matter whether you could make it through or not, Henry. If you say you could, I believe you. But it wouldn't do us the least bit of good. Because we could never use that route to supply Equatoria over the long haul. King Leopold would never allow us to run a permanent supply route through his territory. He has his own ambitions in that direction. You know that, Henry. He's aching to extend the northeastern border of the Congo Free State to the banks of the Nile. Only the difficulty of getting through the Ituri has stopped him so far. Are you listening to me, Henry?" Hutton took Stanley by the arm. "It's ludicrous to imagine that Leopold would allow—"

"Take your hand off me, Hutton."

"What?"

"Take your hand off me and stop blabbering at me like a bloody idiot."

Hutton's face went ashen. He stepped back. "I beg your pardon," he said icily.

"I'm perfectly aware of the objections to this route. I don't need to be lectured on them either by you or by Grant." Stanley turned back to the billiard table and folded up his map. "Now I think we had best get on to the next piece of business." He walked over to the tea table and picked up his valise. He replaced the map in it, then extracted several sheets of paper from it. "What I want to discuss now are the expedition's finances." He sat down at the table and began thumbing through these papers. "I've made some preliminary calculations as regards the cost of the outfitting and so on, but it would help me to know what funds I will actually have at my disposal."

"Henry," Mackinnon said.

Stanley looked up from his papers. None of the men had followed him to the tea table.

"Henry, this route you've proposed—"

"There's nothing further to be said about it."

"I think there is, Henry."

"No there isn't. Not unless you are having second thoughts about who is in command here."

"No, of course I'm not. There's no need to put it on that basis. But you must understand that you've rather startled us by proposing to take this Congo route."

"You weren't listening to me, Mac. I did not propose to take the Congo route."

"Excuse me?"

"I simply described it—and only at your urging, I might remind you—as an intriguing possibility because of the savings in time it would allow. But I said the route you chaps had settled on was the obvious one."

"Then I misunderstood you, Henry. Then I think we all misunderstood you."

"That may be."

"Are you saying you agree with Frank and me?" Grant asked. "The best route to Wadelai is from Bagamoyo?"

Stanley replied without bothering to look at the colonel. "How many times do you suppose I will have to say it before you get it through your thick skull?"

"Don't you speak to me like that! Don't you dare! I won't be spoken to like that."

"Jem, please," Mackinnon hastily intervened. "We've had a momentary misunderstanding, that's all. Let's drop it."

"No, I won't drop it. I won't put up with his beastly rudeness. I don't see why any of us should. I don't see why he can't behave like a gentleman for once in his life."

"Because I'm not a gentleman, Grant." Now Stanley did turn around. "And be bloody glad that I'm not. Because no *gentleman* would have a prayer-in-hell's chance of getting this expedition through to Equatoria."

The meeting lasted another hour. The tension eased somewhat as Stanley outlined the type of expedition he planned to mount, the men and equipment he would need. From time to time de Winton and Grant, drawing on their own African experiences, asked a question or made a suggestion, but neither disputed Stanley on any point; neither believed that he knew better than Stanley what would be required. And whatever would be required, he would have. Mackinnon assured him of that repeatedly. The committee had subscribed in excess of 40,000 pounds sterling; but if that should prove insufficient, additional funds could be raised without difficulty. Stanley need stint on nothing. The stakes were too high to allow a few thousand pounds one way or the other to jeopardize his chances for success. Everyone was agreed that this must be the best-equipped expedition ever to strike into the interior of Africa. And so by the time they broke off in order to let Stanley and Mackinnon get over to Whitehall for their meeting with Lord Salisbury, some of the camaraderie among the men had been restored and the flare-up over the Congo route largely forgotten.

But not by Jephson, because he remembered that mysterious misunderstanding in Delmonico's when the two New York journalists assumed that any return to Africa by Stanley would be on behalf of King Leopold II of the Belgians.

Snow had been falling lightly on and off all day, but by nine that night it was falling steadily, laying down a mantle on the London rooftops and chimney pots, dusting the shrubs and hedges in the parks and the holly wreaths hanging in the doorways, dimming the gas lamps to soft glow. There was no traffic in New Bond Street. Although it ran through the heart of the Mayfair district, where many of the better gaming clubs were located and where, therefore, one might ordinarily expect a parade of hansom cabs and merrymaking gentry at all hours, the street was deserted. Obviously the combination of weather and holiday had kept even the inveterate gamblers at home. Jephson peered through the oval window of his hack, trying to make out the number on the six-story brick building of mansion flats between an apothecary's and a greengrocer's at which the driver had stopped. Mr. Stanley's address was 160, and, yes, this was 160. Jephson glanced up and down the empty street to make sure no roughs were lurking about, then dashed through the snow into the building's dimly lighted vestibule.

Instantly he stepped back with a start.

"*Iko* Bula Matari," a gruff voice had called out of the darkness. "Who's there?"

"*Huyu ni nani?*"

"I say, Who's there? Step out into the light where I can see you."

A man in a reefer jacket and a workman's wool cap emerged from the shadows, but before Jephson could properly appraise him he realized someone else was back there in the darkness.

"Who's that you've got behind you?"

"*Njoo hapa, toto.*"

The other person now moved out into the light. It was a little boy, nine or ten years old, dressed in knickerbockers and vest, a woolen cape, and a long striped scarf, but his round, pretty face was as black as ebony, and golden earrings hung from his ears. By God, a perfect little blackamoor.

"The name's Troup, sir. John Rose Troup. And this here's Baruti. We're waiting for Mr. Stanley." The man doffed his cap to reveal a head of bright red hair. He also had a huge handlebar mustache, which might have seemed fierce except that the red color gave it a slight comic-opera air. A cigarette dangled from his lips. He was about forty years old. "Have you come for Mr. Stanley yourself? Baruti and me, we've been waiting for him the better part of two hours now. We'd just taken to sitting down back there when you stepped in, that's why you didn't see us right off. I'm sorry if we gave you a fright."

"He's not here then?"

"No, sir, he ain't."

"He expected to be here by nine. Well, I suppose he's been detained by the Prime Minister. But there's no reason to hang about down here. Why haven't you gone up to his flat?"

"Ain't no one there."

"No one? Surely Mr. Stanley's butler is there."

"Mr. Stanley don't have no butler, sir."

"Really? How odd. Are you sure?"

"Oh, yes, sir. Mr. Stanley don't keep servants of any kind."

"Well, I say, that's bloody inconvenient."

The man said something to the little blackamoor in a language incomprehensible to Jephson and the boy scooted back into the shadows and, wrapping himself snugly in his cape, sat down against the wall there.

"What language was that?" Jephson asked.

"Swahili."

"Swahili? Is the boy from Zanzibar?"

"No. He's from the Upper Congo, a village called Yambuya.

But they all speak Swahili up there since Tippoo-Tib moved into the region."

"Is he your servant?"

"Oh, no, sir." The man smiled and put his cap back on. "Baruti belongs to Mr. Stanley. He picked him up two or three years ago. The little fellow's kin were taken by Tippoo-Tib's slavers, but somehow he got away. Clever little bugger. Mr. Stanley found him hiding in the bush around Yambuya, and he's looked after him ever since. Sort of adopted him. He's been with me only since Mr. Stanley went off on his tour to America. I was meant to look after him until Mr. Stanley got back. But he's got back a lot sooner than any of us expected, ain't he?"

"Yes. Because of the Emin Pasha expedition."

"Yes."

"Have you come to see Mr. Stanley because of that?"

"To tell the truth, sir, I ain't really sure. I got a cable from him asking me to come by, but he didn't say anything in it about why. I haven't seen him since he left for America."

"Are you a friend of his?"

"Oh, I don't know I'd say *friend* exactly. But I've known him a long time. I worked for him in the Congo Free State when he was opening up the river for King Leopold. I was his transportation and supply officer."

"I see." Jephson walked over to the vestibule's entrance and peered out into the snow-blanketed street. There was no sign of Stanley. He rubbed his hands together briskly; he was getting rather chilled waiting around like this.

"Begging your pardon, sir, but do you mind my asking who you are?"

Jephson turned around quickly. "Oh, I'm terribly sorry, Troup," he said. "How awfully rude of me. My name is Arthur Mounteney Jephson. I've been engaged as secretary to the Emin Pasha Relief Committee. Actually I've spent the last two weeks with Mr. Stanley. I went over to New York to invite him to take command of the relief expedition and returned to London with him last night."

"Pleased to make your acquaintance." Troup shook Jephson's extended hand. Then he said, "Well, if you're here on account of this Emin Pasha business, could be so am I."

"Oh, yes, I'd think that very likely. Would it please you if it were?"

"It would." Troup removed the cigarette stub from his mouth

and flicked it out into the street, then took out a tobacco pouch and some paper and started rolling himself another. "It sure as hell would. Nothing'd please me better than to get back in the bush with Mr. Stanley again."

Jephson watched him make the cigarette, the deft, swift way his strong capable hands worked, then asked, "Did you say the boy . . . Baruti, did you say he comes from Yambuya?"

"Yes, sir." Troup lit his cigarette and left it dangling in the corner of his mouth.

"I think I know where that is."

"Oh, I kind of doubt that, sir. It's a bloody remote place."

"Isn't it where some other river—what was its name? the Aruwimi?—where the Aruwimi joins the Congo?"

"That's right. Good for you. How'd you know that?"

"Mr. Stanley mentioned it while going over the map with the relief committee this afternoon. It's right there at the edge of that big green patch in the middle of the map, the Ituri forest."

"That's it, sir. That's where Baruti comes from."

"Have you ever been in the Ituri forest, Troup?"

"In it? Well, I've been in Yambuya, and I suppose you're in it when you're there. It begins right there, you know."

"No, I mean have you actually gone into it, trekked through it?"

"Oh, no. No one has ever done that."

"Why not?"

"Shit." Troup grinned. "You'd never ask that if you'd ever once seen that green hell."

"You don't think anybody could get through it, I mean get clear through it and come out on the other side at Lake Albert?"

"Shit no." Troup burst out laughing.

"Not even Mr. Stanley?"

That stopped Troup. He removed the cigarette from his mouth. "Why do you ask that?"

"Mr. Stanley said something this afternoon about going through the Ituri."

Troup shook his head. "No," he said. "You didn't hear him right. Mr. Stanley couldn't have said anything like that."

Jephson studied Troup's suddenly very serious face. He wasn't sure whether he ought to press the matter, considering that Sir William had asked that what had been said at the committee meeting that afternoon be treated as confidential. But he didn't have to decide, because just then Stanley arrived and the little blackamoor went bounding across the vestibule and leaped into his arms.

"Hey, little monkey. *Hujambo. Habari? Uhali gani?*" Stanley, laughing, hoisted the child high on his chest and ruffled his woolly head. And then, with a bounce, he perched him on his hip so that he could look past him into the vestibule. "And where's Bwana Troup? What have you done with Bwana Troup, you little monkey? Haven't you brought him with you?"

Troup went toward Stanley instantly.

"There you are, John Rose Troup. There you are, you red-haired devil." Stanley stuck out his free hand. "How have you been faring? Has this monkey been giving you grief?"

"Not a bit, Bula Matari," Troup replied, grinning from ear to ear. "Not a bit."

The two men shook hands vigorously, almost violently; and although their faces were stretched wide by affectionate smiles, they stared into each other's eyes with an extraordinary fierceness.

"And Arthur," Stanley said, at last turning away from Troup. "I'm sorry to be so blasted late. An immense amount of hogwash at Whitehall. Damn near the whole Cabinet felt obliged to have their say. I expected the Queen herself to turn up to give me the benefit of her regal advice. I've got a terrible reputation with the lot of them. They're certain I'll start a war. Ah, to hell with them. Let's go on up and get something warm in our bellies." And still carrying the little blackamoor on his hip, he fumbled for his keys and led the way to the lift.

Stanley's apartment on the top floor was jammed in under the roof beams, a part of the building's attic space. To the left of the entry foyer were a drawing room, a library, and leading off from the latter the master bedroom and bath; to the right was the kitchen and pantry and behind that the servant's room. But it was perfectly obvious that no servant lived in the place. The apartment, or at least what Jephson saw of it when Stanley turned up the lamps, was a mess. The furnishings in the drawing room and library were decent enough—a few high-backed chairs standing against the walls, a sofa in front of the fireplace, a worn padded leather chair with an ottoman, some sturdy tables, shelves crammed with books, a sideboard, a grandfather clock, a pair of cabinets with glass fronts, a rolltop desk, heavy velvet curtains, Oriental rugs. But none of the pieces bore any stylistic relationship to any other; they all seemed to have been picked up at random and set down in the same thoughtless manner. And an astonishing clutter of stuff was scattered all over the place. Papers spilled from the tables or were piled on the chairs; packing crates were pushed in corners; a gun case stood open in the foyer; there was a jumble of brass instruments (Jephson recognized a telescope, sextant, and compass among them); a clutch of spears, canoe paddles, a ferocious mask, ebony carvings, some hide shields, and other such African artifacts leaned against the walls; a small stuffed cheetah guarded the door; the head of a horned water buffalo hung over the fireplace and that of a kudu adorned the space between the windows; lengths of cloth were draped over the sofa; the tanned skins of various beasts were scattered on the rugs; and in the middle of all this shambles stood one of Stanley's steamer trunks, still unpacked, with a Winchester repeating rifle propped up against it. The apartment had the look of a gypsy encampment, a temporary place between arrivals and departures, not anywhere a man actually made a permanent home.

Stanley, with Baruti riding happily on his hip, strode through the mess without any thought of offering an excuse for it. He swept some papers from the sofa to make room for his guests to sit, added a few lumps of coal to the fireplace and stoked up the embers, then stepped over an African drum to reach the sideboard, upon which stood an array of liquor bottles and glasses.

"First you, my little monkey. What will you have? Something sweet? Let me see. How about cherry brandy?" He poured that into a small glass and handed it to the child. "And Jack, old boy. For you and me it'll be Irish whiskey to fight the fever, eh? And you, Arthur, what will you have?"

"I'll join you and Mr. Troup in the whiskey."

"Fine." Stanley poured out three tumblers. "Here you are, lads. To warm the heart on a cold night."

Jephson and Troup sat down on the sofa in front of the fireplace. Stanley took the leather chair facing them, Baruti on his lap, his feet on the ottoman.

"Happy Christmas, lads. Happy Christmas, my little monkey." He clinked glasses with the child, then drank off nearly a third of his whiskey in a single swallow. "It's good to see you, Jack." With one hand resting on Baruti's head, he scratched the child absently as he might a pet dog while the boy nestled closer, sleepily. "Jack was with me in the Congo Free State for damn near five years, Arthur. One of my best lieutenants there. No, by Christ, the best of them." He raised his glass to Troup and took another generous swallow. "And he stayed another year after I cleared out. He only got back this summer. Six years on that bloody river. And bloody it is too, eh, Jack?"

"And getting bloodier all the time," Troup replied, grinning.
"How's the malaria?"
"It's run its course."
"No more attacks?"
"Not one since you've been in America."
"So you're fit for work. Have you found employment yet?"
"I've a chance at something. At a shipping line."
"Which one?"
"Where you put in a word for me. The British India Steamship Company."
"What kind of work does Mac have for you?"
"In the mail department, mostly having to do with the packets sailing for Zanzibar."
"That sounds fine. Doesn't that sound fine to you, Jack?"
"To tell the truth, it don't."
"No? Why not? What would you rather do?"
Troup stubbed out his cigarette in an onyx ashtray on a deal table by the sofa. "Well, if you're asking me, Bula Matari, I'll tell you. What I'd rather do is go up there to Albert Nyanza with you and save that Turk from the dervishes."
Stanley gave out a bark of laughter. "Christ, man, what's the matter with you? Haven't you had enough of Africa yet?"
"No more than you have."
"Come now, Jack. Here you have a chance at some honest employment for a change. Here you have a chance to settle down and earn decent wages and maybe find yourself a nice wife and have some kids and lead a respectable life. What the hell do you need to go back to Africa for and risk your neck another time?"
"I could ask the same of you, Bula Matari."
Stanley laughed again.
"And the answer would be the same," Troup said.
Stanley shook his head, still smiling, "I suppose it would," he said. "Well, in that case, John Rose Troup, welcome to the Emin Pasha relief expedition."
"Goddamn," Troup exclaimed and stamped his foot. "Goddamn, Bula Matari."
Sprawled in the leather chair, the child on his lap, his granite face wreathed in his most winning smile, Stanley held out his glass to Troup. "Drink your whiskey down, man. Drink it down to the bottom and that'll seal the bargain."
Troup threw back his head and poured the contents of his glass down his gullet without pausing for a breath.

"You're my first gunman, Jack. You're the first one I've signed on."

"Is that right?" Troup gasped, his eyes tearing from the hit of the whiskey. "But what about Mr. Jephson here? Ain't he going?"

"Are you going, lad?" Stanley asked.

Jephson sat up with a start at the question.

"No, he ain't going," Stanley said. "No, Jack, I ain't signed nobody on yet except you." He leaned forward as he said this and began gathering up some of the papers he had swept to the carpet to make room for Jephson and Troup on the sofa. "No, Jack, it's just you and me so far. But we've got plenty of chaps who want to go with us."

Troup watched Stanley gather up perhaps thirty of the sheets.

"Do you know what these are?" Stanley asked, handing the stack to Troup. "They're letters of application from chaps who want to go with us. They've been arriving in the post by the score every day. There are hundreds of them by now. Look around. There, over there. Literally hundreds of them from every part of Britain, from all over the world. From men of every condition and station in life. Soldiers, sailors, engineers, waiters, mechanics, cooks, servants, spiritual mediums, magnetizers, somebodies, nobodies. They're all mad to go with us, Jack, to save the noble Turk from the dervishes, to win glory, to escape wives, to make a fortune, to gain publicity, to test their skills, to discover their manhood, to become heroes. What do you say, Jack? Let's sort through them and pick out the best and take them along with us."

Troup dropped the sheaf of papers on the carpet without looking at them. "No," he said.

"Why not? Among so many, there are bound to be some who would be suitable for this adventure."

"We already know who would be suitable for this adventure."

Stanley sat back in his chair idly petting the dozing black child in his lap. "Who?" he asked.

Troup leaned forward. "Hoffman," he said. "Willie Hoffman, for one."

"Where is he?"

"Here in London, living in the East End. He got back a month before I did. I saw him a week ago. We had a drink together in a Cheapside pub the day the newspapers announced you were going after the Turk."

"What's he doing?"

Troup shrugged. "Only the Lord ever knows what Willie

Hoffman's doing. He's doing what he knows best how to do. Something different every day, I suspect."

Stanley nodded. "Can you get in touch with him?"

"Sure."

"Get in touch with him then."

"Sure."

"All right. Who else?"

"Leslie."

"Yes, Leslie. We'll want Dick Leslie."

"He's also back in London. He's set up a surgery in Harley Street. I know where it is. I can get in touch with him too."

"Do that. How about Bertie Ward? Is he around?"

"No. He's still on the Congo. Last I heard he was at Equator Station. His contract's got another year to run, I think."

"That doesn't matter. I'll buy him out of it. I want him with us. Get word to him. Tell him what's on. He can go straight around the cape from Banana and meet us in Zanzibar. We'll let him know when."

"I'll do that."

"Good. Who else?"

"That's five, counting you and me. Were you figuring you'd need more?"

"Yes."

"Well, if you don't mind me saying, Bula Matari, that's something I couldn't hardly know, on account I ain't got a clear idea what kind of expedition you've got in mind. All I know about it is what I've been reading in the newspapers and that ain't much. They ain't written a word about the route even let alone how big a caravan you mean to drive or how many white men you'll need to drive it."

"You're right, Jack. I tell you what. It's getting late. Let me put this monkey to bed and then I'll sketch out the expedition I'm planning so you'll have something to worry about overnight, and we'll go over details tomorrow." Stanley stood up carefully, so as not to wake the little blackamoor in his arms.

"This is bloody marvelous," Troup exclaimed, jumping up from the sofa once Stanley had left the room. "No bloody office job for you, Jack Troup. It's back to Africa, back into the bush where you belong." He began pacing around the cluttered sitting room, grinning, stroking his big red mustache.

Jephson couldn't help smiling at his pleasure. "Is it really so splendid in Africa, Troup?" he asked.

"Eh?" Troup stopped pacing. "You've never been there, have you, sir?"

"No, but I always rather fancied it was a beastly place, you know, full of savages and wild animals and snakes and insects and diseases—and that awful climate. Jesus, anything but splendid."

Troup laughed. "Yes, it's beastly like that, all right. But it's also splendid, in other ways. And anyway, whatever it is, it suits me a sight better than being cooped up in an office from morning till night. Whooee, I had a narrow escape there." He resumed his pacing. After a bit he stopped at Stanley's steamer trunk and picked up the Winchester rifle. "Maybe that's what I like best about it," he said, fiddling idly with the rifle's repeating mechanism. "Not being cooped up. You can't ever get cooped up in Africa. There's so much of it out there. It goes on forever. There are places out there where you can be the only white man."

"And not just the only one. *The first one*," Stanley said, pausing in the drawing room's doorway; he had put Baruti to bed in the servant's room behind the pantry.

It was quiet for a moment, the only sounds those of the jets hissing in the gas lamps, the coal crackling in the fireplace, the grandfather clock ticking. Jephson hoped Stanley would say something further. The idea of being the first white man somewhere—it gave him gooseflesh. But Stanley went over to a big mahogany table that dominated one end of the drawing room and began rummaging through the papers scattered on it.

"Come here, Jack." Stanley found what he was looking for: a map. "Let's have a look at this," he said, clearing the rest of the papers from the table so he could spread it out.

Jephson went over as well and watched as Stanley sketched out the expedition's route for Troup.

It was the route the relief committee had agreed upon at the Athenaeum earlier in the day: from Zanzibar across to Bagamoyo, northwestward to Msalala at the southern end of Lake Victoria, westward along the lake's southern shore to the Karagwe country, then the wide arc north through the Nkole and Nkori country to Lake Albert. While tracing the route, Stanley made various observations about its difficulties and advantages, and to all of this Troup, lighting one cigarette after another, made few comments, and those only by way of elaboration and agreement, understanding everything quickly and easily.

When Stanley finished, he fell silent for an instant, staring at the map, and Jephson thought he would now say something about the other route that he had had in mind, the one through the Congo. But, oddly enough, he didn't. When he began speaking again it was to describe Emin Pasha's position or at least as much of it as was known—much of which Jephson had already heard at the Athenaeum that afternoon. And this too Troup followed with only occasional interjections or questions, tugging on his mustache, taking in the situation that Stanley described with a practiced eye.

"Well, there you have it, Jack," Stanley said. "What do you think?" He went over to the sofa where Troup and Jephson had been sitting and lay down on it, throwing his legs up on the cushions. "Nothing to it, eh?"

Troup too walked away from the map and sat down on the steamer trunk, picking up the Winchester rifle again. "This is a beauty," he said.

"We'll have plenty of them," Stanley said.

"It'll be a lark with stuff like this." Troup sighted along the rifle's barrel, pointing it down between his shoes. "As long as we move fast enough." He placed the rifle across his knees and leaned forward. "That's the only real problem, ain't it, Bula Matari? Moving fast enough. Them dervishes ain't going to hold off once they get wind a relief expedition is on the way. It's going to be a race then, ain't it?"

Stanley, his hands behind his head, nodded, looking at the ceiling.

"So what we want is a column big enough to carry the supplies the Turk needs but not so big that we can't make good speed," Troup continued. "What were you figuring? A thousand *pagazis?* No more than that. You break the stuff down into sixty-pound loads, and a thousand porters will handle it just fine. Along with maybe thirty, forty baggage animals."

"Something like that."

"Well, hell, then me and Hoffman and Ward and Leslie is all we need. We can manage a column that size, no trouble. We've managed them bigger in our day. We hire on half the *pagazis* in Zanzibar, right? Five or six hundred Wanyamwezi with a solid cadre of their chiefs and headmen and pick up however more we need from time to time in fresh relays along the way. Mpwapwa, Tabora, Msalala."

"And who'll manage the askaris?"

"What askaris? I didn't say anything about askaris."

"Well, you should have." Stanley swung his legs off the sofa and stood up. "Christ, man, are you getting soft in your old age?

On an operation like this you had better reckon on having at least two companies of askaris with you. We're not likely to run into much fighting on the first leg, up to Msalala, I'll give you that. But once we start through the Nkole and Nkori country, we'll need professional troops escorting the column."

"The Nkole and Nkori? What are you talking about? They ain't any kind of real trouble."

"What do you know about them?" Stanley snapped. "What do you know what those kaffirs might not try? A valuable caravan like ours loaded with ammunition and stuff, Christ, it's bound to tempt them. And I tell you, Jack, I don't aim to lose time fighting them off every step of the way with nothing more than a pack of scared Wanyamwezi porters. I aim to get through to that Turk in time. And two hundred askaris armed with weapons like that"—he pointed at the Winchester in Troup's lap—"they'll get me through. They'll keep the kaffirs off at a respectful distance." He turned away from Troup and walked over to the sideboard. "And for that I'm going to need two or three Regular Army officers," he said. "You and Hoffman and the rest of our boys can take care of the *pagazis* all right. But I need a couple of veteran Army officers with experience in Africa to handle a tough troop of professional soldiers who can fight their way through the worst country for me."

Troup's face was a mask of bewilderment. He patently didn't agree with what Stanley was saying and Jephson was sure he would argue about it. But he didn't; he looked down at the rifle on his knees and said nothing.

"They would have to take leave from their regiments if not resign outright," Stanley was saying, reaching for the bottle of Irish whiskey on the sideboard. "They couldn't go with us in any official capacity and, God forbid, compromise Her Majesty's Government. But that shouldn't be difficult to arrange. Not with the furor this thing has stirred up. Wolseley will cooperate. I'll go over to the War Office and talk to him about it." He poured himself another glass of whiskey. "All right, Jack, that's how we'll do it. You get hold of Hoffman and Leslie and send word to Ward, and I'll see about finding us a couple of good soldiers to manage the askaris. Here, let me have your glass."

"No," Troup said, standing up. "I'd best get on my way. I have an idea where I can still catch up with Hoffman tonight."

"Have a last nip for the road."

Troup hesitated.

"For Christ sake, Jack." Stanley walked over to Troup and

poured a finger of whiskey into his glass. "It's good having you aboard, Jack. It's good to be working with you again."

"Same here, Bula Matari."

Stanley clinked Troup's glass and broke into a wide grin. "Christ, Jack, it's good to be on the move again, ain't it? Setting off for Africa again. Leaving all this smoke and snow and shit behind. Oh, Christ, we're going to have us some fun before we're done, ain't we? We're going to do some things and see some places the likes of which ain't never been done or seen before. We're going to make them sit up and take notice. We're going to show them we ain't finished yet. We're going to amaze those bastards one more time before we pack it in. Drink up, John Rose Troup, and let's get this bloody adventure under way."

· THREE ·

JEPHSON SAW Willie Hoffman as soon as Baruti opened the door. It was impossible not to see him; he was huge, well over six feet, surely more than twenty stone, rather more beefy than muscular but unmistakably powerful by virtue of his great fleshy size. But what was most startling about him was that he was completely hairless. At first Jephson thought that he merely kept his head shaved—it was an ugly scarred pink cannonball of a head—but when Hoffman turned to see whom Baruti had let into the flat, Jephson realized the man had no eyebrows or eyelashes either; his dull blank stare seemed eternally unblinking, like that of a fish.

Hoffman too had served with Stanley on the Congo; but although Jephson never did learn the details, he had also been with Stanley on other journeys and on his own in other parts of Africa before that. Now he stood huge and hairless by one of the drawing room's windows, wearing a slightly soiled shirt under a short leather coat, and heavy boots into which his trousers were tucked. Evidently, he had nothing to do, nor did he make any pretense of doing anything. He simply lounged in the window frame, his big meaty hands hanging at his sides while his dull unblinking eyes roamed around vacantly, from Jephson's face to the snow falling outside to Dr. Leslie sitting on the couch.

Dr. Richard Leslie was an ordinary-looking man, seeming neither more nor less than what nowadays he represented himself to be: a family physician with a struggling practice in Harley Street. The fact that he, like Troup and Hoffman, had served with Stanley in the Congo Free State—in his case as medical officer at the innermost station at Stanley Falls, where he had gained an almost magical reputation for his cures against the fever—did not in the least show in his physical appearance or bearing. He was small and birdlike, sallow in complexion, with a pince-nez perched on his sharp beak of a nose, a brush of a mustache under that, his gray hair thinning away on top; he sat quietly, almost timidly, on the couch in front of the fireplace in Stanley's drawing room, his hands folded neatly in his lap. Stanley sat next to him, talking intently. Troup hovered nearby, occasionally putting in a word of his own.

Hoffman and Leslie had arrived at the apartment an hour or so in advance of Jephson, and Stanley had already described the Emin Pasha relief expedition and invited them to join it. Hoffman had agreed on the spot; he was down on his luck, had nothing better to do. Leslie, however, was a different case. Since returning from the Congo more than two years before, he had married, had had a child, had moved into a nice house in Norbury, and had bought a share in a medical practice in London, which he was working hard to build up; and therefore understandably he regarded the idea of chucking all this over to go off on an expedition to Africa as quite out of the question.

Stanley's argument, at the point where Jephson came into the flat, seemed in the main to be that Leslie would not have to chuck everything over; he would only need to take a leave of absence, so to speak, of several months. Leslie, for his part, speaking softly, somewhat haplessly, was trying to explain that the sort of life he now led could not reasonably be interrupted even for that length of time. Perhaps if he were more securely established . . . but under the circumstances . . . after all, he had his responsibilities. He would certainly lose his patients to another physician while he was away and would have to start his practice from scratch when he got back, and that was to say nothing of the adverse effect his absence would have on his wife and baby. Stanley's answer to that, given with a bark of laughter, was that Leslie's participation in such a widely publicized enterprise as the Emin Pasha expedition would make him one of the most famous physicians of his time; patients would flock to his surgery upon his return, his practice would boom, and his wife and child couldn't help but regard him with ever more respect and adoration as a result. And so it went, back and forth, argument countered by argument, objections raised and rebutted, Leslie looking up from his folded hands from time to time to face the fiercely intense gaze of Stanley's narrow gray-green eyes and his appealing, irresistible smile.

From what Jephson heard of the exchanges, it seemed to him that Leslie had the best of the argument. All logic was on his side, all common sense ruled against his signing on for the expedition. And yet, almost from the start, Jephson knew that Leslie would sign on. He couldn't say why. It wasn't that Stanley made some finally persuasive argument that was able at last to overcome the strongest of Leslie's objections. The actual back and forth had very little to do with it; indeed there was something rather mechanical, even ritualistic about it, as if it were being conducted merely for the sake of appearances, an obligatory procedure to be gotten through in order to demonstrate that men made choices like this for sensible reasons. No, what worked on Leslie, assailed his position, prevailed against his logic, what lured him however reluctantly toward capitulation occurred beneath the surface of the talk, apart from the formal exchanges of logical argument. It was something unspoken, perhaps unspeakable, a tension that bound the doctor and Stanley, and Troup as well and probably also Hoffman and even the little blackamoor Baruti, and it involved memories and longings that Jephson could only guess at but not share. He looked around the cluttered room, this gypsy encampment of a room, at the shiny brass explorer's instruments, the much handled maps, the spears and warrior shields against the walls, the rifle, and he wondered about those memories and longings of Africa that he could not share.

Troup sat down on the couch on Leslie's other side, squeezing the doctor closer to Stanley. And then Stanley, in a surprisingly feminine gesture, took Leslie's hands and held them in his own. "We need these, Doctor Dick," he said in his rough, low voice. "We would not be safe without them."

Leslie looked down at his hands, allowing Stanley to hold them. "You will be the death of me yet, Bula Matari," he said with a sigh. "I thought I had escaped you." Then he withdrew his hands and used them to polish his pince-nez on his cravat. "What shall I tell my wife?" he asked. "What shall I tell her, the poor dear? She never bargained for this." He closed his eyes, obviously not expecting a reply.

Stanley leaned back. Troup, grinning broadly, threw an arm around Leslie's shoulders and hugged him to his chest. "Goddamn, Doctor Dick!" he exclaimed. "I knew you wouldn't want to be left behind. I wouldn't have gone without you, you know. I told that to Mr. Stanley. I told him I ain't going unless we got Doctor Dick to take care of us. Ain't that what I said, Bula Matari?"

Leslie didn't look at either Troup or Stanley. He had worn galoshes because of the snow, which he had removed when he arrived, and he bent down now and began pulling them on. "I've got to get back to my surgery," he said. "There must be a mile-long queue of patients there wondering what's become of me."

He stood up, stamping his feet into the overshoes. "I've got to make arrangements for them. I've got to find a physician to look after them. Good Lord, I've got a million things to do." He put on his Inverness coat and a deerstalker cap, and picked up his walking stick. "I'll be back in a few days."

"Whenever you can manage," Stanley said, getting up from the couch. "But be a good chap and look in on Messrs. Burroughs and Wellcome in the Snowhill Buildings on your way home today, won't you? Just give them an idea of the medicines and supplies you'll be wanting. Get them started on that."

"Yes, all right."

"You needn't stint on anything. Order whatever you feel is necessary. Money isn't a factor in this."

"Very good."

"And also I was thinking we ought to have everyone inoculated before we actually strike into the interior, so you'll keep that in mind too, won't you?"

"Yes, yes. I know what's wanted. I know everything that's wanted. That's why you talked me into this lunatic enterprise, isn't it? Because I know everything that's wanted."

"Yes, that's why," Stanley said, and he put an arm around Leslie and accompanied him to the door. And there, before allowing the doctor to depart, he said again, "We are in your hands, Doctor Dick. If we survive this, if we come home alive, it will be because of you."

The plans and arrangements for the askaris, as well as for the military supplies to be brought to Emin's relief, were held in abeyance for the moment. Stanley first wanted to recruit the two or three Regular Army officers that he intended to have on his staff so that he could tap their expertise for that part of the job. But with Troup, Hoffman, and Leslie signed on—and Herbert Ward cabled in Africa and expected to join the expedition—work could proceed on organizing and outfitting the rest of the caravan.

Stanley and Troup drew up lists of the equipment needed. Most of the items, like the medical supplies for which Leslie went to Messrs. Burroughs and Wellcome, could be acquired in England. For example, Stanley put in an order at Messrs. Forest and Sons for a galvanized-steel boat of his own design, twenty-eight feet long, six feet in the beam, and two and a half feet deep, that could be disassembled into twelve sections, each seventy-five pounds in weight, for easier porterage. Messrs. Fortnum and Mason of

Piccadilly were commissioned to pack up forty loads, each sixty pounds in weight, of tea, coffee, liquor, meat extract, jams, and other choice provisions to supplement and enliven the diet of the white men. The order for the tents went to Messrs. John Edgington and Co. of Duke Street with instructions that the canvas be specially treated with a preservative of sulphate of copper to withstand the African rains. And hunting guns and ammunition were to come from Messrs. Kynoch and Co., Birmingham, and Messrs. Watson and Co. of Pall Mall.

But what perhaps was the most important item of all could not be had in England, and that was the "currency," or trading goods, with which the caravan would purchase provisions, principally food of course, during the journey itself. Obviously there was no earthly way the expedition could supply itself at the outset with enough food to feed more than a thousand mouths for several months. Some of it, the fresh meat, would be gotten by hunting, but the staples—the cassava and manioc, maize and yams and rice, the plantains and bananas, the poultry, eggs, and milk—on which the caravan would live from day to day would have to be bartered for with the tribesmen of the lands through which it would pass. The medium of this barter, called *mitako*, differed from locale to locale. It was cloth and beads of various colors, materials, and sizes in some places; brass or iron or copper wire, either in coils or cut into eighteen-inch rods, in others. The experts on what was negotiable currency and where could only be found at the firms that serviced the Arab trading caravans that had introduced the concept of currency to the African interior. So a cable was sent to Zanzibar to Messrs. Smith, Mackenzie and Co., the agent for one of the largest of these firms, placing an order for nearly 30,000 yards of cotton cloth and sheeting, 4,000 pounds of beads, and over 2,000 pounds of wire.

In addition, the Smith, Mackenzie agency was instructed to put word out to the Wanyamwezi chiefs and headmen of the island that 600 *pagazis* would be wanted from among their people. The Wanyamwezi, although natives of Zanzibar, Swahili speakers, and Moslems like the Muscat Arabs who ruled the island, were not themselves Arabs but of a mixed race, descendants of black Africans from the interior who had been brought down to the coast over the centuries by Arab slavers and ivory hunters. They were great travelers. Perhaps because of a touch of the Arab in their blood, but in any case unlike the pure Africans of the interior, they were willing to journey stupendous distances from home.

Strong, intelligent, and peaceable, they regularly served as porters in the Arab trading caravans and had served as well with Burton, Speke, Grant, Livingstone, and Stanley himself on their famous journeys of exploration. They were to form the backbone of the expedition. It was understood that in various stretches along the way, depending on the nature of the terrain and the difficulties of the march, additional *pagazis* would be required, often as many as 500 or 600 more, and they would be hired from the local tribes as needed and paid off when they refused to go any farther. But the Wanyamwezi would be taken on for the entire journey; they were meant to travel the full distance to Wadelai and back, and their selection was a vital business. Willie Hoffman was put in charge of it, and he departed for Zanzibar on December 28.

Jephson at first was given the job of looking after the paperwork—keeping the minutes of the relief committee meetings, writing up requests to the War Office and the Admiralty, handling the transactions with the banks, drawing up the contracts for the expedition staff, and so on—but after a few days Stanley also had the youth lend Jack Troup a hand in following up on the orders to the various outfitters and suppliers. Jephson liked working with Troup. The redhead, with his slightly comical brigand's mustache, was a wonderfully sweet-tempered man. His competence was impressive, the enormous skills and experience that he brought to the job were evident in the ease and sureness of everything he did; but out of an innate modesty or because of his absolute confidence in his ability he ungrudgingly shared his knowledge with Jephson as if there were nothing special about it. He always had time to answer the youth's questions, to explain why a particular piece of equipment was needed, how it would be used in the field. In an offhand good-natured way he took Jephson under his wing and became his tutor in the arcane business of mounting an African expedition. And although he was ever mindful of the difference in their class and showed Jephson the deference a member of the aristocracy could expect from a workingman, an easygoing friendship grew up between them.

All the equipment was shipped out to Zanzibar as soon as it came ready, but not all of it came ready at the same time. Standard items such as billhooks and axes could be had in sufficient quantities in a matter of days straight off the suppliers' shelves; but others—the tents for example, which had to be made up from the specially treated canvas—took considerably longer, and the galvanized-steel boat with its complicated disassembly design took longer still. In addition, Stanley insisted on inspecting samples of every item and not infrequently found something wrong or improvements that could be made and had the work done over, adding to the delays. Thus there was a dizzying array of deliveries to be kept track of, intricate shipping schedules to be worked out, warehouse space to be booked on the docks in London, Southampton, Plymouth, and other ports, outfitters repeatedly visited and hurried, bills of lading and invoices checked and filed, payments made. And so Jephson was sent rushing about to consult with shipping agents, talk with sea captains, call on manufacturers, wait at the telegraph office for cables from Africa, and sift through blizzards of paper at Stanley's flat. It was the most work he had ever done in his life. Moreover, Troup was scheduled to follow Hoffman out to Zanzibar within the fortnight to supervise the purchase of the trading *mitako* and baggage animals; and it was altogether likely that he would depart before all the equipment came ready, which meant that it would be left to Jephson to see that the last bits and pieces were shipped out safely. And that was the most responsibility he had ever been entrusted with in his life. Men's lives would depend on it, literally. That fact both awed and exhilarated him, and he threw himself into the work with an enthusiasm bordering on panic.

He couldn't tell what Stanley thought of the job he was doing. Stanley never had a word of praise for him or for that matter for anyone. He came and went in a whirlwind of activity himself, barking out orders impatiently, looking furious or harassed or preoccupied. He was endlessly drawing up lists on scraps of paper and revising them on backs of envelopes, checking and double-checking the supplies and equipment that were being ordered and always adding to them (to Troup's consternation) and scattering these scraps of paper wherever he went. He was a fireball of energy, a bulldog of determination, possessed by the need to get the expedition under way, to reach Emin Pasha's beleaguered garrisons in time.

On the morning of the last day of 1886, when only Stanley and Jephson and the little African boy Baruti happened to be there, Captain Robert Harry Nelson of Methuen's Horse turned up at the New Bond Street flat. He was dressed in the blue uniform of his celebrated cavalry regiment, a sandy-haired man in his early thirties with a deep suntan, somewhat above the average in height, with a grand physique, rather like that of a middleweight prizefighter, his mustache waxed and twisted upward and his sideburns barbered on a slant in what was then the fashion among cavalry officers; over his left breast pocket he wore two rows of combat decorations and campaign ribbons. He was standing at attention when Baruti opened the door and never batted an eyelash at the sight of the little golden-earringed blackamoor, as if he had expected nothing else.

Stanley, in shirt-sleeves, looked up. He had just cracked open a case of tenting canvas and with Jephson's help was about to pay out the material for inspection. He studied the figure in the doorway long enough to decipher the regimental flash on the chap's uniform. Then, getting to his feet, he said in apparent surprise, "Methuen's Horse? Is that Captain Nelson?"

"Yes, sir. How do you do, sir? It is a great honor to meet you, Mr. Stanley."

"But how in blazes did Wolseley get hold of you so quickly?" Stanley walked over to the cavalry officer, dragging the tenting canvas after him. "He told me you were garrisoned in Cape Town."

"I was, sir. But I've been back in Eugland since the first of the month. On detached duty at the Pentworth barracks. Apparently the War Office files aren't quite as up to date as they might be."

"Well, I say, this is a stroke of luck. I'm delighted to see you, Captain. Lord Wolseley speaks very highly of you. Come in. This is Arthur Mounteney Jephson. He's secretary to the relief committee, but just at the moment I'm having him do some donkey work helping me determine the quality of this canvas that Edgingtons have sent around for my approval."

"Edgingtons usually do excellent work in that line of equipment, I've found," Nelson said. "We've used their tents in the Kalahari, and they've stood up smashingly."

"Is that so? How does this stuff strike you?" Stanley handed over the canvas he was holding.

Nelson tucked his visored cap under his arm, took the material from Stanley, and crumpled a patch of it in his hand. "A bit stiff," he said after a moment. "Copper sulphate treated, is it?"

"That's right."

"Depends on the conditions under which you mean to use it, I'd say. Wouldn't do at all for us in the Kalahari. Far too dry there for this. But I daresay it would be just fine if you were reckoning on heavy dampness and rains."

Stanley nodded. "That's precisely what I am reckoning on, Captain." He took the canvas from Nelson and returned it to its case, dumping it in an untidy heap.

"In the lakes region, that would be, I suppose," Nelson said, following Stanley into the drawing room. "Plenty of rain and damp there."

"Yes, there certainly is." Stanley cleared some clutter from the sofa in front of the fireplace and gestured to Nelson to sit down. "Would you care for some coffee or tea, Captain? Or perhaps a glass of port?"

"No, thank you, sir. But do you mind if I smoke?"

"No, of course not. Here. Try one of these. They're American, from Havana."

"Thank you." Nelson took a cigar from the box Stanley opened on the table in front of the sofa. "You will be making for Equatoria through the lakes region then? Through the Buganda and Bunyoro country?"

"Somewhat to the west of that," Stanley replied, taking a seat in his leather chair. "Karagwe, Nkole, Nkori, through there."

"Ah, yes."

"Do you know that country?"

"I've never been that far north myself, sir, but I've heard of it."

"And? What do you think?"

"It's bound to be easier going than through the Buganda and Bunyoro. Those kaffirs have turned ugly, haven't they? Not like they used to be when you first went through there."

"So it seems." Stanley stretched his legs out on the ottoman. "Tell me, Captain, how far north of Cape Town have you been?"

"Not terribly far, I'm afraid, sir. There's no call for British troops much beyond the Limpopo River, you know, but I did once make a trek through Bechuanaland to the Zambezi with a small detachment. Chasing Zulu marauders."

"Ah, yes, Lord Wolseley mentioned that. You fought in the Zulu wars, didn't you, Captain? In '79 and '80. With the Cape Mounted Rifles."

"Yes, sir."

"And with some distinction, I gather."

"Thank you."

"That's the decoration there, isn't it?" Stanley pointed at one of the ribbons on Nelson's chest. "The Victoria Cross."

Jephson, who had been fiddling with repacking the tenting canvas with Baruti's help, turned around with sudden curiosity. Jesus, the Victoria Cross! He looked at Nelson's leathery tanned face with new interest.

"What was that all about?" Stanley asked.

"Oh, just the usual sort of thing, sir. Our unit got into a spot of trouble with the kaffirs at Rorke's Drift and we had a bit of hot fighting to pull ourselves out of it."

Stanley sat forward waiting for Nelson to describe the skirmish. But Nelson chose that moment to light his cigar. He took a long time about it. Stanley watched him; so did Jephson. But when Nelson at last blew out his match, he still didn't say anything, a pleasantly bland expression on his face.

"I take it you don't care to avail yourself of this opportunity to do a bit of bragging, Captain," Stanley said with a smile.

"Oh, I promise you, Mr. Stanley, there's nothing to brag about," Nelson replied. "It was a minor action, I happened to be mentioned in dispatches. A bit of luck."

"That's not how Lord Wolseley tells it, Captain," Stanley said. "By his account—and I must say he provided me with a most vivid account of that 'minor action'—what was involved was not luck at all. Luck never won anyone a Victoria Cross, Captain. Only heroism, the most extraordinary kind of heroism, has."

Nelson took a puff on his cigar, trying to maintain his blandly composed expression, but there was no question that beneath his deep tan a blush of color had risen to his cheeks. He looked acutely uncomfortable.

"Very well, Captain, we shall leave it at that if you wish and get on with the business at hand." Stanley, still smiling, stood up and went to the sideboard to pour himself a glass of port. "But I should like you to know, Captain, that I am quite impressed by your record of service. And by your modesty."

"Thank you, sir."

"Are you sure you won't have a glass of port?"

"I'm sure, sir, thank you."

Stanley returned to his chair with his glass and sat down with his legs on the ottoman. "I take it you know why Lord Wolseley asked you to come around and see me."

"Yes, sir, I do."

"And? What is your feeling on the matter?"

"Mr. Stanley, it would be an enormous honor for me to serve under you in this campaign."

"Why?"

"Why, sir?"

"Yes, Captain, why?"

"Well, sir, at the risk of sounding maudlin, may I confess to having been an ardent admirer of yours since my cadet days. I was a new boy at Sandhurst the year you found Livingstone, and more than anything else it was your account of that expedition that set my heart on serving in Africa. I have followed all your activities avidly ever since, read all your books with utmost fascination." Nelson took a puff on his cigar and looked around awkwardly, not sure what further he should say. "Actually, this isn't the first time we've met, sir," he finally went on. "There is no reason for you to recall it, but I was stationed at the Zanzibar barracks in '77, on my way out to Cape Colony for my first command with Buller's Horse, when you stopped there on your return from your discovery of the course of the Congo River. We paraded for you at the Sultan's palace. It was the last day of November. We were all immensely excited about seeing you. You and Consul Kirk messed with us that day."

Stanley sipped his port, peering at Nelson over the rim of the glass with narrowed eyes.

"I've been very nearly ten years in Africa," the captain continued haltingly, "but all I've seen of it in all this time are the southern regions, south of the Zambezi. I very much want to go upcountry into the interior. I want to see the forests and savannas and lakes and people I've been reading about all these years in your books. The chance of doing it under your command, well, sir, it would be a boyhood dream come true."

Stanley closed his eyes momentarily. Then he said, "You're not married, Captain?"

"No, sir."

"And you've no other attachments?"

"No, sir."

"Good. Because I would be happy to have a soldier with your record with me, Captain."

"Thank you, sir. Thank you very much. I shan't disappoint you."

"I'm sure you won't," Stanley said, setting his glass of port on the carpet and getting up. "When do you think you can get started?"

"As soon as you wish, sir. Tomorrow? I'm sure I can put my affairs in order by the end of the day today and be here first thing in the morning. Oh, that's New Year's Day. I say, what a smashing way to begin the new year. But perhaps you will be making a holiday of it, sir."

"No, we can't afford any holidays just now. By all means come around tomorrow if you can manage it. I'd like to get you started ordering up the armaments we'll be needing for ourselves and Emin."

"Very good sir," Nelson said. "I'll be here." He shook Stanley's hand. "I can't tell you how pleased I am about this, Mr. Stanley. Awfully nice meeting you, Jephson." He shook Jephson's hand vigorously, then started toward the door.

"By the way, Captain," Stanley said, accompanying him, "do you happen to know a Major Barttlelot?"

"Barttelot, sir?"

"Edmund Musgrave Barttelot, Seventh Royal Fusiliers."

"Oh, Ted Barttelot. Wasn't he Lord Wolseley's aide-de-camp on the Nile campaign?"

"He's the one."

"Fought at Kandahar in the Afghan war too, didn't he? Yes, Ted Barttelot. I don't know him personally, sir, but I've heard a good deal about him. Rather a spectacular sort of chap, by all accounts, isn't he? Lots of dash. Quite young for a major. Twenty-six or twenty-seven. Brilliant future, they say."

"Yes, that's what they say," Stanley said. "You wouldn't happen to know where he's garrisoned?"

"At the Stopham barracks, sir. The Seventh Fusiliers are stationed at Stopham just now."

"That's what I thought. That's what Wolseley told me. But perhaps the War Office files are as out of date on Major Barttelot as they were on you."

"I wouldn't think so, sir. I know for certain that the Seventh Fusiliers are at Stopham. I've a chum in the regiment. They're not expecting to be reposted for another few months. To Bombay, they're guessing. Ted Barttelot is bound to be with them."

"Odd then that he hasn't dropped by to see me."

"Oh, has Lord Wolseley recommended him for a place on your staff as well?"

"Yes."

"If you permit me to say so, I think he'd make an excellent choice."

"Do you? He'd outrank you, you know, Captain."

"I wouldn't mind, sir. I'd gladly serve under him. By all accounts, he's a capital chap and a splendid officer. Did marvelous work on the Nile campaign. Repeatedly mentioned in dispatches.

Fought like a bloody demon at Tell el-Kebir. If it had been up to him, they say, the column would have gotten through to Gordon in Khartoum in time."

"Yes, I've heard that. Very impressive. Still, it is curious that he hasn't come to see me as yet. Actually I was expecting him to turn up long before you. After all, I was under the impression you were in Cape Town while Major Barttelot was a mere few hours away at Stopham. In fact, just before, when I saw Baruti open the door to an Army officer, I was certain it was the major. It wasn't until I had had a good look at your uniform that I realized that wasn't the case."

"He may be delayed at Stopham on some regimental business."

"Yes, I suppose he may be, although it is hard to imagine a regimental commander otherwise deploying an officer when he has had instructions from the commander-in-chief to release the man to come up to London on more pressing business."

Nelson did not reply to that.

Stanley stopped at the door of the flat and rested a hand on its brass knob. "Ah, but it doesn't matter," he said suddenly, expansively. "We've got you, Captain, and I'm awfully pleased about that. We can get started on the military aspects of this venture now. I look forward to working with you. You will try to come by tomorrow then?"

"Yes, sir. I most assuredly will." Nelson put on his visored cap.

"And, oh, by the way, Captain," Stanley said, opening the door.

"Sir?"

"There's to be a New Year's Eve ball tonight at Sir William Mackinnon's. As you know, he's chairman of the Emin Pasha Relief Committee and he's invited all the members of the expedition staff to attend. And that now includes you. By all means, try to come. It should be a lively affair."

"Thank you, sir. That's very kind of you. But I doubt if I'll be able to get back up to London tonight, what with all the things I have to do."

"Yes, of course. I understand. Until tomorrow then."

· FOUR ·

SIR WILLIAM'S BALL took place in his town house in Belgravia, a huge imposing pile of a mansion set in its own park. It had a grand marble staircase separating two immense reception rooms, in each of which an orchestra had been installed; and some of the most distinguished members of London society were there—royalty, aristocracy, Cabinet ministers, members of Parliament, the Lord Mayor of London, admirals and generals, bankers and merchant princes and landed gentry, ambassadors and foreign dignitaries of every description; even His Royal Highness Edward, the Prince of Wales, and his usual boisterous retinue were expected. It was a glittering affair, the women decked out in their most gorgeous gowns, sparkling with jewels, fluttering fans; the men brilliant in bemedaled uniforms or elegant cutaways decorated with satin sashes; footmen and waiters scurrying to and fro, the music of violins enlivening the gay chatter and laughter and tinkling of crystal, the glow of chandeliers shining on the vast expanse of marble and polished wood and flushed and happy faces. It was socially the most important affair of the season because, more than merely marking the turn of the year, it was being held in celebration of the brave men who were going off to Africa to rescue Emin Pasha. Henry Morton Stanley, of course, was the guest of honor.

Apart from Stanley, however, none of the other brave men of the expedition were present. Jack Troup had declined to attend. He claimed he had some equipment deliveries to see to that night; but Jephson, having tried to talk him into leaving that business until the morrow, realized that the real reason was the redhead's painful shyness of what he called high-class toffs. Nor was Dr. Leslie there. His problem was his wife, who had been hysterical ever since learning of her husband's decision to join the expedition. She had run off with their baby to her mother's in Sussex, so he was obliged to spend New Year's Eve there. Captain Nelson was back at the barracks in Pentworth putting his affairs in order, Willie Hoffman was in Zanzibar hiring *pagazis*, and Herbert Ward was on the Congo making his way down to the coast to catch a ship around the Cape; and so by default Jephson turned out to be the only other person at the gala who had any actual day-to-day working association with the expedition and, as such, was the object of almost as much attention as Stanley. It pleased him immensely; it was precisely what he had hoped when he had accepted Sir William's offer of the post of secretary to the relief committee in the first place. The glory and glamour of the grand adventure were rubbing off on him; by his close involvement with heroes, he could be mistaken for something of a hero himself.

Sir William and Lady Mackinnon, the James Huttons, Colonel Grant and his wife, Colonel de Winton, and three or four other members of the Emin Pasha Relief Committee, including the Baron Burdett-Coutts and the Countess de Noailles, were manning the receiving line, but Stanley himself had drifted away. He was leaning on the balustrade of the marble staircase, engaged in conversation with Lord Wolseley. The general was a tall, heavy-set man, resplendent in his magnificent red uniform covered with medals and shining with gold braid; yet somehow the smaller, more plainly attired Stanley appeared the dominating figure of the two. His white tie and tails were unadorned. He might have, in fact, worn a chestful of decorations awarded by European monarchs and royal geographical societies for his stupendous feats of African exploration, but he had chosen not to; and the simple uncluttered lines of his short cutaway jacket showed off his muscular arms and shoulders and powerful chest. His close-cropped iron-gray hair, newly barbered for the occasion, emphasized the granite strength of his head. He stood, hands on hips, legs planted wide, looking down, listening to Wolseley, his Oriental eyes lost in the shadows of his high cheekbones. A number of people milled about a few paces away, darting glances in his direction, whispering about him but not daring to approach. His pose and the hard mask of his scarred face were too intimidating, and Jephson held back as well, awaiting a chance to greet him.

But before he got the chance, Lord Wolseley suddenly exclaimed, "Well, wouldn't you just know it, Henry. Speak of the devil. There's the chap now."

"Where?"

"Just coming in. With Dolly Tennant on his arm."

Jephson as well as Stanley turned in the direction Wolseley pointed.

Dorothy Tennant, Jephson's cousin, was regarded as one of the great beauties of London society; and although nearly thirty and still unmarried, she was that only by her own capricious choice, because she was relentlessly courted by the most eminently suitable men. And seeing her now entering the Mackinnon mansion, Jephson could appreciate why. She was ravishing. Her shining auburn hair crowned with a diamond tiara was swept high upon her head, exposing her long, slender neck, her creamy white shoulders, and the deliciously full decolletage of her satin burgundy ball gown. Her wonderful gray eyes caught the light of the chandeliers and sparkled like jewels; her lovely face, still stinging from the snow and wind of the winter night, was radiant. She was laughing, and from every direction admiring men moved toward her as if drawn by her seductive laughter.

But as breathtaking as she looked, it was on her escort that Jephson's eyes riveted. Major Edmund Musgrave Barttelot of the Seventh Royal Fusiliers was the handsomest man Jephson had ever seen; indeed, except for the risk of being misunderstood, one might have said he was beautiful. He was tall and slim, long-legged and narrow-hipped, but with broad shoulders, a rangy athlete's physique fitted elegantly into the white-and-gold uniform of his famous regiment. He had the head of a Greek god, a mass of tight, dusky blond curls, perfectly chiseled features unmarred by mustache or beard or sideburns, and eyes as brilliantly blue as precious stones. He too was laughing as he unbuckled his saber and handed it causually to an attending footman.

"Over here, Ted," Lord Wolseley called and, smiling like a proud grandfather, went toward the couple. "Dolly, my dear, how extravagantly stunning you look. It is enough to make an old man behave like a schoolboy." He bowed deeply, kissing her hand. "And where in blazes have you been hiding yourself, Ted?" he said to the major. "No one has seen hide nor hair of you for a week, I'm told."

"Just enjoying the holiday sir," Barttelot replied, showing a row of strong white teeth in an easy grin as he shook the general's hand familiarly.

"I'm sure you were, knowing you, my boy. Well, anyway, come along. There's someone I want you to meet. You too, Dolly." Wolseley took Dolly Tennant's arms and brought the couple forward.

Jephson started toward his cousin, meaning to greet her. But he checked himself abruptly. The laughter had suddenly fled Dolly's face. She was staring with a most peculiar expression. Jephson turned in the direction of her stare. Dolly was staring at Stanley. And with his hands clenched in fists on his hips, Stanley was returning the stare and holding it with such shocking ferocity that for an instant it seemed as if the violence of his piercing eyes would do her harm. And then Jephson remembered when, at Delmonico's in New York, Stanley said he knew Dolly Tennant. And he also remembered the expression that had crossed Stanley's face when he had said it. This was the same expression.

Dolly, however, quickly recovered and, freeing her arm from Lord Wolseley, went to Stanley. Brushing by Jephson, she extended her hand. "Henry," she said softly.

He took her hand without a word.

"It's been a long time, Henry."

"Yes," he replied and released her hand, but went on staring at her with such unnerving intensity that she was obliged to turn away.

"Arthur, dear, how are you?"

"Happy New Year, Dolly." Jephson exchanged kisses with his cousin.

The Mackinnons and Huttons and Grants, Colonel de Winton and the Countess de Noailles and a few others came over from the receiving line.

"Do you all know Major Barttelot?" Dolly asked, and a round of introductions followed. "And this is my cousin, Ted. Arthur Mounteney Jephson. Major Edmund Musgrave Barttelot."

"How do you do."

"Pleased to meet you."

"And, Ted, this of course is Mr. Henry Morton Stanley."

"Mr. Stanley," Barttelot said, turning gracefully away from Jephson. "It is a great honor to meet you, sir. For those of us who have served in Africa, you are the exemplary soldier."

Stanley's eyes had remained fixed on Dolly. Now he shifted them to Barttelot. "Major," he said. He did not take Barttelot's proferred hand.

Barttelot held it out a second longer, then let it drop to his side and studied Stanley's scarred, rock-hard face with a trace of puzzlement, perhaps even amusement. And these so sharply contrasting yet, each in his own way, physically striking men might have gone on staring at each other in silence for some time hadn't Lord Wolseley intervened.

"Well, we've got hold of your elusive second-in-command for you at last, Henry," he said cheerfully. "But he's been worth the wait, I can tell you. Splendid officer. You won't find better in the whole of the British Army."

Stanley looked at Wolseley, then back at Barttelot, his expression as hard and closed as before. Then, placing his hands on his hips, he said very quietly, "I take it you're aware of the Emin Pasha relief expedition, Major."

"Why, yes, sir, of course I am. Who isn't?"

"And I take it you're also aware that Lord Wolseley has recommended you for the place of second-in-command."

"Yes, sir, I am."

"But I take it you're not especially interested in the assignment."

"Oh, no, sir, quite to the contrary. I'm immensely interested. It sounds a jolly sporting bit of business."

"Does it?"

"Yes, sir."

"Then I don't understand why you haven't presented yourself to me before this, Major."

"I apologize for that, sir. I can understand your annoyance, but I must ask you to excuse me. I've been deucedly tied up these last few days putting my affairs in order."

"I see. And are your affairs in order, Major?"

"They are, sir."

"Then can I expect you to present yourself now?"

"You can, sir."

"Shall we say tomorrow then, at my apartments at 160 New Bond Street."

"Tomorrow, sir? Tomorrow is New Year's Day."

"I'm aware of that, Major."

"But, sir, I'm sorry, I've accepted Dolly's—Miss Tennant's—invitation to join her party at Broadmoor for the day. I shouldn't like to disappoint her."

Stanley turned his stone-hard expression on Dolly. "No," he said. "Nor should I like you to disappoint her." He looked back at Barttelot. "Do you spppose you'd be able to make it the day *after* tomorrow, Major?"

"Certainly, sir. When would be most convenient?"

"As early as you can manage."

"I'll be there first thing in the morning."

"Very good. And now, Miss Tennant, ladies, gentlemen, if you'll excuse me." Stanley made a curt bow and turned on his heels.

"Henry," Dolly called out, startled by the sudden departure.

He stopped and she went to him. It wasn't possible to hear what she said; she spoke quickly, in a low voice, her cheeks flushed, frowning. He listened to her without replying and then bowed again and continued on his way.

"Jesus, what was that all about?" Jephson asked.

"He's in love with her," the Countess de Noailles replied.

"What?" Jephson turned to her. "He's in love with Dolly?"

"You didn't know, Arthur? Why, you sweet little innocent. All London knows he asked for her hand just before he left for America. Everyone says that's why he left, in fact."

"What do you mean that's *why* he left?"

"She turned him down, of course."

"For that popinjay?"

"Popinjay? Which popinjay?"

"Major Barttelot."

"Oh, now don't you start rumors, Arthur. Major Barttelot didn't have anything to do with it."

"Well, what did?"

"Oh, you know. Dolly couldn't ever quite accept the facts of Mr. Stanley's . . . well, you know, his *background*."

Major Barttelot arrived at the New Bond Street flat, very probably intending to make a point by it, virtually at the crack of dawn on January 2, while Stanley was still asleep and before any of the others were there. He was accompanied by his batman, a short, balding, pug-faced cockney sergeant-major of indeterminate age (more likely closer to fifty than forty) by the name of William Bonny. Baruti let them in, and when Jephson arrived nearly two hours later they were still waiting for Stanley to put in an appearance. The sergeant-major had taken a straight-backed chair at a window in the drawing room and was gazing vacantly out at the lightly falling snow, obviously uncomfortable. Barttelot, however, was sprawled leisurely on the sofa in front of the fireplace having coffee and biscuits, which Baruti had brought, and carrying on an animated conversation with the little blackamoor in Swahili. He looked completely at his ease and every bit as shockingly handsome as he had at the ball, even though this morning he was in mufti.

Since Jephson was the only one who had met him before, in Stanley's continuing absence it fell to the youth to introduce Barttelot to Nelson, Troup, and Leslie as each came in.

Leslie had to leave right away; he had dropped by only to pick up some papers. He was always just dropping by and rushing off again in a fluster of agitation. The crisis with his wife had abated somewhat—she had bowed to the inevitable and had agreed to stay with her mother in Sussex for the duration of the expedition—but now the doctor was in a state over the arrangements he had made with another physician to look after his practice. He had found an older retired man who was willing to lend a hand, but the fellow had turned out to be as deaf as a doorpost, which made the business of reviewing patients' files with him maddeningly time-consuming. Leslie explained this in a harried outburst to no one in particular, and barely had he shaken hands with Barttelot and nodded in Bonny's direction than he was out of the flat again.

Troup didn't stay around much longer. He immediately identified Barttelot—by the cut of the major's elegant suit, the perfection of his clean-shaven profile, the indolent slurring of his speech—as the archetype of the upper-class toff who never failed to strike him dumb with shyness. And when in addition he discovered that Bonny, with whom he tried to have a few words, was of the stiff-necked, tight-lipped breed of sergeant-major who responded to any attempt at conversation with short monosyllabic barks, he took the first opportunity to slip off to his work.

Captain Nelson too had chores to attend to. The military equipment to be ordered and tested, which he and Stanley had agreed upon the previous day, the captain's first on the job, included 510 Remington rifles and 100,000 rounds of Remington ammunition, two tons of gunpowder and 350,000 percussion caps, 50,000 Winchester cartridges for the 100 Winchester repeaters Stanley had ordered from America, plus a Maxim automatic gun. But the stolid, plain-faced cavalry captain was openly delighted to meet Barttelot. Unlike the others, he knew of and had reason to admire the quite spectacular young major, at least by reputation; and having ingenuously said as much, he accepted Barttelot's invitation to keep him company over a pot of coffee until Mr. Stanley showed up. And so the two officers were pleasantly engaged in exchanging Army gossip and reminiscing about past postings and campaigns when Mr. Stanley finally did appear.

It was after nine, an astonishingly late hour for Stanley to be starting the day. And even so he still wasn't properly up. He came into the drawing room from his bedroom wearing a loosely belted dressing gown over silk pajama trousers, his face unshaven, his hair matted, his eyes raw and red and sticky, the picture of a man who had spent most of the night awake. It was two nights since his encounter with Dolly Tennant. What he had been doing during those two nights, Jephson had no idea. Carousing with whores as he had done in New York perhaps, certainly drinking heavily, by the look of his ravaged face. But whatever it was, Jephson reckoned, they were all in for another rough, short-tempered day with the man.

"Good morning, Mr. Stanley," Barttelot said, getting up from the sofa.

Stanley nodded at him, but his first words were to Baruti, whom he sent to the kitchen to fetch him breakfast. Then, still ignoring Barttelot, he took Nelson into the library, which had come to serve as the expedition office since the drawing room had been turned into a disordered storeroom of half-opened crates of equipment samples.

As soon as Stanley closed the library door, Barttelot sat down again. He took a cigarette from a silver case, placed it in an ivory holder, lit it, and leaned back in the sofa to wait, unperturbed. Fully an hour passed before Stanley reappeared, but even then he did not approach Barttelot. He escorted Nelson out of the flat, giving him some last-minute instructions, then turned to the breakfast tray Baruti had set on a deal table by the fireplace. He prepared a cup of strong tea for himself and drank it off, spread some marmalade on a slice of toast and popped it into his mouth. And when at last he spoke to Barttelot, he spoke to him with his mouth full.

"Awfully sorry to have kept you waiting, Major," he said.

"That's quite all right, sir," Barttelot replied. He stubbed out his cigarette but did not bother to stand up again. "I can see how busy you are." He gestured at the general mess in the drawing room, the boxes and crates, papers scattered everywhere, the jumble of instruments and weapons and African artifacts. "It's no wonder you couldn't take the time to come out to Miss Tennant's yesterday."

"Ah, yes, Miss Tennant." Stanley fixed himself a sandwich of scrambled eggs and toast. "Did you have a pleasant day with her, Major?"

"Rather. That's a lovely cottage she has at Broadmoor, and the grounds are really quite marvelous. But you know the place, Mr. Stanley. You've visited there often, haven't you?"

"I have."

"And doesn't she have just the finest string of polo ponies

you've ever seen," Barttelot went on conversationally. "I'm awfully keen on polo myself. Play it every chance I get. I captained a splendid team in Cairo when I was stationed there, and I've got a capital bunch of chaps with the Fusiliers at Stopham now. But do you know, the very best I've ever played was in Kandahara. What bloody demons those Afghans are on horses. Do you ride yourself, Mr. Stanley?"

"No." Stanley took a bite of the sandwich while walking over to the leather chair that stood facing the sofa. "Not at least what you would call riding, Major." He studied the handsome, immaculately groomed officer for a moment. Then he said, "I ride asses. Asses and donkeys and mules. I used to ride horses, in the American West, in the Indian wars, but horses don't do well in those parts of Africa where I've been traveling these last few years, so I've pretty much given up on them. I myself think it's the tsetse fly that destroys them; but whatever it is, horses don't last but a few months south of the Sahara. Actually, mules and donkeys ain't all that reliable either. They'll break down on you too after a while. I've found the only really sure way to travel in Africa–in those parts where I've been traveling anyway and where I'll be traveling now—is to walk." He shoved the rest of his sandwich into his mouth. "Did you know that, Major?"

"I suspected it might be the case."

"It is, Major." Stanley continued staring at Barttelot for a moment longer. Then he fished a handkerchief from the pocket of his dressing gown and wiped the egg grease from the gray unshaven stubble of his chin. And while he did this, looking nowhere in particular, he said, "Who the hell is that?"

"Sir? Oh, I say, how dreadfully impolite of me. Billy Bonny is my batman, sergeant-major in the Seventh Royal Fusiliers. Sergeant, this is Mr. Henry Stanley."

Bonny, who had been standing ever since Stanley first entered the room, pulled himself to attention and clicked his heels. Stanley looked at him, then turned again to Barttelot. "Do you go everywhere with your batman, Major?"

"No, as a matter of fact, I don't, Mr. Stanley." A small smile curled Barttelot's handsome mouth. "I brought Sergeant Bonny along this morning with a particular purpose in mind."

"And what might that be?"

"I should like you to sign him on for the expedition. He has my highest recommendation."

"Oh?"

"Sergeant Bonny served with me on the Nile campaign with quite extraordinary distinction, especially at Tell el-Kebir. I don't mind saying that the decoration I won in that fight was largely due to him. And he also fought with me in Alexandria during the Arabist uprising, for which action he was mentioned in dispatches as well. He is an outstanding soldier, sir, as brave and steady as they come, and he's a bloody demon in keeping your troops up to the mark for you and getting the most out of them. He made my job a hundredfold easier throughout the Nile campaign, and he'd do the same for me on this one."

Stanley, who was still standing, leaned on the back of the leather chair.

Barttelot waited a moment, thinking Stanley would say something, and he used that moment to light another cigarette. But, when it was clear that Stanley intended to remain silent, he went on. "It is my understanding, sir, that what I'll have on my plate in this campaign is the command of a military column in escort of the relief caravan. I realize that Captain Nelson will be with me in this, and I want to say that I'm delighted by the prospect. Although I've had the pleasure of meeting him for the first time only this morning, I have of course heard of his marvelous record in the Zulu wars. But even so, sir, and I should say that Captain Nelson agrees with me in this, it would be desirable, if not to say necessary, to have a veteran sergeant-major like Billy Bonny with us to take charge of the day-to-day drill and discipline of the ranks. And especially in this case, when the ranks will be native troops. I assume they will be native troops. I shouldn't think Her Majesty's Government would allow British soldiers to enlist wholesale for the expedition. It would rather alter its nature, wouldn't it, make it seem something of an official campaign."

Stanley walked around his chair and sat down, throwing his legs up on the ottoman.

"Sergeant Bonny has had a wealth of experience handling native troops. In Egypt and the Sudan and before that in Afghanistan. Askaris, sepoys–he's whipped them all into disciplined fighting men. He'd be an enormous asset, I can assure you, Mr. Stanley. He'd make all of our lives a lot easier."

"Excuse me, Major, but I can't help noticing that you speak as if *your* participation in this expedition is settled and what we're here to discuss is whether or not you shall have the convenience of bringing your batman along."

Barttelot felt the cut of that remark and once again a small sardonic smile curled his lips. He removed the cigarette from its ivory holder and carefully stubbed it out. "Perhaps I've misunderstood," he said evenly, "but, yes, sir, I was given to understand that the matter of my participation in the expedition had been settled."

"Given to understand by whom, Major?"

"By Lord Wolseley of course."

"I see." Stanley said nothing further. He slipped his hand inside his dressing gown and scratched himself.

The contrast between the two men in appearance and manner could not have been more striking: the one young, tall, lithely athletic, smooth as silk, and handsome as a matinee idol; the other grizzled, stocky, muscular as a bog hauler, scarred by time and experience. But as if that weren't enough, Stanley seemed deliberately to have gone out of his way to emphasize the contrast between them by presenting himself unshaven, unwashed, half dressed, and edgy from lack of sleep. It was as if he wanted to demonstrate the difference between this well-born gifted Army officer and himself, the bastard workhouse boy, the crude adventurer; the hostility he radiated in the continuing silence was almost unbearable.

It was Barttelot who could abide it no longer. "Evidently, I did misunderstand Lord Wolseley," he said. "Allow me to apologize for anticipating your decision in this regard. It was foolish of me. Of course this is your decision to make, not Lord Wolseley's. But perhaps you will understand that my mistake was born of an eagerness to join your expedition, not of an arrogance about my qualifications."

"An eagerness to join this expedition, Major? Do you know anything about this expedition, Major?"

"Sir?"

"Do you know anything more about this expedition than that, as you put it the other night, it probably would be jolly good sport?"

Again Barttelot couldn't help but grimace, but he answered briskly. "As a matter of fact, Mr. Stanley, I know a great deal more about it than that. Lord Wolseley was kind enough to outline the enterprise in some detail; and as I am quite familiar with the situation in the south Sudan generally and with Emin Pasha's plight in particular from my service in Egypt and on the Nile compaign, I did not have any special difficulty grasping the salient points. In my opinion– But excuse me, sir, you didn't ask for my opinion."

"No, go ahead, Major. What is your opinion? I'd be interested in hearing your opinion."

"In my opinion, the expedition stands a decent chance of succeeding. I don't believe the dervishes mean to move against Equatoria in anything like the foreseeable future. I don't think they've ever really been all that keen about mounting a major military push against the province. It's just too damn far south for them. It raises all the worst kinds of supply and communication problems. It means moving out of the desert and fighting in an alien terrain of grasslands and forests. Certainly they want to be rid of this last remnant of foreign rule on their soil, but I'd say they expect to accomplish that simply by maintaining their siege, keeping Emin's garrisons cut off, and eventually starving them out. Now obviously once the dervishes get wind that a relief expedition is on the way, they will have to make a move. But I'm confident we can beat them to the punch. As long as Emin can fight a reasonable delaying action, retreating up the Nile from fort to fort, I am certain we can get there in time."

Stanley shifted in his chair, pulling his dressing gown closed and rebelting it. "Anything else?" he asked.

"In what regard, sir?"

"In any regard. In regard to the route. In regard to the military escort. In regard to anything on which you might hold an opinion."

"Well, sir, I am not so arrogant as to have an opinion in regard to the route you have chosen. I've looked it over on the map and of course find it eminently reasonable. But how could it be otherwise? On such matters, Mr. Stanley, you are the master. As for the caravan's military escort, yes, I do have an opinion on that."

"Yes?"

"If I'm correct in thinking that political considerations disallow the use of British soldiers and that what we are considering here are native troops, askaris—"

"We are."

"Then I'd recommend Sudanese. I expect you will recruit the bulk of the caravan, the porters and cooks and service personnel generally, from among the Wanyamwezi of Zanzibar, and quite possibly you'd want to put weapons in the hands of some of them as a sort of militia; but for the main fighting force I'd recommend Sudanese. Niggers, you understand, not Moslems, those who've been fighting the dervishes right along in this beastly business, with Gordon and Hicks and Baker and Lupton and Slatin, those who're manning Emin Pasha's barricades right now. I know them pretty well. They fought with us in the Nile campaign. They're good boys, intelligent, quick, brave, especially under the eye of a tough sergeant-major like Billy Bonny. There are hordes of them left over from the war, you know, hanging about in the souks and bazaars of Aden, from Gordon's Black Battalion, the Mudir of Dongola's *bashi-bazouks*. I could go over to Aden and pick the best of the lot and give them a bit of shaping up with Captain Nelson and Sergeant Bonny, then bring them around the Horn to Zanzibar. Fit them out with Remingtons, I should think, but I'd put Winchester repeaters in the hands of the better boys and make corporals of them under the sergeant-major. They'd make a bloody fine fighting force, quite capable of handling anything you might run into on the dash to Equatoria."

Stanley leaned forward and took a cigar from the box on the deal table. "You seem to have thought this through in quite some detail, Major," he said.

"I have."

Stanley busied himself for a few seconds preparing and lighting the cigar. Then he said, "Sergeant Bonny."

"Sir." The sergeant-major, who had remained standing all this time with a studiedly unhearing expression on his pug face, snapped to attention again and marched over to Stanley.

"Sergeant, I gather from Major Barttelot that you have some interest in joining my expedition."

"That I do, sir."

"Do you have any idea what this expedition is about?"

"The major explained it to me, sir. We're to rescue some Turkish chap from the dervishes in the south Sudan."

"And do you also have some idea what your duties would be?"

"Yes, sir. We're to have a column of native troops as escort for the relief caravan and it'll be my job to keep them on the march and up to the mark."

"And you reckon you can manage that?"

"Yes, sir, I reckon I can."

"And you reckon it would be jolly good sport?"

"Sir?"

"Why do you want to do this, Sergeant?"

"Why, sir? Well, I've served under Major Barttelot for four years now, and I'd just as soon go on serving under him as do anything else. If he's off to rescue the Turk, I figure I ought to be off to rescue the Turk with him."

"You've certainly got yourself a loyal batman there, Major," Stanley said, glancing at Barttelot. "But, Sergeant, do you realize that in order to join this expedition you'd have to take leave without pay from your regiment?"

"Yes, sir. The major explained that to me and I've done it already."

"You have? How very prescient of you." Again Stanley turned to Barttelot. "And I suppose you have as well, Major?"

"Yes, sir, as a matter of fact I have."

Stanley took a long drag on the cigar and let the smoke curl out very slowly. Then he said, "You know, Major, there ain't going to be a hell of a lot of glamour in this. There ain't going to be any cavalry charges or flags flying or trumpets blaring. There ain't even going to be any very interesting fighting. Mostly all there's going to be is some long, hard, dirty walking in the sun."

"I know that."

"Do you? Do you really know just how long and hard and dirty it will be?"

"Yes, sir, I think I do."

"Very well then. I want you to work the next few days with Captain Nelson getting the military hardware together. Make sure everything you think we're going to need is on the list Nelson and I drew up. Keep me informed of any changes or additions you want to make but feel free to make them. We must have everything we need to insure that we succeed in this. Because we are going to succeed, Major. Do you understand that? I intend to succeed."

"Yes, sir."

"When you're satisfied that nothing has been overlooked, I want you to get off to Aden and start recruiting those Sudanese troops you mentioned. You can take Sergeant Bonny with you. Captain Nelson will finish up ordering, testing, and shipping the military matériel and then follow you out. But I want you to get away as soon as possible, within the week in fact. Do you think you can manage that?"

"Yes, sir."

"All right," Stanley said and stood up. "Now if you'll excuse me, I had best get shaved and dressed. I'm expected at the Foreign Office this morning."

"Sir, could I have a word with you in private?" Barttelot said, also standing up.

"In private, Major? Why? We're not going to have much privacy on this expedition, you know. Anything we'll be wanting to say from now on, we'll be saying pretty much within earshot of everyone."

"This is a personal matter, sir. It has nothing to do with the expedition."

"What does it have to do with?"

"Miss Tennant."

Stanley paused a moment. Then he said, "I don't believe there's anything we have to discuss about Miss Tennant, Major."

"Please, Mr. Stanley." Barttelot, looking at Jephson and Bonny pointedly, lowered his voice. "I fear there may be a misunderstanding about my relationship with Miss Tennant that may have a bearing on your atttitude toward me."

"Major, I don't give a tinker's damn about your relationship with Miss Tennant. And I can assure you that whatever it is, no matter what it is, it doesn't have the slightest bearing on my attitude toward you. That will be based solely on your merits as a soldier, on your performance on this journey."

"I'm glad to hear that, sir."

"I should think you would be. And now if you'll excuse me."

"Sir, just one last thing."

Stanley turned back to the major.

"Miss Tennant would very much like you to pay a call. She's quite anxious to see you, sir. She asked me to tell you that."

"Did she? How very flattering," Stanley said and strode off to the bedroom.

· FIVE ·

WELL WITHIN the deadline of a week that Stanley had set for him, working with an impressive easygoing skill, Major Barttelot completed the tasks assigned to him and was ready to depart for Aden on January 6. He was to take the train from Charing Cross station to Liverpool that night, where he'd catch a mail packet for Lisbon and there board a Portuguese merchantman bound through the Suez Canal into the Red Sea. Sergeant Bonny had been sent on to Liverpool earlier in the day to make sure the accommodations aboard the packet were in order, and Dolly Tennant gave a farewell supper that evening at her town house in Richmond Terrace. It was a lively, informal affair attended mainly by Barttelot's chums from the Seventh Fusiliers, although a number of his new colleagues from the Emin Pasha relief expedition were also on hand. Stanley too, of course, had been invited; indeed, Dolly had made a special point of doing so and all throughout the festivities kept casting an expectant eye toward the door to see when he would arrive. He never did.

Jack Troup left a few days later, on the tenth, to join Willie Hoffman in Zanzibar. Stanley had had every intention of accompanying Troup to the Fenchurch station to catch the night express to Plymouth, from where the Zanzibar mail packet departed. In fact, several days in advance he had made arrangements for them to have supper in the railway station pub, a quiet occasion for Stanley and his most trusted lieutenant to talk over final details of the expedition, reminisce about previous adventures, and get a little drunk together. Both men were looking forward to it. But then something came up; Stanley was called away at the last minute. He never had a chance to explain what it was about, it happened that suddenly; but it must have been something extremely urgent, otherwise he would never have canceled out on the arrangement with his friend. Jephson, unwilling to let Troup depart alone, decided to see him off in Stanley's place.

Although by this time the bulk of the expedition's supplies and equipment were en route to Zanzibar or were waiting to be shipped on the docks of various ports, a number of key items—the sectional steel boat, for example, about which some problems had arisen—had still to come along, and then too there were the weapons and ammunition, including the Maxim automatic gun, which Nelson had ordered and was testing but which, once the captain also left, Jephson would be responsible for shipping. So Troup spent most of the farewell supper at the Fenchurch station pub giving the youth last-minute instructions, reminding him what had yet to be done, what must not be overlooked.

And Jephson spent most of that supper nodding and saying over and over again, "I know, Jack. Yes, of course, I won't forget that. No, I won't forget that either. Jesus, Jack, you've told me that a hundred times." And then: "Really, Jack, you don't have to worry. I'll look after everything. I know what's wanted. You've taught me well. You've been a splendid teacher."

"Well, if it comes to that," Troup said, letting up at last, "you've been a splendid pupil. For a toff, you've got a quick head for this sort of thing. It's been a pleasure having you around." The meal was done, the dishes pushed aside and they were having brandy and soda. Troup looked at his pocket watch. "We've time for one last snort. What do you say?"

"I say yes indeed." Jephson signaled the barmaid, then turned back to Troup. When would he see this man again? Not for months, perhaps not for years—if, indeed, ever again. For who could say what fate awaited Troup on the journey to Equatoria? And in a rush of sentiment he said, "I'll miss you, Jack. It won't be the same around New Bond Street without you."

"I'll miss you too, lad," Troup replied. "To tell the truth, I ain't never understood why you didn't sign on with the rest of us yourself. You'd have had a jolly good time of it, I promise you."

"Come on, Jack. How can you say that? You know that was never in the cards. I was only meant to be secretary for the committee. Mr. Stanley would never consider taking me along."

"Did you ever ask him?"

"What do you mean, did I ever ask him?"

"Just that. Did you ever ask him?"

"No. But, Jesus, Jack, I know what his answer'd be."

"I wouldn't be so sure."

Jephson looked at Troup in amazement. The redhead was grinning at him. "Did he ever say anything to you about it?"

"Not in so many words. But I know Mr. Stanley. I've been around him a fair number of years, you know, and I usually have a pretty good idea what's going on in his head. I get the impression he's taken a liking to you."

"Really, Jack? You really think so?"

The barmaid arrived with the fresh drinks and set about fussily clearing the supper dishes from the table.

"Leave it, love," Troup said and looked at his pocket watch again. Then he said, "Tell me something, Arthur. Do you want to go?"

Jephson shrugged. "I don't know. I never gave it any thought. I never considered it a possibility."

"Well, why don't you give it some thought now?"

Jephson didn't answer right away. Then he said, "No. I don't want to go."

"Why not?"

Again the youth hesitated, and when at last he spoke he looked away from Troup. "I'm afraid," he said and picked up his brandy and soda. "Yes, that's it, I guess. I'm afraid."

"Afraid of what?"

"I don't know. Of the savages maybe. Of the animals. Of getting killed. Of breaking down and not being able to keep up. Of being left behind. Of not measuring up. I don't know. Of the whole thing. Of Africa."

"We're all afraid of Africa, Arthur. We're all always afraid of that place. To tell the truth, if I let myself think about it, I'm afraid of it right now. But that's the trick of it, lad. To go even when you are afraid. That's the fun of it. It wouldn't be worth doing if you weren't afraid."

Captain Nelson left for Aden on Friday, January 14, and this time Stanley managed to be on hand for the departure. So were Jephson and Dr. Dick Leslie, and the four of them enjoyed a leisurely supper together at the Griffin on Villiers Street before going over the road to the Charing Cross station for Nelson to catch the night express to Liverpool.

Stanley was in an unusually buoyant mood. Nelson's leaving pretty much brought to a close the expedition's preparatory phase. The problems with the portable steel boat had been solved and the last of the loads were on the docks awaiting shipment aboard the first available vessels. Except for Stanley and Dr. Leslie, the expedition's officers were deployed in the field or on their way there—

Nelson now to join Barttelot and Bonny in Aden, Herbert Ward coming from the Congo to join Troup and Hoffman in Zanzibar—and within a week Stanley and Leslie would be on their way as well. Just that morning Stanley had fixed their departure date for January 20, and Jephson had gone around to the shipping agents and booked passage for the pair aboard a steamer of Mackinnon's British India line, the SS *Navarino*, that would depart Southampton for Africa on that night.

There was no mistaking Stanley's relish at the prospect, his eagerness to be on his way at last; and at supper at the Griffin he spoke of Africa with a good-humored, almost boyish enthusiasm that Jephson hadn't witnessed in him before. And in nothing that he said was there anything in the least bit frightening. He made it all sound a boy's grand storybook adventure, of nights out under the stars, roughing it in the wilds, of climbing and swimming and blazing trails, muscles hardened, cheeks tanned, of limitless hunting, stalking gazelle and impala on the savanna, shooting hippo in the rivers, of dusky maidens dancing in the firelight to the beat of jungle drums and the moan of kudu horns—and Jephson couldn't help but feel a pang of envy for those lucky enough to share in such adventures with him.

Slightly tipsy from the wine they had drunk and the high spirits of their conversation, the four men had a hard time negotiating the snowdrifts and traffic in Villiers Street to get across to the Charing Cross station.

"Have you got everything, Captain?" Stanley asked as Nelson got ready to board the train.

"Yes, sir, I think so."

The locomotive whistle shrieked.

"Your saber. Where's your saber, Captain? You've not left your saber behind, have you?"

An expression of consternation flashed across Nelson's face, and instinctively his hand went to his side where the saber would have been had he been wearing a dress uniform. But almost immediately, seeing Stanley's broad grin, he himself burst into laughter.

"Listen, Robbie," Stanley suddenly said in dead seriousness and grabbed Nelson by the shoulders. "Get me good men. Get me the toughest, bravest askaris you can lay hands on in Aden. Get me killers, Robbie, bloody killers. I'm counting on that."

"Yes, sir."

"I want an army of killers that nothing can stop, that can clear a path through hell for me if necessary."

"We'll get them for you, sir. I'd wager Major Barttelot has already got them. He knows the Black Battalion. He knows the Sudanese. He's probably picked the hungriest of the lot and is halfway down the road to shaping them up into a bloody fine fighting force by now."

"Yes. Major Barttelot," Stanley said. He smiled. "Yes, he probably has—the brilliant officer that he is."

The whistle shrieked again. The conductor jumped up on the train, waving his lantern, calling a final all aboard.

"Go on up, Captain," Stanley said. He shook Nelson's hand. "Good luck. God's speed."

The train was moving, picking up speed; it was well down the platform by the time Nelson got to his compartment and yanked open the window to look out and wave. Jephson and Leslie waved back; Stanley, standing with his hands on his hips, merely grinned, watching the train carry the quiet straightforward cavalry captain with the Victoria Cross off into the darkness.

As they were leaving the station, pushing their way through the crush of travelers in the waiting room to get at the cabs drawn up at the curb outside, someone called Stanley's name. Stanley's face was widely recognized, appearing as it did almost daily in the newspapers; and frequently total strangers accosted him on the street.

"Mr. Stanley, sir." A traveler dressed in mufti but holding himself with an unmistakable military bearing stuck out his hand. "The name's Davis, sir, and I want you to know all England stands behind you in this noble task you've undertaken. I was with Wolseley on the Nile, sir, and it is a shame we must live down. Save Emin Pasha, sir. Don't let him go the way of Chinese Gordon. Redeem England's honor, sir. Erase this shame. You have our blessings."

Stanley shook Davis's hand affably, and others in the crowd, emboldened by his example, also pressed forward to make little congratulatory speeches and shake the great man's hand. Leslie looked at Jephson and pulled a face. Clearly, Stanley was in a mood to enjoy this attention and adulation and, smiling beguilingly, shook hands left and right, replying to each of his admirers with charming pleasantries. Leslie tapped his foot impatiently for a minute, then slipped away to catch a cab on his own. He was wise to do so. It took very nearly an hour before Stanley was released by the crowd and he and Jephson found a hack for themselves. Once settled in, the carriage rug pulled up over their knees, Stanley lit a cigar and looked out the hack's oval side window, his rock-hard profile falling alternately in and out of the light of the streetlamps as the carriage jounced along on the cobblestones.

"Another week," he said after a few moments, smiling pleasantly to himself. "Less than a week and I'll be out of all this muck, sailing for Africa, sailing to the sun."

"Yes, sir."

"And what will you being doing, lad?"

"Oh, I'm not quite sure, sir. I was thinking of going over to Deauville and having a bit of a holiday with some chums."

"Ah, yes, that should be fun. The casinos are splendid in Deauville this time of year. I shall think of you doing that. I shall think of you at the gaming tables while I'm struggling through the bush." Stanley gave a bark of laughter and continued watching the street slip by.

Ask him, Jephson suddenly thought. Ask him.

Did you ever ask him? Jack Troup had said. I get the impression he's taken a liking to you.

But what if he laughs in my face? What if he finds the whole idea ridiculous? What if you were wrong, Jack Troup?

Or what if he says yes?

Jephson shifted uncomfortably in his seat. That was it, of course, if he was honest with himself. The other didn't matter. He would get over a rebuke. No one would even have to know that he had asked to go along. It wouldn't kill him. But if Mr. Stanley said yes—that could kill him.

Stanley turned to him, the pleasant smile still on his face, and looked at him with friendly curiosity.

Ask him. You can't count on ever finding him in an easier, more approachable mood than this. Just ask him.

Jephson cleared his throat.

But just then Stanley said something.

Jephson didn't immediately comprehend what it was, it was so unexpected, so thoroughly out of the blue. "Sir?"

"I say, she's your cousin, isn't she?"

"Who, sir? Who's my cousin?"

"What's the matter with you, lad? Have you gone deaf? Dolly Tennant."

"Oh, yes, sir, that's right. She's my cousin. Her mother and my mother are sisters."

"So you know her fairly well?"

"Well, yes, I suppose I do. She's a bit older than I am and

we've never moved in the same set, so I couldn't say we're particularly close. But we do see each other at family gatherings and that sort of thing."

"What do you think of her?"

"Sir?"

"Do you like her?"

"Well, yes of course, I like her." Jephson knew enough to realize that this wasn't just idle chitchat, that there was a purpose to it, but he did not know enough to discern what the purpose might be. And that made him uneasy; he was worried he might say the wrong thing. And so he added, somewhat inanely, "She's very pretty. A bit frivolous, I always thought, but I suppose that's the prerogative of a pretty woman."

"Frivolous?"

"Oh, you know, the way she flits and flirts about and never takes anything seriously and seems interested only in the most superficial sort of things like what's going on at Court and so on. She really is something of the worst kind of snob, don't you know?"

"By Christ, lad, that doesn't make it sound as if you like her one bit."

"Oh, I don't mean to be hard on her. I *do* like her. It's just that I've never understood where she ever got the idea that anyone of real merit and accomplishment could possibly take her seriously."

Stanley didn't reply to that.

"I mean," Jephson went on, "I should think she would be content to find herself an equally snobbish chap from her own set with all the proper credentials and titles and such—God knows, London is chockablock full of them, just falling over each other vying for her favor—and marry him and settle down and lead a perfectly useless life."

"And why doesn't she, do you suppose?"

"Because of the ridiculously inflated opinion she has of herself. No ordinary chap from her own set is ever going to be good enough for Dolly Tennant. She fancies herself making a stunning catch, marrying someone really quite remarkable, someone at the center of the world's attention, someone who would make her the envy of London society."

"You're dead wrong there, lad," Stanley said. "I thought that once myself. And I was dead wrong." For a moment he studied the long ash on his cigar, then broke it off with a flick of his little finger. "I asked her to marry me and she turned me down. Did you know that?"

"Yes, sir, I did."

"Of course you did. Everybody does." Stanley took a long puff on his cigar and looked out the window. "I don't mind saying that when I made that marriage proposal I regarded myself—How did you put it, lad?—I regarded myself as quite remarkable enough for Dolly Tennant, otherwise I never would have risked it, I can tell you. But I was dead wrong. I saw it in her face when I asked for her hand. By Christ, she looked at me as if I had taken leave of my senses. Perhaps I had, expecting her to accept the likes of me for a husband." He turned back to Jephson. "But that's all history, lad. That's not what's interesting. What's interesting is, Why is she pursuing me now?"

"She is?"

"I'll say she is. Something fierce. Even though I'm still the same bastard workhouse boy I always was."

· SIX ·

THE NEXT DAY Stanley vanished.

No one realized it right away, of course. When Jephson went around to the New Bond Street flat in the morning and found Stanley gone, he simply assumed that he had left for the offices of the British India Steamship Company. A meeting there of the relief committee and the Prince of Wales was on the schedule for the day; His Royal Highness had taken a lively interest in the expedition and had requested to be brought up to date on the latest developments now that the preparatory phase was virtually complete and Stanley was within a few days of departing for Africa.

Jephson had understood that the meeting was to occur at a luncheon, but it seemed altogether reasonable that Stanley would have gone over a bit earlier to discuss with Mackinnon and the others what would be said before the Prince arrived. And so, giving it no further thought, Jephson puttered about the flat, putting files in order, drafting replies to some unanswered letters, and generally tidying up the library and drawing room. Later he realized he ought to have suspected that something was amiss from Baruti's behavior. The little blackamoor quite uncharacteristically—he always had something to occupy himself with, some mischief to get into—followed him around the flat all morning, never once letting him out of sight.

At two in the afternoon Sir William Mackinnon arrived at the flat with James Hutton and the two colonels, de Winton and Grant, in tow, all looking extremely annoyed and making no effort to conceal it. Stanley, it turned out, had not showed up at the steamship line's offices for the luncheon with Prince Edward, and His Royal Highness was furious. They had managed to cool him down a bit and to put the meeting off until suppertime by making up some lame excuse for Stanley's unpardonable, incomprehensible absence; and now they all started badgering Jephson for information as to the man's whereabouts.

"The earth didn't simply open and swallow him up, Arthur," Mackinnon cried out in exasperation. "He must have had something bloody urgent to do to stand up His Royal Highness. What was it? You must know. He must have said something to you. You're in touch with everything he's been doing."

"I can't imagine what it might be, sir. Really I can't. We had some trouble with the steel boat, but that's all been sorted out. All the equipment's been shipped, even the Maxim gun. That went to Liverpool yesterday. Let me see . . . Passage had to be secured for Mr. Stanley and Dr. Leslie aboard the *Navarino*, but I've already looked after that."

"But there must be something. For God's sake, *think*, boy."

Jephson shook his head helplessly and looked around the drawing room hoping to see something there that would jog his memory. Hutton and Grant, with much the same idea in mind, had started rummaging through bills of lading and invoices, peering into file boxes, reading letters, examining maps and sketches. Then Hutton went into the library and began going through the drawers of the rolltop desk. It made Jephson uneasy; he felt it was his duty to protect the flat from this sort of cavalier prying, that Mr. Stanley would expect it of him.

"I say, what's this?" Hutton called from the library.

Jephson, followed by the others, went into the library.

Hutton had removed from a drawer of the desk a leather-bound foolscap-size folio secured by a small brass lock. "Do you know what Mr. Stanley keeps in here? It looks like some sort of correspondence."

"I don't know, sir, but if you'll excuse me, I don't think we should be going through Mr. Stanley's effects in this way," Jephson replied.

Hutton ignored him. "Where's the key to this damn thing?" he said, fiddling with the lock in an attempt to spring it. "This may give us a clue as to where that man has got off to."

"Really, sir, I must protest. I feel it is my responsibility to look after this office in Mr. Stanley's absence, and in good conscience I simply cannot allow anyone to make free use of it like this without his permission. I must ask you to return that to the desk."

"The lad's right," Mackinnon said. "We've no business rummaging around in here. Put that back where you found it."

"Just a moment, Mac," Colonel Grant intervened. "This could tell us just what we're trying to find out. Obviously there is something important in it. Otherwise why is he keeping it under lock and key?"

"You ask him that, why don't you, Jem," Mackinnon replied, somewhat testily. "He's bound to turn up in the next few hours and you can ask him why he happens to be keeping a particular set of letters under lock and key. I should think that would be far preferable to his asking you how you happened to break into his private correspondence behind his back. Don't you agree?"

Grant's face flushed and he started to say something in his defense.

But Mackinnon cut him off. "For Lord's sake, Jem, be sensible. Don't you imagine Henry is likely to have certain affairs he prefers to keep locked away from prying eyes? Don't we all? Let me have that," he said to Hutton, taking the leather folio from him. "Where did you find it? Here? All right. Now, Arthur, listen to me. When Mr. Stanley gets back, I want you to tell him that we were all utterly flabbergasted by his unforgivable rudeness to His Royal Highness. Fortunately, however, the Prince has agreed to meet with us again this evening. He will be arriving for supper at the Athenaeum promptly at eight, and under no circumstances would it do to keep him waiting a second time. We expect Henry to be there at the very latest at seven-thirty."

"Yes, sir, I'll tell him that."

"Seven-thirty, Arthur. Seven-thirty at the very latest."

After the men left, Jephson went into the library and sat down at the rolltop desk. It felt odd, after these three hectic weeks, to have nothing pressing to do; the apartment itself seemed an unfamiliar place without the constant comings and goings of the expedition's officers, without the constant deliveries and removals of boxes and crates, without the mess and bustle and Stanley's bulldog energy driving them on. Jephson could not remember ever having been in the flat when it was so quiet, when no one else but Baruti was there. And even Baruti was quiet now. He had followed Jephson into the library and stood by a window, keeping an eye on Jephson as if needing reassurance that someone was still there. Obviously the little fellow had had a scare. Perhaps the child had awakened in the morning and gone into Mr. Stanley's bedroom with the breakfast tray and found Mr. Stanley gone. Or perhaps he had lain awake all through the previous night waiting for Mr. Stanley to come home—and he hadn't.

Was that possible? Had Mr. Stanley not come back to the flat the previous night after he had seen Nelson off? But where would he have gone, where would he have spent the night? Jephson looked at Baruti silhouetted in the window against the gray light of the winter afternoon. He wished he could speak Swahili properly so he could question the little blackamoor on this. It would make a difference if Stanley hadn't come home last night, if he had spent the night elsewhere. For he might still be there.

Jephson looked around the library at the shadowy shapes of furniture in the fading silvery light of the passing afternoon; he looked at the desk in front of him. Then he leaned over and opened the desk's bottom drawer on the right side and took out the leather folio Hutton had found. It was curious that he hadn't been aware of its existence until today. After all, he had been through the desk so many times, filing things in it, searching through its drawers for errant documents, rearranging things. He ought to have come across it a hundred times. But perhaps the folio hadn't been there until today; perhaps Stanley had placed it there only when he knew Jephson and the others would no longer have occasion to bother with the desk. He turned it over in his hand, fiddled with its lock, tried to peer into it. Hutton was right. It did appear to contain letters, a private correspondence of some sort, kept under lock and key. He returned it to the drawer and stood up.

"*Njoo hapa*, Baruti. *Lazima niende sasa, toto.* I go out now," he said in his broken Swahili, squatting in front of the boy. "*Nitarudi upesi.* I come back soon."

He pinched the little blackamoor's cheeks and smiled at him in what he hoped was a reassuring manner. And although the child looked at him with big sad eyes, not seeming in the least reassured, Jephson fetched his topcoat and bowler and hurried down to the street and hailed a passing hack. He gave the driver Dolly Tennant's address in Richmond Terrace.

Dolly was not receiving. Her maid looked at him with grave suspicion at his calling by at such an inappropriate hour and muttered some excuse on her mistress's behalf. At first Jephson thought she was saying that Dolly wasn't in. Then he gathered that she was in but she was indisposed, which, after a bit more wrangling with the girl, translated into the intelligence that Dolly was having a nap and had left strict instructions not to be disturbed. Jephson was not to be put off. He pressed his visiting card on the maid and sent her packing up to Dolly's bedroom with the message that his visit was of an extremely urgent nature.

He remained in the foyer in his topcoat and hat, since the maid had refused either to relieve him of them or usher him into the sitting room. But after a moment, increasingly annoyed at what he presumed to be Dolly's shenanigans, he removed his coat and bowler, flung them over the balustrade of the staircase that ascended to the upper-floor apartments, and marched into the sitting room on his own. He didn't stay there long, however. The house was very still, and thinking he might be able to hear what was going on up in Dolly's bedroom, he returned to the foyer and listened. He couldn't hear a thing. He went a few steps up the staircase and craned his neck around trying to get a glimpse of the first-floor landing. Still there was no discernible sound of voices, either male or female. He stole up a few more steps. But then a door opened and he beat a hasty retreat.

It was the maid. "Miss Tennant will be right with you," she said snippily and clattered off to some other part of the house.

Dolly followed a few moments later. "Arthur dear, how awfully nice of you to pop by," she said, sweeping down the staircase, holding her hand out to be kissed. She wore a rather showy dressing gown over a pretty silk chemise with a long train, but her face was without makeup and her hair quite obviously had been quickly combed and pinned. There was no doubt that she came straight from her bed. "Though I must say this isn't the hour that I'm usually at home to anyone, you know."

"Yes, I do know and I apologize for bursting in on you," Jephson said, taking her hand. "But this is quite urgent, I assure you."

"So Mary said. What is it? I wonder." She led Jephson into the sitting room. "Has someone died?"

"No."

"Well, that's a relief." She walked toward the fireplace as if meaning to warm herself by it but then turned away abstractedly. "What time is it? I was asleep. Is it teatime? Would you care for tea, Arthur?"

"No, thank you."

"Well then, what *can* I do for you?" She faced him, her hands clasped in front of her waist.

Jephson, not having been invited to sit down, also remained standing. "I have a message for Mr. Stanley," he said.

"For Mr. Stanley, Henry? You have a message for him?"

"Yes, and it is quite urgent."

"Well, deliver it, dear boy. Deliver it by all means." She

glanced down at her hands, then up at him again, suddenly frowning. "Am I somehow preventing you from doing so?"

"Dolly, listen. The Prince of Wales is expecting to meet with Mr. Stanley this evening at eight at the Athenaeum."

"Henry and Prince Edward? How very exciting."

"Mr. Stanley doesn't know about this meeting though. The arrangements were made in his absence. But you can understand how important it is that he be told. It would be an awful embarrassment if he failed to turn up."

"Of course."

"It isn't necessary that I tell him myself. In fact, under the circumstances, I can quite understand why it might be preferable that I didn't. The only important thing is that he be told."

"What are you talking about, Arthur?"

"Dolly, I should like to think that I can rely on you to pass this message on to Mr. Stanley."

"On me? How? What in heaven's name *are* you talking about, Arthur?"

"Please, Dolly. You can count on my discretion, I assure you. My only interest is in seeing that Mr. Stanley keeps his appointment with His Royal Highness tonight."

"I haven't the vaguest idea what you're talking about, dear boy. And quite frankly I'm not sure that I want to. As a matter of fact, I think it best that we terminate this conversation right now—before you find yourself saying something you will regret." She turned away from him. "I should be glad to renew my offer of tea, Arthur, but if you are still of a mind to refuse it, well then, you must excuse me. I am attending the Clarendons' fancy dress ball tonight, and I really ought to begin pulling myself together." She started out of the room.

"Dolly, there's no need for playacting. I know he is here."

She whirled around.

"I know how you've been pursuing him ever since he returned from America. I know all about your letters. In my position as his secretary, certain matters come to my attention, inescapably. I can't say that I particularly approve of what you're up to, Dolly dear, or what you want of this man now that he is again so much in the public eye, seeing how you have already once turned him down, and rather to his humiliation, I might add. But I am perfectly aware that it's none of my business. He certainly doesn't need me to protect him from you. He can handle you well enough himself, I am sure. My only concern is that he learn that he is expected at the Athenaeum tonight at seven-thirty to meet with the Prince. As I say, you can count on my discretion entirely as to how exactly he happened to learn of it."

"Not another word." She came toward him, her cheeks flaming, her fists clenched at her side. "I do not want to hear another word from you, you filthy-minded little twit."

Jephson involuntarily stepped back in the face of her fury.

"What do you take me for? A shopgirl? A slut? How dare you suggest I would have any man, let alone your Mr. Henry Morton Stanley, visting with me secretly in my chambers in the middle of the afternoon with no one else about but the house servants? What cheek. I demand an immediate apology. Do you hear me, Arthur Mounteney Jephson? I demand an immediate apology."

Jephson said nothing.

And Dolly slapped him across the face. "Get out of my house. Get out of my house this instant."

Jephson put a hand to his stinging cheek and watched her fly out of the sitting room in a swirl of silk. It was a convincing performance, but was it only a performance? Or was he wrong? Was Stanley really not here? But if he wasn't here, where was he?

Scotland Yard was called in.

Mackinnon had resisted taking such drastic action for as long as possible (actually it was Hutton's idea) in fear that, once it was officially acknowledged, word of Stanley's disappearance would spread like wildfire and cause the enterprise considerable embarrassment. But by Monday morning, the seventeenth of January, Mackinnon conceded the risk had to be taken. Stanley had been missing for two full days by then. De Winton and Grant, both moderately fluent in Swahili, had questioned Baruti interminably during that time, but all they managed to learn was that when the little blackamoor last saw Stanley he was leaving the flat and it was dark. This meager scrap of information provoked a raucous debate. Grant and Hutton argued that it signified that Stanley had slipped away in the middle of the night on some disreputable errand. Mackinnon, however, pointed out that "dark" could just as easily mean the dark of winter's early morning, when Stanley usually was up and about anyway. For his part, de Winton held that what the boy most likely was talking about was the dark of the Friday evening when Stanley had left to see Nelson off at the Charing Cross station; obviously he had not returned to the flat afterward, and the only explanation was that he had met with an accident. It was this prospect that finally persuaded Mackinnon to call in the police.

That night after supper they assembled once again at the New Bond Street flat to discuss what to do. By then, Scotland Yard had run a preliminary check of hospitals, clinics, surgeries, and the morgue to no avail. They had also started an investigation into the possibility that Stanley had been kidnapped, and they were planning to make a sweep of the places he was known to frequent, as well as checking on all train, boat, and coach departures from London in the last seventy-two hours on the off-chance he had left the city or even the country during that period. But so far none of this had turned up anything either; and Mackinnon and the others, slowly and with extreme reluctance, were coming around to the idea that they might have to start thinking about making alternative plans. Could they find a new leader for the expedition at such short notice? Or did they have to face up to the fact that they might have to call the expedition off?

None of them was yet willing to face the appalling consequences of calling the expedition off. The popular uproar would be horrendous, the political embarrassment for Her Majesty's Government almost certainly fatal and the material losses to the relief committee in monies already spent to outfit the expedition considerable. Not to mention the blow of failing to establish the Imperial British East Africa Company in Equatoria they so eagerly wanted. But the alternative of finding a replacement for Stanley was no less problematical. The most immediate obvious choices, because of their previous experience in Africa and their present association with the enterprise, were Grant and de Winton. But neither felt himself suited for the job nor, for that matter, especially keen on taking it on. Grant's age was against him (he was over sixty) as well as the fact that it was now nearly thirty years since he had made his epic journey to the source of the Victoria Nile with Speke. As for de Winton, although younger by a decade, his African experience had been in the establishment and administration of coastal stations, not in pioneering and exploring the interior, not in the kind of dangerous and grueling travel through unknown wildernesses that the relief expedition would entail.

Hutton suggested Joseph Thomson, who barely three years before had headed into the interior from Mombasa on the East African coast in an attempt to reach the lakes region. But, as de Winton pointed out, he never got there; he gave it up and turned back in defeat somewhere beyond Kilimanjaro in Masai Land, and what they needed here was a man who couldn't be defeated and turned back.

Other names were mentioned; indeed, in the course of the next hour in Stanley's drawing room, surrounded by the weird and wonderful artifacts he had collected in Africa, they mentioned all the names of those elite few, those singular daring Englishmen who had penetrated the heart of the dark continent where this expedition would have to go—Sir Richard Burton, Captain John Speke, Sir Samuel Baker, the Reverend Doctor David Livingstone—now all dead or old or broken in health by their own amazing journeys.

"Well, who then, for God's sake?" Hutton demanded impatiently. "There must be somebody. You can't be saying there's only one man who can do it."

No one replied. Mackinnon had gotten up and gone to stand by a window. De Winton was smoking his pipe. Jephson had served the gentlemen brandy, and now Grant, who had taken Stanley's leather chair, took a swallow of his, looking away from Hutton.

"That's complete rot. That's balderdash," Hutton said. "Stanley's not a god. What is the matter with you chaps anyway? Of course there's someone else." He looked at them belligerently, waiting for an answer, but again no one bothered; each was lost in his own thoughts. And as if stung by their silence, he suddenly said with startling venom, "I hate that bastard. I hate that guttersnipe. Look at the mess he's gotten us into. And it serves us right too. We should have known better than to associate ourselves with a son of a cheap whore. Look what's come of it."

"Oh, for God's sake, Hutton, you're not going to start on that again," Grant said sharply, peering around the wing of Stanley's leather chair. "I don't much care for the bugger myself, you know, but cussing him out endlessly hardly helps solve our problem."

They fell into silence again. Jephson, leaning against the sideboard, wondered whether as surrogate host he should offer the gentlemen another round of brandy.

But then Mackinnon turned back from the window. "You've got to do it, Frank," he said.

De Winton shook his head.

"We've no other choice."

"This isn't for me. This isn't my cup of tea, Mac."

"It's either that or we scrap it."

De Winton continued shaking his head. "This is a killer, Mac.

I've never handled anything like this. Maybe I could get a caravan up to Msalala, following the Arab trails. But after that, through Karagwe, through the Nkole and Nkori country, where there are no trails, where no one has been before . . . I don't know how to do that sort of thing. I'd make a dreadful botch of it."

"No you wouldn't. You'd get through."

"It's not just a question of my getting through. I'd have to get through in time. Time is everything in this, Mac. As soon as the caravan strikes upcountry, certainly once it reaches Lake Victoria, the dervishes are going to know about it; and then, as Henry said, the race will be on. They'll attack then. They'll throw their entire force at Emin then. I'd never get through before his garrison fell. It would be Gordon and Wolseley all over again."

"It doesn't matter. You've got to try it anyway. It's better than nothing." Mackinnon came over to the sofa and sat down on its armrest by de Winton. "You know very well I can't go to Salisbury and tell him we're calling it off. He's counting on us. His government's survival depends on this expedition. We're honor-bound, at the very least, to make an attempt for him. It almost doesn't matter whether we succeed or not so long as the attempt is made."

De Winton set his pipe down on the deal table and rubbed his eyes. He kept his hands over them while Mackinnon went on quietly trying to persuade him.

"Frank, listen. Just take the caravan up to Msalala and see what your chances are of getting through to Wadelai in time. If you think you can, splendid, go ahead, and we'll get everything we had hoped for. But if not, if you see it's out of the question, all right, turn back. Just turn back. Leave it at that. No one can be faulted. We've done our best. We've kept our promise. We sent a relief expedition into the heart of Africa, we tried the impossible and failed. It's a tragedy but it can never be said that England abandoned that noble Turk, that we didn't make the attempt to rescue him."

"So that's what it has come down to has it?" Hutton put in. "A charade. A piece of theater. That's what we've been reduced to, thanks to Mr. Henry Stanley."

Mackinnon ignored him. "Look, Frank, chances are that Henry will turn up in good time. He didn't vanish into thin air. We're pretty sure he wasn't murdered or kidnapped. He's bound to turn up. But if he doesn't, if for some reason that we can't imagine . . . Frank, this is our only realistic recourse under the circumstances. We're honor-bound to make a show of it, to get Salisbury off the hook. We've got to at least run a caravan up to Msalala before packing it in. You can do that. You said so yourself. You can do at least that much."

De Winton removed his hands from his eyes. "How large is the caravan meant to be?"

Jephson did not realize the question was addressed to him. He had followed the exchange between Mackinnon and de Winton, and although it disheartened him he understood perfectly well that the expedition, this erstwhile grand adventure, this once glorious vehicle for heroism, was to become a mere political gesture meant less to rescue Emin Pasha than to save Lord Salisbury. And so he assumed that what Colonel de Winton was asking was simply how large a caravan would be required to make the attempt appear credible.

"Arthur," Mackinnon said.

"Sir?"

"Colonel de Winton asked you how many porters Mr. Stanley planned for the caravan."

"Six hundred, sir."

"Only six hundred?" de Winton said.

"Not in total, sir. Six hundred are to make the entire journey. Jack Troup and Willie Hoffman are hiring them in Zanzibar. Wanyamwezis. Whatever additional *pagazis* will be required, perhaps five hundred or six hundred more at different stages depending on the terrain, Mr. Stanley planned to recruit as they are needed, along the route of the march."

"I see. And the armed escort? He also planned to have an armed escort with him, didn't he?"

"Yes, sir." Jephson left the sideboard. "Two hundred, sir, Sudanese askaris. Major Barttelot and Captain Nelson are recruiting them in Aden. Mainly from the remnants of General Gordon's Black Battalion and the Mudir of Dongola's *bashibazouks*. Major Barttelot thinks highly of them. He had them under his command during the Nile campaign."

"And they're to get the Remingtons?"

"Yes, sir, although some will be selected to serve as noncommissioned officers under Sergeant Bonny, and they will be equipped with the new Winchester repeaters."

"I see."

"Have the lad sit down, Frank," Grant said.

"Yes of course. Draw up one of those chairs, lad."

Jephson pulled a straight-back chair up to the deal table. Grant was on his right in the leather chair, de Winton on his left at one end of the sofa, and Mackinnon went around and sat down at the other end, pushing Hutton closer to de Winton, thus completing a circle around Jephson. Ironically, the youth, who had joined the enterprise and indeed had served it until now as its least important, most junior assistant, had emerged by force of the peculiar circumstances as the only person available in London with enough detailed knowledge of the expedition to provide a new leader with the information he needed. At first Jephson confined himself to answering de Winton's questions. But soon enough he found himself anticipating the questions and addressing himself to questions de Winton didn't think to ask; and then, with the others' encouragement, he simply launched into a briefing on his own.

It lasted the better part of two hours and was an impressive performance. Jephson himself, as a matter of fact, was impressed by it. This was the first time he had had a chance to review what he had learned during the past few weeks, and to his tremendous delight he discovered that he had learned everything. He had done his work diligently, paid attention carefully, and because he had been involved in virtually every aspect of the expedition's preparations—assisting Barttelot and Nelson on military matters, deputizing for Troup in the ordering and shipment of the caravan's equipment and supplies, even running errands for Dr. Leslie—he very possibly knew more about it overall (with the obvious exception of Mr. Stanley himself) than any one of them. And the confidence and authority that this gave him showed in his voice as he ran through the multitude of details, as he instructed de Winton and the others clustered around him who were hanging on his words, relying on his knowledge. A subtle but distinct change occurred in their attitude toward him during those two hours, and when he finished they acknowledged this by the way they remained silent for a few moments, waiting attentively until they were sure he had nothing further to tell them.

Mackinnon broke the silence. "What do you think, Frank?"

De Winton picked up his pipe. It had gone out and he stabbed a pipe knife into the bowl and knocked out the dead ashes. Then, with something of a sigh, he said, "All right. I'll give it a go."

"Wonderful, Frank. I knew you wouldn't let us down."

"But I have to have the lad with me."

"There's no problem with that."

"But, sir—"

"I quite need you along, Arthur," de Winton said. "Your familiarity with all these details makes you absolutely essential. I couldn't possibly catch up with all of it in the time that's left. You will be my aide-de-camp and keep an eye on everything for me. I can't imagine carrying this off otherwise."

"That's very kind of you to say, sir, but I wasn't meant to go along, you know. Mr. Stanley never had it in mind for me to go."

"The situation is rather different now."

"I realize that, sir, but I've not made any preparations."

"Well, you'll just have to make them then, won't you? As I will."

"Yes, sir, but, you see, I've no experience with this sort of thing. I've never even been to Africa, let alone gone on an expedition of this sort. You have, sir. All the others have. I'd be the only one without any experience at all."

"What's the matter with you, Arthur? Don't you want to go?" This was Mackinnon. "I should have thought you'd jump at the chance. A young chap like you. What an opportunity this represents to show your mettle. Why, I'd wager, any one of your chums would give an arm and a leg for the chance to exchange places with you."

"I suppose they would," the youth replied. This was happening too quickly, too suddenly, too unexpectedly. He looked at Mackinnon's reproving expression; he could imagine what the man, what all these men, must be thinking of him. "I didn't say I didn't want to go."

"Well, I should have hoped you didn't. I should have hoped you were more of a man than that."

"Of course I want to go. It was just that—"

"It's settled then."

Jesus; Jephson's stomach lurched at those words.

"It's settled, Frank," Mackinnon repeated, rubbing his hands together. "Take the caravan up to Msalala. Do the best you can from there. But however it works out, not to worry. At least we made a show of it."

"Yes," de Winton replied with somewhat less enthusiasm. "We'll make a show of it. But that's the best I can promise."

After the men left—it was nearly midnight by then—Jephson sat on the sofa in the drawing room as if felled by a blow. His mind was in a whirl. The one idea he tried to hold on to was that the expedition was to be a charade, as Hutton had put it, merely a long walk to Msalala. He was sure Colonel de Winton would go no farther than that, would judge it impossible to get through to Equatoria in time, making the expedition a far less dangerous affair. But, oddly, this wasn't quite the comfort it ought to have been, because Jephson hated the idea that all the hard work and planning of the past few weeks were to be used for an empty political gesture, hated to concede that Emin Pasha was to be betrayed and not only Emin Pasha but also Troup and Hoffman and Leslie and Ward and Nelson and Barttelot and Bonny, who had willingly come forward to risk their lives for the sake of a grand adventure, who had unhesitatingly volunteered to undergo brutal hardship for a chance at authentic heroism. They too were to be betrayed.

Jephson stood up. There were any number of practical matters he should have been thinking about—booking passage for himself aboard the *Navarino*, getting his personal kit together, sending cables to Aden and Zanzibar informing the others of the change in leadership, making arrangements for Baruti. Yes, there was that too; the little boy couldn't just be left alone in Stanley's flat. Some arrangement had to be made for him.

"How could he have done it?" Jephson said aloud. "How in God's name could he have done this?" He was speaking of Stanley of course because it was Stanley who had betrayed them.

He went into the library. Later he would tell himself his intention had been to start drafting cables to Aden and Zanzibar. But he didn't start drafting cables. He didn't even bother to look for pen and ink. He sat down at the rolltop desk and went directly to the desk's bottom drawer on the right side, opened it, and took out the leather folio of Stanley's private correspondence. As before, he jiggled the lock in vain for a few seconds. He hesitated hardly at all, and although his heart started racing, he felt he had the right. Stanley had betrayed them; Stanley could be betrayed. He picked up a metal paper knife and inserted it under the brass lock and twisted it and sprang the lock.

A sheaf of letters, perhaps a dozen. But they were not letters from Dolly Tennant. They were in French. They were from Leopold II, the King of the Belgians.

"What are you doing in there, lad?"

Jephson recognized the rough, low voice instantly and whirled around. He heard Stanley striding across the drawing room directly toward the library, and it appeared inevitable that he would catch Jephson red-handed in the act of pilfering his private correspondence, except that at the last moment, thank God, Baruti diverted him. The child, perhaps lying awake with worry or tossing unhappily in the grip of an anxious dream, had heard him come in and now, his woolen nightshirt flying, his face contorted by an expression of unbelieving joy, he came racing down the hallway from his room behind the pantry and flung himself into Stanley's arms. The surprise of it spun Stanley around, and giving out a bark of laughter, he tumbled onto the sofa and let the boy crawl all over him like an ecstatic puppy, affectionately roughhousing with him there long enough to let Jephson shove the letters back into the folio and the folio back into the desk.

"Where have you been? In God's name, Mr. Stanley, where have you been?" Jephson cried. He slammed the drawer shut and bounded out into the drawing room. "Do you realize what a panic we've all been in since last Friday? I mean, you were meant to meet with the Prince of Wales last Friday. No one had the first idea what had happened to you. Scotland Yard's been called in, you know. We thought you must have been murdered or kidnapped or something."

Stanley managed to quiet Baruti, and still sprawled on the sofa and hugging the child to his chest, he looked up and listened to Jephson's agitated rambling with a bemused smile.

"For a while there it actually seemed as if the expedition would have to be scrapped," Jephson went on. "But no one was in favor of that. Everyone agreed that that would only make matters worse. The expedition had to go forward, whatever had happened to you. A new leader had to be found. Everyone agreed that we had to find a new leader to replace you."

"And did you?"

"Yes. Colonel de Winton."

"Colonel de Winton? Oh, for Christ sake."

Stanley's smile, his apparent lack of concern for all the trouble he had caused irritated Jephson. "Colonel de Winton wasn't all that keen on taking on the assignment, but he was sporting enough to give it a go, seeing how you had vanished into thin air and left us all in the lurch."

"Oh, that's ridiculous. Frank could never make a go of it in a million years. What in blazes could the man be thinking? He's never done anything like this in his life. And besides he doesn't know a blasted thing about the expedition."

"That's not true," Jephson shot back. "Actually he knows a great deal about it. I provided him with a detailed briefing just a few hours ago. I filled him in on pretty nearly everything he needs to know. And what's more, I've agreed to accompany him and keep an eye on everything for him. He asked me to serve as his aide-de-camp."

"Did he?"

"Yes," Jephson replied defiantly.

"Well, I must say he showed some good sense in that at least." Stanley shifted Baruti from his chest and sat up straighter. "You'd make a fine aide-de-camp, Arthur. No doubt about it. I congratulate him for thinking of it."

Jepson hadn't expected this. In fact, quite the contrary, he had braced himself for some cutting, sarcastic remark; and when just the opposite occurred, when he heard the warmly flattering words, all of his irritation with Stanley evaporated.

"I've been thinking much the same thing myself, you know," Stanley went on. "The last week or so I started thinking I really ought to have that lad along with me. It'd make my life a hell of a lot easier, having him around to keep an eye on things for me."

Jephson positively beamed.

"You've done a good job, lad. You've kept on top of everything. You'll make a damn fine aide."

"Thank you, sir."

"But even so, even with you along, lad, Frank wouldn't stand a prayer in hell's chance of getting through to Equatoria in time."

"Well, actually sir, I don't think he really thought so himself. No one did, not really. Everyone agreed you were the only one who had any chance at all of making it. But the feeling was that an attempt had to be made anyway. Emin couldn't just be abandoned without at least a show being made of it. So Colonel de Winton agreed to take the caravan up to Msalala, but I don't think he reckoned on getting much farther than that. That would just have to be good enough."

"To get Salisbury off the hook."

"Yes, sir."

"But not to secure Equatoria for the Imperial East Africa Company."

"No, sir."

"They'd given up on the royal charter company, had they?"

"Yes, sir, pretty much."

"I don't suppose they were very pleased about that."

"No, sir, they weren't, but they didn't feel they had much choice once it seemed you had vanished."

"Ah, but you see, I haven't."

"Yes, sir, and they'll be awfully relieved to know that, I can tell you."

Stanley slumped back in the sofa and turned toward Baruti. The child, snuggled up against his shoulder, had fallen asleep.

"Do they know that, sir? Do Sir William and the others know that you're back?"

"No."

"Don't you think they should be told? I could run around to Sir William's."

"It's too late. Time enough tomorrow."

"Oh, I'm sure he wouldn't mind being disturbed. It certainly would improve his night's sleep knowing you're back and we're going ahead as planned."

"Ah, but we're not."

"Sir?"

"We're not going ahead as planned." Stanley's face was turned toward the sleeping Baruti. "There's been a change in plans."

"What is that, sir?"

"The route." Stanley now looked at Jephson. "We're going by a different route."

Jephson didn't say anything.

"We're going by the Congo, lad," Stanley said.

"That was the route you originally proposed."

"That's right. I'm glad you remember. It was always my first choice."

"But Sir William and the others– Well, as I recall, they objected to it quite vigorously."

"That's right. You recall rightly."

"But I don't understand, sir. Won't they still object?"

"Very probably. But it doesn't matter. Because I'm going by the Congo, or I'm not going at all."

• SEVEN •

"BY JOVE, SIR, this is blackmail," James Hutton said. "This is nothing but the cheapest kind of blackmail."

Stanley shrugged. He was leaning against the mantelpiece in the drawing room, hands jammed in the pockets of his dressing gown, staring at the four dumbstruck gentlemen of the relief committee who had rushed over to his flat first thing that morning. They were still in their overcoats; none had sat down.

"Is this an ultimatum, Henry?" Mackinnon asked.

"You can always have Frank lead the expedition."

"That's what I call blackmail," Hutton said again. "There's no other word for it."

"Shut up, Hutton. For God's sake, just shut up," Mackinnon snapped, then turned back to Stanley. "But why, Henry? Why?"

"It's the best route, the fastest. It gives me a decent chance. I've always felt that."

"But if you've always felt that, why didn't you insist on it when you first proposed it?"

"It had a serious flaw, which I only managed to set right in the last few days."

"Oh, don't tell me," Hutton burst in again. "Don't tell me we're actually going to be allowed to know where Mr. Stanley has been for the last few days."

Stanley ignored him. "Obviously, the great advantage of this route is the Congo River," he said, "or, more accurately, the more than one thousand miles of navigable river from the Pool to Yambuya. But, equally obviously it is an advantage only if I can actually travel on it, which is to say only if I can get hold of enough riverboats to transport the men and supplies of the expedition up it."

"You don't say," Hutton muttered under his breath.

"Well, quite frankly at the outset I wasn't sure I could. That's why I didn't press the point. If I couldn't, the river was useless to me. But I never put it out of my mind. It haunted me, nagged at me. The advantage of traveling on the river could make all the difference between success and failure. The caravan could travel five times, ten times, faster on the river than it ever could marching overland, and in a race with the dervishes that could make all the difference. So how could I put it out of my mind? I had to see if I could get hold of enough boats to exploit the advantage the river offered. So I went to Brussels."

"Brussels?" someone croaked; it probably was Hutton.

"Yes, I've been in Brussels these last few days, discussing my problem with King Leopold. And I am happy to report His Majesty has agreed to put at my disposal the entire fleet of Free State steamers he has plying the Congo between the Pool and the Falls."

"He has what?" Hutton cried out. "Excuse me, but I don't think I heard you correctly, sir. Did you say King Leopold has agreed to put his Congo River fleet at the expedition's disposal?"

"That's what I said."

"Why? Don't tell me he has taken a humanitarian interest in Emin Pasha's plight. Please don't tell me that."

"All right. I won't tell you that."

"You *were* going to say that? I don't believe it. By Jove, you actually were going to stand there and say that that monster, has decided to assist in the rescue of Emin Pasha out of the sheer goodness of his black heart."

"If you don't mind, Hutton," Stanley said very quietly, "I'd just as soon you didn't refer to King Leopold in such terms. You seem to forget that I served His Majesty for a number of years in the founding of the Congo Free State and that I regard him as a friend."

"I don't give a damn whether you take offense at my terms or not," Hutton retorted hotly. "I have already taken offense—at your vanishing act, at your blackmail attempt, and now at this contemptible insult to our intelligence. What kind of fools do you take us for? That blackguard couldn't possibly be moved to do *anything* for humanitarian reasons."

"I am going to ask you one more time, Hutton," Stanley said in a low, rough whisper. "Shut your mouth, or I will shut it for you."

"Of course. Naturally. Knock the other chap on the head. That's your idea of how to handle anything. That's what you were taught in the gutters where you come from."

Stanley stepped away from the mantelpiece, a single step. In the same instant his right arm shot out and he seized Hutton by the throat; and with amazing ease, so powerful was his arm, he sent him stumbling wildly backwards across the room.

"Good Lord," Mackinnon shouted, dashing between the two men. "What are we to have now, an ale-house brawl?"

Hutton slammed into a wall and slid down it, collapsing like a rag doll, his face ashen, his eyes popping in fright, a trickle of blood showing in the corner of his mouth where he had bitten his lip. Grant rushed to him, kneeled at his side and offered him a handkerchief. De Winton took this occasion to sit down on the sofa; still wearing his overcoat, he crossed his legs and looked at Stanley with a quizzical expression. Mackinnon had thrown an arm around Stanley's shoulder and, leading him away from Hutton, was talking to him earnestly. Stanley listened quite calmly. This was what attracted de Winton's puzzled attention—Stanley's calm. He didn't seem in the least bit riled; all the fury, which one had to suppose he must have felt to manhandle Hutton in that way, didn't show in his face.

"But surely you see Hutton's point," Mackinnon was saying. "Even you have to concede that Leopold, what with all that we now know about how he has been raping the Congo Free State. . . . Well honestly, Henry, he is hardly someone from whom a disinterested gesture of this sort could be expected. Surely he demanded something in return for the use of his steamers."

"You're damn right he did," Hutton croaked from his sitting position against the wall, dabbing at his bleeding lip. "He demanded plenty. And Stanley's given it to him too. All of it."

"Will you stop it, Hutton," Mackinnon snapped.

"No, I will not. He's sold us out to that blackguard. You mark my word. He's made a deal with that monster, and I know what it is."

"What is it?" Stanley suddenly jerked around toward the crumpled figure on the carpet.

"You two are not going to have at it again." Mackinnon gripped Stanley's arm. "I won't allow it. I'll scrap this whole bloody expedition before I allow this kind of brawling between grown men."

"Don't worry yourself, Mac," Stanley said. "I just want to hear what deal Hutton supposes I've made with Leopold. Go ahead, Hutton. Tell us."

"I'll tell you all right," Hutton replied, scrambling to his feet, holding the handkerchief to his mouth. "Leopold, your darling Leopold, wants to extend the northeastern border of the Congo Free State through the Ituri forest to the southern Sudan. He has been aching to do that ever since the Berlin Conference. Isn't that right? How many times has he tried to send an expedition through the Ituri to lay claim to the territory between the Upper Congo and the Upper Nile? And how many times has he failed?"

"What's your point?" Mackinnon demanded, fearful that Hutton might say something to trigger Stanley's temper again. "Make your point."

"My point is that Mr. Stanley has agreed to make yet another attempt for him, using the relief expedition by which to do it," Hutton replied. "That's the deal he's made with that blackguard. In return for the use of the fleet of Congo riverboats, he has agreed to lay claim to all the territory the expedition passes through, from Yambuya on the Upper Congo to Wadelai on the Upper Nile, in the name of Leopold the Second, King of the Belgians, King of the Congo Free State."

Stanley walked back to the mantelpiece and leaned against it, folding his arms across his chest.

Mackinnon looked at him, expecting him to say something. Then, after a long moment, he cleared his throat. "Henry," he asked, "is this true?"

"What difference does it make?" Stanley replied.

"What difference does it make?" Hutton sputtered. "I'll tell you what difference it makes. For one thing, what happened to the route you were going to open up for us to connect Equatoria to the outside world, the route by which we were going to be able to keep our royal charter company supplied over the long haul? I don't care how cozy your relationship is with Leopold, you know damn well the Congo's no good for that. You know we can't have our trade passing through the domain of a foreign monarch, dependent on the whims of that monarch, and especially *that* monarch. We'd be bloody lunatics to put ourselves into a position like that. We've got to have our own route, a route firmly under our own control."

"And you shall have it too," Stanley shot back. "I'll open it up for you on the way out."

"On the way out?"

"Yes, on the way out. I propose to lead the expedition *out* of Equatoria precisely by the route we originally planned that I lead it *in*." Stanley moved away from the mantelpiece. "Once I've reached Emin, once I've relieved his garrisons and secured his position and am no longer in a race with the dervishes, then I'll have all the time in the world to open that route, pacify the kaffirs, make treaties with their chiefs, build stockades and supply depots, and blaze the trail for the caravans of the Imperial British East Africa Company to follow."

"It sounds like a good plan, Henry," Mackinnon said after a long pause. "Yes, it does that. I can't quarrel with that. But there still is this other matter, what sort of arrangement you made with Leopold in order to be able to carry it off. I mean, I'm not at all sure we could countenance lending the relief expedition to an arrangement of the sort Hutton has described, laying claim to territory in the name of a foreign monarch, carrying a foreign monarch's flag, that sort of thing. It raises all kinds of sticky diplomatic problems and foreign policy considerations, you understand. It is something I would have to discuss with Lord Salisbury, I'm afraid, if it is indeed the deal you've struck with Leopold as Hutton supposes."

"Of course it is," Hutton interjected furiously. "It is exactly the deal he has struck."

Stanley suddenly whirled toward Hutton. "I don't want to hear another squeak out of you, Hutton. Do you understand? I don't give a damn what you suppose. I'm the one who is going to have to march into hell, not you. I'm the one who is going to be fighting through the African darkness while you're sitting here safe and sound by your fire, reckoning your profits. So I'm the one who's going to decide how to go about it. It's none of your concern. All you need concern yourself with is whether or not I bring back your prize, whether I get the royal charter company for you or not." He turned to Mackinnon. "And don't you start raising elegant objections with me either, Mac. I don't want to hear about the niceties of diplomatic considerations and Lord Salisbury's foreign policy problems. Just tell me. Do you want me to go in there and get Equatoria for you or don't you? If you do, then get the hell out of my way. Otherwise let's call it quits. Frank can take command of the expedition. I've set it up for him. He can take the lad here and do whatever the hell he likes with it, and I'll return to America and resume my tour. I don't need this bloody expedition. I don't need to put my life and reputation at risk yet another time. But if I'm going to, then I'm going to do whatever I see fit to make sure I succeed. Because I tell you, my friend, I mean to succeed." He turned again to Hutton and started toward him; and

Hutton, in a panic, scurried around the sofa to put it between himself and Stanley. But all Stanley was after was the cigar box on the deal table. He took out a cigar, bit off its tip, spat that on the floor, and stuck the cigar into his mouth. "So what will it be?" he asked. "Are you going to get out of my way and let me go or aren't you? I've only two days left before the *Navarino* sails."

"Let him go," de Winton said. "Let Bula Matari go."

"Yes, yes, of course we want you to go, Henry. I didn't mean to suggest anything else," Mackinnon said hastily. "It's just that I don't know what I can say to Lord Salisbury to explain the change in route."

"Just say I'm taking the Congo because it's the surest, fastest way to rescue Emin Pasha and get Her Majesty's Government off the hook."

"But what about the arrangement with King Leopold? What am I to tell him about that?"

"What arrangement with King Leopold? Did you hear me say anything about an arrangement with King Leopold?"

"But Hutton—"

"Hutton's a fool and talks rubbish."

"Be reasonable, Henry. Salisbury is bound to ask me why Leopold has put his fleet of riverboats at the expedition's disposal. How am I to reply to that?"

"His humanitarianism, Mac. Leopold has been moved by the noble Turk's plight and is anxious to assist in his rescue."

Mackinnon shook his head haplessly.

"All right," Stanley said. "Now all of you get the hell out of here. The lad and I have work to do."

No one moved. Mackinnon studied Stanley's face, as if searching for some sign there, as if asking another question. But there was nothing to be learned from Stanley's rock-hard expression, and reluctantly Mackinnon turned away and started for the door. Hutton and Grant followed him. De Winton stood up from the sofa.

"If you don't mind me saying, Henry," he said, "I think it's a mistake, tactically."

"Is that so?"

"Yes, I still think that the time you will gain traveling on the Congo you will lose a hundred times over trying to get through the Ituri forest. That's a nasty place, Henry. You know it. I know it."

Stanley took de Winton's arm and escorted him to the door.

"But there's no dissuading you, is there?" de Winton went on. "You're dead set on going through the Ituri. You've been dead set on it from the beginning. I saw that the first day. But I haven't been able to figure out why."

They reached the door. Mackinnon, Grant, and Hutton had gone down the corridor to call for the lift.

De Winton turned to Stanley. "Is it hubris, Bula Matari? To be the first man to get through that beastly forest? To accomplish one last spectacular feat of exploration to cap your career?" De Winton looked hard into Stanley's gray-green eyes. "Or did Leopold give you no choice?"

Remarkably, there was far less work to do in order to reroute the expedition than Jephson had expected. Admittedly, there would have been a considerable saving had the hardware and equipment from England been shipped directly to the Congo, and now too a vessel had to be engaged to transport the supplies and men not merely across the strait to the African mainland at Bagamoyo, but clear around the Cape of Good Hope and up the West African coast to the Congo's mouth. In addition, a number of cables had to be sent: one to Herbert Ward, who was then at Banana Point on the Congo estuary awaiting a mail packet to take him to Zanzibar, telling him to remain where he was; and another to Jack Troup, instructing him to proceed straight away to join Ward on the Congo and begin arranging for the fleet of Congo riverboats and making other preparations in advance of the expedition's arrival. But in the overall scheme of things, these were really minor adjustments. It was as if Stanley had planned for this contingency all along, as if he had expected to take the Congo all along.

Dick Leslie, the birdlike doctor, returned to London from Sussex on Wednesday, the day before the *Navarino*'s departure. Stanley was away; he had gone to Sandringham with Mackinnon to keep at long last his appointment with the Prince of Wales. Jephson and Leslie spent the bright cold day overseeing the cartage of the various steamer trunks and medicine chests and gladstone bags and portmanteaux and duffels and boxes and crates to the Charing Cross station. Leslie was good company. Jephson had come to think of him as something of a comic character, what with his air of being relentlessly harassed by wife and child and mother-in-law and patients, his constant rushing off to quell some disturbance in his disorderly private life. But in the course of that day Jephson saw that this comedy was just a pose. Leslie was nowhere nearly as harassed or befuddled as he liked to make out for the amusement of others. For all his nervous darting about and sharp-tongued complaints, the little doctor knew exactly what needed to be done and how to do it. Having him along saved Jephson an immense amount of time and bother.

For his part, Leslie was mildly astonished to discover that Jephson had joined the expedition. But he didn't make much of it. He simply commented, on noticing Jephson's gear among the luggage they were having sent to Southampton, that sooner or later, he supposed, everyone fell under Stanley's spell. At the time, Jephson misunderstood the remark; he took it to be a reference to one of the workmen from the cartage firm who was patently awestruck by the fact that he was actually handling the famous explorer's steamer trunk. But toward the end of the day, Leslie made another oblique reference to the matter. They had just come out of the baggage office at the Charing Cross station and had decided to stop for tea at the station cafe.

"Well now, we're all set to be blooming heroes," Leslie remarked, taking a seat at a table by a window that looked out on the tracks. "By tonight our luggage will be aboard the *Navarino* and by tomorrow night we'll be aboard her ourselves. Then we'll be in for it. No turning back then. We'll be off to be heroes, whether we like it or not."

Jephson smiled weakly. The thought didn't particularly please him at the moment.

"I myself have been a hero any number of times," Leslie went on. "Whenever one travels with Mr. Stanley one quite automatically becomes a hero, you know. But you, lad, I take it this will be your first time. You shall enjoy it, I assure you. I congratulate you on badgering Mr. Stanley into giving you this opportunity to be one."

"I wouldn't say that I *badgered* Mr. Stanley for the opportunity exactly."

The waitress arrived with the tea and sandwiches. Leslie took the chit from her, waving aside Jephson's attempt to pay, then set about playing "mother." Jephson watched his hands, small and thin but obviously strong, pouring out the tea carefully. Jephson remembered how Stanley had said that they would all be safe in those hands, that they all would come back alive because of those hands.

"Actually, I have to admit, I really didn't much seek the opportunity at all," he said.

"Don't tell me, lad—cream and sugar?—don't tell me Mr. Stanley offered you the place without your specifically requesting it?"

"Yes. Well, actually Colonel de Winton offered it to me first, while Mr. Stanley was still missing and he had agreed to take over the command. And then when Mr. Stanley returned, he said he thought it was a good idea, that it was something he had been thinking about himself and especially now that the route was changed—"

"Hey, hold on there a moment, lad," Leslie interrupted. "What are you talking about? What's this about Mr. Stanley missing and Colonel de Winton taking over command and the route being changed?"

"Oh." Of course, Jephson realized, Leslie knew nothing of the confused tangle of events of the last few days. He had been away in Sussex.

"Would you mind filling me in on what this is all about, especially about the change in route. What change in route?"

"Well," Jephson started. He wasn't sure what he should say exactly. There was so much in this that was still a mystery. "Mr. Stanley disappeared for nearly three days, dropped completely out of sight, without a word to anyone, right after we saw Captain Nelson off Friday night. He only returned Monday night."

"Where had he been?"

"That was the terrific mystery. No one had the least idea."

"Brussels," Leslie said.

"What?"

"He'd been to Brussels. To see King Leopold."

"Jesus, Doctor Dick. How did you know? No one else had the least idea."

"And the change in route is to the Congo."

Jephson was about to exclaim again, something about Leslie being positively clairvoyant. But then he saw the expression on the doctor's face. In an instant he had been transformed from a pleasant comic character into a fiercely angry man.

"We are to take the Congo River up to Yambuya, then follow the Aruwimi River through the Ituri forest to Lake Albert. That's it, isn't it?"

Jephson said nothing, shocked by Leslie's expression. The doctor clearly knew something that none of the others knew. Perhaps Jack Troup and Willie Hoffman and Herbert Ward knew it as well. Perhaps all those who had served with Stanley in the Congo knew it.

"That's it, isn't it, lad? Speak up. Answer me."

"Yes."

Leslie looked away, looked out the cafe window at the train tracks, and closed his eyes. Then he said, "Where is he?"

"Mr. Stanley? He went to Sandringham with Sir William to meet with the Prince of Wales."

"When is he due back?"

Jephson glanced at the cafe clock. "Well, actually, he ought to be back by now."

Stanley was at the New Bond Street apartment in his bedroom changing into tails for a banquet that was being given that evening at the Guild Hall in honor of the relief expedition, and he was half dressed, just about to step into his trousers, when Leslie and Jephson burst in on him.

"You can count me out, Bula Matari," the doctor said. "You can strike me from the rolls. I've no intention of committing suicide."

Stanley didn't pull on the trousers. He flung them on the bed and, wearing only long woolen drawers, his muscular shoulders and powerful chest bare, he placed his hands on his hips and stared at Leslie with an amused expression. "What's this all about, Doctor Dick?" he asked. "Has the missus been giving you a bloody time of it again?"

"This has nothing to do with the missus. You know damn well what it has to do with. The Ituri. I'm not going through there. I never agreed to that."

"Now hang on, Dick. You're going off half cocked," Stanley said, reaching for his dressing gown. "Let's sit down and talk this over quietly."

"There's nothing to talk over. There's only one thing you can say and that is whether or not what I've heard is true."

"I've no idea what you've heard."

"The lad here has told me you were summoned to Brussels and capitulated to Leopold's demand to carry his flag through the Ituri to the Nile."

"I beg your pardon, Doctor," Jephson interrupted. "I never said any such thing."

"All right, you didn't. Not in so many words. All you said was that Mr. Stanley had been to Brussels and when he came back he changed the route to the Congo. I divined the rest for myself." He looked at Stanley again. "It wasn't all that difficult to do."

Stanley said nothing. He slipped on his dressing gown.

"That doesn't surprise you, does it, Bula Matari? The lad was surprised. He was flabbergasted. But you're not surprised, are you?"

"No," Stanley said. "But listen here, Dick—"

"There is nothing to listen to. I have no intention of committing suicide. If you mean to go up the Congo and then try and hack your way through the Ituri, you can count me out. I would never much enjoy the idea of killing myself in the Ituri under any circumstances. But I'll be goddamned if I do it for Leopold. And neither should you. You don't have to. You don't have to any more than I do."

Stanley smiled.

"I mean it, Bula Matari," Leslie pressed. The indignant tone left his voice; an earnestness, a pleading replaced it. "Stay with the original route. Go in from the Indian Ocean coast. Go like the blazes. You'll get to Emin in time. It will be a magnificent triumph. The world will never have seen its like. You don't need the Congo, even less the green death of the Ituri. You don't owe this to Leopold."

"Except . . ." Stanley started but then glanced at Jephson and seemed to think better of it. An odd smile flickered across his lips. He began pulling on his trousers. "But that's not the point anyway, Dick. I prefer the Congo route. I've always preferred it. It's the surest, fastest way to get to Emin."

Leslie's expression hardened again. "That's shit," he spat out angrily. "And you know it and you know I know it, so don't hand me that. All right, take the Congo route then. Kill yourself taking it. Try and get through the Ituri and kill yourself trying. But don't kill everyone else, Bula Matari. You haven't got the right to do that. You haven't got the right to take Jack and Will and Bertie Ward and this lad here and everyone else into that green death just because you think you have to."

"Shut up, Dick. Shut up now."

"Yes, all right, I'll shut up."

The two men stared at each other for a long moment.

Then Leslie said quietly, "They trust you, Bula Matari. You shouldn't betray them in this way." And he turned on his heels and walked out of the bedroom.

Stanley watched him go and continued watching him even when he was no longer in sight, listening to his footsteps hurry through the library and then through the drawing room and out to the foyer. Then the door of the flat opened and slammed, and the sound of that seemed to awaken Stanley from his reverie.

"He's lost his nerve," he said. "Too much wife, too much kid, too much mortgage payments. Too much soft living. Well, good riddance to him then." He resumed dressing.

"But you were counting on him so, Mr. Stanley," Jephson said. "I mean, I remember you saying we wouldn't be safe without him. That if we came home alive, it would be because of him."

"Yes, I said that, lad. But that was before I knew he had lost his nerve. He's no good to me without his nerve. I don't want him that way. I wouldn't take him that way." Stanley pulled a starched shirt over his head and turned to the youth. "Don't look so damned worried about it, lad. We'll do splendidly without him. You'll see. We'll find someone else." He started to turn away but then looked back and narrowed his eyes and peered closely at Jephson. "Or is something else bothering you?"

"Sir?"

"You haven't lost your nerve too, have you, lad?"

"Oh, no, sir. No, of course I haven't."

"Good." Stanley broke out into his most captivating smile. "Now get the hell out of here. I've got to get dressed. The Lord Mayor is giving me the key to the city tonight. Much good it will do me on the Congo."

"Yes, sir," Jephson said, also smiling.

But that night, the last he would spend in London, he had a nightmare.

PART TWO
On the River

· ONE ·

THE OCEAN WAS stained with red mud; and clumps of vegetation carried out to sea by a strong current floated past the ship, souvenirs of the land through which the Congo had coursed on its tremendous journey from the heart of Africa to the Atlantic. Ahead, as the oppressively humid mists of early morning burned away, two sandy peninsulas, about ten miles apart, came into view, arcing out from the coastline like the opposing pincers of a giant crab's claw to form the river's mouth. Beyond it, the landfall was flat. Farther up the coast to the north, red clay cliffs ran along the beach; but they fell away abruptly here, and mangrove forests on both sides of the river stretched inland eastward across a maritime plain to the horizon, where the craggy pastel-blue outline of the Crystal Mountains could be seen shimmering in the rose-tinted haze of the African sunrise.

The SS *Madura* sounded her foghorn. It was March 18, 1887.

Jephson had been on deck since before first light and, except for some Wanyamwezi *pagazis* asleep in the *Madura*'s lifeboats, he was alone. He had on knee-high riding boots into which his cotton-twill trousers were tucked; and the uniform khaki tunic, which he wore like a jacket over a blue collarless shirt, was open to the waist, revealing the holstered Smith and Wesson pistol buckled on his belt. He had removed his chalked sun helmet and set it on the forward rail and rested his chin on it as he watched the approach of the Congo coast with intense interest. For here the adventure was truly to begin; here, two months after departing England, after very nearly circumnavigating the entire African continent, the race to rescue Emin Pasha would now at last get under way.

The voyage out to Aden aboard the *Navarino*, with calls at Alexandria and Suez and a side trip to Cairo so that Henry Stanley could pay his respects to the Egyptian Khedive, had taken a bit more than three weeks. Jephson's concern over Dick Leslie's desertion had been eased to a degree when a Captain Thomas Heazle Parke of the Army Medical Department joined the expedition in Aden. Apparently, Stanley had not been quite as indifferent to the loss of his physician as he had appeared and had made inquiries about a replacement at every port at which the *Navarino* had called. There had been no dearth of candidates; as a matter of fact, medical men in Egypt and Aden, military and civilian, British and otherwise, had eagerly volunteered for the glory-bound campaign; and Stanley had chosen Parke, who was stationed at the British garrison in Aden, as the most promising of the somewhat motley lot.

Surgeon Parke, just thirty years old that month, was Irish and handsome in the dark Irish manner, with close-set brown eyes, a shock of coarse black hair, and a full black mustache. He had been stationed in Egypt since the Arabist uprising and had served with the expeditionary force sent out in '84 to save Gordon in Khartoum, during the course of which, at Aswan, he had met Major Barttelot, and that had counted very much in his favor. Stanley felt that Parke's knowing someone on the staff would help him overcome the various practical and psychological disadvantages of joining the expedition so late in the game. Other than that, Parke's service record was in no way particularly distinguished, but it was the best of all the last-minute applicants unblemished by any glaring blunders, bespeaking at least competence and diligence if not dash and daring. As soon as he came aboard the *Navarino* in Aden, he took charge of the medicine chests in Leslie's unoccupied cabin, supervised their transshipment to the SS *Oriental*, which was to take them from Aden to Zanzibar, and at the first opportunity during that voyage set about inoculating all expedition members who came aboard at Aden with lymph.

At Aden, Major Barttelot, Captain Nelson, and Sergeant Bonny also boarded the *Oriental*, along with the Sudanese askaris they had recruited, and trained there. There were 200 of them, veterans of Gordon's Black Battalion and the Mudir of Dongola's *bashibazouks*, and they were a fierce-looking lot. When Jephson first saw them, they were mustered out in two companies on the Aden quay awaiting the lowering of the *Oriental*'s gangway—big men, black as night, sweat gleaming on their hard-bitten faces from the pounding of the Arabian sun. The corporals, squad leaders, and sharpshooters among them had been armed with the Winchester repeaters, the ranks shouldered the Remingtons, and they were uniformed only to the extent of having been issued these weapons plus ammunition, Royal Army tunics, water bottles, blanket rolls, and rations. Apart from that, they wore and carried whatever they pleased. Most had hooded burnooses or sleeveless *abbas* slung over their tunics; red fezzes, khaki kepis, white turbans or just plain rags covered their close-shaven skulls; many were wrapped in brightly patterned *kikois* and *kangas* in place of trousers. All sorts of knives and sabers, *Shirazi* blades and axes, bandoliers and tribal fetishes hung from their persons, the remnants and loot and odd bits of equipment of other campaigns. The effect of all this was to give them the appearance of a buccaneer battalion embarked on some murderous brigandage, both thrilling and unnerving to see. They came aboard the ship in a column of twos behind a bugler, a drummer, and a standard bearer, the last carrying the red flag of Egypt. Nelson, in crisply pressed tropical khakis, puttees, whitewashed pith helmet with its puggaree lowered to protect his neck from the sun, a holstered revolver strapped around his waist and attached by a rope lanyard to the front of his tunic, marched at the head of the column. The pug-faced Bonny, barking commands in the traditionally unintelligible manner of British sergeant-majors throughout the Empire, followed a stride behind. Barttelot—also uniformed smartly in khakis and a spiked topee but wearing riding boots instead of puttees, the top clips of his stiff collar casually unfastened and showing a blue bandanna, a swagger stick tucked under his arm—watched from the quay. Only when Bonny had brought the troop to parade rest on the *Oriental*'s fantail deck did he come aboard himself. He was deeply tanned, which suited his striking good looks, emphasizing the brilliance of his blue eyes, the whiteness of his smile, and his now sun-bleached blond hair. He went directly to Stanley and saluted, then shook hands with him.

"You're looking mighty fit, Major," Stanley said. "This affair seems to be agreeing with you."

"It's been jolly good fun so far, sir. I'll say that for it. I've even managed to get in a spot of polo with the chaps at the garrison here."

"Have you? How awfully nice for you."

Nelson came over and he too saluted and shook hands with Stanley, then turned and greeted Jephson warmly.

"All right, let's have a look at the soldiers you've found for me, shall we, gentlemen?"

"Ten-hut," Bonny bellowed at the officers' approach; and the ranks, in a rattle of weapons and equipment, snapped to attention.

"Well, there you have them, sir," Barttelot said. "What do you think? A savage enough looking gang, wouldn't you say?"

Stanley went over to Bonny. "Good afternoon, Sergeant."

"Sir. Yes, sir." Bonny saluted.

"Have the men stand easy, Sergeant."

"Yes, sir." Bonny barked the order.

Stanley, wearing a white linen suit and a panama, put his hands on his hips and studied the askaris for a long moment. It was nearly four in the afternoon, but the desert sun was still high and harsh, and the askaris were sweating profusely, their tunics stained black by it, a pungent smell rising from their bodies. Some stared back at Stanley with a certain curiosity, but most kept their eyes averted. All, however, had their lips drawn back, showing filed teeth in something that wasn't a smile.

"Sergeant, how long have these men been waiting to board ship?"

Bonny didn't reply.

"What was that, sir?" Barttelot asked, coming over.

"When did you muster these men to board ship, Major?"

"This morning, sir. Crack of dawn."

"They've been waiting on the quay since the crack of dawn?"

"Yes, sir."

"Well then, I'd say they've had quite enough of it for the day. I'll look them over another time. Sergeant, have these men fall out to their quarters in the hold. And you had best make that on the double."

"Just a moment, Sergeant."

Stanley turned to Barttelot.

"Excuse me, sir," the Major said, "but the parade's not over yet. I had it in mind to put the troop through a close order drill. I'd quite like you to see what kind of shape we've whipped them into."

"It will have to wait, Major. I want these men out of the sun. Sergeant, give the order to fall out to quarters."

"Mr. Stanley, these troops are under my command."

"And you, sir, are under mine. So be so good as to do what I tell you. Before we have a goddamn mutiny on our hands."

The passage from Aden around the Horn of Africa and south down the Indian Ocean coast, with calls for mail and water at Lamu and Mombasa and a lively midnight party to mark the crossing of the equator somewhere offshore of Somaliland took another ten days; and the SS *Oriental* put into the Bay of Zanzibar on February 22.

It was ten in the morning, a Tuesday, and the heat was already stupefying but made tolerable by a beguiling clove-scented breeze that wafted across the water from the spice plantations of the island. But there would be little chance to explore the charms of Zanzibar. For anchored in the crowded harbor that morning was the SS *Madura*, chartered for the voyage around the Cape to the Congo's mouth, watered and provisioned and ready to take the expedition aboard. And waiting on the bustling quay, with the army of Wanyamwezi porters he had recruited and the tons of equipment and supplies that had been purchased in Zanzibar or shipped out from England, was Willie Hoffman, ready to go aboard.

Jephson had forgotten about Hoffman; and seeing him again standing on the end of the pier waiting for the lighter from the *Oriental* to put Stanley and his officers ashore, the youth was repelled anew by the grotesque hairlessness of the man, his monstrous size, the fishlike unblinking expression of his lashless eyes. He wore a pair of grease-streaked trousers, fastened about the waist by a length of rope from which hung a long hunting knife, a sweat-blackened red bandanna around his thick neck, and that was all. He was bare-chested, without any kind of hat to protect his bald bullet-shaped skull; and his beefy hairless flesh was burned brick-red by the sun and peeled from ugly blisters on the shoulders and scalp. He grabbed the lighter's painter and extended a hand to Stanley to help him onto the dock, and that gesture, the perfunctory handshake of it, was the extent of his greeting. He didn't bother to extend even that much of a greeting to the others. One might have supposed he would have had at least a passing curiosity in the men with whom he was to serve on this perilous journey into the African interior and whom, apart from Jephson and Baruti, he had never met. But apparently not. He turned away and escorted Stanley up the pier to where the Wanyamwezis were waiting.

There was a tremendous mob of them, a thousand at least, probably more. In fact, though, only some 600 (620 to be exact, counting the wives and children of chiefs and headmen who were coming along as domestics and body servants for the officers) had been hired for the expedition; the rest were relatives and friends who had come down to the wharf to see them off. They were a remarkably mannerly crowd, given their number, of much lighter skin color than the Sudanese and more aquiline in feature, betraying their Arab blood; and the men and boys were clad in long white shirts and pantaloons and white skullcaps or turbans in the Arab fashion. They lounged patiently among the huge crates and packing cases of the expedition's supplies, smiling, carefree-seeming, chatting contentedly among themselves. But they broke off their chatter and stood up from their places and moved forward eagerly when Stanley approached, and a soft excited murmur rippled back through their ranks.

"*Huyu ni yeye*," they told one another. "*Ndiyo, huyu ni yeye.* It is he. Yes, truly, it is he."

Stanley ambled up the pier, his hands clasped behind his back under the tail of his white linen jacket, nodding, grinning broadly, pleased but not really surprised to find himself remembered by these people, remembered by those who had served with him before and remembered also by their sons who only had heard of the stupendous journeys he and their fathers had made together; to find Livingstone, to locate the true source of the White Nile, to map the great lakes of Central Africa, to discover the course of the Congo. And as he came into their midst now after so many years, he glanced this way and that, looking for faces he too might remember from those grand adventures. Then he stopped dead in his tracks.

A tall, slender older man with a close-cropped beard of snow-white wiry curls came forward through the crowd. Two bandoliers were crossed on the front of his white robe, over which he wore a short embroidered vest; a tasseled maroon fez on his head covered a mass of the same tight white curls as his beard, and he carried at his side, holding it loosely by the trigger guard in an oddly negligent way, an old Snider rifle. Two younger men, with long wicked-looking *pangas* resting on their shoulders, walked beside him; and the rest of the crowd moved away to give him room. Clearly he was a chief.

"*Jambo*, Bula Matari."

Stanley stared at the man with an expression of disbelief. Without turning to Hoffman, he asked in a rough undertone, "Is that Uledi, Will?" But he did not wait for Hoffman's reply. "Is that Uledi?" he asked again, but this time he shouted it, made a whoop of it. "Is that you, Uledi? Is that you, goddamnit? By Christ, I do believe it is!" And then, breaking into a broad grin, he plunged forward and grabbed the old man by the shoulders and a torrent of Swahili burst from him as he took the man into an embrace and hugged him fiercely against his chest. "Uledi, you old devil. Ah, but I'm glad to see you again. *Uhali gani, kukuu rafiki?*"

All around, the Wanyamwezis pressed forward to witness the reunion, smiling, laughing, slapping their thighs and each other's backs; and Jephson and the others pushed up the pier to get a better view of what was going on.

Stanley released the old Wanyamwezi from his embrace but held on to him by the shoulders at arm's length, looking him over with eyes full of affection. "Where did you find him, Will?" he asked but again did not give the big impassive Hoffman a chance to reply. "Where in God's name did he find you, Uledi? You, you old man. You should be on your shamba with your wives and children and grandchildren. What are you doing here? And with your rifle! Do you mean to come with me again, *mzee?* Have you not had enough of the safari?"

Uledi, grinning now as broadly as all the rest, put his free hand on Stanley's where it gripped his shoulder in a lovely gesture of friendship. "You too are an old man, Bula Matari," he said in a soft, lilting voice. "You too should be on your shamba with your wives and children and grandchildren. When I heard it said Bula Matari was coming here to make another safari I did not believe it. I told everyone this is nonsense. Bula Matari is too old for such traveling. He is in the land of the *wasungu*, the white man, very rich and very honored and telling tales of the Bundu to his Queen, not coming here. Still I thought why not come down to the quay this morning and see this impostor who arrives in Unguja bearing the name of Bula Matari."

"Well, Uledi, you see it is no impostor."

"*Ndiyo.* I see it is no impostor."

"And what do you say to it? Will you come with me again? Will you make safari with me again?"

"Ah, Bula Matari, I have no choice. I must. You would not find the way without me."

Stanley gave a great bark of laughter at that and, letting go of the old chieftain at last, turned to the horde of Wanyamwezis crowded around them. "And who else will come with me?" he called out. "Who else will make safari with Bula Matari?"

He was answered by a thunderous, jubilant roar.

The loading of the *Madura* commenced that afternoon, after Stanley and his officers made a courtesy call on the Sultan of Zanzibar, Seyyid Barghash bin Said. It went on throughout the rest of that day and all of the next, and most of the one after that as well, a back-breaking labor in the humid heat, involving as it did the movement of very nearly 200 tons of hardware and supplies—not to mention fifty pack and riding mules and donkeys plus their saddles, harnesses, and tack, and more than 800 people and their personal gear. Thus, it wasn't until late in the evening of February 24 that the work was finally done. Then, even though most of the others, bone weary, retired directly to their cabins after mess, Jephson jumped a lighter and went ashore. He had no special errand to run, and he was as tired as the others, but he wanted to get a better look at Zanzibar, perhaps pick up a souvenir or two from this fabled isle before the *Madura* departed the following morning. And so, once ashore, he set off aimlessly, strolling along the waterfront, wandering through the bazaars, watching a snake charmer, a juggler and a fire eater in a street fair, looking into shops and coffeehouses, following narrow walled streets at random back into the town, quite thoroughly enjoying himself despite his fatigue, delighted with the throbbing hubbub of this exotic port, delighted to be there. And then, making his way back around to the wharf again, he unexpectedly came on Stanley and Hoffman.

They were seated with three Arab merchants on low stools in the open doorway of a mercantile establishment behind the customhouse, where they could catch the salt-and-spice-scented breeze from the bay. The Arabs—bearded, turbaned, in flowing white robes, each with a curved ornamental dagger at his waist—were smoking hookahs. A Negro serving girl came and went, bringing cups of coffee and plates of figs and sweetmeats on a brass tray. Stanley, absently fingering the fruit, was doing the talking. Jephson hesitated, thinking perhaps he ought not intrude, but then he realized that Hoffman had noticed him. The huge bald man, wearing a loose-fitting shirt (perhaps as a concession to the evening hour or the handsome attire of the company he was in, but still barefoot and in the same soiled trousers) stared at him with blank eyes. Jephson went over.

"Arthur, my boy," Stanley said, breaking off his conversation and looking up at the youth. "Are you chaps done loading the *Madura?*"

"Yes, sir, right down to the last hook and bolt."

"And everything checks out?"

"Yes, sir. I've gone through our lists and invoices three or four times, and I must say the suppliers did a bang-up job. Everything we ordered has turned up safe and sound."

"Splendid." Stanley turned to the Arabs and, in introducing Jephson, also translated his remark, which brought an appreciative murmur from them. Very likely they were among the expedition's suppliers, probably of the trading *mitako*, and so could regard Jephson's words as a gracious compliment. The serving girl came out of the shop with another stool and coffee cup.

"Sit down, lad," Stanley said, "and try this coffee. It's bloody marvelous. Thick as molasses and twice as sweet."

"If I'm not intruding, sir."

"Not at all. These gentlemen are from the firm of my old friend Hamed bin Mohammed—Tippoo-Tib, as everyone calls him. He's one of the biggest of the Zanzibari traders in the interior, the biggest by far between Lake Tanganyika and the Upper Congo. He's got stations and depots all through there, Ujiji, Nyangwe, Kasongo, Stanley Falls, clear over nearly to Yambuya. I met up with him in Nyangwe in '71, when I was first trying to get down the Congo. He spends most of his time at Stanley Falls nowadays, these chaps tell me. He's there right now, as a matter of fact, and they've had a caravan from him just this last week, so they are in possession of some fairly current information on conditions in that region. It's a region we will be passing through, you know."

"Yes, sir, I know."

"Taste your coffee, lad, and let us know what you think of it."

Jephson took a sip of the syrupy liquid. "Oh, my, yes, that's quite . . . unusual."

Stanley, grinning, relayed Jephson's comment in Swahili, but apparently gave it a slightly more complimentary interpretation, because the three Arabs again responded with appreciative murmurs. One had a string of amber beads coiled around his palm which he toyed with ceaselessly; the other two sucked on their bubbling hookahs, smiling at the youth pleasantly. There was an awkward pause. They seemed to be waiting for him to speak, as if for reasons of etiquette they granted him the newcomer's prerogative to choose a topic of conversation that interested him. The pause went on a bit too long. Hoffman drained off his coffee cup and began mashing the grinds and sugary residue at its bottom with his silver spoon.

Jephson turned to Stanley. "I'm afraid I'm preventing you from getting on with your business, sir. Will here is fairly chomping at the bit to get on with it."

"That's right, mister," Hoffman said. "We ain't got all night, Bula Matari. Let's get on with it. Find out what tribes Tippoo-

Tib's got running with him these days. Manyema? Or has he got local kaffirs with him? I hope to Christ he's got local kaffirs with him. Them Manyema are a bloody lot. They'd be hell driving through the Ituri. They probably wouldn't go." And without waiting for Stanley to reply, he suddenly switched into Swahili and began speaking directly to the Arabs.

They seemed taken aback by this. Their pleasant smiles faded.

"Hey, go easy, Will." Stanley reached across the table and put a hand on Hoffman's arm.

"I'll go easy after we get through the Ituri," Hoffman replied and started at the Arabs again.

"Goddamnit, man, you listen to me now."

"No. You listen to me, Bula Matari." Hoffman swung his bullet-head around. "You want to go through the Ituri. All right, we'll go through the Ituri. It don't make no difference to me. I signed on thinking we was going in from Bagamoyo, up through the Karagwe country. Turns out, no, we're going up the Congo, through the Ituri. All right. What the fuck. It's all the same to me, the Karagwe, the Ituri. I ain't giving you no shit about it the way Leslie done, right? And I ain't aiming to neither. But if you're asking me to drive *pagazis* through that fucking forest for you, I want to know what kind of *pagazis*. If you're counting on Tippoo-Tib providing you with them *pagazis*, I want to know what kind of *pagazis* he's got running with him. And these here blokes can tell me. So I don't want to sit around here all night talking about the fucking *unusual* quality of their coffee. All right?"

A trace of a smile flickered across Stanley's lips. "Yes, Will, all right," he said. "But I think you had best leave it to me." And keeping a restraining hand on Hoffman's arm, he turned to the Arabs and addressed them softly, almost apologetically; and after a few soothing sentences, the one with the amber worry beads replied. The conversation, which Jephson had interrupted, resumed.

Although they spoke slowly, most of what they said remained well beyond Jephson's rudimentary grasp of the language. And besides, he made no great effort to follow it. His mind was elsewhere; Hoffman's outburst had distracted him. He had never heard this meaty hulk of a man speak so much in a single go or with so much emotion.

What the fuck, he had said; it was all the same to him, the Karagwe or the Ituri. But it *wasn't* all the same to him. That outburst, that uncharacteristic show of emotion, the nervy turning on

Stanley, were testimony to that. He might not quit the expedition as Dick Leslie had done—because he was braver? because he cared less for his life? because he had no alternatives anyway?—but his feelings about the Ituri, about the change to the Congo route, were the same as Leslie's. Jephson was sure of that. He picked up his coffee and, sipping the thick sweet liquid, studied Hoffman over the rim of the cup. The man wasn't talking now; he was leaving it to Stanley; but he listened to the exchanges with a terrible intensity, turning his head from Stanley to the Arabs, from the Arabs to Stanley. When, during the voyage from Aden to Zanzibar, Stanley had discussed the change in route with Barttelot and Nelson, and then later with Parke and Bonny, their reaction had been one of only mild curiosity. There hadn't been anything charged or significant in it for them. How could there be? They had never been anywhere near that part of Africa. But Hoffman had. Hoffman had been on the Congo. He had seen the Ituri forest. He had shared the secrets of Stanley's campaigns on King Leopold's behalf. As Dick Leslie had. As Jack Troup had. Jephson drank off the last of the sweet coffee. Yes, Jack Troup. What about Jack Troup, awaiting them now at the mouth of the Congo? What had he made of the change in route?

At daybreak, February 25, a Friday, the *Madura* sailed from Zanzibar. She was twelve days in the Indian Ocean to Simon's Bay, a British naval station in South Africa, where the expedition staff dined with the commanding admiral, Sir Hunt Grubbe, at the Royal Naval Club, and there was another break at Cape Town, where mail and coal were taken aboard. Then came the passage around the Cape of Good Hope and the haul north up the Atlantic coast of Africa. It was an uneventful voyage. The sea was calm and the weather decent, clear and hot during the day, balmy and washed with stars at night, an occasional thundershower blowing through. The days and the nights blurred one into the other, languorous, lazy, boring.

Jephson passed the time learning Swahili. At first he attempted to use Baruti as his teacher, but as the little blackamoor knew so little English and anyway would not sit still, Jephson took to hanging about with the Wanyamwezis, asking them questions, having them name objects for him, engaging them in childlike practice conversations. Although they laughed at his bumbling attempts, they proved a friendly, cheerful, cooperative lot. They had their quarters in the ship's aft hold and had settled themselves down there into village and family groupings around their traditional chiefs and headmen. They led a busy, contented life aboard ship, very much, Jephson suspected, as they might have done at home.

Hoffman continually kept tabs on them. He was present at the distribution of their rations and often skipped the regular officers' mess topside to take his meals with them and sometimes bedded down among them, dropping his blankets in an unused corner of the hold and curling up for the night. It was difficult to tell what the Wanyamwezis made of him, but if in the regulation of their day-to-day affairs they looked to Uledi and the *nakhudhas* and *mariaparas*, they clearly recognized Hoffman as a greater power in their lives and treated him with wary respect.

Robbie Nelson and Tom Parke struck up a friendship. As much a military man as a doctor, Parke naturally gravitated to the company of the other professional soldiers on the expedition. One might have expected him to take up with Ted Barttelot, seeing how they had served together at Aswan during the Nile campaign; but these two, it turned out, were of very different temperaments. Parke was a cardplayer, an irrepressible chatterer, a gossip really, and rather a tippler too; and once he had completed the program of lymph inoculations on those who had been added to his care in Zanzibar, he was perfectly content to avoid any further employment and simply to enjoy the enforced idleness of the voyage. That wasn't Barttelot's nature at all. This aristocratic officer, this darling of society who had been promoted well ahead of his Sandhurst class just because of his dash and daring, craved activity and action. Idleness was alien to him and repugnant; it made him edgy; he didn't know what to do with it. Besides, in this case, he was sure it would undermine the fighting fitness of the Sudanese askaris. By the time the *Madura* had rounded the Cape, he had given up as impractical, because of the ship's cramped quarters, holding full-scale parades, but otherwise he ran the troops along strict conventional military lines—posting round-the-clock guards on the expedition's stores, drawing up daily duty rosters, conducting drills and inspections—he could be seen at all hours, slapping his riding crop against his thigh, nosing about the askaris' quarters in the forehold, finding things amiss and meting out punishments.

He tended to take out his restlessness on Bonny, sending the faithful cockney sergeant-major scurrying around on a dozen petty chores each day and rarely ever being satisfied with what the man accomplished. He wasn't above pulling his rank on Nelson too and, albeit in the most correct manner, often called the stolid, straightforward captain to task for duties unperformed or assignments unfulfilled. Nelson was too much the good soldier ever to raise a word of protest, but it wasn't difficult to see by the set of his strong, homely face that he regarded the major's relentless activities as foolish projects done for their own sake and of no real military value. On one occasion—Barttelot had barged in on a card game in Parke's cabin to complain that the Maxim automatic gun hadn't been properly cleaned that morning—the jaunty, gabby Parke ventured to suggest that all this scurrying about wasn't in the least bit healthy in this climate and that everyone would do himself a sight more good, medically speaking, just taking it easy and saving himself for the time when it would be necessary. At which Barttelot lost his temper and said a number of rude and stupid things about the laziness of officers setting a bad example for the ranks. It was a disproportionate reaction and might have led to some trouble except that Nelson calmed him down and even persuaded him to join the card game, which Barttelot then proceeded to play with such skill and verve that he wound up with all the winnings. But that evening his restlessness again came to a boil when at mess he tried to engage Stanley in a discussion about the specific responsibilities of the various officers once they reached the Congo—and Stanley rather peremptorily brushed him off.

Perhaps, in fact, this was what really was at the root of Barttelot's edginess. He was extremely conscious of his position as Stanley's second-in-command and, not unreasonably, expected to participate closely with him in planning the operational details of the campaign. Indeed, he had thought that this time of idleness during the voyage up the Atlantic coast would be put precisely to that use and had imagined himself poring over maps with Stanley in his cabin, working out the order of march of the caravan, the disposition of the troops, the bivouacs and campsites, the stretches of terrain where additional *pagazis* would have to be hired, the number and type of boats needed for the ascent of the Congo, and so on. But Stanley repeatedly cut short all discussion of these matters and not only with Barttelot, it must be said, but with everyone. It was as if he did not want them to think about these things; it was as if he wanted them to use these days of idleness to rest, to settle their affairs in their own minds and to gather their strength for what lay ahead.

· TWO ·

AT THE MOUTH of the Congo, on a spit of land arcing out from the coastline, stood the settlement of Banana Point. On its ocean side, above a strip of beach where the surf crashed glistening in the early-morning sunlight, were the residences of the settlement's European traders: ramshackle bungalows of thatch and bamboo with sprawling verandas and screened-in passageways, set among palms and mangroves. On the river side a row of brick buildings with corrugated iron roofs—warehouses and chandleries and a customhouse—fronted a wharf of weathered gray piers on which now, with gulls and sea eagles screaming overhead, a mob of people gathered to witness the arrival of the SS *Madura.* John Rose Troup was among them, a cigarette stuck in the corner of his mouth.

Jephson, peering down from the *Madura*'s forward deck, did not at first recognize him. Troup had grown a full flaming orange beard. He was dressed in a loose blue collarless shirt and dark serge trousers, these last stuffed into woodsman boots and held up by red braces, and he had a pistol shoved in the waistband. He also had a raffia straw hat with a wide, ragged brim, an item clearly of local manufacture, but this he had removed and was shielding his eyes against the sun with his hand, watching the *Madura* ease toward her mooring. Jephson waved at him, but he didn't see him; he was looking up at the ship's bridge, where Stanley was standing.

Everyone was topside now, and the noise was tremendous, the decks aswarm with askaris and *pagazis*, sailors and stevedores, milling about in a state of high excitement, Sergeant Bonny's piercing commands slicing through the din as he mustered the Sudanese in parade formation. No such effort, at least not for the moment, was being made with the Wanyamwezis, and they crowded the rails vying for a view of the port. Some of them had been here before, ten years before, for it was here, in 1877, that Stanley had ended his epic journey of discovery of the Congo's course; and it occurred to Jephson to wonder what those who had been with him then might be feeling now on their return. He looked around for Uledi. The tall white-bearded chieftain was on the lower deck. He and a few of his *nakhudhas* were talking with Hoffman. Then Hoffman, barefoot and half naked as usual, not waiting for the gangway to be lowered, vaulted the deck rail to the wharf. Troup put on his straw hat and went over to him. The two men didn't shake hands. Troup pointed out to the river, and following the direction of his arm, Jephson saw a small paddle-wheel steamer anchored in the roadstead. Then Troup pointed in another direction. But this time Jephson did not look to see where he pointed, because Stanley had come down from the bridge; and also not waiting for the gangway to be lowered and with amazing agility, he too leaped to the dock. He was in uniform—a blue military jacket with gold-braid frogging, white jodhpurs, riding boots, a white spiked pith helmet, a holstered Webley revolver underneath the jacket. He went straight to Troup and shook his hand and then, with Troup and Hoffman on either side of him, strode up the wharf. He was in a hurry.

From its mouth on the sea, upriver for one hundred miles eastward into the interior, to the settlement of Matadi on its left bank, the Congo is wholly navigable. At Matadi, however, the Crystal Mountains rear up, a sparsely wooded granite range ending the maritime plain; and for the next 200 miles the river for the most part is impassable, torn to pieces by a series of thirty cataracts, collectively known as Livingstone Falls, which crash down through those mountains from Stanley Pool. Thus this leg of the journey would take place in two parts: the trip from Banana Point up the Congo estuary to Matadi, then the march around Livingstone Falls through the Crystal Mountains to Stanley Pool. For the first part, Jack Troup had chartered five riverboats from the British, Portuguese, and Dutch trading houses at Banana Point and from the Congo Free State station at Boma; and the next seventy-two hours were devoted, round the clock, to the transfer of the expedition's equipment and supplies from the *Madura* to those boats. On the night of the third day, March 20, Stanley and his staff, able to relax at last, dined at the residence of the chief agent for the British trading company, a Mr. Cobden-Philips, along with the other leading citizens of Banana Point, the Portuguese and Dutch traders and the Flemish harbormaster.

The arrival of the expedition, and especially of Mr. Henry Stanley, who was known to these men personally, represented a much welcome diversion in the otherwise dreary routine of the mosquito-ridden river settlement and Cobden-Philips had taken the opportunity to make a gala occasion of it. The food and drink were excellent and lavish, the spirits high, and the conversation boisterous in an amusingly vulgar way. But Jephson was unable to enjoy any of it; he was not feeling at all well at the time. He had no appetite and picked desultorily at his food; and although the dining room was a screened-in porch with its jalousies open on all sides, he felt hot and clammy and nauseated. He had been feeling vaguely ill since arriving on the Congo, and it worried him. He hoped he hadn't contracted some African fever already. What a bloody disgrace it would be if he broke down and had to be convalesced home before the journey into the interior even got under way. He looked around the table. No one else seemed to be suffering any discomfort. They were eating and drinking with apparent gusto and exchanging news and gossip of Europe and Africa with hearty animation. Jephson looked out the window. Cobden-Philips's bungalow, set in a lushly overgrown garden of frangipani and bougainvillea, was situated a few dozen yards from the ocean, and from where he sat Jephson could see the surf breaking on the beach, glittering in the cool light of a newly risen moon; and the fronds of the palm trees there rustled in an inviting breeze blowing off the sea. So when the coffee and brandy were served and the men began lighting up their cigars and pipes and the room became intolerably stuffy and Jephson felt in danger of being overcome by nausea, he excused himself and went out to get some fresh air.

Troup followed him out. "Are you all right, Arthur?"

"Yes, I guess so. Jesus, I don't know what it is, Jack. I just suddenly felt bloody awful. I hope to God I haven't picked up something this early in the game."

"No, don't worry about it. It ain't that. It's the Congo. Everybody reacts to it like that at first." Troup went to the ocean's edge and soaked his handkerchief in the foam of the surf. "It takes a bit of getting used to," he said and mopped Jephson's face with the wet cloth. "You'll be all right in a few days. You'll see. You'll season up just like the rest of us."

"Jesus, I hope so."

"Sure you will. Don't worry yourself. You ain't going to have any cause to regret taking my advice and asking Mr. Stanley for a place on the staff."

Jephson inwardly winced at that but decided there was no

point bothering to explain, this much after the fact, that he had never actually asked Mr. Stanley for a place on the staff. "Jack, there's something I've been wanting to ask you."

"What's that?"

"It's about the change to the Congo route."

"What about it?"

"Well, I was wondering what you thought about it."

Troup shrugged.

"I mean, Dick Leslie . . . Jesus, Jack, he didn't like it at all, you know. He quit on the spot when he heard about it."

"Yes, I know."

"He thought it was a dreadful mistake. He said it was suicide. I was there. He told Mr. Stanley that trying to get through the Ituri forest was just plain suicide."

Troup didn't say anything.

"Do you think it's suicide, Jack?"

"Come now, man, don't be an ass. Of course I don't think it's suicide. Do you think I'd be going along if I thought it was?"

"But you once said yourself that nobody could get through the Ituri. I remember that. It was when we first met, in London. We were waiting for Mr. Stanley to get back from Whitehall. I asked you if you thought anyone could make it through the Ituri forest, and you said straight out no. You laughed in my face and said straight out shit no. You said I'd never ask a question like that if I'd ever once seen the place. Don't you remember?"

"Yes, I remember." Troup looked down at the toes of his boots. Then after a few moments, still looking down, he said, "Listen, Arthur, it will be a rough bit of traveling. It will be that for sure. I won't say otherwise. But we'll make it through. Mr. Stanley knows what he's doing. If he thinks we can make it through, we'll make it through."

"How rough?"

"Huh?" Troup looked up.

"When you say it will be rough traveling, how rough do you mean? Rougher than anything else you've ever done?"

"Yes. Rougher than anything else I've ever done. Or anyone else has ever done."

"Then why the hell are we doing it? Why didn't Mr. Stanley stay with the original route? Why did he switch to this at the last minute?"

Troup's red-bearded face was close to Jephson's but in the

dark of the garden it was difficult to see the expression on it. And he didn't say anything. He simply started walking back to the bungalow.

The next morning, March 21, the expedition's fleet of riverboats one by one set off upriver into the interior. The first to leave was the *Albuquerque*, a wood-burning steamer chartered from the British trading house; it departed for Matadi at six-thirty with Hoffman, Uledi, 400 of the Wanyamwezi *pagazis*, thirty tons of cargo, and the pack and riding animals. A half-hour later the Dutch steamer *K. A. Nieman*, carrying Nelson and Parke, 100 of the Sudanese askaris, and sixty tons of cargo, followed. Then Stanley and Troup, with the remaining *pagazis*, sixty tons of cargo, and Baruti sailed on the *Serpa Pinto*, a paddle wheeler chartered from the Portuguese. They, however, made for Boma, the capital of the Congo Free State, halfway up the estuary on its right bank, where they planned to call on the governor-general before proceeding on to Matadi. Next to leave were Barttelot and Bonny on the *Kacongo*, a Portuguese gunboat, with the rest of the askaris and thirty tons of cargo, mainly the arms and ammunition for Emin Pasha. Jephson followed them aboard the Congo Free State's yacht, the *Heron*, with what remained.

The river narrowed. Its mouth, more than ten miles wide between the spits of land that enclosed it, gave the misleading appearance of a bay, just another of the coastline's many inlets from the sea; and it wasn't until the *Heron* had sailed some miles upstream from it, leaving the sea behind, that Jephson had the sense of actually entering into a river. Even so, it was a great river, never less than a mile or two across, often as much as four or five. From time to time, large wooded islands appeared in the stream, and the *Heron* had to find her way cautiously through the tricky channels between them; and in those stretches, hemmed in by the overhanging branches of the trees of the islands, in their humid, shadowy closeness, there was a sudden momentarily unnerving reminder that one truly was embarked on a voyage upcountry into the interior of a dark continent. But more usually the vistas were bright, indeed blindingly so, and exhilarating in their openness. Only one bank was ever clearly in view; whichever one the *Heron*'s captain favored for reasons of safe navigation, the other then would be so far away as to be nothing more than a smoky blue smudge along the horizon, and the river flowing between them seemed a vast shining sheet, glittering like molten silver under the blazing African sun. Flowering palms and giant ferns and mangroves with weirdly twisted exposed roots forested the banks; monkeys and parrots, hidden in the brilliant foliage, chattered raucously at the boat's passage; crocodiles sunned in the black ooze at the river's edge; long-legged white water birds, suddenly frightened, fluttered into flight. Occasionally a village would come into view—mud and thatch huts, plots of manioc and bananas, some goats and chickens, a few head of cattle drinking in the river, fishermen in their long slender dugout canoes pausing in the act of casting their nets to watch the boat pass by. And beyond them, seen from the *Heron*'s high bridge, where Jephson leaned against the rail listening to the captain describe the sights, were the sun-drenched meadows and gently rolling hills of the maritime plain—covered in yellow elephant grass, dotted with stands of acacia and baobobs, populated with great herds of zebra and antelope and other wild game—stretching away to the blurred shapes of mountains on the eastern horizon.

This stretch of river, the captain explained, the hundred miles of its estuary from the sea to the mountains, had been known to Europeans for more than 300 years. To be sure, the cataracts of Livingstone Falls and the ruggedness of the Crystal Mountains had blocked the discovery of the rest of the river until Stanley had found the way through them ten years before; but white men had been trading and trafficking on the estuary itself ever since a Portuguese caravel captain seeking a sea route to the Indies had happened upon it at the end of the fifteenth century. A great African kingdom, the kingdom of Kongo, existed on the estuary then, so great a kingdom that it was thought at first to be the legendary realm of Prester John. Its royal capital, Mbanza Kongo, was situated on a hill over there somewhere on the river's southern bank, and one could still hear stories of its magnificence—its palaces and cathedrals, the elaborate rituals and splendors of its court, the bravery and nobility of its kings, the Manikongos, dressed in the most beautiful cloths, almost like velvet and damask although woven from the fibers of the raffia palm, adorned in jewelry cast from copper, and leading hundreds of thousands of warriors plumed in the feathers of eagles and armed with weapons forged of the finest steel . . . Ah, but those were just stories. The captain made a dismissive gesture with his hand. None of it existed any longer, not a trace. It all had been destroyed long ago. The slaving had destroyed it. For, from the first, and for almost 300 years after that, the white man's main trade and traffic on the river had been in slaves.

Yes, there still was slaving on the river, the captain said in reply to a question from Jephson, the slaving of the Zanzibari Arabs; but that was on the farthest reaches of the Upper Congo, beyond the effective jurisdiction of the Congo Free State, not here on the mainstream, not since abolition. Here the chief traffic and trade was in rubber, also in ivory and palm oil, but chiefly in rubber—although it was hard to say that represented much of an improvement from the natives' point of view.

The captain laughed when he said that and stepped away from the rail. They were drinking beer from brown bottles, and he fetched himself another from the water-filled bucket and removed its cork with his teeth. What did he mean by that? Jephson wanted to know. The captain shrugged, wiping his mouth with the back of his hand. The rubber grew in the wild, he explained, in the forests, and the local tribesmen were sent out to harvest it. They brought it to King Leopold's agents at the State stations along the river, from where it was transported to the docksides and warehouses of Matadi and Boma and Banana Point for shipment to Europe aboard oceangoing vessels. They were paid for the latex they brought in of course, but even so . . . Shit, they were lazy bastards, they hated to do the work. So they had to be forced. You'd never get anywhere nearly enough rubber out of them if they weren't forced; they'd just go out in the forest and lie about all day. So you had to force them. The captain turned and leaned on the rail and took a last pull on his beer. Leopold's agents forced them, he said and dropped the empty bottle over the side.

· THREE ·

Sheer limestone cliffs, blinding white in the harsh glare of midday, reared up on both sides of the river. Massive granite boulders—jagged outcroppings seamed with glittering quartz and tourmaline crystals, precarious rock overhangs to which clung the gnarled trunks of dwarf thorn trees—thrust into its waters; and the estuary narrowed to a few hundred yards. Ahead was the gateway of the gorge through which the Congo, thundering over the last of the thirty cataracts of Livingstone Falls, called the Cauldron of Hell, emerged from its 200-mile journey down the Crystal Mountains and flowed out into the maritime plain. And on the left bank, a half-mile or so downstream of the Cauldron, where the river still swirled in muddy eddies and one could hear the muffled roar of the cataract hidden within the walls of the gorge, stood Matadi.

Matadi was less than two years old, still just a skeleton of a village. The original European settlement at this farthest reach of navigation up the estuary, Vivi, was on the opposite bank. In the preceding year, however, the Congo Free State had undertaken to build a road around Livingstone Falls—eventually to be followed by a railway line—and had decided that the terrain through the mountains along the river's southern bank posed fewer geological obstacles. Once construction started, the European traders in Vivi began transferring their operations to that side of the river. So far, though, only the Portuguese had established themselves there in any permanent way, with a brick factory on the waterfront and a bungalow in the grassy foothills of the mountains above the river. There also was an American Baptist mission school up in those hills. The British, Dutch, and French traders there had only a few tin-roofed sheds on the newly built wharf, and the Free State's establishment consisted merely of a tent camp for the surveyors and engineers of the road construction crew. But on this bright hot

Tuesday when the *Heron* sailed into the rock-walled cove that served as Matadi's harbor, the settlement had the look of a thriving entrepot because of the presence of the Emin Pasha expedition.

The *Heron* was the last of the expedition's boats to reach Matadi. The others had arrived either the evening before or early that morning; and the *Albuquerque*, the *K. A. Nieman*, and the *Kacongo*, their cargoes discharged, had already departed. Only the *Serpa Pinto* was still tied up at the wharf, in the process of being unloaded. The crates and boxes and barrels and steel-belted bales stood everywhere along the riverside; and hundreds of half-naked men, sweat streaming down their shining black bodies, swarmed over them, breaking them open, beginning the work of repacking everything—the tools, the stores, the trading *mitako*, the ammunition—into the hundreds of individual loads of roughly sixty pounds each, which the *pagazis* would carry. Farther back from the river, among the acacia and fever trees, tents were being pitched and rude shelters erected of branches and leaves and mud; a kraal had been built of bamboo and brush to pen the pack mules and riding asses, and their restless braying carried out to the river like the cries of so many naughty children. Cooking fires were burning where the Wanyamwezi women were preparing the midday meal; and the armies of men hurrying back and forth raised clouds of dust that mingled with the smoke of the fires.

Willie Hoffman met the *Heron* with a gang of Bakongo porters. The Bakongo were the dominant tribe of the region, descendants of the great kingdom that was said to have once existed along the estuary's banks; but there was precious little grandeur about them now. Their centuries of contact with the white man, with the slavers and ivory hunters and missionaries and rubber traders, had robbed them of whatever native majesty they might once have had. They were dressed in a comically pathetic hodgepodge of European and native clothing—their *mariapara* wore a bowler, a discarded naval jacket with a gin bottle tucked in its pocket, and a woven raffia skirt—and many among them obviously were half-breeds, the blood of some white trader evident in one's light eyes, in another's flaxen hair, in the ugly blotched texture of still another's skin. Short and stocky, docile almost to the point of obsequiousness, they were part of a gang of nearly 600 Bakongo Troup and Herbert Ward had hired from neighboring villages, at a sovereign per load, to reinforce the caravan on the overland march around Livingstone Falls to Stanley Pool.

The caravan was organized into eight companies. Two were

made up of the Sudanese askaris who—because no hostilities were anticipated in the relatively well traveled and pacified country of the Crystal Mountains—were to be deployed simply as advance and rear guards, under Barttelot, Nelson, and Bonny. Scheduled to march between them were two companies of Wanyamwezi porters and two companies of Bakongo. Hoffman, with Uledi as his chief deputy, would be in charge of the Wanyamwezis, Troup and Ward of the Bakongo. But since Ward was not in Matadi—he had gone back up to Stanley Pool some weeks before the expedition arrived on the Congo to see about the State steamers that were to take the caravan from there to Yambuya—Troup would have to go it alone on this leg of the journey. Leading the caravan would be the seventh company, Stanley's headquarters company, consisting of the officers' kitchen, surgery, commissariat, and command tents; Wanyamwezi servants and orderlies to man these; *pagazis* to carry the medical supplies and the personal baggage of the officers; a bodyguard of askaris; the Sudanese drum and bugle corps; plus locally hired Bakongo and Houssa scouts, trackers, and interpreters. Parke and Baruti would march with them. As for Jephson, he was given command of the eighth company, the boat company.

Troup told him this. They were standing in the choking heat of the waterfront; and Troup, his ragged straw hat clamped well down over his eyes, swatting away at the plague of mosquitoes and black flies that swarmed up from the swampy river's edge, had to shout to make himself heard over the din of the work going on around them. Even so, Jephson could not believe he heard him correctly. He had always assumed that throughout the journey he would be attached to Stanley as his aide-de-camp and jack-of-all-work, as he had been in London and on the voyage out; and so when, shortly after arriving in Matadi, Troup called him aside, the last thing in the world he expected to be told was that he had been put in command of anything. He made Troup repeat it.

"I tell you, lad, you've drawn the boat company," Troup said again, smiling through his orange beard.

"You must be joking, Jack."

"Why the devil would I be joking?" Troup replied, but went on smiling merrily. "This ain't nothing to joke about. Come along. I'll show you."

The boat company—which would march near the head of the caravan, behind the headquarters company and the advance guard—consisted of sixty Wanyamwezis, three pack mules and a riding donkey, rations for four weeks, miscellaneous stores and field equipment, and, of course, the portable steel boat. The boat, as Jephson knew, dismantled into twelve sections; each weighed about seventy-five pounds and each was designed to be carried by four porters. Assembled, she measured twenty-six feet long, six feet in the beam, with a 2½-foot draft. She was propelled by ten oarsmen—who, when not on the water, would also serve as porters—and was capable of carrying 100 passengers or ten tons of cargo or various combinations of both. On this leg of the journey, from Matadi to the Pool, her main use would be as a ferry. Streams and rivers flowing into the Congo from the southern bank crossed the route of the march, and in those instances where they were too deep to ford or where their bridges had been washed out the boat would be assembled to ferry men or goods or both across in relays. In addition, wherever there were clear navigable stretches between the cataracts and rapids in the Congo itself, the boat would be put into the water to spell marchers, perform scouting duties, and provide emergency transport. Jephson had been put in charge of her because of his familiarity with the boat's design and workings from his involvement in her construction in London.

Jephson glanced sideways at Troup as he explained all this and it suddenly occurred to him why the redhead was smiling so merrily. He had put Mr. Stanley up to this; he had talked the man into turning over this assignment to his young friend and was pleased as all get out with himself at having succeeded.

"Those are your boys, Arthur."

They had reached the Portuguese warehouse, and Troup pointed to a gang of Wanyamwezis working on its loading platform, cracking open the crates that contained the boat sections. Most of them, stripped down to loincloths or baggy white pantaloons, were familiar to Jephson from his Swahili lessons on the *Madura*. As he came up to them now, they broke off what they were doing and turned to him with smiling, friendly faces. One of their number, obviously their *nakhudha*, carrying a Snider rifle, got them back to work with a sharp command.

"They're a good lot," Troup said. "I had Uledi handpick them for their loyalty, experience, and even tempers. You oughtn't have any trouble with them."

Jephson nodded.

"And I also had him handpick the coxswain. That's him over there. He's Uledi's son. Sudi, *njoo hapa*."

The chap with the rifle jumped down from the loading platform and trotted over. He was a tall and slender yet impressively muscled youth, probably around Jephson's own age, with sleek coffee-colored skin, a neat small head, and aquiline features.

"*Huyu ni*, Bwana Jephson, Sudi," Troup said to him. "*Yeye meli* bwana. *Unanifahamu?*"

"Yes, sah. Good afternoon, sah," the Wanyamwezi replied in a bell-like mission-school English.

"*Shikamoo*, Sudi," Jephson said. "*Nimefurahi kuonana nawe.*"

"Oh, *vizuri*, Bwana! *Unasema kiswahili vizuri.*"

"*Ahsante sana.*"

"He's a good boy," Troup said. "Ain't you a good boy, Sudi?"

"Yes, sah."

"And you're going to help Bwana Jephson, ain't you?"

"Oh, yes, sah, I help bwana. I help bwana plenty."

"He will too, lad. You shouldn't have a scrap of trouble."

"I'm sure I won't."

"What you want to do now is get all this stuff uncrated and repacked into porter loads as fast as you can. Then have them assemble the boat and put her in the water and give her a test run. See if any damage has come to her since London. We don't want any surprises later on."

"No, of course not."

"You probably won't be able to get to that today. But there's time enough. Do it tomorrow. We won't be heading out of here until the day after anyway."

"Fine."

"Right then, I'll leave you to it. If you've any questions, I'll be over at headquarters company." Troup started away.

"Jack."

The redhead looked back.

"I want to thank you for this, Jack."

"*Si kitu.*"

"It's a great chance for me, Jack. And I'm going to do my damnedest to make something of it."

"I know you will, lad." Troup studied Jephson's face for a moment. "So what are you looking so grim about? You ain't worrying about this, are you? Don't. This leg of it, up to the Pool, is going to be a lark."

"How long is it meant to take?"

"Four, five weeks. Closer to four. We'll be pushing. That's the one thing about it. We'll be pushing pretty hard. Mr. Stanley wants to make good time. There's no sense in any of this if we don't make good time, you know."

• •

The rumor about the steamers at Stanley Pool started the following day. It began when a native runner arrived at the expedition's riverside encampment at dawn with a message for Stanley from Bertie Ward, but Jephson didn't catch wind of it until much later in the morning. Full of a sense of his new responsibilities, he had rousted out the boat company before first light and had been preoccupied with them ever since. The work was going well. Sudi and the Wanyamwezis were proving as good as Troup had promised, but there was an awful lot to do before the company would be ready to march the next day. Nearly half the supplies had yet to be repacked into the individual porter loads, and the boat still needed to be assembled and put into the river and tested for leaks. So Jephson, devoting all his attention to these chores, did not realize something was amiss until he saw the *Serpa Pinto* depart the Matadi wharf around eleven that morning. He was on his knees at the time, examining the decking of the portable steel boat's aft section with Sudi. He stood up and watched the paddle wheeler turn downriver. Stanley, Barttelot, and Troup were on her.

"Bula Matari go Mboma," Sudi said.

"Boma?"

"*Ndiyo*."

"Why? What for?"

Sudi shrugged. "*Sijui*."

"No, that can't be right, Sudi. The caravan is meant to leave here first thing tomorrow morning. Mr. Stanley would never get back from Boma by then."

Sudi shrugged again.

Jephson looked up and down the riverfront in some puzzlement. The work of unpacking crates and making up porter loads was going on with the same noisy urgency as before. Hoffman, shirtless, barefoot, was supervising a gang of Bakongo on the next pier, where the *Heron* was still docked, and Jephson considered going over to him and asking if he knew what Mr. Stanley was up to. But he hated talking to the man; the answer he would get would be grudging at best and probably uninformative into the bargain; and then he spotted Captain Nelson and didn't have to bother with Hoffman.

"Hey, Robbie."

Nelson was with a detachment of Sudanese; they had the Maxim automatic gun hitched to a mule and were heading into the hills above the river for some test-firing and target shooting.

"Hey, Arthur," he called back, allowing his gun crew to continue under the command of a big Sudanese corporal. "What's the matter?"

"I just saw Mr. Stanley head downriver on the *Serpa Pinto* with Jack and Ted."

"Yes, they're going to Boma."

"But that's a long trip, Robbie. They won't get back here until noon tomorrow."

"If then."

"But we're supposed to march out of here at first light tomorrow."

"Oh, you didn't hear? That's off. We're not leaving until Friday. Mr. Stanley has put it off until Friday."

"Why? What's happened?"

"I'm not sure exactly. Apparently there's some sort of problem about the steamers. That runner who came into camp this morning had a message from Bertie Ward to that effect."

"Which steamers? The ones that are supposed to take us from the Pool to Yambuya?"

"Yes." Nelson looked around for the gun crew. They had stopped in the shade of some acacia trees.

"What kind of problem?"

"Seems there ain't enough of them. Or at least not enough in working order."

"No, that's not possible, Robbie. Mr. Stanley arranged for those steamers directly with King Leopold. He would never have chosen this route except that he had King Leopold's assurance there'd be enough steamers to take us to Yambuya."

"Well, maybe I got it wrong then. I did only hear it at second hand from Ted. And frankly I don't think he actually got to see Ward's message himself. What he said though was that they were going to Boma to raise hell with the governor about there not being enough steamers."

The unexpected delay in the departure from Matadi, with the extra day it provided, whatever else its significance, proved a boon for Jephson in his eagerness to make a good showing in his first command. Not only did it allow him to get his company's supplies repacked in plenty of time, it also gave him a chance to check the steel boat and drill his boys in her assembly and disassembly and in sailing her. He had them at this all Thursday morning, putting the craft together on the Matadi embankment, rowing her across to Vivi, taking her apart there, putting her back together again, returning to Matadi, until they could damn near do it in their sleep. And then in the afternoon, with time still on his hands and no one certain when Stanley would be back from Boma, he decided to test his boatmen's skill under more difficult conditions. He directed them to row upriver into the mountain gorge where the Livingstone Falls ended.

They were in midstream at the time, on a return trip from Vivi. Sudi was at the tiller in the stern, Jephson in the prow; and the oarsmen and passengers—the entire company was in the boat to approximate an actual ferrying situation, but the loads had been left ashore in the event of a mishap—looked back and forth from the coxswain to the white man with some surprise when they realized what Jephson wanted to do. Sudi himself seemed taken aback by it.

"*Kuna nini*, Sudi?"

"*Kumradhi*, Bwana. *Wapi? Tunakwenda wapi?*"

"*Kule.*" Jephson again pointed to the limestone cliffs that formed the gateway to the mountain gorge.

"*Kule?*"

"*Ndiyo*, Sudi. *Kule*. There. What's the matter with you?"

"But, sah, there is the Cauldron of Hell."

"I know that. I wish to see it."

Sudi pulled a long face.

"Come now, man. Let's go see the Cauldron of Hell. Get these boys to put their backs into it. *Upesi-upesi.*"

Sudi, his uneasiness written all over his face, started up the chant marking the beat of the stroke, and the steel boat swung slowly around and headed into the mountains.

Almost immediately the air chilled. At this hour in the afternoon the sun no longer reached into the gorge, and the zigzagging corridor of broken stone walls lay in cool translucent blue shadows. The river was barely forty yards wide in here, chopped up by boulders and sandbanks and vagrant dead logs. It swirled around these in muddy sucking pools and broke over them in crystal sprays and cascades, but it was navigable enough. The oarsmen, although pulling measurably harder, made decent headway, slipping through the calmer channels. This was not yet the Cauldron; that lay farther upstream, still hidden behind the precipitous cliffs and slabs of jagged rock that cut the river into separate reaches. Its roar, however, grew steadily louder as they proceeded, echoing in this stone canyon.

Sudi stood up and pointed out a crocodile on a mudflat. Jephson had taken it for a log, but at the boat's approach it slithered into the river. Sudi hooked one leg over the tiller to hold the course, picked up his Snider rifle, and watched the crocodile. A creature like that could take it into its dim brain to attack the boat, and in this increasingly tricky water that could cause trouble. But the beast submerged and swam to the opposite bank and rested there on the sand and gravel of the shallows, only its eyes and snout above water. Sudi put the rifle down and gripped the tiller with both hands and remained on his feet. A blue egret stood stock-still in a clump of giant fern, not daring to move. But a small animal, moving too fast to be identified, a monkey perhaps or some kind of water rodent, scampered away and disappeared into a fissure in the rocks. Sudi said something, but Jephson couldn't make out what it was. He realized that the roar of the hidden cataract was growing quite loud. He glanced back to the stern and then, because of the expression on Sudi's face, turned around quickly and looked upstream again. Just ahead this reach of river was abruptly cut off by a massive black boulder, and where the river emerged from behind the boulder the water was white, foaming.

One of the oarsmen shouted just then; and as he did, the boat suddenly lurched, as if the river had dropped out from under her, and she slipped sideways and banged against some submerged logs. Only by a supreme effort of hard pulling at the oars, Sudi hollering the beat at the top of his lungs, was the craft prevented from spinning all the way around. She shot into a safe channel. But soon this channel began to trail off; the oars on both sides of the boat scraped bottom.

"It becomes most difficult, sah," Sudi shouted above the noise of the cataract.

"Stay with it, man. Let's see how much farther we can get."

"*Tafadhali*, Bwana," Sudi protested.

"Keep going, man. *Nenda kule.*"

Jephson, now standing also, braced his legs against the gunwales of the prow, holding himself against the pitch and buck of the roughening water. He was excited by the chill invigorating air, the thunderous roar of the cataract, by the sight of the turbulent river ahead. The Cauldron was there, beyond the boulder, in the next reach of the river, and he wanted to see it. The boat lurched and slipped again, and a rotted tree trunk swirled out of an eddy and slammed against her bow, then rushed away, turning end over end. Jephson dropped to his knees, gripped the gunwales, and crouched over the prow like the craft's figurehead. He was smiling; his heart was racing; he was exhilarated, scared maybe, but scared in a thrilling way. Jesus, this was adventure. This was what it was all about. This was what it was to be in the wilds, deep in a mountain gorge, moving up a dangerous stream, seeking a way around the next bend, accompanied by faithful savages, lured on by that which you have never seen, by that which for some irrational reason you were determined to see.

And then, there it was to be seen.

Jephson never rightly knew how Sudi managed to get the oarsmen to slip through the perilously narrowed channel, but all of a sudden they did. His admiration and affection for them soared as the boat banged up against the boulder and with a final stomach-sinking lurch—the boat spinning sideways under the impact of the foaming white waters rushing out from behind the boulder, the boatmen frantically shipping their oars and grabbing for handholds on rocks and overhangs and branches to keep her from being flung back downstream—they were facing the Cauldron of Hell. It stopped Jephson's heart; it took the breath out of him by its tremendous violence, its primitive beauty, a reach of river, perhaps a quarter-mile in length but choked down by the canyon cliffs to no more than ten yards across, leaping in vicious blue-silver waves thirty and forty feet high, whirling down into dreadful black fathomless holes, crashing over limestone reefs, boiling against granite boulders, tearing away at the soil of the shores, a reach of river in a state of never-ending explosion. Jephson, letting the lash of its spray soak him like a rainstorm, looked up along its raging surface to the top of the reach where the river first plunged into the Cauldron in a sheet of water as thick as steel, and above that to the jungle of foliage that the eternal rain of its spray had grown on the riverbanks, and above that up the sheer walls of the gorge to the small patch of crystalline blue sky that roofed it. An eagle was soaring there. And seeing it, the youth began to laugh, a laugh of pure irrational joy like a bubble bursting in his chest, and Sudi, momentarily nonplussed but then understanding it, feeling it burst in his own chest, joined in, and so did the oarsmen and the passengers, throwing their heads back, understanding the joy, laughing. But their laughter could not be heard above the thunder of the cataract.

Returning downriver, emerging again from the chill blue shadows of the gorge into the bright hot sunlight of the maritime plain, Jephson saw the *Serpa Pinto* steaming upriver, making for the Matadi wharf; and still full of the excitement of the adventure to the Cauldron, still bubbling with laughter, he ordered the boatmen to race the paddle wheeler to the mooring, and they, recognizing the sense of play in this, still grinning cheerfully themselves, put their backs into it and took up Sudi's spirited chant marking the beat of their swiftly pulling oars, like warriors off to battle. After the gorge, after the Cauldron, the relatively smooth water of the estuary was nothing to them; they flew. Jephson only hoped that Stanley was on the paddle wheeler's deck watching them.

He was. Troup and Barttelot were with him, leaning on the rail grinning.

"Stand off, you bloody lunatic," Troup suddenly called out, waving his straw hat.

But Sudi had seen the *Serpa Pinto*'s paddle wheel reverse direction and begin to churn up a mass of water that could swamp the smaller boat and had already leaned hard to port on the tiller. The steel boat veered neatly away and, with the boatmen skillfully shipping their oars, glided up to the wharf, winning the race. Jephson leaped out.

"Take her apart, Sudi," he commanded. And standing on the wharf, his legs planted wide apart, one hand resting on the stock of the pistol at his waist, the other on his hip, his pith helmet cocked back, his tunic soaked through by the cataract's spray, a smile of sheer elation on his sunburned face, the youth watched the oarsmen and passengers scramble from the boat and haul her up the muddy embankment and begin unscrewing the bolts that held her sections together.

"A very pretty showing, lad," Stanley said, coming down the *Serpa Pinto*'s gangway.

"Thank you, sir."

Stanley put a hand on Jephson's shoulder and watched with him as the Wanyamwezis went about disassembling the boat. "Yes, lad, I'll say this for you, you seem to have brought these kaffirs right up to the mark."

Jephson beamed.

"Hey, Jack, what do you think of this?"

Troup and Barttelot had come down from the paddle wheeler; and Troup, beaming almost as much as Jephson, clearly taking personal pleasure in his young friend's good showing, said, "Nothing wrong with it that I can see."

"Very nice indeed," Barttelot added.

Stanley nodded and turned back to the boat. The Wanyamwezis had her half-disassembled. "Seems like my design works right enough, eh, lad? The sections fit together just fine. She looks perfectly watertight."

"She is, sir. She's a tight, tidy little craft."

"Yes, a tight, tidy little craft." Stanley raised his eyes from the boat and, squinting, looked up the estuary to the limestone cliffs that hid the Cauldron of Hell. He remained silent for a minute, studying the river, the cliffs, the mountains through which they would march. The slap of the river against the wharf's pilings, the creak and squeak of its plankings suddenly seemed quite loud. In the distance, up in the hills, there was a burst of gunfire, Nelson testing the Maxim. Stanley removed his sun helmet and wiped his forehead with the sleeve of his tunic. "Have you given her a name yet, lad?"

"Sir?"

"We ought to give this darling little craft a name. I have a suspicion she's going to be doing a lot of hard work for us. She deserves a name."

"Yes, sir, she does."

"That of a beautiful woman," Major Barttelot put in. "Wouldn't you think so, sir? It would seem most appropriate."

Stanley looked at him.

"Miss Tennant, perhaps?"

The muscles in Stanley's jaws tensed.

"I'm sure she would be greatly flattered. The *Dorothy?* Or perhaps the *Lady Dorothy?*"

Stanley looked away. "I want everybody in the command tent on the double. Major, would you be good enough to get hold of Captain Nelson and Sergeant Bonny. Jack, fetch Will. I'll get hold of Surgeon Parke. He's probably in the surgery. And you come with me, Arthur. I want you to hunt up our maps. We're marching tomorrow with first light."

They came hurrying into the command tent straight from the field. Like Jephson, who still was wearing the tunic that had been drenched in the cataract, they too had no chance to change or wash up. They gathered around the field table in the center of the tent where Stanley awaited them. Unshaven since the previous day, the stubble on his chin seeming exceptionally gray, he leaned over the field table, a detailed surveyor's map of the route from Matadi through the Crystal Mountains to the Leopoldville Station at Stanley Pool spread out in front of him.

"As the crow flies, gentlemen," he said, "the distance to the

Pool is about two hundred miles. On the ground it's probably closer to two fifty. But whatever the exact distance, I want us to cover it in not much more than three weeks."

Three weeks! Jephson glanced across the field table at Troup. The redhead had estimated four, even five.

"It's an ambitious pace," Stanley went on. "Ten, twelve, fifteen miles a day. With the tonnage of goods we're transporting, that's an ambitious pace. But it can be done." He paused a moment. Then he said, "No, that ain't the way to put it. The fact of the matter is, gentlemen, it must be done."

He stepped back from the table and glanced about, becoming aware of the blue gloom of dusk that was invading the tent. He reached up for the hurricane lamp that was fastened to the tent's centerpole, pulled it down over the map, lit it, and spent a few moments adjusting its wick. Then he turned to his officers again and put his hands on his hips.

"Yes, gentlemen, it must be done. This is our great task now. This is our great test. Later on we'll have greater tasks. More terrible tests will be made on our skill and courage. But that doesn't concern us now. Now our only concern is to drive this caravan at the fastest possible pace. We must exploit this route. We will never see another as good. We must make time. Time is everything in this. We can perform Herculean feats. We can meet and defeat armies. We can move mountains. We can cut down entire jungles and cross the wildest rivers. But none of it will matter if we are not in time, if we are too late. That phrase rings in my ears. That phrase which haunts Lord Wolseley to this day. *Too late*. Gentlemen, I will not be too late to the relief of Emin Pasha in Equatoria as Lord Wolseley was too late to the relief of Chinese Gordon in Khartoum."

He stopped speaking, and just then there was a distant rumble of thunder. Heads turned in surprise; Jephson glanced out of the tent. A storm was gathering in the northeast over the mountains. A breeze whirled up a dust devil on the parched embankment outside.

"All right, gentlemen, that's it then. We start tomorrow with first light," Stanley said. "We won't be seeing a great deal of each other in the next few weeks. This probably is the last time we will all be together in the same place at the same time until we reach the Pool, so I want to wish you all good luck and God's speed." He went over to one of the boxes of special provisions that Fortnum and Mason had packed for the expedition and pulled a magnum of

French champagne from it. He smiled genially at the buzz of appreciation this evoked from the gathering. "I've got some glasses over there," he said, bringing the bottle back to the table. "Baruti, *tupatie bilauri.*"

"Mr. Stanley," Barttelot said.

"Yes, Major?" Stanley began easing the cork out of the champagne bottle.

"Don't you think, sir, this would be a good time to talk to the men about the problems we seem to be having with the steamers at the Pool?"

But just then there was another roll of thunder, a bit louder this time, and again all heads turned. Troup went over to fasten the tent's front flaps.

"What was that, Major?"

"I was hoping, sir, seeing how, as you say, this is likely to be the last time we will all be together for a while, you would take the opportunity to discuss with us what you heard in Boma about the number of steamers at the Pool and what your plans are if their number is insufficient."

Stanley removed the champagne cork without much violence, merely a festive pop; but as the wine was warm, it came foaming out of the bottle in a messy gush and he jerked it away from himself in mock panic and began pouring it out quickly into the first of the glasses that Baruti had fetched for him.

"Most of us haven't a terribly clear picture what's happening in that regard, you know," Barttelot went on. "Even though I was with you in Boma, I have to confess I've only the dimmest notion myself as to what the situation is at the Pool. An explanation from you would be most welcome. I'm sure everyone here would agree. It certainly would help put an end to the rumors that have been circulating."

"What rumors are those, Major?" Stanley asked, handing the first glass of champagne to Barttelot.

"Well, for one thing, Captain Nelson tells me he heard—"

"What did you hear, Captain?"

"Sir?" Nelson looked around, distinctly uncomfortable at suddenly becoming the center of attention. "Well, sir, what I heard was that there are no steamers at the Pool and we're going to have to make the trek to Yambuya overland."

"Where did you hear that, Captain?"

"I'm the source of that, Mr. Stanley," Parke piped up. "One of the Sudanese askaris, a corporal I was treating for powder burns, told it to me. Apparently he had spoken with that runner who came down from the Pool yesterday with the message from Mr. Ward. He asked me about it. He seemed terribly worried."

"What did you say to him?"

"I said it was complete rubbish."

"Good for you, Doctor. It is complete rubbish."

There was an expectant pause, everyone waiting for Stanley to go on. But he didn't.

· FOUR ·

THE CARAVAN, in march order along the embankment, was more than three miles long, very nearly 1,500 men, women, children, and animals stretching away, from Jephson's vantage point, quite out of sight into the early-morning mist rising off the river.

There had been a great deal of hurry-up-and-wait since the bugler had awakened the encampment at dawn that Friday, March 25; and now, as the sky steadily lightened, evolving from blue to rose to orange over the mountains to the east, there was more waiting going on. A conference of some sort was taking place at the head of the column; Stanley, Troup, and Barttelot were talking with a Portuguese trader from Vivi who from time to time pointed to the river. The *Heron* and the *Serpa Pinto* had departed about an hour before, but the harbor was crowded with the fishing pirogues of local tribesmen; and local tribesmen had also gathered along the bank, to gawk at the colorful pageant that the mustered expedition presented, to say goodbye to friends and relatives among the Bakongo porters, and to do some last-minute trading with the Wanyamwezis and Sudanese. Their presence played havoc with the discipline of the column as the wait dragged on. Hoffman, Bonny, and Uledi—occasionally Parke and Nelson and even Jephson himself—had to chase after their men and order them back into line, and their irritated commands rang out in the chill mist-laden air. But then at last the trader left. A moment later the bugler sounded the advance, an urgent blaring two-note bugle call repeated once, twice, three times; and Troup came trotting back down the line to rejoin his company. It was 6:15 A.M.

Stanley led the way, mounted on a tall black mule, a bandolier slung across his blue military jacket, his holstered revolver strapped on around it, his white pith helmet cocked well forward against the rays of the sun that were now glinting over the mountains. Baruti, clad in a long white shirt, glancing back with an excited grin, walked beside him, holding the mule's reins; and after them came the standard bearer, the bugler, the drummer, the contingent of Houssa and Bakongo scouts, stripped down to loincloths and carrying spears. Then came Surgeon Parke, also astride a mule, leading the bodyguard of handpicked Sudanese riflemen in brightly colored *kangas* and hooded burnooses, followed in turn by the rest of the headquarters company: men in Arab-style pantaloons with bales and boxes perched on their heads, women in flowing dark robes carrying pots and gourds and baskets and trussed-up chickens, boys leading pack donkeys and herding goats, all of them tramping up the road out of Matadi, climbing into the mountains.

The next company in the column was the advance guard of Sudanese askaris, with Major Barttelot, mounted as well, his big mule roan in color, at their head. But, as per orders, he waited for the last of the headquarters company to reach the crest of the first rise in the road and disappear over it, thus putting a comfortable interval between his company and Stanley's. Then, standing in his stirrups and looking back, he gave the cavalryman's signal, pumping his right arm in the air twice; and settling back in the saddle, he applied his spurs to his mount. Sergeant Bonny, on foot behind him, red in his pug face, the veins popping in his forehead, bellowed the command; and the askaris, their weapons and equipment jingling, moved out in a column of twos with a fair semblance of imperial British military swagger.

Jephson made a quick check of his company; they would be next. The twelve disassembled sections of the steel boat (the *Lady Dorothy*, as Jephson was beginning to think of her), looking like open-ended bathtubs, rested on their bottoms in a single file. Four Wanyamwezis stood by each section ready to hoist it on their shoulders by the wooden poles that were run through iron rings attached to the gunwales. Each of these porters, many of whom would double as oarsmen when the boat was in the water, carried in addition four days' rations of rice, his own kit and bedding, and some kind of weapon—a *panga* or an antique flintlock or a spear—strapped to his back. Waiting behind them in double file were twelve more *pagazis*, each of whom, along with his kit, rations, and weapon, carried a sixty-pound load of trading *mitako*, ammunition, field equipment, or miscellaneous stores. These loads were also grounded. Next down the line were three women and a boy, attached to the company as cooks and domestics, burdened with the paraphernalia of their jobs. Then came two muleteers in charge of the company's string of three pack asses loaded with sacks of meal and salt, water bags, and other provisions. There was also a riding donkey, a fuzzy-faced moke with big liquid eyes, intended for Jephson's use; but the youth didn't like the look of the beast—he seemed a balky, ill-tempered creature—and had turned him over to one of the muleteers, a boy named Juma. Perhaps later on he would try his luck with the animal; but as he didn't relish the idea of making a spectacle of himself at the very outset by either being bucked off the donkey or finding it impossible to get him to move, Jephson had decided to start the march on foot. Sudi had cut him a stout walking staff of ironwood for the purpose.

"*Twende zetu sasa*, Bwana?" the young Wanyamwezi asked when Jephson returned to the head of the company.

Jephson looked up the road. The mule-drawn Maxim automatic gun, which brought up the rear of Barttelot's company, was just reaching the top of the first rise. Jephson glanced back down the river embankment. The next company in the column was Uledi's; but Troup had come up the line to talk to the white-bearded chieftain, and now, with a broad reassuring grin, he gave Jephson a good-luck sign. Jephson looked back up the road into the mountains. The Maxim had reached the crest and in a cloud of dust vanished over it.

"*Haya*, Sudi. *Twende zetu sasa*."

"*Vyema*," Sudi shouted without looking behind him. "*Anza*."

Loads were swung up onto woolly heads, boat sections lifted by their poles like sedan chairs, the mules were given kicks in their flanks, and the company marched out of Matadi. Jephson, letting Sudi take the lead, watched them file past, leaning on his walking stick, a thumb hitched in his cartridge belt. Then he removed his sun helmet, smoothed down his hair, put the helmet back on, adjusted it to a sharp angle over his forehead, said a brief prayer, and fell in at the company's rear where he could keep an eye on everyone and prevent any lagging or malingering.

The road veered away from the river, more easterly than northeast; and once the first rise was reached, the landscape opened up on steeply rising and falling hills piled one on top of the other, the next always higher than the last. They were covered in yellow shoulder-high elephant grass, dotted with stands of acacia and fever trees and the occasional lone silver baobob, scarred by outcroppings of jagged granite, quartz, and limestone. The Congo, always farther away to the left and lying always at a lower elevation as they climbed, was apparent only because of the richer, greener foliage that grew along it.

The day warmed quickly. By midmorning the chill had burned off, the mist had congealed into a soupy humidity, and the sky had turned white in the blaze of the sun. Flocks of weaverbirds whirred in the branches of the acacia trees, clouds of butterflies came up from the elephant grass, and here and there were the castlelike structures that the driver ants build, but no game was to be seen. The road, at least this stretch of it, considering it was the work of the Free State's construction crews, was something of a disappointment. Although broad enough and obviously cut through the hills so as to minimize ascents and descents, it was not only unpaved but ungraded and much strewn with cinderlike stones and sharp-edged broken rocks that punished bare feet cruelly, and even those in boots, and often caused the mules and donkeys to stumble, loosening miniature landslides and raising spumes of red dust.

On the other hand, the pace of the march, at least so far, proved less demanding than Jephson had expected. For the youth himself, burdened with nothing more than his pistol, ammunition, water bottle, and walking staff, it was, as Troup had promised, little more than a hot brisk hike. But even the Wanyamwezis, despite their loads, seemed to take to it without much difficulty. Sweat streamed down their bodies; now and again one or another would trip, even fall, especially on the descents; every once in a while there was a sharp cry of pain, an oath flung at some obstacle in the path, a dropped load; and there was always much grimacing and complaining on the ascents. But they moved on, kept the pace, chattering ceaselessly to one another, making jokes, commenting on the scenery, a graceful fluidity in their gait. And then Sudi started up a song—"Are you there, Wanyamwezis?" he sang and they answered, "We are here." "How great is the safari, my brothers?" "It is great."—and Jephson began to relax and enjoy himself; and after a while, he went up to the head of the company and marched alongside Sudi.

At three in the afternoon, the goal of the day's march, the Mpozo River, came into view. It ran from south to north through a narrow valley on its way to join the Congo, the vegetation along its banks marking its twisting course through the rolling yellow hills. A bridge of bamboo and vines spanned it; and when Jephson, coming up over the crest of a razorback, first saw it lying in the valley far below, Stanley's company had crossed the bridge and Barttelot's was just in the process of doing so. It was, however, another hour, making their way cautiously down the steep decline, before he and his men reached the river themselves; and by then

Stanley's and Barttelot's companies had downed their loads and spread out into the adjoining fields and under the trees along the bank.

In the course of the next two hours, the rest of the caravan reached the Mpozo. Most also crossed the bridge before falling out to make camp; but the last to arrive—some of Hoffman's people and all of Nelson's rear guard—remained on the near side of the river. Cooking fires were started; the officers' tents were pitched and shelters for the Sudanese and Wanyamwezis erected; inventory was taken of each company's loads to see if any had been lost, damaged, or stolen, and guards were posted on them; scouting parties were sent out to reconnoiter the countryside and hunt game; and women went to the nearby villages to barter wire or cloth or beads for fowl, goats, fresh fruit, and vegetables. As the sun dropped behind the mountains, casting the narrow valley into shadow, the officers began gathering in twos and threes to exchange gossip and experiences of the day's trek. Parke came down the line on his donkey to see if his medical services were needed by any of the companies. Jephson accompanied him back to Troup's encampment, and leaving him there to treat a *pagazi* with a broken ankle, he went with Troup to report to Stanley.

The command tent was set up in a grove of eucalyptus and palm on the Mpozo's right bank about a half-mile upstream from the road. Stanley had had a swim in the stream with Baruti; and now washed and shaved and changed, he sat in shirt and braces in a canvas folding chair in front of the tent, smoking a cigar, the little blackamoor sprawled at his feet. Barttelot was with them. He too had had a chance to clean up and change clothes; and with a map unfolded on his knees was going over the route of the next day's march with Stanley when Troup and Jephson, both still smeared with the sweat and dirt of the road, came up.

"Christ, lads, you look a sight," Stanley said, grinning, obviously in a good mood. "I don't suppose you'd say no to a drop of this." He produced a flask of brandy and handed it to Troup. "*Viti*," he shouted over his shoulder, and one of the Wanyamwezi women fetched two more folding chairs from the tent. "Sit down, boys. Put the load down. You've earned it. You've done a good piece of work today. We all have. And we're going to do better tomorrow. I was just telling Major Barttelot we ought to reach the mission at 'Palla tomorrow. Eh, Jack, don't you think?"

"Sure." Troup took a long pull on the brandy flask. "The construction ends there, don't it?"

"Yes."

"Might as well make use of it while we got it." Troup took another swallow of the brandy, then passed the flask to Jephson. "Ain't but four, five miles beyond Kulu anyway," the redhead said and started rolling himself a cigarette.

Jephson sat down and drank off a stiff shot of the brandy. It was wonderful, pure luxury, to sit down in a chair, to feel the brandy explode in his chest, to have the sun out of his eyes. He stretched out his legs and arched his back, feeling the brandy flow into his knotted muscles, into his weary bones, into his sun-beaten brain.

"Hey, lad, don't hoard that."

"Oh, I'm sorry, sir." Jephson passed the flask back.

It went around again while Stanley, Troup, and Barttelot talked about the next day's road. Jephson listened, staring up at the sky. The fiery colors of the sunset were fading, and thunderheads were gathering over the mountains. He knew he ought to get back to his company before the rain started to make sure the camp had been made, the rations distributed, the meal started, his tent ready. But when the flask came around to him again, he took another long pull on it and stayed where he was, sprawled out in the chair, feeling terrific—about aching in muscles he never knew he had, about sitting in a camp in the African hills with soldiers and explorers, about having earned the right to be sitting there with them, about simply having made it through the day.

The next day's march was measurably more difficult—the pace quicker, the rest breaks fewer, the distance covered greater, the hours on the road longer, the road itself rougher, climbing more steeply into the mountains—but at the end it seemed worth the effort because they reached the Livingstone Inland Mission at Mpalaballa by nightfall. This was a lovely place, a cluster of brick buildings situated in a pretty wood on a high hill, where the air was palpably less humid and one had a splendid view of the thundering cataracts of the Congo. The missionary, a Mr. Clarke from Devon, thrilled to have the famous Mr. Stanley's expedition camp on his grounds, arranged lodgings for him and his officers in the parsonage, served them a sumptuous dinner, and afterward treated them to a hymn sing by the children of his church school.

The following morning it rained, and the start of the march was delayed for several hours. And then it rained again during the afternoon, a sudden cloudburst blowing through from north to south, sending the *pagazis* scattering into the bush to find shelter.

And after that it rained almost every morning and at least once during the day and usually again at night; for with the beginning of April, they entered the season of the long rains in this part of Africa.

At first the rain was allowed to halt the caravan; but as the days passed and the rain became more frequent and of longer duration—it would become progressively worse until May—and the delays they caused threatened to wreck Stanley's three-week timetable for reaching the Pool, word came down the line to keep the caravan moving even in the foulest weather. This was tricky business, further complicated by the fact that the Free State's road had ended at Mpallaballa and the route they now traveled consisted of narrow footpaths and game trails winding sometimes seemingly at random up and down the rocky, grassy hills between villages and marketplaces and hunting grounds. In clear weather, these paths and trails were not difficult to follow. But when the rains came in blinding sheets, the sky blackening into night, thunder and lightning crashing all around like an artillery barrage, pack animals bolting, men slipping and sliding and falling in the mud, then the way could be lost. The land turned to swamp, leeches emerged from the ooze, torrents gushed over the hills, and the trails washed out.

One storm knocked out the bridge over the Lunionzo River, and a runner was sent back to fetch up the *Lady Dorothy* for ferrying duty. Thankfully, it wasn't raining at the time, so Jephson and his company were able to move up the line with a fair show of speed; but by the time they got to the riverbank where the headquarters company and Barttelot's askaris were waiting, it had been discovered that the steel boat wasn't needed after all. The river, about thirty yards wide here, making a sharp bend through a wood of dripping mangroves, could be forded. A trading caravan had arrived on the opposite bank, just after Stanley had sent back for the boat, and its leader, a French agent for the Free State, shouting through cupped hands, had informed Stanley of the ford and then had started his own caravan across to show its precise location. When Jephson came up, the Frenchman's *pagazis* were still in the process of crossing, a hundred or so Kabindas and Houssas balancing ivory tusks and baskets of raw rubber on their heads and stepping cautiously through the swollen, fast-running river, which at points was chest high. The Frenchman himself had been carried across on a litter and was chatting with Stanley, Barttelot, and Parke on the near bank.

He was from Port Francqui on the Kasai, a tributary of the

Congo, and the ivory and rubber he was transporting had been harvested in that region. He had brought it downriver aboard one of the State's steamers, the *Royal*, to Leopoldville Station on the Pool, where he had got up this caravan for the trek around Livingstone Falls. He had been under way for three months now, seven weeks since leaving Leopoldville, and looked it. His black beret in which a fish-eagle's feather was stuck, his black beard, his fringed hide jacket, his hands gripping a long rifle, even the brass ring in his left ear were caked with mud, and he stank. From time to time he glanced over his shoulder to check his *pagazis'* progress across the river and shout an obscenity in French at them.

"Where is the *Royal* now?" Stanley asked. "Is she still at the Pool?"

"No, no more. She turn round and go back upriver after me."

"When is she due back?"

The Frenchman shrugged. "I don't think for some while, Bula Matari. She go to Bolobo and then Equator Station. There is much rubber waiting at Equator Station, I hear."

"What steamers are at the Pool?"

"Pardon?" The Frenchman had glanced at the river again; the last of his *pagazis* were across.

"How many steamers were on the Pool when you left there, monsieur?"

"How many? Besides the mission steamer *Peace?*"

"Yes, besides her."

"Not many. Let me see. The *Florida*, she was there. But she is not in good shape. I do not know what is wrong with her. Something about her propeller. In any event, she was on the beach when I was there. And . . . yes, the *En Avant*. She was there. But she is no longer a proper steamer, you know. She has no engine. They use her now only as a barge."

"What happened to her engine?"

"They put it into the *AIA* last year."

"Where is the *AIA?* Is she at the Pool?"

"No, she is on the Kasai. She stays on the Kasai these days."

"What about the *Stanley?*"

"Oh, yes, the *Stanley*. You are right, Bula Matari. She was not there, but she was expected. She comes down from the Ubangi. She could be there by now."

"And?"

"And?"

"Which others?"

"Which others? No others, Bula Matari. No, no others. The *Florida*, the *En Avant*, maybe now the *Stanley*. That is all."

"I see." Stanley looked around. The Frenchman's *pagazis* had downed their ivory tusks and baskets of rubber and were mingling with the Sudanese and Wanyamwezis. "Yes, well, thank you, monsieur. I mustn't detain you any longer. You'll be wanting to get on your way. And I ought to start my boys across the ford now myself."

"*Bien sur.* You have a long way to go. You see the ford all right now, *n'cest ce pas?* You will have no difficulty with it?"

"No, I see it clearly. I will have no difficulty, thanks to you."

"*Bon.* Then go with God, Bula Matari."

"Thank you, monsieur." Stanley shook the Frenchman's hand.

"*Bon chance, messieurs.*" The Frenchman shook Barttelot's, Parke's, and Jephson's hands in turn, then strode off, shouting at his *pagazis.*

"Surgeon Parke, let's get the headquarters company formed up and started across the river."

Parke didn't immediately respond. He glanced at Barttelot.

"Mr. Stanley," Barttelot said.

"And, Major, you might as well get your askaris on their feet too. It won't be but a half-hour before it's their turn."

"Mr. Stanley, this news—this isn't exactly the news you were expecting, I wouldn't think."

"What news, Major?"

"About the steamers, sir. What that Frenchie just told us. That there are only three steamers at the Pool and two of them out of commission. You were counting on at least five steamers, weren't you, sir, and all in good working order."

"That news is seven weeks old, Major. A great deal has happened in the seven weeks since that Frenchman left the Pool. You will see that when we get to the Pool. So let's get to the Pool. Get your men on their feet. Surgeon Parke, start the headquarters company moving."

The pace quickened. Each day Stanley set a more distant goal to reach. Each day he pushed harder, farther, longer. Each day the pressure to keep up, to keep going became more punishing. There were more accidents, more injuries. Loads were dropped and broken, loads were dropped and lost. A donkey shattered its forelegs going down into a ravine and had to be shot. Fording the Inkissi, a cookboy was swept away in the torrent; and his father, a headman, trying to save him, also drowned. The steel boat overturned in the Nkalama; and although all hands survived the mishap, a case of ammunition was destroyed. A Wanyamwezi woman came down with fever; she could be heard screaming all through one night, and in the morning she died. An askari was left behind in a village with foot ulcers, unable to walk, and a group of Bakongo porters deserted and returned to Matadi. Straggling and malingering increased; the caravan grew longer, more disordered, winding back across the hills five, eight, ten miles, different sections of it struggling along different trails or along no trail at all, often out of touch with each other. At day's end it never quite caught up with itself and at day's start never properly reassembled. And it rained.

It was still raining; there had been a violent storm at three in the afternoon—high winds, lightning shattering trees—but after the worst of it passed, the sky did not clear. A milky soup of clouds and mist remained hanging low over the hills, and a steady drizzle kept falling. Jephson, mounted on his donkey, rode in the lead of the company, forcing the pace. The canvas poncho he wore covered him to his knees, and he had lowered the puggaree of his pith helmet and tucked it into his collar; but even so he was soaked to the skin. He kept his head lowered, watching the sodden trail under the donkey's hooves, on the alert for an obstacle—a leech or rock, snake or log—that might cause the animal to shy and stumble. For all their reputation for surefootedness, these damn beasts were constantly shying and stumbling. Jephson had already been dumped into the mud twice that day, and in this bloody awful soup chances were that he was in for a third. And besides, what was the point of looking up? He couldn't see anything farther than fifty yards off anyway. He certainly couldn't see any sign of the rest of the caravan; he couldn't even see the whole of his own company. It straggled away behind him into the mist and rain and growing darkness, plodding along sullenly up the endlessly climbing trail.

Sudi came up from the rear of the company, emerging from the mist like an apparition, his hooded djellaba soaked and spattered with mud and hanging around him like a shroud. He took hold of the donkey's bridle as if meaning to lead the animal, but really only to lean against it and be pulled along by it and so rest for a bit. But the grip annoyed the beast, and it twisted its head and nipped at his arm, so the young Wanyamwezi released the bridle and, dropping back a step or two, placed his hand on the donkey's withers and walked alongside Jephson, resting this way. He didn't say anything, but Jephson knew what was on his mind. It was on Jephson's mind as well: When would the day's march end? It was nearly six o'clock; in less than two hours it would be night, and there still was no sign of a runner from Stanley calling the halt for the day. It was possible, Jephson realized, that a runner had been sent back but hadn't been able to find them in this soup.

He wasn't all that sure he was on the same trail as the headquarters company anyway; in the storm that afternoon he might very well have taken a trail farther to the south and so now would be bypassed by a runner coming down the other trail. He would give it another hour, then send up a runner of his own to see what was going on. He couldn't imagine that Stanley would insist on pushing on after dark. He glanced at Sudi out of the corner of his eye, not wanting yet to confront him on the issue. The young Wanyamwezi looked awful but probably no more awful than Jephson himself looked; he hadn't shaved or bathed or changed clothes or had a hot meal or a dry night's sleep in nearly a week.

"Soon there is *kijiji*, sah," Sudi said and pointed ahead with his rifle.

Jephson couldn't see anything. Now and again the curtain of rain and mist parted, revealing the ghostly outline of a tree or outcropping of black boulders, but there was no sign of a village.

"It is Nselo." Sudi did not have a map, but Jephson knew there was no need to check his information against one. The young Wanyamwezi kept close track of the countryside, gathering information at the villages and marketplaces where they traded, sending scouts for miles up the trails in clear weather; and if he said Nselo was up ahead, Jephson had no doubt it was. "We make camp there for tonight, sah?"

Jephson didn't reply.

"I have two hurt boys, sah, and one woman who is sick in her stomach. They have trouble going on. They must rest. I must rest too. You must rest. We all must rest now, sah. We rest well in *kijiji*."

Jephson still did not reply. He did not know what to reply. The prospect of spending the night in a village was irresistible. There would be dry firewood, a hot supper, a hot bath, decent shelter against the storm that surely would blow down on them again during the night. But what if Stanley pushed on for another hour or so? He would be furious if Jephson decided on his own to quit the march here. On the other hand, how would he discover it? There was damn little chance for the company to catch up with the head of the column that day anymore.

Jephson, standing in his stirrups, looked back down the line of his company. What he could see of it—the men straggling through the gloom and drizzle, bent under their loads, dragging one foot after the other through the swamp and slime—made a pitiful sight. Sudi was probably right: They should quit here, they all needed to rest. He sat back in the saddle and looked up ahead again and went on riding in silence, hoping with all his might that a runner from Stanley would show up and make the decision for him. Sudi went on walking beside him for a bit longer but then taking Jephson's silence for a decision, stepped away from the donkey and began dropping back to the rear of the company again.

And just then Jephson saw the conical thatch roofs of a village emerge through a tattered patch of mist.

"*Haya*, Sudi," he called back over his shoulder. "Let's have a word with the chaps in Nselo. Let's see if they'll put us up for the night."

"No one there, sah," Sudi said, trotting back up to the donkey's side, a big grin on his face. "*Kijiji tupu*, Bwana."

"*Tupu?* Empty?"

"*Ndiyo*. All people gone away. Market woman tell me so this morning. We can take *kijiji* for our camp tonight. No one there to stop us."

"How come? What happened?"

"There was trouble in *kijiji*, market woman tell me, and Force Publique soldiers make all people go away."

"What sort of trouble?"

Sudi shrugged. "*Sijui*, Bwana. I don't know. Trouble. Trouble about the rubber maybe. Market woman did not tell me. Maybe people in *kijiji* did not bring enough rubber to agent. That sort of trouble. There is always that sort of trouble. Anyway Force Publique come and send all people away for punishment."

"When did this happen?"

"Oh, many weeks ago, sah," Sudi replied, taking hold of the donkey's bridle again but this time not to rest but in fact to lead the animal. "People may not come back anymore, market woman tell me, so *kijiji* empty since then. It make good camp for us, sah."

Jephson relaxed his grip on the reins and let Sudi lead the donkey toward the village. It was a sizable village, as villages in these parts went, situated on a wooded knoll and enclosed by a sturdy palisade of bamboo pikes. The gate through this palisade, swinging slightly from the buffeting of the rain, stood open on a broad path that led down between two rows of round mud huts, each topped by a tall, graceful cone of thatch, to the chief's compound at the other end. There were perhaps thirty of these huts, neatly arrayed on each side of the path; and a group of four more, within its own bamboo palisade, formed the chief's enclosure. They were handsome structures, their mud walls plastered with lime, woven raffia mats covering their doorways, little verandas around each, gardens of bananas, pineapples, maize, and manioc behind them, and an orchard of guava and lime trees. Jephson had Sudi halt the donkey as soon as they passed through the gate. He dismounted and stood in the mud for a minute surveying the scene. Two or three hundred people must have lived in this village once, and now there wasn't a soul, not a goat or a vagrant hen. It was eerie. Cracks had appeared in the walls of some of the huts, the thatch of their roofs had gone unrepaired, the path and the gardens and orchard were overgrown with grass and scrub. The rain drummed down into a graveyard silence. Jephson walked over to the first hut on his right, ducked under the low-hanging eave of thatch, and reached for the raffia mat covering the doorway. He hesitated, feeling a sudden shiver of fright at what he might see behind it. But when he pulled the mat aside, there was nothing to see. The hut was empty, a round dark room stripped of whatever belongings its occupants might once have owned. Jephson stepped into it. It gave off a dank, moldy odor; but it was dry, and Jephson stood there for a minute relishing the experience of being out of the rain at last. Yes, this would make a good camp, he thought. They would rest well here, and they would take to the march in the morning all the stronger for it. But still . . .

"Sudi," Jephson called, ducking back out into the rain. "Fetch the company up. We will camp here."

"Yes, sah." Sudi slipped through the gate in the palisade and vanished into the mist, leaving Jephson alone.

But still . . . Jephson thought again, turning around to look down the path toward the deserted village to the chief's kraal. He couldn't help feeling there was something ghoulish about this, taking over homes from which the rightful owners had been driven, harvesting their gardens, exploiting their misfortune, benefiting from their misery. The poor buggers—where were they now? Where were they spending this night of rain?

Jephson started down the path toward the chief's compound, looking to the left and right at the abandoned huts. What could these people have done, what terrible trouble had they caused so that King Leopold's agent should have visited such a cruel punishment on them?

Jephson stopped abruptly in his tracks. Something had moved up ahead. He slipped his hand under his poncho and gripped the butt of his pistol and stared hard into the darkness. It was an animal of some sort; no, there were more than one. They had been prowling around something at the entrance to the chief's compound but had fallen still at the sound or scent of Jephson's approach. Crouched in the foggy gloom, they stared back at him. He saw their eyes, orange eyes. Scavengers of some kind, hyenas probably. Jephson brought his pistol out from under the poncho and cocked it. Hyenas were nothing to be afraid of, he told himself; they would scatter at any loud noise, at a pistol shot. He took a step forward cautiously, and the animals moved back, watching him. There were three of them that he could see, three pairs of orange eyes. He advanced another step. Ugly beasts, the size of dogs, with spotted yellow fur.

"Bugger off, you curs."

They backed away still farther but reluctantly, loath to leave whatever carrion it was that had drawn them there.

And then Jephson saw it. At first he did not recognize what it was. He was still several yards from it; the rain and mist obscured it, and he was wary of the hyenas grouped around it. He took another step forward, squinting, puzzled, trying to make out what it was. And then he saw what it was and whirled away.

"Jesus!"

For the longest time he stood with his back to it, horrified, unable to bring himself to look at it again. But then, bracing himself, he did.

It was a basket filled with hands.

· FIVE ·

Stanley Pool—a magnificent natural reservoir formed by the damming of the Congo by the Crystal Mountains, fifteen miles at its widest, more than twenty miles long—is the end (or the beginning, depending on how one chooses to look at it) of the river's single longest navigable stretch—the more than one thousand miles of unimpeded waterway that snakes through the heart of Africa and upon which the expedition was to sail to Yambuya aboard a flotilla of steamers provided by King Leopold's Congo Free State. But on the Friday afternoon, April 22, when the expedition at last reached Stanley Pool, nothing resembling a flotilla of steamers was to be seen. The graceful pencil-slim silhouettes of hundreds of native fishing pirogues dotted the Pool's shimmering surface, but the only European vessel of any size on that vast mirrorlike expanse was a broad-beamed side-wheeler, with two iron stacks and two covered decks, tied up at the jetty of Leopoldville Station.

Stanley had built the station some seven years before, but it still had the look of a raw frontier settlement. It was located on the downstream end of the Pool's southern shore, barely a mile above the first cataract of Livingstone Falls, and was surrounded on its landward sides by a largely unexplored wilderness of forested hills and scrub-covered grassland. Its main structure was a two-story log blockhouse with a corrugated iron roof, a wide veranda circling it at ground level, with seven-pounder Krupp guns on either side of the wood planking that led up to it from the jetty where the lone steamer was moored. A blue flag with a gold star that marked it as a district headquarters of the Congo Free State was flying over it. Behind it, along one side of a grassy field, which served as a parade ground, were a score of single-story buildings, some also of logs but most of lime-washed baked clay with thatch roofs—the guardhouse and barracks of the Force Publique (the

State's local gendarmerie), the bungalows of station officials and State agents, a hotel for itinerant traders and hunters, warehouses for the rubber and ivory brought in from still more remote outposts, stables for pack animals, a clinic, blacksmith and carpentry shops, and various dry goods and provisions stores—all enclosed within a stockade at the two outer corners of which stood twenty-foot-tall watchtowers, guarding the landward approaches.

Outside this cantonment was a native quarter, the scruffy shantytown of the Krooboys and Houssas and Kabindas and half-castes who hired on for the rubber and ivory caravans to Matadi and the supply caravans back. It was a noisy, smelly jumble of sheds and huts that sprawled down to the Pool's reed-choked, mosquito-ridden embankment, where amid discarded oil drums and paraffin tins, broken barrels and rusting machinery, a hull was beached and a derelict steam launch lay overturned.

A quarter of a mile farther up the embankment was a second cluster of European buildings; these belonged to an English Baptist mission and included a clapboard church with a thatch bell tower, a log parsonage with well-tended vegetable gardens, and a long low wooden schoolhouse. There was also a steamer jetty there jutting out into the Pool, but when the expedition arrived only a whaleboat was tied up to it. The mission's steamer, the *Peace*, and the missionaries themselves, the Reverend Mr. Bentley and Dr. Sims, were away at the time, preaching the Gospel at Kinshasa and the other villages of the Bateke tribesmen who lived along the Pool's shore and gathered the raw rubber of the surrounding forests for the station's agents.

A pale, rheumy-eyed Belgian with a forked beard and a hook nose by the name of Liebrichts was in charge of the station. He was an old acquaintance of Stanley's, having served under him in the early days of pioneering on the Congo for King Leopold, but he showed very little pleasure on seeing him again now as he came striding up the wood planking to the blockhouse's veranda. Three white men were on the veranda with Liebrichts—his aide-de-camp, Ensign Dessauer; the commandant of the Force Publique garrison, Major Parmiter; and Bertie Ward. Unlike Liebrichts and the two others, Ward, a scrappy-looking man in his late twenties with a curly chestnut beard and something of an elfin twinkle in his bright eyes, wearing corduroy knickerbockers, a shooting jacket with a profusion of cartridge loopholes, and an Aussie scout hat with the brim tacked up on one side, greeted Stanley effusively, throwing his arms around him. And when Stanley went into the blockhouse with Liebrichts, Ward came bounding off the veranda to bestow a similarly exuberant embrace on Troup.

"What the hell have you been doing, Bert?" Troup said, untangling himself from Ward's hug with a smile. "Where the devil are the steamers you were supposed to have rounded up for us? All I see is the *Stanley*."

Ward shook his head. Barttelot, Nelson, Parke, and Jephson gathered around to hear what he would say. They didn't know him, but Troup didn't bother making introductions. There'd be time enough for that later. Now all anyone wanted to know about was where were the steamers that were to take them to Yambuya.

The State had seven steamers plying the Congo above the Pool–*La Belgique*, *Esperance*, *Royal*, *AIA*, *En Avant*, *Florida*, and *Stanley*. Given the number of people, pack animals, and loads to be transported on this leg of the journey, Stanley had been counting on at least five of these. But according to Ward only three were then at the Pool.

"Three? What do you mean three?" Troup asked. "I only see the *Stanley*." He indicated the side-wheeler tied up at the station's jetty. "Which are the other two?"

"*En Avant* and *Florida*."

"Well, where the hell are they?"

Pulling a sour face, Ward pointed to the hull pulled up in the reeds of the Pool's swampy embankment. That was the *En Avant*, he said. She was without machinery; her engine had been cannibalized to repair the *AIA*'s and she could now be used only as a barge. And the *Florida* was the derelict launch lying overturned in the mud beside her. Her bottom was holed through in two places below the waterline and her propeller was irreparably bent; she couldn't even be used as a barge.

"Jesus. How does Liebrichts explain this?"

Ward shrugged. "He doesn't. He claims he never received any instructions from Brussels about making the steamers available to us. I told him that was shit. I told him Bula Matari had personally spoken to His Royal Highness about them. But he just dug in his heels and said he'd never been told anything."

"But what about the cable Bula Matari sent to Brussels from Boma? He must have had a reply to that by now."

"No. He says he hasn't heard a word, not a word."

"Well, fuck him then. He's had word now. Bula Matari's given him the word. He's just going to have to round up those steamers and get them back here in a hurry."

"Come on, Jack. You know better than that. Those boats are scattered all over the river basin. The *Royal* is at Port Francqui. The *AIA* is hundreds of miles up the Kasai. The *Esperance* is on the Ubangi. And God knows where *La Belgique* is. There's no way of getting word to them; and even if you could, it'd be months before any of them could get back here."

No one said anything after that for a minute.

Then Jephson broke the silence. "Well, what are we going to do then?"

"Pack it in, I suppose. Pack it in and go back down to the coast." This was Barttelot. He fitted a cigarette into his ivory holder. "Not much else we can do, I shouldn't think. There's no way we can get to Yambuya, let alone to Emin Pasha, in anything like a reasonable amount of time without the steamers. No, I'm afraid we're just going to have to pack it in and march back down to the coast like a bunch of damn fools. Rather humiliating, I must say. Getting stopped before we're even half started."

"What about the *Peace*, Bert?" Troup asked, ignoring Barttelot.

"She's due back tonight. But you can forget about her too. I've been at Bentley for weeks, trying to get him to give us the loan of her. But he won't do it. The pious son of a bitch, he just won't do it. You know what he thinks of Mr. Stanley."

Troup nodded and looked up at the blockhouse. Ensign Dessauer and Major Parmiter were still on the veranda, leaning on its rail, talking quietly to each other. Stanley and Liebrichts were still in the blockhouse, presumably talking not so quietly to each other. From the distance the sounds of the caravan clearing ground and cutting brush, pitching tents and building shelters, could be heard.

"Hard to imagine how he could have gotten himself into a stupid fix like this."

This was Barttelot again. Like all the rest of them, he was filthy and unshaven, his uniform sweated through and caked with mud from the road. None of them had had a chance for a proper clean-up during the hard marching of the last two weeks. But somehow this only made Barttelot look that much more the dashing soldier, the ivory cigarette holder clamped between his strong teeth, a slightly amused expression on his face.

"You'd have thought he would have made damn sure he had the steamers nailed down before he ever committed himself to this route. But surely once he heard in Matadi what the situation actually was up here, why in blazes did he go ahead and march us all this way anyway? What possibly could he have had in mind? Eh, Troup? What do you think? What could he possibly have had in mind?"

"Something."

"Something?" Barttelot smiled.

"Yes, something, Major. You can be damn sure he had something in mind. Because I can tell you he ain't going to be stopped. He ain't never been stopped before, and he ain't going to be stopped now. You can bet your life on it."

The next day Ngalyema came. The ceremony that accompanied his arrival was terrific, as wildly savage as anything Jephson could have dreamed of in his wildest fantasies of Africa.

Ngalyema was the paramount chief of the Bateke tribe that inhabited the forests around the Pool; and like almost everyone else in this part of the world, he knew Stanley. They had first met in 1877, when Stanley discovered the course of the Congo. Indeed, Stanley was the first white man Ngalyema had ever seen. Stanley was in dreadful straits at the time; he had been fighting his way clear across the whole of Africa for three years by then, and Ngalyema had saved his life. They met up again four years later, when Stanley returned to the Pool to build Leopoldville Station. Things did not go quite so smoothly between them that time. Ngalyema wasn't at all keen on having a white man's fort and trading depot set up in the middle of his domain, but after a few skirmishes Stanley talked him around to accepting the idea and signing a treaty that put his lands under the sovereignty of King Leopold's Congo Free State. And now, having heard Stanley had returned to the Pool a third time (actually Ward had gotten word to him on Stanley's instructions), Ngalyema came to meet him once again. He came from his *banza* in Kinshasa.

Thousands of his warriors preceded him—big, loose-limbed blue-black brutes, their faces tattooed with fierce cicatrices, their naked torsos painted half white and half orange, wearing grass skirts, their hair braided in Medusa-like plaits, carrying bows and arrows, coming down the paths out of the forest in a weirdly rhythmic dancing gait to the beat of drums and the eerily mournful cries of kudu horns. They filed through the postern gate in the station's stockade under the guns in the watchtowers and formed themselves into a great semicircle on the parade ground facing the back veranda of the station's blockhouse. Force Publique gendarmes took up positions around them. The Houssas and Kabindas and Krooboys of the station's shantytown crowded into the cantonment to see the spectacle. And all the station's Europeans gathered on the blockhouse's back veranda, as if on a reviewing stand.

Stanley stood at the center of the front rank of these, wearing his blue military jacket with gold-braid frogging, white jodhpurs, a freshly chalked sun helmet, and a severe expression. On his left Liebrichts, in the gold-piped white uniform and kepi of a district commissioner, kept up an incessant stream of nervous chatter in his ear, which Stanley acknowledged only occasionally by nodding. On his right, watching the proceedings with unconcealed disapproval, were the two Baptist missionaries, the Reverend Mr. Bentley, a brawny Englishman with a black spade beard that came down to the middle of his chest, and Dr. Sims, a plump little man with wispy blond muttonchops, both returned to Leopoldville aboard the *Peace* the previous evening. Ranged on either side of them along the veranda railing for the best view of things were the officers of the expedition (except Bonny and Hoffman, who were looking after the caravan) as well as Baruti, holding Troup's hand. And grouped behind them were the principal officials and residents of the station—Ensign Dessauer, Major Parmiter, a Swede by the name of Shagerstrom who was captain of the *Stanley*, a Mr. Walker who was that steamer's engineer, an American ivory hunter by the name of Swinburne, his Irish assistant Roger Casement, several Dutch and German and Russian traders, and agents and storekeepers.

Formed in their semicircular ranks, the Bateke warriors squatted on their haunches, creating a sort of amphitheater of the parade ground. Then the drumming ceased and kudu horns fell silent. An expectant hush fell over the cantonment. It went on for about five minutes. Then there was an ear-splitting blast from a single kudu horn, the drummers started up a furious blood-quickening beat, and a double file of ten Bateke appeared at the stockade gate. They were chiefs in their own right, vassals of Ngalyema, decked out more elaborately than the warriors, in headdresses of gray and green parrot feathers, monkey skins draped from their shoulders, carrying spears and painted hide shields; and as they pranced down the length of the parade ground to the beat of the drums, they rattled their spears against their shields, making a sound very much like machine-gun fire. They entered the clear space in front of the veranda, formed a smaller semicircle of their own there, and raised their spears in salute to Stanley and the other white men. And again the drumming stopped and there was another long, expectant pause.

When it was broken, when the drummers and the kudu horn players struck up their primitive music again, a cluster of women came through the stockade gate. They were naked except for leather aprons, and the Europeans on the veranda pressed forward for a better view. Jephson glanced at Stanley. His expression was as clenched and as rock-hard as before, but the spade-bearded missionary Bentley on his right grimaced at the sight of all these bare breasts and voluptuous hips jiggling tantalizingly as the women danced through the warrior ranks carrying baskets of fruit and calabashes of palm wine on their heads, swinging live fowls from their undulating arms, leading strings of goats. They brought these to the center of the circle, then withdrew behind the honor guard of chiefs, except for one girl who remained to tend the livestock. And again it became quiet.

Then a tremendous shout went up from the warriors. The women broke into a spine-shivering ululation. The drummers and trumpeters started up again, and the chiefs dropped to their knees. Jesus, what a show! The chief of chiefs of all the Bateke was borne through the gate in an ebony sedan chair enclosed in a beautifully made little hut of woven raffia, carried thus unseen through the adulatory shouting and howling and dancing of his people, borne to the center of the amphitheater and set down there. Immediately it was dead silent again. The sedan-chair bearers stepped back and prostrated themselves. The chiefs bowed their foreheads to the ground. The girl with the goats clung to the neck of one little beast to keep it from bolting. And nothing happened. The suspense was delicious.

And then without warning Stanley strode down from the veranda. Jephson turned at the sudden clatter of his boots on the steps and saw Barttelot start to follow him, but Liebrichts seized his arm and held him back. Stanley took up a position directly in front of the sedan chair, legs planted wide apart, hands on hips, and said something softly, too softly for Jephson to hear. But whatever it was, it had its effect. Without fanfare, one side of the chair's enclosure was flung open and Ngalyema stepped out. There was an audible gasp on the veranda—Jephson himself gasped—and a huge sigh rippled across the parade ground, but otherwise the silence was strictly maintained, all eyes riveted on the tremendous figure of the paramount chief. He was six feet and six inches at the very least, with mammoth shoulders and chest, a terrific barrel of a stomach, and pillars for legs, and all this gigantic blue-black flesh was naked except for a loincloth. He wore no feathers or skins or trinkets or fetishes, his body was unpainted, he carried nothing in his hands, neither scepter nor spear; but on his head, crowning it, was fully half the body of a crocodile, its mouth open, showing its dreadful teeth. Mockingly or perhaps as a gesture of savage courtesy, Ngalyema mimicked Stanley, planting his legs wide and placing his hands on his hips, and the two men contemplated each other for a long moment.

Then Ngalyema turned away and surveyed the prostrate forms of his vassal chiefs. He raised his arms above his head and spread wide the fingers of his huge hands. And then he shouted; it was a stupendous, growling basso of a shout: "Bula Matari."

The chiefs leaped to their feet and, rattling their spears against their shields, echoed the cry: "Bula Matari."

"Bula Matari," Ngalyema shouted again, this time to the hundreds of warriors squatting in the field.

They too jumped to their feet and responded, a tremendous deep-throated roaring response: "Bula Matari. The Rock Breaker."

"Bula Matari, Bula Matari, Bula Matari," Ngalyema cried out to every quadrant of the parade ground.

And every quadrant responded, the warriors and the chiefs and the women, raising their piercing voices in that nerve-tingling ululation, and then even the Krooboys and Kabindas and Houssas of the shantytown who had come to witness the meeting of two fabulous men: "Bula Matari. Bula Matari." And it went on deafeningly, the roaring and shouting and shrieking and the rattling of spears like gunfire; and while it went on, Ngalyema turned back to Stanley and stepped up to him and embraced him, and the drums began again, and the kudu horns and the savage dancing.

"You shouldn't allow this, Liebrichts," Bentley said. He had taken Stanley's place at the railing beside the district commissioners. "This isn't the old days. He doesn't have the run of things here anymore."

Liebrichts looked at him with his rheumy, bloodshot eyes but said nothing.

"He will cause trouble for all of us. I warn you, Liebrichts, if you let him go on in this way, he will cause serious trouble."

Liebrichts shrugged and looked back to the parade ground.

The presentation of gifts had begun. Ngalyema was leading Stanley around among the various baskets of fruits and vegetables, gourds of wine, and trussed-up chickens that the women had brought, selecting examples of each and handing them to Stanley so that he could see for himself that they were of the finest quality. When he came to the goats, he touched the head of the girl who had been left behind to tend them, and she stood up shyly, keeping her eyes lowered. Ngalyema chucked her under the chin to get her to raise her head and show her pretty face and said something to Stanley and they both smiled. Then, smiling still, the chieftain took hold of the girl's bare breast and bounced it playfully on his massive palm; and it dawned on Jephson that, yes of course, in this too he was proudly displaying a gift of the finest quality. The girl was as much a gift to Bula Matari as were the goats and the guava and the palm wine. As he had done with those others, Stanley appreciatively appraised this one as well, allowing Ngalyema to press his hand to the girl's breast.

"Dear God, look at the brute! The man is utterly shameless," Bentley growled. "He is every bit as much a savage as any of these poor benighted heathen. Look at him. Just look at him, will you. How dare he participate in such wickedness. I tell you, Liebrichts, you must put a stop to this."

"My dear Monsieur Bentley, how should I put a stop to this?" Liebrichts replied in a weary voice. "What would you have me do?"

"Good Lord, man, you're the commander of this station. It is for you to know what to do. You can't just let him bully us about."

The others on the veranda began taking an interest in this exchange and awaited Liebrichts's reply. But again Liebrichts said nothing, only shrugged fatalistically.

"You've got to stand up to him, man," the missionary said. "We've all got to stand up to him."

"Well, you certainly have, Reverend." This was Jack Troup, and he intruded into the conversation with a sharpness that surprised Jephson. "No one will ever be able to say you let Mr. Stanley bully *you* about."

"I wasn't speaking to you, Mr. Troup," the missionary replied and turned back to the proceedings on the parade ground.

The time had now come for Stanley to reciprocate Ngalyema's gifts, and at a signal from him five Wanyamwezis filed out from behind the blockhouse, carrying bales of brightly colored cloth, crates of coiled trading wire, and barrels of shiny beads on their heads. They were led by Uledi, wearing his tasseled fez and his short embroidered vest over his long white robe and pantaloons, but without his bandoliers and rifle. Once the *pagazis* had set down their loads, he came over to stand by Stanley, a wooden box in his hands. Stanley put an arm around Uledi's shoulder and said something to Ngalyema. The Bateke chieftain studied his Wanyamwezi counterpart, bringing his face almost nose to nose with Uledi's, then gave out a great holler of recognition. They knew each other of course. Uledi had been coxswain of Stanley's boat on that first epic journey down the Congo, and after they had embraced and exchanged a number of hearty back thumpings, Uledi handed Ngalyema the wooden box he carried. The gigantic chieftain prized it open with his powerful fingers and withdrew from it a brightly polished brass spyglass. Jephson thought that now a bit of comic business must ensue while the savage tried to figure out what the instrument was. But not at all; Ngalyema knew perfectly well not only what it was but how to use it. He raised it to his eye and, deftly adjusting its focus, peered through the glass at the white men on the blockhouse veranda.

Once all of Stanley's gifts had been presented, two of the Bateke women unrolled a large woven-raffia mat on the grass beside the sedan chair, and Stanley and Ngalyema sat down on it facing each other, their legs crossed à la turque. The Bateke chiefs gathered behind Ngalyema, Uledi squatted down next to Stanley, and the *shauri* began.

It was impossible to hear what was said. At first Ngalyema did most of the talking, gesturing elaborately as he did so, pointing east toward the *banza* of Kinshasa, pointing behind him toward the forests beyond the stockade, pointing up at the white men on the blockhouse veranda, often with such vigor as to knock his crocodile headdress askew, and Stanley listened intently, his chin in his hands, his elbows on his knees. But after a while he began speaking as well, interrupting Ngalyema, leaning forward to touch him on the leg or arm. Soon the *shauri* became a conversation, and as Ngalyema's chiefs also joined in, a general discussion, lively, agitated, punctuated with bursts of laughter and shouts of anger, always with much animated gesturing. At one point Ngalyema got up and walked away, and Stanley went after him and brought him back. The talk continued, the two men leaning their heads close together as if conspiring. At another point they both stood up and paced around for several minutes arm-in-arm, out of earshot of even the chiefs and Uledi.

Jephson watched all this with fascination, although from time to time his eyes couldn't help but stray to the naked girl sitting among the goats absently stroking the nose of the littlest one of them. She seemed totally indifferent to what was going on around her, simply a gift, quietly waiting to be taken away.

"How much longer is this hocus-pocus going to go on?" Barttelot suddenly asked. He had been leaning with his elbows on the veranda railing, his ivory cigarette holder clamped between his teeth, but now he straightened up and looked around in annoyance. "We've been hanging about here twiddling our thumbs doing nothing since yesterday, thanks to this muddle he's marched us into. And now he decides to waste another day palavering with a blasted nigger. What the devil is that supposed to do for us in our fix?" He put the question into the air, more in way of venting his irritation than in expectation of a reply.

But he got one. "I don't know what it's supposed to do for you, Major," Bentley said, "but I can tell you what it will do for us here at the station. Cause trouble. No end of trouble. Ngalyema's just been waiting for a chance like this; and now that he's got it, he's going to voice every last one of his complaints against us, you can be sure of that."

"Complaints about what?"

"About everything, Major. About the rubber quota being too high. About the Force Publique being too cruel. About my mission interfering with his pagan rites. He has complaints about everything. It's an endless list, and now thanks to your Mr. Stanley he has his chance to voice them and make demands about them and rile himself up into a fury over them. And that will cause trouble, no end of trouble, mark my words."

"But what's the sense in complaining to Mr. Stanley? He has no official authority here."

"Precisely. That's precisely my point. That's precisely what I've been telling you, Liebrichts. He has absolutely no official authority here, and yet you let him carry on as if he did. Look at him. Good Lord, just look at him, will you, whispering in that savage's ear. Bula Matari indeed! Don't think Ngalyema doesn't believe he's the big chief here again. He does. Of course he does. Why shouldn't he? Everyone else does, the way you've let him bully us about. Oh, I warn you, Liebrichts, this will cause trouble. He'll rile those savages up more than they already are. He has to be stopped before it's too late, I tell you. He has to be put in his place."

"Is that why you refused him the loan of the *Peace?*"

"What?" The missionary turned to Troup.

"I said, Is that why you refused Mr. Stanley the loan of the mission's steamer, Reverend? To put him in his place?"

"No, Mr. Troup, that is not why. That most certainly is not why. As you are perfectly well aware, sir, I've patiently explained my reasons to Mr. Ward on several occasions and then again to Mr. Stanley when I returned last night."

"You cannot spare her."

"That's right, Mr. Troup. I cannot spare her. I have urgent work of my own for her to do. After she's watered, reprovisioned, and refueled, Dr. Sims and I will sail across to Mbe on the northern shore. We have medicines to bring to our parishioners over there, and we also intend to preach the word of our Lord Jesus Christ to them on Sunday. You may not agree, Mr. Troup. I am sure Mr. Stanley does not, but I regard God's work as far more important than assisting Mr. Stanley in yet another of his smash-and-grab adventures into the interior."

Troup stared at the missionary for a moment, his face a mask of rage and frustration. Then he said, "You pious hypocrite."

"What? How dare you!"

"I say there, Troup. Mind your manners, will you?"

Troup shot a sharp look at Barttelot.

"You've no call speaking to Mr. Bentley like that," the major went on. "We never counted on the use of his vessel. He's not to blame for the fix we're in. If you want to complain about it, speak to the man who is responsible—Mr. Stanley. He's the one who marched us all this way for nothing. He's the one who put his trust in Leopold and refused to heed the reports we've been getting ever since Matadi." Barttelot's voice was quiet, but he spat out the words with contempt. "So if you want to complain about it, old boy, why don't you screw up a bit of nerve and speak to him."

"Ted." Nelson put a hand on Barttelot's shoulder. "No need for that. That ain't going to help any."

Barttelot glanced at the captain. "You're right, Robbie. Nothing's going to help any."

That night—after the *shauri* ended, after Ngalyema had made a ceremonial departure by torchlight and the drumming had faded into the forest and the kudu horns had sounded their last mournful notes and the moon had come up to shine on the Pool's glassy surface and jackals had started yowling in the hills—the expedition's officers dined with Liebrichts in the district commissioner's mess on the second floor of the blockhouse. It was not a happy occasion. Stanley was in a black mood, and it dominated the gathering. He sat on Liebrichts's right at the head of a rough-hewn oak table in the stuffy overly furnished room, the flickering light from the lamps that hung from the rafters showing the angry workings of his jaw muscles. He kept his eyes fixed on his plate throughout the meal and said nothing to anyone; and what little conversation did spring up from time to time among the others was strained and humorless and quickly trailed off. The sound of silverware clinking against crockery, as white-jacketed negro stewards came and went bringing and removing the courses, seemed loud in the long uncomfortable silences. But when the brandy and coffee were served, Stanley at last came to life. He took a cheroot from the cherrywood box one of the stewards had placed on the table, lit it, and turned to Liebrichts.

"All right, now let's get a few things straight, Commissioner. I'm taking the *Stanley*."

"Yes, of course, Bula Matari. You are welcome to her. I only wish–"

"She's in good shape. I looked her over with Shagerstrom and Walker. She can carry two, three hundred of my people and probably sixty tons of cargo."

"Yes, that is true, monsieur, but that still doesn't–"

"Just shut up, Liebrichts and listen to me. I also mean to float the *En Avant* and use her as a barge. Have the *Stanley* tow her. She can do that, can't she?"

"I don't know, monsieur. It depends."

"On what?"

"On how heavily she's loaded."

"I'm reckoning on putting ten, twenty tons of cargo on her and maybe two hundred people. The *Stanley* can tow that."

Liebrichts shrugged. "Perhaps, monsieur. But if so, just barely."

"All right. Now tell me something else. The *Florida*. Those holes in her hull, they ain't too bad. They can be repaired. You've got plate and rivets and a blacksmith here. We can patch her up and float her as a barge as well."

Liebrichts nodded, fingering his forked beard.

"All right. Now what I want to know is can the *Stanley* tow her too?"

"Along with the *En Avant?*"

"Yes."

"Oh, no, monsieur. *Mon Dieu*, no. Even if the *Florida* didn't have a stick in her, the *Stanley* would tear herself apart attempting that. No, she could never do that."

"But the *Peace* could."

"The *Peace?*"

"Pay attention to me, Liebrichts. Pay close attention. What I'm asking you is, Could the *Peace* tow the *Florida* with the rest of my caravan—say another hundred tons of cargo and three hundred people—distributed between the two of them?"

"Is that a hypothetical question, Mr. Stanley?" Barttelot put in.

Stanley turned to him.

"I mean, sir, considering how adamantly Mr. Bentley has refused you the loan of the *Peace*, the question strikes me as rather hypothetical."

"But it isn't, Major. It isn't hypothetical at all."

"Oh, *mon Dieu*, Monsieur Stanley! Please, don't say such a thing. Don't even think such a thing. You must put such an idea out of your mind. It is completely out of the question."

"Let me be the judge of that, Liebrichts."

"Oh, no, monsieur. I cannot let you be the judge of that. I must be the judge of it. I am the commissioner of this station. The mission is under my protection. They are my responsibility."

"I will relieve you of the responsibility. I'll arrange matters so that it's out of your hands."

"No, no, no, monsieur. You go too far with this. I have tolerated a great deal from you these last two days. I realize that you hold me to blame for your predicament, that you feel it was the State's duty to make the steamers available to you, so I have been willing to tolerate a great deal. But this I cannot tolerate. Absolutely not. You go too far with this. *Mon Dieu*, it would be a scandal. I would never hear the end of it. Oh, no, monsieur, I draw the line here. I will not permit this."

"Listen to me, Liebrichts." Stanley reached across the table and seized the Belgian's wrist. "Listen to me carefully. I don't care what you permit or don't permit. There's only one thing I care about, and that's getting my caravan upriver to Yambuya. And I *am* going to get them upriver. One way or another, I'm going to scratch up enough boats and get them to Yambuya. You can be sure of it. Nothing is going to stop me. Not you, not Bentley, not the King of the Belgians."

"I must say, sir," Barttelot broke in, "what you seem to be contemplating sounds very much like an act of piracy."

"Call it whatever you like, Major."

"I'll call it piracy then."

"And? Does it offend your sensibilities?"

Barttelot shrugged.

"Because if it does, Major, you can get the the hell out of

this right now. And that goes for all of you." Stanley looked around the table. "This expedition is going to the rescue of Emin Pasha, come hell or high water, and anyone who's got second thoughts about that had best sign off right now and catch the next trader's caravan down to the coast." He turned back to Barttelot. "Well, Major?"

"I always heard your methods were unorthodox, sir. I just hadn't imagined they'd be quite as unorthodox as this."

"All right then, get out. Anyone else?"

"No, Mr. Stanley, you misunderstand me. I signed on for this expedition with the knowledge that I would be expected to obey your orders. And if these are your orders, sir, I'm prepared to obey them. And, besides, these orders do rather promise to provide us with a bit of fun."

"Fun?" Liebrichts cried out. "You think it will be *fun*, Major? Oh, no, it won't be fun, I assure you." He stood up from the table. "Monsieur Stanley, I understand your predicament, and I will confess that to a degree I even sympathize with you over it. But, monsieur, I must warn you. It is my sworn duty as commander of this station to defend all those who are under its protection. Make no mistake about this, monsieur. I and my garrison will not stand idly by while an act of violence is committed against the property or persons of Mr. Bentley's mission."

"Oh, I didn't expect you and your garrison to stand idly by, Liebrichts," Stanley replied. "No, not at all. I did not expect that for a moment."

· SIX ·

DRUMS AWAKENED JEPHSON. His billet was in a room of the station's hotel; and lying on the truckle bed there, still caught in the confusion between sleep and waking and gazing stupidly through the bed's mosquito netting at the pale stripes of dawn showing through the shutters of the window, he did not at first recognize the distant throbbing sound. He thought it was thunder. But then he remembered Ngalyema's drummers and sat up. This was a very different beat though, not the wild and complicated drumming of the *shauri* but something far simpler, three identical beats repeated over and over, first by one set of drums, then more softly by a second set, the one echoing the other, the one at a great distance from the other somewhere back in the forested hills.

"Robbie."

Nelson shared the room, sleeping on the mate to Jephson's truckle bed a few feet away. He was curled up on his side like a baby, his head half buried under a pillow, the sheet tangled around his ankles, his mouth open, snoring lightly. At the sound of his name, he rolled over on his back but did not wake up. Jephson unfastened his mosquito net and reached over and shook him by the shoulder.

"Huh?" Nelson opened his eyes and closed his mouth.

"Listen, Robbie. . . . What do you make of it?"

Nelson remained on his back, staring up at the thatch roof. Then he said, "Kaffir drums." He listened a moment longer. "Talking drums, I'd wager."

"Talking drums?"

"Sounds like it. The Zulus had them." Nelson undid the mosquito netting around his bed and, in his singlet and drawers, went out on the hotel's veranda.

Troup and Ward were already there.

It was not yet truly morning; although the moon had long set and there was a faint luminous glow in the east over the Pool, the sky was still full of stars and the air chill, but the cantonment was stirring to life nevertheless. The light of bull's-eye lanterns appeared in the windows of the blockhouse, and men in nightshirts were coming out on the verandas of the buildings along the edge of the parade ground.

"You figure them for talking drums, Mr. Ward?" Nelson asked.

"Yes," Ward replied.

"I thought so. Heard enough of them in the Drakensberg to last me a lifetime."

"What are they saying?" Jephson asked.

Ward shook his head. "I don't know. I've never heard them like this before."

"I think we better get dressed," Troup said.

The soldiers of the Force Publique garrison, mainly Bangalas from the upper river, dragging Mauser rifles, stumbled sleepily out of their barracks to the barking commands of two Flemish sergeants. Their commander, Major Parmiter, was on the guardhouse veranda in his shirtsleeves, pulling up his braces with one hand, clutching a holstered Enfield revolver and cartridge belt with the other, while traders and agents and various craftsmen and functionaries of the station, most still half dressed, gathered around him. Surgeon Parke emerged from the clinic, where he had his billet, buttoning up his tunic against the morning chill, looking around in puzzlement. He caught sight of Troup, Ward, Nelson, and Jephson hurrying from the hotel and trotted after them.

"What's going on, chaps?" he asked, falling in step beside Nelson. "What's all this racket? Are the niggers on the warpath?"

"Those are talking drums, Tommy," Nelson replied.

"Talking drums? What are they talking about?"

Nelson shrugged, and the five of them joined the crowd around Parmiter.

"It's Ngalyema. Who did you think it was?" Parmiter was saying. "Up to his usual deviltry."

"It's Ngalyema, all right, but it ain't the usual deviltry, Parmiter," one of the traders retorted. It was the American Swinburne. "I've been hunting in these parts damn near four years now, and I ain't never once heard the drums going on like that."

"Them's war drums," a Dutchman said.

"Don't be a bloody fool, Vanderwycken," Parmiter snapped. "Of course they ain't war drums. And I don't want you going around here saying they are. Jesus Christ, that's all we need, an alarmist in our midst."

"Well, if they ain't war drums, what the hell are they then?" the Dutchman persisted.

"Talking drums. Jesus Christ, that's got to be perfectly obvious to anyone who's spent even one day among the Bateke."

"You're right, Parmiter, they're talking drums all right," Swinburne said. "But what are they talking about? That's what I'd like to know."

"I'll find out soon enough," Parmiter replied. "If you people would clear the hell out of my way and let me get on with my duties, I'll find out soon enough what those drums are talking about, don't you worry." He strode down from the guardhouse veranda and went over to the barracks, where his soldiers were mustering into platoons. The two white sergeants saluted.

Now Commissioner Liebrichts appeared on the scene, hurrying over from the blockhouse. His aide, Ensign Dessauer, followed at his heels. The traders and agents immediately converged on him.

"Messieurs, please, calm yourselves. There's no need for such excitement." Liebrichts raised his hands as if fearing he would have to fend these agitated men off physically. "One at a time. I will get to you all, one at a time. Major Parmiter."

Parmiter came back and saluted.

"What is it, Major? Have you found out what it is?"

"Not yet. But I mean to. I'm taking a patrol out."

"Taking it out where?"

"Kinshasa."

"Kinshasa? For Christ sake, Parmiter," Swinburne cut in, "that drumming ain't coming from Kinshasa. They're back up there in those hills somewhere."

"Please, Monsieur Swinburne," Liebrichts said. "Major Parmiter knows where they are. He can hear where they are as well as you. He isn't deaf."

"But what's up there?" This was the Dutchman again. "There aren't any *banzas* up there. There's nothing up there but the rubber forests. What are they doing up there?"

"I don't know, Vanderwycken," Parmiter answered. "But Ngalyema does. You can be bloody sure of that. That's why I'm going to Kinshasa."

"Yes, very good. And how many do you take with you?" Liebrichts asked.

"Just the patrol. Ten boys and Sergeant Glave."

"Ten? Ten?" This was Swinburne again. "Are you crazy, Parmiter? Ten aren't enough. There could be hundreds, thousands of kaffirs in those hills."

"Jesus Christ, Swinburne, I said I'm only going to Kinshasa. I'll find out there if ten ain't enough. If it ain't, I'll—"

"Yes, yes, all right, Major. . . . Let me speak to the men. I don't want any unnecessary violence." Liebrichts took Parmiter by the arm and led him to the barracks, leaving the traders to gabble excitedly among themselves.

The expedition's caravan was camped on the shore of the Pool, in the reedy rubbish-strewn stretch between the station's wharf, where the *Stanley* was tied up, and the mission's, where the *Peace* was now moored. The big white marquee of the headquarters company, the commissariat tent, and two smaller gray ones were pitched on the high ground to the west of the mission's wharf, out of the stench of the shoreline's mud. Lower down, erected in rows, every score or so with a cooking fire that had been kept burning through the night to drive the mosquitoes away, were the wattle huts and grass lean-tos of the *pagazis* and askaris; and the kraals and pens of the pack animals and livestock stood at the water's edge in the swirling mists of the early morning. The bugler had not yet sounded reveille, but the caravan was up, awakened like everyone else by the drumming.

The caravan's strength was now down to less than 800. The Bakongo porters who had been hired for the trek around Livingstone Falls had been paid off and sent home. In addition, seven Wanyamwezis and Sudanese had died of fever or by accident during the trek from Matadi, three had deserted or become lost along the way, three others had had to be left behind at missions and villages because of illness or injury, and four more were presently laid up in the Leopoldville clinic unlikely to be able to proceed. The number of loads too had been reduced. Thirteen tons of rice had been consumed since leaving Matadi; very nearly as much *mitako* had been bartered off for fresh food; and several boxes of equipment had been lost or stolen or irreparably damaged in the roughest terrain and worst weather of the march. These, however, were replaceable from the station's stores; and once the caravan had been paraded and had breakfast, Uledi took a gang of porters up to the cantonment and began lugging down burlap sacks of mealie meal, hogsheads of palm oil, bales of cotton sheeting, barrels of trading wire, and boxes of biltong and added them to the crates and packages of expedition supplies already stacked along the Pool shore.

A detachment of askaris stood guard over these, the Maxim gun prominently displayed, pointing up the embankment toward the shantytown to discourage pilfering, while the remaining Sudanese, armed with axes and crosscut saws and leading strings of mules, went out to collect firewood for steamer fuel. The repair of the *Florida*'s hull was started; her damaged plates had to be cut away, new ones hammered out in the blacksmith's forge, rivets made, and a slipway of logs laid down to the Pool on which to launch her. Meanwhile, 200 Wanyamwezis were put to the job of launching the *En Avant*. The *Lady Dorothy* was assembled and put into the water with the idea of having her also serve as a barge. In the din and dust of all this—the chanting and hammering and chopping, the crying of donkeys trudging under loads of firewood, the stamping feet of hundreds of porters bringing the new provisions, orders being shouted back and forth, the curses of askaris shooing off the local kaffirs who came down from the shantytown looking for trade or employment—the sound of drumming back up in the hills was drowned out and momentarily forgotten.

The day came up hot and muggy. Fishing pirogues put out on the Pool's glittering surface trailing nets from cove to cove. Flocks of cranes crossed the sky to the north, where clouds gathered above the forested hills. Hippopotamuses sported in the ooze of a nearby backwater, and hordes of mosquitoes and gnats and horseflies swarmed up from the marshy embankment to plague the working men. At midmorning the *En Avant* was launched. Several experiments were made with different kinds of rigging, then the *Stanley* took her in tow and, with the barge yawing to the larboard, steamed up the Pool for a trial run. She came back an hour later, hooting her whistle to announce the success of the test; she docked at the station's jetty, and the *pagazis* began loading both vessels. Matters did not go so smoothly with the *Florida*, though. The first time she was put in the water, a third puncture in her bottom was discovered and she had to be manhandled back up the slipway and overturned for further patching. And before the efficacy of this repair could be tested, a thundershower came storming down across the Pool, sending everyone scrambling for shelter.

Jephson ducked into the headquarters company command tent. A moment later Ward followed him in. They had been working on the *Florida* and were soaked to the skin, not from the rain but from their repeated wadings in and out of the Pool with the leaky hull. Ward hunted up some brandy from the Fortnum and Mason boxes stored in the tent, and he and Jephson stood at the tent flap passing the flask back and forth while watching the torrential downpour with its fireworks display of thunder and lightning. It did not go on very long, however. This was not a resumption of the long rains from which they had suffered on the march from Matadi but merely nature's way of ridding herself of the oppressive burden of humidity that built up in the course of the day under the relentless pounding of the sun, the so-called short rains which they now could expect more or less like clockwork every afternoon for the next several weeks. Startling in its suddenness, tremendous in its fury—the winds howling with typhoon force, tearing at the tents and churning up ten-foot waves on the Pool—the storm never lasted much more than an hour or so. And when it blew itself out, the sky cleared quickly.

"The drums have stopped," Ward said.

Jephson turned around. Ward was looking off to the south, his head cocked slightly. The distant throbbing beat of the drums could no longer be heard. Others had noticed this—*pagazis* sticking their heads from huts, askaris throwing back the hoods of their burnooses, market women stepping out from under the protection of their stalls—and they turned and looked toward the hills in the south, expectant, curious. A bird began to sing and was answered by another; the tree frogs started their melodious croaking again; a breeze rustled through palms along the shore, and the rainwater dripping from the fronds into muddy puddles tinkled like crystal; but otherwise the sweet quietness persisted.

And then it was rent by a high-pitched hysterical shout: "*Stanley!*"

A figure burst from the front door of the blockhouse. "*Stanley! Monsieur Stanley!*"

It was Liebrichts. He came pelting down the wooden planking that led from the blockhouse between the two Krupp guns to the Pool. Two men clattered after him. One was Ensign Dessauer, but Jephson didn't recognize the other until they were quite close. Then he saw that it was Sergeant Glave, who had gone out on the patrol with Major Parmiter that morning. The fellow was stumbling with each step, trying to hold on to Dessauer for support. His tunic was torn open across the right shoulder. And it was stained black with a sticky substance. Blood, Jephson realized.

"Where is he? Where is Monsieur Stanley?"

"I'm not sure," Ward replied, hurrying toward Liebrichts. "I think he's aboard the steamer. I saw him go up on her before the rain. He may still be there. What's happened?"

Liebrichts didn't respond. He dashed out onto the station's jetty waving his arms, shouting Stanley's name. Dessauer raced after him, less supporting the stumbling sergeant than dragging him along. Ward and Jephson followed them.

Hoffman, in charge of loading the vessel, had just started down the steamer's gangway, and Liebrichts in his hysterical excitement almost bowled into him.

"Is Monsieur Stanley aboard?"

"Up in the wheelhouse."

Liebrichts rushed by.

"Hey, what's your tearing hurry?" But then Hoffman caught sight of the sergeant's wound and turned back and clambered up the ladder to the wheelhouse after Ward and Jephson.

"Monsieur Stanley!"

"Eh?" Stanley was studying a map with the steamer's captain, Shagerstrom.

"This is your doing, Monsieur Stanley."

"What?" Stanley looked around. "What's my doing?"

"This, monsieur, this!" Liebrichts thrust the wounded sergeant into the wheelhouse.

"Good God, Liebrichts. Have you taken leave of your senses?" Stanley reached out quickly and caught hold of the sergeant, who under the impact of Liebrichts's shove reeled sideways, about to lose his balance and fall. "This man's hurt, you bloody fool. He's been speared."

"Yes, exactly. He's been speared."

"Then what the devil have you dragged him over here for? He should be at the clinic." Stanley peeled back the tattered rag of the sergeant's torn tunic, revealing the ugly blackened wound. "By God, that's a nasty slice."

"And it's your doing, monsieur. It's your doing. Monsieur Bentley warned me this would happen."

"I don't know what you're talking about, Liebrichts, but this man better be looked after in a hurry. He's in a bad way. He's still got a piece of the spear head in him. Ensign Dessauer, take him up to the clinic. Surgeon Parke is there. He'll look after him."

"No! Leave him alone. Leave him where he is. I want you to

see with your own eyes what you have done, Monsieur Stanley. I want you to hear it at firsthand what has happened, thanks to you. Tell him, Sergeant Glave. Tell Monsieur Stanley what happened."

"Speared," the sergeant croaked, his face dripping sweat.

"We know you were speared, Glave. But how were you speared? Tell him how you were speared."

"Ambush on the trail from . . ." The sergeant's eyes rolled up into his head in a swoon.

"Listen, Liebrichts, unless you mean to kill him off here and now, you'd better get him straightaway up to the clinic," Stanley said.

"They've all been killed off. And Major Parmiter made captive. Captive, do you hear? Only Sergeant Glave escaped."

"All right. You seem to know what happened. You can tell me about it. But you've got to get this man to the clinic. Dessauer, take him to Surgeon Parke. Get going. Double time."

Liebrichts made no further protest. The steam of agitation had gone out of him, and he stared blankly as the wounded man was led from the cabin. Then he turned to Shagerstrom. "Let me have some whiskey, Captain."

"Why don't you sit down?" Stanley indicated the captain's swivel chair bolted to the deck beside the ship's wheel. "Sit down and tell me calmly what the devil this is all about."

"I don't want to sit down." Liebrichts jerked away from Stanley and took the bottle of Irish whiskey Shagerstrom had fetched from the locker under the ship's compass. He uncorked it and drank a long pull straight from it. "I have no time to sit down. Soon none of us will have any time to sit down." He turned to the wheelhouse windscreen. "All the warriors are gone from Kinshasa," he said and gestured up the Pool shore with the whiskey bottle. "All of them. And Ngalyema with them. They must have cleared out during the night. Only the women and children and old men were left when Major Parmiter got there with his patrol this morning."

He stepped closer to the windscreen and peered out. "I don't know what he could have been thinking. He should have returned to the station immediately he saw the situation. He said he would return if he needed more men. But he didn't. I don't know why. Sergeant Glave thinks it was because of something one of the old nigger men told him. In any event, he decided to go up in the hills as far as the first set of drums. They sounded as though they weren't more than a mile away, and he wanted to have a look, scout around, see what it was all about. So he went up." Liebrichts turned back from the window. "And they were ambushed. Ambushed, monsieur. No sooner had they reached the forest than hundreds of howling niggers fell on them. Two hundred, Glave thinks, maybe even three hundred. They were waiting for them. They knew they were coming. My boys never had a chance. Not a single shot was fired, Glave says. The ten of them were butchered on the spot, speared, hacked to pieces with *pangas*, and Major Parmiter made captive. The dear Lord only knows what will happen to him. Only Sergeant Glave managed to escape, and you have seen for yourself that he is as good as half dead."

"Surgeon Parke'll fix him up."

"Will he, monsieur? And will he also fix up Major Parmiter and those ten kaffir boys?"

Stanley made an impatient gesture.

"Not five miles from this station, practically in the very shadow of the stockade, ten soldiers of the King's Force Publique massacred and a white officer made prisoner. Nothing like this has ever happened before. Never in my worst nightmare would I have imagined that it ever could." Liebrichts took another long swig from the whiskey bottle. "But it has," he said. "Yes, monsieur, it has. Ngalyema's on the rampage. And we have you to thank for it. It is your doing. You riled him up. Just as Monsieur Bentley warned me you would, you riled him up with all your—"

"*I* riled him up? Don't tell me I riled him up. Don't try to put that off on me, Liebrichts. I riled him up? Christ, that's a laugh. You want to tell me he wasn't riled up until I got here. The hell he wasn't. He was so goddamned riled up it's only a wonder he hasn't gone off on a rampage long before this. I sat and listened to him for damn near five hours at the *shauri* yesterday. I heard what's been going on here. I heard what you and your boys have been doing to these poor buggers. I heard how you collect the rubber, Liebrichts." Stanley took a step toward the Belgian. "I heard about the *hands*."

Liebrichts looked away.

"Yes, my friend, I heard about the hands," Stanley said again. He moved still closer to Liebrichts and dropped his voice to a hoarse whisper. "So don't try and tell me *who* riled him up. Just tell me what you intend to do now that he is."

Liebrichts, still looking away, took another long pull of whiskey. His face had broken out in a sheen of sweat, and the hand that gripped the whiskey bottle had begun to tremble.

"You do intend to do something, don't you? You're going to take the garrison out and go after him and see if you can't get Parmiter back, ain't you? Or were you planning to stand there sucking on that bottle and wait until he falls on the station and cuts your throat?"

"Take the garrison out?" Liebrichts replied, slowly, lowering the whiskey bottle. "Yes, of course I am going to take the garrison out. What else can I do? It is what you would have me do, isn't it?" And then suddenly he jerked around to face Stanley. "Why yes, of course it is. *Mon Dieu*, how could I have been so stupid as not to have seen it before? It is precisely what you would have me do. Indeed, it is what you are *counting* on me to do. Take the garrison out of the station and leave you here with a free hand to do . . . to do whatever you wish. That was the whole point of it, wasn't it, monsieur? That was why you called Ngalyema to the *shauri* in the first place. That was why you drew him out on his complaints against us and encouraged him in them and, for all I know, actually plotted with him to act on them. So that there would be a pretext for getting rid of me and Parmiter and the soldiers of the garrison and leave you here with a free hand to seize the *Peace*."

Someone coughed. Jephson glanced around. Shagerstrom pulled out a dirty rag of a handkerchief and covered his mouth.

"Of course that was the whole point of it," Liebrichts went on. "I see that now. How could I have been so stupid as not have seen it before? You made up your mind to have the *Peace*, and nothing was going to prevent you from having her. Nothing. You told me as much yourself. Nothing was going to stand in your way. Not the killing of ten nigger soldiers. Not the killing of Major Parmiter if it comes to that. Not the killing of God knows how many more now when we go up into the forests after those savages. None of that matters. No, all that matters is that you have the *Peace*. That you get your caravan up the river. That you reach Emin Pasha in time. Oh, yes, monsieur, I see it now. It is as it always has been with you. All that matters is that you succeed. All that ever matters is that Bula Matari—"

"That's enough, Liebrichts. That's as much of this rubbish as I'm going to listen to."

"Rubbish? Yes, of course, call it rubbish—"

"I said that's enough!" Stanley's voice was like a pistol shot.

Liebrichts stepped back.

"You can believe that, Liebrichts. You can believe whatever

you want. But let me give you a piece of advice, my friend. That ain't what you should be worrying about right now. What you should be worrying about right now is getting your troops cracking. There ain't much daylight left, and you don't want to be chasing those kaffirs in the forest after dark. And you sure as hell don't want to wait until morning. You know what Ngalyema will do if you give him until morning?"

Liebrichts made no reply.

"Sure you do," Stanley said. "So why don't you be a sensible fellow and get the hell out of here." He turned back to the ship's console, where the chart of the river was spread out.

"You bastard," Liebrichts said.

Stanley turned around fast.

Liebrichts walked out of the wheelhouse.

A hollow silence was left behind. Stanley waited for a moment, as if giving the others–Ward, Hoffman, Jephson, Shagerstrom, perhaps especially Shagerstrom–a chance to comment on the exchange they had just heard. But no one did. The silence dragged on. Oddly, the sounds one would have expected to hear–of men working on the shore, of their chanting and hammering and shouting, of donkeys braying under their loads–couldn't be heard. There was only the soft slapping of water against the steamer's hull beneath their feet, the buzzing of flies above their heads. And then, dimly, there was the sound of drumming back up in the hills again.

One hundred Sudanese, 250 Wanyamwezis, and roughly fifty tons of goods waited on the Pool shore. The rest of the caravan and its supplies were aboard the riverboats. The *Stanley*, with the *En Avant* and *Lady Dorothy* in tow, was standing just off the station's jetty, the steam in her boiler up. Troup and Baruti were aboard her with Captain Shagerstrom, Engineer Walker, and about 250 of the Wanyamwezis; Nelson and Parke were on the *En Avant* with most of the pack animals, fifty Wanyamwezis and a hundred Sudanese. The portable steel boat was loaded to the gunwales with boxes and crates battened down under greased tarpaulins, with Sudi and a crew of ten. The *Florida*, which had been successfully floated after the fifth attempt, was tied up at the station's jetty, listing slightly to the port, ready to be taken in tow; Ward was aboard her, but the Wanyamwezis who were to travel with him on the hulk were among those still ashore. They were waiting with the fifty tons of cargo and the remaining hundred askaris at the mission wharf where the *Peace* was docked. Hoffman and Uledi were in charge of them; Stanley, Jephson, and Barttelot stood among the askaris; Bonny leaned against the barrel of the Maxim automatic gun.

Seeing this, suspecting what was going on, Bentley, with Sims following, came down from the parsonage and immediately began protesting angrily.

"Save your breath, Reverend," Stanley said, going over to him. "Just save your breath and listen to me. I'm taking the *Peace*. That much is settled. The only thing that ain't settled is whether I'm going to take her the easy way or the hard way. That's up to you."

"Taking the *Peace?*" Bentley looked at the mission vessel riding at anchor at the jetty. All her lights were out, but her crew was gathered on the fantail deck, staring down at the askaris and the automatic gun on the shore. The Maxim was pointed at them. "You wouldn't dare," Bentley said, but his voice cracked and he had to start over. "You wouldn't dare. You're bluffing. Or you're mad. You'd be ruined, utterly ruined, if you ever dared do such a thing. I'd see to it. I promise you, sir, I'd see to it. This is piracy. This is a capital crime in every civilized nation in the world, and I'd see to it that every civilized nation in the world knew of it. Your reputation would never recover from the scandal. You'd be known everywhere for the brutal brigand you are. Just think of it, Mr. Stanley. Just think of the disgrace that would greet you when you returned to Europe."

"I'll think of it when I return to Europe," Stanley replied. "But right now I want you to think of this. I have a hundred armed men here, as you can see, and the Maxim. They have their orders. If anyone attempts to interfere . . . But it need not come to that. No one need come to any harm, Reverend, if you behave sensibly."

Bentley didn't say anything.

"Dr. Sims."

The little fat fellow jumped at the sound of his name.

"Dr. Sims, you are going to pilot the *Peace* upriver to Yambuya for me."

"I am?"

"You are. Do you know where Yambuya is?"

"No, sir. I've never been any farther upriver than Kimpoko."

"It doesn't matter. Captain Shagerstrom knows where it is. All you have to do is follow him."

Sims looked down the Pool shore to the station's jetty.

"He will be towing the *En Avant* and my steel boat. Once we get the *Peace* loaded, I want you to take her to the station's wharf and hitch up with the *Florida* there. My boys will lash her alongside, out of the way of your stern-wheel paddle. You can manage that, can't you?"

Sims nodded.

"All right then. Major, Dr. Sims will go aboard the *Peace* now. Be so good as to accompany him."

"Dr. Sims," Barttelot said.

"Major Barttelot," Bentley burst out, "you cannot allow this. You cannot participate in such a foul crime. You, sir, an officer of the Queen."

"I'm serving under a different flag just now, Reverend."

"Oh, no, Major. That won't do. That sort of argument won't save you. You'll be ruined just as surely as this man if you go ahead with this. I promise you. I'll see to it that the whole world knows what you've done here."

"Actually I rather doubt it will much care, Reverend," Barttelot said. "If we get to Emin Pasha in time, if we rescue the noble Turk from the dervishes, I rather doubt the world will much care what exactly we had to do in order to accomplish it. And if we don't . . . well, I rather doubt it will make much of a difference then either. Because we'll all probably be dead. Isn't that how you reckon it, Mr. Stanley?"

"Take Dr. Sims aboard the *Peace*, Major."

Barttelot smiled and turned to Sims again.

"Don't you dare go, Sims," Bentley snapped. "Don't you dare become a party to this."

Sims looked at Bentley haplessly.

"Stand your ground, man. Stand your ground, do you hear?"

"You weren't listening to me, Reverend," Stanley said. "I'll repeat it one last time. There's no point in your kicking up a fuss. You won't accomplish anything by it. Liebrichts and the garrison are gone, out chasing Ngalyema, and those left behind with Dessauer ain't a match for these askaris here. You kick up a fuss and there'll be some shooting and some people will get hurt, but I'll take the *Peace* anyway. So why don't you let me do this the easy way? Stand here nice and quietly so the crew on the vessel and anyone else who might happen by will see you've come to your senses and have agreed to let me have the loan of her. And nobody will get hurt that way. All right?" Stanley peered into Bentley's eyes. Then he said, "All right, Major. Go on up with Dr. Sims."

"There's no fuel," Sims blurted out. "We can't go anywhere. I never had a chance to refuel her."

"There's fuel," Barttelot said. "There's plenty of fuel. Our boys have cut enough for at least two days' steaming. So if you'll come along with me, you can show them where you want it stowed."

Sims looked at Bentley and shrugged. He had tried, he seemed to say. Then he went with Barttelot.

"Start the loading, Will," Stanley called to Hoffman. "Let's go a bit closer, Reverend. I want your crew to see you quite clearly."

The *pagazis* carried the loads up the *Peace*'s gangway without their usual chatter; the askaris, drawn up in two ranks blocking off the landing, stood rigidly at attention. Now and again metal jangled, a bayonet clinking against a bandolier as a soldier shifted position, the hollow thud of a load being dropped when a *pagazi* stumbled, a muted curse, Hoffman or Uledi giving an order. A lantern went on in the vessel's wheelhouse, traveled along the main deck, and disappeared. Deckhands came down to the jetty, threw Bentley a glance, then began working on the steamer's lines. The first tentative puff of black smoke belched from the iron stack, and some machinery began to clank in the boat's bowels.

Stanley pulled a brandy flask from his hip pocket, took a swig, and offered it to Bentley. The missionary ignored him. "Do you want some of this, lad?"

Jephson took the flask, drank off a stiff shot, and handed it back.

"I want you to keep Mr. Bentley company for a bit now, lad," Stanley said. "I'm going up on the *Peace* and see if I can't hurry this along." He turned to the missionary. "You ain't going to do anything foolish, are you, Reverend? You ain't going to make any difficulties for this young fellow?"

"You'll pay for this," Bentley replied through gritted teeth. "You'll pay for this dearly."

"I probably will." Stanley shoved the brandy flask back into his hip pocket. "You've got a pistol with you, Arthur. Use it if you have to," he said and went out on the mission jetty.

Bentley watched him pass through the ranks of askaris and up the *Peace*'s gangway and disappear into the crowd of porters on the main deck. Then he looked up to the wheelhouse, expecting Stanley to reappear there. He didn't. "He'll pay for this," Bentley said again and started to walk away.

"Sir!"

Bentley looked back at Jephson. "You will all pay for this," he said. "You included, Mr. Jephson. You're involved in this as much as anyone. Piracy. Kidnapping. You'll be ruined by it along with all the rest. I'll see to it, I promise you." He turned and started walking away again.

"Sir, please." Jephson went after him quickly. "I have to ask you to remain here. Mr. Stanley was quite explicit about that."

Bentley, however, continued walking.

And the youth didn't know what to do. What could he do? Pull out his pistol? Grab hold of the man? Physically restrain him? Threaten him? But how could he do any of that? This man was a missionary, old enough to be his grandfather, a respectable gentleman he might meet any day in London society, not a lout or a savage. How could he be expected to manhandle or threaten him? Jesus, what an awful situation. He had never dreamed that going with Mr. Stanley would involve him in a situation as awful as this. "Please, sir," Jephson pleaded, trotting after Bentley, "I really must insist."

But it didn't do any good. Bentley kept going down the Pool shore, lengthening his strides, paying no attention to the youth. He was heading for the station blockhouse. Jephson suddenly realized what the man planned to do once he got there. Oh, Jesus, Mr. Stanley would have his head if he let Bentley get away with it. And hating himself for having to do it, hating Mr. Stanley for putting him in a situation where he had to do it, Jephson reached out to grab the missionary's arm.

But Bentley started to run.

It caught Jephson so completely unaware that he did not immediately take up the pursuit. He stood stock-still watching in amazement as Bentley, his coattails flying, his arms pumping crazily, his body tilted forward in wild desperation, ran for the blockhouse.

"Stop him," someone shouted.

Jephson started to run.

"For God's sake, stop that man, Jephson." It was Stanley's voice.

Running at top speed, crying out Bentley's name, Jephson fumbled at his holster for his pistol.

A shot was fired. Bentley went sprawling face forward in the mud.

"Oh, my God." Jephson stopped. He hadn't fired. He had barely got his pistol out of the holster. Someone else had fired. He looked around. People were running toward him—Bonny, several askaris, Stanley. He turned and ran to the prostrate form of the missionary and dropped on his knees beside him. "Are you all right? Where have you been hit?"

Bentley rolled over on his side and pushed himself halfway up on an elbow. His face was smeared with the mud of the embankment.

"Let me help you."

"Get away from me."

Jephson realized he had his pistol out.

"No, no, it's all right." He flung the pistol aside. "I want to help you. Show me where you've been hit."

"Leave me alone."

Bonny and the askaris came running by. Then Stanley.

"You didn't have to shoot him. Why did you shoot him? He couldn't have gotten anywhere. I would have caught him. You didn't have to shoot him."

But Stanley kept running toward the blockhouse.

· SEVEN ·

KINSHASA WAS BURNING.

All through the night it burned; and the flames leaping from the thatch roofs of the Bateke village cast a light that could be seen for miles out on the Pool. Jephson, leaning on the rail of the upper deck of the *Stanley*, stared at it and at the stretch of beach and the forest of mangroves and the muddy waters that it lighted in a violent orange light. At this distance from the shore he could not tell what had happened in the village or what might still be happening there. All he could surmise was that Ngalyema and Liebrichts were at war.

Jack Troup came up from the lower deck and leaned on the rail beside him. Shagerstrom was at the steamer's wheel, Walker in the engine room below, Baruti asleep in one of the cabins behind the wheelhouse. On the *En Avant*, in tow behind the *Stanley*, Nelson and Parke, like Jephson and Troup, stood at the starboard rail watching the fire ashore. The *Peace*, with the *Florida* lashed alongside, followed by less than a quarter of a mile; but there was no way of knowing whether Stanley, Barttelot and Dr. Sims aboard her or Ward, Hoffman, and Bonny on the hull also were watching the destruction of Ngalyema's royal *banza*. A ghostly mist had arisen from the Pool's surface and enshrouded them.

"It didn't have to come to this," Jephson said.

Neither of them, Jephson as little as Troup, was certain as to what exactly Jephson referred—the burning of Kinshasa, the seizure of the *Peace*, the shooting of the Reverend Bentley, the death of Major Parmiter—but it didn't matter. They were all of a piece, bound together inexorably, each the inescapable consequence of the other, stemming from the same source.

"It would never have come to this except for Leopold."

Troup pulled out his tobacco pouch and rolled a cigarette.

"Why did he do it, Jack? Why did he give Mr. Stanley his word on the steamers and then break it?"

"I don't know," Troup replied, lighting the cigarette.

"Don't tell me you don't know!"

Troup turned to Jephson, startled by the sharpness of the youth's tone.

"Who should know better than you? You were with Mr. Stanley on the Congo all the time he worked for Leopold. You know what there is between them. You know their secret. Just like Dick Leslie knew."

"What are you talking about?"

"Don't, Jack. You don't have to pretend with me. I'm not stupid. I've realized for a long time now that Mr. Stanley took the Congo route only because Leopold forced him to. He holds something over Mr. Stanley's head. And he used it to force him to take this route, to go through the Ituri forest and claim it for him and extend the border of the Congo Free State to the Upper Nile for him. I don't know what it is but it must be something terrible to have forced Mr. Stanley to do this against everyone's advice. But what really doesn't make any sense is why, once he got Mr. Stanley to take this route, he didn't give him the steamers as he promised. If Mr. Stanley weren't Mr. Stanley, the expedition would have ended right here at the Pool. We'd never have gone another step farther. It would have all come to nothing. And Leopold would have gotten nothing."

Troup shook his head. "No, Arthur. You ain't got it right."

"Don't tell me I ain't got it right. I was there. I was there when Mr. Stanley went to Brussels. I was there when he came back. Leopold sent for him, Jack, sent for him and threatened him; and when he came back he changed the route to the Congo."

"Leopold didn't send for him. If he went to Brussels, he went on his own. He went to try and arrange for the steamers with Leopold." Troup looked back down river in the direction of the *Peace*. "But, as we see now, he didn't succeed."

"But I was there when he came back. He said—"

"I know what he said. He said Leopold had agreed to put the entire Congo State fleet at his disposal."

"What are you saying? Are you saying he lied?"

"Maybe he believed it when he said it. Maybe Leopold gave him some sort of half-promise that allowed him to believe it. Maybe not." Troup turned back to Jephson. "I don't know where you got the idea Leopold forced him to take this route, Arthur, that he threatened him with some terrible secret. But wherever you got it, I can tell you it ain't right. Nobody threatens Mr. Stanley. Nobody forces him to do anything. You ought to know that by now. No, lad, he took this route for only one reason: He wanted to take it. He's always wanted to take it. If you tell me I know his secret from all my years on the Congo with him, then I'll tell you *that's* his secret. He's always wanted to take this route. He always wanted to go through the Ituri. And this expedition gave him the chance. Maybe he went to Brussels. Maybe he went to Leopold. Yes, he probably did. He would have had to. He would have had to *at least* make it seem that he had arranged for the steamers. Otherwise he couldn't have made any argument at all for taking this route. Without steamers, he would have been considered mad to propose it. And who would have let him go then? Who would have gone with him then? But it never really mattered to him if Leopold gave him steamers or not. He was going to take this route in any case. Even if he had to kill and steal to do it, he was going to come back to the Congo and go through that damn forest."

"But why, Jack? In God's name, why?"

Troup shrugged. "Because he wanted to be the first one to do it? Because he wanted to show the world he could do what no other man could do? Because he wanted to add that feather to his cap?" The redhead turned away again. "Because he's Bula Matari."

The mist burned off at dawn, revealing sandstone cliffs on both shores, gleaming white in the pale rays of the sunrise. Stanley, when he first saw them ten years before, had named them for the cliffs of Dover; they formed the gateway from the Pool into the Upper Congo. Kimpoko was on the left bank, a cluster of grass huts beneath the cliffs, dugout canoes overturned on the beach. At this hour, one could have expected the canoes to be on the river, the tribesmen beginning their day of fishing, but apparently news of the trouble at Kinshasa had already reached them and the village was quiet. Walker, the steamer's engineer, was at the wheel of the *Stanley*—he and Captain Shagerstrom had spelled each other in four-hour tricks during the night—and he made for Kimpoko, where he ordered the engine cut and the anchors dropped. He wanted to give the *Peace* a chance to catch up. Heavily loaded, tilted to starboard by the *Florida* cumbersomely lashed alongside her, and riding deep in the water, the mission vessel had fallen more than a mile behind.

Upriver of the narrow inlet to the Pool formed by the cliffs, the Congo widened to very nearly two miles, running fast between banks that were still quite hilly, with palm and mangrove forests along them climbing up and thinning away into a rolling countryside of acacia groves and fever trees and rocky scrub and yellow grass. But as they sailed farther upstream, these remnants of the foothills of the Crystal Mountains steadily dropped away, the embankments flattened out, and the forests along the water's edge grew richer and denser and greener, tangled with creeping vines and flowering lianas, sprouting ferns and foliage and giant trees seen nowhere else in the world and spreading always farther away from the river to the north and south. Here the river slowed and broadened, swamping the shore, and in every sluggishly winding reach, wooded islands and mudflats and sandbanks appeared in the stream. Crocodiles dozed on the sandbanks; the muddy backs and yawning jaws of hippos emerged from the shallows; antelope drank at the tributaries; and white water birds wheeled in the whitening sky, emitting piercing cries. Often there were villages on the banks and the islands, but they were as silent as Kimpoko had been; and the occasional fishing pirogues that appeared, pencil-slim silhouettes on the horizon, fled on catching sight of the steamers, vanishing into muddy, overgrown backwaters.

The passage was slower than Jephson had expected. The *Stanley*'s top speed was twenty knots; but laden as she was with tons of supplies and hundreds of kaffirs, and towing the equally heavily laden *En Avant* and *Lady Dorothy*, she rarely managed better than nine or ten, her engine laboring cruelly even at that, with the Kabinda firemen in her engine room stoking prodigious amounts of firewood into her furnace to keep the steam pressure up. And the *Peace* was worse. Under the best of conditions her top speed was no more than twelve knots, but from the way she kept falling behind, black smoke belching fitfully from her single iron stack and hanging in the breathless humid air, it was clear she couldn't be doing more than six or seven.

Predictably in midafternoon the rain came; it stormed down from the forests in torrential sheets, accompanied as usual by a spectacular display of lightning and thunder and whistling wind, which so roiled the waters and so hindered navigation that the boats were obliged to stop in the face of it and drop anchors and ride out the hour of its fury. When it blew over, Shagerstrom steered for shore. This came as a surprise. Troup went up to the wheelhouse to find out why. It was still relatively early in the day, and Stanley's orders had been to push on as long and as far and as fast as possible. But it wasn't possible to push on. The steamer was out of fuel; she was burning far more firewood than anyone had reckoned, because of her heavy burden, and what they had believed would be enough for more than two days' uninterrupted steaming had turned out to be less than sufficient for one. More had to be collected. Shagerstrom anchored in a swampy backwater where a small stream marked on his chart as the Black River debouched into the Congo. Two hours later the *Peace* caught up, also in need of fuel.

That became the main work of the upriver journey, gathering and cutting fuel for the steamers. It was grubby work, hunting for deadwood in the fetid forests of the embankments, beating off the biting ants and insects that swarmed up in the marshy shadows, keeping an eye out for snakes, brushing through sticky clinging spider webs, dragging lightning-split trees and worm-ridden rotted trunks through the tangle of underbrush to the swampy water's edge and chopping them up into thirty-inch lengths to fit the grates of the steamers' furnaces—and doing it for hours. Two hundred kaffirs, Wanyamwezi and Sudanese, scoured the woods fetching and carrying, and two score more wielded the axes and crosscut saws, their bodies streaming sweat and covered with flies; they did it from well before sunset to well after moonrise, and it never seemed to be enough. Shagerstrom and Walker and Sims would look over the woodpile, sort out and discard the green wood that was useless, and say there wasn't enough for even a few hours' steaming, the vessels consumed such exorbitant quantities.

At least the *Stanley*, if stoked extravagantly enough, could maintain a reasonable speed; but no matter how much wood was fed into the *Peace*'s furnace, she kept falling behind. Stanley at first suspected Sims of sabotage and had Walker come aboard the *Peace* on the second day's journey to set things right. (Troup took over as the *Stanley*'s engineer.) But it wasn't Sims; it was simply that the *Peace* was preposterously overloaded. She'd get up a good enough head of steam at the outset, fifty-five or sixty pounds, but within minutes would begin losing it, her boiler hissing and snorting and banging, her paddle-wheel barely able to hold its own against the down river current; and every hour or so she had to be halted altogether to be oiled and cleaned as her grates got choked with the buildup of charcoal and ash from the immoderate fueling.

And so they slipped behind schedule. The plan had been to reach Kwamouth by the fifth of May, but they did not put into this state trading outpost for resupply until the tenth. And then the next day the *Stanley* ran aground.

It happened in the afternoon, with a storm advancing on the

river. The steamer was about 300 yards from the southern bank, Captain Shagerstrom making for the lee of an offshore island for shelter. Over the forests to the north the sky had already darkened and the slate-gray sheet of rain was tearing up the river's surface there, but here the sun was still shining brightly. Jephson was on the bridge, lounging against the forward rail in the shadow of the wheelhouse's striped canvas awning, idly watching the boat's progress; and he clearly saw the obstruction beneath the sunlit surface, a wide flat shimmering yellow shape, a submerged sandbank perhaps, or a limestone ledge. The boat was steaming directly toward it. He glanced at Shagerstrom in the wheelhouse. The captain, a yellow meerschaum pipe gripped in his teeth, both hands on the wheel, was peering ahead intently. Obviously he saw it too; it probably was lying deeper in the water than the sun's refraction made it appear. Jephson looked north, feeling the first spray of rain on the gusts of wind blowing from that direction, then looked back to see how far behind the *Peace* had fallen.

But he never saw her; at that moment there was a tremendous jolt and he was pitched on his backside. Shagerstrom burst from the wheelhouse. There was the dreadful sound of metal shearing. Then the vessel stuck fast.

"Cut the engine, Mr. Troup," Shagerstrom shouted. "We've fouled, damnit, we've fouled."

The side-wheels ceased, and with that the steamer began swinging to the larboard as if on a pivot jammed into her bow; and the *En Avant* and the *Lady Dorothy* in tow behind her swung with her in a wide arc, the steel boat banging into the barge.

"Drop anchors."

A terrific clanging racket of anchor chains was heard, and then men were running, shouting, cursing. Nelson came clambering hand over hand along the line from the *En Avant*.

"Get below. See what the damage is."

Jephson scrambled to his feet and went clattering down the ladder from the wheelhouse. Nelson had vaulted onto the steamer's lower deck and was pushing his way from the stern through the mob of panicked Wanyamwezis, shouting at them to sit down and keep still; the boat was in danger of capsizing with all their wild rushing about.

"The forward hold, Arthur." Troup's soot-blackened bearded face popped out of the engine room. "That's where she took it. Get some men down in there and start bailing for all you're worth."

"Uledi," Jephson cried, running forward.

Some deckhands were at the forward hold already on their knees, unfastening the hatch cover. Uledi and Nelson raced up. And just then there was a blinding flash of lightning, an ear-splitting crack of thunder; and a whistling rain-soaked squall swept the deck.

"Oh, Jesus," Jephson groaned, jumping down into the hold after Nelson and landing in at least a foot of water.

The vessel had been pierced by a limestone reef in three of her nine forward compartments, and the river was pouring through them fast. Nelson and Jephson started a gang of Wanyamwezis shifting the hold's cargo to the stern, hauling and heaving boxes and crates out of the flood, while Uledi set a bucket brigade bailing fast. Although they couldn't make any headway against the water already in the hold, they at least managed to keep the river from gaining on them; and then, when the full force of the storm reached them, the typhoonlike wind slamming the ship broadside, it was as if the great hand of God grabbed the vessel and wrenched her from the ledge.

Shagerstrom immediately seized the opportunity. He bellowed for full speed astern. Troup opened the throttle. The paddle wheels slashed at the river. There was no time to weigh anchor; and with a terrible scream the chains dragged over rock and snapped explosively, and their amputated ends went slashing across the deck, ripping up planking. More hull plate sheared with that dreadful grinding noise, and, with a terrible lurch the steamer broke free into deep water. Now calling for full speed ahead, Shagerstrom ran for shore. He had no choice. To attempt to wait out the storm with the anchors gone and the steamer taking water like a sieve was to risk sinking outright; and so, despite the thunder and lightning and caterwauling wind, despite the fact that he couldn't see a dozen feet in front of him in the howling rain, counting on memory and luck to find his way around the reefs and mudbanks, bucking against five-foot waves, he ran for shore.

Uledi kept the men bailing, and Nelson and Jephson threw themselves into the work, filled with a fear that the boat would hit another rock. She'd never survive another accident, Jephson was sure; a few more holes in the already punctured compartments, a few new holes in the unpunctured ones, and no amount of bailing could keep her from wrecking, and wrecking the *En Avant* and *Lady Dorothy* with her.

And then suddenly, with a tremendous shudder, she did run aground again. The bailing stopped. Dropped buckets sloshed away in the two feet of stinking water in the hold, banging against the bulkheads. Jephson looked up, waiting for some catastrophic sound, an explosion, a bursting of compartments, a final splitting of the hull, a deluge of water as the vessel overturned. But there was nothing. The engine was cut. Nelson dashed upon deck. Jephson followed him. The rain was thundering down at the height of its fury now, and in the storming darkness the youth couldn't make out where they were or what had happened.

"You son of a bitch, Shagerstrom." Troup burst from the engine room and clambered up the ladder to the bridge. Shagerstrom stepped out of the wheelhouse grinning. "You goddamn son of a bitch," Troup shouted and flung his arms around the captain. "You've got to be the goddamnedest luckiest son of a bitch in all creation. You made it, man. You beached her like a bloody angel."

When the rain let up, Shagerstrom went into the forward hold to assess the damage. The *En Avant* was untied and anchored separately in the offshore shallows, and the *Lady Dorothy* was pulled up on the beach and unloaded. Shagerstrom had landed them in a secluded cove on the southern bank, some two miles downriver of a village marked Bolobo on his chart, and there was some concern that the *Peace* wouldn't see them and would pass them by. So while camp was made—they obviously could expect to be here for a while—Jephson took the steel boat out with Sudi and ten oarsmen to flag the mission vessel down.

She was still far downriver. Sudi spotted a puff of her smoke at the head of the reach, nearer the right bank than the left; there was a second puff and a third, then nothing, and the smoke diffused into a gray smudge against the white sky. Apparently she had stopped. Sudi started the chant of the stroke; and with the aid of the downriver current they reached the mission vessel in a half-hour, coming up alongside the *Florida* on her starboard.

"Hey, Arthur. What the devil are you doing here?" Bertie Ward reached down from the *Florida*'s rail and gave Jephson a hand up over it. "Where's the *Stanley?*"

"We put in four, five miles upriver, just below Bolobo."

The *Florida*'s deck was jammed with Wanyamwezis sprawled on the boxes and crates and sacks and bales of their loads, and Jephson had to pick his way through them to get across to the *Peace.* Ward followed him. Hoffman, who had been sitting up on the hull's prow, also came over.

"What'd you put in for?" Ward asked. "Run out of fuel?"

"No. We had an accident." Jephson leaped the short distance between the *Florida* and the *Peace* and climbed the latter's rail.

"What kind of accident?" Stanley stepped out the doorway of the *Peace*'s engine room, wiping his hands on a wad of cotton wool. He was stripped to the waist, and his face and chunkily muscled torso were streaked with soot and oil. Walker was with him, also half naked and equally as filthy. Obviously they had been working on the engine.

"We ran aground, sir. Fouled on a reef just before the storm."

Stanley stopped wiping his hands.

"Captain Shagerstrom thought he had plenty of clearance. He said he's steamed through that channel a hundred times and never had a speck of trouble. He realized how heavily he was loaded this time, but he said he usually clears those reefs and ledges by five, six feet, so he reckoned he had at least three feet to spare. But he didn't. We stuck fast. The *Stanley*'s drawing very nearly eight feet of water because of her load, sir. Captain Shagerstrom said we were lucky she didn't break up and sink on the spot."

Ward and Hoffman had also hopped across from the *Florida*.

"But when the storm came up, the wind yanked her free, and he made a run for it. It was as pretty a piece of sailing as you'd ever want to see, sir, Captain Shagerstrom running blind in the storm. He beached her in a cove four or five miles upriver from here, just below Bolobo."

"What's the damage?"

"She's holed in five places in three of her forward compartments. There are a few others scattered about, but Captain Shagerstrom says we can live with those. The five though, they've got to be patched up."

"What's going on?" This was Barttelot. He ambled over from the cabin behind the wheelhouse, where evidently he had been shaving; there was a fleck of soap in one ear, a towel around his neck. "What are you doing here, Arthur? Anything wrong?"

"The *Stanley* ran aground."

"Oh, good God! Not that too!" Barttelot burst out laughing. "I say, this is turning into a bloody farce."

Stanley shot him a poisonous look.

"This tub can't keep up a decent head of steam and now the flagship of our marvelous fleet has run aground."

"Mr. Walker, start the engine."

"What can we look forward to next, do you suppose? The *Florida* capsizing? Why not? Just look at the way she's heeled over."

"Stow it, Major."

"Sir?"

"You heard me. Stow it. I ain't in a mood for your witty observations just now."

"No, I don't expect you are. Seeing how it looks as if the game is up."

"The game ain't up, Major."

"Come now, Mr. Stanley. There's no sense fooling ourselves. It was a jolly good try. No one can fault you on that. But this scratched-up flotilla of yours—it's a joke. We can count ourselves lucky if it all doesn't just sink to the bottom of the river before we ever reach Yambuya, let alone get us to Emin Pasha in time, the rate we're going. You know it yourself, Mr. Stanley. This tub's going to break down and surrender the ghost any moment the way she's loaded. And now the *Stanley!* What in God's name are we going to do about that?"

"Patch her up, Major. Mr. Walker, I said start the engine. Arthur, get up to the wheelhouse and show Dr. Sims where that cove is."

The *Stanley* was unloaded and pulled farther up the beach and turned broadside to the river. A trench was dug around her bow, uncovering three of the five punctures in the hull. Shagerstrom cut patches from oil drums and beat them flat, painted one side of each with red lead, stuck a piece of canvas to that and coated it with a layer of minium to assure water-tightness. Meanwhile, working inside the hold with hammer and chisel, Walker punched out bolt holes around each puncture. Then the prepared patch was held in place while the spots for the bolt holes were marked on it from the inside and corresponding holes punched into it. Finally the bolt holes were aligned, bolts slipped through them, and the patch screwed fast to the outside of the hull with nuts.

Once that was done—and it took the better part of two days—the vessel was pushed back into the river to see where water leaked through the remaining punctures. The procedure was repeated, although this time with considerably more frustration. Shagerstrom had to dive under the vessel with a prepared patch and hold it against the outside of the hull for Walker to mark the bolt holes; and when those were punched through, he had to go back under and hold the patch in place until Walker could slip the bolts through and screw them fast. To facilitate the alignment of the bolt holes in the patch with those in the hull, twine was threaded through; but as often as not, Shagerstrom ran out of breath before

Walker could complete the operation, or Walker dropped a bolt and lost it in the hold's muddy bottom, or the piece of canvas on the patch twisted askew and covered the bolt hole, or the minium layer came unstuck, or some other aggravating mishap occurred and the whole thing had to be done over three or four times before it was gotten right. And so it wasn't until May 15 that the expedition was able to resume the upriver journey.

They traveled even slower than before. Because of the accident, the steamers now kept each other in sight all the time so that in the event of more trouble one could go quickly to the assistance of the other; and since the *Peace*, her engine toiling pitifully under her heavy load, her boiler plagued by asthmatic rises and falls in steam pressure, limped forward only in fits and starts, the *Stanley* had to hold back to a snail's pace. But even if that hadn't been the case, Shagerstrom wouldn't have pushed the vessel faster. The grounding had given him a bad scare. He wasn't entirely sure of the repair that had been done on the vessel, and he put a crewman on permanent duty in the hold checking for leakage; but mainly what made him proceed with ever greater caution now was the fact that the river was growing increasingly treacherous.

It continued to widen to four, six, and in some reaches as much as ten miles across, a truly mighty river by any measure, pouring nearly two million cubic feet of water every second down to the ocean, in this respect the second most powerful river in the world, a bloody inland sea; but, perversely, as if bent on perpetrating a sinister deception, it did not show itself in this way to the travelers on it. For with each passing day, with each slowly gained mile, more and more islands and sandbars and shoals and reefs mobbed its great expanse and more and more tributaries, some nearly as large as the Congo itself—the Kasai, the Sangha, the Ubangi—debouched into its powerful flow, creating a maze of subsidiary embankments and divergent waterways, so that instead of a single, broad river, they seemed to be steaming up small streams and serpentine creeks, losing and finding their way in muddy narrow channels and stagnant fetid backwaters, thickly overgrown with luxuriant foliage, stinking of rotting vegetation, swarming with insects and mined with rocks, pushing their way through a bewildering network of watery alleyways into the heart of the very land itself.

A dull routine settled on the voyage. Each morning at five, to the chattering of monkeys and the screeching of gray parrots, while the mist still smoked on the river, hovering among the twisted roots and vines and low-hanging trees of their previous night's anchorage, they would set off, the *Peace* usually leading the way, with Walker relentlessly tinkering with her boiler, and for a while the mission vessel would manage to make decent headway. But long before the last of the mist had burned off in the day's gathering heat, she would begin losing pressure and speed in fits and starts again, and the *Stanley* would overtake her and steam ahead into the killing blaze of the rising sun.

Shagerstrom lounged half in and half out of the wheelhouse, swatting mosquitoes away from his sweat-sheened cheeks, a sweat-soaked bandanna tied around his throat, his meerschaum clamped between his teeth, glancing back occasionally to see how the *Peace* was faring but looking ahead again quickly to guide the vessel into yet another dangerously winding channel between islands, around some more mudbanks thrown up by a tributary, making for yet another forested horizon where the river turned again and where they would have to wait for the *Peace* again. Much of the time Baruti was with him, naked except for a white loincloth, fooling with the compass, peering through the spyglass, taking a hand at the wheel himself in the more open stretches; the rest of the time the little blackamoor was down in the engine room with Troup learning the mysteries of the ship's machinery or making a pest of himself with Uledi and the Wanyamwezis on the lower deck or chasing the butterflies that followed the boat.

Jephson envied him his energy and put it down to the obvious, that this was, after all, the little monkey's native habitat. But it certainly wasn't his; Jephson felt seedy all the time. There was something about the river here above the Pool beyond the cliffs, moving now into the center of its vast drainage basin nearly a thousand miles from the sea, there was something here that seeped into him like a miasma and sapped him, enervated him—the pounding heat of the sulfurous sun, its cheerless glare on the water, the oppressive weight of the breathlessly humid air, the shocking greenness of the forests, the endlessness of the white sky, the emptiness of the villages they passed, the silence of the river.

Barttelot switched places with Nelson and came aboard the *Stanley* after Bolobo. His relations with Stanley had grown just too prickly for them to comfortably share the one stateroom on the *Peace*, and Jephson, yielding to rank, let the major have his cabin on the steamer and took the quarters Nelson had shared with Parke on the *En Avant*. There was some fever back there among the askaris, malaria probably, and to guard against its spreading, Parke administered doses of quinine each morning not only to the kaffirs but also to the white men on all the boats. Then he'd return to the *En Avant*'s fantail deck and break open a bottle of brandy and a pack of cards. While Nelson had been aboard the barge, he and Parke had passed the time with two-handed skat games but Jephson wasn't interested. He didn't have the energy for it, and he spent the days of the grinding slow voyage slouched listlessly in whatever patch of shade he could find, listening to the slap and splash of the paddle wheels and the drone of insects, vaguely ill and feverish, watching the ever-changing, always repeating landscape of forest and river and swamp glide by.

But soon enough, and often sooner than expected—sometimes they ran low on firewood only a few hours after setting off because much of what had been collected turned out to be green; rarely did they ever have enough to last from sunrise to sunset—Shagerstrom would sound the steamer's whistle, interrupting the youth's torpid reveries, and he and Parke—and Troup and Barttelot on the *Stanley*—would rouse the dozing kaffirs and, to the cry of the leadman sounding the fathoms and the scurrying of deckhands heaving ropes and the rattle of the anchor chains, they would put into land for refueling. If the work went on until after dark, which it usually did, that would be the end of the day's journey, because, since the accident, Shagerstrom absolutely refused to sail after dark, and the caravan would make camp, in a forest clearing, on a spit of beach, in the mosquito-ridden cove of yet another swampy island.

On the first of June they crossed the equator.

· EIGHT ·

"SHE'S STOPPED AGAIN," Parke said.

Jephson didn't bother to look back at the *Peace*. He was sitting on a box of Winchester ammunition, his legs on the barge's rail, wondering where exactly the equator was.

"They're putting a boat over the side."

Now Jephson did look back. Parke had left his cards and brandy and was standing at the rear rail peering downriver through field glasses. "Who's in it?" Jephson asked, getting up.

"Mr. Stanley. And Bertie Ward."

"Let me have a look."

Stanley was standing in the prow of a small flat-bottomed dory, the *Peace*'s lifeboat. Ward, seated behind him, was rowing. Shagerstrom had ordered the *Stanley*'s engine cut as soon as he realized that the *Peace* had stopped again, and he was letting the steamer drift back downriver on the current, so it was only a few minutes before the dory passed the *En Avant* and came alongside the *Stanley*.

"Let's find out what's going on." Jephson handed the field glasses back to Parke and hurried forward to the bow of the barge, where he clambered the hundred feet or so over the ropes and hawsers that attached her to the steamer.

Uledi and a couple of Wanyamwezis ducked under the rail of the lower deck and grabbed hold of the dory's gunwales. Troup came from the engine room and, kneeling at the rail, extended a hand to Stanley to help him aboard. But he ignored it; he stayed in the lifeboat, grasping the steamer's rail. Shagerstrom and Barttlelot came down the ladder from the bridge.

"Mr. Walker can't get up any more than ten pounds of steam, Captain," Stanley said. "And he don't dare hold even that much for anything more than a few minutes. He says he'll blow the boiler sky high if he does."

"I thought it might be something like that," Shagerstrom replied, squatting down at the rail; Barttelot remained standing a step or two away. "I didn't think you had fouled on a reef or anything."

"No."

"It was bound to come to this sooner or later, you know, Bula Matari. She's overloaded and overworked. We need another steamer to transport this much stuff."

"I don't have another steamer, Captain," Stanley replied but he wasn't looking at Shagerstrom; he was looking at Barttelot. The major didn't bat an eyelash.

"Do you want me to go back and see what I can do?" Shagerstrom asked.

"No point in that, Captain. You're just going to have to tow us in, that's all. How far do you make it to Equator Station? A half-hour?"

Shagerstrom grimaced and shook his head. "Ain't no way I can tow her and the *Florida* in, Bula Matari. I'm having enough trouble as it is with the *En Avant* here and that steel boat of yours."

"I'm not asking you to tow all of us, Captain. What I want you to do is go on up to Equator Station and unhitch the *En Avant* and the steel boat and unload this vessel, then come back and fetch us. We'll lay at anchor here and wait for you."

Shagerstrom, still squatting, looked downriver at the *Peace*.

"You can tow the *Peace* and the *Florida* with this vessel unloaded, can't you?"

Shagerstrom removed his pipe from his mouth. "Yes, I suppose so," he said.

"Go on then and get back here as fast as you can. You don't want to be towing us in the dark."

"Hell no." Shagerstrom stood up. "All right, Mr. Troup. Let's get up a full head of steam."

Stanley looked again at Barttelot. The major was smiling. Stanley waited a moment, as if expecting him to say something, as if, in fact, hoping he would. But then the *Stanley*'s paddle wheels began turning again and Uledi and the Wanyamwezis shoved the lifeboat clear.

Equator Station was located a half-mile north of the equator on a swampy, low-lying headland formed by the confluence of the Ruki River with the Congo. It was the last of the Free State's trading depots on the Congo's mainstream (actually Stanley, five years before had established a station at Bangala, a couple hundred miles farther upcountry, but it had long since been abandoned), and all there seemed to be of it, seen from the foredeck of the *Stanley* as she pulled up against a rickety jetty jutting out into the Ruki, were a tool shed and storehouse at the water's edge and a bungalow of lime-plastered clay with a dried-grass roof and veranda a few hundred yards up the slope of the embankment on the cleared sun-beaten high ground of the headland. A white man was sitting on the veranda of that building.

"Hey, Van Gele," Shagerstrom shouted from the bridge and yanked the cord of the steamer's whistle.

The white man came down from the veranda, placing a battered panama on his head. He was dressed in a white linen suit, soiled and rumpled but complete with buttoned jacket and waistcoat, shirt and tie; he was barefoot, however, and his trousers were rolled to his knees.

"Get some of your niggers down here, Van Gele, and lend me a hand."

The crew of the *Stanley* were scampering around heaving ropes, dropping anchor, jumping over the side onto the jetty and into the muddy shallows of the Ruki, making the steamer fast. Sudi had cut loose the *Lady Dorothy*, and his oarsmen were rowing her to the beach while the *En Avant* was being untied and anchored independently on the downstream side of the jetty. The white man on shore, however, made no move to assist them; he merely stood in front of the station house, his naked toes curled in the dust, staring as if stupefied by all the activity. Others, though, began appearing on the knoll around him, blacks dressed in the uniform of Force Publique gendarmes, carrying rifles.

"What's the matter with you, Van Gele? The sun got you?" Shagerstrom hopped over the rail onto the jetty. Barttelot and Troup followed him; then Jephson and Parke hurried over from the *En Avant*. "Come on, man. Get a move on, will you. I've no time to waste."

"What the devil are you doing here, Shagerstrom?" Van Gele started down the slope toward the jetty. "I wasn't expecting you. I've no rubber for you."

"I ain't here for rubber."

"What then? What the devil is all this? Who are all these people?"

"The first half of the Emin Pasha relief expedition."

"The what?"

"Bula Matari's leading an expedition to the relief of Emin

Pasha's garrisons in Equatoria. Surely you've heard about it, you old soak. You ain't that much out of touch, are you? I'm taking them up to Yambuya, and they're going to cut their way through the Ituri to Albert Nyanza from there."

Van Gele's face didn't lose its expression of bewilderment. Seen close up, it wasn't a pleasant face: narrow and sharp-featured with caved-in cheeks and a sunken mouth that suggested it had very few if any teeth left in it. His chin was grizzled with a stubble of a beard and smeared with some kind of grease.

"Monsieur Van Gele, chief of Equator Station," Shagerstrom said. "Major Barttelot, Bula Matari's second-in-command; Dr. Parke and Mr. Jephson, officers of the expedition; and you know Jack Troup."

Van Gele shook hands all around, a limp handshake, and by the continuing blank look on his face, Jephson realized that he had indeed never heard of the Emin Pasha expedition, that he was in fact that much out of touch, stuck out here in the middle of nowhere. The idea caused an uncomfortable shiver to run down Jephson's spine, and he looked around the dusty clearing of this last outpost of white civilization on the river.

There was more to it than had at first appeared, but not much more, a few mud-and-wattle sheds and storehouses like those down at the jetty and another lime-plastered clay building behind the first with a flagpole in front and a Krupp gun pointed toward the surrounding forests at back, apparently the barracks of the Force Publique detachment. The gendarmes who had come out of that building at the blast of the *Stanley*'s steam whistle watched their chief and the visitors from a distance, their khaki uniform shorts and shirts disagreeably stained and torn and hung with odd bits of beads and cowrie shells and other fetishes, their faces scarred with tattoos. Behind them, near the edge of the forest that ringed the clearing, were a scattering of native huts where a group of dirty, ragged women and children, some of the latter clearly half-breeds, had gathered. Scrawny, yellow pariah dogs cowered at their feet. There were no other white men; Van Gele was alone at the station.

"Where's Bula Matari?" he asked.

"On the *Peace*. They've had a spot of trouble and need a tow. I'm going back to fetch them. That's why I want you to round up your boys. I've got to unload my boat first. The *Peace* has got the *Florida* lashed alongside and there's no way I can tow them both, loaded up the way I am. You can see how much water I'm drawing. Damn near eight feet."

"But there's no rubber here."

"How's that?"

"I've no rubber for you, Shagerstrom. None at all, I tell you."

"What's the matter with you, Van Gele? Ain't you been listening to me? I said I didn't come for rubber."

"The *Royal* took it. Martin came with the *Royal* and took it all. There ain't none left. It was only a month ago that he was here, maybe two . . . no more than two, and I ain't had time to collect any more. How much rubber do those bastards want anyway? How much rubber do they think I can collect? You can't squeeze blood from a stone, Shagerstrom. I sent down seven thousand kilos on the *Royal*. You'd think that would satisfy them. But no, they want more. They always want more. Well, I ain't got any more. I got hands, but I ain't got any more rubber."

Shagerstrom looked at Troup. Troup raised his eyebrows.

"You can have all the hands you want, Shagerstrom. I've got plenty of hands. You see that shed back there?" Van Gele pointed to a small windowless mud-and-wattle hut beside the barracks. "It's filled with hands. Filled to the rafters. How many do you want? You can take them all. Take them down to Leo and dump them in Liebrichts's lap. Maybe that'll satisfy him. I'll fetch them for you."

"No. That's all right, Van Gele. Forget it," Troup said. "Leave him be, Captain. We can manage this with our own men."

After the *Stanley* was unloaded and Shagerstrom and Troup had departed on her, the surgery tent was pitched on the Ruki side of the headland, but no camp was made. Jephson considered this a mistake. To be sure, as Barttelot pointed out, it was not yet noon and the *Stanley* could be expected back with the *Peace* and the *Florida* within an hour or two, so there'd still be plenty of daylight left to travel a farther piece upriver before stopping for the night. But that didn't take into account that some pretty extensive repair work would probably have to be done on the *Peace*—for all they knew, her whole damn engine might have to be torn down and overhauled or something—so it was bloodly unlikely they'd be able to get away that day.

"If ever," Barttelot responded laconically.

"All right, have it your way, Ted. If ever. But what I'm saying is we're damn certain to have to spend the night here."

They were standing on the jetty with Parke. Baruti had gone off to investigate the native village, where he had spied a number of boys his own age, and most of the Wanyamwezis and Sudanese had sprawled in the shade of the boxes and crates they had unloaded from the *Stanley*. Some of the women were down at the water's edge washing clothing, and some of the men had waded into Ruki trying to catch fish with makeshift nets. A cooking fire was burning, but no guard had been posted. The riding and pack animals were still on the *En Avant*, their restless stomping and braying and their musky odor mixing in the hot, still air with the buzzing of flies and the river's swampy stench.

"We ought to make camp," Jephson said. "Pitch the rest of the tents and get some shelters up before the rain."

"I don't have any orders to that effect."

"Ted! For God's sake."

"Did you hear him say anything about making camp? I didn't. All I heard him say was unload the *Stanley* and wait for him here. Well, we've unloaded the *Stanley*. So now let's just wait for him and see how he plans to get us out of *this* fix." Barttelot looked around at the station house where Van Gele was again sitting quietly on the veranda. "That crazy coot's got the right idea. No sense waiting out here in this blasted heat." He went up to the bungalow.

"We could at least use the time to gather firewood," Jephson called after him.

Barttelot didn't answer. He slipped into the shadows of the station-house veranda, and Jephson heard him say something to Van Gele and Van Gele, very softly, reply. Then there was the sound of a chair being dragged across the floorboards, Barttelot settling into it, the clinking of a bottle.

Jephson turned to Parke. "What do you think, Tommy?"

Parke shrugged.

"The *Stanley*'s going to need fuel. She's bound to burn up a hell of a lot towing the *Peace*."

"Yes, but . . . I don't know, Arthur. It could just be a hell of a waste of time. I mean, what's the difference anyway? I can't see how Mr. Stanley can hope to go on now. It's all come unstuck, hasn't it? . . . Yes, maybe we really ought to just wait and see, like Ted says." Parke looked around at the station house. "Let's wait up there with Ted. Van Gele's probably got some beer stashed away up there."

Jephson removed his pith helmet and ran his fingers through his sweat-damp hair and watched Parke go up on the veranda. He didn't follow him; he looked again at the caravan sprawled in listless disarray along the riverbank. He could put them to work, he thought; he could go down there and have Uledi start them building shelters and send Sudi out with a gang of axes and crosscut saws to gather steamer fuel. He didn't need Barttelot's consent. But what was the point? Barttelot and Parke probably were right.

Jephson put his helmet back on and let his eyes roam absently around the station clearing. Baruti was playing in the dust with some half-breed children in front of the native village, but the women had gone into the huts and the Force Publique gendarmes into the barracks to escape the blistering noonday heat. The yellow pariah dogs were stretched out like the dead in the shade. His eyes moved on to the windowless mud-and-wattle shed that Van Gele had said was filled with hands. He stared at it for a moment, an innocuous little structure, half falling down and shimmering in the humid haze. It had a door made of wood slats from a packing crate, with a rusty hasp and an even rustier padlock fastened through that. It was a perfectly ludicrous precaution; anyone with a mind to do so could break in without the least effort. The hasp and lock would pull out of the shed's mud wall with the merest tug. He went over to it.

"Get away from there."

Jephson turned with a start.

Van Gele had come over to the railing of the veranda. "Get away from there, young man. No one's allowed in there. That's State property in there. Valuable trading goods."

"Valuable trading goods?"

"Come on up here, Arthur." Parke also came over to the veranda railing and gestured with a beer bottle. "If you don't get out of that blasted sun you'll be as crazy as this chap in a minute."

The boats and the rain arrived at the station at virtually the same moment. Jephson had expected to be forewarned by the smoke from the *Stanley*'s stack, but by then the sky had lowered, dark and leaden, and no smoke could be seen. The first he realized that the steamer was back was when he heard her whistle as she rounded the headland. At just that moment there was a deafening crack of thunder and the rain came crashing down. Deckhands and askaris and *pagazis* spilled off the vessels hauling ropes, and Stanley and the other white men bounded to the jetty and came splashing up the suddenly flooded embankment to the station house.

"Bula Matari."

"How are you, Van Gele?"

"Dear Lord, I never dreamed I'd ever see you back on this

pest-hole of a river again, Bula Matari. I thought you were done with it for good."

"I'm just passing through, Van Gele. Just passing through." Stanley pulled a handkerchief from his tunic and wiped the rain from his face.

"Yes, just pass through. That's the right idea. Don't linger. Because it is worse now than it ever was. It was bad enough when you left, but I tell you it is worse now. Much worse. It is a horror now, Bula Matari. The rubber. The hands. I sent down seven thousand kilos on the *Royal* not two months ago."

Stanley nodded absently; the wind was blowing off the river, driving the rain onto the open veranda, and he went into the bungalow to escape it. "Do you have a kettle on, Van Gele?" he asked, looking around. "Put a kettle on, man. Let's have some tea."

The bungalow consisted of three rooms. One was entirely bare. The second contained an iron bedstead, a worm-eaten wooden bureau, and an open steamer trunk littered with dirty linen. The third, the middle one into which everyone followed Stanley, was the living room. Baskets and boxes stood under the shuttered windows, some spears and canoe paddles and an Express hunting rifle leaned against the wall, but all it had in way of furniture were a few cane-bottom chairs and a wooden table. Stanley, wringing out his wet handkerchief on the plank floorboards, pulled one of the chairs up to the table. The cookhouse was outside, near the locked shed where the hands were supposed to be stored, and Van Gele flung open the shutters of one of the windows and shouted out to a servant to put up water for tea. Then he turned around to Stanley again and resumed his recitation.

"Oh, yes, Bula Matari, if I could find a way out of this horror, I would. It gets worse every day. Rubber. Hands. They're never satisfied. They always want more. I sent down seven thousand kilos with Martin on the *Royal* a month ago, but it wasn't enough. . . ."

Stanley removed his helmet, set it down on the table, and fished out a cheroot from his tunic. Barttelot was smoking a cigarette, and Troup started rolling one of his own. The small room, with all but one window shuttered against the rain, quickly filled with smoke.

"What do they do with the hands, Bula Matari?" Van Gele suddenly asked.

"Eh?" Stanley looked up from the match he was holding to his cheroot.

"I've always wondered about that. I understand about the rubber all right, why they can never get enough of that, why they're always after me for more. Tires, coach tires. Yes, certainly, a marvelous invention. There must be a tremendous demand for it. But the hands, Bula Matari? I've been away from Europe too long, I suppose, but I can not imagine what use they make of them. Is it a new fashion? Like the elephant legs? I often try to imagine how they are used. As candy dishes perhaps?"

Barttelot gave out a startled bark of laughter.

Van Gele turned to him. "No? But it seems possible. Here. Let me show you." He went to a basket under the one unshuttered window.

Stanley took the cheroot from his mouth. "What do you have there, Van Gele?"

"Let me show you," Van Gele said again, bending down to the basket. A woven raffia lid covered it. He lifted that off and extracted a small object. "I've spent a great deal of time trying to imagine how it best could be used," he said, bringing the object over. "And all I can think of is something like a candy dish. See." He placed the object on the table.

"Get that thing away from me." Stanley leaped back from the table, upending it; and the object, along with Stanley's helmet, went flying across the room. "Goddamn you, Van Gele. Get that thing out of here."

Jephson caught a glimpse of the thing as it slithered into a corner. It was a hand, of course, a black shriveled hand.

Stanley stormed after it and picked it up by the thumb and flung it through the open window out into the rain. "Do you have any more of them, you goddamn lunatic?" He went to the basket under the open window and grabbed it and flung it out as well; and yes, it was full of hands, small, large, children's hands, women's hands, men's, some with fingers missing, some partly putrefied, some smoked to preserve them, all stiffened into claws; and they scattered on the mud outside like so many giant spiders or crabs. "Now you get out of here too, Van Gele. Get out of here before I throw you through the window too, you bloody lunatic."

Van Gele backed against a wall.

"Do you hear me? Get out of here, you disgusting animal."

"But it was you, Bula Matari—"

Stanley grabbed Van Gele by his shirt front and yanked him forward, lifting him from his feet, then threw him back, sending him stumbling toward the veranda. "Get out. Get out of here, damn you. I don't want to see your filthy face."

Van Gele retreated to the veranda. He was out of sight there, and that seemed to satisfy Stanley. He turned back into the room. His face was white with rage; his eyes narrowed to slits, the muscles of his jaw jumping with agitation.

Barttelot was grinning. "Candy dishes, by Jove! Nigger hands as candy dishes in all the best London salons. I like that."

"But what *are* they for?" Jephson suddenly cried out. "Why did he collect them? He's got a shed full of them out there. He says it's filled to the rafters with hands. Why?"

"Why?" Stanley whirled toward the youth. "Why the hell do you think? To terrify the niggers. To terrify them into harvesting the rubber. That's why. Those poor buggers know if they don't bring enough rubber into the station Van Gele's gendarmes, those ugly brutes out there, will go after them and find them and chop off their hands."

"Jesus! That's awful!"

"Sure it's awful. The whole bloody Free State is awful, from King Leopold on down. But that ain't my concern anymore. I'm just passing through. I got other things to concern me now."

Stanley turned away from Jephson, and noticing the table he had upended, he set it right with a ferocious bang. Then he fetched his helmet and put it on, hunted around the floor until he spied his cheroot, stuck it back in his mouth, and relit it. Then he pulled up his chair and sat down and took off his helmet again and slammed it on the table.

"Where the hell's that tea, Van Gele? Get that goddamn tea in here."

They heard Van Gele, still on the veranda, call to the servant in the cookhouse. Then he put in a timid appearance at the bungalow's doorway. "He'll be here with it in a minute, Bula Matari."

"Get your ass in here, Van Gele. I want you to hear this. I'm leaving part of my caravan here, and I expect you to make all the amenities of this godforsaken station available to them."

"You're doing what?" Barttelot blurted out.

Stanley turned to him. "I'm splitting the caravan, Major." He dropped his cheroot on the floor and ground it out with his heel. "As you were the first to point out so goddamn perceptively, it's plain we can't get everybody up to Yambuya on the boats we've got. So I'm leaving Bertie Ward and Sergeant Bonny here with about half the loads and three hundred of the men. That ought to lighten us up enough to make some decent headway. When we get to Yambuya, we'll unload and send the boats back to fetch them up."

"And how long will that take?"

"How long will what take?"

"For the boats to come back and fetch them up to Yambuya."

"Five or six weeks."

"So we're going to have to wait in Yambuya for five or six weeks?"

"Not all of us, Major. I said, I'm splitting the caravan. A flying column will set out through the Ituri as soon after we arrive in Yambuya as is feasible. That's unexplored country, the Ituri. No white man's even been through it, so a trail will have to be blazed and the tribes pacified in advance of any attempt to move a caravan of our size through it. It's a job that would have to be done in any event, whether we had this trouble with the boats or not, and it might as well be done sooner than later. There's nothing to be gained by putting it off five or six weeks. This advance column will travel light and fast and well armed. What I have in mind is maybe two hundred Wanyamwezis, carrying just enough supplies to get the column through the forest, and a hundred askaris as escort with the Maxim and the portable boat. Meanwhile the rest of the caravan will wait in Yambuya for the boats to get back with Bert and Sergeant Bonny and the others we'll be leaving here. Then they will form up and follow on the advance column's trail. This rear column will consist of the bulk of the equipment and relief supplies, some four hundred Wanyamwezis and a hundred askaris, reinforced, of course, as was the case for the march from Matadi to the Pool, with about six or seven hundred locally hired porters."

"Tippoo-Tib's slavers?" Troup asked.

Stanley turned to him. "Yes, Jack. Tippoo-Tib's people in Zanzibar told me he's sure to be at Stanley Falls about now with a few thousand of his Manyema. In that country he'll be our best bet. I doubt if we could get any of the local Basoko to go through the Ituri."

Troup nodded.

Stanley looked back at Barttelot. "I will command the advance column, Major."

"I could have guessed as much. And the rear column?"

"You're my second-in-command, Major."

"Yes, I could have guessed that too." Barttelot placed his hands behind his head and looked up at the ceiling. Then he said, "I suppose it's just as well, putting a bit of distance between us."

"You'll be five, perhaps as much as six weeks behind me, Major. And you'll have four times the number of men and loads. On the other hand, I'll have to hack out every step of my way through that damn forest, and you'll have the track to follow. So there's every reasonable expectation that you will catch up with me before I get to Wadelai. In fact, I'm counting on it."

"Who will I have with me? Apart from Bonny and Ward."

Stanley turned away from Barttelot and let his narrowed eyes move from one to another of the expedition officers standing and sitting around the room, Ward and Bonny, then Nelson, Parke, Hoffman, Jephson, and Troup. His eyes stopped on Troup. "Jack," he said.

Troup nodded.

"You know how important this is, Jack. You know the whole thing will come to nothing if the rear column doesn't get through in time."

Troup nodded again and closed his eyes.

· NINE ·

THE ARUWIMI enters the Congo from the east at latitude 1 degree, 15 minutes north and longitude 24 degrees, 12 minutes east. The Congo here, describing a great sweeping arc away from its original course, flows now from the south, and a day's journey farther upstream in that direction are the Stanley Falls, a series of white-water cataracts over a stretch of sixty miles that put an abrupt and tumultuous end to the 1,100 miles of navigable river from the Pool. But that was of no concern to the expedition, because on June 20, having traveled at almost twice their previous speed since leaving Ward and Bonny, 300 men, and half the loads at Equator Station, the steamers left the Congo and turned into the Aruwimi.

The river was alive with huge dugout canoes, each containing thirty or forty oarsmen and warriors, the former standing, their long paddles topped with balls of ivory, the latter smeared in red camwood war paint, wearing caps of wildcat skins, bones pierced through their nostrils, their ears grotesquely distended by tufts of grass stuck in holes bored around the edges and armed with spears and bushbuck-hide shields. These were the Basoko; they had been alert to the approach of the steamers since dawn and their massed armada now blocked the Aruwimi's mouth. But when the *Stanley*, leading the way into the tributary by a channel along its northern bank, shrieking her whistle repeatedly, pressed on nevertheless, the canoes suddenly turned tail and with amazing speed fled upriver and disappeared around the first sharp bend.

Where it empties into the Congo, the Aruwimi is about a half-mile wide, but this is misleading, because in fact it is one of the lesser tributaries of the Congo, and within the first few miles of its course it narrows to less than 500 yards; and by the time the steamers had rounded that first sharp bend where the Basoko canoes had vanished, they found themselves inching their way up what was little more than a fast-running stream—barely 200 yards from shore to shore, bowered over with fruit and raffia palms, eucalyptus and gum copal, and stands of giant ferns and bamboo, from which hung ghostly veils of gray-green orchilla weed—blocked to any further passage by boats of their size by rocky cascades and foaming rapids tumbling out of a solid dark wall of jungle to the east. The south bank here was high, a clay bluff rising steeply from the water's edge to a height of almost fifty feet, and atop this bluff was a village. This was the village of Yambuya, nearly 1,400 miles from the Atlantic, the farthest point inland that the expedition could travel by steamer, the point from which it would launch its overland strike into the Ituri forest.

It was a large village as African villages go, or more accurately a succession of villages, stretching a half-mile along the Aruwimi's southern bank, with a population of perhaps a thousand people. The dwellings were of a design not seen before, extremely tall pointed cones made of palm leaves overlapping one another layer upon layer like shingles. They stood in orderly rows along a rectangular grid at right angles to the river. They were surrounded on the landward side by fields of manioc, at this time of year just ripening. The greater portion of Yambuya's population—a short, stocky people of lighter skin color than those on the lower river, jaybird naked except for necklaces of crocodile teeth and skirts of shredded leaves—had lined the bluff, brandishing their spears and shields as they watched the expedition's flotilla approach.

The steamers and barges came abreast of the village but stayed close to the opposite bank, out of range of the spears, and cut their engines. All the askaris were on the *Stanley* now; they had exchanged places with the Wanyamwezis when the expedition set off that morning in preparation for the landing at Yambuya and were mustered along her starboard rail on the lower deck, rifles at the ready. Barttelot was with them. Nelson also had boarded the *Stanley* with the Maxim gun and gunners, and they were up on the wheelhouse deck, the automatic gun positioned to rake the village if necessary. Baruti, in the meantime, had gone over to the *Peace*. Yambuya, of course, was the little blackamoor's home, where Stanley had found him orphaned after Tippoo-Tib and his slavers had come down the Congo from Stanley Falls on one of their periodic raids against the Basoko; and he was now to serve as go-between and interpreter in the expedition's attempt to establish a base camp for the rear column there. Stanley had dressed him in his best European clothes—a peaked sailor's cap, a naval cadet's short jacket with two rows of brass buttons, narrow-cut blue trousers—and along with Willie Hoffman, who also spoke the Basoko vernacular, Stanley and the boy got into the *Peace*'s lifeboat. It was just past eight in the morning when the dory was put over the side.

Seeing this, the warriors on the bluff began rattling their spears against their shields, and an elephant-tusk horn gave out a fearsome blast. Hoffman, at the oars, ignored this warning outburst and rowed to a cluster of rocks roughly in midstream and made the dory fast there against the rush of the lively current. The strongest of the Basoko probably could have hurled a spear that distance with some effect, but generally they were still out of harm's way. Stanley and Baruti went up into the dory's prow to open the palaver. The boy removed his cap and waved it and shouted something in Basoko; and whatever it was, it stopped the warriors rattling their spears, and the elephant-tusk horn fell silent. Baruti went on, his child's soprano singing out across the stream like a bird's call in the jungle. He was identifying himself and relating his history. A murmuring arose among the people on the bluff, and many of the women and older men behind the phalanx of warriors pressed forward to have a better look at the oddly dressed little fellow. Then someone shouted something back, a curt angry phrase. Baruti answered it, his sweet voice rising with an almost tearful insistence. A few minutes went by, and then all of a sudden a figure appeared on the beach beneath the bluff: a girl, nude, young, a child really by the shape of her figure, perhaps only a year or two older than Baruti himself. It was impossible to tell how she had made her way down the high bluff, but she came to the water's edge, waded into the stream up to her ankles, and cupping her hands to her mouth, called to Baruti. Baruti responded with a great shout of joy, a single word, very likely a name: "Yalisula."

The girl dropped her hands in surprise and glanced back to the top of the bluff. Then, with a wonderful skill in one so young, she selected one of the smaller fishing pirogues on the beach, righted it, launched it, and standing unashamedly revealing her pretty little naked body, paddled out to the dory. The warriors started rattling their spears again but rather halfheartedly and stopped soon enough; they were as interested as everyone else to see what would happen.

Baruti leaned out over the dory's prow and extended a hand to the girl, meaning to draw her alongside; but she refused to take it and, feathering her paddle adeptly, stood off a few feet in the pirogue and spoke to the boy rapidly and severely. Baruti flashed a broad grin and quickly undid the brass buttons of his jacket and, when he had stripped it off, proceeded to remove his shirt as well.

Then he turned and showed his bare back to the girl. She paddled a bit nearer, throwing a wary glance at Stanley, and peered at it, crinkling her nose. Then she reached out and touched it tentatively, ran her fingers down it wonderingly. There was a scar on Baruti's back, a blue-black welt that went from his shoulderblade to just under his armpit, where as an infant he had been bitten by a crocodile; and on seeing it now the girl gave out a piercing little cry. For here was certain proof that this was indeed Baruti, a long-lost brother thought to have been taken away or killed by Tippoo-Tib's slavers. The boy turned quickly and flung his arms around her; and in that extremely awkward position, each in a different boat and hers gliding away downstream, they embraced.

Stanley waited a decent interval, then put an end to the touching scene by taking the boy's arm and saying something to him in Swahili. Baruti repeated it in Basoko to the girl. She shook her head vigorously and began speaking herself. A hurried animated conversation ensued between the two children, which Stanley couldn't follow; and as he couldn't get Baruti to break off and tell him what it was about, he called Hoffman forward to translate. The hulking hairless man listened for a moment without expression, then repeated what he heard. Stanley pulled a face and spoke again to Baruti. The boy nodded eagerly. Hoffman interjected a remark, and Stanley looked around at the Basoko atop the bluff. Then he spoke at some length to Baruti, gripping the boy's bare shoulder, shaking him a bit, lecturing him, and again the boy nodded vigorously. And then he slipped from Stanley's grasp and clambered into the girl's pirogue. Stanley called after him sharply, holding out the naval jacket and shirt the boy had removed. But Baruti didn't turn back. Stripped to the waist, his eyes fixed on Yambuya, he took the paddle from the girl and, with a skill not lost in the years spent in London, smoothly negotiated the swirls and snags and stones in the quickly rushing stream and headed for shore. Seeing this, the women on the bluff gave out a sustained joyful ululation, and the elephant-tusk horn blared a sort of fanfare of welcome; and from somewhere back in the village an unseen drum started up a lively, rhythmic tattoo.

And the wait began.

The sun rose. Although it could not penetrate the dense canopy of leaves and flowering vines and orchilla weed that enclosed the stream except in vagrant glittering rays, its effect was to make of the embowered backwater a suffocating steam bath, cloying with exotic smells, thick with clouds of gnats and butterflies.

Stanley and Hoffman remained in the dory in midstream while those on the steamers and barges loafed against the rail, sluggish in the humid heat. When Baruti and the girl had beached the pirogue, Jephson, on the *En Avant*, had watched to see by what path they'd ascend the high steep bluff. But the two children ran off into a thicket and disappeared. Jephson then looked up to the top of the bluff, expecting to see them reappear there. They didn't, but after a few minutes it was evident that they had arrived, because the Basoko women began their ululating again; and they and the older men and children withdrew into the village, leaving only the warriors on the edge of the bluff.

An hour passed, two; the morning slipped away. Jephson looked at Stanley in the dory. He did not appear impatient; perhaps he had reckoned that it would take this long for Baruti to explain the purpose of the expedition, that it was neither a Free State party hunting rubber nor a caravan of Tippoo-Tib's gunmen hunting slaves. Jephson went to his cabin for a drink from his canvas water bottle.

"Get steam up!"

Jephson bolted from the cabin.

"Get steam up, Captain Shagerstrom."

Stanley was signaling with his helmet from the dory. Hoffman had taken up the oars and was pulling for shore. Jephson glanced to the top of the bluff. All the warriors had cleared off.

"Bring her across, Captain Shagerstrom. Bring her across."

Troup popped out of the *Stanley*'s engine room and called up to Shagerstrom on the bridge. The steamer's side wheels were turning, the boat was edging upstream toward the rapids above the village. When she was just within a few yards of the white water and in danger of fouling on the rocks there, Shagerstrom shouted to Troup, and the redhead dashed back into the engine room. The paddle wheels reversed; and catching the current, the vessel began crossing the river at a slant, more broadside than backwards.

"What happened, Tommy?" Jephson called to Parke.

"I don't know. The niggers vanished, from one minute to the next. Mr. Stanley's landing the askaris."

Jephson ran forward on the barge and scampered over the lines to the steamer. Barttelot had paraded the askaris by company in double file at the gangway.

"Hold your fire, Major," Stanley called to him from the dory. "Hold your fire until it's absolutely unavoidable."

Barttelot nodded. He unholstered his revolver, spun the chamber once, and cocked the hammer.

"Did you hear that, Captain?" Stanley shouted up to Nelson on the bridge with the Maxim. "Cover us, man, but I don't want you shooting that bloody thing unless we're actually attacked. I ain't sure what these buggers are up to. And Baruti is back in there with them somewhere."

"Yes, sir."

"Right then. Let's go, Major. Let's take this village."

With a final strong pull on the oars, Hoffman beached the dory and Stanley leaped out in a half-crouch, holding his pistol at chest level. At virtually the same moment, the steamer bumped aground broadside on the muddy flats where the Basoko canoes lay overturned. The rail gate was flung open, and with Barttelot in the lead the askaris went splashing through the shallows. When they hit the beach, at Barttelot's bellowing command they spread out along the foot of the bluff. They were exposed there, in range of the spears; but even if the Basoko warriors had suddenly reappeared at the top of the bluff, a burst from the Maxim would have driven them off. They didn't reappear. Stanley and Barttelot started up the bluff almost simultaneously, here and there losing their footing in the soft crumbly clay; and the first company of askaris, most armed with the Winchester repeaters, holding the weapons high and out in front, scrambled after them, eyes darting anxiously in every direction, expecting the first spear to come flying at any moment. Barttelot reached the bluff's summit first and threw himself prone, gripping his revolver with both hands, bracing it with his elbows jammed into the ground. But in the next split second he was back on his feet; and waving the weapon above his head, he charged into the village and out of view. Stanley was a step behind him, running, shouting for the first wave of askaris to follow. The second wave was halfway up the slope by then, and soon it too went over the top and disappeared from sight.

Jephson leaned far over the rail, straining to see what was going on, listening for the first shots to be fired. Shagerstrom had maneuvered the steamer closer to shore, and Hoffman, still in the dory, caught hold of her line. One of the anchors was dropped, then Troup cut the engine and came over to the rail beside Jephson and Parke. Shagerstrom left the wheelhouse and stood behind Nelson at the Maxim. The *Peace* and the *Florida* were still anchored near the opposite shore, waiting for the signal to also come over. But there was no signal; there were no sounds of any kind. The landing party seemed to have vanished into the forests around the village.

And then Stanley reappeared at the edge of the bluff. His pistol was back in his holster. He scanned the river's embankments, hands on his hips, then called down to Hoffman. Hoffman let go of the steamer's line and started rowing across to the *Peace*.

"Is that it, do you suppose?" Jephson asked.

"For the moment," Troup replied. He squinted up at Stanley on the bluff's summit. Then he said, "Come on. Let's get the boats unloaded while we have the chance."

Yambuya was deserted. The askaris had scouted down the streets, beaten through the fields of manioc, poked nervously into the huts. Chickens wandered about unconcerned. Here and there goats were tethered and wicker bins were filled with sugarcane. Gourds and clay pots, mats, wooden scoops, stools, manioc pounders, and a variety of other implements and tools had been left behind; but the Basoko themselves, and Baruti with them, were gone. Hoffman took out the best of the Wanyamwezi trackers, along with a squad of Winchester-armed Sudanese, to see if any trace of them could be found. But it was a perfunctory gesture; there was very little expectation of success. The Basoko could have gone anywhere, upriver or down or into the forest to some other village. Or, for that matter, they might still be somewhere in the vicinity, watching the expedition land from the darkness of the encircling trees where not even the best tracker was likely to find them.

Still there was no great worry about Baruti's fate. The Basoko were his tribesmen, his family; he had gone over to them willingly, and they would do him no harm. No doubt, in the first happy flush of his homecoming, the boy would want to stay with them and run with them, renewing blood ties and friendships, remembering the old ways; but after a few days, Stanley was sure, he would slip away and return. In the meantime though there was work to do. Yambuya was to serve as the base camp for the expedition's rear column for perhaps as much as six weeks—until the steamers fetched up Ward and Bonny and the men and supplies left at Equator Station—and in view of the apparent unfriendliness of the Basoko, it had to be made secure for that.

The officers' tents were pitched in a close tight circle not a hundred yards from the edge of the bluff; and the nearest of the Basoko huts were taken over as billets for the Wanyamezis and Sudanese and for use as storehouses. But all the rest—and there were hundreds of them—Stanley ordered razed to the ground so that there would be a clear field of fire from the camp to the surrounding forests and no cover for any hostile force that might try to sneak up on the camp and take it unawares. In addition, construction was started on a ten-foot-high stockade around the camp's landward sides with a moatlike ditch around that, six feet wide and five feet deep and spiked with sharpened bamboo spikes. Then too a stepped path had to be cut in the face of the steep bluff down to the riverside to facilitate bringing up the loads and pack animals from the boats; and the chickens and goats and stores of sugarcane that had been left behind by the Basoko had to be collected and the ripening manioc in the fields harvested so that the camp would have a reserve supply of food in the event of a siege or any other trouble. Teams of axmen under guard had to be sent out into the forest to chop firewood for the steamers' return to Equator Station, and equipment and supplies had to be sorted out and repacked into special loads for the trail-blazing advance column. It was work that would occupy the officers and men of the expedition for several days, and they started on it on the afternoon of the landing. But there was one further and extremely crucial matter that had to be attended to before Stanley could set off with the advance column into the Ituri. And that was the hiring of those 600 additional porters that Barttelot and the rear column would need when they followed out on Stanley's track six weeks hence. So the following day, after she had been unloaded, the *Stanley* steamed back down the Aruwimi to the Congo and then upriver to Stanley Falls to pay a call on Tippoo-Tib.

Hamed bin Mohammed—the people of the forest had given him the nickname Tippoo-Tib, saying it was the sound made by his guns—was the most prosperous and powerful of the Zanzibari Arabs then hunting ivory and slaves in the African interior. He had been at the bloody trade for more than thirty years, first as an apprentice in his father's caravans, then on his own, year after year pushing always deeper inland from the Indian Ocean coast. Stanley had first met him at Nyangwe on the western shore of Lake Tanganyika when attempting his epic descent of the Congo in 1876; but in the decade since, using the slaves he captured to carry the ivory from the elephants he killed and selling both slaves and ivory in Zanzibar, he had vastly expanded his field of operations, westward across the Congo to the Lomami and northward down the Congo to Stanley Falls; and he was now the sultan of a region larger than Great Britain, the commander of an army of tens of thousands of gunmen, mainly cannibal tribesmen from the Manyema forest, and the lord of hundreds of lesser Arab sheiks and vassal African chieftains. His settlement at Stanley Falls, called Singatini, reflected his terrible greatness.

As the *Stanley* steamed up the Congo on the afternoon of the next day, June 22, quite all of a sudden on the river's right bank, just below the thundering white water of the Wagenia cataract, the last of the Stanley Falls, in the midst of what was one of the world's most savage wildernesses, a miniature Zanzibar hove into view.

The principal buildings were two stories high, handsome white-washed villas with brass-studded doors and intricately carved balconies, set in lush gardens of bougainvillea and frangipani and hibiscus. The minaret and dome of a mosque could also be seen among the trees, and there were dozens of lesser buildings as well, tembes for the servants, harems for the odalisques, barracks for the soldiers, shops and kiosks of every description, coffeehouses and stables and warehouses filled with ivory lining high-walled crooked alleyways and jumbled around little parks and squares. Behind them, hacked out of the jungle itself, were miles of plantations of sweet potato, rice and onion, maize and banana, orchards of lime and mango and pawpaw and pomegranate; and in front of them, along the sandy beach of the riverbank, in the shade of a promenade of palm trees, a grand bazaar was spread out beneath brightly colored awnings. And there, amid throngs of slaves and gunmen and market women, a score of stately Arabs clad in white linen, over which they wore long embroidered cloaks, gathered to watch the steamer's approach.

"Which one is he?" Barttelot asked.

"Oh, I wouldn't think he'd come down himself," Stanley replied. "But that's his brother, Selim. And over there, that's his nephew, Rashid, one of the bloodiest bandits of them all. And that one there is his eldest son, Sefu."

They were standing on the *Stanley*'s forward deck, each scanning the promenade through field glasses while Shagerstrom eased the vessel toward the low, sloping embankment. Jephson was with them. Walker was down in the engine room, and there was also a squad of ten Sudanese askaris aboard; but the rest of the officers and men had remained on the Aruwimi completing the entrenchment and fortification of the base camp at Yambuya. A mixed lot of slaves and half-castes and Manyema waded out into the river to help the vessel's deckhands with the mooring.

"Well, I'll be damned," Stanley suddenly said, still looking through his binoculars. "We're being accorded a signal honor, gentlemen. There he is. Coming out of that garden over there. Do you see him?"

Barttelot hunted about with his field glasses for a moment. Then he said, "Oh, yes."

The two men watched through their glasses as a figure walked slowly from the main buildings of the settlement down to the promenade. Jephson had neglected to bring his glasses with him and so could make the figure out only to the extent of seeing that he was taller than the others, turbaned and wearing a black cloak, and that he was accompanied by a bodyguard of musket-armed retainers. As he approached the river's edge, the crowd made way for him, the sheiks bowing and touching their foreheads.

"Have a look, lad." Stanley handed his binoculars to Jephson.

Jephson fiddled with the focus for a moment, then Tippoo-Tib's face leaped into view. It wasn't what he had expected. He really didn't know what he had expected—a pirate, a smuggler, a slaver of infamous cruelty, a beast—but what he saw was a face of unmistakable intelligence and refinement. He was a shade darker-skinned than most Arabs—evidently there was a touch of the African in his heritage—and his full curly beard was snow white, giving him the appearance of a sage or scholar. He was in his fifties, but his bearing was that of a younger man, proud and strong. His black cloak was embroidered with silver thread, the haft and sheath of the ornamental Shirazi dagger he wore in his girdle were silver-filigreed and studded with precious stones; and gold rings adorned his long tapered fingers. There was the air of the mosque and the palace about him, of Arabian nights, luxurious, cultivated, sensuous, utterly out of keeping with his savage history, utterly at odds with this savage geography. Only his eyes betrayed him—they were heavy-lidded, hooded—but the menace and cunning in them were dispelled when he smiled as he smiled now, watching Stanley come down the gangplank of the steamer.

"Bula Matari," he said and raised a hand to his heart, his lips and then to his forehead.

"Hamed bin Mohammed," Stanley replied and repeated the gesture of salutation. "*Salaam aleikum.*"

"So you have come back, Bula Matari. It is a great joy to see you again."

Stanley bowed his head.

"But I am not surprised. You shall always come back, I think. For you love this place as I do, this river, these forests, the sky above our heads, this Africa; and as long as you live, I think, they shall beckon to you with their memories and draw you back. Is that not so?"

Stanley nodded again with a smile.

"Ah, yes, it is so. And why should it not be so? It is here, after all, that you put your youth aside and came to manhood. It is here, on this river, in your terrible trial of discovering the course it ran and in the blood you spilled into its waters that you found your greatness. It is here that you became Bula Matari, and it is here in the heart of Africa that you shall forever be Bula Matari, the rock breaker. I greet you. *Salaam aleikum*."

Stanley grinned, not without pleasure but also not without a trace of irony. He was dressed in his gold-frogged and epauletted blue officer's jacket and freshly laundered white riding breeches, and his spiked topee was newly chalked. Barttelot too was attired specially for the occasion, wearing the parade-dress uniform of the Royal Fusiliers and all his decorations. He had marched the guard of Sudanese onto the beach, then had come up to stand beside Stanley. Jephson stood on Stanley's other side, also dressed in his Sunday best. None of them was armed. A few of the principal sheiks—Selim, Rashid, Sefu among them—had moved up behind their sultan, but the others and the general populace of the settlement remained at a respectful distance. Shagerstrom and Walker watched from the steamer's bridge.

"Is this your son, Bula Matari?" the slaver asked, turning to Barttelot.

"What? Oh, no. I regret to say I am not as fortunate as Tippoo-Tib. I have no sons."

"Then who is he, Bula Matari? Tell me. Who is this beautiful soldier who accompanies you?"

"Major Edmund Musgrave Barttelot, sir," Barttelot replied for himself. "Her Majesty's Seventh Royal Fusiliers."

"The major is second-in-command of my expedition, Tippoo-Tib. And this is Mr. Arthur Mounteney Jephson, my aide-de-camp."

Tippoo-Tib nodded at Jephson, then returned his heavily lidded eyes to Barttelot and studied him with a peculiar interest, a sort of measuring, a shrewd-eyed attempt at judgment.

"You know of my expedition, Tippoo-Tib, do you not?"

"I know of it, Bula Matari."

"I was certain you would. Very little passes in these regions that Tippoo-Tib does not know of."

"That is so, Bula Matari."

"I am in need of your assistance for this expedition and that is why I come to you now, Tippoo-Tib. Do you know that as well?"

"I know that as well, Bula Matari." The slaver at last took his eyes from Barttelot and turned to Stanley again. "Your need is for *pagazis* to carry the loads of your expedition through the forest of the Ituri. You cannot engage the Basoko for this work. The Basoko do not trust the white man since the business with the rubber began, and besides, they would never go into the heart of the forest of the Ituri, as they fear it most dreadfully. So you have come to me for my Manyema, who will go anywhere that I command them to go no matter what their fear."

Stanley bowed his head again and smiled.

"You yourself will go first through the forest with a small column of your men to break the trail. Some weeks later the main caravan will follow from Yambuya with the heavy loads. It is for this that you need my Manyema."

Again Stanley nodded, but his smile stiffened perceptibly. It was, to say the least, surprising that the slaver should have quite such detailed information about a plan made only a few weeks before. A possible explanation was that someone in the expedition was in Tippoo-Tib's pay, that when Hoffman hired on the Wanyamwezis in Zanzibar, Tippoo-Tib's agents there had slipped a man of their own among them to keep their sultan informed of the expedition's intentions and progress. But Stanley did not remark on this now; for the moment anyway, he saw no harm in it. And so he merely said, "And, Tippoo-Tib? How do you respond to this need of mine?"

"We shall speak of it, Bula Matari. We shall speak of it later. But you have journeyed far and are tired and hungry." Suddenly he raised his voice in mock anger. "What sort of guest are you, Bula Matari, that you would have Tippoo-Tib appear so inhospitable as to keep you here at the riverside in palaver when you are tired and hungry? It will not do. First you shall rest and eat. Then we shall speak of these matters. Come along, Bula Matari. Come along, beautiful soldier." He reached for Barttelot's hand.

The gesture nonplussed the major and he drew back.

"What is it, Major? Are you not hungry?" Tippoo-Tib asked. "Ah, but I shall raise an appetite in you, an appetite of the like you have never known," he said. "Come along, my beautiful soldier. Come along." He took Barttelot's hand, and in the Arab fashion, hand-in-hand, strolled with him to a large multicolored marquee set up in the bazaar.

This tent had been readied as a *barazan*, a reception area. Persian carpets covered the ground, and silk pillows and bolsters and mats were scattered on them. Tippoo-Tib indicated the places that had been prepared for his guests and, releasing Barttelot's hand, adjusted the skirts of his djellaba and reclined in accustomed ease among the cushions. Stanley, Barttelot, and Jephson followed suit. The sheiks came in and seated themselves cross-legged in a semicircle facing them, while the bodyguard of musketeers formed a phalanx at the tent's entry to keep the people of the bazaar from drawing too close. Then Tippoo-Tib clapped his hands.

The odalisques appeared. They were Nubian and Abyssinian girls mostly, although some were astonishingly fair in complexion, wearing billowing pantaloons and short embroidered vests over filmy chemises, the lower halves of their faces veiled, their naked arms bangled from wrist to elbow. There were golden chains around their necks, and their jet-black hair was done up in different styles and fastened with flowers. Moving with a sinuous grace, they brought in heavy brass trays and platters heaped with steaming food—goat kabobs and rice, curried chicken, vermicelli, plantains fried in ghee, various peppered meats, and spiced vegetables not so immediately identifiable—and bowls of fresh fruit and gourds of palm wine and cassava beer and urns of coffee and tea. They set these on the carpet in front of their sultan, then moved quickly back in a whisper of silk to the walls of the tent with downcast eyes. Tippoo-Tib invited Stanley to begin the feast; and Stanley, complimenting the repast, saying he hadn't set eyes on such since leaving Zanzibar, and warning Barttelot and Jephson to go slow lest they upset their stomachs on the unaccustomed rich fare, picked up a charred piece of spiced meat from a salver, which turned out to be antelope, blew on it, and popped it into his mouth. There were no plates or utensils; each man ate with his fingers and by turn, according to some unstated protocol—Stanley first, then Tippoo-Tib, Barttelot, and Jephson, then the brother Selim, the nephew Rashid, the son Sefu, and the lesser sheiks—each selecting whatever pleased him from the array of platters and bowls. Tippoo-Tib, however, often made recommendations, genially urging this or that morsel on his guests, and he personally served the drink with which to wash it down and cool its spicy bite, pouring out cups of wine or coffee, beer or tea, depending on the food.

From time to time Jephson threw a surreptitious glance at the harem girls. How could he resist? Of course they fascinated him, standing there so demurely in their silks and jewels, slaves to the passions of the slaver. They excited his imagination to flights of the wildest fantasies. And one in particular attracted him. She was slim and long-legged, yet very buxom, the fairest in complexion of the lot, almost white, an Egyptian perhaps or Turk or Circassian. Because of her veil, the youth couldn't tell if she was pretty, but unlike the others, she looked up occasionally to study the white men. Then he saw her eyes, and they were huge, dark, lustrous as a deer's and shining with what he fancied was the sorrow of her tragic situation.

Barttelot too, Jephson saw, noticed her, once even caught her glance and tried to hold it, but she had lowered her lids immediately then, and the major's attention was distracted by Tippoo-Tib offering him some tea. Jephson, however, went on watching her and, after a bit, saw that she did look up again; and although Barttelot was then engaged in conversation with Stanley and the slaver and therefore did not realize it, she looked at him.

"Will you smoke, Bula Matari?"

"Yes but only tobacco."

"And your officers?"

"The same."

Tippoo-Tib clapped his hands.

And the odalisques hurried forward, some to clear away the platters and dishes, others bringing the hookah pipes. There was one of these for each of the men and a girl with each to prepare it. The fairest skinned knelt at Tippoo-Tib's feet and deftly filled the hookah's jar, sprinkling a greenish powder on the tobacco leaves, inserting a glowing coal in the bowl beneath the water chamber. Jephson watched her, the swift movement of her hands like birds, the long lithe curve of the back of her neck as she bent forward, the smooth patch of white skin above the waistband of her pantaloons when her short vest rode up with the movement of her hands. Tippoo-Tib said something to her in Arabic or perhaps Amharic. She glanced up at Barttelot. Then she went to him on her knees and, nudging aside the girl preparing his pipe, took over the task herself.

Stanley immediately leaned over and grasped her wrist. "*Hapana*," he said.

"What is it?" Barttelot asked.

Tippoo-Tib broke into a mischievous grin. "Ah, Bula Matari, where is the harm?"

Stanley shook his head.

"You are like a mother hen, protecting her chicks from the

vultures," Tippoo-Tib said, chuckling, and took up the long coiled hose of his hookah.

"What is it?" Barttelot asked again.

"Hashish, Major," Stanley replied. "They are smoking hashish."

Tippoo-Tib lounged against his pillows and placed the amber mouthpiece of the hookah between his lips and drew deeply on it, letting his hooded eyes again rest on Barttelot with a kind of greedy curiosity, evidently captivated by the major's good looks. Barttelot turned away with an annoyed, uneasy shrug and took up his pipe. So did the others. The harem girls withdrew. It was now late in the day. The sky to the north was darkening with the coming rain, and the light inside the tent was growing dim. The soft gurgling sound of smoke bubbling through the water in the several pipes was like that of a flock of pigeons contentedly roosting, sheltering from the coming storm.

"So you will go through the forest of the Ituri, Bula Matari," Tippoo-Tib said after a period of quiet smoking.

Stanley nodded.

"No one has ever gone through the forest of the Ituri, Bula Matari. No one has ever ventured more than several leagues into it."

"I know."

"And that is the reason you go, eh, Bula Matari? To be the first one to do it. Again to be the first one."

"No," Stanley said and laughed. "Not this time, Tippoo-Tib. This time I travel on a different errand. I bring relief supplies to the beleaguered garrisons of a brave soldier of my Queen, Emin Effendi, Pasha of Equatoria."

"Ah."

"And for this I require your assistance. I shall pay handsomely for it."

At this point, the sheik Selim leaned forward and whispered in Arabic to his brother. Tippoo-Tib listened without averting his gaze from Stanley. Then he said, "What Selim says is true. There is a spell on the forest of the Ituri."

"A spell?"

"Yes, Bula Matari, there is a spell. This is the reason no one ventures into it. This is the reason no one has ever gone through it. There is a spell."

"That was also said of the Congo, was it not, Tippoo-Tib? Did you not yourself tell me so in Nyangwe, these many years gone, that no man would ever discover where this mighty river ran, because there was a spell on the river."

"And you broke the spell."

Stanley said nothing.

"And now you would break the spell of the forest as you broke the spell of the river."

"With your help, Tippoo-Tib."

Again Selim whispered in his brother's ear. Rashid, the nephew, and Sefu, the son, moved closer to hear, their black eyes, pinpoints now under the influence of the hashish.

"Yes, Bula Matari," Tippoo-Tib said after this consultation. "You would break the spell of the forest as you broke the spell of the river. Yes, I believe this. It is just as you say. But would it be a good thing? Was it a good thing?"

"What are you asking me, Tippoo-Tib?"

"Listen, Bula Matari, and I will tell you. I did not believe you in Nyangwe. I gave you *pagazis* then and even went with you myself for a way, but I did not believe you. I went with you for fifty marches down the Congo, and then I turned back because I did not believe that any man could find the course of this mighty river, that any man could break this mighty river's spell. And when I left you, I was certain no word would ever be heard of you again. I was mistaken. You found the way down the Congo. You broke the river's spell. But was it a good thing?"

Stanley did not reply.

"For when you broke the spell of the river, the white men came, did they not?" Selim again was whispering in Tippoo-Tib's ear, but he waved him aside impatiently with a bejeweled hand. "They followed after you, Bula Matari. Wherever you have gone in Africa, wherever you have broken the ancient spells, the white men have followed after you, have they not? building their forts and trading depots, taking the land and its riches for themselves. They followed after you on the Congo. And once you break the spell of this forest, they would follow after you there as well, would they not?"

"As would you, Tippoo-Tib?"

The slaver raised his eyebrows.

"Did you not also follow after me down the Congo, Tippoo-Tib? Once you had learned that I had broken its spell, did you not bring your men and guns down the river for the ivory and slaves to be had on its shores? And would you not do the same in the Ituri? If I break the forest's spell, would you not follow after me for the ivory and slaves to be hunted there?"

The slaver sucked deeply on the hookah's mouthpiece and, letting the pungent smoke seep out slowly from his nostrils and between his lips, smiled.

"You would, Tippoo-Tib," Stanley said, smiling in return. "So there would be profit in it for both of us."

Now Rashid and Sefu as well as Selim pressed closer to Tippoo-Tib and whispered conspiratorially to him.

"I require six hundred of your Manyema, Tippoo-Tib, and I am prepared to pay handsomely for them. Six pounds sterling the head to Albert Nyanza. And the chance for you to learn the way through the Ituri as you learned the way down the Congo."

"I do not have six hundred men to spare here in Singatini, Bula Matari. I would need send to Kasongo for them."

"Send to Kasongo for them then."

"When would you require them?"

"In six weeks' time. I will set out myself tomorrow or the day after with the advance column to break the trail, but it will be six weeks before the steamers bring up the men and loads I had to leave at Equator Station. Only then will the rear column set off after me. That should give you time enough to send for your men in Kasongo and deliver them to Yambuya."

"To Major Barttelot in Yambuya?"

"Yes, to Major Barttelot in Yambuya. He will command the rear column."

"Ah," the slaver said and, sucking on the hookah, again shifted his heavily lidded eyes to Barttelot. It was impossible to know what, if any, effect the hashish was having on his sensibilities; but the hooded gaze he fixed on the handsome major now was openly lascivious, shockingly depraved. From the distance came the first faint rumble of the thunder of the approaching storm.

"Will you stay the night, Bula Matari?"

"No. I will start back for Yambuya directly after the rain."

"A pity. I should have seen to it that your stay here would be a pleasure."

"Oh, I know, Tippoo-Tib," Stanley replied and burst out laughing. "Good Lord, do not think I do not know just how great a pleasure it would be. I have stayed with you before, Tippoo-Tib and I know the pleasures you offer. But I dare not stay this time to enjoy them. For then I might never leave. And I must." He leaned forward and peered into the slaver's hooded eyes, his own strange eyes narrow and gleaming. "The forest of the Ituri awaits me."

PART THREE
The Forest of Death

• ONE •

THE ADVANCE COLUMN set off into the Ituri forest on June 28.

Stanley, after returning from Tippoo-Tib's, had delayed the departure from Yambuya for four days. Ostensibly there were things that had to be done before they could get away—the completion of the camp's fortifications, the dispatch of the steamers and barges to Equator Station to fetch up Ward and Bonny and the rest of the rear column, the sorting and repacking of the advance column's equipment and supplies—but mainly what he had done during those four days was wait for Baruti. There had been no sign of the little blackamoor or, for that matter, any of the Basoko since the expedition had landed at Yambuya. That they were there though, somewhere in the jungles surrounding the camp, there could be no doubt. At night one heard the beating of their drums, the moan of their elephant-tusk horn, the weird hoots and cries they made in imitation of the nocturnal birds; and in the morning Stanley sent Hoffman and Uledi out with the Wanyamwezi trackers in an attempt to contact them. He hoped to establish peaceful relations and trade with them for the sake of the rear column, which would be camped in their midst, to acquire guides from them to point the advance column's way through the forest, and to get a message to Baruti. But they were never to be found. During the night of the 27th, however, the boy returned on his own.

An askari on picket duty at the western end of the newly built stockade caught him trying to sneak into camp. He wasn't immediately recognized. He had stripped off the last of his European clothing and was wearing only a skirt of shredded palm leaves and a necklace of crocodile teeth; white circles were painted around his eyes, a yellow stripe ran from his forehead down his nose, and he carried a small cane bow and a clutch of arrows. The Sudanese corporal of the guard took him for a Basoko spy, bound his wrists, and brought him to Barttelot. Even the major didn't realize who he was at first; and when he did, laughing at the child's savage appearance, he had him untied. At that, however, Baruti made a dash for it, and in the mad scramble that followed the entire camp was awakened. Barttelot tackled the boy just before he could slip out of the stockade gate. Taking firm hold of his ear, he marched him back into camp.

"Let go of him, Major."

"That's the last you'll see of him if I do, Mr. Stanley. He doesn't seem awfully keen on rejoining the expedition."

"Just let go of him." Stanley, barefoot and in a nightshirt, stood at the entry flap of the command tent, his hands on his hips.

"As you wish." Barttelot released Baruti's ear with every expectation that the boy would bolt again.

But Baruti stayed where he was, looking down at his toes. Jephson, Troup, Nelson, Parke, and Hoffman, also in various states of undress, their eyes sticky with sleep, had come out of their tents, Nelson with his revolver, having mistaken the commotion for an attack on the camp.

"*Njoo hapa, toto.*"

Baruti, still looking at his feet, scuffing them in the dirt as he walked, went over to Stanley. Stanley dropped to his knees in front of the boy, took his chin in his hand and raised his head. The boy kept his eyes downcast. Stanley said something to him, but the boy didn't reply. Stanley studied his painted face, turning it from side to side by the chin, then touched the yellow stripe that ran down the nose. The boy jerked his head back as if fearful the man would smear the paint. Stanley took his hand away and rested it on his knee and again spoke to the boy softly, questioningly. But again the boy did not reply. Troup took a few steps toward them, and Stanley looked up at him, raising his eyebrows.

"*Kuna nini*, Baruti?" Troup asked. "*Unaweza kuniambia?*"

Baruti said nothing, nor did he look at Troup; he continued staring at the ground, placing one small bare foot on top of the other. Stanley ruffled his woolly hair affectionately, then stood up and went back into the command tent. When he came out, he had Baruti's peaked cap and the short naval cadet's jacket with the brass buttons with him. He kneeled in front of the boy again and popped the cap on his head. The boy didn't move. Stanley fooled with the cap for a moment, adjusting it to a slightly rakish angle, then draped the jacket over the boy's shoulders. And then, quite all of a sudden, he pulled the boy into an embrace. At that, Baruti dropped his bow and arrows and flung his arms around Stanley's neck and buried his face against the man's chest. But it lasted only a moment. Stanley gently pushed the child away and picked up the bow and arrows and handed them to him.

"*Nenda sasa, toto,*" he said, getting to his feet. "*Nenda nyumba*, my little monkey."

Baruti, the peaked cap perched above the fearsomely painted face, the cadet's jacket hanging askew from one naked shoulder, looked up at Stanley hesitatingly. Then he raised his bow and arrows in a kind of salute. And then he spoke at last. "*Kwa heri*, Bula Matari," he said in a small sweet voice.

"*Kwa heri*, Baruti."

"*Nakupenda sana*, Bula Matari."

Stanley smiled ruefully. "Yes, my little monkey. I know. I love you too. But go now. And go quickly. Before you break my heart."

Baruti turned to Troup. "*Lazima nienda sasa*, Bwana Troup."

"*Fahamu*, Baruti. I understand."

"*Kwa heri*, Bwana Troup."

"*Kwa heri, toto.*"

Now Baruti turned to Jephson, and Jephson saw that his eyes had filled with tears. The boy said nothing. He probably could not see very clearly.

"*Kwa heri*, Baruti," Jephson said to him.

The little fellow nodded silently, the tears now streaming down his cheeks, and looked around at the others, at Barttelot, Nelson, Hoffman, Parke. Then he turned back to Stanley and again raised his bow and arrows. And then he ran out the stockade gate.

"Where is he going?" Barttelot asked.

"Home," Stanley replied, turning away. "He's going home, Major. He only came back to say goodbye."

The next morning at first light the advance column formed up at the stockade gate in single file. It consisted of 100 Sudanese, 210 Wanyamwezis, ten pack mules, and a riding donkey for each of the five white officers. There were no women or children in the caravan, and this had caused something of a furor, since it meant separating wives from husbands, sons from fathers, sisters from brothers; but Stanley had decided the journey would be too hard and dangerous for them until the trail was blazed and the forest tribes pacified. He, of course, would lead the way with Uledi as *kirangozi*, the foremost man, in charge of the scouts and trackers and a pioneer company of twenty Wanyamwezis wielding axes and billhooks and *pangas* to clear the path and blaze the trees.

Next in line was a front guard of thirty Winchester-armed askaris under Nelson's command, and then came Jephson with Sudi and the boat company. The backbone of the column was made up of the pack mules and 150 *pagazis,* divided into groups of ten, each under its own headman and captained overall by Hoffman. Their loads had been stripped to the bare essentials—ammunition, trading *mitako,* tools, medicines, a minimum of field equipment (only the command and surgery tents, no camp beds or mosquito netting or any other such luxuries for the officers), and such staple provisions as tea, coffee, brandy, mealie meal, rice, salt, sugar—in order to speed the pace of the march and in anticipation that whatever else might be needed could be traded for at villages along the way. Bringing up the rear and guarding the flanks were the remaining seventy askaris and the Maxim gun under Parke's command.

Based on a comparison of their known longitudes, Wadelai, Emin Pasha's headquarters on Lake Albert, at 30 degrees, 30 minutes east, lay roughly 380 statute miles east of Yambuya at 25 degrees, 3½ minutes. How much of this distance was enclosed in the Ituri no man could say for certain, for no man had ever traveled it; but Stanley was working on the premise that probably damn near all of it was. And since the only practical way through terrain of that sort was by the native paths that connected the villages of the forest one to the other, and since such paths were unlikely to travel in anything resembling a straight line, let alone directly to the east, one had to reckon that the actual distance they would cover could be as much as 450, possibly 500 miles.

"Six, eight, maybe ten miles on some days with luck," Stanley said. "I figure we should break out of the forest and reach Lake Albert by the second week of September." Ready to set off on the journey, he stood by his big black riding donkey at the head of the column, his officers gathered around him. "But you'll do better than that, Major. With our trail to follow, ten miles a day ought to be your minimum, and if you put your back into it, there's no reason the rear column can't make fourteen, fifteen miles a day."

Barttelot nodded. He had stopped shaving since arriving at Yambuya, and the week's growth, a shade darker than the sun-streaked blond hair of his head, made him look perceptibly older but no less handsome. Indeed, if anything, it seemed to emphasize the classical cut of his chiseled features, the astonishing brilliance of his blue eyes. He watched Stanley with a faint smile.

"I expect you to get away from here no later than the second week of August," Stanley went on. "The steamers will have fetched up Ward and Bonny and the rest by then. Tippoo-Tib will have brought in his porters. Even if it takes you seven weeks to get through, you should catch us up on the shores of Lake Albert by the end of September, and we can rejoin forces there for the last dash to Wadelai."

"If nothing further goes wrong."

"Nothing further will go wrong, Major."

"If the steamers don't break down or run aground again. If Tippoo-Tib makes good on his promise. We've had those sorts of troubles before, you know, Mr. Stanley."

"And we've overcome them, Major."

Barttelot inclined his head noncommittally, still smiling wryly.

"The steamers will get back here in time. You needn't worry about that. With their reduced loads, they'll have no trouble. They'll be back in six weeks, maybe less. As for Tippoo-Tib, Major, you heard him. You were there. It's in his interest to deliver those porters, to follow me into the forest. There are riches in the forest for him to hunt."

"I'll remind him of that. I'll go up to the Falls and remind him of that in a week or two, just in case."

"No, Major!"

"Sir?"

"Stay away from the Falls, Major. Stay away from that place. You just wait here for the porters. Tippoo-Tib'll deliver them here." Stanley turned to Troup. "Do you hear that, Jack? I don't want any of you going up to the Falls. I don't want anyone messing about in that sinkhole of temptation."

Troup nodded.

Stanley turned back to Barttelot. "You can count on Tippoo-Tib, Major. He ain't bloody likely to miss out on this chance of discovering the way into the forest and opening up a new hunting ground for himself. He'll deliver the porters all right. So just wait for them here. You'll only make trouble for yourself if you don't . . . Right, then. Clear your people away from the caravan. We're ready to march."

The men and women being left behind in Yambuya had gathered with their friends and relations in the advance column to exchange final farewells, and they separated from them now with shouts and cheers and a great show of tearful emotion.

"Good luck, Major. We'll see each other again in three months' time. Jack"—Stanley grabbed Troup's hand—"come after me fast. Come after me as fast as you can."

"I will, Bula Matari."

"Everything depends on that, Jack. It'll all come to nothing if the rear column doesn't get through in time."

"I know."

Stanley held Troup's hand a moment longer, then turned away abruptly and mounted his donkey. "Take command of the front guard, Captain Nelson. Will, Arthur, Dr. Parke, join your companies. We march. Uledi, *kirangozi, safiri.*"

Troup fell into step beside Jephson as the youth hurried back down the line of the column to his place at the head of the boat company.

"Jesus, but I wish you were coming with us, Jack," Jephson said.

"So do I." Troup turned away. Uledi and the trail-blazing pioneers were filing through the stockade gate. Stanley, a Winchester repeater in his saddle holster, his donkey moving at a slow walk, followed close on their heels. Troup turned to Jephson again. "But don't you worry, lad. It'll be all right. He'll get us through. He got us this far. He'll get us the rest of the way."

"Do you really believe that, Jack?"

"Yes. Goddamnit yes, I do. I know that man. Whatever else you can say about him, this much is certain. He always gets through."

Jephson looked to the head of the column and watched as Stanley rode out of the stockaded camp, erect in the saddle, one hand on the butt of his holstered Webley revolver, bandoliers crossed on his chest, his sun helmet tilted well forward, a calm, set, determined expression on his square, rough-hewn face. Striking off into the unknown, once again striking off into a wilderness where no white man had ever been before. He had made a lifetime out of such journeys. Why? What did he seek in all these mysterious regions? What did he hope to find on the other side of all these unpassable places? What did he dream would come to him at the end of all his endless wanderings? He disappeared into the forest, the thick tangled curtains of its foliage closing behind him. Now Nelson, also mounted, giving the cavalryman's signal for the advance, started his riflemen through the stockade gate. In a moment it would be the boat company's turn.

"Sudi."

The young Wanyamwezi came forward. Juma, the mule boy, followed a step behind leading Jephson's riding donkey.

"We go now, Sudi."

"Yes, sah."

Jephson took the donkey's reins from Juma and swung up into the saddle. "Jack, take care of yourself."

"You take care of yourself, Arthur."

Jephson reached down from the saddle and grasped Troup's hand. "Until Albert Nyanza, *rafiki*."

"Until Albert Nyanza."

Jephson straightened up in the saddle and wheeled the donkey toward the sunrise. "*Anza*, Sudi. *Anza, rafiki zangu. Safiri*."

The path into the Ituri from Yambuya, leading more or less eastward along the Aruwimi toward the next Basoko village on the river's left bank, tramped out by generations of tribesmen and scoured into a shallow gutter by the rains, was barely a yard wide. It wound between the forest's close-growing mammoth trees—oak, mahogany, ebony, red cedar, cotton, palm, teak, gum copal, rubber—some 100, some 200 feet tall, and was cast into an eerie perpetual aquamarine twilight by the tier upon tier of branches and leaves that intertwined overhead and roofed out the sun and sky. Setting off on it was like stepping down into the underworld. Rattan creepers, flowering lianas, coiled vines as menacing as snakes, and veils of gray-green orchilla weed as spooky as shrouds hung down on every side. Here and there the rotting pulpy trunks of recently fallen trees, slimy with moss and sprouting monstrous orchids, lay like breastwork barriers across the way; and everywhere thorny thickets of twenty-foot-high underbrush, the bush and bramble and bamboo and giant fern of secondary growth and the exposed tangled roots of mangroves encroached underfoot, snagging and clutching like animate beings.

Although Uledi's pioneers tirelessly slashed away at this nightmare riot of vegetation with their axes and billhooks and *pangas*, singing out with every cut, the *pagazis* still had constantly to duck and twist, climb and crawl in order to negotiate their loads through it. Streams and creeks crossed the path, and where they did the ground turned to sponge. There was a swamp that took two hours to cross, the men and mules floundering up to their necks in the stinking malarial ooze and emerging on all fours covered with leeches and beating off the attacks of fire ants. Lesser tracks intersected the main one from time to time, some man-made, forking off to villages in the south, others game trails littered with the spoor of rhino and elephant and bushbuck and warthog; but because of the racket the pioneers made clearing the way and the crashing of the caravan through the undergrowth behind them, no animals were seen. But there were birds and monkeys in the trees screaming at their passage and plagues of insects swarming up at every step—mosquitoes and flies and beetles and grubs and flying worms. In the huge silken webs spun everywhere through the foliage, innumerable black-and-white-spotted spiders fed on the brilliantly colored butterflies trapped in them.

The temperature rose steadily, relentlessly, from the reasonably pleasant mid-seventies of the dawn into the hundreds by noon, a stifling, cloying, steaming heat. Although it did not rain, it might just as well have, for the oppressively dank air dripped; moisture trickled down the boles and vines, and every leaf and petal seemed to weep, splattering the marchers with coin-sized drops of dew, soaking their clothes, mixing with their sweat, raising an acrid odor. It became hard to breathe. The singing and chattering and raucous bantering among the men petered out. Nature seemed to take on a vengeful aspect the deeper they penetrated the forbidding primeval gloom.

At four in the afternoon, more than ten hours but less than ten miles from Yambuya, the path they followed unexpectedly widened and became a surprisingly straight leaf-strewn avenue for a distance of about a hundred yards; and at the end of it stood a village that was very much like Yambuya, a collection of tall conical huts of overlaid palm fronds; and its warriors, just as at Yambuya, in war paint and feathers, had assembled in hostile array in front of it to block the caravan's approach. About a hundred of them, armed with spears and shields, formed a phalanx across the path; behind them, defending the village's western perimeter, were perhaps another two hundred with bows and arrows. They waited in the green sun-speckled shadows of the towering trees, unmoving, not making a sound.

Uledi halted the pioneers. Stanley dismounted.

"Will, get some of the *mitako* up here. A few yards of *merkani*."

The *pagazis* downed their loads and began bunching up the path to see what had caused the halt. Hoffman chased them back, then broke into one of the bales of trading cloth, extracted a length of blue cotton sheeting, and trotted up the line to Stanley with it.

"Captain Nelson, form your guard into a firing line."

"Yes, sir." Nelson snapped an order and the askaris mustered into two ranks across the path, those in front dropping to their knees, those behind standing with rifles raised, taking aim down the broad avenue over the heads of their mates. Nelson dismounted and unholstered his pistol.

"But hold your fire, Captain. I don't want to scare these buggers off if I can help it. We're going to have to make friends with them sooner or later, and we might as well start here. They've got goats and fowls we're going to need, and I want to try and get a few guides out of them besides."

"Yes, sir."

"And get word back to Surgeon Parke to send up some of his men just in case."

Nelson slapped the shoulder of one of his corporals, and the big black dashed back down the line toward the rear guard. As he passed, Jephson dismounted and, handing off his donkey to his muleteer, went up to the head of the column. He also unholstered his pistol.

"Send some scouts out, Uledi. Find out if there's another way into this village."

"*Haya.*" The Wanyamwezi chieftain consulted hurriedly with a group of his trackers, then one slipped off into the woods to the right of the path and another made for the river to the north.

"All right, Will. Let me have that."

Stanley took the blue cotton trading cloth from Hoffman and, unfurling it, holding it up for the Basoko to see, started down the widened avenue toward them. Hoffman, usually unarmed except for his hunting knife, grabbed Stanley's Winchester from the big black riding donkey's saddle and followed him. But they hadn't gone more than a few steps before Hoffman suddenly seized Stanley's arm and yanked him back.

"What?"

Hoffman dropped to a knee at Stanley's feet and brushed aside some of the leaves that were strewn on the path. A bamboo skewer protruded from the sodden earth directly in front of Stanley's boot. Hoffman pulled it out. It was about six inches long, sharpened to a vicious point and notched halfway down so that once it penetrated an unsuspecting foot it would break off and work its way into the wound.

"Son of a bitch. You'd better start wearing shoes, Will."

Hoffman went on brushing away leaves in an arc around himself, uncovering several more of the ugly skewers. "They're everywhere," he said. "They've spiked the whole goddamned road."

Stanley peered down the path; once you knew what to look for, the skewers, despite the camouflage of leaves, were not all that difficult to spot. "Uledi."

The Wanyamwezi nodded, and in a minute he had the pioneers spread across the path; and imitating Hoffman, they went down on their knees and began inching forward, clearing away the leaves and yanking out the spikes.

And seeing this, realizing their trap had been detected, the Basoko warriors, until then immobile and silent, suddenly sprang to life, bursting out in a chorus of angry shouts, those in the front rank rattling their spears against their shields, those behind brandishing their bows and arrows. Jephson's hand tightened around the butt of his pistol. Behind him he heard the rapid clicking of Winchester bolts being drawn.

"Steady, askaris," Stanley called over his shoulder. "Hold them steady, Captain. Go on, Uledi. Get those damn things out of here."

The pioneers resumed crawling forward, reaching in every direction for the skewers, but they glanced up repeatedly, warily appraising the Basoko's intentions. Stanley followed them, again holding up the length of blue trading cloth, showing it as a peace offering. Hoffman walked beside him, the Winchester tucked under his arm, the barrel pointed down. Jephson took a tentative step forward, not sure if he should go along, not particularly eager to do so. He looked back at the firing line of askaris for reassurance, at Nelson standing easy but alert, his revolver in his hand, his hand hanging at his side.

"*Sen-nen-nen-neh*."

Jephson spun around.

It was Hoffman, calling to the Basoko in their vernacular. They stopped their awful racketing at this. Uledi and the pioneers had cleared the path nearly halfway down to the village; and Stanley and Hoffman, now little more than fifty yards from the phalanx of spearmen, moved up in front of the kneeling Wanyamwezis, intending to open up a palaver.

And a spear was thrown.

It came arcing out of the trees, five feet long, ornamented with windings of brass wire and with a three-foot flanged iron head, sharp as a razor, flying swiftly and as quietly as a bird. With a lethal thump, it buried itself a good ten inches into the sodden soil of the path, vibrating with an audible hum, not two feet from where Stanley was standing. He jumped aside reflexively, dropping the blue trading cloth. Hoffman swung up the Winchester. The Wanyamwezis scrambled to their feet and started to run.

"*Simameni*," Stanley barked.

The Wanyamwezis froze, crouching, eyes wide, trembling. Stanley turned back to the Basoko. The spearmen were poised, shields held well forward, arms up over their heads, all of them ready to throw now; and those behind them had slipped arrows into their bows and drawn back tautly on the bowstrings, threatening but for the moment only threatening, holding themselves as taut as their bowstrings, ready but not yet willing to launch an attack, clearly counting on the quivering threat of their postures to turn the strangers away. Cool as ice, Stanley bent down, picked up the blue trading cloth, and checking his footing to avoid the bamboo skewers still in the path, started toward them again.

And another spear whizzed out from the warrior rank. It thudded into the earth directly in front of Stanley, much closer than the first, less than a foot away, beautifully aimed for maximum effect and the least harm. Stanley didn't flinch; he had expected it this time, but he stopped in his tracks.

"Stupid bloody buggers," he shouted. "They don't know what rifles can do. They've probably never seen any. I think we better show them. Captain Nelson." He shouted this while facing the Basoko, as if he were shouting at them, scolding them. "Fire over their heads, Captain. Two volleys, no more. That ought to be enough to educate them."

And it might have worked—the Winchester rounds shattering the branches high in the trees and sending flocks of weaverbirds scattering in screaming alarm. That might have impressed the Basoko sufficiently to make a palaver possible, but no one would ever know, because just then, just when Nelson gave the order for a second volley, Tom Parke came running up the line with thirty of his own askaris. He had heard the first fusillade; and now seeing the Basoko arrayed across the path, spears poised, shields held high, arrows drawn back, he yanked out his pistol and fired.

"No," Stanley screamed, whirling around.

Fired from the hip, on the run, Parke's shot was wild. Jephson saw it kick up a spurt of damp earth well short and wide of the Basoko phalanx. But the damage was done. The askaris from the rear guard, confused anyway as to what exactly was going on, took Parke's shot as an order to fire. They opened up. That panicked Nelson's Sudanese. And in a flash their Winchester repeaters were spitting bullets into the Basoko ranks, splintering their bushbuck-hide shields, ripping through their naked bodies, tearing up the leaves and brush and branches of the forest around them, turning the air blue with the smoking stink of gunpowder. Jephson flung himself to the ground.

"No. No. No." Stanley raced back, flailing his arms futilely, risking getting cut down in the crossfire.

For the Basoko had hurled their spears. Jephson saw one at the very moment it found its target. The iron spearhead smashed into the back of a fleeing Wanyamwezi, broke down through the muscled thickness of his torso as if through butter, and emerged from his groin in a hideous explosion of red and yellow gore. The man fell forward, pinned, and his crazed cries inflamed the other pioneers in their blind, hectic dash for cover. A black cloud burst overhead, a cloud of hundreds of arrows, each a foot long, feathered with palm leaves, needle sharp, beastly things whining like dreadful dragonflies, pattering through the foliage like hail, zinging into trees. An askari took one in the throat. He flung his arms apart, throwing his rifle away, then clutched at his neck as if to strangle himself, blood gurgling from his mouth, and toppled over backwards.

Jephson, on his belly, grappled with his pistol. He didn't care what Stanley was shouting. The situation was out of control. At any moment the bloody savages would charge. He was sure of it. He had to defend himself. He raised the pistol, held it out in the direction of the village, not really aiming, eyes half closed, flinching in anticipation of the weapon's kick, and squeezed the trigger. It didn't fire. The blasted thing was jammed. When he had flung himself down, he must have jammed mud into the barrel or cylinder. He banged the weapon on the ground, trying to unstick it, his breath coming in short, hot, harsh gasps, sweat streaming into his eyes. He was certain he was going to be killed. Spears and arrows were flying all around him, gunfire and blood-curdling screams rang in his ears. He raised the pistol and pulled the trigger again. The goddamn hammer wouldn't trip. He had to get out of there. He sprang to his feet.

And saw that the Basoko were running away. They couldn't stand against the rifles with their spears and arrows. The murderous fusillades were blowing them apart, cutting them to pieces, butchering them. Grotesquely mangled and bleeding corpses were sprawled everywhere, twisted in the brush, smashed against the trees, hanging half erect from branches. A score, two score. It was a massacre. The living were running for their lives.

And Hoffman was running after them. He had dropped the Winchester and with long lumbering strides chased them toward the village. Suddenly he fell. A bamboo skewer had pierced his bare foot. He rolled over with an animal grunt and scratched at it. Then he was up again. With an elephantine lunge he tackled one of the Basoko, crashing his meaty hulk on top of the brute, locking a huge arm around his throat. Stanley ran by him. Nelson, Parke, and now Jephson too, in a wild kind of elation, caught up in the madness, knowing he wasn't going to be killed, askaris on every side firing, stormed into the village.

The Basoko were gone.

"The river," Stanley shouted and dashed to the edge of the bluff overlooking the Aruwimi, a dozen askaris in his train.

Nothing was there. The beach beneath the bluff was empty; there was no sight or sign of the tribesmen's canoes. Stanley turned back to the village. Askaris were running down the streets kicking into the huts, charging through the surrounding fields of manioc and sugarcane, shooting into the forest. But there was nothing. Everyone had vanished; everything was gone—the canoes, the furniture and implements in the huts, the stores of food, the goats and fowls. The Basoko had cleared out with all their movable possessions.

"Goddamn you, Parke."

"Sir?" Parke spun around, his smoking pistol in his hand, his tunic torn open at the throat.

"You goddamn bloody fool."

"I don't understand. What have I done?"

Stanley went toward him, his face white with rage, the muscles in his jaw working furiously. "Who told you to fire? You goddamn bloody fool, who gave you the order to fire?"

"But I thought—"

"You thought? What did you think? Don't think. I don't want a bloody fool like you thinking."

"But I say, Captain Nelson had fired." Parke, flushing crimson, backed away from the maddened bull-like figure bearing down on him. "All the front guard was firing."

"I gave Captain Nelson the order to fire. I gave the front guard the order to fire. But I didn't give you any such order."

Nelson came over quickly. And it suddenly occurred to Jephson that Stanley, in a towering rage, intended to lay hands on Parke, do him some violence. But Nelson got between them. He didn't say anything or do anything, but the homely good sense of the man—his steadiness, his quiet professional composure, the simple direct way he looked at Stanley—had the effect of checking Stanley's fury, bringing him to his senses. Askaris were trooping back from their futile reconnaissance. Uledi and the pioneers were coming into the village. It would never do to have them see two white men go at each other. Stanley turned away from Parke and spat on the ground.

"We got one of them anyway, Bula Matari."

Stanley looked up.

Hoffman limped over, a hand gripping the back of the neck of the Basoko he had tackled, shoving him forward. He was an ugly brute, his body greased with palm oil and reeking with sweat. An animal bone pierced his nostrils, his ears were distended to twice their size by tufts of grass jammed into holes bored in their edges, his face was painted half red, half white, and a massive necklace of crocodile teeth hung down on his tattooed chest.

"Tie him up. We'll get to him later. Dr. Parke."

"Sir?"

"Have a look at those buggers out there." Stanley pointed to the score or more of mangled Basoko bodies sprawled along the village's western perimeter. "See if any of them are alive and can be patched up."

"But what about our own chaps, sir? We've taken some casualties too, you know. Don't you think I'd better have a look at them first?"

"Just do what I tell you, Doctor. Get over there and fix up any of those poor bastards that you can. We need guides. And Arthur, bring in the caravan; the loads, the wounded, the dead. Don't leave any of the dead outside. Get a move on. Uledi, the manioc, the sugarcane, whatever else is in these fields. Collect as much as we can carry. And Captain Nelson, I want a zareba built around this place. Use brush, branches, rocks, tree trunks. Make it sturdy and get it up before dark. And post a guard. There's a chance these buggers might take it into their heads to come at us during the night."

Night fell swiftly in the forest, the last of the sunlight suddenly winking out and an inky blackness rushing in. When it fell, the drumming began; and the sudden unnerving blasts of an elephant-tusk horn and vagrant hoots and howls and menacing shrieks could be heard all around in the impenetrable darkness of the jungle. The Basoko had returned. They now ringed the village, hiding in the trees; and from time to time throughout the night two voices sang out a repetitive, haunting refrain:

"This country has no welcome for you."

"No welcome for you."

"All men here are against you."

"Against you."

"And you surely will be slain."

"Will be slain."

Three of the column had been killed—one askari and two pioneers—and six injured, counting Hoffman. Parke cut out the broken bamboo skewer from his instep, doused the wound with carbolic, and bandaged it; and Hoffman hobbled off, not bothering to put boots on. Of the others, four had been slashed by spears or nicked by arrows but would be all right. For the fifth, though, Parke held out little hope; he was the askari Jephson had seen take an arrow through the throat. As for the Basoko, forty-eight had been left behind in the carnage at the village's western perimeter, of whom three were alive. Two, however, died before sunset. Parke worked on the third for several hours in the surgery tent, shooting him full of morphine and digging two bullets out of the poor bastard's guts. But he knew it was a vain exercise, at least as far as the savage's use to the caravan was concerned; for even if he survived, he wouldn't be able to travel. So Hoffman's captive was the only guide they would have.

Jephson watched Stanley and Hoffman question him in the flickering light of a campfire. They had him sitting on the ground behind the command tent, his wrists tied in his lap, his legs stretched out, the ankles bound together. Stanley sat on a tree stump in front of him. Hoffman squatted at his side, and as he translated the questions that Stanley put about the lay of the land, the location of villages, he also—casually, almost absentmindedly—stripped the savage of his warrior adornments. The necklace of crocodile teeth he toyed with for a bit as if admiring it, then broke it from the brute's neck with a sudden sharp downward yank. The animal bone through the Basoko's nostrils—Hoffman eased that out slowly, leaving a trickle of blood running into the black's mouth. Then one by one, causing little ugly spurts of blood with each, all the while translating Stanley's questions softly, insistently into the vernacular, Hoffman plucked the tufts of grass from the rims of the savage's ears. With each, the Basoko winced but said nothing, made no sound, his eyes downcast, staring at his hands in his lap, stony-faced, resigned to his fate. Only when Hoffman started on the war paint did the Basoko react, jerking up his bound hands to protect his face. Hoffman seized him by the throat to hold him still and with a big meaty paw wiped off the red and white paint and in this way, step by step, transformed the once ferocious warrior into nothing more than a cowering boy. Jephson turned away.

A brushwood zareba had been thrown up around the village with pickets posted every ten yards; Nelson patrolled along it, peering out into the inky darkness, trying to assess the sounds in the forest, the changing tempo of the drumming, the chances of an attack. The loads were stacked in the center of the village, also under the guard of askaris, with the pack animals and riding donkeys tethered nearby. Cooking fires were burning in front of several of the abandoned huts. The Wanyamwezis had buried their speared companions in the floor of one of the huts with a certain amount of ceremony, but the Sudanese had dumped their dead mate into the river. They believed the Basoko were cannibals and for some reason considered it preferable that the body be devoured by crocodiles than dug up and eaten by men. A group of them squatted in front of the surgery tent waiting to dispose of the askari with the arrow through his throat in the same way.

Jephson went over there. "Tommy."

Parke was seated on a medicine chest, his head in his hands. He looked up abruptly. In the flickering yellow light of the lantern his face appeared drawn and sickly.

"Are you all right, Tommy?"

"Yes. Are you?"

"A bit fagged out."

"Yes, me too." Parke stood up and came out of the tent. He was holding a flask of brandy. In the tent's shadows, the two wounded men, the askari and the Basoko lying side by side, moaned softly. A dreadful stench came from them. Parke took a swig of the brandy. "Do you want some of this?"

"I was just going to get something to eat."

"There's nothing to eat."

"What?"

"There's nothing to eat. And I'm to blame. Don't think I haven't been told. Don't think Mr. Stanley hasn't had at me about it. You can be bloody sure he has. According to him, we're all going to starve because I *panicked* and drove off the niggers before he had a chance to palaver with them."

"Oh, for Christ sake, Tommy. Don't talk rubbish. Nobody's going to starve. Mr. Stanley never said any such thing. There's no fresh meat, that's all. But we've plenty of plantains and manioc out of these fields. And we're carrying biltong and mealies. So come on. Let's get some of it. I'm famished." Jephson started toward the cooking fire of the boat company.

Parke didn't follow him.

Jephson turned back.

"Those niggers wouldn't have traded with us, Arthur. Any more than the niggers at Yambuya would. All these niggers want to do is kill us, Arthur. That's all. Just kill us. Listen."

The screeches, the chilling yelps and howls, the whistling, the strange yammering and moaning—it was impossible to tell which were the natural sounds of the nighttime jungle and which were those made by the savages hiding in the trees. Only the hollow nerve-beating drumming, rising and falling, advancing and retreating, pounding in the forest like the pounding of the surf of an unearthly ocean, only that was sure, only that and the haunting tireless refrain: "And you surely will be slain."

· TWO ·

FOR THE NEXT seven days—the Basoko captive showing the way, his wrists tied in front of him, leashed to Uledi by a length of rope around his neck and prodded along by the stock of the Wanyamwezi chieftain's Snider rifle—the column followed winding narrow trails from one village to another deeper and deeper into the muggy gloom of the jungle. The villages were spaced at irregular intervals, and the trails between them were of varying difficulty—some trodden as smooth and hard as asphalt, others descending into neck-deep bogs crawling with leeches; some breaking out into relatively open clearings of scrub and elephant grass, others badly overgrown with creepers and blocked by rocks and lightning-blasted trees or pocked with deadfalls and flooded by streams or riven with ravines and choked with rotting vegetation, hot and stinking, brush and bramble whipping at the men's faces as they scrambled down one side and up the other, sweating and cursing and dropping loads. As a result, on some days a village wasn't reached until long after the sun had set, while on others they'd pass through three or four before making camp for the night.

But in every case the villages were deserted.

Word of the slaughter at the first preceded the column, and the forest people cleared out in the face of its advance. They spiked the paths in and out of their villages before fleeing and carried off all the goods they could; and at night, when the column was encamped within a hastily built zareba and sentries had been posted and cooking fires were burning, they started up their infernal drumming and howling and trumpeting in the surrounding darkness. But they did not attack. They had learned the lesson of the rifles, so there were no fights, no more killing, and that was a relief. But there also was no chance to trade, so there was no fresh meat.

On the morning of the eighth day, not quite seventy miles

from Yambuya, the Basoko captive quit. They had spent the previous night in a village composed of only five of the conical palm-leaf huts, the smallest they had come upon so far. Nelson had gone down to the river before daybreak in hope of shooting game; but because the Aruwimi here was still wildly turbulent with rapids, no big animals came down to drink, and all he brought back was a clutch of guinea hens, some weaverbirds, and a small bushbuck. These were put aside for the evening meal; breakfast again was manioc pudding and fried plantains. Then the fires were kicked out, the two tents struck, the village's fields and gardens looted of their fruit and vegetables, and the men, grousing about the monotony of the diet, collected their kit and fell into line. Jephson took an inventory of his company's loads, then mounted his donkey and waited for Uledi and the Basoko to lead the column out of the village.

The Basoko refused to move. Uledi poked him with his rifle, but the brute wouldn't get up. He sat on the ground, his arms wrapped around his drawn-up legs, his head pressed against his knees. Uledi kicked him in the ribs, and the black gave out a groan but only huddled down further.

"What's going on here?" Stanley rode over on his mule, letting the big animal nudge up against the Basoko. "Get to your feet, boy. Don't play games with me."

Hoffman came up the line in a skipping, hopping sort of a run; the skewer wound hadn't healed yet and was giving him trouble.

"What the devil's ailing this bugger, Will?"

Hoffman limped over to the Basoko, and the Basoko threw up his tied hands in obvious terror of the hulking hairless man and began jabbering away in the vernacular. Hoffman grabbed the rope around his neck and jerked him to his feet, The column fell into disorder as men inched forward to see what was going on. Jephson and Nelson came over and listened, without comprehending, to the exchange between Hoffman and the agitated savage.

"Well?" Stanley asked after a bit.

"This is the end of the Basoko country, Bula Matari." Hoffman released the rope around the captive's neck, and the fellow immediately slumped to the ground again. "Beyond this village are the Babukwa, he says. And he won't go there. He says we can kill him but he won't go there."

"The Babukwa? Have you ever heard of them?"

Hoffman shook his head.

Stanley looked down at the Basoko. "Ask him where the next village is. How far it is."

"No use in that, Bula Matari. He don't know. He ain't never been there. He says he ain't never even been this far from his own village."

"You believe that?"

Hoffman nodded.

Stanley puffed out his cheeks and expelled his breath in a sigh of exasperation. Then he looked around abruptly. "What the hell's going on here? What do those men think they're doing? Captain Nelson, Mr. Jephson, get back to your companies. Get this column in march order." He turned to the Basoko again. "Let him go, Uledi."

Uledi signaled to one of the pioneers, and the Wanyamwezi came over with his *panga*. The Basoko, misunderstanding this, pulled away in wide-eyed panic, thinking he was to be killed. Uledi had to hold him so the pioneer could cut the thong that bound his wrists. Then the rope was removed from his neck.

"All right, boy. Bugger off. *Ondoka*."

The Basoko looked at Stanley, then at Uledi, then at the pioneer with the *panga*. Then he jumped to his feet and began to run. He got halfway down the column before he realized he wasn't going to be chased. He stopped then and, rubbing his wrists, pulled himself erect and walked off slowly, with dignity, into the forest.

The only trail that could be found exiting the village meandered southeastward and thus away from the Aruwimi, passing through a field of head-high sugarcane that was aswarm with ticks. Within minutes of entering it, every man in the caravan was infested with the filthy things; and even after they had cleared the field and were once again in the dismal gloom of the forest, they went on scratching and clawing at themselves, digging in their ears and mouths and the humid membranes of their nostrils where the vicious little mites burrowed and lodged.

It grew dark. In the closed-off vegetable cathedral of the forest, under its roof of intertwined foliage, there never was any way of knowing the actual nature of the day, the weather in the world outside; but now, within, there was a steady deepening of the gloom, a thickening of the gray-green watery twilight. A warm clammy breeze sprang up and sloughed through the branches and the leaves; the endless shrieking of the birds and monkeys in the trees ceased, and the marchers too fell silent. There was a distant peal of thunder. The trail pinched out in a quagmire clogged with duckweed.

Stanley dismounted and went down to the edge of the stinking bog. He took his rifle with him. Uledi came up beside him and they stood together staring across to the wall of trees on the other side. Something was there. Jephson was sure of it; he could feel it in his bones, in the hair prickling at the back of his neck, in the way Stanley and Uledi stood listening. Savages were there, invisible in the thickets, watching them. The Babukwa? Who were they? Neither Stanley nor Hoffman had ever heard of them.

"Captain, I think you had better give us some cover on this crossing."

"Yes, sir."

A word to Nelson was always enough and usually unnecessary. An experienced soldier, quietly sure of himself, uncomplicated to the point of simplicity, almost boyish in his dedication to his tasks, he was always thinking ahead, assessing the situation, anticipating what Stanley would want next. In this instance he had already divided the front guard into two squads and had deployed the first in a crescent-shaped skirmish line along the bog's near shore. Now, pistol held above his head, he led the remaining fifteen askaris into the swamp's muck. Uledi and the scouts followed, then Stanley and the pioneers.

Jephson set out to make the crossing on his donkey's back; but not halfway across, the damned beast mired, snout down in the stinking water, snorting and braying hysterically. He had to dismount, and immediately he went neck-deep into the disgusting scum. Behind him his boatmen were having the devil's own time of it, slipping and stumbling under their loads. Hanging on to the donkey's reins with one hand, he grabbed with the other for the vines and creepers that dangled from the trees over the swamp; and feeling for footholds in the ooze of the bottom, trying not to imagine what creatures might be creeping around down there, shaking his head madly to keep off the wasps and mosquitoes stirred up from the duckweed, he half swam, half pulled himself and his donkey across, crawling out through a tangle of weeds, dripping with slime.

The askaris were deployed in a skirmish line on this side as well, mirroring that of those on the other side, their rifles sweeping a wide arc of the forest to the north, east, and south. Stanley and Nelson stood at the apex waiting. Uledi and the scouts had gone ahead in search of the continuation of the trail. Lightning flickered from time to time, pale sheets of momentary illumination in the steadily deepening darkness, scattering the jungle's shadows, creating illusions.

Uledi and the scouts came back, and the column re-formed; but the track they followed now—bearing always more to the south, always farther away from the Aruwimi—was no longer man-made. It was a game trail, elephants probably; the trees along it were rubbed clean of bark where the huge animals had stopped to scratch their backs.

"Look!" That was Nelson.

And with startling suddenness, Stanley whipped up his Winchester from the saddle and let fly a shot from his mule's back.

Three savages were crouched on the trail a hundred yards ahead. Youngsters, boys—no, one was a girl—children. Stanley's shot, well in front of them, kicking up a spume of dirt, brought them scrambling to their feet in wild surprise.

"*Sita! Simamemi!*" Stanley fired again, this time to the north of the trail, high into the trees, cracking a branch, bringing down a shower of leaves.

The children looked in that direction in amazement, then bolted.

"Goddamn you. Stop, I say." Stanley's third shot, aimed now, the Winchester at his shoulder, winged one of the boys, spinning him full around, dropping him to his knees. "Grab him. Don't let him get away."

Uledi and the scouts were racing down the trail. The girl and the other boy stopped to look back at their fallen friend. The bullet had clipped him high on the right arm; he was clutching himself there, blood seeping through his fingers. The girl dashed back for him. Stanley kicked his mule and lunged forward, overtaking Uledi. But the girl got to the boy first, pulled him to his feet, and dragged him off the trail into the forest where the mule couldn't follow. Uledi and the scouts crashed after them, slashing out with their *pangas* at the dense undergrowth; but Stanley reined in abruptly and turned and barked a sharp warning to Nelson and Jephson, pointing at the trail, waving them off.

There, where the children had been, where the blood of the boy could be seen splashed on the grass, was an elephant trap, a wedge-shaped pit a good eight feet deep, spiked with bamboo skewers and covered with branches and brush. Apparently the three little savages had been checking if any game—elephant, rhino, bushbuck—had fallen into it overnight. But none had. And the children, possible guides, were also gone. Uledi and the scouts re-emerged from the trees badly scratched by brambles, their pantaloons and shirts torn, empty-handed.

Stanley muttered a curse and dismounted.

"There must be a village back in there somewhere," Nelson said, gesturing into the forest where the children had fled; he climbed down from his mount. "Those tykes probably ran for it."

"Not necessarily." Stanley shoved his Winchester back into its saddle holster. "They may have made off that way deliberately to lead us astray. But even if not, it's no use to us anyway. It's in the wrong direction." He looked around, narrowing his eyes. The lightning flashed more frequently now, the thunder rumbled closer, and the wind was picking up, fluttering the vines and the gray-green draperies of moss that hung from the trees. "No, Captain, I think we'd best make camp here before this storm breaks, and count on getting to a village tomorrow."

But they didn't. Nor did they the day after. The elephant track brought them to a chain of stagnant pools thick with water lilies and fern, frogs croaking in the slime, clouds of mosquitoes making the crossing a pesky hell. And on the other side the track wandered off to the south, losing itself in the undergrowth, then reappeared much diminished fanning out into a network of competing game trails that crisscrossed a marshy meadow. That was July 7; and it rained again that day, this time catching the column on the march, the darkness of night descending without warning, thunder and lightning suddenly cracking in deafening salvos and the wind swirling up with tempest force. For a few minutes, though, the rain itself beat on the forest's dense canopy overhead without wetting the marchers on the trail below; but then it broke through in a torrent, bringing down leaves and branches and vines with it, and turning the trail into a river.

It never became light again that day. The storm lasted for four hours; and when it stopped, it was night—dank, chilled, unrefreshed. Stanley had pressed on beyond the marshy meadow to make camp on somewhat higher ground; and it was well past midnight before the last of the column, slogging through the muck and mire, trying to follow the pioneers' blazes in the darkness, came in. Several of the loads, including a medicine chest, had been dropped or flung aside during the storm; and Hoffman took a detachment of *pagazis* back to fetch them. A half-dozen askaris of the rear guard failed to turn up. A corporal was sent out to find them, firing his rifle at intervals as he went, hoping by this to show them the way. The tents were pitched; a rude zareba of brush and brambles was built and heavily picketed, but there were no cooking fires that night. Not a stick of dry wood could be found. The men huddled down in disconsolate groups against the trees—wet, bedraggled, too tired to erect shelters for themselves—and munched on uncooked mealies in a cheerless silence.

The silence was everywhere. The natural sounds of the jungle night—nocturnal birds, the soft guttural growls of animals on the hunt, frogs croaking, the humming of insects in the grass—all had been stilled by the storm. And there were no drums either, no horn blasts, no menacing howls of savages in the darkness. The silence was complete, the forest all around seemingly devoid of life. Jephson stood at the flap of the surgery tent listening. Parke was inside. They had shared a tin of sardines, some biscuits, and cold Liebig's beef tea from the special European provisions; and now Parke was curled up in his damp bedroll with a flask of brandy, drinking himself to sleep. A lantern burned in the command tent a few yards away, the only light showing in the inky darkness. Stanley was in there with Nelson, but if they were talking, no sound of it could be heard. And where Hoffman was, the youth hadn't the slightest idea. He shivered suddenly. It was as if momentarily he were alone, cut off by the silence and darkness . . . where? Did they know where they were? They had been following whatever trails they could find. Did they know where these had led them?

A clammy mist shrouded the camp the next morning. Fingers of blue vapor curled wraithlike through the matted mass of luxuriant growth; and the men, gathering their kit, loading the pack mules, striking the tents, forming up by companies, moved about in it like ghosts. Their voices were strangely muted, as were their complaints and rude jokes, the jingling of their gear, the orders of the headmen and officers, the unhappy braying of the donkeys, all echoing flatly, disembodied in the dully glistening wet. If the sun had risen that morning, there was no seeing it down here on the forest floor; its drying rays did not penetrate to this sodden vegetable underworld.

They backtracked to the marshy meadow, now ankle-deep in water, where they had left the elephant track the night before; but none of the game trails that crisscrossed it proved of any use. Uledi, the scouts, and Stanley himself followed down the most promising of them; but they all either pinched out in the undergrowth after a few hundred yards or headed south or west, away from Lake Albert. Stanley returned to the meadow, where the column was taking a midmorning break—some enterprising fellows had managed to get a fire started; and Jephson, Nelson, and Parke stood around it drying their clothes—and rode along the wall of the forest, scanning it through his field glasses. Then he dismounted and handed off his mule to one of the pioneers. Uledi and the scouts gathered around him; Hoffman joined them. Jephson, Nelson, and Parke, thinking a consultation was in progress about how best to proceed, hurried over. But before they reached him, Stanley turned away and, on foot, struck off to the east straight into the trees where there was no trail.

And now day after day, they marched eastward by compass bearing through a trackless wilderness. Occasionally there were open stretches, a grassy clearing, a natural avenue between the mammoth trees, a thinning of the bush where lightning had ignited a fire or young growth had choked itself to death by its very profusion. But mainly it was a matter of the pioneers hacking out virtually every step of the way, the column bunching up behind them, waiting in suffocating heat or pouring rain while they did this work, then lurching forward again, pulling along the miserable pack animals, eyes fixed on the ground watching for rough footing, with creepers and twigs slashing at their faces, snagging their loads, ripping their clothes, and the company behind quickly losing sight of the one ahead in the dense bush, picking out the way by the blazes on the trees—only to come bunching up to a stumbling halt again a few minutes later while the pioneers cut and chopped and tunneled a new path through the strangling gloom. It was brutal going and excruciatingly slow. Three or four hundred yards in an hour was considered good progress, half a mile a veritable dash.

There was another problem. It was now well over a week, nearly two, since they had left the last village and had last stocked up on the plantains, beans, and manioc from that village's fields; and these were running low. The trackers, ranging in every direction well in advance of the column, turned up no sign of any more villages or any place where fresh food supplies could be had. Apparently they had wandered into an utterly unpopulated region of the forest; and since there was no telling when they would get out of it, Stanley put the caravan on half rations. It wasn't too bad. Doubtless it was sufficient technically—a pound of mealies, a pound of rice, and three biscuits per day per man plus a quarter of a cup of salt for every ten. But what with the lack of fresh meat and the punishing labor of the trek, it left everyone with the vaguely annoying feeling of always being hungry; and during the breaks and interminable waits while the path was being cleared, men drifted off into the jungle to forage and hunt, and the constant petulant, irritating effort of rounding them up again further slowed the column's progress.

They came to a broad stream flowing north over a white sandy bed. This was one afternoon in the second week of the trackless march; and although much earlier than usual, Stanley called a halt for the day there so that he could use the remaining hours of daylight to explore where this stream ran. He took Uledi, the scouts, and ten askaris with him, leaving Nelson to fall out and encamp the column as it straggled in.

The Sudanese looked awful. The Wanyamwezis were scratched and tattered, aching in every bone and as tired as hell; and they flung down their loads and went about tethering the mules and erecting shelters and starting cooking fires with much restive, unhappy muttering. But there was life in them yet, a resilient strength, and in no time they recovered their easygoing spirits and were splashing in the stream, washing themselves and their clothes, catching lizards and frogs, fishing. The Sudanese, on the other hand, looked beaten. Unlike the Wanyamwezis, they were not used to this climate. They came from a dry open desert land; and when they had been recruited, before the switch to the Congo route, they had expected to travel to Wadelai across the high savanna plateau from the Indian Ocean coast. The cloying, enervating humidity of the jungle and its relentless malarial gloom were steadily taking a toll on them. Their once glossy ebony complexions had gone a sickly gray, and they went about their chores listlessly, gazing dully like churlish dogs out of yellow bloodshot eyes. Several had fever. Two were missing.

The Europeans didn't look much better. With the exception of Hoffman of course—and in this he stood out as something inhuman—they all had several days' growth of grimy stubble and, Hoffman included, rents and tears in their trousers and tunics, cuts and abrasions on their faces and hands, and myriad pink welts and blood-encrusted bites from lice and ticks and mosquitoes all over their bodies. And they stank appallingly.

In addition, Hoffman had the trouble with his foot; the skewer wound had ulcerated. A number of the Wanyamwezis also suffered from this condition. Although some, like Hoffman, had stabbed themselves accidentally on the bamboo skewers sown in the paths of the villages, actually any nick or scrape to bare feet tramping the moist, rotten jungle floor quickly became infected and started festering, the tissue disintegrating with alarming rapidity, putrefaction eating down to the bone. These were hideous-looking afflictions. Parke did his best to treat them, but he had never seen anything like them before and really didn't know what to do. His hands shook as he poured carbolic acid into the ugly yellow-green sores and swabbed out the pockets of pus. He too had a touch of fever.

Jephson went down to the stream. From a little way off, it promised refreshment, but in fact it was heavy with mud, tepid in temperature, and swarming with water bugs. Nevertheless, he stripped and went in and gave himself a good wash, examining himself while he did so. He was perfectly two-toned—his face and neck and forearms burned bronze, his chest and legs milky white—and hard as a board. There wasn't an ounce of excess flesh on him; whatever bulk he had had, had been hammered into muscle and sinew by the rough traveling. He waded out of the stream, pulled on his trousers, and sat down on the sandy embankment to inspect his boots. They were taking a terrific beating now that he was no longer riding the donkey, cracking along the edges from the repeated soakings and drying out, the soles working loose. It wouldn't be long before they fell apart. He'd be all right though; he had two more pair and he was glad as hell for it. Having seen the ulcers on Hoffman's and the Wanyamwezis' feet, he'd certainly hate to have to go barefoot. He pulled the boots on and went over to the boat company's encampment, meaning to get one of his boys to put up a kettle so he could shave.

But then there was a rifle shot.

Sudi, sitting on a log by the boat company's cooking fire, mending a shirt, stood up quickly and looked north. The shot had come from downstream, where Stanley had gone. Jephson's first thought was that Stanley had spotted game, was hunting. But then, all of a sudden the rattling crack of a fusillade erupted, several rifles firing at once in rapid succession. Nelson shouted and began to run. A bunch of askaris ran after him. The Wanyamwezis came scrambling out of the stream clutching for their clothes. Sudi snatched up his Snider rifle. Jephson looked around wildly. He was unarmed. He had left his pistol in the surgery tent. He glanced back there, debating whether there was time to get it. Then he caught sight of a boatman's *panga*, grabbed it, and went racing after Sudi and Nelson and the askaris, down the stream's sandy bank, stumbling over tangles of exposed mangrove roots, holding up the *panga* to ward of overhanging branches.

And there was the Aruwimi.

They had come back to the river; Stanley had led them back. Or, more likely, in its serpentine course through the forest the river had come back to them, far larger here than it had been at Yambuya, now in flood from the rains, rushing swiftly between high wooded banks and wholly free of rapids. Dugout canoes were making their way down it. And Stanley and the askaris were firing on them.

Three were directly abreast of the bank where Stanley and the Sudanese, on their knees, were banging away with their Winchesters. Downstream, where the river made a sharp bend to the south, two others were just disappearing from view when Jephson rushed up, and there were three more upstream. The kaffirs in them were standing and paddling into the current, trying for all they were worth to keep the river from sweeping them back into the murderous fusillade. And there was a ninth, caught on a snag of dead trees and rocks in midriver, in which a woman with a baby in a sling on her back was screaming hysterically while a man leaning over the prow desperately tried to free the craft with his paddle. These weren't war canoes. None of their occupants were shooting back; none had anything to shoot back with. Each carried only two or three people, as many of them women and children as men, along with goats, chickens, raffia baskets, earthenware jars, bundles of manioc, strings of fish—evidently on their way to or from a market. Uledi and the scouts had scrambled down the high bank to the river's edge and were swimming out into the stream to get at them.

Two of them made for the snagged canoe. The woman in it screamed a warning, and the man spun around and began flailing madly at the Wanyamwezis with his paddle. They backed off and swam around to the other side of the craft, getting some footing on the rocks and tree trunks of the snag. The man dashed to that side, swinging the paddle. And then with a convulsive jerk he fell back; half his face was blown away. The woman with the baby on her back jumped over the side. She went under; a moment later she surfaced, rolling in the flood like a porpoise, the baby on her back waving its little arms. Then they went under again and didn't come up. There was someone else in the canoe, an old man crouched on the bottom, and now he also tried to get out. But the two scouts hauled themselves up over the gunwales, very nearly capsizing the craft in the process, and one flung himself at the old man before he could escape while the other wrenched the paddle from the dead kaffir's hands and pushed off from the snag.

Another canoe, sucked into an eddy and twisting bow around stern, no one paddling her, slammed into them broadside. Three children were standing along the gunwale screaming and crying; two adults were sprawled on the bottom, unmoving. The scout with the paddle lunged for it just as Uledi and two other scouts swam up and grabbed its prow. They started to scramble in. The children jumped out. Uledi immediately dropped back into the water and went after them, catching hold of one by the hair, stroking hard with his other arm to keep from being swept downstream. He went under. When he came up spluttering, looking around, the child was gone. The scouts were paddling the two canoes to shore.

Those were all they captured, those two canoes. The other seven escaped, upstream and down. Stanley ordered the askaris to stop firing and climbed down the bluff of the embankment to where Uledi and the scouts were beaching the dugouts. Nelson went after him, leaving the askaris in the charge of a corporal. The Sudanese who had raced up to the river with Nelson had not participated in the shooting. Nelson hadn't permitted them to; in his opinion, the ten with Stanley had provided far more than enough firepower against the handful of unarmed kaffirs, and he had angrily waved off his men when they had started to raise their rifles. Now, as the corporal formed the two groups into a single rank, those who had been with Stanley boasted to Nelson's men of their marksmanship while the latter grumbled about having been kept out of the fun. Jephson moved away from them, staring out to the river. It had been a duck shoot; those poor bastards had been picked off like ducks on a pond. There was no sign of any of their canoes, but here and there in the river's reach the youth could still see their bodies bobbing in the stream. Mr. Stanley must have tried to palaver with them; he must have hailed them and tried to get them to put into shore and trade. Of course he must have, but those stupid bloody bastards . . . Jephson looked down at the beach beneath the bluff.

The dead from the captured canoes—the man with his head half blown away from the first, a man and a woman from the second—had been laid out side by side facedown in the mud; and the one living, the old man from the first, wrapped in a piece of bark cloth and shivering, squatted by them keening his heart out while the Wanyamwezis sorted through the goods from the craft. Three live goats, a dozen trussed chickens, four smoked monkeys, a mess of carplike fish on a line, several jars of palm oil, palm-leaf-wrapped cassava cakes, baskets of crocodile eggs, ears of maize, bunches of bananas. It was a welcome haul, a needed haul. It would renew the column's morale, shore up its strength. Maybe it was reason enough for the killings.

"Arthur, get the steel boat up here."

"Sir?" Jephson moved closer to the bluff's edge.

The Wanyamwezis had overturned the two canoes, and Stanley was on his knees inspecting their bottoms. Nelson clambered up the bluff.

"What did he say, Robbie?"

"He wants you to bring the *Lady Dorothy* up. He's going to scout the river, see how far up it's clear of rapids, where there's a village, if we can get more canoes. Get a move on."

There was less than two hours of daylight left by the time the *Lady Dorothy* was assembled and launched, Sudi at the tiller, Stanley, Nelson, and Jephson in the prow, ten Wanyamwezis at the oars, and the entire front guard of thirty Sudanese askaris squeezed together on the thwarts, their Winchesters between their knees. Hoffman and Parke watched from the muddy strip of beach as they pulled away, the rest of the caravan in march order on the bluff above.

It was a relief to be on the river, to be out of the suffocating closeness of the forest, to have the sky overhead once again and an uncluttered vista opening away before the eyes. The Aruwimi here flowed almost directly out of the east, out of the slowly gathering evening, in a long sweeping silvery blue reach of perhaps three miles, unbroken by rapids, in some places as much as five hundred yards wide, the embankments ten and fifteen feet high, a few wooded islands in the stream. They moved up it cautiously, staying close to the southern bank. The oarlocks had been wrapped with strips of cloth and emitted only muffled squeaks and groans as the boatmen pulled, Sudi chanting the beat of the stroke in a low voice, the oars feathered on every stroke, splashing gently. Clouds of gnats and mosquitoes hummed along the water's surface, and now and again there was the sound of an askari swatting at one, cursing. Then it was quiet again, all eyes on the lookout, darting from shore to shore.

They rounded the head of the reach.

"Sudi."

"I see it, Bula Matari."

"*Nyuma*."

"*Ndiyo*, Bwana." Sudi, leaning hard against the tiller, ordered the oarsmen to quit pulling; and the steel boat, drifting back on the current, angled toward the bank, slipping under the leaves and lianas overhanging a swampy backwater.

At the start of the river's next reach, on a rocky bluff jutting into the water from the southern bank, was a village. It was the first they had seen in weeks and was unlike those lower down the Aruwimi. Instead of the tall conical palm-leaf huts, the dwellings here, perhaps a dozen, built at regular intervals on both sides of a broad street that paralleled the river, were haystack shaped and of wattle and mud.

"*Nenda*, Sudi," Stanley said. "But slowly, *rafiki*, slowly."

Sudi nodded. "*Moja. Mbili.*"

The oarsmen leaned well forward and pulled once, feathered, then pulled again; and the boat glided forward close along the bank, ferns and reeds hissing against her side, the leaves of overhanging branches brushing the passengers' faces.

There was a tremendous bustle in the village. Fires were burning along the riverside, and people were rushing back and forth from the huts carrying bundles and baskets of every kind down to a dozen or so dugout canoes and fishing pirogues beached there. It was clear what was happening. The two canoes that had escaped upriver from the askaris' rifles had brought word of the column's approach, and the people were abandoning the village, fleeing with all their belongings. Three of the canoes, already loaded, were pushing out into the stream, making for the opposite shore in the apparent belief that the danger would come only from this side. Four much larger canoes, war canoes—one with a high curved prow about 60 feet long—had also put out on the water, but their paddlers held these close to the bank. Twenty or thirty warriors stood in each. They were short, stocky brutes, perfectly naked except for weird tall hats of basket weave from which monkey tails hung down. Armed with bows and arrows, they were keeping watch over the proceedings on the shore, the firelight gleaming on their camwood-painted flesh.

"*Simameni!*"

Again the Wanyamwezis shipped their oars.

Stanley grabbed hold of a low-hanging branch and pulled the boat snug against the marshy embankment. "All right, Captain."

Nelson nodded and went quickly down the length of the boat selecting askaris, tapping their shoulders. One by one, they went over the side, first knee-deep into the river, then up the slippery slope of the embankment. Twenty of them, they formed up in double file, leaving their ten mates behind in the boat. Then Nelson slipped over the side himself.

"Robbie, listen to me." Stanley took hold of Nelson's shoulders. "We need those canoes. We need anything we can lay our hands on in that village, but the canoes, Robbie, that's the main thing. As long as this river stays clear of rapids and keeps flowing out of the east, it's a better trail for us than any we can hope to find in the forest. We can make time on it. There'll be villages along it. It'll save us a hell of a lot of wear and tear. But it's no use to us without those canoes. You understand that."

"Yes sir, but—"

"What?"

"Well, sir." Nelson, the swampy backwater lapping at his knees, averted his eyes, clearly uncomfortable in what he wanted to say.

"What is it? Go on."

"Well, I was thinking, sir, couldn't we try to palaver with them first? I mean, I could go on in there and see if I can't make friends with them and—"

"No." Stanley's reply was quick, harsh. "There's no point in that. We'd waste precious time and it'd come to nothing anyway. These kaffirs don't want to palaver. We've seen that. And besides, they'd never palaver for their canoes. They need them as much as we do."

Nelson said nothing.

"Right then. I'll wait until I hear your rifles. Then I'll come at them from the riverside."

The twenty askaris slipped off into the forest, Nelson leading them in a wide arc through the trees that would bring them to the village on the upriver end where they'd be least expected. Jephson watched them until the last man—a corporal, hunched down to get under a tangle of vines and branches—vanished into the blue shadows of the falling dusk. Then he looked at Stanley. The man was as filthy and tattered as the rest of them, his hair hanging down greasy and matted from under his pith helmet over the frayed collar of his tunic, which was plastered to his back by sweat. He had placed his Winchester stock down on the decking of the boat's prow and gripped its barrel with both his big gnarled hands, leaning on it lightly and staring with narrowed eyes through the overhanging foliage of the bank in which the steel boat was effectively concealed from the village. He seemed icy calm, but his thin lips under his scraggly mustache were moving, as if he were counting to himself.

Two more of the fishing pirogues had put out from the village, each carrying four or five people plus a mound of baskets and bundles. They made for the opposite shore, where a fire had been started and the first three canoes were drawn up. But at least ten others still remained on this bank besides the four big war canoes. The biggest of these, the sixty-footer, had drifted downstream a bit toward the *Lady Dorothy*. An elder of the warriors in it, a man with snow-white hair under his monkey-tail headdress, probably the chief or headman, had stepped out onto the beach to hurry a group of women struggling to load some goats into a canoe. But for all the rush and bustle, there was an orderliness about the evacuation, no sense of panic among the villagers. Obviously they believed the column wasn't likely to be on the march in the evening hours; and besides, scouts and war parties doubtless had been sent to sound the alarm in case it was. They had no way of knowing about the steel boat or that the main body of the column had been ordered to come up only after it heard the shooting start.

Stanley pulled out his pocket chronometer. Jephson reflexively did the same. It was just coming on to six o'clock.

"Get into the stern, Arthur. I want all the askaris up here."

As Jephson moved aft on the boat, the ten Sudanese went to the front and clustered on both sides of the prow behind Stanley. They were tense and excited in an eager animal way, drawing their lips back, showing their filed teeth.

"One stroke, Sudi," Stanley whispered.

The steel boat eased forward, nosing her prow, bristling with the Winchesters, out through the foliage.

"Now hold." Stanley again grabbed an overhanging branch to steady the boat against the current.

Jephson, standing next to Sudi at the tiller, unholstered his pistol and spun the cylinder. He didn't want the bloody thing jamming again. He cocked the hammer and, gripping the weapon at his side, peered over the askaris' shoulders toward the village. The white-haired warrior had got the women and their goats safely off in the canoe and was walking up the beach, hurrying others along.

And then the shooting started.

Incredibly, for an instant the scene remained unchanged. There was the rattling crack of the rifles shattering the silence like a sudden shower of hail, but it was as if the villagers didn't hear it. They kept on with their chores; the white-haired chief continued on his way up the beach. But then Nelson and the askaris exploded into view, rushing out of the trees, storming down the street between the huts, firing to the left and right as they came, as much in the air as at anyone in particular, creating a frightening racket; and at last the village erupted in a pandemonium of yells and screams, and people began running wildly in every direction, flinging aside bundles, scrambling into the huts, clambering down the bluff, jumping into the river. A hut unaccountably burst into flames. Then another, lighting up the twilight. Jephson saw the white-haired chief dash back to his canoe. The warriors in the others leaped for the shore and, slipping and sliding in the mud, let loose a ragged barrage of arrows.

"Now, Sudi. *Vuta. Vuta. Vuta.*"

Sudi picked up Stanley's chant, roaring it at the top of his lungs, and the oarsmen bent their backs to it. The steel boat came flashing out of the foliage, bucking against the current, racing for the village.

Stanley planted his left foot on the prow's decking, braced his left elbow on that knee, his left hand gripping far down the Winchester's barrel, its stock at his right shoulder, his cheek pressed against it, a grim smile pulling at the corners of his mouth. He squeezed off a round, and the ten askaris, straining over the prow with much the same mirthless grin on their lips, followed suit. This first fusillade cut down three of the warriors on the beach. The others spun around, a pitiful expression of disbelief on their faces at this unexpected development.

"*Tena,*" Stanley barked. "Again, askaris. Again."

Two more warriors dropped as the beach and water all around them exploded with shot.

"Stand off now, Sudi. Stand off."

Sudi threw his full weight against the tiller, and the boat came swinging around broadside, not a hundred feet from the shore. The askaris scrambled for positions along the starboard gunwale and loosed off another volley. Jephson didn't fire. He couldn't bring himself to. It was point blank-range, slaughter. Another half-dozen warriors went down, falling face forward into the river. But they didn't break and run. All around them women and children were scrambling for dear life, trying to push off in canoes, capsizing, spilling bundles and goats and babies into the fast-running stream. Another hut went up in flames. But the warriors held. The white-haired chief raced up and down the beach, holding them, forming them into a phalanx. He pointed up to the village.

Nelson and several of the askaris had reached the edge of the bluff and were immediately met by a swarm of arrows. One of them pitched forward and came tumbling down, head over heels, breaking his neck. The bowmen restrung with astonishing speed and another cloud of the vicious missiles whined up the bluff. Nelson dropped. Jephson gasped. But Nelson had only dropped to his knees firing his pistol with both hands, his face glowing like a demon in the firelight. His askaris, charging to the bluff's edge, lined out on either side of him, kneeling, falling prone, firing. Front and rear, from the forest, from the river, the phalanx of bowmen was being cut to pieces. But it held; with lunatic courage it held, defending the village.

And then an amazing thing happened. The white-haired chief jumped into the big war canoe; fifteen or twenty of his warriors jumped in after him. Five others grabbed the stern, throwing their shoulders against it, and pushed off; and the canoe came flying out into the river straight for the *Lady Dorothy*, straight into the spitting lead of the Winchesters.

Jephson fired then.

The paddlers stood ten to a side digging into the river with maniacal determination, howling the beat of the stroke. The white-haired chief climbed up on the high curved prow, and his warriors crowded around him, their bows drawn, howling to wake the dead.

"*Tena*, askaris," Stanley shouted into the din. "*Tena*."

Two of the paddlers, one on each side, suddenly jerked up their heads like marionettes on a string and plummeted into the river. Two of the warriors next to the chief fell back into the arms of their mates. But the canoe kept coming. And then the arrows were fired, thick as a swarm of hornets.

The aft-most Wanyamwezi oarsman on the starboard side abruptly turned around and looked at Jephson and Sudi in the stern as if expecting an order from them. An arrow was sticking out of his left eye; the eye was running out down his cheek.

Jephson dropped to his knees, braced his pistol with both hands on the boat's steel bulwark, and emptied its chambers. All the shots were low, splintering into the canoe's side, kicking up the river. The askaris, thank God, were doing better. Four or five more bowmen went down; three paddlers that Jephson could see were crumpled over the canoe's gunwale. But the canoe came on, kept coming on, closing fast. The white-haired chief was waving his bow above his head, exhorting his warriors; and clouds of arrows erupted like smoke, pinging off the *Lady Dorothy*'s side, banging about her innards, biting into flesh. As askari slumped forward clutching his belly and slid slowly into the water. The boatmen jerked their oars from the locks and raised them to use as weapons.

The fusillade from the Winchesters became ragged as askaris fell back to reload. Then the white-haired chief was hit. He was hit several times. Jephson saw the spouts of blood explode from his naked chest. But he remained standing, his arm still in the air, still shouting. Then his basket-weave headdress and the top of his skull were blasted away in a plume of gore. As he toppled over the side, a younger man leaped to his place on the prow, taking up his blood-curdling cry. Jephson fumbled at his cartridge pouch, desperate to reload.

The canoe rammed the *Lady Dorothy*.

Jephson looked up. He had just that much time to look up and see the howling savages leaping from their canoe, boarding the *Lady Dorothy*, throwing themselves at the askaris and oarsmen, using fistfuls of arrows as stabbing knives.

Then he was in the river.

· THREE ·

Someone was talking. From off in the distance came the occasional crack of rifle fire. There was the smell of smoke. For some time Jephson had been vaguely aware of these, but now he heard a bird singing. He opened his eyes. He was naked, covered by a wool blanket, lying on a bed of palm leaves in a small dark hut. The misty gray light of the dawn showed in the hut's circular doorway. Tom Parke was outside talking in an urgent whisper to Nelson. In raising his head to hear what they were saying, Jephson became conscious of a dull, throbbing pain all down his left side. He let his head drop back while he considered this. Then he turned aside the blanket. It was too dark in the hut for him to see anything; but gingerly exploring his thigh and hip and ribs and chest with his fingers, he felt the rough, scabbed abrasions, now sticky with a film of ointment, where the river had battered him against the rocks. He remembered the current sucking him under, swirling him around, dashing him against the rocks, but not how he had gotten into the river in the first place. Had the *Lady Dorothy* capsized when the savages boarded her? Men were splashing wildly on every side, shouting, striking out. He had come up once choking, grappling for the boat; but she wasn't there, and then the river had swept him away.

"Shut up!" Nelson's tone was fierce. "Just shut up, for God's sake. I don't want to hear any more about it."

Parke stopped talking. Three rifles, far away, fired one after another. Nearer, in the trees by the hut, several birds were warbling sweetly, welcoming the morning.

"You've got to get a grip on yourself, Tommy," Nelson said after a few minutes in his more usual, gentle voice. "You've got to pull yourself together, old boy. We've an awfully long way to go still."

"I'm not going. I tell you, Robbie, I'm not going a step farther with that lunatic. I'm going back."

"You're not going back. Stop talking nonsense. He's not going to let you go back. And you can't go back on your own."

"You come back with me. We can get the askaris to come back with us. They'd leap at the chance. You hear how they're talking. They see he's just going to get us all killed. Let him go on alone if he wants. He won't get far. He'll have to turn back too."

"He'll never turn back. Don't be a damn fool. That man'll never turn back."

Nelson walked away. Jephson couldn't tell whether Parke went with him, but it was quiet again except for the birds and the intermittent firing of rifles. Jephson sat up cautiously, wincing from the pain of his bruises, wondering if he had broken anything. He felt around on the dank dirt floor of the hut for his clothes. They weren't there, so he wrapped himself in the blanket and ducked out through the hut's low doorway into the ghostly mist of the morning.

The village was a smouldering ruin; it was the village they had attacked the night before, and the fight to take it must have been long and brutal for it to have been so thoroughly leveled. Most of the huts were burned to the ground, the smoke still hanging like a pall over them, mixing with the lingering stench of gunpowder. Along the street between the huts, among the litter and wreckage of the battle and the looting that had followed it—smashed pots and gourds and stools and drums—fifty or sixty bodies were laid out like cords of wood. These were mostly women and children and warriors of the village, but there were also some Sudanese and Wanyamwezis among them, and the sweet, sickly stench from them mixed with the smoke and the cloying dampness of the mist. The living—*pagazis* and askaris making ready for the new day's trek, Nelson shouting orders to them, the pack mules fidgeting under their loads—stirred up hordes of flies wherever they moved. Once they moved on, the flies resettled in black crawling carpets on the faces of the dead. Parke stood in their midst, his hands in his pockets, staring down at them vacantly.

"Tommy."

Parke looked up. His eyes were bloodshot as if from a lack of sleep or too much to drink.

"Do you know where my clothes are, Tommy?"

"Arthur. Had a sound sleep, did you? I should think you did. That was a nasty crack you took to your head."

Instinctively Jephson raised his hand and discovered a thick bandage behind his left ear.

"Five stitches," Parke said, coming over, speaking with an odd shrill cheerfulness. He *had* been drinking. "What you've got to do now is try and keep the damn thing clean. Wouldn't do to let it get infected, although God only knows how you'll keep it clean in this muck."

"Who fished me out?"

Parke shrugged. "Mr. Stanley? Sudi? I don't know. You were already on the beach when we got here, bleeding like a stuck pig. I thought you were dead." His voice suddenly went flat. "I thought we all were dead, Arthur, the way those niggers were fighting." He gestured toward the river. "The way they're still fighting."

Three of the big war canoes were on the river a quarter-mile or so up the reach, fifteen, twenty warriors in each; and beneath the bluff of the embankment on the muddy strip of beach, a squad of Sudanese were taking potshots at them. But it was strictly a symbolic exercise; the kaffirs were well out of range and seemed inclined to stay there. Stanley was also down on the beach with Hoffman and Uledi, inspecting the spoils of the war: the bundles and baskets and livestock of the dead villagers plus the sixty-foot war canoe and five smaller fishing pirogues. Amazingly, despite the ferocity and suddenness of the attack and the superiority of weapons, the majority of the village's canoes had gotten away. Jephson could see some of them, the three war canoes at the head of the reach, a few of the smaller ones slipping through the mist among the islands in the river and along the opposite short. Still, counting the *Lady Dorothy*, which had survived the fight and was drawn up beneath the bluff, and the two canoes that had been captured earlier downriver, they were now in possession of a flotilla of nine craft.

"This is crazy, Arthur."

Jephson turned back to Parke. "What's crazy?"

"All of it." Parke made a sweeping gesture, taking in the burned-out village, the corpses, the surrounding forest, the river. "It's completely crazy. He thinks he can get through this godforsaken wilderness by shooting his way through. But he can't. No matter how much killing he does, he'll never get through. Nobody can. Nobody ever has."

Jephson said nothing.

"We should turn back, Arthur." Parke's voice dropped to a conspiratorial whisper. "Listen to me, Arthur. I was telling this to

Robbie. We should turn back now, while we still have the chance."

Jephson looked away, back to the beach where Stanley was moving around among the canoes, kicking their sides, discussing them with Uledi and Hoffman. Then Hoffman scrambled up the bank's bluff and began rounding up the *pagazis* and sending them down to the river with their loads.

"I better find my clothes," Jephson said. "It looks like we're moving out."

The caravan was divided into a land party and a river party.

Of the 315 men who had started out in the advance column, 296 were left. Fourteen had been killed in the fights with the natives (four at the first Basoko village beyond Yambuya, ten here), two had died of other causes, and three had disappeared along the way. In addition, twelve were down with fever or otherwise sick, and nine had been injured seriously enough in the fights or during the trek to have difficulty keeping up. They were put with the river party, the big sixty-foot war canoe serving as a hospital ship and carrying, as well, the medicine chests, twenty Wanyamwezis to paddle, and ten askaris as guards. Parke was in command of her, assigned to bring up the flotilla's rear.

The *Lady Dorothy* took the lead with Jephson and Sudi, ten oarsmen, twenty *pagazis*, most of the headquarters company's kit and supplies, and a front guard of twenty askaris. The seven smaller pirogues, strung out in a line between these two, were each capable of carrying half a dozen men or so plus their loads, bringing the river party to a total of 147. The intention was to commandeer additional canoes in the days ahead; but in the meantime, the remaining 148 men of the column, not counting Stanley, plus the donkeys and pack mules and Maxim would have to continue slogging it overland, staying wherever the terrain permitted in sight of the river and the flotilla, Uledi as *kirangozi* leading the way with his trackers and pioneers, Nelson commanding the askaris, and Hoffman driving the *pagazis*. For his part, Stanley planned to alternate between the two parties as conditions demanded; and on the first morning leaving behind the charred hulks of huts and the fly-covered corpses of the destroyed village, he pushed off in the *Lady Dorothy*.

The mist burned away slowly, unveiling a dull, muggy day, the sky overcast and threatening rain, the river under that sky a greasy pewter gray. Stanley stood in the prow of the boat peering upriver at the three war canoes at the head of the reach. He too must have been dumped into the river during the fight the night before and battered about on the rocks. His jaw was swollen, the grubby gray stubble covering it was encrusted with dried blood, and his clothes were still damp and caked with mud. From time to time he glanced back to check the disposition of his little fleet or to keep track of the land party slogging along the shore, then he resumed watching the war canoes ahead with narrowed calculating eyes. Doubtless he coveted them, was aching to lay his hands on them—those three alone would relieve seventy or eighty men in the land party and their loads—but no opportunity presented itself. As the *Lady Dorothy* advanced, the three canoes retreated, darting from bank to bank, slipping in among the river's islands, disappearing into its coves and backwaters, then reappearing, always well out of range.

Three more war canoes appeared on the river.

Jephson was sitting in the stern with Sudi, using a bale of trading cloth as a backrest, a 577 Express hunting rifle across his lap—he had lost his pistol in the river the night before—watching the forested banks glide by when the canoes emerged from the reeds at a confluence with a minor stream and slipped silently into the flotilla's wake. He first thought they were the original trio, which in their endless flitting about somehow had managed to get behind them. But when he looked upriver, he saw that the first three were still there.

"Mr. Stanley."

Stanley turned around, and Jephson pointed to the three new canoes trailing them. Stanley nodded and in his turn pointed to an island lying off the port. Two more canoes were lurking under the cover of the marsh grass of the island's swamped shoreline. Jephson raised his field glasses and studied the newcomers: short, stocky, muscular, their nakedness ocherous in color from camwood, their basket-weave caps adorned with monkey tails, small cane bows and arrows in their hands—obviously of the same tribe as those who had put up the bloody fight at the village. Persistent buggers, Jephson thought a shade uneasily, and he looked around to locate the land party.

They had started out nearly two hours earlier than the river party; but there was no trail along the bank—clearly the kaffirs hereabouts used the river for their road—and they had been steadily falling behind throughout the day. Now they were no longer in sight. The brush and thickets and brake along the high embankment screened them from view, and the crash and slash of the pioneers' axes and billhooks hacking out a path carried only faintly out to the water.

There was the sharp metallic clicking of rifle bolts. Jephson looked back. The askaris had stood up, and Stanley was signaling downriver to Parke and the others to bunch up and get closer to the bank. More canoes had appeared.

The river made long sweeping bends, and in each of these bends and sweeps canoes now were waiting. Where they came from was unclear; but by midafternoon a score or more were shadowing the flotilla, following in its wake, running ahead of it, skulking in the mouths of creeks, slipping out of murky backwaters, hugging the far forested shore, providing an ever-present ominous escort.

Jephson didn't immediately see the next village. What he did see, though, were a dozen small dugouts and pirogues suddenly scurrying like frightened water bugs across the river from the south bank. Obviously there was a village on the south bank and the kaffirs were abandoning it to make for the opposite shore. Five huge canoes, twenty or thirty warriors in each, stood in midstream guarding the evacuation. The *Lady Dorothy* slowed; the Wanyamwezi oarsmen, peering nervously over their shoulders at the array of war canoes now hovering all around them just out of range, faltered in their stroke. Parke's hospital canoe drew alongside, the askaris in it crowded forward, rifles at the ready, Parke with his pistol drawn, the sick and injured up on their elbows, craning their necks to see.

Jephson went up into the bow beside Stanley. "Who are they?" he asked. "Babukwa?"

"No," Stanley replied. "We passed the Babukwa country long ago."

"Who are they then?"

"I don't know. Someone else." Stanley turned back to Sudi. "Pick up the stroke, *rafiki*. Make for shore and get the boats out of the water. I don't want to risk losing any of them." Stanley vaulted the *Lady Dorothy*'s gunwale and waded ashore; and as the men shipped oars and paddles and pulled the steel boat and the captured canoes well up on the beach, he walked into the village.

The huts were nestled shoulder-to-shoulder in groups of seven or eight around small muddy squares open on one side to the river. In the center of each was the remnant of a communal cooking fire, and each was connected to another by a narrow street following the bend in the river. A head-high palisade of bamboo pikes ran along the landward side; outside it, spreading back to the dark wall of the forest, fields thick with ripening manioc and maize dripped with the clammy dew of the close, humid day, while within it were small gardens of spinach, tomatoes, pumpkins, tobacco, and peppers, and groves of plantains and bananas. But everything else of value had been carried away. Stanley ducked into one of the huts; and although he remained inside for several minutes, when he came out he was empty-handed. He looked around with narrowed eyes, the muscles tensed in his grizzled swollen jaw. Then he went over to the charred remains of a cooking fire and kicked around in its ashes with the toe of his boot. Broken gourds, clay jars, cracked milling stones, cornhusks, fruit rinds, animal bones, that sort of rubbish was scattered on the cold coals. Stanley squatted on his haunches and rummaged through them. Jephson came up behind him.

"Cannibals."

"Sir?"

Stanley picked a bone out of the ashes and turned it over in his hand. "This is human." He tossed the bone back onto the ashes. "They're cannibals, this lot, whoever else they are." He stood up and looked out to the river.

The war canoes had gathered along the opposite shore. Jephson counted twenty-seven of them but there could have been more, obscured by the low-hanging trees over there or hidden behind the islands. Twenty or thirty warriors in each, maybe seven or eight hundred altogether; cannibals. They stood in their canoes watching, waiting.

"How are you feeling, lad?"

The question startled Jephson.

"Are you feeling all right?"

"Yes, sir. I'm feeling fine."

"That cut ain't bothering you?" Stanley reached for the bandage behind Jephson's left ear and peeled away the sticking plaster. He studied the wound, the blood-scabbed black stitches, the purple swelling. "It'll be all right," he said after a moment and smoothed the plaster back in place. "You're doing fine." He dropped his hand to the youth's shoulder and, with a quick, unexpected smile, gave him a friendly squeeze. "You know that, don't you, lad? You're doing just fine."

"Thank you, sir."

Stanley took his hand away and looked back to the river. "We're all doing just fine," he said quietly. "My guess is we've come a good third of the way already. More, maybe. Now if this river would only stay clear of rapids and keep coming out of the east and we could lay our hands on some more canoes . . ." His voice trailed off, but he continued staring out at the Aruwimi. Then he said, "All right, lad. I'm leaving you in command."

"Sir?"

"Get the boat and canoes unloaded and all the gear up on the high ground and make camp. Post half the askaris in a firing line on the beach and picket the rest in a perimeter up here around these huts. Don't bother with the tents. We'll use the huts. And no fires. Let the headmen dole out the rations and have the boys collect as much as they can out of these fields and gardens, but we'll do without cooking fires tonight. No sense giving those buggers any unnecessary targets. And for God's sake, don't let anyone wander off."

"But where are you going, sir?"

"Downriver. I want to see if I can't hurry up Robbie and Will. I'll feel a hell of a lot better when we've got the Maxim up here."

Jephson expected Stanley to round up a few Wanyamwezis and Sudanese to take with him, but he didn't. He simply strode off, the stock of his Winchester tucked under his arm, a bandolier across his chest, his pistol on one hip, his water bottle on the other. Jephson watched him vanish into the forest. Then he looked back at the river and counted the war canoes again. Twenty-six, one less than before, but he didn't trust the count. It was getting too dark. He went down to the beach to carry out Stanley's orders.

It started to rain. There was nothing spectacular about it this time, no thunder or lightning, no furious tempest of wind. As dusk approached, the dirty gray overcast of clouds merely lowered and a steady rain began to fall, and it fell and fell as if there would never be an end to it. Jephson, draped to the knees in his canvas poncho, a piece of oilskin wrapped around his pith helmet, carrying the Express rifle, walked up and down the line of askaris he had posted on the beach, sloshing through ankle-deep puddles, keeping watch on the canoes on the river. They were almost impossible to see now through the sheets of rain. If they should take it into their heads to attack before the land party got there with the Maxim, if they stormed ashore now under cover of the rain and darkness, it could be one hell of a bloody mess. He had forty askaris at most, counting the hurt and sick, with Winchesters and Remingtons, maybe another thirty rifles of various vintages and reliability in the hands of Wanyamwezis, plus an assortment of *pangas*, knives, billhooks, axes, and spears against nearly a thousand cannibals . . . He stopped walking and looked back at the askaris he had picketed around the huts and along the palisade: a miserable lot, hunkered down in their soaked abas and burnooses. Everyone else—a reserve guard of askaris, most of the Wanyamwezis, and Parke—had taken shelter in the huts. No lights showed; they had had something to eat and gone to sleep. In a while, though, Jephson would fetch Parke and they would change the guard. The youth reached under his poncho for his pocket watch, remembered that it too had been lost when the *Lady Dorothy* capsized, and once again turned to the Aruwimi.

The steady drumming of rain on the water, the soft splash and rush of the current—those were the only sounds to be heard. He went closer to the river's edge. As best as he could make out, the canoes were still clustered along the opposite bank, sheltering under the leaves and branches and dripping curtains of moss there. He wiped the rain from his face and rubbed his eyes; his head ached, every bruise and cut and battered bone in his body ached in the chill penetrating wet.

There was a rifle shot. He looked around quickly. It came from behind him but not from any of his men, from somewhere far to the west in the forest, downriver. There was a second and a third, then after a pause a fourth, fifth, and sixth in rapid succession, faint distant cracks miles away in the darkness, barely audible above the ceaseless pattering of the rain. Only those outside heard it; the askaris on guard turned, a few Wanyamwezi headmen sorting through the rations looked up. No one came out of the huts. Jephson walked in the direction of the shots, as if getting a few steps closer to them would make any difference. The Sudanese corporal of the guard followed him, and a pair of Wanyamwezi headmen came over. One of them was Sudi, carrying his Snider rifle. The quartet stood staring off into the trees, listening for more shots. After a long interval they came—three, then three more, each trio again in rapid succession.

"That's not a fight," Jephson said.

"No, sah," Sudi answered. "The land party signal to us, sah. To show them the way."

Jephson nodded.

"They do not know where we are, sah. We must reply."

Jephson nodded again slowly. "Yes," he said. "But I'd sure as hell hate to set those savages off by it." He glanced back to the river, wondering if the cannibals in the canoes had heard the firing.

Some of the askaris on the beach had broken ranks and were drifting over to see what was going on. "Corporal, get those men back on the firing line. And keep them alert. This might set off the whole blasted works." He looked back into the trees: and when he heard the next trio of shots, he fired his Express rifle three times in reply.

These shots awakened the camp. Men bolted out of the huts. Parke, in shirtsleeves, barefoot, immediately drenched to the skin, bounded over.

"What is it? What the hell's going on?"

"Tommy, get down to the beach. Take all the askaris with you. I don't know what those savages will do. They might attack."

"Attack? Sure they'll attack, shooting your gun off like that."

"The land party's out there somewhere. I think they're lost."

Just then Sudi fired his Snider into the air.

Parke whirled toward him. "What's he doing? Stop him. He's going to spook those damn niggers."

"For Christ sake, Tommy. I just told you. Mr. Stanley and the others are out there. We've got to signal them."

Again a crackle of shots sounded from deep in the woods, this time from several rifles, each at some distance from the other. Sudi immediately answered them.

"I'm going to take Sudi and a few of my boys and see if I can find them. They sound lost. You round up all the askaris and get them down on the beach, just in case."

Parke looked around uncertainly. Then he said, "All right. I'll get my clothes."

"Jesus, Tommy, forget about your clothes. Just get down on the beach and make sure those savages don't try to come ashore."

"Don't give me orders, Arthur."

Jephson hesitated a split second. Then he said, "I am giving you orders, Tommy. Get down on the goddamn beach."

Parke stared at the youth, his hair plastered over his forehead by the rain, the rain running down in his scraggly beard. For a moment, it seemed as if he meant to defy Jephson. But then all of a sudden his angry expression crumpled, his mouth going as slack as a baby's—for a startled instant Jephson thought he was about to cry—and he turned and dashed to the river, shouting for the askaris to follow him.

"Come on, Sudi. Get hold of our boatmen and let's go. *Upesi-upesi.*"

• •

They ran into Nelson about an hour out of the village, struggling through the jungle almost directly from the south. He had about fifteen askaris with him, some of Uledi's pioneers and trackers, a crowd of *pagazis*, and six of the pack mules.

"How far to camp?" he asked.

"About a mile."

"Which way?"

"Practically straight north. Didn't you meet Mr. Stanley?"

"Mr. Stanley?" Nelson looked around as if expecting to see Stanley. He was wearing a waterproof mackintosh, his pistol belted on around the outside of it, his face scored with innumerable scratches. The drenched long shirts and pantaloons of the Wanyamwezis were torn to ribbons, the Sudanese peered out from the folds of their sodden hoods like hunted beasts. "Show these boys to the camp, Arthur. I'm going back for the others."

"Where are they? What happened?"

"Nothing happened. What the hell should have happened? We got lost, that's all. There's no way of keeping the river in sight in this blasted jungle, and we got lost."

In dribs and drabs, in total disorder, the land party straggled into the village all through the raining night. Stanley came in with three pack mules and a riding donkey—the donkey had a shattered foreleg and had to be destroyed—then went out again with Uledi and some trackers, firing his rifle at intervals as he went. Hoffman brought in the Maxim, and Nelson set it up on the beach, pointing it out into the pitch-black darkness of the river, and then they too went back again in search of those still missing. Thirty-one were still missing at midnight. The firing of rifles to signal them was almost continuous. Parke set up an infirmary in one of the huts to treat the injured—cuts, sprains, one broken arm—and the lantern burning in there struck Jephson as dangerous. The cannibals on the river almost certainly could see it. Nelson returned with ten askaris of the rear guard and took them down to the beach. Uledi came back with some more mules and *pagazis*. When Stanley came back, it was still raining steadily; but there already was a hint of the coming day, the false dawn silvering the lowering clouds in the east. He went down to the beach where Jephson and Nelson stood beside the Maxim gun watching the river.

"You'd best get ready, Captain," he said. "It'll be light soon. If these buggers are planning anything, that's when they'll do it—at first light."

Nelson issued the order, and the Maxim's gunner got down

behind the weapon's shield, straddling the support brace, his legs stretched out in front of him, both hands on the trigger grip. Two askaris kneeled in the mud on either side of him, one to guide the feed and the other the ejection of the ammunition belt. There were now about seventy askaris in line on the beach; and seeing the gun crew make ready, they repositioned themselves, dropping to their knees, fiddling with their rifles.

"Let them get close to shore, Captain. Let them get close enough so we can lay our hands on their canoes. We've got to get hold of at least ten more if we don't want to go on slogging through this bleeding forest any longer."

"Yes, sir." Nelson went over to the gunner and stood directly behind him, resting a hand on his shoulder.

They resumed their watch on the river. Hoffman was still out in the forest hunting for the last of the land party's stragglers, and they could hear his rifle going off from time to time as slowly, almost imperceptibly, shapes began taking form in the growing gray light of the coming day.

The river was empty.

The sight of it shocked Jephson; had the dawn revealed hundreds of canoes packed solid from bank to bank filled with howling savages he would not have been more shocked. His eyes darted upriver and down, squinting through the rain, unbelieving. The river tumbled by in a silvery flood with no sign of life upon it. The canoes and the hundreds of cannibals had vanished during the night. Where had they gone? He looked at Stanley.

Stanley had turned away. Hoffman was coming down the beach. "All safe and sound, Will?"

"No," Hoffman replied. He was limping badly; and when he got to Stanley, he reached down and squeezed the curled toes of his ulcerated foot. "We're missing four *pagazis* and two mules."

Stanley watched Hoffman massage a cramp out of the foot—it looked awful, blackening, swollen—but said nothing. There was no point telling Hoffman to wear boots now. He turned to Nelson. "How about the askaris, Captain?"

"All accounted for."

"Good. Get some food into them and have them dry out their powder and oil their weapons and patch up their kit. We'll move out at six."

"That's less than two hours, sir. Most of these men haven't had any sleep since yesterday."

"They'll get some sleep later. We'll all get some sleep later.

Right now the smartest thing we can do is get the hell out of here."

"Yes, sir."

"I'll go with the land party today. Will, you can take my place in the boat. Rest that foot up for a bit."

"I'm all right."

Stanley looked down at the ugly, misshapen foot, at the way Hoffman stood, keeping his weight off it. "You sure?"

"Look, Bula Matari, you got to have three white men with the land party. Otherwise the same fucking thing's going to happen today as happened yesterday. Those stupid bastards are going to stray all over, and we'll spend the whole fucking night trying to round them up again."

Stanley turned to Jephson. "Do you think you can manage the river party with just Surgeon Parke, lad?"

"Yes, sir, I can manage."

"Right then. Here's what I want you to do. Push on upriver until noon. Fire your rifle every half-hour or so to give us a sighting, and at noon put in to shore and wait for us to catch you up. When you see us, you can go on, and at the first village you come to around three make camp and wait for us there. But keep on signaling every half-hour. And make damn sure you hear me reply. Don't ever get out of earshot of my rifle. If you do, if you don't hear me reply, stop right where you are and wait and keep on firing until you do."

"Yes, sir."

"And, Arthur. Keep your eyes skinned for a chance to get hold of some more canoes."

"I will, sir. But where are they? Where the devil have they got to?"

"They're around." Stanley looked out onto the river. "You can be bloody well certain of that. They're around somewhere. You'll see them again soon enough."

But he didn't—not that day or the next, not for day after day. And the rain kept falling all through those days, sometimes only as a fine drizzling mist, other times hammering down, with thunder rumbling above the forest and startling flashes of lightning illuminating the smothering clouds. There was no getting dry anymore. The men huddled in the steel boat and in the following canoes wrapped in odd strips of canvas or sheeting, as often as not waist-deep in water and bailing listlessly while Jephson stood in the prow watching each bend and twist in the river, certain he must see them on this day, in the next reach, around the coming bend, lurking in the dripping gray moss, in that tangle of vines beyond the mist-bound spit of the next headland. But they were never there; eastward, day after day, deeper and deeper into the heart of the continent, the Aruwimi was as silent as a grave.

But they *were* there. Every tingling nerve in his body cried out that they were, lying in wait. But where? Goddamnit, where? In which creek? Behind which island? Hidden by which stand of marsh grass along which twisting flooded shore? The never-ending rattle of rain on the water, the monotonous splash of the oars and paddles, the rumble of distant thunder, the whispering of the wind in the trees, the sudden piercing cry of a fish eagle, all these only underscored the nerve-racking quiet, only exacerbated the unnerving sense that they were being drawn steadily, remorselessly into a trap and that at any moment around any bend the trap might be sprung.

The land party was having a beastly time of it. The only paths to be found were game trails; and although the temptation to follow them was great, they invariably led away from the river and pinched out in bogs and impassable thickets deep in the jungle, and the job of hacking the way back was murderous. But the job of hacking a way along the embankment was no less so, and rarely a day went by that didn't see some toll taken, some damage inflicted, some loss incurred in men, mules, loads, time. Again and again, Jephson had to put his little flotilla into shore and lie up and wait, firing his rifle, straining to hear a reply, far downriver or deep in the forest; and at the night's camp—as often as not in the open on a sodden beach or in a dripping wood of mangroves—he'd find himself waiting uneasily for hours for the land party finally to appear, exhausted, soaked, sullen, shivering with fever, hurt and ravenously hungry, but with only a mess of vegetables looted from abandoned villages to look forward to. The goat and fowl captured downriver were now long gone and no resupply was to be begged, borrowed, or stolen in this wretched deserted stretch of river. Stanley rotated the personnel of the two parties every so often to spell the marchers, and quarrels broke out every time he did over whose turn it was to go on the river; and then at last he halted the journey entirely for forty-eight hours to allow them all to rest and have their injuries looked after and mend their clothes and kit and try their luck at hunting and fishing and give those who had fallen behind a chance to catch up. Then on yet another chill gray raining day they set off again, although with not much better heart.

That day Jephson spotted canoes.

This was either the fifteenth or sixteenth of August. Jephson had lost track in the endless sameness of rain, river, and jungle; but he remembered thinking that it was just about the time Major Barttelot, Jack Troup, and the rear column would be setting out from Yambuya and wondering how they would fare. It was a Sunday or Monday, late in the afternoon, and the rain was falling in a light misty drizzle when he was on the lookout for a likely place to camp. The only village he had seen in the last hour or so had been on the opposite embankment; but now as they rounded a sharp bend to the north, a large island loomed up out of the mist almost exactly in midriver with a cluster of huts on the near end. To get the land party over to it would require a ferrying operation; but because of the considerable size of the island—it practically blocked the river entirely, dividing it into two narrow, fast-running channels—the distance between the village and the southern bank wasn't more than a few hundred yards. The *Lady Dorothy* and Parke's big hospital canoe together, once unloaded of their present loads and passengers, could make reasonably quick work of the ferriage. Besides, nothing on the near shore—low-lying, swamped, thickly overgrown, and mosquito-ridden—offered anything nearly as inviting.

Then he saw the first canoe.

It was pulled up on the island's beach just below the village. It might have been a vagrant log, a piece of driftwood tossed up by the river's current, even a crocodile. But it was a canoe. He studied it through his field glasses. Then he raised the glasses and carefully swept the island, the jumble of mud-and-wattle huts, the dense dripping tangle of vegetation behind them, the strip of pebble-strewn beach curving upriver into the mist. Another canoe was there. It also was pulled up on beach, a bit farther upriver, also apparently abandoned. He wiped the rain from the glasses and made a second careful reconnaissance. Two canoes, of medium size, transportation for another ten, fifteen men and their loads.

"Do you see them, Sudi?"

"Yes, sah."

"What do you think? Is it a trap?"

Sudi shook his head. "No, sah. I think they are no good. I think they have been left there because they are broken."

"Let's have a look."

"What is it?" Parke pulled alongside in the hospital canoe and grabbed the *Lady Dorothy*'s gunwale to steady himself. "You plan to make camp in that village?"

"Yes, maybe. But there are a couple of canoes on the beach there. I'm not sure what they mean. I think I better go over and have a look first."

"I'm not sure you should do that."

"Why not?"

"Listen." Parke's bloodshot eyes flicked upstream. He didn't look good. He was dosing himself regularly with quinine and chlorodyne but there was no question he had fever. His cheeks were sunken, his complexion a ghastly yellow, and his hair and beard stuck out all over his head in greasy unkempt tangles. During the two-day halt, all the others had taken the opportunity to shave and trim their hair. Parke hadn't. It was even questionable whether he had made any effort to wash; a foul odor emanated from his body. His breath stank of brandy. "What's that noise?"

"What noise?"

"Listen," Parke said.

Jephson looked upstream. He couldn't see far; the sharp bend in the river, the large island, the misty drizzle blocked the view. "It's thunder," he said after a few minutes.

"That's not thunder. It's too constant for thunder. It sounds like a railway train."

"Tommy, for Christ sake."

"Or drums."

Jephson looked upriver again. Then he looked at Sudi. The young Wanyamwezi had his head cocked, his eyes closed. Some of the other Wanyamwezis—the boatmen and the *pagazis*—and all the Sudanese were listening in the same way. There *was* something, an odd, steady sort of murmuring, very soft, perhaps very far away, hard to make out over the slap of the river against the boat, the patter of rain on the river.

"Come on," Jephson said. "Let's put into the bank here and I'll go over to the island with my askaris and have a look around. You and your boys can cover me from here."

"Hang on a minute, Arthur. What if something happens to you? What am I supposed to do?"

"Nothing's going to happen to me. Mr. Stanley can't be more than a few miles off. He'll catch us up soon. You'll hear his rifle." Jephson went up into the *Lady Dorothy*'s prow. "Let's go, Sudi. But slowly, *rafiki*, slowly."

They made for the downstream tip of the island; and when they were fifty or so feet from it, just off where the first canoe was pulled up, Sudi called a halt to the stroke to give Jephson a chance to study the terrain through his field glasses. Even at this closer distance there was nothing new to see. The village appeared utterly abandoned. The huts leaned at rakish angles, as if beaten that way by the rains, the thatch of their roofs sagging, the blackened pits of the cooking fires in front of them filled with water. They went closer. A reef jutted out from the island; and when they reached it, Jephson, clutching his Express rifle, jumped over the side and waded to the canoe. He stopped and looked quickly toward the village. The fronds of some palm trees there had rustled. Now they were still. Monkeys perhaps, or just the rain. He glanced around. From beyond the upper end of the island came that peculiar low deep-throated beating sound, from downriver the intermittent firing of Parke's pistol trying to raise the land party. Nothing else. He looked down at the canoe. It was overturned, but he saw right away that Sudi's guess had been correct. It had been abandoned because it was damaged. A ragged split ran almost half the length of its bottom. He dropped into a squat beside it and examined the split, pressing his fingertips into the sodden wood, testing if it would give. Actually, it didn't seem too bad. It probably could be repaired. Caulk the split with rags and pitch, brace the sides with rattan rope, and the canoe probably could be made to carry a few men and their loads. They couldn't be picky; anything that could float would be a help to those poor bastards slogging it through the jungle.

Nothing seemed wrong with the second canoe. Drawn only halfway up on the beach, it wasn't overturned; and as a consequence its bottom was awash with two or three inches of rainwater, but otherwise it looked in fine condition. There were even two paddles in it, floating in the rainwater. Jephson kicked its side. It was a carved-out iroko log, and it rang sound. He walked around and kicked the other side. "I wonder why this was left behind," he said to Sudi. "It looks all right."

"I do not think it was left behind, sah."

"Eh?"

Sudi was looking into the jungle of vegetation behind the village. "I think someone still here, sah."

"Where?"

Suddenly Sudi jerked up his rifle.

"Don't shoot! For God's sake, don't shoot." Jephson spun around. "Don't anybody shoot!"

The askaris, evidently catching sight of whatever Sudi had seen, had also raised their rifles. On Jephson's sharp command, they drew back.

"Where, Sudi? I don't see anyone."

But just then he heard a weird squeaking sound and in the same instant caught sight of a small figure scampering through the trees.

"It's a monkey," he cried out. "Jesus, Sudi, it's nothing but a monkey."

"No monkey, sah. *Msichana*. Look. There."

A little girl, no more than eight or nine, stark naked, her hair done up in dozens of pickaninny pigtails, emitting terrified little squeaks just like a monkey, was hopping up and down in a veritable panic farther up the beach, beyond the second canoe. When Jephson now turned to her, she scampered into the river, knee-deep, and began scooping out handfuls of water and pouring them over her head.

Jephson couldn't help breaking into a wide grin at that. She looked so silly in her pitiful fright, yet so endearing. "What in blazes is she doing?"

"She make sign so you do not harm her."

"*Njoo hapa, toto*. No one will harm you." But when Jephson started toward her, smiling, holding out a hand in what he hoped would be understood as friendship, she scampered away again, splashing in the shallows still farther up the beach. Jephson stopped; she stopped and resumed the silly business of pouring water over her head. "What's she doing here all alone anyway? Why did they leave her?"

"I do not think she is alone, sah." Sudi was again looking into the trees where he had first spotted the girl. "I think there is someone else. I think she wishes to lead us away from him."

"Let's have a look."

As Jephson and Sudi started into the trees, the little girl resumed her panicked monkeylike behavior; and with each step they took her desperate squeaking grew louder, her hopping up and down more agitated. She rushed back down the beach to where the second canoe was pulled up. Jephson looked at her. She stopped, jumped up and down, squeaking like crazy, splashed water over her head, then scampered up the beach again, for all the world trying to draw him after her, away from whoever else was in the woods.

It was a miserable old man, nothing but a wrinkled bag of

bones, propped up against the bole of a palm tree, trembling from the damp or fear, staring at Jephson and Sudi with milky clouded eyes. He was as naked as the girl except for a basket-weave cap with a monkey tail trailing down the back, obviously of the same tribe they had fought downriver. A cannibal then; but seen close up, helpless like this, there was nothing terrifying about him, just a pitiable old man cowering in the forest. Jephson could see how he had gotten there; the tracks were fresh and clear in the rain-soaked ground where the little girl had dragged him from one of the huts in the village, probably upon seeing the approach of the *Lady Dorothy*.

Jephson kneeled beside him. "Don't be afraid, *mzee*."

The old man turned to the sound of the youth's voice but evidently did not see him.

"It is the river blindness, sah," Sudi said.

"What else is the matter with him?"

Sudi shrugged. "He is just very old. He cannot travel anymore, so when they heard us coming they left him here with the little girl to look after him."

Jephson pulled out a handkerchief and wiped the rain from the man's face. He shrank back at the touch. The little girl's squeaks and shrieks increased in pitch. She had come back down the beach and stood by the small canoe but didn't dare come any farther. The askaris and boatmen watched her with amusement.

"Let's get him into a hut out of this damn rain. Surgeon Parke'll look him over and do whatever he can for him." Jephson got up and, taking the old man under one arm while Sudi grasped the other, lifted him gently to his feet.

The sight of this thoroughly panicked the little girl; obviously she believed they were going to kill and, God only knew, eat the old man and she began hollering and screaming and jumping about like a maddened monkey.

"Stop it! You silly little creature, stop it. Nothing is going to happen to grandfather, so just stop that infernal racketing."

The girl stopped it.

Jephson grinned. "That's better."

The girl stared at him.

"Come here, *toto*. Come here now." The old man was as light as a feather, so Jephson let Sudi take him back to the village while he started toward the girl. "Come here, little one. There's nothing to be afraid of. We're going to take good care of grandfather."

The girl remained motionless, staring at him silently, watching him approach. Jephson's smile broadened; he thought he had won over this little pickaninny. But when he was perhaps ten feet away, she turned and, quick as a flash, grabbed hold of the small canoe, pushed it out into the river, and jumped in.

"Hey!" Jephson started to run.

She snatched up one of the paddles; and with a last terrified glance over her shoulder as if to confirm there was nothing any longer that she could do for the old man and must now think of saving herself, she shot out into the stream and made off upriver with amazing speed. Jephson raced up the beach after her, shouting, waving his arms like an idiot, furious that he had lost the canoe, even more furious that a little girl would run away from him as if he were some kind of monster.

And then he stopped running. He had reached the upper end of the beach. From there he could see where the river above the island became a single broad stream again, making a sharp bend, flowing down from the north. The little girl in the canoe was swiftly disappearing up it into the drizzling mist. And from there, with a view of a mile or so upriver, he saw the source of that faint distant peculiar drumming sound that they had been hearing. Stretching full across the Aruwimi and blocking it off entirely was a thirty-foot-high horseshoe-shaped waterfall.

· FOUR ·

THE PORTAGE around the waterfall took five days. A twelve-foot-broad track was cleared through the jungle along the southern embankment, strewn with boughs and branches and leaves; and the steel boat—kept all in a piece to save time—and the now nine canoes were hauled and dragged and carried up the steep, rocky, perilously slippery incline. It was three-quarters of a mile; it took sixty men for the steel boat alone and ten separate trips back and forth to manhandle up the loads and pack animals. But there was no other way. The waterfall was impassable, plunging over the God-made dam of mammoth boulders and granite ledges through four thundering chutes, each at least a hundred yards wide, throwing up towering spumes of roaring yellow water, filling the air with an unending storm of spray and roiling the river below with spitting waves and boiling gouts of foam and bottomless black whirlpools for a half-mile or more downstream. There was another waterfall five miles farther, which would also have to be portaged—Uledi and the trackers had scouted it—but the river could be made use of again at least until then.

The reunited caravan set off at six in the morning after a day of rest. The rain had finally let up; and the sun, a ghostly white disc rising out of the dripping trees, beat down through a shimmering sticky haze. The worst of the sick and hurt—they numbered twenty-nine now—were put in the hospital canoe with Parke, and the steel boat and other canoes were stowed with as much of the equipment and supplies as they could carry; but they were occupied by only enough men to paddle, pole, and steer them. Stanley's idea was to move up all the goods and incapacitated men by water and to allow the pack animals and the rest of the column to make the overland trek to the next waterfall pretty much unburdened. This meant two trips for the flotilla, but it was worth it. The terrain along the river here was particularly hard—densely overgrown, cut up by creeks, jagged outcroppings, and innumerable ravines, and constantly ascending—so the only way loaded men and animals could have proceeded would have been by detouring God only knew how far inland. But Stanley was anxious to keep the river party and the land party close together.

He went ahead with Uledi and the pioneers to blaze the trail. Hoffman, because of his bad foot, remained behind with twenty askaris and the Maxim to guard the loads that would be brought up on the second trip, while Nelson commanded the main body of the column, marching them along the rough, rocky high ground above the river.

Although relieved of their loads, they marched without spirit. The climb around the waterfall, the weeks of hard trekking before that, the miasma of fever steaming out of the bogs and swamps of the jungle, the foot ulcers many of them suffered, perhaps most of all the poverty of their diet—the everlasting dreary meals of rice and manioc and banana, the scarcity of fresh meat—all of it was telling on them, grinding them down. There was a gauntness in them, a vacancy in their eyes, resentment and despair in their expression. The sullenness of the Sudanese was spreading to the Wanyamwezis. There were frequent cases of malingering and constant complaining. They had to be prodded and threatened and sometimes beaten to be kept going.

Once clear of the falls, the river calmed again and opened up, marshy creeks debouching into placid scummy pools where half-submerged crocodiles dozed in the ooze. The flotilla—Jephson in the lead in the *Lady Dorothy*—made good headway, running well ahead of the struggling land party. But as they began to near the next waterfall, to hear the faint rumble of it, they had to slow down. The water roughened first in riffles and flecks of foam, then with swirling eddies and gurgling spray, splashing over reefs, rocks, and jams of driftwood that forced the vessels always closer to shore. The river narrowed, from 400 to 200 yards, from 200 to 100, and the embankments on both sides rose higher, slate and shale sheering up steeply from the water's edge.

Around two in the afternoon, with the sun glistening harshly on its surface, the river made another sharp turn to the north; and they entered a deep blue-shadowed canyon where at first breath it was wonderfully cool and at the top of which stood the second waterfall. Three flat giant steps of stone, smoothed by the ageless flow of water, climbed up like a fairy-tale stairway from the canyon floor as if to an invisible palace hidden somewhere within the brilliant green of the jungle from which the river tumbled in gorgeous cascades of shining silver sheets and cotton-white foam. Stanley was waiting for them there, poised high on a limestone ledge that jutted out over the boiling water, leaning on his rifle, motionless as a statue.

When he saw the *Lady Dorothy* turn into the canyon, he sprang to life, waved, hopped down to a lower ledge like a mountain goat, and waved again. Jephson glanced back. The land party, picking its way precariously along the canyon's precipitous wall, was strung out in a wavering line for a mile or more, some of the men down at the river's edge, others a hundred feet above, the rest scattered between. Nelson was at the tail end, thrashing the rump of a balky mule while the animal's driver tugged at its halter. Jephson looked back at Stanley. He had climbed down to the river's level and was now shouting at them through cupped hands, but because of the roar of the cascades he could not be heard. Jephson looked around again, unable to see what was agitating Stanley. Then it suddenly struck him. They were in a trap. He jumped out of the boat and ran for the bank.

"Sudi! Put in to shore. Tommy, all of you, put in to shore."

The canyon was a trap, the trap into which he had feared they might be drawn. Now it was to be sprung. No European general could have planned it with finer cunning, waited for the chance with greater patience. The column in disarray, stumbling over impossible terrain, worn out and off guard, the Maxim miles away, and not an acre of flat ground anywhere on which to assemble and make a stand.

"Get the boats out of the water."

"No!" Stanley was running down the embankment, leaping from rock to rock, teetering on windfalls of rotted logs. "Keep going another hundred yards, to the cascades."

Parke stood up in the hospital canoe, unable to hear what Stanley or Jephson were shouting. He began shouting himself. Nelson left off beating the mule and started down the canyon wall toward Stanley, digging in his heels to keep from sliding, unholstering his pistol. Then he stopped, looked across to the opposite bank, and abruptly pitched forward and tumbled the rest of the way down to the river head over heels. He lay there for a terrible instant, his face in the stream. Then, as though revived by the cold water, he jumped to his feet. An arrow was sticking out of his chest. He looked down at it, startled, a small thing, not eight inches long, and went to yank it out. It snapped in his hand. He flung the shaft aside and started shooting.

They were everywhere; as mysteriously as they had vanished, they now reappeared by the thousands, on the ledges and rocks above the cataract, along the edge of the canyon wall across the river, in the trees and brush of the opposite embankment, in scores of canoes suddenly flying upstream out of all the creeks and coves and hidden backwaters, raining arrows as they came, howling, an eerie keening howl high-pitched above the thunder of the cataract.

Jephson dropped to a knee and fired his rifle. A warrior in the lead canoe jerked his head up, then crumpled over the side. It astonished Jephson. He had shot a man. Without aiming or even thinking, he had shot a man, maybe killed him. He hadn't expected that, hadn't actually intended it. A hot wave of excitement rushed to his head, his cheeks flushed, his pulses began hammering. He looked for the warrior's body, as he might look for a partridge he had brought down, but couldn't find him. His eyes were swimming, his head spinning. He thought he was going to throw up. Singly, shots cracked and sang, rattled and whined in sharp echoes in the stone chamber of the canyon. The column was trying to defend itself. He cocked his Express rifle and fired again.

Stanley was suddenly beside him shaking his shoulder. "Move the boats up," he screamed in the youth's ear. "Can't you hear me? Move them up to the cascade, goddamnit."

"Captain Nelson's been hit."

"Don't worry about him. Just move the boats up to the cascade. There's space behind the falls where they can be stowed. Uledi's there. He'll show you. Get going. The last thing we want to do is lose the boats and loads."

Stanley dashed off downstream, crouched over, trailing his rifle. Suddenly a pack mule came crashing down from the top of the canyon wall and splattered on the rocks in front of him. The next instant, the muleteer followed, got up, looked around in surprise, and fell backwards, cracking his head open on the rocks. Stanley jumped over them, shouting at Nelson, pointing upriver. Nelson looked, nodded, and started scrambling back up the canyon wall, waving his men toward the cataract. Stanley kept going, down the rocky embankment, through the hail of arrows, half in and half out of the river, skipping from stone to stone, ducking this way and that, until he disappeared around the river's bend out of the canyon.

Jephson leaped back into the *Lady Dorothy*. "*Vuta, rafiki zangu. Vuta, vuta, vuta*, you buggers. Pull for all you're worth."

Uledi and the pioneers were on the bank at the foot of the falls, those with rifles or bows and arrows firing into the mass of savages on the rocks above them. Uledi splashed out into the river waist deep waving his rifle, signaling the *Lady Dorothy* to keep on coming. Jephson couldn't for the life of him see where. The river was a witch's cauldron of boiling foam. But Sudi saw what Uledi was getting at. He slammed the tiller hard to port so that the boat's prow angled straight at the bank, then jumped out, shouting at the oarsmen to follow him. Shipping their oars, they leaped into the river; and floundering in the waves, hanging on to the gunwales, slipping and sliding on the rocks, they heaved and hauled the boat to the bank. And then Jephson saw it too.

There under the cataract behind the sheet of water falling down the last step of the cascade was a sandy cove fronting on a pool of miraculously still water, a cavern of sorts, like a child's magical hideaway, cool as an icehouse, enclosed by the steep rocky embankment at its back, curtained by the silvery sheet of falling water in front, and large enough for the boat and the canoes and a hundred men besides.

Jephson scrambled out of the boat and ran back downriver calling to Parke and the following canoes. One after another, men jumped out of them, and they were towed and shoved through the spitting foam and swirling rapids toward the cavern. The trickiest job was with the hospital canoe; the wounded and sick had to be gotten out and left lying helplessly exposed on the bank while it was wrestled to safety. By then, though, Nelson had most of the askaris and some of the rifle-armed Wanyamwezis up at this end of the canyon. They were mustering in squares and firing lines, on the bank, behind rocks, in the trees, on the higher ground, pouring a steady barrage of covering fire into the attacking savages.

The river filled with them, shot from their canoes, blasted off the rocks, cut down on the bank. But there were always more. Those in the canoes posed the greatest threat. Oddly, the savages on land did not charge the vastly outnumbered column. They fired their vicious little arrows from massed black phalanxes jammed shoulder to shoulder along the jungle wall; and whenever one fell, another quickly took his place; but for the moment at least they stayed where they were. The canoes, however, were a different story. They rushed up the river straight into the boiling foam of the cataract, five and six abreast, negotiating the torrents with amazing skill, wave after wave, unloosing swarms of arrows before being beaten off by the killing fusillades of the guns.

Jephson sprawled behind a rock firing and reloading and firing as fast as he could. Nelson raced up and down the embankment positioning the askaris and the armed Wanyamwezis, herding the muleteers and pack animals and *pagazis* behind the falls; and each time he ran back toward Jephson, the youth saw the shockingly bright red flower of blood from his wound blossom larger and larger on the chest of his tunic. Parke was in the cascade-curtained cavern, where he had helped drag the injured and ill, and Jephson didn't expect to see him reappear while the fight was going on. But he was being unfair. Almost immediately, in fact, Parke dashed back out shouting and made for Nelson.

"The bloody things are poisoned, Robbie!"

Nelson didn't hear him and started scrambling up the canyon wall toward a group of Wanyamwezis trapped on its face. Parke ran after him, grabbed at the skirt of his tunic, dragged him back. Nelson spun around in angry surprise and wrenched himself free. But Parke wouldn't let him go, and something of an idiotic pushing and pulling brawl ensued.

"Goddamnit, Robbie, I'm telling you those bloody things are poisoned. Uledi says they're poisoned. You've got to let me get it out of you."

Jephson suddenly realized what Parke was talking about. The arrows—they were poisoned arrows. Several were lying near him. They had no metal or stone arrowhead as such; the slender shaft of cane wood was merely sharpened to a needle point, but on that point a sticky glob of some copal-colored substance had been baked, and three or four inches below it the shaft was notched. When Nelson had yanked the one from his chest, he doubtless had snapped it at the notch, leaving the point with its lump of baked poison in his chest. Jephson glanced at him. Parke had managed to pull Nelson down behind a boulder and was ripping open the front of his tunic and shirt. Curiously, once the crimson-soaked cloth was pulled away, there didn't seem to be much damage. Just a black hole, a small puncture emitting a trickle of blood a bit to the left of the middle of Nelson's chest. Parke probed at it with his fingertips.

"You've got to come back in there with me, Robbie, where I've got my things. This wound's got to be cleaned out."

"There's no time for that. You can do it later." Nelson started to his feet.

Parke pushed him down and then, astonishingly, thrust his face against Nelson's chest and began sucking at the wound.

"For Christ sake, Tommy, leave off." Nelson seized Parke's hair and jerked his head away. "There's no time for that now, I tell you. I'll be all right." He rolled over on his stomach and started shooting around the boulder.

Jephson saw Parke spit out a mouthful of blood.

The fighting stopped abruptly. After how long Jephson couldn't tell. Time hadn't existed for him during the turmoil of it, the maddening noise, the gunsmoke, the desperate fury of frightened murderous men. While it was going on, it might have been forever. But now that it stopped, he realized that probably no more than an hour had passed. The shadows in the canyon were longer and bluer, but there still was broad daylight in the patch of sky above. It was still afternoon, quiet again, if not to the ear exactly because of the ceaseless rumble of the cataract, quiet then to the eye as the massed black phalanxes of savages melted back into the forest, as their war canoes one after another dropped back down the river, as the men of the column slowly, apprehensively lowered their weapons and looked around, not convinced that it really had stopped, certain that it had not stopped for long.

The savages had suffered considerable losses in that hour. Corpses littered the opposite bank; and even though most of those who had fallen into the river had been swept away by the current, Jephson could see a score of black bodies pinned against rocks, half washed up on reefs, turning grotesquely in eddies. A war canoe that had grounded on a snag of driftwood in midstream was filled with sprawled dead. By comparison, thanks to the terribleness of their guns, their own losses were slight—five or six killed, ten or so wounded—but comparison wasn't the point. They couldn't afford even those losses, and this wasn't the end to the losses either. Surely the savages had broken off the fight only to lick their wounds and rethink their tactics. They'd be back.

Crouching, Jephson darted over to Nelson. He had taken off his pith helmet and was sitting with his back to the boulder, his pistol in his lap, gazing up at the ledge that formed the top step of the cascade. Parke had run back in to the cavern behind the falls and now returned lugging his canvas medicine bag. Uledi came with him. Everyone else, however, held their positions behind cover, waiting for the fighting to begin again.

"Potent stuff, Uledi says," Parke muttered, fumbling in the canvas bag. "He says they boil it out of the petals of some flower.

A species of arum would be my guess, lilies maybe, from the smell of it."

"You're making a fuss over nothing, Tom," Nelson said quietly. "I feel perfectly fine."

"No, Bwana." That was Uledi. He moved closer to peer at the ugly little puckered puncture wound that Parke uncovered, pulling Nelson's tunic and shirt open. "It is strong poison, Bwana. These people hunt the elephant with it. It kills even the elephant."

"I'm stronger than an elephant, *rafiki*," Nelson replied, but he rested his head against the boulder and let Parke work on him.

"There it is. I see it. An inch, an inch and a half in, that's all. Not bad." Parke probed the wound with a pair of forceps. "That hurt?"

Nelson didn't say anything, merely closed his eyes.

"I'll give you a half-grain of morphia, old boy."

Jephson watched Parke administer the injection, then resume probing for the arrow point. His hands were visibly trembling and a torrent of sweat broke out on his face so that from time to time he had to stop to wipe it from his eyes. Jephson pulled a rag of a handkerchief from his tunic pocket and mopped Parke's brow. Parke looked at him, raising his eyebrows, meaning to say something to Jephson. He cocked his head at Parke questioningly, but Parke turned away and returned to his task.

"It'll work its way out on its own," he suddenly said and dropped the forceps back into the canvas bag. "The thing to do is let it work its way out on its own."

Nelson opened his eyes.

"What we want to do, though, is give it a good washing out." Parke took a syringe from the bag, filled it with a solution of carbolic acid, and injected it directly into the wound. Then he reversed the plunger and sucked most of it back out and squirted it on the ground. It was brown with blood.

"Why aren't you taking it out?"

"It isn't necessary. It'll work its way out on its own." Parke repeated the washing process. "Foreign matter, old boy. The body will reject it. You'll see. In a day or two it'll pop out on its own."

"You *can't* take it out. Is that it, Tom?"

Parke looked up at Nelson. "It's in an awfully awkward spot, Robbie. Very close to the heart. It's best not to fool around with it in there."

Nelson didn't say anything. Parke finished washing the wound and fastened a wad of cotton gauze over it with sticking plaster, then pulled a brandy flask from his canvas bag and handed it to Nelson. Nelson took a long pull. When he handed it back, Parke took a long pull himself.

"Uledi, collect the wounded and get them back in there behind the falls so Surgeon Parke can attend to them too."

"*Ndiyo*, Bwana."

"You'll see, Robbie," Parke said again, packing up the canvas bag. "In a day or two you'll be free of the damn thing. It'll pop out on its own."

"Yeah, I'm sure. Now get on back there and look after the others."

Parke took another swallow of the brandy before returning the flask to the bag, then scurried off.

"Well, Arthur, what do you think?" Nelson asked, looking up again at the rocks and ledges at the top of the cascade. "What I think is they're going to try to get behind us. They're going to start up all that howling and racketing again down here to keep us occupied while a bunch of them cross the river up there above the cataract and try to slip around behind us."

Jephson looked where Nelson looked.

"I don't think we should let them do that," Nelson went on calmly. "There'd be hell to pay if we did. I think I'd better get up there with a squad of Winchesters."

"Do you feel up to it?"

"Sure. I'm fine." Nelson started to pull himself together. "Damn that Parke. He's popped all my buttons." Nelson adjusted his cartridge belt so that it held his shirt and tunic closed over the bandage and got to his feet. For an instant he was unsteady. He shook his head, clearing his brain. "Blasted morphine," he muttered and clapped his helmet on his head and reholstered his pistol. "Another thing, Arthur. We ought to try and get hold of that canoe out there." He indicated the war canoe snagged in midriver and filled with corpses. "We could make jolly good use of it."

"Yes, of course. I'll get it. But, Robbie—"

"Not to worry, Arthur. All we need to do is hold fast until Mr. Stanley gets back with the Maxim."

The savages attacked again while Jephson and Sudi and a gang of boatmen were on the river going after the grounded canoe. The attempt itself may have triggered the attack; the savages probably wanted to save the canoe, or perhaps they were incited by the way the dead in it were treated. Bent over double, desperately aware how exposed they were, barely able to keep their footing in the rough water and wildly anxious to get out of there as soon as possible, the Wanyamwezis simply dumped the bodies into the river and let the current carry them away.

The first fusillade of arrows killed two of the Wanyamwezis still in the river.

And they charged this time. They tried to cross the river above the cataract, as Nelson had predicted; but they also swarmed into the river below, streaming down the wall of the canyon opposite, splashing into the foam, scrambling across the reefs, leaping from rock to rock, sailing their canoes straight into the bank, disgorging from them. Nelson had positioned the riflemen well; and the riflemen, both Sudanese and Wanyamwezi, backed to the wall, fought well, with steel nerves and iron courage, and so the carnage they inflicted with their guns at the always closer and closer range of the charging savages was horrendous. But still they came, howling black hordes of them, wave after wave of them, as if there never could be an end to them; and there was no telling how long the riflemen would have held, for all their nerve and courage, how long until their lines would have been overwhelmed, how long before they would have broken and run if the Maxim hadn't saved them.

Stanley himself worked the infernal machine, raking the river to murderous effect from a vantage point high on the canyon wall.

Above the waterfall, atop the first step of the cascade, the Aruwimi turned against them, as narrow there as it had been at Yambuya, as broken with rocks, as white with rapids, and, most discouraging of all, flowing out of the north. Stanley went off in the steel boat with Sudi and a dozen askaris to see if its nature and direction changed farther on, while the last of the loads and canoes and pack animals and wounded and dead were hauled up from the canyon below.

They had left a charnel house in the canyon below. More than two hundred of the savages had been butchered down there before they had finally grasped the full horror of a weapon like the Maxim and broke off the attack and fled. And all through that night, while the column waited for them to return, using the darkness to reinforce the lines and retrench the riflemen and salvage the canoes the savages had abandoned, vultures and hyenas had come into the canyon to feed on the dreadful profusion of corpses. But the savages hadn't returned; like the Basoko and Babukwa before them, these nameless cannibals too had learned the lesson taught by the white man; and so another stretch of the route through the Ituri could be said to be cleared, another tribe along it pacified. In the morning at first light Jephson had taken the *Lady Dorothy* and six of the canoes downriver to fetch up Hoffman and the loads that had been left at the lower cataract.

That was yesterday. Now it was raining again, making the climb out of the canyon so much more difficult. Five additional canoes had been acquired in the fight, bringing the flotilla to fifteen, and put with the others on the rocky embankment. Back in the woods the dead of the column—eleven Wanyamwezis, five Sudanese—were buried by their mates in unmarked graves to keep the cannibals from getting at them. The newly wounded huddled around Parke's surgery tent, sheltering from the rain under plantain leaves, straw mats, blankets, strips of canvas, cotton sheeting, waiting their turn for treatment. There were twenty-three of them, some suffering very much more than others, their faces contorted in speechless pain, an awful rigidity taking hold of their limbs.

This, however, wasn't necessarily a measure of the degree of their wounds—indeed, a number who suffered the most had only been nicked by the savages' arrows—but rather, as Uledi explained, a consequence of the freshness of the poison on the arrow that had nicked them. The more recently it had been cooked up, the more quickly did it seep into the bloodstream and bring on the onset of lockjaw.

Nelson apparently had had a bit of luck on this score. The poison on the arrow that had found him must have been rather old, or perhaps it was because Parke had sucked most of it out; but in any case, he seemed to be bearing up somewhat better than the others. His face was drained of color and his hand repeatedly went to his chest, as if trying to help his body eject the arrow tip embedded beneath his heart. But by and large he was capable of handling his chores, posting pickets, supervising the construction of a zareba, making camp on the level rocky ground above the cascade. Actually, of the Europeans, it was Hoffman who was in the sorriest shape. He had fashioned crutches for himself to take the weight off his ulcerated foot, but with every step as he struggled up out of the canyon driving the last of the pack animals, the dumb expression of agony on his face not unlike that on the sorely-tried beasts, he left an imprint of pus and blood behind him.

Stanley returned at four in the afternoon. He had been gone nearly twelve hours but had managed to explore upriver barely six or seven miles. Although no sizable falls or cataracts had blocked the journey, rapids, boulder-clogged channels, shoals and shallows, and turbulent bends had required repeated portaging; and the swiftness of the current against him had made a knot or two good headway even in the calmer stretches. There was one piece of good news though. Two miles up, the river turned and again flowed out of the east for what appeared a considerable distance.

"I think we should stay on it," he said, going into the command tent. "I think it is still our best way."

Nelson, Jephson, Parke, and Hoffman, the chiefs and headmen of the Wanyamwezis, and the Sudanese corporals crowded in after him, soaked to the skin. The four whites took seats on the crates of special provisions stored in there, the blacks stood along the canvas leaning on their rifles. Stanley, removing his helmet to scratch through his hair for lice, paced about in the small muggy space in front of them, never quite looking at any one of them as he spoke, speaking more or less to himself.

"I think we should stay on it for as long as it keeps taking us to the east. It'll be hard pulling what with all that damn white water but, given the number of sick and wounded we've got, not nearly as hard as hacking through that bloody forest. And who can tell? The river might calm and broaden farther on. It did between here and Yambuya. Maybe it will again. I think it's worth chancing." He stopped pacing. "Eh, Captain? Don't you agree?"

The question came as something of a surprise. Stanley wasn't in the habit of consulting on matters of this sort. Ordinarily he made his decisions without a word to anyone, quickly, on the spot, and then pressed on, leaving the others hurrying to catch up. But now he looked at Nelson and waited; and there was a trace of an appeal in his expression, perhaps even a shadow of doubt in his eyes. The ambush in the canyon had shaken him.

Nelson, startled by this, started to stand; but the abrupt movement jarred the arrow point in his chest, causing him a stab of pain and, he decided to remain seated. "Yes, sir. By all means. Let's stay with the river as long as it's humanly possible. God knows, most of the sick and wounded couldn't go on otherwise. We'd have to leave them behind. And with them their loads. There'd be no one to carry their loads. As it is, we've more loads than we have men to carry them. The loads of our dead."

"Yes." Stanley went to the tent flap and looked out at the encampment, at the hunched figures clustered in front of makeshift shelters trying to get cooking fires started in the rain, at the tethered mules and donkeys with ears laid back in despair and ribs protruding from weeks without proper forage, at the loads ragged and battered and scattered helter-skelter along the rocky embankment, at the Maxim gun pointed back out over the thundering cascade where vultures and kites flapped and circled above the corpses in the canyon below. "Well then, we're agreed on that."

"Are we, sir?" That was Parke.

Stanley looked at him.

"I mean, sir, in view of what's happened and what we can expect to go on happening—the niggers, sir, these attacks, the losses we've suffered. Surely, Mr. Stanley, there must be some question whether we should go on at all. On the river or otherwise."

"No, Doctor, there's no question about that."

"I think there is, sir. I think if you'd consult with these men here, you'd discover there is." Parke indicated the blacks standing along the tent wall.

It was difficult to tell how much of the conversation they understood. Uledi and Sudi and a few others with a good command of English obviously understood it all, but the others too seemed in no doubt about what was under discussion, that their fate was being decided.

"Uledi?"

The Wanyamwezi chieftain shrugged.

"Will you follow me, Uledi?"

"You need not ask me that, Bula Matari. Have I not always followed you faithfully?"

Stanley nodded and looked at the other blacks. He had spoken with Uledi in Swahili, so there was no doubt that they had understood him. They said nothing, however, simply stared at him with stony faces. He again looked out the tent flap.

"What's our muster, Captain? Fifty hurt and sick? Two hundred and thirty more or less fit? Ten mules?"

"About that, sir."

"And we've enough canoes now for . . . What? Pretty nearly all the loads, I should think, and a hundred fifty men besides."

"Yes, sir. Something like that."

"All right then. That's how we'll form up. All the hurt and sick will go on the river with, say, a hundred of the fit. That leaves a land party of about a hundred thirty. We'll spell them every few days, but as they won't be carrying loads except for their weapons and personal kit, and those on the river will be breaking their backs portaging more often than not, I don't want to hear any grousing about who goes with which party." Stanley looked back into the tent. "You'll go with the river party, Captain."

"That isn't necessary, sir. I'm quite able to march."

"I'm sure you are. But I want you to go easy for a few days. Until that arrow works its way out of your chest. Surgeon Parke will take your place."

"Sir?"

"You'll march with me and Will Hoffman in the land party for a few days, Doctor, in command of the rear guard."

"But what about the sick and wounded, sir? Don't you think my place is with them? There are several in rather serious condition, you know. I'm afraid we can expect to have a number of tetanus cases on our hands from the arrow wounds, besides the pleurisy and dysentery and malaria and infections and foot ulcers and broken bones and God knows what else we already have."

"You'll be able to look after everybody at the nightly camps."

"No, sir." Parke suddenly stood up. "That wouldn't do at all, sir. I must be with them at all times. There's no telling when they might be in need of treatment. Take Captain Nelson, for instance. There's no telling when that arrow will begin poking its way out. It could happen at any time, and I must be on hand to cut it out when it does."

"Why don't I take Captain Nelson's place, Mr. Stanley?" Jephson said.

"Actually there's no need for anyone to take my place."

"Yes, why doesn't Arthur take Robbie's place? That would seem the more sensible arrangement. He'd have no difficulty making the march. He's fit. He's certainly fitter than I am. I mean, apart from my responsibilities to the sick and wounded, there's that too, Mr. Stanley. I've had fever for weeks, you know. Malaria, most likely. It's taken all my strength away. Look. You can see for yourself." Parke stuck out his hands, revealing how badly they trembled. "I don't know what to do about it, Mr. Stanley. I've tried everything. Quinine. Chlorodyne. Nothing seems to help. I've no strength left at all. It isn't possible for me to march in this condition. You really must let me go on the river, sir, as much as one of the sick as their physician. Arthur would be the far better choice . . ." His voice trailed off under Stanley's steely gaze.

There was a moment of embarrassed silence in the tent. Then Stanley looked away from Parke and said, "We'll spend another day here to rest up and put our gear in order. We'll set out the day after tomorrow. With any luck, it'll have stopped raining by then."

"*No!*"

All eyes turned to Parke.

"I'm not going. I'm not going in the land party. I'm not going in any party. I'm not going at all. I'm going back."

"Tommy!"

"You can have my resignation, Mr. Stanley. I submit my resignation." Parke jerked to attention and saluted. It was a ludicrous, frightening gesture. "Thomas Heazle Parke, Army Medical Department, requests permission to resign from the staff of the Emin Pasha relief expedition, sir."

"For God's sake, Tommy. Are you drunk? You're behaving like an ass."

"You're the ass, Robbie, not me. You're the ass if you go another step on this insane enterprise. You're the ass—you're all asses, every last one of you, if you think you'll ever see Wadelai. Wadelai? Where is it? Does anyone know where it is? Does Mr. Stanley know? A hundred miles? Two hundred? Five hundred? There to the east, up the river, through the forest? Where? But it doesn't matter. It doesn't matter a bloody damn, because you'll never get there, not one of you. Do you hear me? Not one of you will ever lay eyes on the place. The niggers will kill you before you do. And if not the niggers, the forest. And if not the forest, the river—"

"That's enough, Dr. Parke."

"Yes, sir, it's enough. It certainly is enough for me. More than enough." Parke turned sharply as if executing a parade ground maneuver and started from the tent.

Nelson jumped up.

"Let him go, Captain."

"Yes, let me go." Parke stopped at the tent flap and looked back. His face was a sight, the scraggly beard, the tangled hair, dripping with sweat. "Let me go," he said again and stepped out into the rain.

But he didn't go, of course. There was nowhere to go.

• FIVE •

Although by a tortuously serpentine course, the Aruwimi continued flowing out of the east. Whenever it pulled them so far either to the north or south that Jephson thought that now at last they would have to abandon it, it unexpectedly twisted back as if it had played a joke it suddenly regretted. But it never opened up again into the broad navigable river it once had been. To the contrary, mile after mile, day after day, it steadily narrowed pouring down through a close leafy tunnel of embowering trees, crashing over boulders and reefs and mudflats and hoorah's nests of driftwood in an endlessly recurring series of rapids and cataracts. Making way up it was a brutal struggle. Not a day went by that the boat and canoes didn't have to be taken out of the water, unloaded, and hauled around some treacherous obstacle—and not once but several times, and not just for a few hundred feet but on occasion for miles. It was miserable, punishing work, exhausting the already exhausted men. To keep them at it was a constant fight. Again and again, they would quit, and Jephson and Nelson and Sudi had to go after them, arguing, pleading, cajoling, threatening, striking out at them in sudden fits of frustration and fatigue.

In the third week of September—when by Stanley's original calculation they should have reached the shore of Lake Albert—the column crossed longitude 28 degrees east. In a direct line, this was 185 miles from Yambuya, but they actually had come probably more than twice that distance. They had at least that much more yet to go.

The Aruwimi forked here or, more accurately, met the confluence of another river. This other river, the fork to the left so to speak, nameless, unknown, emptied into the Aruwimi from the north, while the Aruwimi itself continued flowing out of the east. The second river was by far the larger of the two. At its mouth on the Aruwimi it was a good 300 yards wide and—as far as the eye could see up its muddy, sluggish, invitingly navigable but unfortunately useless course—never less than two hundred yards from bank to bank. By comparison, the Aruwimi appeared to be the tributary, not the other way around, and a rather minor one at that, hardly twenty-five yards wide at this point and, where it joined the other river, foaming violently over yet another stretch of rapids that would have to be portaged. Jephson waved the flotilla to shore. They had spent the better part of that afternoon fighting their way around a bad patch of broken water not a half-mile downstream, and the idea of starting the whole blasted business all over again so soon struck Jephson as intolerable. Besides, a storm was brewing.

"We'll make camp here, Sudi."

"Yes, sah."

Jephson hopped out of the *Lady Dorothy* and waded back down the shallows to where the hospital canoe was putting in to the pebble-strewn beach. "Robbie, there's another mob of white water up ahead, and what with this rain coming on . . . Well, we might as well call it quits for the day here, don't you think?"

Nelson didn't reply. He was helping hand out the wounded and sick from the canoe; but when he started ashore himself, he seemed in as much need of help as any of them. He walked with a stiff-legged gait in something of a half-crouch, holding his head at a peculiar angle, one shoulder hunched slightly higher than the other. His wound had healed—it was nothing now but a hard lump covered by a black scab, and there was no sign of infection—but the arrow point was still in there, floating around his heart, not working its way out as Parke had predicted. And the poison was still in him, coursing through his bloodstream, circulating to his vital organs. For the past several days he had been experiencing sharp shooting pains in the nape of his neck and fits of nausea. Jephson recognized these symptoms. He only had to observe the others in the hospital canoe who had been wounded in the canyon at the same time. Most were in dreadful straits by now and getting worse, stiffening along the spine, limbs swelling grotesquely, racked by horrid spasms. Seven had already died. One Sudanese had gone so rigid in the throat and jaw that he had been unable to swallow; and although his mates had tried to feed him a soupy gruel of mealie meal, he had wasted away to a skeleton before their eyes and died of starvation. The effect on Nelson, traveling in the hospital canoe with them, must have been awful, but he never commented on it. It was as if he refused to notice or make the connection between those poor devils and himself; and he went on participating in the grueling work of the river party, unsparing of whatever was left of his strength, unmindful of his pain. He was all right, he insisted repeatedly, and indeed the first time Stanley had paraded the river and land parties and sorted out the newly sick and injured from the malingerers and had the healthy in each group exchange places, Nelson had prevailed on him to let him rejoin the land party and resume his command of the rear guard and have Parke take back his place in the hospital canoe.

That arrangement, however, had lasted only one day. When Nelson came into camp that night after very nearly thirteen hours on the march he hardly could speak.

Now he stumbled on the pebbles of the riverbank, and an askari grabbed hold of his arm to prevent him from falling. He shook the fellow off irritably and stood for a moment bent double, still ankle-deep in the water, both hands resting on his knees as if he were about to vomit.

"I'm going to scout upriver a ways and see how far before we get quiet water again," Jephson said as matter-of-factly as he could, trying to keep the concern he felt for the man out of his voice. "But I'm pretty sure there's no sense in starting the portage today anymore. It looks to be at least a couple of miles."

"Hang on a minute." Nelson's words came out as a hoarse, shockingly strangled croak. He cleared his throat and spat into the water at his feet, but when he spoke again there wasn't much improvement. "I'll go with you."

"There's no need for that. And anyway one of us ought to stick around here and see about setting up camp."

"You do it then."

"What? Oh, sure, I'll do it if you prefer."

"What does that mean? If *I* prefer?" Nelson straightened up. His eyes were glazed, his face a mask of pain. "Don't patronize me, Arthur. Don't treat me like a bloody invalid."

"Robbie, I'm not—"

"For God's sake." Nelson suddenly bent double again, a hand going to his chest. "Oh, for God's sake."

"Robbie." Jephson started toward him.

"Leave me alone."

Jephson stopped and stared at Nelson in a kind of horror.

After a minute, still bent over, Nelson said, "Go on, Arthur. Scout the river. I'll look after making camp."

Jephson hesitated.

"Go on, old boy. I'll be all right."

Jephson fetched Sudi and four of the askaris, and they followed the Aruwimi up along its southern bank for about a mile. It remained a solid stretch of rock and torrent throughout that distance, nowhere in the least navigable. But what was worse, the terrain on both sides, in addition to the damnable trees and brush and roots and vines and clumps of thorny thickets in which it was jungled, ascended so steeply that by the time they stopped they found themselves standing a good hundred feet above the river, and there was still more climbing ahead.

The portage would be punishing. The track to be cut would be uphill all the way; trees would have to be felled to serve as rollers over which to haul the canoes; the *Lady Dorothy* probably would have to be taken apart. They'd be days at it.

Jephson clambered out on a ledge of lavalike stone overhanging the river in the hope of seeing where it calmed and the portage would end. He didn't. Another half-mile or so farther up, the reach ended; and the river, rushing around a sharp bend from the southeast, was hidden from view beyond that by still higher and steeper clifflike embankments. Jephson studied the spot through his field glasses. The countryside grew progressively so much more hilly to the east, north, and south that the place where the river issued into view—a foaming steel-gray ribbon under the lowering clouds of the approaching rain—looked like the mouth of a mountain gorge.

He buttoned the field glasses into his tunic to secure them, hopped from the ledge, and scrambled down to the riverbed. Sudi and the askaris followed, setting off landslides of shale and pebbles and chips of flint, clutching at shrubs and branches and exposed roots to keep from pitching headlong into the water. As they made their way farther along the bank toward the gorge at the head of the reach, they heard the sporadic crack of rifle shots, Nelson signaling to the land party the camp's location.

"Sah."

Jephson stopped.

"It is finished, sah."

They had reached the mouth of the gorge. Jephson took a few steps into it and stared. The river here had narrowed to less than fifteen yards and, at the top of the gorge, disappeared. There was only a waterfall, a single almost perfectly cylindrical plume bursting over a lip of limestone and plunging down in a straight unbroken line from a height of more than 200 feet into the basin of the gorge below. It was at once a beautiful and terrible sight. The perpetual cloud of spray it raised, smoking up from the basin's boiling pool, had forested the gorge's sheer black rock walls with balsam and flowering liana and magenta orchids and hairy gray-green curtains of moss through which now in the waning daylight hundreds of small snipelike birds flew.

"The river is finished for us, sah," Sudi said again.

Jephson shook his head. He didn't want to believe it. "Up above, Sudi," he said after a moment but with little conviction. "Above this fall, maybe there the river . . ."

"No, sah. It is finished. We can no longer travel on it."

Jephson did not argue.

The rain had begun by the time they got back to the encampment, fat tepid drops splattering in the cooking fires, slowly extinguishing them. No zareba had been built around the partially cleared site, no pickets had been posted. Most of the men, beaten and exhausted, had retreated from the rain into the shelters of leaves and grass they had erected for themselves helter-skelter along the river embankment. The surgery and command tents stood among them forlornly, sagging between their poles. It was a badly made camp, testimony to Nelson's condition, and the land party had not arrived yet. Apparently they were having troubles of their own. Jephson found Nelson in the command tent fully clothed, covered by a damp blanket, asleep. He looked utterly done in, his mouth open, his breathing labored. He coughed in his sleep and tried to turn over, but the effort proved too much for him and he fell back and lay still again. Jephson decided not to disturb him. Perhaps he should have awakened him and helped him out of his filthy clothing and persuaded him to have some supper, but he decided the best medicine was simply to let him sleep. And anyway, he wasn't anxious to tell him what he had discovered about the river. Tomorrow would be soon enough for that.

He went to the surgery tent and took off his boots. These were his third pair. He had thrown away the first, thoroughly rotted through, and now alternated the remaining two every few days in the belief that this somehow would make them last longer. Sudi brought in a plate of food—the wing of some unidentifiable bird, rice porridge made with condensed milk—and hunkered down in a corner of the tent and watched Jephson eat.

"Have you had something yourself?"

"Yes, sah."

Jephson polished off the bird wing greedily, sucking the juice and marrow out of the bone—Christ, he was hungry; he was hungry all the time now—then started on the gluey mess of porridge with his fingers. "Is anything the matter, *rafiki?*"

Sudi didn't answer.

Jephson looked up from his plate. The young Wanyamwezi had been staring at him, but when their eyes met he lowered his. Jephson studied him. He was a good chap, as good as any of the headmen ten years older, as good as any of the Europeans—intelligent, capable, loyal, tireless, uncomplaining. But it would be foolish to imagine he had no complaints. God knew, they all had. They were being pushed too hard, tried to the very limits of their endurance, and there was no end to it in sight. Of course they had complaints. But it was just as well not to inquire into them too closely, because there was nothing to be done about them anyway.

Jephson set the plate aside. "Come on, old boy. We'd best signal the land party again. They can't be too far off now." He got up and went out into the rain.

"How is he, Tommy?"

Parke picked up his canvas medicine bag and came out of the command tent.

"Will he be able to walk?"

This was the next day, a clear day, the sun beating down out of a cloudless sky. Nelson was in the command tent sleeping like the dead.

"He's going to have to walk, Tommy. You've got to fix him up so he can walk."

Parke stared off into space. A sour stench wafted from his torn and rumpled uniform, lice crawled in his greasy matted beard. He was probably drunk.

"Are you listening to me, Tommy?"

Parke turned back to Jephson. "Walk, Arthur? Where would you have him walk?"

"Tommy!"

"What do you want from me, Arthur? In God's name, what do you want from me? I'm the one who said we should go back. I'm the one who said we should go back before we die. And we still could go back if you hadn't scuttled the canoes."

"Mr. Stanley—"

"He told you to. Of course he told you to. And why? Why, do you suppose?" Parke moved closer to Jephson, breathing on him foully. "I'll tell you why. Because he was afraid that as long as we had the canoes the men wouldn't go on. They'd steal the canoes and go back." Suddenly he clutched at Jephson's sleeve. "Tonight, Arthur. That was their plan. I heard them talking."

"Who?"

"All of them. The askaris mainly but plenty of the others too. They're on the brink of mutiny, Arthur. One of these days they're going to leave us stranded."

Jephson pulled his sleeve free of Parke's clammy grasp. "You're crazy, Tommy. You're imagining things."

"No. It's true. Ask Mr. Stanley. He got wind of it. That's why he had you sink the canoes. So there'd be no way back. So we'd have to go on."

And the next day, mustered once again into a single party, a land party, lined out in Indian file under the harsh sun of yet another cloudless morning, they went on, up along the Aruwimi's southern bank into the jungled hills above the waterfall. There they veered off, south by southeast, and headed inland, giving up on the river once and for all. It was doubly worthless to them now. Not only could they no longer travel on it, but worse, they had scant prospect of replenishing their much-diminished stocks of food along its craggy cliff-steep shore. Villages with fields of manioc and maize, groves of plantains and bananas, gardens of greens and beans were more likely to be found, if they were to be found at all, inland. Indeed, Stanley and the land party in their struggles through the forest in the last few days had come across paths and trails a few miles back from the river that appeared to be man-made; and the hope now, as they once again chopped their way into the claustrophobic vegetable gloom of a trackless jungle, was to find one that would take them to the east through an inhabited cultivated region.

The first day Stanley halted the march on the bank of a small creek that tumbled out of the hills northward back to the Aruwimi. Darkness had fallen before the last of the column, carrying torches of dried plantain stalks by which to see the blazes the pioneers had cut on the trees, straggled in. These were mostly the sick and injured, those who had traveled in the hospital canoe until now, a ragged, pitiful bunch hanging on to each other like mendicants from an institution, as well as a few muleteers driving cruelly overloaded half-starved pack animals. Nelson was with them. He had started the march in command of the rear guard but had been unable to keep up. Jephson hurried back to lend him a hand.

"I'm all right," Nelson said, but when Jephson put an arm around his waist his knees buckled.

"It's only a little farther, Robbie. You can make it."

Nelson gritted his teeth and, leaning heavily on Jephson, allowed himself to be dragged the last few hundred yards to the creekside camp. "Don't let me lie down. Just prop me against something. I'm afraid I won't want to get up again if you let me lie down."

Jephson selected a smooth-barked palm near the command tent and lowered Nelson into a sitting position against its bole. "How's that?"

Nelson's legs stretched out uselessly in front of him. "Take off my helmet, will you." He spoke in that strained, almost inaudible croak Jephson had gotten used to. When his pith helmet was removed, he let his head drop back against the tree and closed his eyes.

Stanley and Parke came over. Parke remained standing; Stanley got down on his knees next to Jephson. From a distance, Hoffman, hanging on his crutches, watched them for a moment, then hobbled away.

"You did fine, Captain," Stanley said.

Nelson opened his eyes.

"It'll be easier going tomorrow. We're sure to strike a trail tomorrow, probably even a village."

Nelson nodded. He was sweating profusely.

"How did the others with you do? Did we lose anyone?"

"A tent boy. Foot ulcers. He couldn't get up after the last break."

"I'll send back for him."

Nelson shook his head. "No sense in that. He's dead by now. The buzzards were already there when we left him."

"I see." Stanley leaned forward and brushed away the flies that gathered in the rivulets of sweat streaming down Nelson's haggard face. "Do you want a shot of morphine?"

Nelson didn't reply. He had closed his eyes again.

"Let Surgeon Parke give you a shot of morphine, Robbie. It'll help you sleep." Stanley stood up. "Dr. Parke."

Jephson also stood up. Willy Hoffman had come back; he had fetched a bowl of rice gruel from the command tent's cooking fire and handed it to Parke as Parke kneeled down beside Nelson. Jephson walked off a few paces with Stanley.

"Couldn't we fix up a litter for him, sir?"

"Sure we could. But who did you have in mind to carry it? There ain't a fit man in this column not already carrying more than his fair share. And you'd need four for a litter."

"We could leave some of the loads."

"Oh, we could, could we? Like which ones?" Stanley's voice was suddenly harsh with irritation and fatigue. "The rations? The ammunition? Or maybe the medicines."

Jephson didn't say anything.

Stanley looked back at Nelson. After a long moment he expelled his breath in a weary sigh and said, "All right, lad, we'll see. We'll see how he does tomorrow. But I'll tell you this. Once you start carrying a man, he goes quickly. He becomes like a baby. He loses his will."

The column was infuriatingly slow getting under way the next morning. Uledi and the trackers were off well before daybreak in search of a trail upstream along the creek, but the rest of the men, grumbling sullenly, had to be routed out of their shelters with shouts and threats. Hoffman went among them poking and prodding with his crutches, but even so, three couldn't be gotten up at all. One, a victim of the arrow poison, had died during the night; the other two simply lay in their bedrolls with dumbstruck eyes, barely conscious, unable to fend off Hoffman's blows. They were left behind. Nelson, mercifully, was not one of them. He was already on his feet when Jephson awoke, leaning stiffly against the tree under which he had spent the night sitting up, watching as camp was broken and the column paraded, making no move to participate in the work, waiting only for the trek to begin again, conserving all his energy for that. There was no question of his resuming command of the rear guard. Parke was put in charge of them, and Nelson marched with Jephson's company.

This was rougher, hillier country now, the forest floor climbing out of its swampy sink in sudden jagged ridges and steep rocky rises toward some distant jungled upland. As the morning wore on, Nelson's pace faltered and he dropped back. Jephson dropped back with him.

"Lean on me, Robbie."

Nelson shook his head. He didn't speak at all now. He couldn't. It was more than he could do just to keep going, lifting one foot and setting it down in front of the other, his breath coming in wheezing gasps, his expression fixed in a rigid death's-head grimace, staring blindly ahead. The column pushed by him, ignoring him, each man grimly absorbed in his own terrible labor of keeping up, keeping on, going only God and perhaps Stanley knew where.

Just before eleven word was passed down the line that the scouts at last had picked up a trail, and although no order to that effect was given, the men seized on the news as an excuse to take a rest break. Jephson and Nelson had by then fallen back among the last of the other haplessly struggling sick and injured. As Jephson was damn sure Parke wouldn't come down the line to see how they were faring, he forced Nelson to go on. It was more than a mile to the head of the column. Nelson couldn't make it. Jephson got him as far as the boat company and left him there with Sudi and went the rest of the way alone.

A bridge, a ford really, of rotted moss-slick logs lashed together with vines crossed the creek where the pioneers and front guard had halted. A narrow path, the trail that had been found, emerged from the forest from the west, passed over the ford, and continued eastward into the trees on the other side for another hundred feet or so. And there it entered a village.

Or what had once been a village. It was burned to the ground. All that was left of it was a blackened clearing spotted with the charred husks of fifteen or twenty huts, the broken remains of a palisade, the stubble of ravaged fields. The smoke of the fires that had destroyed them, faint but distinct, still hung in the heavy humid air above the clearing. Stanley, Hoffman, and Uledi had crossed the ford into the village; and the askaris of the front guard were drawn up in a double firing line on the creek's near bank, covering them. Parke was with the askaris. He jerked around nervously at the sound of Jephson's footsteps.

"Jesus, Tommy, what happened here?"

"No one seems to know. Some kind of fight. One tribe of niggers making war on another probably." Parke looked across the creek. "There are probably thousands of niggers on the warpath back in there. And that madman is going to march us straight into the middle of them."

Down the path through the trees on the other side, Jephson could see Stanley rummaging about in the ruins of one of the huts, stirring up puffs of gray smoke from the still-smoldering ashes. The devastation, whatever its cause, had occurred that recently, possibly no more than a few hours before. Hoffman and Uledi, apparently searching like Stanley for a clue to what had happened, were at the far end of the village, where the path re-entered the forest to the east. But there was no other sign of life, only the shrilling of insects in the day's steadily mounting heat. Jephson went over the ford.

Stanley spun around, leveling his Winchester.

"Hey, hold on." Jephson threw up his hands.

Seeing who it was, Stanley lowered the rifle, but without a

trace of humor about his mistake or embarrassment about his jumpiness. He looked around the clearing with narrowed eyes, as if he suspected the footsteps he had heard had been made by someone else.

"Bula Matari." That was Hoffman. "Over here, Bula Matari." He had laid his crutches aside and was kneeling in the scrub of the path. Uledi had come up behind him and was looking over the naked bulk of his sun-blistered shoulders. Evidently he had found something.

Stanley went over quickly. Jephson followed.

He saw the corpse right away. Hoffman was straddling it, so his big fleshy torso blocked most of it from view; but there was the head, a kaffir's, glassy eyes open in an expression of final terror, the mouth full of blood, and an outflung arm, its hand stiffened into a claw. Farther up the path, deeper into the woods were four more; they were sprawled facedown. Hoffman apparently had turned this one over and now, Jephson suddenly realized with a shiver of disgust, was probing into its chest with the point of his hunting knife, unmindful of the swarms of flies he was stirring up or the sickening stench, his hands as bloody as a butcher's. While Jephson watched with horrified fascination, Hoffman dug an object out of the leathery flesh and held it up on his palm to Stanley.

A mashed lump of dull gray metal—lead, a bullet.

"Shot?" Jephson blurted out stupidly. "He was shot?"

Stanley picked up the slug.

"But who shot him? Our men didn't shoot him, did they? Uledi, did one of the trackers shoot him?"

Uledi shook his head.

"I don't understand." Jephson looked again at the other corpses. They too must have been shot; from their sprawled facedown positions they appeared to have been shot while trying to escape up the path into the woods from whoever had attacked and destroyed the village. But who had attacked and destroyed the village? Not other kaffirs. Kaffirs didn't have guns. Who then? Who besides the men of the column had guns in this godforsaken wilderness?

"Tippoo-Tib," Hoffman said, wiping the knife's bloody blade on his trouser leg. "Eh, Bula Matari? It's Tippoo-Tib's work, ain't it?"

Stanley, absently jiggling the spent slug in his hand, once more was surveying the destroyed village. It must have been pretty once, a cluster of huts nestled on the bank of a fast-running creek, probably even prosperous by native standards. To the north, beyond where one side of the ruined palisade had stood, were fields of manioc or perhaps maize, groves of plantains or maybe the elais, plots of what might have been tobacco or beans. It was difficult to tell, because those too had been reduced to ashes by the fires.

"It's Tippoo-Tib's work all right," Hoffman said again and re-sheathed his knife. "Slavers' work. I'd wager my last quid on it."

"No," Jephson said. "No, that can't be."

Hoffman, ignoring him, got back up on his crutches.

"It can't be Tippoo-Tib, Mr. Stanley. How can it be?"

"A gang of his anyhow."

"But I thought the slavers never came into the forest. I thought no one did. I thought no one dared."

"Yes, so did I." Stanley looked at the slug in his hand, then let it drop. It landed near the outflung arm of the corpse. "Seems we were wrong."

"But what about the rear column then? What about Jack Troup and Major Barttelot? How are they going to come after us with the relief supplies? They won't have enough porters. I mean, if Tippoo-Tib already knows the way into the forest, if his slaving gangs are already here, he won't provide them with the porters he promised. He only promised to provide those porters in order to learn the way into the forest, didn't he?"

Stanley, as if unhearing, gazed blankly at the corpse at his feet, the face crawling with flies, maggots, and other vermin already eating into the new wound Hoffman had opened in the chest, the whole putrefying mess bloating in the midday heat.

"He didn't have any other reason to promise them, did he?"

"I don't know," Stanley finally answered and with the toe of his boot nudged the corpse over onto its face.

"You don't know?"

Stanley looked up. "That's right, lad. I don't know." And in that moment he seemed very old, played out, his face grizzled with stubble, slack with exhaustion, lined and worn and battered by responsibility and care. It was the business with the steamers at the Pool all over again, Jephson realized with a shock. Stanley had gambled the expedition's success on Tippoo-Tib's providing porters for the passage through the Ituri just as he had gambled it on King Leopold's providing the steamers for the voyage up the Congo—and again had lost.

"But we can't worry about that right now. We've got other things closer to hand to worry about. Uledi, take the trackers out. Those slavers are bound to be still lurking around here somewhere. I want you to find the bastards."

"No need for that, Bula Matari," Hoffman interjected. "The bastards have found us."

A short distance back into the forest, just beyond where the other corpses lay, a half-caste of some sort—part Arab, part African, possibly part something else—had stepped out onto the path. He was mahogany-skinned, bearded, as sharp-featured as a hawk and rail thin. His soiled white ankle-length djellaba was belted with colored cloth, a Shirazi dagger in the belt. Bandoliers were crossed on his chest, an old muzzle-loader was on his shoulder, and his head was wrapped in a filthy blue turban. He was the very picture of a cutthroat bandit; and he had a band of cutthroats with him—ugly blue-black brutes, ten or fifteen of them, dressed in long white skirts, naked above the waist, also turbaned and similarly armed. They were Manyema, those cannibal tribesmen from the forests of the Upper Congo whom the Zanzibari Arabs employed as gunmen and porters in their ivory and slaving caravans. They remained half hidden in the sun-dappled gloom of the trees, peering out at the white men, so unexpectedly come upon. Beyond them, deeper still in the forest's speckled shadows, Jephson could make out other human shapes and forms, perhaps a score or more, herded closely together, some huddled on the ground; they were making low keening sounds. It took him a moment to realize who they were: the men and women and children who had been captured by the slavers in the raid on the village. Each one was yoked and trussed.

"Will, bring the front guard over the creek and have the Maxim fetched up. I don't want this bastard thinking it's just the four of us."

"Who are you, *wasungu?*" Calling out in the singsong of coast Swahili, cocky, insolent—*wasungu*, white men, not Bwana—the half-caste started down the path toward Stanley. "Where do you come from? Where do you go? How is it that you find yourself in a place such as this, so far from the comforts of your home?"

"I would ask the same of you, slaver. I did not know the dogs of Tippoo-Tib strayed this far east of the Congo."

"Ah." The half-caste stopped. Stanley's quick uncowed belligerence surprised him, put him on his guard. He decided to keep his distance. "How rudely you reply, *wasungu*. Why is this? What quarrel do you have with me? Are we not both but simple travelers met by chance in a savage corner of the universe we share? Surely we intend no harm, the one to the other." Here he smiled, a thin, crooked, predatory smile that showed the points of his yellow teeth and did little to enhance the sincerity of his words. "For my part, *wasungu*, I willingly declare I intend you no harm."

"Nonetheless, you do me harm. Your very presence in a region where I would travel does me grievous harm." Stanley pointed to the corpse at his feet. "Tell me, slaver, how much death like this will I now encounter on my way to the east? How many villages like this will lie in my path? How many fields of manioc and maize like these will I find burned to the ground, and how many groves of plantains and bananas and palm raped of their fruit? Tell me, slaver, what will I find standing on which to feed the people of my caravan in a region where a dog of Tippoo-Tib has been before me?"

The half-caste didn't answer. His attention had been diverted. The askaris of the front guard were filing into the village at a fast trot. Word of the presence of slavers in this part of the forest had spread among them like wildfire; and the catastrophe they knew it portended showed in their eyes, intent, apprehensive, darting about, registering the destroyed huts, the shot-down corpses, and most especially the wantonly ravaged fields from which they had counted on replenishing their depleted stores. Hunched over, rifles at high port, they deployed quickly around what once had been the village's market square. In a minute the Maxim would be with them. Hoffman was back on this side of the creek, barking orders at the gun crew hauling the weapon over the half-sunken slippery logs of the ford.

"Tell me, slaver, will I find anything? Or have you like the locust devoured everything and made a wasteland of the forest where I would now go?"

The half-caste looked at Stanley. His smile was gone. The realization that he and his band were outgunned, that they had stumbled into a situation where they for once were the ones at the disadvantage in arms and in danger of suffering the sort of treatment they were in the habit of meting out, had wiped the smirk from his hawk-sharp face. "*Wasungu,*" he said, and a wheedling aggrieved note crept into his voice, supplanting the earlier arrogance. "You must not mistake the servant for the master, a mere captain for the general, these few poor soldiers you see with me for the army."

"The army, slaver? What army?'"

"The army of my master, Abed bin Salim, known to all as Kilonga-longa, sheik in the household of Hamed bin Mohammed, known to all as Tippoo-Tib—may his name be praised—an army of more than a thousand guns."

"Ah, you threaten me with an army of a thousand guns?"

"Oh, no, no, for the love of Allah, I do not threaten you in any way, *wasungu*. I mention this army of my master, I mention Kilonga-longa and his thousand guns only to explain that it is he who rules in these forests, *wasungu*, not I. It is he who commands, from his fort in Ipoto, the things that are done here, this destruction of which you complain. You must not hold me to blame for it, *wasungu*. I am but his humble servant, one only of his many captains, a Waswahili of no account. Believe me, *wasungu*, I intend you no harm."

As he spoke, the half-caste backed a few steps away, his face wet with sweat, all the swagger gone out of him. For the Maxim had been set up in the center of the village square, and its gleaming sun-struck barrel was aimed directly at him.

"And where is this Kilonga-longa, slaver? Where is this Ipoto? Where is this fort with its army of a thousand guns of which you boast?"

"To the east from here, *wasungu*." With a jerk of his bearded chin, the half-caste indicated the forest behind him. "To the east and northeast by this path, on the bank of a river the Washenzi of the Ituri call the Ihuru."

"How many marches to the east?"

The half-caste shrugged. "That depends. Ten? With poor luck, fifteen perhaps."

"A hundred miles." Stanley said this in English. "A hundred mile, more or less. And between here and there—what? Nothing, I suppose, nothing but more of this death and destruction."

The half-caste didn't understand.

"Will."

Hoffman, issuing a last order to the Sudanese corporal in charge of the gun crew, came swinging over on his crutches.

"Have you ever heard of Abed bin Salim, Will? Also known as Kilonga-longa. One of Tippoo-Tib's henchmen."

Hoffman scrutinized the half-caste with his lashless eyes, then said, "This ain't him. This ragpicker don't claim to be him, does he?"

"No."

"Yes. I heard of Kilonga-longa. A murdering shit. Last I heard of him, though, he was at the Falls."

"Well, seems he ain't there anymore."

"Where is he?"

"A place called Ipoto. A hundred miles or so farther on into the forest."

"Since when?"

Stanley turned back to the half-caste, who at the approach of Hoffman's monstrous hairless hulk had retreated still farther up the path. "How long is it since Kilonga-longa took his leave of the household of Tippoo-Tib, slaver? How long is it since he led his caravan out of Singatini?"

"A year, *wasungu.*"

"A year?"

"A full year and more. For seven months we journeyed to the east from the Congo. For seven months we fought our way into the green hell of this forest. Then at last we came to Ipoto in the valley of the Ihuru, where Kilonga-longa decided to build his fort, and seven months have gone since then."

"And this was done with Tippoo-Tib's knowledge, I suppose. Kilonga-longa came into the forest with Tippoo-Tib's blessing and consent."

"Oh, yes, *wasungu.* It was Tippoo-Tib himself who sent Kilonga-longa into the forest. Many times before, Tippoo-Tib had sent caravans into the forest; many times before, he had chosen a trusted one of his sheiks and instructed him to go and break the spell of the Ituri and open up new hunting grounds for him here. But only Kilonga-longa succeeded. All the others found the curse of the forest too terrible and returned—when they returned at all—in defeat. Only Kilonga-longa succeeded."

"And Tippoo-Tib knows of this? He has been informed of Kilonga-longa's success?"

"No, *wasungu,* not yet, but soon. Soon now he will be informed. For it is my task to inform him. You have met me by chance on my way back to Singatini to inform Tippoo-Tib of Kilonga-longa's success."

"So, that's it then." Stanley looked around at Jephson. "There you have it, lad. There's your answer for you."

"Sir?"

Stanley flashed a wolfish grin, his scarred, battered old face coming alive, youthful again. "We're all right. Yes, by Christ, we're still all right. The rear column's got the porters. Tippoo-Tib delivered them. I'm sure of it. He delivered them long before this, and they must be well under way on our track by now. Don't you see? The cunning bastard was covering his bet. That's what it was all about. He obviously had more faith in me than in this Kilonga-longa. He reckoned I'd get through whether this Kilonga-longa did or not. And I will get through. By Christ, I will."

The trail to Ipoto was blazed. The slavers had blazed it, marking it out in the forest's confusion of game tracks and false paths with distinctive oblique *panga* slashes on the trees every twenty yards or so, head high, a hand's breadth in width, emitting a faintly garlicky scent from the peeled bark. Anxious to take advantage of this and make up for lost time, Stanley drove the men along it at a merciless pace. He stayed well out in front, in advance even of Uledi and the pioneers, two Sudanese sharpshooters, and two of the best scouts dogging his heels. A burst of new energy was in him, a ferocious urgency like a spiritual second wind that conveyed itself to the weary men of the column as something akin to madness or panic as they hurried after him in the dismal twilight of the trees, climbing higher into the jungled hills to the east and north, scrambling over massive granite outcroppings made slick by lichen, threading along the lips of precipitous ravines, skirting bogs and deadfalls, passing through villages clustered on the banks of streams. Like the first, all of these villages were burned to the ground, their fields and groves plundered, their streets littered with the skulls and bones and still rotting corpses of those who had tried to resist or escape the slavers.

They had entered Kilonga-longa's raiding circle, a realm of ruin and desolation, radiating in every direction from its center at Ipoto. It was a realm that Stanley reckoned, from his experience with other Tippoo-Tib henchmen—Muni Mohara on the Upper Congo, Bwana Nzige on the Lumami, Ugarrowwa on the Lulua, Mtagamoyo at Lake Ozo, Tippoo-Tib himself among the Manyema—might be as vast as thirty, forty, even fifty thousand square miles.

Within it the great enemy was hunger; within it starvation began to haunt the column's steps. For ironically, despite the nightmare profusion of monstrous growth, very little grew in the jungle that was fit for man to eat.

The bastard jack fruit, the *mabengu* or nux vomica, the red berries of the *phrynia*, the *matonga* and cardamom, the oblong bitter pear of the *amona*, a species of wild forest bean encased in a leathery brown rind that had the taste of acorn and could be ground into a flour and made into cakes or porridge, some varieties of mushroom and root and rock tripe. From the start, hoarding what remained of their stores of rice and mealies and biscuits, knowing there was little hope of finding even one unspoiled garden in this slaver-ravaged wasteland, Stanley had the men forage to eke out their niggardly rations, and for grubs and the slugs that burrowed in the bark of trees and caterpillars and beetles and snails and white ants. These were meat. Because of the violently disturbed state into which the forest had been thrown by the slavers and now the added disturbance of the column's hectic passage through it, there was almost no chance for game—an occasional rat or bat or civet cat, a guinea hen that was mostly feather and bone. It was a repulsive, despicable diet, besides being cruelly insufficient. The five Europeans still had some of the special provisions left—tea, coffee, condensed milk, brandy, sago, a bit of beef extract, tapioca, arrowroot—to blunt the filthiness of it. But the Wanyamwezis and Sudanese, already worn out and undernourished from the weeks of hard trekking on half-rations that had gone before, weakened and sickened on it at an appalling rate.

Nelson was carried. He had managed to keep to his feet and struggle on for a few days after the meeting with the slavers, then gave out and collapsed in Jephson's arms. Although his eyes often were open and he asked reasonably lucid questions intermittently about the column's progress, he actually was unconscious most of the time after that. A litter was made of a strip of tent canvas sewn between two of the *Lady Dorothy*'s oars; and some loads of spare parts for the steel boat that Jephson judged they could do without—extra bolts, oarlocks, caulking material—were dumped to free men to serve as bearers. But the same could not be done for the other sick and injured. There were too many of them; too many loads would have to be jettisoned to provide enough bearers for them. And so one by one they died. One by one they fell behind and died or wandered off into the woods and died or failed to rouse themselves from sleep and were left behind and died, in pathetic silence, in the throes of screaming agony, of lockjaw from the arrow poison, of dysentery, of fever, of broken bones gone gangrenous, of festering foot ulcers, of melanosis, of pleurisy, of too little to eat, of loss of heart. The rest collected their gear and moved on eastward, ever eastward, into the Ituri.

· SIX ·

TEN MARCHES, the slaver had said; with poor luck, fifteen. But after ten marches, after fifteen, there was no sign of Ipoto. The blazed trail ended at a river.

It was the largest they had come to since leaving the Aruwimi, and it now barred the way, plunging down out of the hills from the southeast between hundred-foot-high black granite embankments, rushing northwest over jumbled masses of boulders and driftwood thirty or forty yards wide where they came to it, thundering with rapids, turbulently in flood. A suspension bridge of rattan hawsers and split-bamboo planking once had swung between the high banks, but it either had been washed out by the rains or, as with everything else man-made within the slavers' raiding circle, deliberately destroyed. Its ends, still anchored to trees on both sides, hung down the jagged rock walls of the embankments in frayed tangles, and the center section was completely gone. When Jephson came up, Stanley was going into the river to see if it could be repaired.

Stripped to his drawers, his clothes piled at the water's edge, a rope tied around his waist and held by Uledi and four of the pioneers, he grabbed the bridge's broken vines for support and stepped into the boiling stream. The men of the lead companies had clustered along the edge of the bank above to watch him. It was tricky going. The fast strong current pulled and pushed at his ankles, swirled around his knees, smashed at his thighs as he cautiously made his way forward, probing out tentatively with each leg at every step, feeling for bottom or anything solid beneath the foaming surface. On the fifth step, when he was waist-deep, he lost his footing. For an instant he managed to hang on to the bridge's vines, but the power of the river broke his grip and he was swept under.

A horrified gasp went up from the onlookers. Uledi shouted, and the four pioneers, digging in with their heels, bracing their legs, hauled hard on the rope; and with a sudden jerk, Stanley resurfaced some yards downstream, spitting water, shaking his head like a drowned dog, momentarily disoriented. The rope held him. With waves chopping and surging around his ears, it was difficult to tell whether he was standing or treading water. Then, with those powerful shoulders and arms of his, he plunged in against the current and swam back to the remnants of the bridge. He again grabbed hold of some vines and, swinging hand over hand along them, finding whatever footholds he could on rocks and logs and gravel-strewn reefs, occasionally going down on all fours, resumed working his way out to midriver in search of the bridge's missing center section.

Meanwhile the rest of the boat company straggled in and, putting down the big sections of the *Lady Dorothy* and their other loads, crowded up along the bank with the others to see what was going on, where they had come, whether they had reached Ipoto at last. The litter bearers set Nelson down beside Jephson. His silky dirty-blond beard made him look very young and innocent, an adolescent boy's beard; or perhaps it was because he had grown so thin and frail, the bones of his cheeks pressing sharply against his stretched, sallow, mosquito-bitten skin, his eyes sunken and enormous and as bewildered as a child's. He watched helplessly as Jephson knelt next to him, put a hand under his head, raised it gently, and held a water bottle to his parched lips. He sucked at it avidly but actually drank very little. He couldn't swallow without terrible pain, and most of the water dribbled out the sides of his mouth. He turned his face away and muttered something. Jephson bent closer to hear what it was.

"Ipoto?"

"Soon, Robbie. It can't be much farther now."

Sudi, bringing up the rear of the company, came over.

"You better get the boat assembled," Jephson said to him. "It looks as if we're going to have to ferry here."

Sudi studied the river for a moment, then shook his head. "No, sah. We do not ferry here. This water is too rough, too strong. There are too many rocks in this water. We lose the boat if we try to ferry here."

"Well, we're just going to have to risk it." Jephson stood up. "That bridge is gone for good, I'm afraid."

Stanley, in fact, had given up on the bridge and was working his way to the opposite bank. He crawled up on a ledge of slate there, rested a moment, then removed the rope from around his waist and climbed farther up the bank to the tree line. He picked out a sturdy gnarled scrub acacia and tied the rope to it, tested it with a few sharp yanks, then hollered back over the river's roar to Uledi. The Wanyamwezi chieftain and the pioneers selected a tree on the near bank and tied their end of the rope around it.

When it was secured, when all the slack had been taken up and the rope spanned the river tautly, bowing down from the banks to just a few inches above the boiling surface at midriver, Stanley waded in again and, hooking an arm around the rope, using it as a sort of handrail, improvising a ford of the boulders and logjams and reefs, half swimming, half pulling himself along, started back.

"Get the boat put together, Sudi," Jephson said and clambered down the embankment to the water's edge.

Stanley came out of the river snorting and spitting. He grabbed up his shirt from the pile of his clothing on the bank and used it to wipe his face.

"I'm having the boat assembled, sir. We'll have it down here in a few minutes."

"No, don't bother with that. She's no use to us here."

"We can give her a go, sir. There's no salvaging that bridge, is there?"

"No, but– Sudi, can you ferry this river?"

Sudi was still standing at the top of the embankment next to Nelson's litter. He hadn't bothered to order the men to start assembling the boat. They stood crowded around him, looking down. "No, sah," he replied.

"No, not bloody likely. Christ, just look at that blasted torrent. No, we'll do better fording it, the way I just did, using the rope." Stanley started putting on his clothes.

"But what about the loads, sir? You didn't have a load with you. It won't be that easy with a load."

"We'll manage."

"And the injured men? The sick?"

"I said we'll manage." Stanley pulled on his boots. "We've got about five hours of daylight left. If we step lively, we might just be able to get the whole lot across before dark."

The first to cross were the trackers and pioneers. Led by Uledi, carrying only axes or billhooks, *pangas* or spears, their personal kit strapped to their backs or tied around their waists, moving agilely, slipping occasionally, they went over without too much fuss and vanished into the woods on the other side to hunt for the continuation of the trail to Ipoto. The askaris of the front guard, the next to go, although not much more heavily burdened—their rifles slung, the barrels plugged with scraps of cloth, their rucksacks and blanket rolls hoisted high on their shoulders—had more trouble. The first of their number—a tall, skinny sharpshooter with a Winchester, his boots hanging by their laces around his neck, his saronglike *kikoi* tucked between his knees—stepped into the river, reached for the rope, and missed it. He went under. A hoot of derisive laughter from his mates on the bank greeted him as he popped to the surface sputtering and lunged for the rope again. And missed it again. And then the laughter abruptly died. For suddenly he was being swept downstream at a terrifying rate tumbling backwards in the roaring current, kicking wildly, flailing his arms frantically. He slammed into a rock with a sickening thud, hung there for a moment, his pack snarled on a branch, then was torn free by the pounding waves, swirled around in an eddy, and was sucked under again. His boots came up but he didn't. Those on shore stared at the spot in stunned silence. The boots ran away downriver as if in a panic.

"You. *Nenda kule. Upesi-upesi.*" Stanley grabbed the arm of the Sudanese second in the file. "What are you waiting for? Go across."

The askari glanced at Stanley and then at his mates with frightened eyes, as if beseeching them to intervene and save him from this ordeal.

"What's the matter with you? Are you an old woman? There's nothing to fear. You must only be careful, not like that clumsy fool. You must only watch where you put your feet. Come, I will show you." Stanley shifted his grip to the askari's wrist and, stepping into the river himself, tugged the fellow in after him. "This is nothing for a brave man to fear. This is nothing more terrible than taking your morning bath. Come along. Take hold of the rope. Here, take hold of it. Hold it strongly. *Haya. Vyema.* Now go on. Go across." Slipping around the man, letting him pass between his arms, Stanley gave him an encouraging thump on the back. "Keep on going. You're doing fine. You are well on your way." Knee-deep in the swirling torrent, he watched as the Sudanese inched crabwise into the river, fishing for footholds, gaining confidence. "That's it, askari. You are already nearly halfway there."

The askari, barely five yards from the bank, hanging on to the rope for dear life, looked back and showed his filed teeth in a nervous grin.

"Eh, askari? You see. Didn't I tell you there is nothing to fear?" Stanley turned back to the bank. "Now you, askari. You are next. You are no less brave than your brother. Come." He grasped this Sudanese by the wrist and guided him to the rope and, keeping up his jollying patter, started him on his way across as well. And then he returned to the bank for the third man.

It went slowly, frustratingly, Stanley having to coax each askari into the river in turn, sometimes going as much as halfway across with one before the man was willing to be left on his own, then coming back for the next one. He was tireless, inexhaustible, relentless. There was another mishap. When nearly to the other side, an askari tripped on a snag of spindrift; and although he managed to catch hold of the rope again and save himself, his rifle and pack were torn loose and lost in the waves. The remaining Sudanese turned balky again and Stanley had to threaten and cajole and strike and kick to get them going again.

Jephson watched it from atop the steep embankment, standing beside Nelson's litter. He had sent Sudi off into the surrounding forest with about half the boat company to forage; the rest of the men, no longer interested in what was happening in the river, lay sprawled by their loads a few feet back from the bank, waiting listlessly for their turn to cross it. They were a sorry sight, their clothing in tatters, many plagued by foot ulcers or shivering with fever, filthy, smelly, fagged out, and hungry—that most of all, hungry.

Askaris were still in the river when Hoffman's *pagazis* began trudging in. They were as pathetic-looking as the boatmen, dragging themselves and the pack animals along wearily, staggering under loads that seemed to weigh tons. Sudi and his men had by then returned with a sizable cache of wood beans; and the new arrivals gathered around them to watch as these were skinned, the leathery rinds scraped out, and the gluey brown stuff within pounded into flour for patties. They might have gone out and collected some for themselves—the bean apparently grew in profusion here—but they were too exhausted to consider it. Later they'd go; later their headmen would force them to go. Now they simply squatted on their heels and watched the boatmen enviously.

"Sudi, we go now."

Stanley had crossed to the opposite bank with the last of the front guard. Uledi had reappeared there; and the two of them were standing at the water's edge, heads together in consultation, while above them the pioneers and askaris could be seen going about the business of setting up camp. Evidently Stanley planned to spend the night by the river and pick up the trail to Ipoto in the morning—if there was a trail to pick up. The trackers were still out hunting for it.

"Captain Nelson goes first."

The bearers carried Nelson down the embankment, slipping and stumbling on the jagged decline, so that Nelson, wincing, raising his head in alarm, had to grip the litter's sides to prevent himself from being pitched out. But once at the river's edge, they didn't go farther.

"What are you doing? Pick up the litter."

"Sah."

"Get them moving, Sudi. We haven't all day."

"But, sah, they can't carry—"

"Of course they can."

"No, sah."

"They can, I tell you. By God, they had better. Come on." Suddenly thinking to emulate Stanley's tactics, Jephson went into the river himself. He went in backwards, in order to better rail at the bearers, but the current immediately snatched at his legs. Nearly losing his balance, he turned quickly and grabbed for the rope. "Come on, I say. Pick up the litter and come on. This is nothing for a brave man to fear. Come on, goddamnit."

But it was impossible. The two bearers, front and rear, on the downstream side of the litter could hang on to the rope with their free left hands and thus brace themselves against the terrific rush of the river while they fished with their feet for footing. But the other two, on the litter's right side, upstream of the rope, with nothing to grab on to, instantly were in trouble. The fellow in front hadn't taken three steps when he suddenly twisted around and went in up to his neck and in a panic to save himself let go of the litter. The sudden jerk this caused unbalanced the other bearer on the upstream side; and although gamely trying to hold up his end, his legs went out from under him and he sat down in the shallows. At that, Nelson started rolling off. Jephson lunged for him. Sudi dashed into the river. But now the two bearers on the downstream side were also floundering.

"All right. Go back. *Go back!*"

Fortunately they had managed to get only a few yards from shore; and with Sudi replacing one of the fallen bearers and Jephson holding on to Nelson, they scrambled to dry land without any further disaster. Jephson dropped to his knees beside the litter. Nelson pushed himself up on an elbow and looked around, unsure what had happened. The bearers sprawled on the rocks, half in and half out of the river, gasping wildly, not so much from any effort they had made as from the scare they had gotten. The rest of the company was lined up along the embankment by their loads looking down at them. So were the *pagazis* of Hoffman's company. Hoffman himself was now also there, having brought in the last of his men. Slumped on his crutches, he surveyed the situation expressionlessly.

"Bula Matari calls to you, sah," Sudi said.

Jephson looked across the river. Stanley was standing ankle-deep in the water on the other side shouting through cupped hands. What he was shouting couldn't be heard above the roar of the rapids, but Jephson didn't need to hear it. He could guess well enough what it was.

"Bula Matari wants—"

"I know what Bula Matari wants. What I want is rope."

"Sah?"

"Rope, man, rope. Get a full coil. *Upesi-upesi.*"

"Yes, sah."

"Robbie, are you all right?"

Nelson nodded and began to let himself down from his elbow.

"No, no. Sit up." Jephson put an arm around Nelson's shoulders and held him. "Robbie, listen. You're going to have to ford this river. The boat's no good to us here, and you saw what happened when we tried to carry you across."

Nelson looked at Jephson blankly, his eyes unfocused.

"It'll be a bit chancy, but you can make it. I'm going to go with you. Do you understand?"

Nelson continued staring blankly for a moment. Then, as if he had at last absorbed what Jephson was saying, he nodded again.

"Right, then. On your feet." Jephson slipped his right arm around Nelson's waist, got that shoulder under Nelson's left arm, and lifted him from the litter. He was light, shockingly so. He couldn't have weighed more than nine or ten stone, he had lost that much weight. But it was all deadweight. Jephson had to bear it all. Nelson couldn't stand. "Where's the rope?"

Sudi hurried over with a coil of heavy rope.

"Tie it around us. Tie us together. And I want a half-dozen of the strongest men we've got hanging on to the end of it."

"Yes, sah."

"Hold on to me, Robbie. Hold on hard."

But Nelson was too weak. His left arm rested limply over

Jephson's shoulders, the right hung uselessly at his side; his knees were like jelly. Jephson tightened the grip of his right arm around Nelson's waist; and when Sudi completed looping the rope around them and fastening it securely, he half dragged and half carried Nelson to the water's edge and reached for the fording rope with his free left hand. Sudi followed closely behind as the six Wanyamwezi boatmen he had selected payed out the line.

"All right, old boy, here we go." Jephson glanced across the roaring stream and saw Stanley, now with his hands on his hips, waiting for them at the other end of the fording rope. The pioneers and askaris on that shore had stopped their work to watch. "We'll make it, Robbie. You'll see," Jephson said and stepped into the torrent.

Nelson was sufficiently in command of his senses to understand what was wanted of him, and he made a gallant effort. But he was as helpless as a rag doll. On the first impact of the powerful current his legs were swept out from under him and banged into Jephson's. Jephson immediately stumbled, caught himself, and paused, his heart racing like mad, while he tightened his grip both around Nelson's waist and the fording rope. Then he moved forward again, very slowly, wading in deeper, blindly exploring the river's rocky bottom with his feet, searching for purchase, terrified of slipping, bringing Nelson along in jerky hops beside him. Sudi still followed them, one hand on the fording rope, the other just behind them on the lifeline. In hard-slapping waves the water rapidly rose around them, to their knees, their thighs, their hips, their waists. When it reached their chests, Nelson partially floated. It made him lighter, less of a deadweight; but buoyant, pummeled by the current, he twisted in Jephson's grip, and again his legs swam out in front of Jephson and interfered with his progress. Sudi came up closer, reaching out along the lifeline. Jephson found footing on a gravelly reef where the water was only knee deep and dragged Nelson up on it.

"We're doing fine, Robbie. Just fine."

They had come only a few yards. The worst of it was still in front of them. Stanley had advanced deeper into the river, coming toward them along the fording rope. Jephson glanced at Nelson out of the corner of his eye. The poor bastard's face was contorted with pain.

"We're doing just fine," Jephson repeated and, hitching Nelson more firmly against his hip, started forward again.

And went under.

He didn't know how it happened. One moment he was probing out with a leg feeling where the reef they stood on ended, testing how sharply it fell off, where he might safely gain another foothold and the next moment his legs were flying out from under him, knocked away like a pair of duckpins. His stomach lurched in wild panic. A fist of water punched into his mouth, and choking, he was sucked down into a roaring darkness. For an instant he still had hold of the fording rope. Then it was torn from his grasp as the murderous current rushed him downriver. Nelson came with him. He tried to yank his right arm, the one around Nelson's waist, free in order to swim, but Nelson rolled on top of him and sank him deeper; and together they were slammed against rocks, ripped at by the branches of submerged trees, dragged along the jagged bottom, again slammed into some obstruction and either that or the Wanyamwezis on shore hauling on the lifeline that bound them together halted them with a sudden bone-rattling jar. But they were still under and drowning; and Jephson, now struggling like a maniac to save himself, his lungs exploding, on the brink of losing consciousness, his one arm still pinned by Nelson, clawed with the other for the surface. He burst clear, gulped frantically for air, but was immediately pulled back under by Nelson, who in his own desperate need to get at air was attempting to climb up over him. Jephson fought him off in a frenzy, striking at him with his free arm, and once more he managed to thrust his face to the surface, and then realized he was also fighting with Sudi.

"Grab my legs!" That was Stanley. He had come all the way across on the fording rope; and now hanging from it with both hands behind his head, he was letting the current pull him downriver so that his legs extended toward Jephson. "Grab 'em, damn you. Grab 'em."

Jephson lunged for them, but they were out of reach. Swallowing another mouthful of the river, he started going under again, a terrible blackness rushing into his vision. He was passing out. But then a hand, Sudi's, grabbed a fistful of his hair and yanked his face up, and he was breathing again. He lunged for Stanley's legs again and this time caught hold of an ankle as the Wanyamwezis hauled on the lifeline, twisting him broadside to the current, dragging the now awfully still deadweight of Nelson along with him back to the bank.

Nelson was alive, although just barely. Stanley, barking orders angrily, had him slung facedown over a barrel of trading beads, then rolled him on it with hard rhythmic strokes. Jephson, more than half drowned himself, prostrate on the shingle, hawking and spitting and coughing uncontrollably, watched conscience-stricken through bleary, stinging eyes. It was a dreadful sight. Nelson's frail body seemed as if it must snap in two under Stanley's rough pressure. The water that spewed from between his shriveled lips was bright with blood; his face had turned a ghastly blue. If he dies, Jephson thought . . . But then, thank God, in a gagging explosion of slimy spittle, his legs suddenly thrashing spasmodically, Nelson started gasping for air. Stanley snatched him up and hurriedly fished his tongue out of his mouth and held him upright in his arms until the breaths came regularly. Then he lifted the limp form from the barrel and set it back down on the litter.

He turned to Jephson. "You all right?"

Jephson nodded and got to his feet.

"That was a damn-fool stunt you pulled, you know."

Jephson shrugged. "I couldn't think what else to do."

"Yes . . . well, we've wasted enough time by it. Don't let's waste any more. Parade your company."

"But, sir, what *are* we going to do?" Jephson pointed at Nelson. Lying on his litter, his hands on his chest, his eyes closed, his face drained of all color, he might have been a corpse; except that in his drenched clothes he was shivering convulsively. "How *are* we going to get him across?"

"We're not."

"Sir?"

"I'm afraid we're going to have to leave him."

"Leave him? Oh, no. No, sir. You can't mean that."

"Look, Arthur. You tried. You tried the best anybody could, and you damn near drowned him, and yourself besides. It can't be done. A blind man can see that. Not with the river in flood like this. Not with him as weak as he is. Maybe in a few days, in a week, the river'll be down or he'll be stronger and we can try it again then. We can send back for him and try it again then. In the meantime—"

"A few days? A week? What are you talking about? If you leave him alone here that long he'll be dead."

"And we'll be dead if we don't keep moving. We'll all be dead if we don't get to Ipoto pretty damn soon, I can promise you that. So let's get moving. We're wasting the daylight."

"No. Wait a minute. There must be someplace we can get him across. There must be an easier ford someplace else."

"Where? Show me where."

Jephson glanced around, his eyes darting up- and downriver frantically searching the boulder-clogged rapids, the sheer cliffs of the embankment, the dark wall of the jungle crowding along their edges. "Send the trackers out. They'll find something. They're bound to find an easier ford someplace. Maybe there beyond that bend, downstream a ways, in the next reach or—"

"For Christ sake, Arthur, don't be a bloody idiot. We've no time to go exploring."

"But we can't just leave him."

"Arthur, listen to me. I don't fancy this any more than you do. But we've no choice. We've just about run out of our rations. The rice is completely gone. We've barely enough mealies for three days, four at the most. The biscuits won't last us another week. Our only chance for resupply is Ipoto. Our only hope to keep from starving is Ipoto. We've got to get there. I don't know how much farther it is. If you want the truth, I don't know *where* it is. We've lost the trail. The trackers can't find it. We may have gone wrong somewhere. I don't know. But we've got to find it. We've got to get to Ipoto. Otherwise we're finished. Do you understand? Finished. We might just as well never have left London."

Stanley kept his voice low, a hoarse, harsh whisper, so as not to be overheard—Sudi, the litter bearers, and the six boatmen who had hauled them in on the lifeline stood only a few paces away—but his expression was that of a man shouting. The cords of his neck bulged, a vein throbbed in his forehead, his face was flushed. He was shouting inside his head. Hoffman, eyeing him curiously, started down from atop the embankment; and Jephson wondered, seeing how clumsily he negotiated the jagged decline on his crutches, whether he'd be able to ford the river or whether he too would have to be left behind.

"We'll send back for him once we reach Ipoto. Once we've resupplied and got some decent food into us, we'll come back and see what we can do for him. He won't be the only one. God knows, there must be a dozen, two dozen men in the caravan who ain't in any kind of shape to make this crossing either. I'm going to have a camp set up for them here and leave them a fair share of the rations. They'll be all right. They'll have a chance to hunt and fish and forage and get some rest. They won't be any worse off than they'd be dragging on through this bloody wilderness. Christ, they'll be better off. And we'll send back for them as soon as we can."

Hoffman came over. "My boys are ready to go, Bula Matari. You want me to start them across?"

"No. The boat company's next. They're going now. Arthur."

For a moment Jephson just stared at Stanley. Then he began shaking his head. "You won't come back," he said. "You say you will but you won't. You'll just keep going."

"Parade your men, Arthur."

Jephson backed a step away, still shaking his head. "Yes, you'll just keep going. That's all that matters to you—to keep going, to get through the forest, to reach Emin Pasha in time. Nothing else matters to you—not Robbie, not anything, not anybody. Just that—to succeed."

Stanley turned away. "Sudi."

"Sah."

"Parade the boat company. Parade them in single file and bring them down to the river one by one."

Sudi hesitated, looking sideways at Jephson.

"*Nenda kule. Sasa. Upesi-upesi.*"

"*Ndiyo*, Bwana."

Having witnessed the near drowning of Jephson and Nelson, the boatmen hoisted their loads and started down to the river with extreme reluctance.

"Will, have Captain Nelson taken back up on the embankment. I want a shelter built for him up there. And get him out of those wet clothes."

"No, leave him alone."

"Arthur!"

"I'll do it."

By the time the last of the boat company was across and Hoffman had started his *pagazis* into the river, Parke and the rear guard and a handful of the sick and injured who were still managing to keep up straggled in. Parke went over to the shelter that had been built for Nelson and looked in. Nelson was asleep or unconscious on a bed of palm leaves, clutching his blanket up to his chin like a child. Jephson sat by his side, resting a hand lightly on his forehead. Parke made no comment. Nor did he make any move to examine Nelson or administer to him medically. He merely looked at him, then at Jephson, and then back out to the river and the desperate efforts of the men crossing it. There was something monkeyish about him—his bandy legs, his hairy face, the way he stood with his arms hanging loosely at his sides and his head thrust forward on his scrawny neck.

"We're leaving him behind, Tommy," Jephson said.

Parke didn't reply. A struggle was going on in the river with a pack mule a few yards from the embankment. Two Wanyamwezis, their heads barely above water, were pulling on its lead harness while Hoffman, hanging on to both the animal's tail and the fording rope (God only knew where his crutches were) butted and shoved against the mule's rump; but the beast, petrified by the foaming torrent, its eyes rolling wildly, refused to budge. It might have been comical, except that the mule was carrying some of the column's last bags of cornmeal. Stanley started into the river to lend a hand.

"Did you hear what I said, Tommy?"

"Yes."

"And?"

Parke looked back at Jephson. "And what?"

"For God's sake, man, don't you have anything to say about it? Doesn't it bother you? Don't you care? We're leaving him here in the middle of nowhere, Tommy, dying."

Parke muttered something and looked away.

"What? What did you say?" Jephson stood up. "No, damn you, no! It's not probably for the best."

"Hey, hold on. I only meant—"

"I know what you meant. I don't care what you meant. I—" And all of a sudden Jephson was in a towering rage. All of a sudden he hated Parke. All of a sudden he hated the very look of the man, his filthy habits, his lice-ridden beard, the foul stink he gave off, his whining complaints, the drunken stupor in which he was perpetually sunk. All of a sudden he saw Nelson's plight as Parke's doing. "It's your fault," he cried out. "You know that, don't you? It's all your fault. You let him die. You left that arrow in him. Any halfway decent surgeon would have got it out of him. But you didn't. You couldn't. You left it in him, and it's killed him."

It wasn't fair. It wasn't true. In some part of his brain Jephson knew that. But he didn't want to be fair; he didn't care what was true. Blind, senseless rage overwhelmed him, rage against everything, against anything, against Parke's wretchedness, against Nelson's plight, against the jungle and the river and the rain and the heat and the hunger and the fever and their countless other miseries, against Stanley's insane, ruthless ambition that had led them into all of it. "You killed him," he shouted. "You killed him."

"What are you talking about? Have you gone crazy? Hey! Stay away from me. What are you doing? *Get away from me!*"

Stanley, knee-deep in the river, spun around at the sound of that shrill hysterical scream, and saw Jephson leap at Parke.

Parke went down on his back, his head slamming against the ground, his helmet flying, Jephson on top of him grappling at his throat. Everywhere along the embankment, askaris and *pagazis* froze at the sight.

Stanley came charging up the embankment. "What the hell's going on here? Get off him. Goddamn you, get off him." On the run, Stanley hooked an arm around Jephson's neck and yanked him off Parke, sent him sprawling.

Parke, his nose spouting blood, skittered away on his back like a crab. "He's crazy. He's gone crazy."

"I won't have this. Goddamnit, I won't put up with this sort of thing. Do you hear me? Anybody starts this sort of thing again, by God I'll make him regret it."

"I didn't do anything. He jumped me. He jumped me for no reason. He's gone crazy."

"Shut up. I don't want to hear another word out of either of you. Christ, this is just what I need. I don't have enough on my plate. I need this too. You goddamn stupid bastards. You start fighting with each other, how long do you suppose it'll be before everybody in this caravan will be fighting with each other? And then where will we be?"

"He said I killed Robbie. He had no business saying that."

"I told you to shut up. Clear these men away from here. They've got work to do. I want shelters built for all the sick and injured who can't make it across the river. I want a proper camp built for them here. Go on, step lively."

Parke got to his feet, wiping his bloody nose on his sleeve. "It isn't right. He shouldn't be allowed to say a thing like that."

"Get on with it, will you? And you, mister." Stanley strode over to where he had flung Jephson, took hold of the front of his tunic, and jerked him to his feet. "You join your company."

Jephson pulled away.

"I'm warning you, mister. Don't give me any more problems than I already have. I want you across the river. And I want you across right now. All your people are across. Your place is with them." He grabbed Jephson's arm.

Jephson pulled away. "I'm not going. I'm not going across the river. I'm not going anywhere. I'm staying here with Robbie. I'm not going to leave him here like this. You can. You can do whatever the hell you please. There's nothing I can do about that. But I'm going to stay here with him."

Parke was still there a few paces away, watching, listening. He hadn't started his men—the askaris of the rear guard, the injured and sick and stragglers—on the work of building an encampment; so they too were still there, scattered about, also watching and listening. Stanley, however, ignored them.

"I see," he said. "So you're quitting on me."

"What?"

"I thought you were made of better stuff than that, Arthur. I thought you had the stuff to stick it, no matter what. I guess I was wrong. Well, quit then. Go ahead and quit."

"I'm not quitting. Don't tell me I'm quitting. I'm staying here with Robbie is what I'm doing. That's a lot different than quitting. When you come back, *if* you come back, you'll find me here. I'll be here with him." Jephson turned and started for Nelson's shelter.

"And what do you think you're going to do for him here?"

Jephson looked back.

"There's nothing you can do for him, Arthur. Not a thing."

"Yes there is. Yes, by God, there is. I can keep him company if nothing else. I can keep him from being alone. I can do that for him. I can keep him from being alone in this godforsaken place. I can—" But suddenly uncontrollably, tears sprang into Jephson's eyes and he averted his face.

"Arthur. For Christ sake, Arthur." Stanley advanced a step, and Jephson, wary of his intentions, retreated a step. "I understand how you feel, Arthur. But listen to me, lad. He's a soldier. He's been in situations like this countless times. He knew what would happen if he couldn't keep up. Just as I would know if I were in his shoes. Just as you would know."

Jephson, his face still averted, surreptitiously rubbed his eyes.

And now Stanley did turn to Parke. "What are you gawking at, Doctor? Didn't I tell you I want a camp made here? Get on with it. Put those men to work. The daylight'll be gone in an hour."

Parke moved off.

"Christ. Look at him. Just look at him, will you."

Jephson uncovered his face. He saw what Stanley meant: Parke's uncertain movements, his confused expression, the inept way he set about rounding up his men.

"I need you, Arthur."

Jephson turned to Stanley. Stanley had spoken so softly, almost inaudibly, that he wasn't certain he had heard him correctly.

"I can't afford to lose another officer, Arthur. Nelson's gone and Parke's next to useless. I can't go on with just Will. The two of us can't drive this caravan alone. We need you." When Jephson made no reply, Stanley said, "It's going to get worse before it gets any better, Arthur. It's going to get a lot worse, I'm sorry to say. And when it does, there's going to be trouble with the men. I've got to have another officer. I won't be able to handle them just with Will."

"But Robbie—"

"He knows how you feel, lad. He knows you don't want to leave him. He knows you'd like to help him, that we all would. But he knows we can't. He's a soldier, lad. He wouldn't have it any other way."

Jephson started shaking his head back and forth and kept on shaking it. And then he turned and ducked into Nelson's shelter. He dropped to his knees beside the bed of palm fronds and looked back out. He half expected Stanley to follow him. But Stanley remained where he was; he had placed his hands on his hips, that aggressive commanding stance of his, but there was little aggression in him now, little command. He just seemed awfully tired.

"Robbie." Jephson slipped an arm beneath Nelson's shoulders and raised him from the bed.

Startled by this, Nelson opened his eyes. For a few seconds he didn't seem to recognize Jephson, perhaps didn't see him at all. But then his cracked and blistered lips parted in what Jephson realized was meant to be a smile.

"Oh, Robbie."

"Not to worry, old boy." Nelson mouthed these words, unable to make a sound. "Not to worry. I'm all right."

Jephson, holding Nelson in his arms, again looked out the shelter. Night was falling quickly now, and Stanley's figure and those of Parke and the men making camp were vanishing into its shadows. How terrible to be left alone in that night, Jephson thought, how terrible to vanish into those shadows.

"Robbie, listen to me." He hugged Nelson closer, spoke into his ear. "I'm coming back for you. In a few days I'll be back to fetch you. Do you hear me? I'll be back. I swear it. So wait for me, Robbie. Please wait for me. Don't die."

· SEVEN ·

THE MUSTER was this: 151 Wanyamwezis, seventy-two Sudanese, four Europeans, eight mules, 168 loads, the Maxim gun, and the portable steel boat. Five Wanyamwezis, three Sudanese, and a mule had drowned fording the river; twelve loads had been dropped and swept away; and thirty-two of the variously sick and injured, unable to make it across, had been left behind with Nelson.

But now the desertions began.

The way was lost. Day after day the jaded, battered column followed whatever paths or tracks could be discovered leading more or less to the east. These were unmarked, narrow, stifling, vine-snarled tunnels snaking through the twilight labyrinth of the giant trees, often twisting back on themselves after only a few hundred yards or leading into the cul-de-sac of a ravine or turning into flooded gulleys when it rained or pinching out in massive tangles of undergrowth without reaching any apparent destination, so that eventually each one had to be abandoned and new ones tried. Uledi and the scouts, ranging a good day's march in advance of the column, could find no trace of the blazed trail that had brought them to the river or any sign of the slavers' settlement of Ipoto where relief could be had. Perhaps they had bypassed it in their aimless wandering. Perhaps it lay yet another ten or fifteen marches ahead. Perhaps it didn't exist at all. For who could say for certain that the half-caste hadn't lied?

Oddly, shamefully, Jephson found that with each passing day he missed Nelson less and less, forgot about him more and more. Partly this was because of his own wretched condition, his own clawing hunger, his own never-ending exhaustion, the sporadic bouts of fever he now experienced that numbed his brain. But there was also something else, that curious saving quality of mind that refused to acknowledge the horror of the deed, that prevented him from fully accepting the fact that he had abandoned his friend, that allowed him to pretend that Nelson was really still with the column, marching with another company, up ahead or far behind, and would be met up with again at the end of each day's torturous trek if only he kept on. And so he kept on and kept his men going on, following Stanley as if in a dream, no longer clear where they were going or to what purpose, only going on as if there was no purpose other than this endless going on.

And then the rations ran out and the desertions began.

It wasn't mutiny. There was no sense that a conspiracy had been hatched or even that those who deserted had given much thought beforehand to what they would do, where they would go, how they would survive in this never-ending wasteland of wilderness once they were on their own. Overcome by hopelessness, made reckless by despair, they simply slipped away at night while the camp slept its exhausted, deathlike sleep, or during the day when the column was stretched out to its greatest length and in a chaos of disorder, or under the cover of blinding sheets of pouring rain. They slipped away singly, in pairs, in groups of never more than three or four—some taking their loads, others leaving them behind—and disappeared into the fetid shifting shadows of the jungle. Indeed, it occurred so quietly and unremarkably that it wasn't immediately recognized for what it actually was or what dreadful catastrophe—in the loss of the precious irreplaceable supplies that were carried off, in the diminishing number of fit men to carry those that were left behind—this silent hemorrhaging of the column's strength foretold. After all, a man missing at a morning muster could mean anything. He had injured himself during the previous day's march; he had lost his way in the woods while foraging for food; he had dropped back to help a mate among the growing number of pitifully hungering stragglers. Chances were he'd turn up again before nightfall. But he didn't. Search parties were sent back. A case of Remington cartridges was found cracked open and looted but not the man who had carried it. A cask of lamp oil, stove-in and upended in a pool of its own contents; a bale of trading cloth floating in the marshy shallows of a creek; a coil of rope dangling from the low branches of a tree; the splintered haft of a billhook; a shattered lantern or cooking pot—remnants like these were occasionally found, but the men who had carried them vanished without a trace. Whatever track they may have left was swallowed up as thoroughly by the thickets of the forest as the wake of a small boat is swallowed up by the waves of the ocean.

In four days, nine men disappeared; by the end of a week, thirteen. Stanley had the column paraded and went through the ranks with his officers, chiefs, headmen, and corporals of the guard, closely questioning each of the men. Fifty-three were singled out. They were those whose loyalty was open to question, whose reliability no one was willing to guarantee. Their weapons were taken away from them in the perfectly sensible belief that no one would venture off into the jungle unarmed. In addition, the most valuable of the loads—the ammunition, the medicine, the best of the *mitako*—were lashed together in series of eight to make their theft more difficult. But these precautions did little good. Indeed, not twenty-four hours after they were instituted another man was discovered gone. He was Juma, Jephson's mule boy. He had taken the mule.

It was coming on to dusk of a day that had been sweltering and rumbling with the threat of a storm. Stanley and the lead companies had made camp on a cleared knoll where a village once had stood, its half-dozen huts reduced to ashes by slavers, a field of Indian corn trampled into mush. The main body of the column was still on the road, winding back two or three miles into the dark green oblivion of the forest. Jephson, in the lead of his company, looked back down this serpentine line and counted his people as they labored up the knoll toward the camp. He realized that the mule boy was missing even before the last of his men had come in. It was because he couldn't see the mule. He immediately set off back down the trail.

"Where's Juma?" he shouted to Sudi, bringing up the rear of the company. "Where's he got to with our bloody moke?"

Sudi instinctively glanced behind him, then back at Jephson. "He is not with you, sah?"

"No."

"I thought he was with you, sah."

"Oh, great."

"I counted him in the muster at noon, sah. He was in his place at noon."

"What about after that? When did you last see him after that?"

Sudi ran a hand across his brow, wiping sweat from his eyes. When he took the hand away, his expression was grim, pained. He shook his head slowly.

"Jesus, I don't believe it. The little bugger's made off." Jephson looked down the trail from where they had come, where the first of Hoffman's *pagazis* were now emerging from the trees. "Well, he can't have gotten very far. Not with that mule in tow. Come on. Maybe we can still catch him."

They found the mule about a half-mile back. The sudden startled beating of buzzards' wings revealed its location in a clearing fifty yards or so off the trail. It had been slaughtered and butchered for its meat. The mule boy, obviously working in terrible haste and unable to carry as much as he would have liked, had made an awful mess of the job. The animal's throat had been slit to bring it down, then a leg up to its haunch hacked off and the gut opened to get at the liver. The rest of the poor beast lay in a slimy pool of its own blood, one eye gazing haplessly at heaven, the jaw dropped open and overhung by a lolling tongue. Despite Jephson's and Sudi's presence, the buzzards remained hovering about it, big black crow-like creatures perched in the low branches of the trees, hopping clumsily on the ground, flapping their wings sluggishly, squawking irritably, wary of the men but loath to leave the still steaming rubbish heap of hide and flesh and spilled entrails that had attracted them. Jephson stared at it with revulsion. He couldn't imagine how the mule boy, who had fed and groomed and doctored the animal for so many months, who must have developed some tender feelings for the sorely tried moke in all that time, could have had the heart to cut it down and cut it up in such grisly fashion. There was something faintly cannibalistic about it.

"We take this to camp, sah?"

"Huh?"

Sudi had dropped to his knees beside the carcass and, shooing off the carrion birds, was making a closer inspection of it. He ran a hand across a bloody flank. "It is not yet spoiled, sah. There is still much good meat here. It can make a meal for many men." He stood up. "I fetch some of the *pagazis* to carry it to camp?"

"Wait a minute." Jephson walked around the carcass. He could see where the haunch had been dragged through the brush, then where the mule boy must have hoisted it to his shoulder and stumbled on into the forest. What else was the little wretch carrying? The mule had been loaded with four boxes. What with shouldering the haunch, the boy couldn't possibly have managed to make off with even one of them. Where were they then? Holding his rifle in front of his face to ward off the tangle of branches and vines and brush, Jephson pushed a few steps deeper into the trees. From his left, fifty yards or so to the trail, he could hear the low grunts and groans and rasping breath and occasional curses of Hoffman's *pagazis* trudging by toward the camp.

"Sudi."

"Sah?"

"Look there."

Sudi came over and peered into the trees where Jephson was pointing with his rifle.

"Do you see? There. It's him, isn't it?"

A breeze had sprung up, rattling the leaves, rustling the draperies of moss and flowering vines in the jungle gloom. Lightning, herald of the approaching storm, flickered faintly from time to time, scattering a multitude of shadows that might be anything.

"Juma. *Njoo hapa*, Juma."

There was no response. Behind them the buzzards again hopped on the mule carcass with a heavy beating of wings. Sudi glanced around at them, clearly more interested in saving the meat than in finding the deserter.

"That's him all right. I'm sure of it. The bloody idiot thinks he can hide there until the column passes by." Jephson moved another step into the tangle of vegetation. "Goddamn you, Juma, come here. Don't make me come and get you." But there still was nothing, only the muted sounds of the passing column.

"I see you, Juma. I see you as clear as day. I have you in the sight of my rifle. I'm going to give you to the count of three. Then I'm going to shoot you. Do you hear me, you little wretch? I'm going to shoot you straight through the heart if you don't come out of there. One, two . . . I swear to you, Juma. I'm going to kill you if you don't come out of there this minute. . . . *Three.*"

That did it. Jephson didn't have to shoot. The boy broke from cover. In fact, though, he hadn't been anywhere near where Jephson had thought. Brush and branches and leaves exploded much farther to the right. Jephson whirled in time to see the boy running fast, crashing through the thickets, his arms flung out in front of him, whatever he may have been carrying thrown away.

"Stop him! Goddamnit, stop him."

The boy never had a chance. Every *pagazi* on the trail in the immediate vicinity joined the chase, dropping loads and rushing into the forest, caught up in the enterprise with a sudden show of hot emotion, a murderous enthusiasm, like hounds on the hunt. It lasted little more than a half-hour. The boy managed to make it back another quarter-mile or so to the west, and there he was run down by a pack of Hoffman's *pagazis*. When Jephson next saw him, his hands were bound behind his back, a rope was looped around his neck, and he was being dragged up the trail by one of Hoffman's headmen. Sudi walked at his side, speaking to him in an agitated undertone, berating him; and he was hemmed in by the

Wanyamwezis who had caught him, jostling and taunting him, as if finding in him a target for all their hurt and misery and frustration, a scapegoat to blame for their desperate plight. Hobbling on his crutches, Hoffman preceded this dismal parade.

"Good show, Will. Thanks."

Hoffman continued up the trail toward the camp, brushing by Jephson without a word; but the others slowed to a stop as Jephson approached. The captured mule boy looked at him with an expression of utter resignation.

"All right, Murabo," Jephson said to the headman. "I'll deal with this. You can take that noose off his neck."

"*Hapana!*" Hoffman swung back. "Leave it, Murabo. Leave it where it is."

"What's the matter with you, Will? I said I'd deal with this. The boy's from my company."

"You won't deal with this, mister. Bula Matari will deal with it. This is for Bula Matari to deal with. *Nenda kule*, Murabo."

The headman yanked on the rope, and Juma, lowering his eyes, shuffled forward obediently.

Stanley was waiting for them in front of the command tent. He was naked to the waist, a towel draped over his shoulders. Apparently he had been about to shave when word of the capture of a deserter had reached him. Uledi stood next to him; and the others already in the camp—pioneers slashing at the grass and brush of the knoll to make space for shelters, askaris constructing a zareba of branches and boulders, trackers and boatmen rooting through the village's burned-out fields to see if anything edible had survived the slavers' destruction—also left off what they were doing and drifted over as Hoffman and Jephson and the motley procession approached.

"*Huyu ni nani*, Uledi?" Stanley asked when the prisoner was brought before him.

Uledi looked to Sudi for the answer.

"Juma, sah," the young Wanyamwezi said.

"Juma."

The mule boy looked up timorously.

"He's from my company, Mr. Stanley," Jephson said. "My muleteer. There's no need for you to trouble yourself about this. I'll deal with him."

Hands on hips, his narrowed eyes fixed on the prisoner, the muscles in his jaw working, Stanley ignored Jephson. Very softly in Swahili he said, "What have you done, Juma? What have you done that you are brought to me bound in this way?"

The prisoner's eyes darted from Stanley to Jephson, to Sudi, to his friends in the crowd that was slowly gathering around him, seeking someone among them to whom he might appeal. There was no one.

"You tried to run away?"

Juma looked back at Stanley.

"They tell me you tried to run away, Juma. They tell me you took your mule and killed him for the meat and then tried to run away. Is this true?"

Juma made an uncomfortable noncommittal movement with his head and shoulders.

"Answer me, Juma. Answer me so that all can hear. Did you try to run away?"

"*Ndiyo*, Bwana."

"So, you tried to run away." Stanley removed the towel from his shoulders and mopped sweat from his face and the back of his neck. Then, still in a quiet voice, he asked, "And why, Juma? Why did you try to run away? Did you believe you had fulfilled your obligations to us? Did you believe there was no longer any need for your services? Did you believe we were so rich in supplies that we would not suffer the loss of the mule you killed and the loads you threw away? Or perhaps you have been ill-treated. Is that the reason, Juma? Have you been ill-treated?"

Juma shook his head.

"Then why did you try to run away?"

The boy shuffled his feet in the dirt uneasily.

"Answer me, Juma. Answer me so that all can hear. Why did you try to run away?"

"*Nina njaa*, Bwana. I am hungry."

"So, you are hungry. Yes, I believe you are hungry. But who among us is not hungry?" Stanley raised his voice slightly. "Is there any among us who is not hungry?" he asked.

No one replied.

"You see, Juma, there is no one among us who is not hungry. We all are hungry. Would you have us all run away then?"

"No, Bwana."

"No? Even though we are all as hungry as you? Even though we are all as tired as you? Even though we too are sick and hurt and afraid of the forest and know not where it will end or if it will ever end, we must go on? Yes, we must go on to the end of this journey. We must remain faithful to one another in this our hour of greatest need. But you, Juma, you need not go on. You may run away. Because you are hungry and tired and sick and afraid, you may steal what you like of our goods and deplete what little remains of our strength and run away. You may abandon us to our fate. You may leave us to die."

Juma lowered his eyes. The gnats and flies and mosquitoes of dusk swarmed in clouds around his face; but because of the way his wrists were tied behind his back, he could do little about them except squirm fretfully. "*Ninasikitika*, Bwana," he mumbled after a moment.

"What do you say?"

"I am sorry, master."

"Yes, you are sorry. I believe you are sorry. I am also sorry."

Juma looked up quickly, as if startled. There was a sudden flash of sheet lightning just then.

"Hang him."

"*Hapana! Hapana*, Bwana! *Tafadhali*, Bwana!"

"Hang him," Stanley said again.

Jephson didn't understand. He didn't know the Swahili word. But Juma's agonized cry, the sudden horror in the others' faces, the way the headman Murabo dropped the rope and stepped aside as if Juma had suddenly become leprous, the way Sudi jerked around and looked at Jephson with an expression of desperate entreaty, the way Uledi's hand shot out and grasped Stanley's shoulder as if to restrain him . . .

Stanley shrugged the hand off. "Hang him, I say. Hang him where all can see him. Hang him where all who pass this way will know what fate awaits anyone who would desert Bula Matari."

"Mr. Stanley, I don't think–" Jephson started forward.

But at that moment Juma bolted. In his blind terror, however, in his unreasoning panic, the stupid little wretch made a dreadful error in judgment. He bolted straight toward Hoffman. Anyone else–the other Wanyamwezis, the Sudanese, even Sudi or Uledi, perhaps even Jephson himself–might have let him pass, but not Hoffman. With an almost lazy indifference, the huge man raised one of his crutches, drew it back, and smashed it across the boy's face. The nose broke. There was an eruption of bone splinter and blood. The boy went down like a stone; and skipping on his one good foot, balancing on one crutch, Hoffman jammed the other crutch into the small of the boy's back and pinned him. A groan of shared pain went up from the onlookers.

"Pick up the rope, Murabo."

The headman stared at Hoffman, frozen.

"You heard Bula Matari. Pick up the rope. We hang him."

Slowly, as if coming back to life, Murabo began shaking his head and backed away. Sudi also backed away. And all the others too backed away, an ugliness coming into their eyes, the shock and horror that had been there a moment before over the enormity of Stanley's judgment, its excessiveness, congealing now into something alarming. Jephson glanced around apprehensively. These, their own men, had suddenly become strangers. Hungry, tired, lost, pushed too far, they had suddenly become dangerous. Most still carried their weapons—Winchesters, Remingtons, Sniders, muzzle-loaders, flintlocks, spears, *pangas*—a murderous array. Backing away, muttering deep in their throats like angered animals, they formed a ring around the three white men, isolating them with the condemned boy. Neither Stanley nor Hoffman was armed. Jephson clutched his Express hunting rifle at his side but couldn't remember whether it was loaded. In these circumstances it didn't matter much whether it was or not.

"Uledi, *hiki ni nini?* You allow this? You, my chief, the chief of all my chiefs, the companion of all my journeys, you allow this defiance?"

"*Kumradhi*, Bula Matari." Again the old Wanyamwezi chieftain put a hand on Stanley's shoulder. "Forgive me, but this what you propose is too hard."

"Too hard, Uledi? You find it too hard?"

"He has done a terrible thing, *rafiki* and must be punished. But not in this way."

"Will, get off him."

Hoffman hopped back. Facedown, bleeding into the grass, his bound hands lying lifeless on his buttocks, Juma emitted a rattling gasp of relief as the spear of Hoffman's crutch was removed from his back.

"Stand up, boy."

Juma made the effort. He lifted his head. He rolled to a side and tried to lever himself up on an elbow. He drew his legs up under his pelvis, stuck up his hindquarters, dug into the ground with his toes; but it was all only the pathetic writhing of a trussed and beaten animal. He couldn't get up; and Stanley strode to him with sudden impatience, grabbed the rope around his neck, jerked him to his knees, and held him there. He had to hold him there. For the boy was barely conscious. His eyes had rolled up into his head. Blood streamed down his face from his shattered nose and bubbled on his lips with each of his tortured, wheezing breaths. He would have toppled forward except for the rope, pulled taut by Stanley. Stanley's bare arm showed the strain of it, the bicep bulging powerfully, a vein slowly swelling and throbbing along that cannonball of a muscle.

"So you would spare him, Uledi. You would show him mercy. Even though he would desert us in our darkest hour, you would plead for his life."

"He is but a boy, Bula Matari. Hungry and far from home."

"No, Uledi. He is our enemy." Stanley looked down at the kneeling boy. His head was cocked awkwardly to one side from the pull of the rope; his mouth had fallen open from its choking pressure. "As much as the wild beasts of the forest, as much as the savages with their poisoned arrows, as much as the hunger that saps our strength, he threatens our lives. In stealing our supplies, in diminishing our forces, in running away when we are in danger, in abandoning us to an uncertain fate in a dreadful wilderness, anyone who would desert us reduces our chances and brings us closer to death. Why should such be spared? Why should we show him mercy? To spare him would be a terrible injustice to those who remain loyal to us and suffer with us in our tribulations. To show him mercy would be a sign of weakness, a foolish encouragement to those who might be tempted to follow his example. Already nearly a score have deserted us. Already we are closer to death by that number. How many more will we allow to go before we put an end to this slow death? Oh, no, Uledi, he cannot be spared. He must not be shown mercy. Do not plead for him, *rafiki*, for he is our enemy and must die."

They could have shot him now, any one of them; they easily could have shot Stanley and saved the boy, but they didn't. They made no move. They stared transfixed, mesmerized, awed, intimidated as if by the sight of some grotesque circus strongman performing a prodigious feat of strength. Naked to the waist, a hand on one hip, legs planted wide apart, every muscle in his powerful bull torso standing out like hewn granite and glistening with sweat, his scarred face rock-hard in terrible concentration, his eyes narrowed to piercing Oriental slits, Stanley slowly, steadily, remorselessly flexed his arm.

The rope cut into Juma's neck. His head cocked farther to one side. The tendons and veins and cords stretched. His tied hands began flapping desperately behind his back, the fingers curling in agony. An awful gurgling sound escaped his throat. His eyes popped. Both knees lifted from the ground. But he wasn't actually lifted.

His helpless deadweight pulled him back down against the relentless, powerful upward pull of the rope. He was strangling.

"Dear God! Oh, dear God!" Jephson hurled himself at Stanley.

With a swipe of his free arm, Stanley batted Jephson aside. But he let go of the rope. Juma fell forward on his face. Sudi rushed over to him.

"Is he dead?"

Sudi flipped the boy over on his back, clawed frantically at the rope, loosened it. "Soon," he replied. His voice was a guttural growl. "Soon he is dead."

"String him up, Will," Stanley said. "String him up where everyone will see him when they come into camp."

Hoffman started toward Juma.

"No. Get away from him. Are you crazy? He's still alive."

"Arthur!" Stanley's voice was like a pistol shot. "Don't make trouble, Arthur. Just do what I tell you. If you don't want to get us jumped and cut to pieces by these kaffirs, do exactly what I tell you."

Jephson glanced around the circle of watching Wanyamwezis and Sudanese.

"We show the least sign of weakness now, these buggers are going to lose their heads and come at us. We back down now, we don't finish this business the way it should be finished, we lose our nerve, we're dead men. Look at them. By Christ, just look at them. Give them half a chance—"

"This didn't have to happen. None of it had to happen."

"Don't tell me what had to happen. Don't try to be smarter than me. Just do what I tell you. If you want to get out of this with your skin, let Will finish this as it should be finished."

Very few slept that night. Standing at the entry flap of the surgery tent, his Express rifle loaded and propped handily against the center pole, Jephson looked out into the rain. The men were huddled in their shelters of sticks and leaves whispering to each other—restless, angry, scared, scary. Hoffman prowled among them, the sudden tremendous flashes of lightning illuminating his figure hulked on his crutches, first in one place, then in another. A lamp burned in the command tent; Stanley also was awake.

"What are they doing?" Parke asked.

"Nothing."

"Not yet."

Jephson looked around. Parke sat on a crate in a dark corner of the tent, his knees drawn up to his chin, his arms wrapped around his legs, hugging himself as if he were freezing, rocking rhythmically back and forth.

"This is the end for us," he said. "You know that, don't you, Arthur? This is as far as we're going to get. This is where we're going to die. Here, in this miserable wilderness, in the middle of nowhere. We marched halfway across Africa to die here, where no one will ever find our bones. We– What's today?"

"I don't know."

"Is it October yet?"

"Of course it's October. It's damn near the end of October."

"More than half a year we've been under way. Very nearly nine months if you reckon from when we left Aden, and this is where we got. Where? No one even knows. And no one will ever know. It's a joke. It's laughable." Parke began to laugh, a soft idiotic laugh.

"Why don't you have some brandy and go to sleep?"

Parke stopped his rhythmic rocking. "That's what they're waiting for, Arthur. That's just what they're waiting for. For us to go to sleep. Then they'll cut our throats."

"Oh, for Christ sake. I'm keeping watch. I'll get you up in time if it comes to anything like that." Jephson looked back out into the rain.

Stanley had come out of the command tent draped in an ankle-length poncho. He had his Winchester with him. "Will."

Hoffman materialized out of the darkness.

"What was that? Did you hear it?"

Hoffman nodded.

"What was it?"

Hoffman shook his head, and the two men stood together for a few minutes listening; but there was only the braying of the pack animals, the sporadic deafening peals of thunder, the steady beating of the rain slashing through the trees.

"Who's there?" Stanley suddenly cried out. "Uledi, is that you? Answer me. Answer me, goddamnit."

No one answered him.

Jephson grabbed his rifle.

Parke jumped up. "It's starting. Oh, dear God, it's starting now. They're coming for us."

Jephson didn't reply. He dashed out into the rain.

Slavers were there.

· EIGHT ·

TWELVE DAYS after leaving Nelson, nearly a month and 200 miles from the razed village where the slavers had first been encountered, the column at last reached Ipoto.

It was a large, thriving settlement set in a shallow, bowl-shaped valley through which, north to south, a muddy stream flowed, the banks thick with fern and coconut palm and orchards of mango and lime trees. The slopes of the hills descending to it were cleared and planted in Indian corn, sugarcane, rice, beans, yams, cassava, onions, and bananas—a veritable oasis in the wilderness. Its buildings—sturdy tembes of mud and wattle with pitched roofs of woven thatch, the wide eaves shading deep verandas, as well as a profusion of huts and sheds, granaries, chicken runs, storehouses, and corrals for livestock—were arranged around a sun-beaten square on the stream's east bank, at the center of which, facing the stream and enclosed by a palisade of bamboo stakes, stood a fort.

It was toward this, guided by the slavers who had found them, that the caravan made on the morning after Juma's execution, while the square around it filled with hundreds, a thousand, perhaps two thousand people. They were Zanzibari Arabs, half-castes of a variety of combinations, Manyema, natives of the surrounding forest, mostly men, armed with matchlocks and muzzle-loaders and spears. There were also some women and children among them; and seeing them well fed, their skins glossy with health, dressed in brightly colored tribal cloths or sparkling white djellabas, Jephson realized with sickening clarity into what a truly pitiful state the column had fallen. Ragged, starving, filthy, afflicted with sores and ulcers and fever, dragged down by their loads, stumbling with every step, their eyes bloodshot and rheumy in their pinched faces and darting about furtively, they gave the appearance of a mob of beggars at the very end of their tether. It was not, under the circumstances, an advantageous impression to give. Stanley halted them in front of the fort in the shade of the palm and mango trees of the riverbank and went up to the gate in the fort's palisade.

A bodyguard of Manyema gunmen blocked the entry. Behind them was a courtyard perhaps sixty feet square, ringed by outbuildings. The fort itself, of baked clay, its dung-colored walls pierced here and there with oblong embrasures for musketry, stood on the far side. On its front veranda, two steps up from the hard-packed earth of the courtyard, Abed bin Salim, known as Kilonga-longa, sheik of Ipoto and ruler of the tens of thousands of square miles of jungle plundered by his slaving gangs, waited.

He was short and fat. He was dressed in a voluminous unbelted white robe and an unadorned white turban. His tiny feet were pushed into beautifully tooled leather slippers; his chubby chocolate cheeks were smooth and hairless as a baby's. He sat on a low carved stool, with his hands resting on his knees as if on overstuffed bolsters, and his body was pitched back as if pushed out of the way by his overflowing belly. He made no gesture of welcome, nor did he signal his bodyguard to unbar the entry. He simply stared with beady pig eyes at the white man who had appeared there. On either side of him stood his captains and chiefs, all more elaborately attired than he, with bandoliers crossed on their chests, Shirazi daggers in their girdles, feathers in their turbans, and leaning lazily on long rifles. There were also some women on the veranda—wives or odalisques, quite pretty actually, although every bit as obese as their master and with their faces smeared spookily in some kind of white paint. There was a band of drummers and horn players, who on some other occasion might have serenaded the arrival of strangers; now, however, they were silent. All were silent. It was a bright clear morning, and there was still a freshness in the air from the rainstorm of the previous night; but in the long-drawn-out, patently unwelcoming silence of Kilonga-longa's scrutiny, Jephson could fell the oppressive heat of the day beginning to rise, the sun beating on his back, the yellow earth of the square baking into dust under his feet, the torment of flies and mosquitoes starting anew.

Stanley had shaved and dressed for the occasion. He wore his blue gold-frogged military jacket and his spiked topee; but the jacket by now was moldy and soiled, the frogging tarnished and frayed, the helmet battered and unchalked, and his cheeks, nicked about by his rusty razor, were haggard and drawn with hunger and fatigue. In comparison with the fat, sleek slaver, he looked little better than a vagabond at his wit's end. Perhaps it was because of this that Kilonga-longa stared so hard at him and with so little show of the vaunted Arabic courtesy.

At last he broke the silence. "Bula Matari." His voice was high pitched, that of a castrato. "I was told to expect you."

"Kilonga-longa," Stanley replied, placing his hands on his hips. "I was told you were here."

"Yes, I am here. What is it you want of me?"

Stanley shifted his right hand to the butt of his holstered pistol and gripped it so that his knuckles whitened. But he kept his expression impassive, his voice quiet and calm. "I do not understand this, Kilonga-longa," he said. "Am I to speak to you from here, across this yard, over the heads of these soldiers who bar my way? You do not invite me into your house? You do not offer me refreshment? Am I not welcome here?"

The Arab glanced up at one of the captains standing at his side. The man bent over to let him whisper in his ear, then slipped away on some unknown errand.

"I ask you, Kilonga-longa, am I not welcome here?"

"And I ask you, Bula Matari, why have you come here?"

"But surely you can see that for yourself. You are not blind." Stanley turned and gestured toward the column. "Look at my men. Look at the poor wretches. For very nearly thirty marches they have trekked through a land laid waste by your slaving gangs. For very nearly thirty marches they have had little to eat but the vermin and bitter fruit of the forest, thanks to the depredations of your people. They are sick and starving. Many have died. Many have lost heart and deserted. Many have dropped by the way. My second-in-command, an officer in the armies of the English Queen, a hero of her wars, lies wounded in the wilderness not a fortnight's march from here, unable to continue. For the love of Allah, why do you suppose I've come here?" Stanley turned back to the Arab, his voice rising. "For food. For rest and succor. For provisions so that I can go on."

"Where do you go?"

"To the other side of the forest. To the great lake, Albert Nyanza, on the other side of the forest."

"Ah, you go far."

"How far?"

The question, fired back testily, surprised the Arab, and his little pig eyes widened quizzically. "You do not know?"

"I reckon that, as the crow flies, another hundred, perhaps another hundred fifty miles still lies before me. But I am not a crow."

"No, Bula Matari, you are not a crow."

"How far is it then for one who is not a crow?"

"You cannot ask that of me. For I also do not know. I have never been to the other side of the forest. I often think it has no other side."

"How far have you been?"

The Arab shrugged. "Fifteen marches. Twenty."

"And in twenty marches you did not come to the other side of the forest?"

"No."

Stanley removed his sun helmet and ran his hand through his matted gray hair. It was a gesture of infinite weariness. "Well, twenty marches then," he said after a moment. "I shall need provisions for at least twenty marches then." He put the helmet back on. "For I must suppose that your people have made a wasteland of the forest for that distance as well."

The Arab didn't reply.

"Arthur, Will, have the *mitako* brought up here."

"*Mitako*, Bula Matari?"

Stanley turned back to the Arab. "I mean to pay for the provisions I seek, Kilonga-longa. For I see that here the hand of friendship is not extended to the sorely tried traveler. I see that here hospitality is not offered to hungering strangers. I see that here, in the darkness of the forest, the injunctions of the Koran are forgotten. Very well. So be it. I do not come to you as a beggar seeking alms. I am prepared to pay for what I need, and pay well."

"With *mitako*, Bula Matari? With beads and cloth and coils of wire?" The Arab all of a sudden gave out a trill of contemptuous, mirthless laughter, then cut himself off as abruptly. "Oh, no, no, Bula Matari," he said. "You must not insult me. You must not imagine me some savage of the forest to be enthralled by such trinkets. Look around you. Do you not see silver and precious stones and silks and cloths of braided gold? Oh, no, Bula Matari, I do not trade for such trinkets. I have no use for such stuff."

"For what then do you have use?"

The Arab stood up. Because of his gross size, he required the assistance of two of his women to accomplish this; but when he came down the veranda steps and crossed the courtyard toward Stanley, he moved with a surprisingly dainty agility. His chiefs and captains followed him. The bodyguard at the palisade gate made way for him.

"I ask you, Kilonga-longa, what will you take in trade for the provisions I seek?"

The Arab brushed past Stanley and out through the palisade gate, where he had an unobstructed view of the column, the ragged ranks of askaris paraded with their Winchesters and Remingtons, the gun crew slouching wearily against the Maxim, the gaunt Wanyamwezis clustered around their battered loads, the bag-of-bones pack animals browsing listlessly on the grass of the riverbank. He scrutinized them for a long moment, his hands folded on the big drum of his stomach, as if appraising their decrepitude, judging their worth. Then he said, "Guns."

"Eh?"

"Guns, Bula Matari. I will trade for guns and cartridges and powder. I have use for such. In my affairs, I always have use for such."

Stanley shook his head. "I do not trade with my guns."

"No?" The Arab unclasped his pudgy hands and pointed at the Maxim. "For that one gun alone I could see my way clear to provision you for—"

"I tell you no, Kilonga-longa." Stanley's tone sharpened. "I do not trade with my guns. I too have use for them. What else?"

The Arab took another long look at the ragtag column. Then he said, "Nothing else."

"Now look here, effendi. Let us not play this game with each other. We are not in a Zanzibar souk. Neither of us has the leisure or inclination to pass the day in haggling like old women in a bazaar. I need food. These men of mine are well nigh to starving. But you can not expect me to be so foolhardy as to trade away my guns for it. I have countless marches still to go through an unknown wilderness, and I will not go without my guns. Who but a madman would? So let us put aside the sport of the bazaar and speak plain to one another. What else will you take?"

"I have spoken plain. Nothing else." The Arab made a derisive dismissive gesture at the column. "You have nothing else," he said and started back to the fort.

"Don't walk away from me. Don't you dare walk away from me." Stanley grabbed at the Arab's sleeve.

And instantly the Manyema guard surged forward and the hands of the chiefs and captains flew to the knives in their girdles.

Stanley withdrew his hand. "You vulture," he said in English. "You filthy bloody vulture. You'd pick the bones of your dying mother if you thought you could get away with it."

The Arab no doubt understood this. Nevertheless he gazed at Stanley with a lordly impassiveness, a lofty disdain, his hands once again clasped contentedly on his belly. He was altogether sure of himself, and with reason. A thousand of his armed men surrounded the column. He waited a moment as if to let this fact sink in. Then he said, "Guns, Bula Matari. It is only for guns that I will trade." And he continued on his way back to the fort.

"*Sita. Ngoja kidoga. Tazama!*"

The Arab looked around in alarm.

Stanley had drawn his pistol.

And again with a sharp sucking gasp the Manyema moved in quick protective anger, swinging up the barrels of their rifles. For an instant, a mad instant, it seemed that Stanley, his pistol aimed straight at the Arab's fat gut, meant to challenge them, dare them in a sudden burst of gunfire, to exchange his life for their master's. But it was only an instant, a flash of terrible frustration, the wild childish desire to strike out in some way, no matter how futile, against a dreadful turn in luck. And in the next instant he spun the pistol by its trigger guard end over end on his finger, grasped the barrel, and shoved it, butt forward, at the Arab.

"Here then. What will you give for this, slaver? How many of my men will you feed for this?"

"Ah." If the Arab had had a qualm of fear, he allowed himself a sigh of relief now. "You come to your senses."

"Or this?" With impatient fury, Stanley unbuckled his cartridge belt and held it out to the Arab. "How much food can I get for this? How many ears of corn will you give for it? Or for a rifle? Or a box of percussion caps? What is the rate of exchange here? How high do you set the price to feed starving men?"

"We must speak of it. Calm yourself." The Arab now was smiling in undisguised triumph. "There is no need to agitate yourself so, Bula Matari. We shall speak of it and reach an arrangement. Come." And holding out his hand in the Arab fashion, he took Stanley into the fort.

The morning passed, mounted into a dusty, scorching afternoon shrilling with insects, weighted beneath a sulfurous sky. Under the pounding of the sun, the crowd around the column thinned out bit by bit, the women drifting off with the children to resume their chores milling corn, weaving cloth, and tilling the fields. The older men retreated to the shade of the tembe verandas to smoke their water pipes and play their board games. But the gunmen remained, the cannibal Manyema, the hawk-faced half-castes. They formed not so much a guard as an intimidating presence. There was little order in their ranks. They lounged on their rifles, lazily swatting away flies and mosquitoes and chattering among themselves; and now and again the Swahili speakers among them tried to engage the Wanyamwezis in conversation. Five to one, Jephson reckoned. They outnumbered the column by at least that much, and in this case the Maxim couldn't be counted on as an equalizer. Not where it was positioned anyway. If there was trouble, if any attempt was made to use it, the slavers, taking a few losses, could easily overrun it, they were that closely packed around. Perhaps he should have it repositioned, moved farther back to give it a clear field of fire. Perhaps too he should reposition the askaris, deploy them in a skirmish line along the riverbank.

But what was he thinking? There mustn't be a fight. Jesus, no. They had come here for food and provisions. Ted Barttelot and Jack Troup and the rest of the rear column, following on their track and suffering all the same frightful privations they had suffered, would also come here for food and provisions. There mustn't be trouble of any sort. They had to stay on the right side of these vultures. They couldn't risk anything that would provoke a fight. They had to wait for Stanley to strike some reasonable bargain with the Arab. And besides, there was now a question about their own men: Would they fight? Jephson slapped irritatedly at an insect whining in his ear as he surveyed them. Since Juma's execution, their mood had turned dark, unpredictable, dangerous.

Their headmen and corporals were gathered in a circle around Uledi. It had the look of a shauri, a palaver, except none of them spoke. Uledi, hunkered on his haunches, traced a design over and over again in the dust between his feet. Was it some kind of a map? He glanced around now and then at the slavers and beyond them at the fields of maize and rice, the stands of sugarcane, the gardens of beans. The others watched him, wordless. It was difficult to make out what it was about. Were they planning something? Sudi was among them. Jephson hadn't spoken to him since the terrible business with Juma the evening before, and he wasn't encouraged to do so now by the hard expression on the young Wanyamwezi's face.

Hoffman was down at the river. Seated on a flat rock at the water's edge, his crutches propped against another, he was letting his ulcerated foot soak in the slowly flowing stream, pulling it out from time to time to inspect and probe the disgusting fist-size wound. He showed no sign of pain, but the pain must have been great. It was amazing, an act of monumental stupidity or astonishing will that he had been able to keep going with such an affliction. Parke watched him from a little distance. He seemed fascinated by what he saw, his mouth hanging open as if awed or appalled by the sight of the vile wound; but apparently it didn't occur to him that he was a physician and could help. When Jephson went over, he got up quickly and moved away like a child caught out in something or trying to avoid being caught out. Jephson ignored him and went down to the water.

"How're you doing, Will?"

Hoffman darted him a sidewise glance, then went back to ministering to his foot.

"Do you need something? Ointment maybe or fresh bandages?"

Hoffman grunted an unintelligible reply and dropped his foot back into the stream.

Jephson set his helmet aside, got down on his knees, and splashed several handfuls of water on his face, then he scooped up another, meaning to take a drink, but thought the better of it. The stream was thick with sediment and vegetation; God only knew what diseases lurked in its depths. He splashed that handful on the back of his neck instead. "Will, what do you think Uledi's up to?"

"Eh?"

"Have a look at him."

Hoffman glanced over his shoulder.

"He's up to something, don't you think?"

"Yes."

"What do you think it is?"

"What do I think what is?"

"Oh, for Christ sake." Jephson rocked back on his heels. There never was any point talking to Hoffman; there never was any getting anything out of him. Whatever he thought or felt or knew, he kept to himself. Perhaps he also kept it *from* himself, believing that to trouble himself about anything except what was most immediately at hand would get in his way, interfere with his work, prevent him from going on. And maybe he was right; maybe it was the only way; maybe you had to become that sort of animal in order to go on. Jephson lay back against the slope of the riverbank and closed his eyes against the harsh sunlight flashing through the fronds of the palm trees and thought of Nelson lying by that other river. The poor devil. But Stanley probably had been right to leave him there. After all, what would have been the use, even if they had been able to get him across that river, of putting him through the torment of these last twelve days of marching, of bringing him here? There was nothing for him here either. No, he really was no worse off there in his shelter of branches and leaves on that rocky embankment above those thundering rapids. He could just as easily die there as he could here.

It was coming on to dusk when Stanley at last re-emerged from the fort. He came out alone. Kilonga-longa was nowhere in sight. A few of the slaver's captains and odalisques stood on the fort's veranda and watched him cross the dusty courtyard and pass through the Manyema guard at the palisade gate. He didn't look good; his expression wasn't encouraging; he walked slowly with a distracted air, a hand resting heavily on the butt of his pistol.

Uledi stood up. One after the other, so did the headmen and the corporals. Hoffman got back on his crutches and started toward him. Jephson and Parke followed, but Uledi and the others remained where they were, watching him approach. He pushed through the crowd of the slaver's gunmen and went straight to where the pack animals were tethered in a forlorn bunch near the stream. He picked out his own, the big black riding mule, and for a minute Jephson had the wild idea that he was going to mount it and ride away, just ride away, just get the hell out of there. But all he did was throw an arm around the haggard beast's neck and lean against it and gaze out over the river, the flesh of his scarred face slack.

"Mr. Stanley."

He didn't seem to hear. After a moment Jephson said his name again, and he turned then.

"Are we getting food, Mr. Stanley? Have you managed to get us food?"

"Yes. We're getting food. I've managed to get us food." He looked back toward the fort.

A handful of slave women had appeared in the courtyard in front of one of the outbuildings, a storehouse. The provisions Stanley had traded for were being handed out of it to them.

It was next to nothing: twelve large baskets of Indian corn, maybe 125 ears in each basket, which worked out to about six ears of corn for each man in the column. Even under the strict niggardly rationing that Stanley had enforced when they had first entered the slavers' raiding circle, this represented provisions for no more than three days. In addition, there were three live goats. And for that, Stanley had agreed to give forty-eight rifles—nearly all the column's spare weapons, those that had been recovered from the men who had fallen by the way or been killed—plus 3,000 rounds of ammunition. At that rate of exchange, twenty days' worth of provisions, enough to see them through to the other side of the slavers' raiding circle, would disarm the column entirely.

The slave women set the baskets and goats in front of Stanley and quickly melted back through the ranks of the encircling gunmen. No one said anything, no one made a move. Despite their hunger, despite what must have been a terrible urge to fling themselves on this the first real food they had seen in weeks, the Wanyamwezis and Sudanese—scattered in little groups along the riverbank, some standing, some kneeling, some squatting on their heels or propped against tree trunks—simply stared in dumb disbelief.

"All right. On your feet everybody. We're getting out of here."

"Sir?"

"Let's get this column in march order, Arthur. We're moving out."

"But it's after five, sir. There's barely two hours of daylight left."

"I don't care how many hours of daylight are left. We're getting out of here. Will, form the *pagazis* up by company. Uledi, get these baskets loaded on the pack animals. Dr. Parke—"

"But what's the sense in that? How far can we get in two hours anyway? Why don't we just stay here for the night?"

"We're not staying here for the night. We're not staying here for another minute. Dr. Parke. Where the devil is that man? Muster the rear guard, Doctor. Uledi, didn't you hear me? I want these baskets loaded on the pack animals."

Uledi hadn't moved when Stanley first called to him. Now he came forward. Sudi and the other headmen came with him. The eyes of all the Wanyamwezis and Sudanese were fixed on them.

"Come on, man. What's this dawdling? Get some *pagazis* over here and have this corn loaded. We're moving out, I say."

Uledi looked at the twelve baskets stacked at Stanley's feet, at the three goats. "Is this all of it, Bula Matari?" he asked quietly.

"Yes, this is all of it." Stanley's reply was quick, edgy, defensive.

"It is very little."

"I know it's very little. You don't have to tell me it's very little. But it was all I could manage without stripping ourselves clean. As it is, it cost us all our spare rifles."

"So this is all of it. *Vyema*. I will distribute it to our people."

"You'll do what? What do you mean you'll distribute it? You'll do no such thing. Didn't you hear what I said? I want this stuff loaded. We're not staying here. We're moving out."

Uledi looked up. He was as gaunt and worn as the rest. His curly white beard, once so neatly trimmed, straggled in greasy, knotted tangles halfway down his chest. His pantaloons were in tatters, exposing his bony, scabbed knees. And somewhere along the way he had lost his maroon fez and now wore strips of sweat-soaked cloth around his head. "The men are hungry, Bula Matari. They must eat."

"They'll eat later."

Uledi shook his head. "No, Bula Matari. They will eat now." He threw a glance over his shoulder.

Sudi stepped forward and reached for one of the baskets.

"Oh, no. You're not going to do this." Stanley grabbed for the basket, knocking it from Sudi's hands, sending scores of unshucked ears of corn spilling in the dust.

Sudi stepped back, casting an uncertain glance at Uledi. But two of the other headmen came forward and, keeping a wary eye on Stanley, staying a bit to the left of him, made a grab for another of the baskets. Stanley whirled toward them, but he wasn't quick enough this time and they managed to pull the basket out of the pile. And that emboldened the others. And not only the headmen. Now the rest of the column started forward. Some restraint had been broken. They wanted their food.

Stanley pulled out his pistol. "Uledi!"

The old Wanyamwezi chieftain looked at the weapon, then into Stanley's eyes.

"I'm warning you, Uledi. Don't do this."

Uledi turned his back on the weapon.

And Stanley fired.

The noise was horrendous. Men jumped, then flung themselves to the ground. The slaver's gunmen whipped up their rifles. People rushed down from the fort's veranda, Kilonga-longa among them. But Uledi didn't stir; the shot had exploded a plume of dirt within an inch of the back of his heels, but he hadn't stirred. In a steady quiet voice he said, "Take the baskets. Take the goats. Distribute them to the people. We shall eat now."

But no one responded. Everyone was watching Stanley. He was gripping the pistol with both hands to keep it from trembling, pointing it at the small of Uledi's back. It was much the same posture he had struck with Kilonga-longa, infused with much the same rage and frustration. But he could no more shoot Uledi than he could have shot the Arab, and for much the same reasons. "Damn you, Uledi," he groaned after a moment and lowered the pistol.

Uledi turned to him then.

"We can't stay here. You know we can't. You know what will happen if we do, even for one night. We'll lose half the men. They'll sell themselves to the slavers. They'll sell themselves for food. And the other half will sell their guns. The column will be ruined."

"That may be, Bula Matari. There are such men among us. They are the men who have lost heart, who no longer have faith in you, who do not believe there is an end to this forest or that you can bring them to the end if there is an end. They are the men who believe that to go on with you is to go on only to die. And so they will sell themselves to the slavers. They will sell themselves for food." Uledi turned around. The men were carrying off the baskets of corn, leading away the goats, and a cooking fire was being started down near the stream. When he spoke again, he spoke watching the men taking the baskets and goats to that fire. "But there is nothing to be done about those. They will desert the expedition and go to the slavers whether we spend the night here or not. They will go from the next camp if not from here. They will go during the march to the camp after that if not from there. They will go during all our marches and from all our camps. They will go whenever and wherever they find the opportunity." He turned back to Stanley. "They cannot be stopped, Bula Matari, not by leaving here tonight, not by any means. Men who have lost heart and faith never can be stopped. No matter how many you hang."

Night came, a moonless night but clear and full of stars. No shelters were built nor were either of the tents pitched. Nothing resembling a proper camp was made; but several more cooking fires were lighted, and these cast dancing shadows from the men moving around them portioning out the provisions Stanley had bought, shucking the ears of corn, grinding the kernels into meal, slaughtering the goats. The four white men watched this activity standing by the tethered pack animals, onlookers, outsiders.

"Aren't we going to get any?" Parke asked. "Aren't they going to give us any?"

No one answered him.

"We're just as hungry as they are, for Christ's sake. We haven't had any more to eat than they have, the lousy niggers. The bloody bleeding niggers." When still no one responded, he said, "I told you this was going to happen, Arthur. I told you these niggers would turn on us one of these days."

"Shut up, Tom. Just shut up."

"All right, I'll shut up. Why shouldn't I shut up? Who the hell am I anyway? What does it matter what I've got to say?" He moved off muttering to himself and sat down.

After a bit Hoffman also sat down. His foot obviously was getting too much for him. Laying his crutches aside, he gripped the ankle and squeezed it and kept on squeezing it as if trying to cut off the pain. Stanley and Jephson remained standing. It was impossible to tell how the men were dealing with the food, whether they were setting any of it aside for the unknown number of days of marching that still lay ahead or whether, famished, they intended to consume all of it this night with no thought for the future—or with a different thought of what the future would bring. That was for Uledi to decide now; he had taken charge of the matter, had taken it out of Stanley's hands.

The air grew chill; fingers of mist rose off the river; there was the soft croaking harmony of frogs, the shrilling of cicadas, the crackling of the fires, the nickering and braying of the donkeys and mules. The slaver's gunmen still formed their cordon around the column, although in the dark beyond the fires they were merely so many shadowy shapes, like the trees. Oil lamps, however, had been lit in the fort; and in that faint flickering light the fat figure of Kilonga-longa could be seen on the veranda.

Then Uledi called to the white men. Places had been made for them at one of the fires; a single slightly rotted tree trunk had been dragged to it, so they were obliged to sit side by side in a row like schoolboys, facing the flames. Tin plates of food were brought—boiled mealie meal containing chunks of broiled goat—and once handed over, the men who had brought them withdrew. Only Uledi, Sudi, and the other headmen remained at the fire, squatting on their heels. They had already eaten.

Parke immediately fell on his food. The aroma, especially of the meat, was irresistible, almost painful; and Jephson was about to plunge in to it too when he saw Hoffman hesitate and look at Stanley. Stanley lifted a sticky glob of the *posho* off his plate, then let it drop back.

"You have served with a generous hand, Uledi," he said.

"Eat, Bula Matari."

"How much is here? Five ears of corn? Six?"

"It is needed. We have gone too long without proper food. It will give us back our strength. It will revive our spirits."

"Have you served this generously to all the men?"

"I have."

"So it is finished then. The twelve baskets are finished. The forty-eight rifles I gave for them are eaten up in one night."

"We will get more tomorrow."

"We will get more tomorrow! Where will we get more? How will we get more?"

"As you have gotten this. With our guns."

"Ah, with our guns." Stanley set his plate aside. "Yes, I see."

"No, Bula Matari. You do not see."

"Oh, yes, Uledi, I do see. I see only too well. I see that you too have lost faith in me and will not go on."

"No, Bula Matari."

"Don't tell me no. Tomorrow when the men awaken and look into the baskets and find them empty, they will cry out to you that they are hungry, too hungry to go on; and so you will trade away forty-eight more of our rifles to fill their bellies as you have filled them tonight. And the next day it will be the same. For *those* forty-eight rifles too will have been eaten up; and the men again will cry out to you that they are hungry, too hungry to go on, and you will trade away more of our rifles to fill their bellies. And, when you have traded away the last of them and we are unarmed and defenseless in this wilderness, then we truly will be unable to go on; and so in this way you will bring our journey to an end here in this slaver's camp, at this slaver's mercy."

"I tell you no, Bula Matari."

"Like hell, no!" Stanley jumped up. "Look there, you fool. Do you not see him there on the fort's veranda? Do you not see how he watches and waits like the bloody vulture he is? Why do you suppose he watches? For what, in God's name, do you suppose he waits? He waits for this, only for this, only for us in our hunger to trade away all our guns and so become his helpless prey. He waits to enslave us."

"No. It will not be so. We will go on. Quiet yourself." Uledi took Stanley by the arm and forcibly seated him. "Sit down and eat. Here." He picked up Stanley's plate and handed it to him. "Eat. All of you, eat. You are hungry and must eat."

Jephson could no longer restrain himself and greedily wolfed into the *posho*, fingering out chunks of the goat meat, jamming them into his mouth, made almost faint by the marvelous forgotten flavor of it. And after a moment Stanley also began to eat; and when he did, so did Hoffman.

"We will go on, Bula Matari," Uledi said. "I promise this to you. Have I not always been faithful to you? And I remain faithful to you now. Yes, we will go on, but not tonight. Not even tomorrow. First we must get more food. Then we will go on. Only then will it be possible to go on. *Sikilizo,* Bula Matari. Hear me. You must get more food for us. Tomorrow you must go to the Arab and get more food for us."

Stanley looked up from his plate; but his mouth was full, and besides, Uledi knew well enough what he would say and forestalled him.

"The devil take our guns. The devil take them, I say. For the love of Allah, what reason is there to save them now? What good are they to us if we starve? What use will they be when we are dead? No, *rafiki.* I tell you you must get more food if you want to continue this journey. You must go to the Arab tomorrow and give him as many guns as he demands for corn enough and goats and fowls for a week's march. A week's march, Bula Matari. Just one week's march."

He moved closer to Stanley and rested a hand on his knee. "Hear me, *rafiki.* I have spoken of this with my *nakhudhas.*" He indicated Sudi and Murabo and the other headmen still squatting by the fire. "As I have said, there are those among us who will not go on in any case. They are broken in heart and health and lost to us no matter what we do. But there are others, Bula Matari. We have spoken of them, my *nakhudhas* and I, and we agree. If we restore their strength, if we revive their spirits, if we allow them some rest, if we give them reason to hope, they will go on. They will follow you. They are well fed now. I have fed them with a generous hand, as you say, and they will sleep easier tonight because of it, and tomorrow they will see the whole matter in a less gloomy light. If then you bring them food enough for a week's march, *rafiki*, just a week's march, if they see they will not starve for at least that length of time, they will follow you. They will not worry themselves unduly about a future that lies much farther off than a week; for, Inshallah, who is to say what fate will bring them in a week?"

"How many of the men?"

"Enough, Bula Matari. Enough to make up a column to take us through the forest."

"I ask you, Uledi, how many?"

"A hundred twenty-five of my people, forty-five of the Sudanese, fifty perhaps."

"A week's provisions for a hundred seventy-five men. That's twenty-five baskets of corn at the very least."

"And goats and fowls."

"He'll want a hundred more rifles for that. More."

"Give it to him."

"And twenty thousand rounds of ammunition."

"Give it to him. Give him as much as he wants. We will manage without it. We will manage with what is left to us. And we will be able to go on."

"And send back for Captain Nelson."

"*Kumradhi?*" Uledi turned to Jephson.

"You must not forget Captain Nelson, Uledi. Once we've got hold of these provisions and the men are fed and rested, we must make up a relief party and send back for him."

Now Uledi looked at Stanley. Stanley had also turned to Jephson. Parke and Hoffman had stopped eating.

"Twenty men, Uledi, and a couple of the pack animals is all. Traveling light like that, they can make it back to the river in half the time it took us to get here, in a third of the time. The trail's cleared and blazed. It'll be easy going for them. Three days, no more than four."

No one said anything.

"*Kunanini?* Why are you looking at me like that? We've got to go back for him. Of course we do. I told him we would. I told him that once we got to Ipoto and resupplied and rested, we'd go back for him. He's waiting for us."

"What're you talking about, Arthur? He's not waiting for us." That was Parke. His beard was speckled with bits of *posho*, slobbered with goat grease. "It's been twelve days. He's not waiting for anybody. He's dead."

"Well, if he's dead, we'll bury him then. But we're not going to just leave him there. We're not going to just leave him there to rot while we sit around here and fill our bellies. We're going back for him. You needn't look at me like that. I'm telling you, we're going back for him. Sudi."

The young Wanyamwezi stiffened.

"You come with me, Sudi. We'll take twenty men, twenty of our best men, and two mules. We'll make good time. Three days there and three days back. We'll set off tomorrow. The column won't be leaving here for a few days anyway. We'll catch them up inside a week."

Sudi turned away.

"Look, Arthur," Stanley said. He put a hand on Jephson's shoulder. "We've got troubles enough of our own now, lad–"

Jephson slapped the hand away. "Don't start on me with that. Don't start on me with your excuses. I don't want to hear them. I knew you wouldn't go back. I knew from the start you never had it in your mind to go back for him." He stood up. "Well, I don't care. I'm going back. I'm going back even if I have to go back alone. I promised him I would."

· NINE ·

IF THE TRUTH be told, Jephson never really believed he'd have to go back for Nelson alone. In his heart of hearts he was sure he wouldn't be allowed to, that the foolhardiness of it would compel someone—Stanley, Uledi, Sudi—even if only at the very last moment, to intervene. But the next morning, with the sun already fully risen, no one intervened.

His mule—a scrawny beast borrowed from Hoffman's company—was already loaded, overloaded, with two sacks of corn flour, two bunches of bananas, and two trussed live chickens—his and Nelson's share of the newly acquired provisions—plus a case of ammunition, a bale of trading cloth, the fly from the surgery tent, blankets, lantern, rope, axe, shovel—a peddler's burro. In addition—having bathed in the river and shaved, wearing newly washed khaki trousers patched in the seat with blue and white checked coverlet, his field glasses around his neck, a cartridge belt around his waist, a water bottle on his hip—he carried a 40-pound rucksack of personal gear on his back. Already he could feel the sting of its straps cutting into his shoulders. In his right hand he held his Express rifle; his left gripped the mule's lead rope. He looked around.

Sudi was standing in front of a shelter he was having the boat company build. Several others, lean-tos battened to the palm trees, were also being built, and the command tent had been pitched. The place was taking on the appearance of a proper encampment; there was a settling in going on, an expectation of several days' rest here. The new rations had been distributed; and the men were sitting around campfires cooking, eating, mending clothes, repairing equipment, picking lice out of each other's hair. Some were fraternizing with the Swahili speakers among the slaver's men and trading what little of value still remained of their personal possessions for additional food. They traded blankets or sandals for a couple of eggs; razors or knives for a few onions; pipes and fetishes, carvings they had made, drums and ornaments they had looted from villages, empty bottles and tins they had scrounged from discarded European stores, caps and shirts, the clothes off their backs, for a bunch of bananas, a basket of dried beans, a handful of mangoes. They broke off to look at Jephson. Parke and Hoffman and Uledi were also looking at him, although as if from a tremendous distance, as if he already was gone. Only Stanley wasn't there to look at him. He was back in the fort with Kilonga-longa negotiating for still more provisions, enough for a week's march. Jephson turned away and, tugging on the mule's lead, started his solitary climb back out of the shallow valley in which Ipoto was located, back into the sun-speckled gloom of the jungle, listening with every step for someone to call to him. But no one did.

As he had anticipated, the going was comparatively easy, what with the trees blazed and the trail cleared and the direction known; and by ten that morning he reached the razed village on a knoll where Juma had been executed. The boy's body still hung from the lowest branch of an ebony tree where Hoffman had strung it up; and passing beneath it, he considered cutting it down and burying it. But it had been exposed to the elements for nearly four days, and the carrion birds had gotten at it. So he averted his eyes and went on. It was enough, he thought, that he'd have to bury Nelson.

He made it back through three of their old camps in the first day. Even as he went, dragging the mule after him, it struck him as almost indecent, a mockery of all they had suffered, this covering in a matter of a few hours ground they had struggled over for days. The landmarks and litter of that struggle were everywhere: the swamp where a mule had floundered and drowned, the stream they had crossed and recrossed a dozen times in search of a way, the false trails they had taken and backtracked, the endless hills they had climbed with no idea what they'd find over the crests, the patch of *matonga* bushes stripped bare where Stanley had allowed them to spend a day foraging, scraps of clothing snagged in the undergrowth, broken-down shelters, bits and pieces of equipment and gear, piles of human waste swarming with butterflies, the remains of dead men. In the third camp, where Jephson had planned to stop for the night, there were three skeletons. What the carrion birds had left, the driver ants had eaten from the bones. There was no way of telling who they were anymore, Wanyamwezis or Sudanese, deserters who had slipped into the camp after the column had gone, or injured men whom the column had left behind. He pushed on for another half-mile to a bit of a clearing by a brook. It was still light or what passed for light in the undersea gloom of the forest. After he unloaded the mule and hobbled it and shrugged out of his rucksack, he investigated the clearing—flat lichen-splattered rocks, tufts of waist-high elephant grass and reeds crowded around by the exposed twisted hairy roots of mangroves, the brook's water running by quick and dark—poking into the underbrush with his rifle, kicking over stones.

He wasn't sure what he was looking for, what he should be worried about, alone in the forest, night falling; but a distinct worry of some sort began seeping into him with the rising chill of the evening mist. When he returned to the center of the clearing, the light was practically gone. He unpacked the tent fly with the idea of stringing it up between a couple of close-growing trees, but suddenly and unaccountably the task proved too complicated for him. He was all thumbs. He couldn't tie knots or untie them. His hands began to shake, and he found himself grappling at the ropes and strings and loops and flaps in desperation, splintering his nails. Then a bird screamed. He spun around. Some kind of horrible bird. He could imagine it, plumed like a maniac, watching him from the trees. He stared into the foliage stupidly, waiting for it to scream again. It didn't.

He looked up through the dense canopy of intertwining leaves and branches and vines overhead. The scrap of sky he could see was clear, pearly blue, not yet night; but the first of the stars, chips of sparkling ice, had come out. And then the bird did scream again, and another, somewhere across the brook, answered it. Then there was another sound, a sound of stealthy scurrying through branches nearby, and then a clicking and a chattering, then hoots and howls and the sudden hysterical laugh of a hyena. The forest was coming alive with the sounds of the approaching night. He let the tent canvas slip from his fingers. The hell with it. It wasn't going to rain anyway. The thing to do was get a fire started, if not for the warmth or to cook on, then for its light to hold back the jungle's darkness, to keep away its nocturnal creatures. But he found he couldn't do that either. He knew where the axe was stowed in the untidy pile of gear he had unloaded from the mule, and where the matches were and the paraffin tin. He knew too where there was a plentiful deadfall of twigs and branches at brookside. But he didn't move. He was rooted to the spot, listening to the frightful sounds all around him, watching the inky blackness close down upon him.

Jesus, how had he got himself into this? What in God's name

was he doing here? Nelson was dead. Nelson was surely dead. He was almost as good as dead when they had left him. What was the point of going back for him? He was only a skeleton now, a heap of jumbled bones. Someone else could bury his bones. Ted Barttelot could. Jack Troup could. They would reach him soon enough. Following blazed and cleared trails, as he had seen for himself that day, the rear column was sure to be making good time. They had started out six weeks after the advance column; they probably were only three or four weeks behind them now. Oh, yes, that was soon enough to bury Nelson's bones. He didn't have to do it. He could return to Ipoto and rest there with the caravan and then just go on with them. That was bad enough. That was duty enough. He didn't have to do this too.

But what if Nelson was still alive?

He crouched down slowly and reached for where he had set his rifle when he had started fooling with the tent fly, keeping his eyes fixed on the brush by the brook. Something was there snuffling. The mule also heard it, stopped browsing, raised its head. Jephson cocked the rifle as quietly as he could. But after a few minutes the thing, whatever it was, went away. He heard it go into the water, heard the soft splash. A snake? A crocodile? He waited. After a bit he smoothed out the tent fly and sat down and waited some more, the rifle across his knees. The night thickened, the last glimmer of gray faded, and the nocturnal noises of the forest took on a repetitive pattern, a steadier, more predictable rhythm—the calling of bird to bird, the grunting of monkeys, the croaking of tree frogs, the whirring of cicadas, the natural sounds and rhythms of the busy life of the jungle's night. The things that were out there either were unaware of his presence or had accepted it. The mule returned to its browsing. Jephson inched over to the jumble of his gear a shade calmer. He would build a fire. He saw the axe. But instead he pulled out a blanket, wrapped it around his shoulders, broke a banana off one of the bunches, sat down on the tent fly, and ate it. Although he dozed off from time to time, he didn't realize it. He believed he sat up on guard throughout the night. And when the first pale light of the dawn made itself felt in the forest, a wash of gray outlining the trees, he loaded the mule and went on.

He reached the river where Nelson had been left on November 5. That morning, the fourth of his trek, while building a cooking fire, he became dimly aware of the faint distant roar of the river's rapids. He didn't at first realize what it was. He couldn't believe he had come so far so quickly and thought it was thunder.

But the sky was as clear as it had been each day now for nearly a week. As he went about preparing his breakfast—a porridge of the corn flour with some mushrooms he had foraged along the way—he listened, puzzled, to that faraway thrumming sound. And then it occurred to him what it was. He wolfed down his food, kicked out the fire, hastily packed up his gear, and set off again. There was a stream to cross. Jephson remembered it as a place where they had had great difficulty with the sections of the steel boat, but he led the mule across now with little trouble, hurrying on toward the increasing roar of the river. By ten, the forest ahead was perceptibly thinning, and an hour later he was catching glimpses through the trees of the boulders and cliffs and ledges of the steep gorge through which the river thundered. He slowed down a bit then, suddenly uneasy about what he would find there.

It was noon when he stepped out of the forest into the blazing sunlight of the river's high embankment and looked across to the camp that had been built on the other side for Nelson and the thirty-two other sick and injured who had been left with him. Vultures and kites wheeled in the still, humid air above it. Jephson looped the mule's lead rope around a bush and raised his field glasses. The huts and shelters and lean-tos of the camp appeared fallen in, beaten down by rain, blown apart by wind, deserted. Except for the carrion birds, swooping in slow sinister circles and alighting from time to time in the treetops, there was no sign of life. Jephson looked down at the river. The fording rope that the column had used to cross it was still in place, a good deal slacker now, a long stretch of its midsection under water, but still usable. Jephson took off his rucksack, slung his rifle, tightened the chinstrap of his helmet, and climbed down the rocky cliff face to the river's edge.

"Robbie, Robbie."

It was ridiculous. No one could hear him above the thunder of the rapids. Certainly a dead man couldn't. He peered through the binoculars again, and this time thought he caught sight of some movement. It was in the corner of his eye. He lowered the glasses quickly and looked, then raised them and looked again. There was something. Yes, definitely, back from the ruined camp, back where the trail vanished westward into the forest, there was something.

"Robbie, it's Arthur. Arthur Jephson."

He buttoned the binoculars into his tunic, took hold of the fording rope, and stepped into the river. It was down a bit, lower than a fortnight before, probably because of the recent spell of dry weather, but that didn't make it much easier to cross. More of the jagged black rocks jutted out of the stream; and the waves crashed over them more violently, pulling at his legs, pounding his body. Coming up on a reef about halfway across, he glanced back to make sure the mule and loads were all right, then again raised his binoculars and scanned the opposite shore. There was no question about it. Someone was over there, maybe more than one, staying clear of the camp, hanging back at the edge of the encircling forest, watching him approach. He checked his rifle to make sure it was loaded, then went on, going in knee-deep, waist-deep, fishing for footholds, half swimming, his left arm looped tightly around the fording rope.

When he reached the other side, he immediately dropped to his knees. This, he hoped, put him out of sight of anyone atop the embankment. He unslung the rifle, checked it again, then dashed forward in a deep crouch to the base of the steep clifflike bank. Here he rested, catching his breath; and then, keeping his head down, his chest pressed hard against the rocks, digging with his toes for purchase in cracks and crevices, his hands grasping at shrubs and ledges, he inched his way up the cliff face. The barrel of his rifle appeared first, then the top of his pith helmet, then his eyes. He leveled the rifle and peered over the embankment's edge, sighting down the barrel. Among the ruin of huts and lean-tos, he picked out the one that had been built first, the one right beside the trail, the one in which Nelson had been left. It was a jumble of sticks and crumbled earth and leaves; nothing resembling Nelson or his remains could be seen among them. But again out of the corner of his eye, he caught a glimpse of a figure or several figures flitting through the shadows of the nearby trees. He pulled himself up over the top of the embankment cautiously, paused a moment on his knees while he swept the ground in front of him with the rifle, then stood upright. The movement scattered a couple of vultures perched in the trees.

"*Hujambo. Yule ni nani? Mimi ni* Bwana Jephson. *Iko wapi* Captain Nelson? *Namtafuta* Captain Nelson. *Unaweza kunisaidia?*"

His words died out in the shrilling of insects. He began advancing slowly toward the wreck of Nelson's shelter, his eyes darting in every direction, jerking his rifle left and right whenever he thought he saw some movement. As he went, here and there he saw the evidence—the usual trash and litter of every abandoned camp—that thirty-three men had actually lived here: splintered boards from a crate, barrel staves, strips of cloth, an empty burlap sack, rotted boots, cartridge casings, blackened fire pits, bean husks, bones. Bones. Another human skeleton. Jephson stopped abruptly, his heart going a mile a minute. It lay by the gray ashes of a cooking fire near where Nelson's hut had stood. Was it Nelson? How could he tell, a skull grinning up at him? But no, it couldn't be Nelson; it was too short; one of the cookboys maybe or a muleteer. But where was Nelson? Where were the rest of them? Where were *their* bones?

Jephson looked up quickly. Oh, yes, there was no question about it. He was being watched from the trees. Again he turned to the river, as if checking on the mule and equipment he had left on the other side. Then, as in a game of hide-and-seek, he turned back suddenly—and saw him.

"Dear Jesus!"

He was a dwarf, a midget, not four feet tall—a pygmy. He was perfectly formed, beautifully muscled, a delightful miniature. His skin was the color of yellowed ivory, his eyes absurdly huge for so small a creature and as lustrous as those of a young gazelle. He wore a breechclout of furry monkey hide and a necklace of monkey teeth. His hair was plaited in a single braid and oiled so it stood up like a horn, and a green parrot feather was stuck through it. His left forearm was covered with a thick padding of bushbuck hide, this apparently as protection against the snap of his bowstring, for he was armed with a cane bow, slung by its rattan string across his chest; and a leather quiver of perhaps fifty arrows, each wrapped in a palm leaf and tipped with stone, was strapped to his back. He stood at the edge of the forest to the north of Nelson's camp and studied Jephson timidly with those huge eyes.

Jephson smiled at him. And then all of a sudden he laughed, laughed out loud. He couldn't help himself. There was something so truly funny about this little man, something so wonderfully ridiculous and precious and magical, something so much out of a fairy tale, that the very sight of him drove the misery from his soul. And his laughter, the harmless gaiety of it, drew another pygmy out of the forest.

This one was wearing a pith helmet.

The effect on Jephson was as if he'd seen a ghost. His laughter choked in his throat. "What's that? What've you got there? Where did you get that?" Anger jumped into him, and he started toward the pygmy quickly.

And they both immediately vanished.

Damn it! What did he do that for? He knew better than that.

He knew how easily the people of the forest spooked. He had to go gently if he ever hoped to catch one. He had to make himself appear harmless, peaceable. He sat down.

And then a most incredible thing occurred. The two pygmies reappeared. But this time, between them, each holding one of his hands, each coming up barely as high as his waist, was a white man.

"Oh, God." Jephson slowly got to his feet. "Oh, dear God."

An old white man, an ancient, a relic, nothing but skin and bones. His clothing, what remained of it, hung in shreds from his emaciated frame; his wispy hair and beard were totally white. Truly a ghost, an apparition. But he was standing on his own. The pygmies, having brought him out of the forest, having brought him to show to Jephson or to show Jephson to him, had released his hands and stepped away. And he stood there on his own.

"Robbie?"

Was he blind? He cocked his head in a peculiar way at the sound of Jephson's voice. Or deaf?

"It's Arthur, Robbie. Arthur Jephson."

"Arthur?"

"I've come back for you, Robbie. I've come back like I said I would."

"Is that really you, Arthur?"

"Yes, Robbie, it's me. Of course it's me."

"By Christ. Oh, by Jesus Christ. It is you. It is, isn't it? It's really you." He took a step toward Jephson, then stopped and turned away abruptly. His eyes had filled with tears. "It's my friend. He's come back for me. I told you he would come back for me. And he has. Do you see?" He was saying this to the pygmies, his voice as shrill as a reed, quavering, cracking, choking with sobs, slightly mad, maybe altogether mad. Whatever the two little fellows made of his words, they surely understood the emotion, the terrible relief, the incredulous joy, the sense of deliverance that had overcome him, and they looked up at him with bright pleased smiles.

"It's a miracle, Robbie. It's a bloody miracle. I never thought—"

"Yes, it is a miracle, Arthur. It is that, by God." He had brought himself under enough control to risk facing Jephson again without shaming himself and turned to him and smiled. Oh, it was a horror, that smile. His teeth were gone and the gums were black. It was a gaping wound of a smile in his shriveled, wrinkled white-bearded face. The poor devil probably had no idea what he looked like. He squared his shoulders and stuck out his hand to Jephson.

"It's a miracle all right. Oh, yes, I can tell you, Arthur, it's a bloody miracle."

Jephson took his hand. He didn't dare actually clasp or shake it. It felt so fragile, a dried leaf that would surely crumble to dust at the merest pressure, so he simply held it and, staring into Nelson's awful aged face, enclosed it with his other hand, feeling his own emotions welling uncontrollably into his throat.

"*Ashante sana, rafiki,*" Nelson said. "Thank you, my friend."

And at that Jephson lost *his* composure, and tears suddenly filled *his* eyes. He pulled Nelson to him and flung his arms around him and pressed his face against his face and, despite the disgusting stink that emanated from Nelson's emaciated body, hugged him and hugged him and began laughing and crying all at once. And this—the sobbing and laughing and hugging and exclaiming—brought more pygmies out of the forest, a whole family of pygmies, a whole little tribe of them, little women as well as men, little girls and boys, tiny little babies, a swarm of them all as beautiful and funny and magical as lucky sprites in a child's enchanted glade, grinning and pointing and hopping around in delight, watching the two tall white men in their desperate loving embrace.

"I knew you'd come back, Arthur. By Christ, I did. I never doubted it for a minute. I want you to know that."

"Of course I've come back. I said I would. And I've brought some stuff. It took us forever to get to Ipoto, Robbie. We'd lost the way and then when we got there— But I managed to get hold of some stuff. Mealies, bananas, a couple of chickens. I've left it on the other side of the river." Jephson released his hold on Nelson's skeletal body and, taking him gently by the shoulders, held him for a moment at arm's length to look him over more carefully. He was a half-starved ruin, a wreck of the man he had been, yes, but the amazing thing was that he was on his feet at all, no longer dying of the arrow poison. "Let me get that stuff over here. These little buggers can give me a hand, can't they? And then you've got to tell me what happened. You've got to tell me everything that happened. I mean, I never thought I'd find you alive."

As it turned out, the pygmies were afraid of Jephson's mule. They had never seen anything like it and wouldn't go near it. When it raised its head and brayed at them unhappily, showing its broken yellow teeth, they scattered like children. So it had to be left on the other side. But they were marvelously adept at getting the provisions and equipment across the river, skipping from rock to rock, carelessly negotiating the worst of the rapids, passing the loads one to another as if making a game of it, having absolutely no need of the fording rope. They brought the stuff to their village a quarter of a mile back in the trees.

No, not a village, a camp. For they were a nomadic people, a people perpetually on the move, roaming aimlessly through the forests in little bands of twenty or thirty, hunting monkeys and other small game with their bows and arrows but living primarily off the honey they bravely poked out of bees' hives high in the trees, building and abandoning their small, primitive huts of sticks and mud from month to month, restlessly going on, going wherever the wind blew them. Nelson had no idea when they had come to the river. Perhaps they had been there all along. Perhaps, watching silently from the trees, they had seen the column arrive, had seen it make its way clumsily across, had seen it leave Nelson and the other sick and wounded behind. But if they had, it wasn't until many days later—how many, Nelson couldn't say—that they made their presence known.

For those many days, Nelson lay on his bed of palm leaves in a nightmare stupor. He understood more or less what had happened, the nature of his predicament. He had overheard, if only as in a dream, the quarrel between Stanley and Jephson before they left him. But in his condition, racked with pain, raging with fever, all his strength gone, he couldn't focus on it, couldn't bring his mind to consider it or shape a plan to deal with it. All he could do, between his bouts of deathly sleep, was listen to the noises outside his shelter—the talk of the men who had been left with him, their moans and groans and arguments, the crackle of their fires, the chopping of wood, the jangle of gear being packed and unpacked, their calling back and forth to each other as they came and went—and try to interpret that, keep track of events by that, forge through that a link to life.

At night, food and water were brought to him. That must have been the first night, because he was given a biscuit and a soupy gruel of mealies from the share of rations Stanley had left with them. A Wanyamwezi boy brought it, one of the tent boys. He came again in daylight but by then—and it probably was only the second day after the column had left—the rations were gone. With no one in authority to control them, the hungry men had eaten everything. The boy brought him only a porridge of forest bean scrapings. He was a good boy, faithful. Or perhaps it wasn't always the same boy. But that much had to be said in all fairness: Nelson wasn't abandoned right away. For many days someone always came into his shelter and awakened him and fed him a share of whatever had been foraged out of the forest that day—bean scrapings, fungus, fruit of the india rubber vine, things he couldn't identify. They gave him water and mopped his brow and then let him sleep again. And in his sleep he went on listening to the noises outside his shelter, hanging onto them as on to life.

A quarrel broke out, a fight of some kind. Suddenly angry shouts. The footfalls of someone running and someone chasing him. Then quiet. And it was night again. And then, all of a sudden Nelson was being shaken roughly awake. The Wanyamwezi boy was shouting at him hysterically. Bula Matari was dead. All the *wasungu* were dead. A terrible catastrophe had befallen the column. Only a few men had escaped. They had returned bringing the news. (Jephson realized that these must have been some of the deserters, telling this tale to justify their desertion.) The boy dropped his head on Nelson's chest, sobbing. *Sisi ni potea*, he cried pitifully. We are lost. Nelson didn't understand. He tried to console the boy. And slept again.

When he awakened, it was bright daylight, but quiet. There were no sounds of the men. Where were they? Nelson tried to push up on an elbow. Then something landed heavily on the roof of the shelter. He looked up. In a moment it lifted off and appeared at the doorway. A vulture. It hopped a few steps into the hut. It folded its huge black wings and, with its bald head sunk into the obscene fleshy folds of its neck, peered at Nelson with one blood-red eye. Nelson screamed at it. It moved a step back and remained there. Another one joined it. And then Nelson realized that there was no living soul outside the shelter, no one to chase the carrion birds away. The men had decamped. Believing Bula Matari to be dead, they had set off to try to find their way home. He had been abandoned, and these vultures had come to watch him die.

"And then these funny little buggers appeared out of nowhere and saved me, Arthur."

They were sitting by a cooking fire in the pygmies' camp, eating the corn porridge and chicken Jephson had prepared from the provisions he had brought. The pygmy men stood around observing everything they did with the greatest interest. The women and children kept a more modest distance but were obviously no less fascinated.

"They did everything for me, Arthur, everything." Nelson spoke in hurried outbursts during pauses between greedily fingering the food into his toothless mouth. "They brought me here.

They gave me a hut of my own. They fed me. They nursed me. They even got that blasted arrowhead out of me. Look." He set his plate aside and unbuttoned his shirt—Jephson had given him one of his and a pair of trousers as well to replace his rags—and he pulled it open to expose his sunken bony chest. The white scar was still there just below the heart, but the hard lump was gone. "He got it out. That one." He indicated the pygmy wearing his sun helmet. "Tommy couldn't get it out, but this little bugger did. I don't know how he did it. It didn't even hurt. He's their witch doctor or chief or something. A cunning little bugger. He poured some concoction into the wound and then I really started getting well. They even gave me one of their women." Nelson looked around, then pointed out a pretty little thing standing by the doorway of one of the huts. "That one," he said, and she looked away shyly, knowing she was being talked about and doubtless what was being said about her. When Nelson turned back, he grinned his horrible grin at Jephson. "I couldn't do anything with her, old boy. Not a thing. But it was nice having her beside me. It was a comfort. The only thing that was awful was the food. Half the time I had no idea what they were feeding me. Half the time I didn't want to know." He picked up his plate. "I can't tell you what this tastes like to me, Arthur. It's . . . I can't tell you."

He resumed shoveling the porridge into his mouth with such avariciousness that Jephson was tempted to tell him to take it easy, that he'd make himself sick eating like that, that in any case they had to be prudent and save enough rations for the trek back to Ipoto. But he didn't have the heart.

After a few minutes Nelson said, "I keep wondering why they did it. Why they went to all the bother. Why they didn't just leave me there and let me die."

It wasn't a question to which he expected an answer. He was already back at the food—the poor devil, his hunger was insatiable—but Jephson looked around at the pygmies and wondered about it too. After a moment he asked, "Do you suppose they'll let you go?"

"What?" Nelson looked up from his plate.

Jephson smiled in order to make light of what he was saying. "I mean, how do we know? Maybe your being white, your white skin . . . well, maybe they think you're some kind of supernatural creature, a god they've saved. I don't know. And they'll want to keep you with them for good luck or something."

Nelson considered this. Perhaps he had thought of it before, perhaps not; but he turned it over in his mind now, could be seen turning it over, heavily, that old man's mouth of his ruminating absently, sucking at his gums for tidbits of food. Then he looked around at the pygmy chief, the one wearing his pith helmet. "*Njoo hapa, rafiki,*" he said and signaled the little fellow to come to his side. And when he did, when he squatted on his haunches next to Nelson, a sweet questioning look in his big eyes, Nelson fingered a piece of chicken from his plate and placed it at the pygmy's lips. A soft gasp of surprise escaped from the others at this, and they pressed closer.

"Open your mouth, *rafiki,*" Nelson said and forced the morsel between the pygmy's lips.

The pygmy let it lay on his tongue, amazed, not daring to bite it or even taste it, staring at Nelson wide-eyed in wonderment, as if he were being asked to participate in some marvelous rite.

"Eat it, my friend, eat it." Nelson pantomimed eating. "It is good, my friend."

The pygmy at last bit down, and pulled a face. Everyone was watching him as if it were a test, as if his bravery were on trial. With his eyes fixed on Nelson trustingly, he bit down again and again and slowly began to chew; and when he swallowed, it was with a terrific gulp of his Adam's apple. And then he broke into a delighted grin.

"You liked that, eh? It was good, wasn't it?"

Nelson picked up another piece and fed it to him and then another. The pygmy ate each of them with an always greater show of gusto, chomping away vigorously, smacking his lips, glancing around at his fellows and grinning at them with a full mouth, with a soaring pride. And they grinned back at him. Everyone grinned back at him—the women and children, Jephson, Nelson. And then all of a sudden Nelson flung an arm around the little fellow's shoulders and hugged him to his chest, and tears of gratitude and happiness and love and a million other emotions filled his eyes.

They started back to Ipoto the next day, and the whole little tribe of pygmies came with them. They got Nelson and the loads across the river with little difficulty, but when it came to packing up the mule, that was left for Jephson to do. Nelson couldn't help. The river crossing, his first real exertion in God only knew how long, had exhausted him; and the pygmies wouldn't go anywhere near the creature. When Jephson set off in the lead with it in tow, they gave it a wide berth, fanning out into the jungle on either side or remaining well to its rear, foraging all sorts of odds and ends as they went along to add to the evening's cooking pot. They were a merry band of lively, playful little folk following their pied piper they seemed to care not where.

Because of Nelson's emaciated condition, their progress was slow, less than half what Jephson had made on his own. Every hour or so the poor scarecrow of a man had to rest; and although Jephson was concerned about getting back to Ipoto before Stanley and the column departed—or at least not too many days after they had departed—he refused to go on ahead and leave Nelson to follow him. Having saved him once, he wasn't about to take the chance of losing him again. And so he would coax him to his feet and have him hang on to the mule's halter so that the animal could help drag him along. Or he would let him fall back to where the pygmies trailed after them so they might lend him a hand, but he never let him out of his sight. When they camped at night, he strung up the tent fly as a shelter for him and made a bed of leaves and ferns in it for him and brought him his rations and sat with him while he ate with that voracious appetite of his. He stayed up with him, often past midnight, listening to him recount again and again the story of his abandonment and his miraculous rescue by the pygmies until he calmed down enough to sleep.

On the morning of the ninth day of the trek the pygmies disappeared. Jephson had slept out in the open that night by the side of their fire, and when he awoke in the misty gray of dawn he realized right away that something was different. He pushed up on his elbows, then threw aside his blankets and jumped to his feet. Nelson was still asleep under the tent fly. The mule was grazing a few feet off in the woods on the other side of the fire. It raised its head to watch as Jephson hurried over to the pile of provisions and equipment. His first thought was that the little buggers had looted the stuff and made off with whatever struck their fancy. It would be a disaster if they had stolen . . . But no, the pile was untouched; everything appeared to be exactly as Jephson had left it when he had unloaded the mule the night before. And on top of it all was Nelson's pith helmet. The little chief had returned it, had placed it carefully on the disorderly stack of gear before leading his people away.

Where had they gone? And why had they gone so suddenly without a word of farewell or forewarning? Had something scared them away? Jephson walked slowly around the campsite peering up and down the trail they had been following and to either side of it, deep into the woods. And then he recognized where they were and understood. The body of the hanged mule boy had scared them away.

He hadn't noticed it in the gathering twilight when they had made camp the previous evening, but they had reached to within a few hundred yards of the village on the knoll where Juma had been executed. No doubt in their ceaseless foraging and gamboling the pygmies had come upon the corpse and taken fright. Jephson fetched his rifle and started up the sloping trail toward the knoll. The body was almost immediately in view; it practically sprang out at him from the clearing, a twisted bundle of decayed flesh and bleached bones. Of course it had frightened the pygmies. It would frighten anyone.

"What's going on, Arthur?"

Jephson looked around.

Nelson was coming up the trail behind him in that old man's shuffle of his, scratching his head, rubbing sleep from his eyes. "What's happened to our little friends? Where have they got to? I don't–" But then he saw the hanged body. He stopped and looked up at it. He looked up at it for a long time. Then he asked, "Who is it?"

"Juma. My mule boy."

"What did he do?"

"Tried to desert. We had a lot of desertions after we left you. But this poor devil was the only one we caught. Mr. Stanley decided to make an example of him."

Nelson nodded slowly, still looking at the corpse. "Yes . . . well, sometimes that sort of thing is necessary."

"No, it wasn't necessary. It wasn't necessary at all. All he accomplished by it was to set the men against him. All of them. Even Uledi."

Nelson looked at Jephson, but he didn't say anything.

"He's a bastard, Robbie, a cold-blooded bastard. He'll do anything, kill anyone in order to get where he's going. That's all that matters to him: to make a success of this expedition."

"No–"

"Don't say no. I know what I'm talking about. Let me tell you something. If it had been up to him, no one would have come back for you, Robbie. Do you know that? For all he cared, you could have waited there by the river forever."

Nelson looked away. "Yes," he said softly. "I sometimes thought that might be the case."

"And I'll tell you something else. He cares as little about me. I'll wager you anything he isn't waiting for me in Ipoto now. He isn't waiting to find out how I've fared, whether I found you or not, whether I got into any trouble, whether I need help. I'll wager you anything, Robbie, that he's just gone on."

And he had.

· TEN ·

IT WAS NINE in the morning of the thirteenth day since he had departed when Jephson led Nelson and the mule back down into the shallow valley of Iopoto and through the cluster of huts and tembes into the settlement's dusty square. There was an air of quietness about the place. The gates of the fort's palisade were closed. Most of the inhabitants were either out working in the fields or off in the forests in roving gangs performing Kilonga-longa's other chores; and unlike the last time Jephson had arrived here, only a few of the Manyema gunmen and a scattering of women, old men, and children were on hand to watch his approach.

The main reason for the quietness was the absence of Stanley and the column. Their camping ground under the palms and mango trees along the riverbank was deserted. The shelters and lean-tos Jephson had seen them build had been pulled down, the ashes of their cooking fires had blown away, and whatever litter they had left behind had been scavenged or cleaned up long before. Studying the remnants, walking slowly among them, kicking here and there at their last traces, Jephson concluded that Stanley and the others had decamped at least a week before. If he and Nelson could now follow their trail at twice their pace, if he and Nelson could make one camp to every two of theirs, it still would take them three weeks, more likely four, to catch them up. *If* they could make one camp to every two of theirs. He looked around at Nelson.

Nelson had slumped down against the bole of a palm tree, his legs splayed out in front of him, his chin on his chest, done in. He looked up when Jephson began unloading the mule but made no movement to help. "Are we staying here for a bit?" he asked hopefully.

"For a bit. Long enough to get some food."

Jephson had no illusions about this. Their share of the provisions that Stanley had acquired from Kilonga-longa, on which he and Nelson had subsisted (supplemented by what the pygmies had foraged for them) for very nearly a fortnight, was pretty much gone, thanks to Nelson's unappeasable appetite. And Jephson knew well enough that there was no sense applying to the Arab for more. They didn't have the barter goods the slaver would demand, they didn't have the guns. All they had was Jephson's Express rifle, and they would need it to defend themselves in the jungle during the three weeks or more of marching that lay ahead of them. No, their only hope was to do what the men of the column had done—try to trade directly with the people of the settlement.

He unpacked the tent fly and spread it on the ground like a market woman setting up in a village bazaar, then began sorting through the loads and baggage for those items he reckoned they could afford to do without. The lantern, for instance, and the tin of paraffin that fueled it. He dusted them off ostentatiously and placed them on the tent canvas, pointedly taking no notice of the women and older men and some of the gunmen who started drifting over to see what he was doing. He got out his "housewife," a pretty teak sewing box that in itself might catch somebody's eye, and neatly set out its contents: bodkins, needles, spools of thread, a pair of scissors. Then there was his dressing case with its variety of bottles and brushes and combs and a handsome ivory-framed mirror. When he turned back to his baggage to hunt up some other potential merchandise—he had in mind a couple of spare shirts, the pair of trousers patched in the seat, a red flannel cholera belt—one of the women squatted down beside the dressing case and picked up the mirror. He smiled at her, she smiled at him and then at her reflection in the glass. Another woman fingered the scissors, then tested it by taking a little snip off the hem of her *kanga*.

Others gathered more closely around. Two of the men—one a skinny old fellow with rheumy eyes, the other a big fiercely tattooed Manyema carrying a monstrous blunderbuss—were attracted to and mystified by the lantern. Jephson went over to them and showed them how it worked. And in this way, his little market slowly got going. As the activity of it increased, as the noise of it rose, more and more people—Jephson noticed some of the men from the column, deserters, but chose to ignore them—a dozen, a score, fifty emerged from their dwellings or left the fields to participate.

They were sharp traders, by Jove, especially the women. Although Jephson, holding up the pair of trousers, extolling their virtues and demanding at the very least a basket of beans for them, artfully concealed the blue and white coverlet patch in the seat, they spotted it quickly enough and offered in turn no more than four ears of corn for them. But there was humor in them as they did it, a good nature, a sporting sense. They obviously expected Jephson to try and cheat them, indeed considered it part of the game and enjoyed the challenge of it and enjoyed even more catching him in it and then besting him at it. The ivory-framed mirror was the great success; it brought four chickens. For the "housewife" and its contents they got enough corn flour to last them a week. And so as the morning wore on, a reasonable amount of provisions began slowly to accumulate.

But then the gates of the fort's palisade were suddenly flung open, and Kilonga-longa appeared.

He was accompanied by his usual retinue, his gaudily accoutered banditry of chiefs and captains, his bodyguard of Manyema gunmen. He himself, as the last time, was unarmed and wore only a simple white djellaba and turban. With his pudgy little hands clasped on his great tub of a stomach, he advanced toward where Jephson was conducting his bazaar with quick, dainty mincing steps. Jephson stood up. The crowd around him immediately melted away.

"Fetch the rifle, Robbie."

Nelson picked up the Express and came over to stand by Jephson's side.

"We don't want any trouble, Robbie. All we want is to get away from here with this stuff. We've paid for it. We've paid damn well for it. So if he tries to take it from us—"

"Yes, all right." Nelson kept hold of the rifle, grasping the barrel just below the front sight, the stock on the ground, leaning on it as if it were a cane; and with what doubtless was an unconscious but nevertheless openly nervous grimace on his withered old face, he watched the fat little Arab come over.

"*Hujambo,* Abed bin Salim," Jephson said. "*Salaam aleikum.*"

The Arab replied with an almost imperceptible bob of his head and a careless automatic performance of the ritual gesture of greeting—touching heart, lips, forehead—then fixed his tiny pig eyes on Jephson with a baleful inquisitive stare. Evidently he remembered having seen him before. After a moment he turned to one of his captains and said something to him in a whispered aside, and the man, a half-caste, stepped forward.

"My master would know why you are here, *wasungu.* Are you not of Bula Matari's caravan? Yet Bula Matari is gone. He is gone already many days. My master would know why you have not gone with him."

The man spoke in Swahili and very quickly and in that singsong version of half-castes which was unfamiliar to Jephson's ear. So he needed a moment to grasp the gist of it and then compose a reply to it. But he didn't get that moment. Nelson replied for him.

"He did not go with Bula Matari, effendi, in order to rescue me."

Kilonga-longa turned to Nelson rather abruptly, as if suddenly seeing him for the first time, as if acknowledging the presence of such a decrepit scarecrow of a man was distasteful to him.

"Robert Harry Nelson, captain of cavalry, Methuen's Horse, Her Majesty' officer, bearer of the Victoria Cross." Nelson straightened himself up with some effort, lifted the rifle's stock from the ground just enough, and brought himself correctly to attention. "I was wounded by a poisoned arrow in an engagement with hostile natives on the River Aruwimi, effendi, and when near to death and no longer able to continue, when I had become nothing but a burden on Bula Matari's caravan and an impediment to its progress, I was left behind. But not to die, effendi. No, not to die, thanks to this noble officer who you see before you, this faithful friend, this truly courageous young gentleman. He separated himself from the comforts and security of Bula Matari's caravan and returned for me. He returned alone and at great risk to himself and, as you see, effendi, brought me to safety."

The Arab looked back at Jephson. It was impossible to tell what he thought of Nelson's rather flowery speech, whether it had impressed him in the slightest. His hands remained clasped on his stomach, his expression was blank.

"And now we go on, effendi, to rejoin Bula Matari and resume our duties with his caravan," Nelson continued. "We have rested ourselves for a bit in your settlement. We have traded for a bit with your people. And now, with your leave, we go on."

Nelson was prepared to say a good deal more, indeed was in the act of saying it in as showy a Swahili as he could manage, but Kilonga-longa wasn't paying attention. Again he whispered something to the half-caste, then suddenly turned on his heels and headed back to the fort. His retinue followed him. The whole thing hadn't lasted ten minutes.

"Jesus. What the hell was that all about?"

"I don't know, but I'll tell you something, Arthur. I think the smartest thing we can do now is just get the hell out of here. Let's not press our luck. I don't like the feel of this place."

"Right." Jephson glanced around. The people he had been trading with had cleared off. He could see a few of them peering at him from around the corner of their huts and tembes, but they obviously had no intention of coming back. The little bazaar was finished. They had gotten all they would get. "Right," he said again and starting packing up the provisions.

But they weren't halfway done when a delegation again appeared from the fort.

"Oh, Jesus, now what?"

Kilonga-longa wasn't with this group. The half-caste led it, followed by a dozen or so of the Manyema gunmen and a few slaves. They approached very quickly, evidently eager to catch the white men before they departed, perhaps anxious to prevent their departure. Jephson and Nelson hurried on with their work, slinging baskets on the mule's back, stuffing Jephson's rucksack, pretending they hadn't noticed.

"*Wasungu! Ngoja.*" The half-caste started running. "*Ngoja kidoga, wasungu.*"

Jephson and Nelson turned around.

A slave boy was following directly behind the half-caste, also at a trot, leading a goat.

"*Mbuzi,*" the half-caste called and took the goat's lead rope from the slave. "This is for you, *wasungu.* It is from my master." He stopped running and dragged the goat in front of Jephson. "It is a gift from my master, in admiration of your bravery and of your fidelity to your friend." He handed the rope to the startled Jephson.

The goat came forward and started nibbling at the toe of Jephson's boot. The gates of the fort's palisade were still open, and through them Jephson could see Kilonga-longa standing on the fort's front veranda. He raised a hand to him in a kind of salute. The Arab made no response.

"Tell your master that I thank him."

"I will tell him."

"Tell him that I thank him from the bottom of my heart. This gift is badly needed."

"Yes, I will tell him."

"Tell him—"

"Yes, yes. I will tell him. I will tell him all of it. But go now, *wasungu*. Go while you may. Go in peace."

Three weeks, four, maybe five. They never knew. They never would know, two white men swallowed up in the incalculable immensity of that forest, two lone travelers drowned forty fathoms deep in that ocean of monstrous vegetation, two mere specks of humanity crawling like insects among the titanic pillars of those colossal trees, following the twisting track left by Stanley and the column, seeking out in the perpetual twilight the blazes cut by Uledi and the pioneers, passing through the wreckage made of the villages by Kilonga-longa's slaving gangs, climbing higher, always higher into the rocky jungled foothills of that forever promised, forever distant upland, the days merging one into another unremarked, undistinguished, unnumbered.

Their provisions ran out. They ran out far more quickly than they should have, far more quickly than Jephson had reckoned, within a fortnight, probably less. It was Nelson's fault. Jephson had tried to keep them to sensible rations, had tried to save the goat, hoard the fowls, eke out the corn flour and beans and onions with foraged fruit and mushrooms and winged ants, that sort of thing, but it hadn't been possible with Nelson. That hunger of his, the terrible craving in him, was unappeasable, insatiable. He was ashamed of it himself and apologetic, knowing what it cost them, but he couldn't help himself. Whatever he ate—and the way he ate it, his desperate greed overcoming his own embarrassment about it, was awful to see—no matter how much he ate, it was never enough. He wanted more, had to have more, jollied Jephson for more, tried to make a joke of it, begged for it; and when he couldn't have it, whenever Jephson got tough with him, he turned irritable, quarrelsome, petulant, morose.

Of course he needed the food, Jephson understood that, needed it more than Jephson himself did and needed more of it, to fatten up his poor decimated frame, to rebuild his strength, to recover from his wound, to keep up with the hard-driving pace Jephson tried to maintain. But as the days went by, as they struggled deeper into the unknown gloom and their bickerings over food took on an edge and grew always slightly less friendly, always slightly more tense and urgent, Jephson saw that it was something more than this. Nelson's long siege of illness, the shock he had suffered at his abandonment, and his nightmare of dying alone in the wilderness had done him as much injury in the mind as in the body. The poor devil, Jephson realized, had become in fact and in spirit the testy, querulous, self-absorbed old man that he so horribly appeared to be in the flesh.

He was full of an old man's petty complaints and aches and pains and excuses and tricks, lagging always farther behind, constantly pleading to rest, and often, with an old man's cunning, dropping out of sight to stop and sit down on his own. So ten times a day, a hundred times a day, Jephson was obliged to wait for him or go back for him and coax him to his feet and force him to go on at least for another mile, a half-mile, frequently by threatening to go off and leave him if he didn't and, indeed, frequently by actually going off and leaving him—a demeaning little game—only of course to return and, fuming, start the whole damn business of coaxing and cajoling and threatening him all over again. Jesus, what a trial he became, this once so plain and gallant soldier, what an onerous burden, what a cruel test on Jephson's patience and understanding and friendship, what a source of mounting anxiety over the prospect of never catching up to Stanley. After all, his own life was at stake here too. And then there was that ongoing trouble with him over the mule.

Nelson wanted to butcher it for the meat. Jephson wouldn't hear of it, couldn't believe that Nelson was daft enough to suggest it. True, by the time Nelson got around to this, the goat and chickens were gone and they were down to one stalk of bananas and their last few ears of Indian corn. But the mule was carrying the bulk of their gear—the box of cartridges, the cooking pot, the rope and tools, the tent fly, trading cloth. How in God's name did Nelson imagine they could get along without them? They couldn't carry the stuff themselves. As it was, Jephson was loaded down under the rucksack, jam-packed with clothes and medicines and blankets. No, it was utterly out of the question, a lunatic idea. Once they ran out of that last bit of maize and banana, they'd just have to forage harder.

Jephson did all the foraging, as he did all the work. Sometimes Nelson followed him, halfheartedly plucking at berries or scraping fungus from the bark of a tree, sniffing at it, and then eating it on the spot. But more usually, sheepishly pleading illness or exhaustion, he remained in their camp and waited for whatever Jephson brought him. And whatever it was, no matter how Jephson fixed it up—he had learned from the pygmies to make a stew of mushrooms and wood beans that actually had a meaty flavor—Nelson complained about it. He ate it all right, he gobbled it right down but complained about it. It wasn't enough, it tasted awful, there was no nourishment in it. Then he would start up again about the mule, going over to the scrawny beast, stroking its withers. Jephson took to watching him. One day, he thought, if he didn't keep a sharp lookout, Nelson was going to have the mule after all.

And after all these weeks, the rain started again to add to their miseries. It came like clockwork each evening at dusk. Throughout the day, as they clambered over the granite outcroppings of the endless hills and through the ravaged clearings of the destroyed villages and down into the vegetation-choked gulleys of the water courses and green-scummed sinks and then up again, the jungle heat thickened. Glistening streamers of mist lowered through the tangle of branches and leaves and vines, and thunder rumbled and lightning flashed; and invariably, before Jephson had a chance to pitch the tent fly, the storm would break with malignant fury and they'd be soaked to the skin, and then soaked again during the night when the screaming wind and pelting downpour tore the tent fly away. Jephson's fever returned with a vengeance; he shivered and ached with the ague; his patience frayed and his temper snapped.

"I'm warning you, Robbie. Don't lay a hand on that animal."

This was one morning after a particularly severe and prolonged rain. Neither of them had slept much that night, and what little sleep they had had been under sopping blankets and with the tent canvas fallen on their faces. Jephson had awakened suddenly, startled from his sleep by a foreboding or perhaps something in his dream, and found Nelson already up, standing by the mule.

"Just stay away from him, do you hear? Just leave him be."

Nelson turned around slowly. Jephson couldn't say there was anything about him to have aroused suspicion. He didn't have the axe or *panga* in hand, nothing like that. He was simply standing by the beast in his wet clothes, a small wan smile on his shriveled old face.

The campsite was a mess, a mudhole running with rivulets and curtained around by a chill gray cloud of fog. It was located at the base of a fairly steep hill, perhaps three or four hundred feet high, the top shrouded in the cloud, a damn-fool place to have camped what with rainwater rushing down upon it in veritable cascades from the hill. But Nelson hadn't been able to make it up the hill the night before.

"I told you to leave that animal alone, Robbie."

Nelson had draped an arm over the mule's shoulders. He took it away quickly. "For God's sake, Arthur, what do you keep shouting at me for? There's no need to shout at me. I haven't done anything."

"Yes, well, just stay away from the mule. Just stay away from him." Jephson picked up the tent fly, shook the puddles from it, and folded it up. Then he started wringing out the sodden blankets. "Why don't you see if you can find some firewood so we can dry out this stuff."

"Firewood? You must be joking. Where am I going to find firewood in this swamp?"

"Have a look around, why don't you? Have a look around. Or I'll have a look around and you pack up the gear. Would that suit you better? Would you prefer that? Yes, I bet you would. Get me out of the way for a bit. Right? Give you a chance to cut down the mule. That's it, isn't it? Have me out hunting for firewood while you butcher the poor bloody animal. That's what you have in mind, isn't it? That's what you're thinking, isn't it? Answer me, goddamnit–."

He cut himself off. He heard his own voice, a shrill unnatural sound even to his own ears, a raving like a madman's. His cheeks were on fire, he was burning up. Every bone in his body ached, and his head behind his eyes pounded with fever. He flung down the blanket and turned away. What difference did it make anyway? What the hell did any of it matter? Nelson was right. There probably wasn't a stick of dry wood anywhere within fifty miles of them. And he probably was right about the mule too. What was the sense in saving it? What was the point in having it lug all this bloody gear? They weren't getting anywhere anyway. They might just as well kill it and eat it as starve. He sat down, sat down right there in the mud, and dropped his head on his arms, his arms on his drawn-up knees.

And heard voices.

He looked up. It wasn't Nelson. Nelson wasn't saying anything, just staring at him dumbly. Besides, the voices he heard were coming from above, in the clouds. Oh, dear God, was he really going crazy? He looked up into the cloud of fog. And then he realized what it was, scrambled to his feet, grabbed for his rifle.

"Savages, Robbie."

Nelson spun around and looked up. There at the top of the hill, three or four hundred feet above them, peering down through the swirls of ghostly mist were a dozen short, stocky, extremely black men armed with spears and shields, their arms and legs adorned with glistening polished bracelets of ironwork.

"Don't shoot. For God's sake, Arthur, don't shoot."

"I'm not going to shoot. I'm not crazy."

"They've got the drop on us. You'd never pick off more than two or three before their bloody goddamn spears skewered us."

"I can see that."

"We've got to try to palaver with them."

But before either of them had a chance to say a word, the tribesmen slipped back again into the curtain of fog. Jephson, however, could still hear their voices; they hadn't gone far. Assuming that they could see him as little as he could see them, Jephson used the moment to seek cover and dodged behind a tree. Nelson followed him.

"Who are they?"

"How the hell should I know? Savages of the forest."

"But we haven't run into any before now. The slavers had them pretty well cleared out."

"Well, maybe we've gotten beyond their raiding circle."

"Hey, maybe we have. Maybe we have at last."

They both looked up again, peering around the tree trunk. A few of the tribesmen had re-emerged from the mist. And they had someone new with them. A taller, slimmer man in white pantaloons, carrying a rifle. An Arab? A Manyema? If so, that destroyed their momentary hope that they might have at last got to the other side of Kilonga-longa's raiding circle and so had a chance of coming across unravaged villages where they could trade for food. On the other hand, if it was an Arab or Manyema, it was unlikely the savages would attack a couple of white men. Jephson wished he had his binoculars so he could get a better look at the fellow. But he didn't; they were over there somewhere in the jumble of their rain-soaked gear. Well, no point hiding behind the tree forever. He'd just have to risk it. He stepped out into the clear.

"Sah?"

"What? What was that?"

"Is that you, sah?"

"Sudi? My God, Robbie, it's Sudi."

They had caught up with the column. It was camped in a huge village, a village of long wooden-plank buildings with gabled roofs set in orderly fashion on either side of a gridwork of streets, a village surrounded by fields of maize and sugarcane, gardens of tomatoes and tobacco, yams and beans, groves of melons and bananas, a village in which the men of the column (God only knew how long they had been there) had grown fat and glossy and strong again feeding on puddings of plantains and goat's milk, kid soup, roast chicken, sweet manioc, and banana fritters, a village of friendly tribesmen who shouted out in greeting as the two new white men entered—*Borrdu, borrdu, brenda, brenda*—adding their voices to the cries of amazement and excitement of the Wanyamwezis and Sudanese at seeing Jephson and Nelson again.

But there was more to it than this. Oh God, yes, much more. Jephson saw that at a glance. For beyond this village's fields, there to the east, the trees thinned out and gave way to a spectacular view: hundreds of square miles of grassland, leagues upon leagues of pastureland stretching away under an open sky to a massive range of mountains at the base of which Lake Albert lay.

It was December 7, 1887. After 162 days, after more than 620 miles, after 189 men had died, been lost, or deserted, they had come through the forest at last.

PART FOUR
Emin Pasha

· ONE ·

HE WAS a small, wiry man, narrow through the shoulders, long in the waist, with a rather solemn face framed by a full black beard and bisected by a sharp spear of a nose, at the end of which bottle-thick wire-rimmed spectacles perched. The much magnified eyes behind them were dark, watery, and sad. He was wearing a European-cut suit of spotless white cotton drill, a high stiff collar of celluloid, a floppy black bow tie, and a tasseled maroon fez. He stood, one hand behind his back, the other resting on the brass knob of a walking stick, at the end of the steamer jetty that jutted out into the Nile from the station's eucalyptus-lined riverfront, watching as the *Lady Dorothy* approached.

Jephson, in the boat's prow, still a good hundred feet off, drifting downriver with the current from the south, stared at him in undisguised amazement. It was late in the afternoon; and the great orange ball of the sun, setting behind the low scrub-covered hill that overlooked the river's left bank and on top of which the station's fort was situated, shone practically straight into his eyes, so that the man was difficult to make out, a puzzling, oddly unimposing silhouette. Next to him at the end of the jetty, towering over him, was a big burly Nubian or Egyptian with an elaborately waxed mustache, dressed in the white riding breeches and red tunic of an Egyptian Army officer, a saber slung from a sash around his thick midriff. Behind them, in the shade of the riverfront's eucalyptus trees, a troop of Egyptian and Sudanese soldiers were paraded, smartly got up in khaki tunics, baggy Turkish-style trousers, and green tarbooshes, shouldering Remington rifles and flanked by a brass band and a color guard. And behind *them*, jamming the crooked streets and dusty squares and flyblown bazaars of the station itself, were crowds of milling disorderly humanity—soldiers, merchants, market women, mule skinners, camel drivers, fishermen, carpenters, blacksmiths, sutlers, harem girls, slaves, children, with scores of scrawny yellow pie dogs yapping hysterically between their feet.

Jephson took all this in, then returned his gaze to the small bearded man at the end of the jetty. Except that it would have been patently rude, he would have used his binoculars to get a better look at him, so sharp was his curiosity, so acute his surprise. What a peculiar-looking little fellow. Surely not a Turk—a Jew perhaps or a Viennese—a physician, a librarian, a university professor, a clerk out for a Sunday stroll—surely he was not the beleaguered provincial governor whom they had been sent to rescue from the dervish hordes, surely not the vaunted general who had done what even Chinese Gordon had been unable to do: stem the advance of that murderous infidel tide.

Jephson glanced back to the stern of the steel boat. "What do you think, Sudi?"

"It is Wadelai, sah."

"Yes, it is Wadelai. But is that Emin Pasha?"

Jephson and Sudi, with a crew of ten oarsmen and an escort of five askaris, had been under way in the *Lady Dorothy* for five days by then, coasting northward along the western shore of Lake Albert from the point where the advance column had first struck it near its southernmost end, coasting northward for very nearly a hundred miles on into its outlet, the Albert Nile, and then some thirty-five miles farther north down the river from there. Stanley had sent them ahead to see what they could discover about the situation in Equatoria, whether Emin and his forts and stations along the Nile were still holding out or whether they had fallen at last to the dervishes, while he led what remained of the advance column overland along the lakeshore.

The trek to the lakeshore from the end of the forest had, certainly in comparison to what they had endured in the forest, been easy. For not only had the nature of the terrain radically changed once they were out of the forest, but the men of the column had been well rested by the time they had set off for the lake across those hundred or so miles of bright open highland savanna that intervened between it and the forest, well rested and well fed and in much revived spirits, having spent a full week in the village where Jephson and Nelson had caught up to them and then another week after that to give Jephson and Nelson a chance to recuperate and recover their strength as well.

That had been a marvelously indolent time, those two weeks,

a time of luxurious idleness of a sort they hadn't experienced since their arrival at the Congo's mouth nine months before. The village, called Ibwiri, lay outside of Kilonga-longa's raiding circle, and as such, it was unmolested and intact, a rich and flourishing place. Its inhabitants, called the Baburu, had proved friendly and generous hosts, providing food in abundance and clearing out their long, low gabled wooden dwellings and turning them over for the column's use. Indeed, all that the Wanyamwezis and Sudanese had to do during those two weeks was eat and sleep, and, by God, they had done both with a vengeance.

It was perfectly wonderful to see how quickly they had grown fat and sleek again under these conditions, how quickly their eyes had recovered their luster, their skins their glossy sheen, their muscles their sinewy tone, how quickly their wounds had healed and their fevers had abated and their quarrels were patched up and how quickly too the bad times had faded from their memory and the comrades they had lost along the way were forgotten. The jungle was behind them; open country lay ahead, and they were alive—that was the thing. Laughter was heard again; there was loud chatter and rude jokes; and around the cook fires at night tales were told and songs sung about the dangers they had faced and the adventures they had survived and the history they had made by being the first to have ever traversed the fearsome Ituri.

Jephson, however, kept himself apart from all this. When he first came into the village, the men had rushed around him crying out in delighted disbelief, as if he had reappeared from the dead. Parke in the forefront of the crush clutched at his sleeve, wanting to shake his hand or throw an arm around his shoulder and thump him on the back, but he shook him off, shook them all off with ill-concealed annoyance. He saw Stanley emerge from one of the huts, drawn out by the jubilant row his arrival had caused, and start toward him smiling. But Jephson ignored him as well and kept on going through the village, through the outlying fields and gardens, kept on going to that place where the last trees stood, where the forest ended, where the open country began.

It was glorious. Hundreds of square miles of grassland stretched away as far as the eye could see in wave upon wave of gently undulating hills and rolling pastures, wafted by fresh breezes, watered by countless streams, studded with pretty little woods and flowering thickets of acacia thorn and mimosa, blue gum and baobob, a great highland plain, three, four, five thousand feet above the elevation of the sea. Stepping out into it, drawing a deep breath of what, after the suffocating humidity of the jungle, tasted like the sweetest drink, was like stepping out of a dank, dark dungeon into the bright new light of freedom. Oh, yes, it was glorious, a destination so long sought, a goal so long dreamed of and yet . . . There was little joy in it for him. His heart did not soar. What he felt was only a dull anger, a bitter resentment. He turned back to the forest.

Stanley had followed him, was watching him from a tentative, respectful distance.

Nelson by now had also scrambled up the hill into the village from their previous night's camp and been surrounded by the shouting, cheering men. Parke hugged him like his best friend, pumping his hand like a long lost brother, chattering away at him like a demented magpie, unbuttoning his shirt to examine his miraculously healed wound. Even the dour Hoffman had lumbered over on his crutches to have a look at him and make sure this aged wreck of a man really wasn't a ghost. A merry scene of happy reunion. Who would have thought that all of them, every last one of them, had been perfectly willing to leave him behind to die, had been perfectly willing to let Jephson go back for him and die too.

"Have something to eat, lad."

Jephson looked at Stanley.

"You must be hungry."

Jephson nodded absently and looked away again. Nelson, that forever insatiably famished devil, was pushing his way through the crowd toward one of the cooking fires, drawn to it by the savory odor of something steaming that Uledi was ladling into a bowl from the cooking pot.

"There's plenty of everything, lad. Meat, fruit, milk, maize. More than you could ever hope to eat."

Jephson nodded again and went on watching as Nelson took the bowl from Uledi and hunkered down over it by the fire and, between voracious mouthfuls, regaled Parke and Hoffman and the rest of the noisy mob with what doubtless was the story of his miraculous rescue by the pygmies. Oh, what great friends they all were now, what splendid concern they showed for him now.

"Arthur."

Again Jephson turned to Stanley.

"There's something I'd like to say to you."

"Sir?"

Stanley advanced a few steps closer. "What you did, you

know—going back for Captain Nelson—well, what I'd like to say is . . . it was a noble thing."

"Thank you."

"I don't mean it as kudos. Kudos don't matter. Not from me anyway. Least of all from me, I realize that. But not from anyone else either." Stanley came closer and hesitatingly put a hand on Jephson's shoulder. "What matters, the only thing that really matters, is that you did it, that you alone of all of us had the character and courage to do it and that you know you did, and will know it and will remember it for the rest of your life."

"Yes," Jephson replied. "Yes, I suppose I will. For whatever that's worth." And shrugging Stanley's hand from his shoulder, he went over to the cooking fire with the others.

There were 132 of them—ninety-two Wanyamwezis, thirty-five Sudanese, and the five Europeans (during the two weeks in Ibwiri, a few who had been thought lost or dead, like Jephson and Nelson, and a few who had deserted to the slavers and had had second thoughts about it, straggled in), plus four surviving mules—and by the time they broke camp and set off on the last leg of the journey to the lake they were restless and eager to go, taking up their loads without complaint, mustering into companies with good-humored bantering, raising their voices lustily in the spirited chant of the safari, and stepping out into the fresh open country at a brisk and lively pace.

This was the country of the Watusi, a very different people from the Bantu Negroes of the Congo forest, a Nilotic people, kin of the Galla of the northeastern lake kingdoms, descendants of the ancient Abyssinians, cousins to the Zulu, an extremely tall people—some stood over seven feet tall—willowy and long-muscled with café-au-lait satin-smooth complexions and, most strikingly, exceedingly fine features: sharp aquiline noses, shapely thin mouths, slender necks, small heads, and the proud carriage of hunters and warriors and herders of cattle. They wore knee-length tunics of beautifully tanned hides, carried spears and long bows and oval-shaped shields centered with spikes like the shields of the ancient Greeks. They adorned themselves with bracelets of ivory, necklaces of lion's teeth, and headdresses of ostrich feathers and the plumage of the eagle and the quail. Unlike the tribes of the forest, perhaps because they lived in a bright and spacious land with grand and distant vistas, not forever hemmed in by masses of suffocating vegetation and moving about in perpetual semidarkness, they showed no fear of the column or any hostility toward it. Quite to the contrary, in their haughty self-confidence they viewed it with bemused curiosity and followed along beside it and welcomed it to their villages and traded with it and provided guides and porters for it and impis of warriors to guard it on its way.

And so the going was easy and the rate of travel swift, often more than twenty miles a day through what surely was one of the most spectacularly beautiful wildernesses in the world. It was a young man's dream when he dreamed of safari, those bright hot days on the high savanna under the infinite blue of the African sky, those numberless herds of water buffalo and eland, springbok and kudu, hartebeeste and zebra, elephant and giraffe, and ostriches running away with dainty ladylike gaits, the magnificently feathered Watusi warriors loping through the tall yellow grass beside them, the villages of tall conical huts and broom-swept streets and herds of lyre-horned cattle and plantations of millet and dhura and maize, the drumming and dancing that greeted them wherever they arrived, and when the sun set in a dazzling blaze of glory, the fresh winds of night and the billions of stars and the smell of wood smoke and the roars of lions in the grass.

And then one day, when it seemed least to matter, when they could just as well have gone on this way forever, they reached the lake. It was ten in the morning on December 19.

There was a moment of confusion. At first no one was quite sure what he was looking at. The plain before them stretched away for a half-mile or so—dotted with mimosa bushes and wind-stunted acacia thorn, a fast little brook rushing down through a shallow ravine to their left, a herd of grazing wildebeeste raising their bearded faces to watch them from a knoll on the right—and then quite literally vanished into thin air. Far off in the distance they could see the pale blue outline of a great range of mountains rearing up into the sky. But between those mountains and the plain there seemed to be nothing but sky.

It was Uledi who was the first to realize what this was. "Nyanza," he said softly. "Nyanza, Bula Matari. Albert Nyanza. *Kule. Iko karibu.*" And then all of a sudden he shouted it, triumphantly, and began to run. "Nyanza, *warafiki.* Nyanza."

And the entire column ran after him.

The grassland ended with startling abruptness, and they found themselves standing on the edge of a fantastic precipice, a sheer dizzying drop of more than 2,500 feet. And there below, shining like a plate of silver in the morning sun, nearly one hundred miles long and twenty-five miles wide, lay one of the great inland seas of Central Africa, source of the Albert Nile. They stared down at it in an awed thrilled silence. Its western shore directly beneath them—from the foot of the fabulous escarpment of massive black boulders on which they stood to the water's edge where surf broke with glittering spray like an ocean upon its beach—was nine miles wide, seeming from this great elevation like a vast park of brilliant green grass, running with myriad marshy creeks, fretted by muddy inlets and bays, dotted with clumps of tamarind trees and tiny fishing villages, alive with millions of birds of every conceivable species, abounding in game. Where this parkland rounded to the south (they had come to the lake about five miles from its southern end), it climbed up into the first of the forested foothills of the Ruwenzoris, that legendary massif of Central Africa, the "Mountains of the Moon." Directly across, the eastern lakeshore was bounded by the cliffs of the tableland of Unyoro, cliffs higher than the one on which the caravan stood and every bit as precipitous but plunging straight down into the waters of the lake without an intervening bank, its face streaked by waterfalls and cascades. And to the north there was nothing at all except this great sheet of silver water stretching away to Equatoria and Wadelai and Emin Pasha.

"You have brought us to the Nyanza, Bula Matari," Uledi said, turning away from the lake. "You have brought us to the Nyanza as you promised you would."

Stanley nodded.

"*Warafiki!* Do you see? Bula Matari has brought us to the Nyanza. He has brought us here as he promised he would. Many times we did not believe him. Many times in the hell of the forest we did not think he would. Many times when we were sick and starving we did not think he could. Many times, oh how many times, we lost faith in him. But you see, *warafiki*, you see. We have reached Albert Nyanza. Bula Matari has brought us here as he told us in Unguja that he would. Cheer for Bula Matari, *warafiki*. Cheer for our great chief."

"No, Uledi."

But the Wanyamwezis and Sudanese burst out into a wild and jubilant chorus of howls and shouts.

"No, my friends," Stanley called out to them, raising his hand. "No, no. Save your cheers. This is not yet the time for them. The time for them will be later. When we have reached the Pasha and rescued him from the dervishes. Pray now only that we will not be too late. For we still have far to go, and the dervishes know we are coming and will surely seek to capture him before we arrive."

But his words had no effect. Indeed, they hardly could be heard. For the men—whatever their reasons, for all their mixed reasons, to honor Stanley, to celebrate their own survival, to express their relief, just to hear the noise—went on cheering and screaming and whistling at the top of their lungs. Stanley watched them for a few moments, then let them be and turned to Jephson.

"Arthur."

"Sir?"

"I'm going to send you ahead in the steel boat."

But Jephson didn't listen to him either. For when Stanley had turned to him, he saw, with rather a shock, that there were tears glistening in the grizzled old explorer's eyes.

· TWO ·

"YES, I AM Dr. Emin." The impeccably neat little man with the black beard and wire-rimmed spectacles probably was in his early fifties but nonetheless appeared wonderfully spry and fit. He reached into the *Lady Dorothy* to help Jephson out. "And what is your name, my boy?"

"Arthur Mounteney Jephson, sir." Jephson hopped up on the jetty and saluted as the Wanyamwezis shipped oars and Sudi made the boat's painter fast to a piling. "It is my great privilege to inform you—"

"Yes, yes, I know. You come from Mr. Stanley. You are attached to the expedition he is leading to our relief. Yes, yes, we have heard for some time now that you were coming. And we are extremely pleased to be able to greet you at last." The little man took both of Jephson's hands in his own. "Extremely pleased, my boy. Oh, yes, extremely so. You bring us life."

He spoke softly, sweetly with a vibrant, altogether heartfelt sincerity but in a curiously precise English that had the unmistakable overtones of a German accent (yet another discordant note, yet another feature jarringly at odds with what Jephson had expected) and went on holding Jephson's hands in a warm fatherly way while the boatmen and askaris scrambled up on the dock. They too seemed thoroughly taken aback by the incongruity of this small professorial-looking man being the vaunted Pasha of Equatoria.

"Allow me to present Shukri Aga, commandant of the garrison here at Wadelai." Emin turned to the burly mustachioed fellow in the Egyptian Army officer's uniform who had been waiting on the jetty with him. "Vakeel, Mr. Arthur Jephson, emissary from Bula Matari."

The fellow, a Nubian by the look of his ocherous, rotund,

rather operatically villainous countenance, clicked his heels together smartly and sketched a bow. "Effendi."

"Vakeel."

"I place my neck beneath your feet, effendi. Your every wish is my command."

"Thank you. And may I . . . Dr. Emin, this is Sudi, headman of my company and coxswain of our boat. Sudi, His Excellency, the Governor of Equatoria."

"Pasha."

Emin, in what apparently was a characteristic gesture grasped both of Sudi's hands with much the same artless friendliness that he had displayed with Jephson, evidently making no distinction between their race or rank. "*Nimefurahi kuonana nawe.*" His Swahili was as fluent if as guttural as his English. "You have traveled far and suffered much in order to come to my assistance. This I know and for this I thank you from the bottom of my heart. I thank you all." Still holding Sudi's hands, he addressed the boatmen and askaris. "I thank you all for your courage and devotion and for the terrible sacrifices you have made on my behalf and on behalf of my people. We have awaited your coming with great hope and welcome you with much joy. *Ahsanteni sana, warafiki.* Come and rest yourselves among us as our honored guests."

He released Sudi's hands and slipped an arm through Jephson's and, in this quite charming Continental fashion, escorted him down the jetty toward the station's riverfront promenade. Shukri Aga preceded them; Sudi and the others, carrying the oars and weapons and baggage from the boat, followed in a kind of respectful bewilderment.

"Tell me, my boy, where is Mr. Stanley now?"

"I'm not entirely certain, sir. I left him at a fishing village just where we first reached Lake Albert. Perhaps you know the place, about five miles from the lake's southern end on the western shore. His plan was to set off overland with the advance column the next day or the day after that at the latest. That was five days ago. I should think he could be nearly halfway here by now."

"Ah, yes. Well, we shall save him the walk. We shall go and fetch him in the steamer."

"The steamer, sir?"

"Oh, yes, I have a steamer. Didn't you know? The *Khedive.* An old tub but still quite serviceable. Sir Samuel Baker brought her up the Nile in a dozen pieces back in 1870 when he was Pasha here; and she's been plying the river between the head of the rapids at Duffile and the Nyanza ever since. She's been extremely valuable to us in these trying times, as you might well imagine. We couldn't possibly have managed without her. She's downriver at Duffile with Captain Casati at the moment, but I expect her back in a day or two. And then we shall go and fetch Mr. Stanley. He has walked far enough."

They had arrived at the head of the jetty, where the troop of Equatorial Regulars were paraded. Shukri Aga, a few steps in advance, barked a command in Arabic and the soldiers snapped their Remingtons from their shoulders and fired a salute. And immediately, while the rifle shots still resounded off the scrub-covered range of hills on the other side of the Nile and the wisps of blue gunsmoke dispersed in the pastel pink light of the sunset, the brass band on the quay struck up "God Save the Queen."

It caught Jephson entirely unaware. He hadn't expected it. He couldn't have said what he had expected, the Khedivial hymn perhaps or some Turkish marching song, in any case not this, not the homey, sentimental, but always comforting and loved strains of the British anthem. The effect on him was uncanny, out of all proportion. As soon as he realized what the blaring brass was playing, he involuntarily shivered and broke out in gooseflesh. He snapped to attention. Jesus, to hear this familiar music, this amiably solemn tune of London parades and school holidays, here on the other side of the world, a million miles from home . . . It was played badly. The tempo was all wrong, slowed down to a dirge, but it didn't matter. The music and all the fond memories it called forth spoke to him with a thrilling potency; and what it said, what it made him realize, was what somehow he hadn't fully realized until the moment he heard it: that they had succeeded. Yes, by God, they had succeeded. They had won through. After all these months and miles and miseries, they had reached Emin Pasha. And they had reached him in time. Here he stood, this peculiar, bespectacled little man with fez and walking stick, alive and well and to all appearances in no imminent danger of being swept away by the dervish hordes. And the anthem played, as if in celebration of the monumental deed.

"My people."

The crowds jamming the streets and alleyways and bazaars of the river station surged forward to hear the words of their mudir, to see more clearly the newly arrived white man with him.

"My people, our prayers have been answered. Our cry for

help has been heard. The message we sent to the outside world of our plight has been received and heeded. For so long we have been tantalized by rumors of a great expedition coming to our relief. My people, these were no rumors. At this very moment, as I speak to you, a caravan is making its way along the Nyanza shore toward us under the leadership of Henry Morton Stanley. Henry Morton Stanley, my people, the great Bula Matari himself. It is his emissary you see standing beside me. We have not been abandoned, my people. We have not been forgotten. Bula Matari comes. We are saved."

One fairly could have expected a tremendous roar of approval at these words, a full-throated explosion of joy. But in fact the response was disappointing: some scattered applause, a bit of whistling, an unintelligible shout here and there, but mostly an uncertain murmuring, a moody, muted muttering, and the continual barking of dogs.

"Come along, my boy."

Again Emin linked arms with Jephson; and as they made their way through the crowded crooked streets of the station toward the fort overlooking it from the hill about a quarter of a mile inland, Jephson became aware of the rather skeptical scrutiny of the milling masses of people around him. Well, he couldn't blame them. He could imagine well enough the sight he made. Despite the good eating and easy traveling they had enjoyed since emerging from the forest and despite the efforts he had made at sprucing up before landing at Wadelai, he realized he must look the perfect ragamuffin in his badly broken boots, his battered sun helmet, his endlessly patched and repatched clothes. And his handful of followers, the boatmen and askaris, clad by now as much in bits of stitched hide and scraps of beaten bark as in cloth and uniforms, hardly made a more inspiring sight. One certainly could forgive these people for wondering just what sort of saviors were these who had come to save them.

A moatlike ditch backed by solidly packed earthen breastworks eight feet high and eight feet thick, with sandbagged mountain guns emplaced at each of its four corners, and posted with sentries, formed the outer defenses of the fort. Within, the area was divided into two separate compounds, the sheds, huts, and buildings of each constructed of a bright yellow bamboo apparently native to the region. Some were plastered with mud and cow dung, others thatched with grass, and all looked exquisitely neat and clean, cool and airy. Those to the south, against the upriver side of the fort's parapet, composed the station's garrison: barracks, orderly room, guardhouse, mess, kitchens, armory, and the huts of the soldiers' families. To the north, on the downriver side—set among flower and vegetable gardens and orchards of lime and orange, custard apple, pomegranate and fig trees—were the houses of the station's officers and officials, lodgings for itinerant traders and other occasional travelers, the administrative buildings of the provincial government, and Emin's living quarters. Between the two was a spacious parade ground ringed around by storehouses, shops, stables, hospital, blacksmithy, other factories, and the *barazan,* that formal receiving room to be found in every settlement of the Islamic Orient from Turkey to Zanzibar that had any pretensions to civilization. Emin escorted Jephson there.

It was a circular structure of bamboo latticework under a peaked thatched roof, open so as to catch the evening river breezes, and furnished with divans and couches, pillows and bolsters, inlaid tables, chairs, and footstools, and carpets of the finest Persian weave. The troop of riflemen formed an honor guard at its entry; Sudi and the men took their places in hushed awe on the brilliantly patterned rugs especially laid out for them, while Jephson, with Emin at his side and Shukri Aga in a leather-strapped chair opposite, sat, lounged, reclined, sank into the luxurious softness of the pillows on the central divan. Then on a signal from Emin, a dainty clap of his hands, servants in spotless white cotton robes and knitted skullcaps brought in refreshments—gourds of *m'tama* beer for the boatmen and askaris, a vessel of frothy curds and whey for Jephson. This latter struck Jephson as an odd choice; but once tasted, he drank deeply of it and with enormous satisfaction. As Emin evidently knew, after so long on a deprived diet, it was precisely the sort of nourishment his body craved.

"There is so much we have to talk about, my boy. There are so many questions that I would like to put to you."

"And I to you, Governor."

"Yes, of course. I can well imagine. And we shall both have the opportunity. Later this evening, once you have settled yourself and feel at home, we shall dine together and gratify our respective curiosities. But I must beg your forbearance a little while longer. I am obliged to put you on display."

"Sir?"

"You are a great prize, my boy. You must understand that.

For us, your arrival here is a dream come true. I cannot keep you to myself." Emin indicated the crowd that had gathered outside the *barazan*.

They were the notables and dignitaries not only of this station but of much of the province as well—after the fall of Khartoum and the death of Gordon, Emin had withdrawn Equatoria's capital to Wadelai from its traditional seat at Lado, 200 miles to the north—army officers, tax collectors, storekeepers, clerks, scribes, factory managers, plantation overseers, technicians, traders of a motley of races and nationalities, Egyptian, Sudanese, Syrian, Tunisian, Turk, Greek, Copt, Druse, as well as the chiefs and headmen of the local tribes. On Emin's handclap, they were admitted one by one, some simply to stand and stare at Jephson with much the same skepticism he had seen on the faces of the people in the station below, while others came forward to shake his hand or kneel at his feet and in the Moslem fashion kiss his fingertips and exclaim some elaborate formula of thanksgiving.

Emin introduced them all with an easy informality, having a few warm personal words to say about each, behaving toward them not in the usual autocratic manner of a mudir toward his subjects or a general toward his troops but rather like a benevolent headmaster toward his pupils. But what most struck Jephson about these men was that all of them, like Emin and Shukri Aga, like the servants and the soldiers, were immaculately clothed in handsomely tailored uniforms or splendidly embroidered robes, and remarkably well nourished and robust in appearance into the bargain. Not one of them looked in dire straits or in any desperate need of rescuing. Quite to the contrary, they seemed in a far better position to rescue Jephson and his wretched men than the other way around.

This queer sensation of everything being just slightly topsy-turvy, of nothing quite fitting Jephson's notion of a Turkish general in a beleaguered outpost fighting for his life, was made all the sharper when Emin finally put an end to the reception and had a servant show Jephson to his quarters, a birdcagelike structure built along the lines of a garden house or gazebo, situated in a grove of flamboyants and fig trees at the far end of Emin's compound. It contained a pillow-strewn divan, a large *angarep* (the Turkish-style bed whose mattress is formed by strips of tightly woven cowhide), mosquito netting, freshly laundered linen, a bureau of drawers with some books and periodicals strewn on top of it, a cloth-draped table set with a bowl of fruit (mangoes, oranges, figs, pomegranates) and candles, a heavy carved wardrobe, two chairs, a full-length mirror. One could hardly have asked for better accommodations in St. James's. And in the middle of it all, placed on a spectacular leopard-skin rug (head and tail intact), was a big iron tub full of steaming water with a variety of soaps, scented oils, ointments, towels, and Egyptian loofahs laid out beside it.

Jephson needed no prompting. As soon as the servant left, he stripped and slid down into the bath with a groan of pleasure and made vigorous use of the roughest of the loofahs to scrub out the months of accumulation of dirt and jungle rot, and then toweled and oiled himself with a sensuousness that under any other circumstances he would have regarded as shameful. Once done, his skin scented and tingling, feeling truly clean for the first time since leaving Yambuya, he couldn't bear the idea of getting back into his smelly tattered garments. The servant had stowed the grubby bits and pieces of his baggage under the *angarep* (almost as if deliberately wanting to get such filthy stuff out of sight), and Jephson rummaged through them to see if he possessed anything tolerable to wear. But of course he didn't; everything he owned was by now disgusting in the extreme.

Well, he'd just put it off. He wasn't meant to join Emin for supper for another hour or so. That would be soon enough to get dressed. He wrapped a towel around his waist and sat down on the edge of the *angarep*. The bureau of drawers stood beside it as a sort of night table, and he took a look at the books on it. Only one was in English, a volume of Shakespeare's tragedies; the others were in Arabic, French, and German. The periodicals were also in German, scientific journals of some sort, *Petermann's Mitteilungen*, *Mitteilungen des Vereins für Erdkunde zu Leipzig*. One of these contained an article that seemed to be about the birds of the Equatorial Nile region written by an Eduard Schnitzer. Jephson made a halfhearted attempt to read it, then gave it up and lay down on the *angarep*, letting his body relax in the indescribable luxury of a real bed.

From where he lay he could see the shiny fruit of a fig tree by the gazebo door rustling in the gentle breeze that wafted up from the river and could hear the peaceful sounds of the fort making ready for evening: women calling children to supper, the changing of the guard on the breastworks, the distant chant of a muezzin from the minaret of a mosque. How strange, he thought, how very strange to have come all this way through so much hardship only to arrive . . . But whatever the thought, whatever sense of unreality it sought to untangle, it was lost in a sweet, drowsy confusion of images as he slipped involuntarily, irresistibly into sleep.

He awakened as if into a dream. It was night, the deep magical night of Africa, bright with moonlight, sweet with the fragrance of flamboyants, still but for the cooing of mourning doves. And in the doorway of the gazebo, bathed in the moonlight, stood a beautiful girl. Oh, yes, a dream, surely. He peered at her langorously through half-opened eyelids so that she would not too soon vanish from his fantasy. She was small but full and shapely, dressed in the manner of a Turkish odalisque in gauze and silk and bangles and jewels, all of it silver in the moonlight except for her hair, shining raven, tumbling to her shoulders, adorned with flowers. It was also difficult in that light to make out the shade of her skin—olive, coffee, perhaps even darker than that, highlighted by the moon—but her features were remarkably fine and delicate and he thought, if she were African, Circassian, Abyssinian, Egyptian, she was likely all of those and of other races as well, perhaps of all the races that down through the centuries had mingled on the Nile. And in finding himself analyzing her so, he realized that of course she wasn't a dream, and he sat up with a start.

"Oh, I have awakened you."

"No, no. That's all right. I should have been up long before this. My God, what time is it? I've kept the governor waiting."

"I came twice for you, but I did not have the heart to disturb you. You slept so deeply."

"My God, yes. I only meant to close my eyes for a moment. But I'm up now. Please, be so good as to convey my apologies to Dr. Emin and tell him I'll be along in a moment." He started to get off the *angarep*, but just in time remembered he was naked except for the towel around his waist. "Oh, good heavens, you must excuse me. I had a bath, you see, and, well, I wasn't all that keen on getting back into my rather ratty things."

"Perhaps you would prefer this." The girl entered the gazebo and went to the big carved wardrobe across from the *angarep* and produced from it an ankle-length loose-fitting white robe. She held it up toward him. "Would you not find it more comfortable than your hard-worn uniform? It is customary here to wear the caftan when the day's work is done. And look, there is this too, surely more comfortable than your heavy boots." "This too" was a pair of tooled leather slippers.

Sitting on the edge of the *angarep*, the towel lying across his lap, he watched in some embarrassment and excitement as she brought these items to him, her bracelets tinkling, her silks sighing, a lovely scent of blossoms upon her person. Jesus, who was she? A harem girl, another example of Emin's generous hospitality, like the bath and soaps and ointments, a recognition of his needs after the hardships he had endured, like the curds and whey, a gift in reward for the mission he had accomplished, meant for his pleasure?

"I shall wait for you outside so that I may show you the way."

"Just a minute. Tell me, what is your name?"

"Faridah."

"Ah, Faridah . . . yes, well, thank you, Faridah. I shall only be a moment."

It was nearly midnight; and except for the sentries manning the mountain guns at the four corners of the earthwork ramparts, the fort was asleep in the moonlight. From the station below came the faint yapping of pie dogs, answering the cries of the jackal and hyena on the savanna. Out on the river tiny spots of firelight could be seen where Loor tribesmen fished from dugout canoes for the Nile's carp and bream. Emin's house, arbored by lime and papaya trees, had a glorious prospect of the river—a moon-silvered ribbon, very nearly two miles wide, winding away to the north—and of the star-crowned hills of its far bank. A deal table, laid with linen and cutlery and crockery and a bowl of orchids, stood on the veranda. Emin himself, now also dressed in a caftan as well as his tasseled maroon fez, which transformed his clerkish professorial look into something rather more grand, an Islamic philosopher, an Arabic astrologer perhaps, was seated in a high-backed wicker chair beside it, reading a small worn leather-bound volume by candlelight.

When Jephson and Faridah appeared, he set the book aside and looked up. "Ah, Mr. Jephson, there you are. I trust you have rested well."

"You must forgive me, Governor, but—"

"No, no. Not a word, my boy. I understand completely. After all you've undergone . . . Actually, I was tempted to let you sleep through till morning, but Faridah was concerned that you hadn't eaten and might awaken in the middle of the night ravenous. And I must confess, for my part, I was eager for our conversation. And now here you are. Excellent. Sit down, my boy. Faridah, *meine Liebe,* see if you can't rouse our lazy servants and have them bring us our supper."

"Yes, Father."

"Father?"

"Faridah is my daughter, Mr. Jephson. You are surprised? Well, I cannot blame you. She doesn't in the least look like me, I know. And thank God for that. What would you look like if you looked like me, *schatz?* A shortsighted little gnome with a furry chin. *Nicht wahr?*"

"Oh, you silly." The girl went over to Emin's chair and leaned against him affectionately.

He put his arm around her slim waist. "No furry little gnome this. Oh no, a true beauty. A great beauty. Wouldn't you agree, Mr. Jephson?"

"Wholeheartedly, sir."

"Yes, a true beauty." Emin looked up into the face of his daughter, and his voice softened. "The very image of her mother, a princess. I mean that quite literally, Mr. Jephson. My wife . . . my late wife, this child's mother, was of the royal house of Axum, granddaughter of the Negus of Ethiopia. She was taken into slavery after the sack of Magdala—that insane business—and I came upon her in the seraglio of Ismail Hakki, Mudir of Antivari, just a snip of a girl then, when I was court physician there . . . Ah, but that is another story, a long story, an old man's story. I shall not bore you with it."

"But I should like to hear it, sir."

"Yes? Well, perhaps another time. Now we must eat. Go on, Faridah. Fetch us our supper."

It was a wonderfully light repast, perfect for the lateness of the hour: sherbets and fruit, honey and a variety of cheeses, drafts of new milk, enormous omelettes, loaves of a delicious fluffy white bread, all of it served in a most civilized manner by two well-trained Loor boys under Faridah's supervision. She stood behind Emin's chair, a hand resting on his shoulder, and kept close watch on the proceedings, not eating herself, making sure that neither Jephson nor her father was ever in want of anything. Indeed, no sooner was a dish consumed or a platter empty, than with a sharp clap of her hands or a stern whisper she had it replenished. Jephson had a hard time keeping his eyes off her and paying attention to his host.

Emin was full of questions, about England, about Europe, about the world at large—he had been cut off and out of touch for more than two years now and eager to catch up on everything—but, understandably, what interested him most was Stanley and the expedition, the supplies it was bringing, the route it had taken. He had, he said, expected help to come, if it were ever to come at all, to come from the south and east not the west—up from the Indian Ocean coast by way of the Karagwe and Nkole country not from the Atlantic and the Congo—and he expressed his amazement and admiration for Stanley's incredible daring in attempting and then succeeding in traversing the forbidden Ituri. He wanted to know, in the kind of detail that could only be described as a scientist's curiosity, everything that had been encountered in that fearsome forest where no white man had ever been, the flora and fauna, the geography and geology, the types and nature and habits of its tribes. But the particular question, which he posed again and again with a somewhat apologetic but pressing insistence, concerned the expedition's origins. Who had sponsored it? And why? There was a mild but unmistakable note of suspicion in the way he asked it.

"When I sent my runners out with our call for help . . . Well, my boy, you can imagine I felt exactly like the proverbial marooned mariner who casts a note in a bottle into the sea. *Mein Gott,* what were the chances of its ever reaching England? Minuscule! Minuscule! But even if it did, even if against all odds it managed to find its way to London, what right had I to hope that anyone would take notice of it? After all, who was I, what was Equatoria in the grand scheme of the British Empire?"

"But, sir—"

"No, no, my boy. I do not say this out of false modesty. I am perfectly aware of my own insignificance, of this province's relative unimportance. Gordon, yes, the great beloved Chinese Gordon. And Khartoum, of course, commanding the confluence of the Blue and White Niles. There a great effort had to be made. There the fate of the entire Sudan was at stake. But once Lord Wolseley failed and Gordon was dead and the Sudan was as good as lost anyway, well, I had to ask myself why—"

"But that's precisely why, sir. It was precisely because Wolseley had failed."

"Please?"

"Don't you see, Dr. Emin? You gave England a second chance, a totally unforeseen second chance to redeem her honor, to make good her failure to save Khartoum, to avenge Gordon's death. You can't know the excitement your message caused. The news that Equatoria was still holding out, that *you* were still holding out . . . By God, yes, here was a second chance. Here was a second Gordon."

"A second Gordon?"

"Yes, sir, a second Gordon. It was how all England spoke of

you. But you were not to go the way of the first. Where England had failed Gordon, it would not fail you. Men volunteered in the hundreds to join an expedition to your relief. Mr. Stanley returned from America to lead it. A committee of leading citizens was got up to raise funds to finance it. It was the matter of the moment, the issue of highest priority, the question of the most intense popular concern. The newspapers wrote of nothing else. The last of Gordon's lieutenants standing alone against the dervish hordes. No matter what the difficulties, no matter how hopeless the situation might appear, Emin Pasha must be saved."

For a moment, Emin said nothing. He sat back in the wicker chair and simply stared at Jephson, his weak watery eyes behind his thick spectacles wide with disbelief. Then Faridah, standing behind him, squeezed his shoulder; and this roused him from his reverie. "I didn't know," he said finally. "I had no idea. I am extremely moved to hear this, Mr. Jephson." He removed his spectacles and began polishing them slowly on the hem of his caftan. "A second Gordon. A second Gordon, you say," he went on in a quiet voice, his head slightly tilted, speaking as much to himself as to Jephson. "So that is the reason, is it? I would never have thought it. No, I would never have thought that Englishmen would undertake such a dangerous and costly business for such a sentimental reason." He smiled a little.

"It was my reason, sir. I can assure you."

Emin replaced his spectacles. "Oh, I am certain it was, my boy. I am certain it was." He reached across the table to pat Jephson's hand. "But for others perhaps, well, for others I cannot help thinking there may have been other reasons."

Coffee had been served—sweet thick Turkish coffee in tiny glass cups fitted into filigreed brass holders—and Jephson took a sip of his as an excuse to look away from Emin's inquiring gaze. For he too could not help thinking that for others there were other reasons, for Sir William Mackinnon, for Leopold II, for Henry Morton Stanley himself, other reasons than the rescue of this odd little man. But those reasons, he felt, were not within his competence to discuss. When he looked up, Emin was holding his coffee cup and saucer at his lips, his eyes partly closed, that small, somewhat sardonic knowing smile still playing at the corners of his mouth.

"But what I was wondering, sir . . . If I may put a question to you."

"Why yes, of course."

"Well, what I was wondering, sir, is what actually is the situation here? I mean, things don't really look too awfully bad, you know." Jephson made a gesture that was meant to encompass the well-set table, the pretty arbor of Emin's *boma*, the peacefulness of the moonlit night beyond. "As a matter of fact, they look rather good, if I may say so, certainly nothing at all like what I had expected."

"Ah, yes." Emin looked around absently. "Yes, I suppose they do. I see your point. But appearances often are deceiving, my boy. And in this case I am afraid they are extremely deceiving. Things are really not very good at all. You see, here in Wadelai, we are more than two hundred miles south of the dervish lines. We are— But perhaps it would be best if I showed you this on a map."

"I'll fetch it, Father."

The table was cleared and the map Faridah brought, a yellowed worm-eaten rectangle of vellum, was unrolled on it. The upper corners were anchored by the candle and some pieces of crockery; Emin held down the lower corners; and with Jephson and Faridah standing on either side of him he mused for a moment about where to begin.

Originally explored and annexed to the Sudan by Sir Samuel Baker in 1870 and developed and administered by Gordon himself until he was appointed governor-general of the entire Sudan in 1877 and Emin replaced him, Equatoria lay, roughly speaking (there could of course be no clearly demarked frontiers in a wilderness like this), between the equator and 6 degrees north latitude and between 29 degrees and 33 degrees east longitude, an area of very nearly 100,000 square miles, fairly neatly bisected by the Nile flowing northward out of Lake Albert. The chain of forts and trading stations along the river, nine in all from Wadelai to Lado, formed its heart and spine; but there also were a few outposts and depots scattered along the borders of the forest kingdoms of the Wanyoro and Waganda tribes to the southeast of the Nile and to the northwest of it in the grasslands of the Makaraka and Dinka peoples, the northernmost of which, Amadi, was more than a thousand miles south of Khartoum and separated from it by the burning wastes and barren mountains of the Nubian desert and the dreadful swamps and papyrus marshlands of the Sudd. Thus, even in the best of times, it was an extremely isolated and inaccessible place. And these were not the best of times.

Even before the fall of Khartoum, the dervishes had invaded it. Under the command of a certain Emir Karam Allah, one of the Mahdi's ablest generals, an army of very nearly 5,000 mounted rifles and an equal number of spear-bearing infantry struck southeast out of the neighboring province of Bahr al-Ghazal—which they had overrun with terrible ease the month before—and laid siege to Amadi. The battle lasted three weeks. Although numbering less than 500, Emin's soldiers put on a tremendous show, fighting with a suicidal gallantry; and it was only when the last of the survivors were on the brink of starvation that they at last abandoned the fort, cut their way through the dervishes' lines, and fled toward the Nile. Karam Allah, in hot pursuit, fell on Wandi and Rimo, two other lone penny-packet garrisons in the Makaraka grasslands; and here again they met with a far fiercer resistance than he had any reason to expect. But ultimately these too were overwhelmed. And the way to Lado, then still Equatoria's capital, was open.

"The prospect was not brilliant," Emin said, running his hand absently over the map. "Not brilliant at all."

For by then, Khartoum had fallen and Gordon had been beheaded and the Nile was closed and it was useless to hope for help from the north. Emin learned this melancholy news in a message Karam Allah sent to Lado under a flag of truce, describing Equatoria's position as utterly hopeless and demanding its immediate surrender. "In the name of Allah, the merciful and compassionate, from the servant of Allah, Karam Allah, to Emin Pasha of Equatoria, may Allah guide you into the path of virtue, amen! Know that the gracious Allah has sent his Mahdi, the looked-for messenger and Messiah, so as to show through him the true faith and by him to kill the infidel. Know that those who believe in the Mahdi and surrender to him will be delivered; but those who do not will be destroyed, as Gordon Pasha of Khartoum and Slatin Pasha of Darfur and Lupton Pasha of Bahr al-Ghazal were destroyed and whose souls Allah has condemned to fire and eternal misery."

Emin had replied, "To me, Karam Allah, it is all one whether Gordon Pasha has been destroyed, whether Slatin Pasha has been destroyed, whether Lupton Pasha has been destroyed. To me, it is all one whomsoever has been destroyed. I am here like iron." And straightaway he evacuated Lado, removed his headquarters to Wadelai, pulled in his troops from the indefensible outposts in the west and, concentrating them—some 3,000 strong—in the chain of stations along the Nile with the idea of fighting a spoiling rearguard action from one to the other upriver to Wadelai, where he intended to make his last stand, braced for Karam Allah's onslaught.

It did not come. Mysteriously, Karam Allah's army withdrew. At the eleventh hour Equatoria was granted a miraculous reprieve.

For it was just at this time that the Mahdi died; and his successor, the Khalifa Abdullah, was more concerned with consolidating his newly won power over the dervish legions and strengthening his hold on the vast territory they had already conquered than with adding this, the Sudan's most distant and inaccessible province, to it. Emin and his people, however—now entirely cut off from the larger world by the dervishes on the north, the jungles on the west, and the great unexplored African wilderness and the warring kingdoms of the Wanyoro and Waganda to the south and east—could not know this. And so a period of tense waiting ensued, of frantic digging in, of nerve-racking expectation that at any time the dreadful fury of the dervish armies would descend upon them.

Food, clothing, shelter were not the problem. It was part of Emin's genius that long before the troubles started he had made Equatoria virtually self-sufficient in the basic necessities. Each of the river stations had its own plantations of maize and *m'tama*, yams and ground nuts, its own vegetable gardens and fruit orchards, its own flocks of fowls and herds of cattle, sheep and goats. Moreover, he had had the foresight to put cotton into cultivation at Wadelai some years before, so that, together with the wool sheared from the sheep, a pretty fair quality and range of cloth and clothing were manufactured there. And native ingenuity found ways of making do with all manner of substitutes, honey for sugar, beeswax for candle tallow, fat and potash for soap, the seeds of the hibiscus plant for coffee. But the hard goods and other merchandise that used to come up the Nile to Lado at regular intervals on the steamers from Khartoum came no more. The medicines, tools, metalware, paraffin; the spare parts for the *Khedive* and other machinery; the beads and wire and other trading *mitako;* the currency and specie and pay packets for the soldiers and officials; and above all the weapons and ammunition so vital to survival in a perilous wilderness in a perilous time and which no amount of ingenuity or Robinson Crusoe-style inventiveness could replace—these began dwindling away.

For two years they waited. For two years the soldiers watched from the ramparts of their forts along the Nile for a renewal of the dervish invasion, or for the arrival of help. There were incidents. Roving bands of dervishes infiltrated the grasslands to the west of the Nile where Emin had withdrawn his garrisons, terrorizing villagers, engaging in guerrilla war; and the tribes there went over to them. Those closer to the river, sensing the shift in Emin's fortunes, turned hostile. There were occasional raids on the river stations, skirmishes in the back country, outbreaks of banditry and freebooting and random violence. Caravans traveling from Duffile, where the rapids on the Nile put an end to river traffic, to supply the northern forts were ambushed and plundered; and the steamer, plying the river between Duffile and Wadelai, often had to run a gauntlet of rifle fire from the banks. Nerves frayed; tempers gave way; a siege mentality took hold. As the days turned into weeks and the weeks into months and the months into years and hope of rescue faded, a dark cloud of despondency settled over the province, and there was talk of desertion, mutiny, surrender. To all it was plain that the dervishes were only delaying their final assault until that time when the garrisons had run so short of ammunition that they would not be able to put up a decent fight and the chain of forts and stations along the Nile could be plucked one by one like rotted fruit from the vine.

But now at last help was on the way.

"And not a moment too soon, my boy. Not a moment too soon." Emin removed his hands from the map and it rolled up with a snap. "For, it seems, the dervishes are on the march once again." He sat down at the table.

Faridah took the map away and ordered fresh coffee to be served. Jephson also sat down.

"It is not absolutely certain of course. Nothing ever is these days. It is just a rumor. Just another rumor. There are always rumors these days. In this case, of quite a large army sailing up the Nile from Khartoum on a flotilla of steamers and barges captured from Gordon. Omar Saleh, the conqueror of Suakin, is said to be in command." Emin took a sip of the fresh coffee and turned to face Jephson directly. "The story is that the Khalifa got wind of Mr. Stanley's relief expedition and decided that he had better attack us now and put an end to us once and for all before it gets here."

Jephson nodded. "It is something Mr. Stanley always expected would happen."

"Yes, well, we shall know for certain when the *Khedive* returns. Captain Casati will have the latest news of the situation in the north." He drank off the last of his coffee and looked out to the moonlit river as if looking out for the steamer's return.

They waited three days for her return, days that for Jephson retained the slightly unreal quality of the first. Sudi, the askaris, and the Wanyamwezi boatmen had been provided with quarters as genial as Jephson's, a *boma* of five huts all their own in the compound of the soldiers' families on the upriver side of the fort. Several of the station's women had been recruited to cook for them and look after their other domestic needs, and bolts of cotton cloth had been given them from which to cut and sew new shirts and pantaloons to replace their pathetic rags.

Nor did the generous Emin overlook Jephson's tattered condition. On his first morning there, two Copts turned up at the gazebo, one a tailor, the other a cobbler. They took his measurements and returned the very same evening with two sets of well-made tunics and trousers of rough cotton, and shirts, socks, singlets, and underdrawers of softer stuff, and a pair of calfskin riding boots. Even so, slipping into a mood of idleness and ease, Jephson found he preferred the cool, sensual, slightly decadent comfort of his caftan and slippers and took to wearing them most of the time while he dawdled away those days, dozing in a hammock in the shade of the fig trees, reading Shakespeare on his gazebo's veranda, dining alfresco above the Nile, strolling about the gardens of the fort and the souks of the station in Emin and Faridah's company or, when Emin was busy with the affairs of the province, with Faridah alone.

She was very young, much younger than Jephson had at first realized, barely fifteen, little more than a child. But she had very little of the playfulness, spontaneity, or silliness of a child. There was a quietness in her, a constraint, an earnest dignity that, while surprising, even amusing in one so young, struck Jephson as altogether befitting her remarkable exotic beauty, indeed as enhancing it; and it made her seem to him, rather disconcertingly he had to admit, less the adorable child than the desirable woman.

When her father was about, she kept herself demurely in the background, never intruding on their conversation, ever watchful of their wants, often anticipating them. And when she was alone with Jephson, she was if anything even more self-effacing, performing the role of his guide with a dutiful, rather humorless gravity, showing him whatever he wanted to see, taking him wherever he wanted to go, answering his questions with a thoroughness of detail that was truly staggering. She seemed to know the name of every tree, plant, shrub, bush, flower, bird, bug, and animal on the land and every fish and reptile in the river. One had to suppose her soberness, her studious seriousness, the lack of all childish gaiety in her were the result of some melancholy history. But what that was—her mother's death, the dervish threat, some tragedy of her racial mixture?—Jephson couldn't discover. There was no getting close to her in that way.

With Emin, on the other hand, the beginnings of a friendship quickly sprang up. Jephson liked the little man instinctively, liked him right from the start for his kindliness, his modesty and generosity, his warm fatherly manner. They took all their meals together; and their conversation was easy, relaxed, amiable, animated. He was a fund of fascinating information and acute observation. From references he let drop in passing, Jephson gathered he had been formally trained as a doctor of medicine; but clearly his quick, curious mind had taken him beyond that into virtually all the natural sciences.

Evidence of his widespread interests were everywhere about his home: shelves jammed with books in several languages; stacks of journals filled with notes written in his tiny cramped hand; bundles of maps he had drawn of places never seen by any other white man; carefully prepared skins of animals and snakes, stuffed birds, dried frogs; collections of butterflies and beetles pinned behind glass; ceramic pots of unusual plants he was growing under a variety of conditions. There was even a basket of human skulls in a room he used as a laboratory, each meticulously measured and labeled according to tribe, sex, age, and cause of death. Obviously it was from him that Faridah had acquired her amazing knowledge. He was very much a teacher, a teacher of the sort one could only wish to have had at school and never did—enthusiastic, interesting, considerate, erudite without pedantry, just slightly, endearingly eccentric. And it was very much as a schoolteacher or, as Jephson had originally noted, a tolerant headmaster that he governed his people.

He was up well before dawn each day to make his rounds at the hospital, inspect the troops and fortifications, check on the level of supplies in the warehouses, see to it that the gates to the fort were opened and the streets swept, examine the livestock being let out to graze and the goods and produce being brought in by local tribesmen to be bartered in the bazaar. The middle of the day, when everyone else retreated from the heat, he devoted to his studies, making notes, taking measurements, sending the children of the soldiers out to catch frogs and bugs for him, and then gathering them around and instructing them on what they had caught. He even kept a little zoo: a tame eagle, a baby elephant and giraffe, some chimps, and some bewhiskered colobus monkeys.

Wadelai was the newest of his stations. Until he transferred his headquarters there from Lado, it had been just another little fishing village of the Loor (a short, thickset, industrious, intelligent but ugly people who plaited goat's wool into their hair as adornment), but in the two years since he had made it into an extraordinary place, a sanctuary of civilization, a wilderness city, a home. He had taught the women how to spin raw cotton on homemade distaffs, built a factory where the bobbins of thread were woven into cloth on spindles and dyed in solutions made from the bruised bark of fig trees. He had devised a process by which potash and animal fats were boiled into soap, introduced the manufacture of salt, erected a drydock where the steamer could be repaired and lighters built; and he now was experimenting with the raising of rice, using a system of weirs and oxen-driven paddle wheels to flood paddies with river water, all of which he showed off to Jephson with touching pride.

Not counting the Loor, but counting the wives and children and concubines of the officers and officials, merchants and soldiers, more than 2,000 people lived there; and wherever he went, they called out to him in greeting, to ask his advice, to tell him their troubles; and he always stopped for them and had time for them. He never seemed to give orders or mete out punishment. He relied rather on reason, logic, persuasion, argument, cajolery, flattery, and, at the very worst, when all else failed, he might fly into a temper and scold.

Because of the profusion of crocodiles and snapping turtles in the Nile, he had had a stockade of bamboo pikes built out in the river to form a safe pen where the women of the station could draw water and wash clothes. One day when he was taking Jephson to meet the local Loor chief (whose name was Wadelai and who was so fat it was said a boy could stand on his stomach while he was sitting down), Emin noticed some girls doing their washing outside this pen. He immediately began shouting and waving his walking stick at them. In his mind they were in imminent danger of being grabbed by the crocs lurking in the shallows. When the girls realized what it was he was warning them about, they burst into gales of giggles and began jumping up and down and splashing about in mock panic, pretending they were being attacked. Emin turned livid at this horseplay and went wading into the river, shoes and all, and dragged one of the girls out by her hair. The others quieted down then and after a minute followed her out. They recognized the genuineness of Emin's concern for them in his somewhat comical anger, the authenticity of his desire to keep them from harm, his worried paternal love for them; and they came up to him one by one, shamefaced, and kissed his hand and begged his pardon and dutifully trooped back into the river to continue their washing within the crocodile pen. Emin beamed at them.

Oh, yes, he loved them; it was plain to anyone with eyes to see how well he loved his people, how well he cared for them. And they responded with an affection of their own; and without in the least being afraid of him or intimidated by him, they invariably obeyed him as students obey a loved and loving master. Jephson couldn't help but compare him to Stanley in this respect, his gentle indulgent patience to Stanley's hard-driving, often ruthless single-mindedness. And he also couldn't help but wonder how such two different men would get on once they met.

But as well as Jephson felt he came to know and appreciate Emin in their few days together, a puzzle remained. Who was he? Despite his name—Mohammed Emin Effendi, to give it in full—Jephson found it impossible to believe he was a Turk or for that matter any other sort of Moslem born. But what he was, where he came from originally, Jephson was never able to gather a clue.

· THREE ·

"THE *Khedive*, Jephson effendi. Look, the *Khedive*."

Jephson, lazing in the shade of the veranda of his pleasant little garden gazebo after a sumptuous lunch, looked up.

"There," Faridah said. "There, you can see her now." And she rushed down from the fort to the station below.

The *Khedive*, a single-stack wood-burning side-wheeler had just rounded the far side of an island in the Nile and was churning crossriver toward the station's jetty, where the *Lady Dorothy* was tied up. Jephson could see Emin and Shukri Aga hurrying out to the end of the jetty to meet her. His immediate reaction was to rush down there too, but he stopped himself. He had to change first. He was, as usual, wearing his caftan and slippers; but the days of idleness were over now, and the work of the expedition was about to resume. He ducked back into the gazebo and quickly dressed in one of his newly made uniforms.

By the time he got down to the river, the *Khedive* had docked and her passengers were disembarking, an unruly mob, mainly women and children and old folks, pushing and shoving their way down the gangplank, calling out to those on the quay. It was apparent at a glance who they were: refugees fleeing from the north, burdened under bundles of household goods and personal possessions. A troop of soldiers from the garrison had formed a cordon along the waterfront to keep those on the quay from surging onto the jetty; but the excitement was too great, and here and there, people broke through, clamoring to hear the news. Jephson pushed his way into the heart of this pandemonium, wondering where Faridah had got to. A soldier snatched at his arm, meaning to stop him, then saw who he was and let him through.

Emin, at the end of the jetty with Shukri Aga, was being shouted at by the steamer's captain, a stocky black-bearded barrel of a man dressed in khaki shorts, high boots, a loose white shirt open at the collar to reveal a hairy chest, a pistol on his hip, and a ragged wide-brimmed panama on his head. This latter he kept removing and waving about, then jamming back on to express various degrees of excitement, anger, disgust, frustration, perhaps even something close to fear.

"Calm yourself, Gaetano. For the love of God, calm yourself. I tell you everything will be all right. Help is on the way. Look, here is Mr. Jephson now. Mr. Jephson, come here. Come here, my boy. I want you to meet Captain Casati. Gaetano, this is Mr. Arthur Jephson, Bula Matari's emissary."

"Captain." Jephson extended his hand.

But the agitated fellow could scarcely bring himself to nod at Jephson by way of a greeting let alone grasp his hand before he resumed his violent tirade at Emin. Jephson couldn't understand a word of it; he was speaking Italian.

"What is it? What's happened?"

"I am afraid Captain Casati brings us unhappy news from the north, my boy."

"Unhappy news? Is that how you call it, Pasha? Unhappy news?" Again Casati removed his hat and slammed it against his thigh. "Jesus Maria, we are finished. That is the unhappy news I bring from the north, Signor Jephson. We are finished. At the end of our rope. And he calls it unhappy news."

"Now stop that, Gaetano. Stop it at once." Emin seized Casati by the arm and gave him a scolding shake. "There is no reason to carry on in this way. Just calm yourself. Pull yourself together."

"Yes, of course. Our world has come to an end and I am to calm myself." Casati jammed his hat back on his head. "I am to pull myself together. I am to be as imperturbable as our beloved Pasha, even though the end is upon us at last."

"The rumors are true then? The dervishes are on the march again?"

"On the march? On the march? Oh, no, Signor Jephson. The dervishes are not on the *march*. They are *here*."

"Now just a moment, Gaetano. That is not true. That is not what you said."

Casati whirled on Emin in a fury. "They have taken Lado, Pasha. Can't you understand that? Jesus Maria, I am telling you, they have taken Lado."

"Yes, yes. But you said that was just a few horsemen, an advance guard or scouting party of some kind. You said the main force—Omar Saleh's army, the steamers and barges and nuggars—is still far downriver, still making its way through the Sudd. It will be weeks before *they* reach Lado, Gaetano, weeks. And besides, what does Lado matter to us? We evacuated Lado long ago. We gave it up to the dervishes long ago."

"Oh, I see. So it is all right then. So we have nothing to worry about then. Oh, yes, of course. How foolish of me to worry. An army of thousands is descending on us. Not one of the forts north of Duffile has enough ammunition to fight for a week. The people everywhere are in a panic. Jesus Maria, Pasha, just look at them, will you?" Again Casati whipped off his panama and this time waved it at the passengers streaming off the *Khedive*. "I couldn't keep them off the boat. They mobbed me. They would have torn me to pieces. And I left hundreds behind, thousands. They are flooding into Duffile from all the stations, from Chor Ayu, from Labore, Muggi, Kirri, Bedden, Rejaf. And they will be coming here next, overland if they have to. They will walk if they have to. They want to get out. They want to get as far south as they can. And they are right, Pasha. They should get out. We all should get out. We should abandon this godforsaken hole now while we still have the chance and retreat to the south before Omar Saleh's army reaches Lado."

"What kind of nonsense are you talking, Gaetano? Retreat to the south? Retreat to the south *where?* Where, I ask you. Tell me that. Retreat to the south where?"

"Into the Nyanza. To the southern end of the Nyanza. Into the Ruwenzoris."

"With ten thousand people? Are you crazy, Gaetano? There are ten thousand people in my charge here in Equatoria. And most of them are women and children. You want me to retreat with them to the southern end of the Nyanaza, into the Ruwenzoris? How? And then what? Even if I can get them there, what will I do with them there? What do you suppose will become of ten thousand people in the wilderness of the Ruwenzoris? Tell me that, Gaetano."

Casati didn't reply. Clearly he wasn't thinking about ten thousand people when he spoke of retreat.

"No, it is nonsense. It is impossible. It cannot be done. If I thought it could be done, I would have done it long before this. There is no point arguing about it. We will not retreat. We will not leave our homes. We will stay."

"And wait like lambs for the dervishes to cut our throats?"

"No. We will fight for each station, for each fort, for every inch of ground. We will fight to the last man, if it comes to that."

"With what, Pasha? Jesus Maria, with what will we fight? I tell you, there isn't enough ammunition—"

"And I tell you help is on the way. If you would only listen to me, Gaetano. If you would only stop ranting for a moment. This young man is Bula Matari's emissary, I tell you. Bula Matari is on his way here with an expedition to our relief."

"Where is this Bula Matari?"

"On the western shore of the Nyanza, perhaps no more than fifty miles from here. We shall go and fetch him in the steamer. We have only been waiting for you to get back. We shall have him here in a few days."

"A few days, eh? A few days?" Casati replaced his panama. "Well, all I can say is that it had better be only a few days."

"It will be, if we don't stand here talking. So let's make the steamer ready. Wood her up. Clear these people off her and wood her up. We will sail first thing in the morning. Mr. Jephson will lend you a hand. We want to load some provisions for Mr. Stanley and his party. They have had a dreadful time of it. Go along with him, my boy."

"Yes, sir."

But Jephson hesitated. A sickening thought had struck him. He realized he had inadvertently misrepresented the situation. He had allowed Emin to believe that Stanley, marching along the lake-shore, was bringing up the *entire* relief expedition not merely the trail-blazing advance column. He had failed to make clear that the massive amount of ammunition and weapons that Emin was counting on to save Equatoria, with which he would stand a fair chance of beating off the dervish invasion, was not with them but with Barttelot and Troup and Bonny and Ward and the rear column and the 600 porters recruited from Tippoo-Tib in Yambuya. And *they* were still at least four, five, maybe six weeks behind.

Emin peered at him quizzically through the thick lenses of his spectacles. "What is it, my boy? Was there something you wanted to say?"

"Sir? Oh, no, I was just thinking . . . But it isn't important." Jephson started down the jetty after Casati. He simply didn't have the heart to start trying to clarify the matter now.

• •

They sailed from Wadelai at eight the next morning—Jephson, Emin, Casati, Sudi, the five askaris and ten boatmen, plus the steamer's crew of six, with the *Khedive*'s hold crammed with provisions for Stanley and his men, the *Lady Dorothy* in tow. Faridah had expected to come (she usually accompanied her father on his journeys) and so had Shukri Aga, along with a color guard, the garrison's brass band and a troop of soldiers to provide Stanley with a welcome to Equatoria of appropriate pomp and circumstance. But as the object of the voyage was to bring back the relief expedition in as few trips as possible, space could not be spared for them aboard the vessel.

She was a small vessel, 108 ton displacement, eighty-five feet long, eighteen feet in the beam with a draft of about five feet. Considering the circumstances (the lack of replacement parts, no proper shipyard overhaul in more than two years), she was in remarkably good condition. Her engine and boilers, however, were badly worn; and Casati, for all his anxiety to get to Stanley as quickly as possible, did not dare force her to make more than five or six knots. So, steaming upriver against the Nile's strong current, it wasn't until sunset that they at last entered the great inland sea of Lake Albert. Here, for lack of powerful enough lanterns with which to proceed in the dark, they anchored for the night in the lee of a small uninhabited island, and took up the search for Stanley and the advance column along the lake's western shore at first light the following day.

It was a beautiful day, the eighth since Jephson had separated from Stanley, as brilliantly clear as a blue diamond, with a spanking wind blowing out of the Mountains of the Moon in the South, raising sun-flashing whitecaps on the oceanic expanse of the lake's steel-gray waters and driving galleons of shining cumulus clouds above the spectacular cliffs that bounded its western shore. The tribal villages scattered on the shore looked positively idyllic, little Arcadian settlements of mud-and-grass nestled in shady glades or amid groves of bright green banana trees, by the banks of creeks or pools of crystal waters fed by cascades, herdsmen lying idly among their flocks of grazing goats, fishermen paddling lazily in and out of craggy inlets in dugout canoes setting nets, women pounding corn and stitching hides and salting fish, children playing hoops and tag or simply dreaming away the day in the warmth of the sun.

The steamer was not unfamiliar to them. Baker and Gordon had brought her into the lake on occasion, and Emin had been there several times mapping the shoreline. But her appearance nonetheless was always a novelty, a splendid diversion; and everywhere she passed people stopped what they were doing and splashed knee-deep into the lake and shouted and waved and broke into good-humored displays of singing and dancing.

This delighted Jephson, watching them through his field glasses from the bridge, and he shouted and waved back at them, and so did Emin, leaning on the rail beside him and offering a running commentary on the customs and habits of these lakeside tribes, and so too did Sudi and the boatmen and askaris on the lower deck. But Casati in the wheelhouse, calling instructions down to the stoker in the engine room or out to the leadsman sounding the fathoms from the forward rail, ignored it all and kept a sharp lookout for some sign of Stanley and his party. He was, it seemed, a man of only two moods: flamboyant outbursts suddenly subsiding into brooding silences.

He had been an officer in the Bersaglieri (his rank of captain referred to that service rather than to his command of the *Khedive*), but whether he was cashiered from that elite Italian regiment or quit on his own no one knew. In any case, he had found his way out to Africa some ten years before as part of a team conducting a survey of the Upper Nile, but he had quit that too for no apparent reason and drifted into the Mobutto country hunting ivory and also, possibly, slaves. With the advent of the Mahdi and the dervish uprising, his traveling became too perilous, and he had made his way to the relative civilization of Lado with the idea of catching a steamer there to Khartoum. But he arrived too late; the dervishes were already astride the Nile and transport to the north was cut off; and so, for lack of any other alternative but with little show of enthusiasm, he threw in his lot with what he regarded as Emin's quixotic attempt to save Equatoria. Emin, grateful for whatever help he could get, had pressed him into service as the *Khedive*'s captain.

"Is that them, signor?"

"Where?" Jephson ducked into the wheelhouse.

"There. On the beach behind that island. No, not there. More to the south. More to your left."

"I see a village," Jephson said. "On the mainland facing the island."

"That is Nsabe. Now look to the left of it, signor, a degree to the left. Is that not a tent? I am sure it is a tent."

"You're right. It's a tent." Jephson kept screwing the eyepieces of the binoculars to improve the focus. "It's our command tent."

Casati yanked the cord of the steamer's whistle, and the sudden screeching blast sent Sudi and the others scurrying forward to see what had been spotted. It also must have been heard on shore, because now Jephson saw figures spring into motion out of the dusky shadows under the cliffs and rush down to the water's edge. Casati sounded the whistle again, and at that Jephson heard the faint distant answering crack of rifle shots and saw more excited movement among the figures on the beach. And then he spied the second tent, the surgery tent, pitched on somewhat higher ground, and also the flickering yellow spots of the firelight of several cooking fires.

"Is it Mr. Stanley, my boy? What do you think? Is it him?"

"Yes, of course. Who else could it be?"

"Excellent. You see, Gaetano. What did I tell you? Take us in, my friend. Take us in."

"I can't take us in much closer than this. That is all shoal water there behind the island. We'll run aground."

"Well, take us in as close as you can and we'll go ashore in Mr. Jephson's boat."

"Sudi." Jephson popped back out on to the bridge and called down to the lower deck. "Bring the *Lady Dorothy* alongside. We're going ashore in her."

Casati remained aboard with the crew to look after the boat, while Jephson and Emin scrambled down a rope ladder into the *Lady Dorothy*. With Sudi at the tiller, the askaris along the gunwales, and the oarsmen pulling with enthusiasm, they made for the mainland's gravel-strewn beach, where the men of the advance column had gathered. Seeing the *Khedive*, seeing the *Lady Dorothy* returning with another white man, they obviously realized that Emin Pasha had been found, and they shouted and cheered and fired their rifles in the air in excited triumph.

Peering at them through his field glasses, Jephson could make out their happy faces, recognize many of them: Uledi, Murabo, some of the other headmen, the askari corporal in charge of the Maxim gun crew, the big bald Hoffman on his crutches towering above them all. But he didn't see Stanley or Nelson or Parke. The camp itself, about a quarter of a mile to the south of the village of Nsabe and a couple hundred yards inland, was pitched on a gently sloping grassy knoll dotted with mimosa bushes. The command tent was at the lower end, the surgery tent above. Between them, Jephson could see the caravan's loads stacked rather haphazardly, the Maxim gun standing barrel down and unattended, the four surviving pack mules grazing contentedly on the lush grass. There didn't seem to be a zareba around the site or any other sort of fortification. Apparently there was no need; the tribesmen of the lake evidently were as peaceable as they looked. Indeed, many of them had come over from Nsabe to watch the *Lady Dorothy*'s approach, and a number of their goats had strayed into the camp to graze among the pack mules. As the steel boat neared the shore, Jephson kept sweeping the campsite with his binoculars, wondering where the devil Stanley had got to. And then he saw him.

He stepped out of the command tent. He must have ducked in there on catching sight of the *Khedive* to change out of his usual khaki field kit, for he was wearing the blue officer's jacket with gold frogging and braid and the spiked topee he always donned for special occasions. And that too apparently accounted for Nelson's and Parke's absence, for they now emerged from the surgery tent changed into what was the best of their clothes, and they hurried after Stanley down to the water's edge.

They made a shocking sight.

Jephson had forgotten. In his days of pleasant idleness at Wadelai, in his caftan and slippers, in the good eating and sleeping and rambling strolls with Emin and Faridah, and now in his new uniform and boots, he had forgotten what they all looked like, what he himself had looked like. He didn't dare turn to Emin to check his reaction. He could only hope that because of his weak eyes and the fast falling dusk Emin didn't see or didn't see quite so clearly what he saw: the ridiculous, pathetic parody of formal dress of Stanley's stained, mildewed, tarnished, and torn uniform; Nelson's toothless mouth and sunken cheeks and befuddled eyes; Parke's disgusting lice-ridden beard and greasy shoulder-length hair; Hoffman's half-naked hairless crippled hulk; the filthy vagabond state of the *pagazis* and askaris; and most of all the poverty of the camp behind them, with its few battered loads, its few scrawny mules, its patched and sagging tents.

But Emin did see. When Uledi and some of the Wanyamwezis dashed into the lake to pull the boat up on the beach, and Sudi and the oarsmen and askaris leaped over the side and raced ashore to greet their friends and tell their news, and Jephson himself jumped out into the ankle-deep water, Emin remained standing in the prow, squinting incredulously through his spectacles at the sight of this decrepit caravan that had come to save him. But it was only for an instant. His innate courtesy quickly overcame his crushing disappointment, and he too vaulted the boat's gunwales and, with both hands extended in front of him in that characteristic gesture of his, went splashing ashore toward Stanley.

"Bula Matari, I owe you a thousand thanks. I do not have the words to express the thanks I owe you for what you have done for me."

"Emin Pasha?" Stanley allowed his hands to be grasped and stared in astonishment at the wiry, clerkish, utterly unlikely little man in the fez. "You are Emin Pasha, sir?"

"Yes, I am Dr. Emin. And my thanks—"

"No, no. Don't mention thanks, Pasha. There's no need for it. It is I who have reason to be thankful, for finding you alive and well, for having reached you in time." Stanley glanced at Jephson, taking in the youth's clean new uniform, his well-made new boots, then let his narrowed eyes run up and down Emin's meticulously tailored white cotton drill civilian suit, his high, stiff collar, his floppy bow tie. There was something slightly disapproving in this perusal, something vaguely annoyed. "I take it I *have* reached you in time. From what I see, I think I can presume you still hold Equatoria."

"Yes, thank God, we still hold Equatoria, Bula Matari. With the exception of some stations to the north and west, we still hold the province, I am happy to say."

"That's splendid news. That certainly is splendid news. I congratulate you, Pasha. You have done a remarkable job." Stanley disengaged his hands from Emin's grasp. "Perhaps, in fact, there was no need for me to come to your relief at all."

"Please? You make a joke?"

"No, I don't make a joke."

"But then I don't understand why you say that?"

"Well, you must admit, it does look rather as if—"

"Oh, no. *Mein Gott*, no. We have been waiting for you on tenterhooks, Bula Matari. We have been counting on you. We have been praying for you. We are in desperate need of your relief. We could not hold out very much longer without it."

"It's pretty much what you always said might happen, Mr. Stanley."

"Eh? What is?" Stanley turned to Jephson.

"The dervishes are on the march, sir. An army of some several thousands is making its way up the Nile from Khartoum right now. Apparently they'd been content to keep the province cut off and wait for the garrisons to run out of ammunition, but news of the relief expedition set them off again, just as you feared it might. Dr. Emin had it confirmed only yesterday."

"So that's it? I see." Stanley turned back to Emin. "Coming up the Nile, are they?"

"They've got hold of Gordon's steamers and barges," Emin replied. "Evidently, he did not have a chance to scuttle them before Khartoum fell."

"How far have they got?"

"A small party of some sort reached Lado a few days ago. But Lado doesn't matter. I evacuated it some time ago as indefensible. The main body of the army is still pushing its way through the Sudd."

"And how long will it take *them* to reach Lado?"

"That is difficult to say. Weeks. In any case, weeks."

"How many weeks? Five? Ten?"

"Well no, not ten. Five perhaps. Five or six."

"And then?"

"Please?"

"I'm asking you what your position is, Pasha. How long can your garrisons hold out once this dervish army *does* reach Lado?"

"But, Bula Matari, now that you are here with the relief—"

"No, not with the relief. Forget about the relief."

"Forget about the relief?"

"What I want to know is how well armed your garrisons are, Pasha. How long do you reckon they can hold out against the dervishes with what they have in hand right now?"

"Right now?"

"Yes, right now. Do they have enough guns and powder and cartridges to put up a decent fight for . . . what? For a few weeks anyhow?"

Emin didn't reply. For a long moment he simply stared at Stanley blankly. Then slowly, very slowly, he began nodding his head. "I begin to understand. Yes, now I begin to understand." He looked away from Stanley to Nelson, then to Parke and Hoffman and Uledi, then to each of the askaris and *pagazis* who in their tattered garments had gathered around him like a band of gypsies. He seemed to count them and only now allow himself to fully recognize the fewness of their numbers. Then he looked beyond them to their small camp pitched in the shadows of the cliffs, the two tents, the four mules, the haphazardly stacked boxes and bales, the Maxim gun. He looked particularly at the Maxim gun, its armor-plate shield dully reflecting the flames of the cooking fires. Then he looked back at Stanley. "Yes, I begin to understand, Bula Matari. I begin to understand. You have not brought the relief."

"No. This is only the advance column. Didn't Mr. Jephson explain that to you? Arthur?"

"No, no. Don't blame the boy. It was my own foolishness. I jumped to a hasty conclusion."

"The relief is with my rear column, Pasha. A thousand men bringing hundreds of tons of ammunition and weapons—powder, percussion caps, cartridges, Remingtons, Winchesters. Our job was to cut the trail for them through the Ituri."

"Yes, I understand. But now you must allow me to put the same question to you that you just put to me, Mr. Stanley. How long will it take them to get here?"

"Well, they set off from Yambuya about six weeks after us. There were some problems with the steamers bringing the supplies up the Congo from Leopoldville that delayed them. And then too some six hundred porters had to be hired and assembled in Yambuya for the overland trek through the forest. But even so, they were meant to get away no more than six weeks after we did."

Stanley looked around to the west, where the sun was setting behind the cliffs, where the grasslands of the Watusi stretched away to the Ituri, where Barttelot and Troup and the others must someday appear. "I thought originally they'd be able to make better time than we did, what with our trail to follow, with the way marked out for them, and that they would come pretty close to catching us up by the time we reached the lake. And for all we know that may yet be the case. Yes, that may very well yet be the case." He turned back to Emin. "But the Ituri is a filthy place, Pasha, far filthier than I had ever imagined. We had an awful time of it there, a bloody awful time of it, and it is only sensible to suppose that the rear column will too. They may not be able to do as well as I had originally hoped. It is altogether possible that they may not be able to catch us up at all. In fact, I am afraid they may very well fall even farther behind. So it could be as much as six or seven, perhaps even eight weeks before they get here. That's why I ask you how long you reckon your garrisons can hold out once the dervishes reach Lado. If, as you say, it will take them five or six weeks to clear the Sudd, the question is, Can you hold them off another two or three weeks after that until the rear column gets here with the relief?"

"Well," Emin replied quietly, "what choice is there, Mr. Stanley? We will just have to, won't we? We will just have to." He looked away and said, "Will you introduce me to your men, Mr. Stanley?"

"What? Oh, yes, of course. You've already met Mr. Jephson and Sudi. This is Captain Robert Nelson of Methuen's Horse. And Surgeon Thomas Parke of the Army Medical Department. And Mr. Will Hoffman, lately of the Congo Free State gendarmerie. And Uledi of Zanzibar, paramount chief of our *pagazis* and *kirangozi* of the caravan."

Stanley moved down the line, naming the other chiefs and headmen and the corporals of the askari guard, and Emin went to each and, in his characteristic way, took each by both hands and said a few gracious words of thanks either in Swahili or English. In Hoffman's case, he also inquired about his injured foot and kneeled down to examine it; but Hoffman jerked it away and hopped back on his crutches with ill humor. Emin looked up at him in surprise.

"Let us go to my tent, Pasha," Stanley said. "We have much to talk over and plans to make and the evening grows chill."

Emin stood up. "I have some provisions aboard the *Khedive* for your men, Bula Matari. Mr. Jephson was good enough to indicate what might be most useful. Cloth, blankets, soap, tobacco, and so forth."

The irony of this, of the relief expedition being the one to receive relief and not the other way around, no more escaped Stanley here than it had Jephson in Wadelai. Jephson saw that in the sudden tensing of Stanley's jaw muscles, his rather thin-lipped smile. But all he said was "That's very kind of you, Pasha."

"Perhaps you would arrange to have the stuff offloaded before it becomes too much darker."

"Of course. Uledi, Will."

While Uledi and Hoffman rounded up a score of *pagazis* and Sudi and the boatmen made ready to take them back out to the steamer in the steel boat, Emin clasped his hands behind his back and, rather like an absentminded professor, wandered off into the advance column's camp. Stanley fell into step beside him. They did not speak. Doubtless Stanley would have—he must have had myriad questions to ask and details to discuss—but Emin's distracted air deterred him. Jephson, Nelson, and Parke followed a few steps behind.

"Good Lord, what a queer duck he is, Arthur," Parke muttered under his breath. "What is he, a Jew?"

"What makes you ask that?"

"That accent, old boy. I thought he was meant to be a Turkish general. But he's no Turk. Good Lord, no. Mohammed Emin Effendi, my foot. That's a made-up name, Arthur. He's a Jew for certain. Or maybe a German. Am I right?"

"I don't know."

"What do you think, Robbie?"

Nelson shrugged.

"He's a Jew or German, all right," Parke went on. "I'd wager my last quid on it. And he's certainly no general, no sort of general I've ever laid eyes on anyway. A runty little chap like that. Looks more like a bookkeeper to me."

"He's a doctor, Tommy."

"A doctor? No joking? Christ. I wonder how on earth he ever got way the hell out here. And why."

Emin stopped at the Maxim gun. Stanley, thinking they were going to the command tent, had preceded him in there and so was obliged to step back out and wait for him. He stood at the tent fly with his hands on his hips and watched as Emin contemplated the weapon.

"This must be a pretty devastating piece of machinery," Emin said after a few moments.

"It is, Pasha. It fires three hundred and thirty rounds per minute."

Emin tilted his head appreciatively at this information and ran his hand down the barrel. "It would be a great help to us. Along with the two mountain guns we have at Rejaf . . ." He looked at Stanley. "Rejaf is our most northerly station now. It is there that I expect the dervishes to come at us from Lado. A weapon like this would be a great help in holding them off."

"You're welcome to it, Pasha. You're welcome to whatever we've got." Stanley looked around the camp. "There's little enough, but you're certainly welcome to whatever there is."

"Thank you."

For a few moments, in the deep blue shadows of the gathering dusk, a chill breeze blowing off the lake, these two very different men looked at each other; and for those few moments, it seemed to Jephson, there was a sympathy and understanding between them. Then Emin turned away and looked across the lake.

"This is very beautiful country," he said. "Don't you think so, Mr. Stanley?"

"Yes," Stanley replied and looked where Emin looked. A flight of cranes, lighted by the last rays of the dying sun, could be seen making for the cliffs of the opposite shore.

"You have been here before."

"Well no, not exactly here. But there, on the other side, in the Waganda and Wanyoro country."

"As, yes, that is also very beautiful. I have been there too. When I first came to Equatoria, Gordon Pasha sent me to the court of Mutesa to try and make peace with the Waganda. You knew him, didn't you? Mutesa, I mean."

"Yes, I knew him. And Gordon as well."

"Yes, of course."

Again there was a silence between them, each doubtless caught up for a moment in his own memories.

Then Emin said, "Yes, it is beautiful country, very beautiful. I didn't think there could be such beautiful country. I was a long time finding it. I came a long way to find it."

"From where did you come?"

"Oh, from the north. From far to the north. From all those busy civilizations in the north—Turkey, Europe, Arabia. You know."

Stanley nodded.

"Yes, I came a long way to find it," Emin said again. "I do not want to be driven away from it now."

· FOUR ·

THEY STARTED for Wadelai the following day—Emin and Stanley, Jephson and Nelson, the Maxim gun and crew, twenty additional askaris and thirty of the advance column's *pagazis.* The rest of the column, in Parke and Hoffman's charge, were staying at Nsabe on the Albert shore to await the arrival of the rear column. The plan was for the *Khedive* to return to Nsabe in six weeks' time and fetch the reunited expedition up to Wadelai.

Hoffman immediately put the men remaining in Nsabe to work building something of a permanent base camp there, while those who had been selected to go on, and as much of the weapons and ammunition as Stanley judged could be spared to reinforce Emin's garrisons without leaving the men at Nsabe defenseless, were loaded into the *Lady Dorothy* and ferried out to the *Khedive.* Jephson oversaw this operation (with Parke doing nothing in the way of help, merely grousing about being left behind). It took five trips; and by the time Jephson himself went out to the steamer on the final trip with the Maxim and gun crew, it was nearly noon of another bright, cloudless day. As he climbed aboard the vessel, he saw Casati on the bridge carrying on in much the same agitated fashion as he had when Jephson had first seen him on the jetty at Wadelai, shouting at Emin in Italian, waving his straw hat around, stomping to and fro. Stanley, also on the bridge, watched him with a steely expression. Jephson could easily enough guess what it was all about. He vaulted the deck rail and Nelson came over with a dozen *pagazis* to help the gun crew hoist the Maxim aboard.

"Is that the last of it, Arthur?" Stanley called down from the bridge.

"Yes, sir."

"Right then, we can weigh anchor now, Captain Casati, and be on our way."

"Be on our way?" Casati whirled on Stanley. "Be on our way

where, Signor Stanley? Be on our way why, Signor Stanley? Tell me that, Signor Stanley. Tell me why we should be on our way anywhere. Tell me what you imagine—"

"Gaetano!" Emin grabbed Casati's arm.

"No, no." Casati yanked the arm free. "Jesus Maria, no. This is ridiculous. This is ludicrous. This is a joke. This is not relief." He waved his panama violently at the lower deck where the column's few boxes of weapons and ammunition were stacked, where the Maxim had been hauled aboard, where the *pagazis* and askaris stood looking up at him in bewilderment. "You call this relief? This is not relief. This is spit."

"Now just stop this, Gaetano. I tell you, in six weeks Bula Matari's rear column will be here."

"In six weeks? In six weeks we will be dead, Pasha. In six weeks all our throats will have been cut by the dervishes. In six weeks—"

"Oh, Christ." Stanley turned away in disgust and came down the iron ladder from the bridge, leaving Emin and Casati disputing like fishwives. He walked the full length of the lower deck to the forward rail and looked out to the lakeshore. Sudi and the oarsmen were on their way back there. The *Lady Dorothy* was remaining with the men at Nsabe. When she beached, Stanley turned around and looked up at the bridge. Emin and Casati were still at it. He pulled a sour face and headed back there.

"Let's get this stuff down in the hold," he said to Jephson and Nelson in passing, indicating the crates and boxes that cluttered the deck, then scrambled up the ladder to the bridge. He broke into Emin and Casati's argument, with sharp impatience. "Now look here, Pasha, are we getting under way or aren't we?"

"Yes, yes, of course. In a moment."

"No, not in a moment, Pasha. If we're getting under way, we're getting under way now."

"Please, Bula Matari, you must understand. This has all come as a great disappointment for Captain Casati."

"I'm certain it has. But we can discuss it just as well while we are under way. So if you please, Pasha, let's not waste any more time."

"Gaetano, really, Bula Matari is right. We must get under way. We are wasting precious time. We will talk about it on the way to Wadelai. I will explain it all to you on the way. You will see it is not as bad as you think."

"Not as bad as I think? Not as bad as I think? What kind of fool do you take me for? How could it be any worse? We are finished. Equatoria is finished. These few lousy guns . . . Jesus Maria, do you think your soldiers will stay at their posts when they see this? Do you think they love you so much? No, they will mutiny. They will run away. They will surrender to the dervishes. And who can blame them?"

"All right. Now that's enough. That's more than enough. I don't want to listen to any more of this. If Captain Casati is unwilling or unable to make steam and weigh anchor, I'll be glad to do it for him." Stanley started for the wheelhouse.

"Just a moment, signor. You stay out of there. I am in command of this vessel. Do you hear me? You have no business in there."

"No, you hear me, Casati. I made a long, hard journey to get here. And I didn't make it, I can tell you, to listen to the likes of you weep and whine. So you either get into that wheelhouse and get this tub under way or I am going to do it for you."

"Pasha!"

"Mr. Stanley, please."

"Make up your mind, Pasha."

"Oh, for the love of God, Gaetano, do what he says. Just do whatever he says."

Sailing with the current and thus making better time than on the voyage out, the *Khedive* entered the lake's outlet well before sunset that evening and reached Wadelai by midmorning of the following day.

The riverfront was mobbed. While still a mile upstream they could see the crowds, like an army of ants, streaming down the hillside from the fort, jamming under the eucalyptus trees that lined the quay, spilling out of the station's alleyways and bazaars, their numbers swollen by the refugees who had been fleeing south ever since hearing the news that Lado had fallen. A cordon of the garrison's troops kept them from swarming out onto the jetty. It looked precarious though, as if at any moment the cordon must give way under the pressure of their unruly surgings, their anxious craning for a look at the steamer, for a first glimpse of the expedition that was coming to save them. But for the moment the cordon held. In fact there was no one at all on the jetty. The delegation of officers and officials that Jephson had expected to meet them, the color guard, the brass band to play them ashore, the squad of riflemen to fire a welcoming salute—apparently they had not yet had a chance to assemble.

Casati sounded the steamer's whistle and swung the wheel hard to the starboard. A large island stood about a half-mile out in the Nile here, almost directly opposite the station; and, perhaps because of a vagary in the current or submerged snags, Casati chose to sail around its far side and approach Wadelai from downriver. Thus, for the next several minutes, the station was out of sight, screened by the island's trees; and then when it came into view again as they rounded the island's northern tip and turned back toward it, they saw the big burly figure of Shukri Aga, a hand clutching his fez, his saber banging against his leg, running out onto the jetty.

Several of the garrison's officers and station officials followed him. A few others tried to slip through the cordon after them but were stopped. A row broke out. There was an angry roar, some scuffling. Then two soldiers were let through. They were dragging someone between them. The fellow, whoever he was, seemed ill or hurt. He kept stumbling, falling to his knees, and getting yanked back on his feet. Halfway down the jetty, Shukri Aga paused to wave them on urgently, then hurried to where the *Khedive* was drawing alongside the jetty, her crew jumping out, tossing lines, making her fast, lowering the gangway. In a minute the jetty was in a state of almost as much noisy milling confusion as the quay.

Emin was the first to disembark. He went down the gangway quickly, his head thrust forward on his narrow shoulders, squinting through the thick lenses of his spectacles, obviously puzzled by all the disorder. By the time Stanley, Jephson, Nelson, and, trailing sulkily behind, Casati got down on the jetty (the askaris and *pagazis* remained aboard, clustered along the deck rail watching the commotion; there was no sense adding to it by having them disembark as well), the two soldiers had dragged up the man they had between them; and Emin, hemmed around by Shukri Aga and the others, was talking to him in Arabic. Or trying to talk to him. The fellow had slumped to his knees again, his chin sunk on his chest, his eyes closed. Shukri Aga gave an order and the two soldiers jerked him roughly to his feet. He was a prisoner. Jephson, coming closer, saw that his legs were in irons, his wrists manacled; although he managed to keep to his feet, his head remained hanging. He was a weird-looking chap, a Nubian of some sort, possibly a Dongolawi from the deserts north of Khartoum, dark-skinned, very nearly black but with sharp saturnine features and the most extraordinary head of frizzy hair done up in a profusion of spiky braids that stood a good foot or two away from his head like a maniac's crown. There was also some kind of band around his head, a strip of split bamboo that might have been an adornment except that it seemed rather too tightly bound. But what was most striking about him was his jubbah. The white ankle-length belted gown was speckled with scores of small rag patches, some black, some green, some red. Emin put a hand under his chin and raised his head. His eyes opened—huge black pools of ferocious defiance.

"What have you done to him?" Emin asked.

Shukri Aga shrugged and glanced at the others, as if hoping one of them would answer for him. But before anyone could answer, Casati barged onto the scene.

"A dervish! Jesus Maria, Pasha, a peacock dervish."

"We know who he is, Gaetano."

"The Mahdi's elite, the worst of the lot, the bloodiest cutthroats of the lot." Casati was again in a state. He made for the man. "Do you see these? Do you know what they signify?" He grabbed at one of the colored patches on the dervish's jubbah and ripped it off. "They sew them on as marks of virtuous poverty. Virtuous poverty! Jesus Maria." He brandished the patch in Emin's face. "They are fanatics, Pasha, the worst kind of crazed fanatics. They are the ones who took off Gordon's head."

"We know that, Gaetano. In God's name, don't you think we know that? So just stay away from him."

"But what is he doing here? Where did he come from? How was he captured?"

But he hadn't been captured. He had come into Wadelai of his own accord. At first light three days before, Shukri Aga explained, the day after the *Khedive* had set off to fetch Stanley and his men, he had been discovered at the gate of the fort in his bizarrely patched jubbah, a multicolored shawl wrapped as a turban around his wild hair, a sword slung from his belt, carrying three spears. No one had seen him approach; no one could say from which direction he had come; he simply was there, leaning on his spears, as if he had materialized out of the damp early morning mists rising off the river. The sentries on the sandbagged mountain gun emplacement at the fort's gate—staring down at him in shocked disbelief, thinking him a trick of the dawn light or their fevered imaginations, expecting him to disappear as mysteriously as he had appeared—had taken several minutes to realize who he was. And then they had seized him. In a sudden frenzy, maddened as much by the fright he caused as the hatred he inspired, they had flung themselves upon him, raising the alarm, awakening the fort, bringing out the entire garrison on the run.

He didn't resist. Perhaps that was what was most unnerving, what more than anything else sent a shiver of terror throughout the station when they heard of it, that he didn't resist, that he made no effort to defend himself or harm his attackers or flee. As passively as he had presented himself at the fort, so unresistingly had he allowed himself to be taken and disarmed. By the time Shukri Aga got to him, he was on the ground, his turban torn from his head, his spears broken, and his sword in the hands of one of the sentries, its curved razor-sharp blade laid across his throat.

Shukri Aga at first refused to believe he had come alone—it made no sense—and immediately sent out patrols to locate the others. But there were no others. All day they waited, the people of the station crowding up into the fort for protection against the attack they were sure the dervish's arrival heralded, the gunners and riflemen on the breastworks scanning the horizon for the telltale dust clouds of the host of horsemen they were sure he had preceded, while the patrols gingerly probed northward along the river and westward into the surrounding hills for a glimpse of the army they were sure would spell their doom. But there was no army; there was no one. At sunset the patrols returned, grimy with sweat, shaken by the mystery. By then the dervish had been put in irons and chained to a stake in the center of the fort's parade ground. The entire population of Wadelai gathered around him aghast, awestruck, in fear. Who was he? A spy? A messenger? A deserter from the Mahdi's army?

He would not say.

"And so you tortured him." Emin indicated the thin strip of split bamboo bound tightly around the dervish's head.

"What was there to do, Pasha?" Shukri Aga replied. "We had to learn why he had come. What he wanted."

"And? Did you?"

Shukri Aga shook his head. "No, he does not speak. He does not say a word. He comes here and puts himself in our hands and does not say a word. See for yourself." And as if in a sudden rage, Shukri Aga grabbed a handful of the dervish's hair. "You son of a whore. You pig-eating dog. Speak. Speak now. This is the mudir, Pasha of Equatoria. Tell him why you have come. Tell him what you want here."

But it wasn't the dervish's hair he grabbed, Jephson realized. It was something hidden in the hair, covered by the wild, greasy locks: a piece of wood. It was slipped through the band of split bamboo around the dervish's head, and Shukri Aga was twisting it as he hurled the foulest possible oaths at him. By twisting it, he was tightening the strip of bamboo, tightening it so that it cut into the flesh of the poor devil's forehead, tightening it so that it seemed it would crush his skull. The pain must have been excruciating. The dervish's eyes shut, then popped open. The pupils rolled up in them and vanished, leaving only the agonized bulging whites, the thin strip of bamboo now actually puncturing the dark sweating flesh, slicing into it so that trickles of blood began to run down his face. But for all that, the man did not speak, did not make a sound.

"Enough."

"Yes, enough." Shukri Aga released the piece of wood, and the dervish again slumped to his knees. His head dropped on his chest, and only the hold of the two soldiers on either side of him prevented him from falling forward on his blood-streaked face. "It does no good in any case. He will not speak. No matter what is done to him, he will not say a word. You would think his tongue has been cut from his head."

"Perhaps it has."

It was Stanley who said this. They all turned to him in astonishment and watched with morbid fascination as he stepped forward and took hold of the dervish's chin and raised his head. The poor devil, no doubt imagining that some further torture was in store, tried to twist his face away. But Stanley's grip was strong, and he knew just where to exert pressure to force open the man's mouth. He then stuck his other hand into the involuntarily gaping, drooling cavity.

And now at last the dervish did make a sound, a grotesque retching sound.

There was no tongue.

Jephson immediately turned away with a rush of nausea. When he looked back, Stanley had extracted his hand and was wiping the spittle off on his trouser leg. Shukri Aga and the others had drawn away from the dervish in stunned horror, and the two soldiers had let go of him as if he were some kind of contaminated creature, allowing him to collapse in a silent heap on the rough splintered boards of the jetty.

Casati broke the silence. "They send us a man without a

tongue, a messenger who can not deliver a message, a spy who does not bother to hide himself, a defector who makes no plea for sanctuary. Jesus Maria, don't you see, Pasha? It is a warning, an omen."

"Shut up, Gaetano. In God's name, what's the matter with you? Do you want to start a panic?" Emin glanced at Shukri Aga and the others. They were drawing still farther away from the dervish, whispering to each other. "Get back on board the steamer, Gaetano, and make ready to cast off. We still have a good eight hours of daylight left for sailing. Go on. Go on." Then he turned to Stanley. "We will go north, Bula Matari. We will go north and see what has happened."

Downriver from Wadelai, northward into the deserts of the Sudan, the Nile narrowed; and numerous islands overgrown with reed and papyrus began appearing in the stream to reduce it even further into a maze of separate twisting, sluggish channels. Now and again, on one bank or the other, it momentarily broadened into a large lagoon where herds of hippo, startled by the steamer's passage, hastily submerged, sending up great jets of spray. But even these patches of relatively open water were choked with tangles of floating vegetation, tangles of lilies and blue hyacinth and snakelike creepers that, floating downriver year after year, century upon century, ultimately piled up to form the monumental tangle of the Sudd. Palmyra palms, ripe with their melonlike fruit, and thickets of ambatch, whose spongy wood the Nile fishermen used to make floats for their nets, dotted the shoreline. The dun-colored foothills of parallel ranges of mountains to the east and west of the river–rocky, sparsely wooded in acacia thorn and wild fig and candelabra cactus–encroached always more closely to the water's edge. This was not yet, strictly speaking, desert; but the farther they steamed northward from Wadelai and the forests and savanna of the Lake Albert region, the more the land on either side of the fertile strip of the river's valley grew ever more arid, ever more barren. A dry pungent smell of dust hung in the baking breezeless air, while high overhead kites and turkey buzzards wheeled and soared, ominous black specks against a sky bleached bone-white by the blaze of the sun.

Jephson, swatting away the flies and mosquitoes that rose up in clouds from the river's swampy islands, lounged in the hot shade of the striped-canvas canopy that covered the steamer's lower deck. Nelson and the *pagazis* and askaris were with him. Casati was in the wheelhouse. Emin and Stanley were on the bridge. Suddenly

Stanley raised his field glasses to study something on the left bank. Immediately Jephson also raised his glasses and looked where Stanley looked.

"What is it?" Nelson asked.

Jephson shrugged. All he could see were giraffes feeding on the upper branches of ambatch trees. There had been no sign of people on the barren shore since leaving Wadelai. He handed the glasses to Nelson and looked back up at Stanley. Stanley had gone to the other side of the bridge and was now scanning the right bank. Jephson looked in that direction; so did Nelson and the *pagazis* and askaris. Except for the throb of the steamer's engine and the hard slap and thrash of her paddle wheels, there was no sound aboard the vessel. A tense silence gripped the men; a sense of unease, of wariness, of something unknown and dangerous in the offing had been mounting steadily among them since leaving Wadelai.

They reached Duffile, the next station north of Wadelai and the farthest north the *Khedive* could go, for here began with Fola Falls a series of cataracts that made the Nile unnavigable for more than one hundred miles northward to Lado, on the evening of the second day after their departure from Wadelai. Duffile was the oldest of the river stations (Samuel Baker had built it at the site of the Bari village where he had reassembled the *Khedive* after hauling her in pieces up over the rapids from Lado fifteen years before), and in many respects it was still the best. It was the most carefully designed, smaller than Wadelai, more compact, more strictly a fortification than a trading depot, laid out on a neat rectangular plan directly at the water's edge. Its three inland sides (the Nile formed its fourth) were enclosed by earthwork battlements twelve feet high and twelve feet thick; and these in turn were enclosed by a ditch twelve feet deep and twelve feet wide. At each of its two inland corners, sandbagged mountain guns commanded the southwestern and northwestern approaches; and in each of the walls of its battlements, south, west, and north, a large postern gate gave out to fields of Indian corn and millet, ground nuts and *m'tama* that stretched across the surrounding plain to the foothills of the arid, rocky western mountains.

The buildings within, divided into three compounds and lining a gridwork of broom-swept streets, were of brick, whitewashed with lime and with corrugated iron roofs and regular doors and windows, a genuine novelty in this part of the world. There was also a mosque, a handsome two-story structure decorated with raffia matting and the shells of ostrich eggs, its minaret towering over the station's central bazaar, where what looked very much like a bandstand—a raised platform covered by a peaked thatch roof, but which in fact was the station's *barazan*—stood in the shade of three giant gnarled fig trees. From it, the station's main street, overarched by Palmyra palms and flowering jasmine trees, ran down to the boat sheds, engineering shops, warehouses, and wharves of the waterfront. And there in the open space of the landing stage circumscribed by these buildings and lighted by lanterns hanging from poles, the station's garrison was paraded, and what must have been its entire civilian population was gathered.

They were unnaturally quiet. Unlike the unruly mobs on the quay at Wadelai, these people awaited the docking of the *Khedive* with a calm fatalism that in the chill blue shadows of the approaching dusk struck Jephson as faintly sinister. The others on board felt it as well. Stanley and Emin came down from the bridge and, with Jephson, Nelson, the *pagazis*, and askaris, took up a wordless watch at the lower deck's portside rail as Casati eased the steamer against the station's pier. The screak of her hull plates along the pilings sounded uncommonly loud in the peculiar silence. And when the gangway was lowered, there was a moment of hesitation, of wary scrutiny of the oddly quiet crowd on the wharf, before they disembarked.

The station commander awaited them in front of the first rank of the dress parade of his troops.

"Hawashi Effendi," Emin said, going forward.

"Pasha." He was an Egyptian, tall and skinny except for a hard tub of a belly, his mahogany skin pitted with pockmarks, a pirate's mustache curling down to join a black sharply pointed goatee. He salaamed, touching hand to chest, lips, and forehead, and mumbled a few words of greeting in Arabic. When he straightened up, Jephson saw that he was wall-eyed, making it difficult to tell at what he was looking. He didn't seem to be looking at Emin.

"I have the honor to present Mr. Henry Morton Stanley, the great Bula Matari of whom we have heard so much and for whom we have waited so long."

Again the fellow sketched a bow and muttered an Arabic greeting. It was a mechanical formality. From behind him, several officers of the Duffile garrison—each like their commander dressed in a dark red tunic, white trousers, and green tarboosh, sabers at their sides—moved up from the parade formation of their troops to stand on either side of him. The civilians of the station—the usual collection of officials, civil servants, clerks, storekeepers, merchants, craftsmen, soldiers' wives, and children—also came closer out of the shadows of the warehouses and boat sheds and trees into the yellow glow of the lanterns. Except for the shuffle of their feet and the rustle of their robes, they maintained their silence. Jephson fancied he could hear the muted sound of their breathing.

"And Mr. Arthur Jephson and Captain Robert Nelson, two officers of the advance column of his expedition, the expedition that he has been leading, at great peril and much hardship, to our relief."

Again the perfunctory bow, the murmured Arabic salutation, the unfocused, wandering gaze of those cocked eyes, looking for something past Emin's head. Jephson glanced around. Casati, having had the *Khedive* made fast to the wharf, was coming down the gangway. But it wasn't at him that the Egyptian was looking. It was at the *pagazis* and askaris. They were still on board, staring over the rail into the quiet gloom of the landing stage. No one had given them the order to disembark; and although this was the end of river navigation and from here on northward they would have to proceed overland, they obviously weren't in any hurry to do so.

"The first installment of that relief, I am happy to tell you, has at last reached us. We have it here, aboard the *Khedive* and shall take it to Rejaf to shore up the defenses there. In six weeks' time, in time enough before the dervish clears the Sudd, Allah be merciful, Bula Matari's rear column, a column of a thousand men, bringing hundreds of tons of weapons and ammunition . . ."

Emin spoke quickly, in something of a nervous rush, obviously affected by the unresponsiveness of his audience. His voice was high pitched but strong enough to be heard not only by Hawashi Effendi and his officers but also by the ranks of soldiers and the civilians around them as he explained the situation in detail: the arrival of the advance column at Nsabe, its task of blazing a trail through the Ituri, the probable location of the rear column following this trail, the certainty that the supplies it brought would be more than sufficient to turn back the dervish hordes. He spoke quickly in order to overcome all doubts and put heart and steel into these people for the one last desperate fight they would have to make until relief at last arrived. Jephson only half listened to him, more concerned with the effect of his words than with the words themselves (much of it was in Arabic anyway), scrutinizing the blank faces in front of him, trying to fathom what was going on behind the mask of their inexpressive silence.

And then all of a sudden there was a shout. Two words, in Arabic, not loud, but in the unnatural quiet sounding very loud, harsh, rude. Emin immediately stopped speaking and turned sharply in the direction they had come from. It wasn't clear who had shouted them, someone over to the left, perhaps in a back rank of the soldiers or farther over, among the civilians clustered on the steps of one of the long brick warehouses. But now it was quiet again. Emin looked at Hawashi Effendi. The Egyptian hadn't reacted. Nor had any of his officers. It was as if they hadn't heard or, having heard, weren't surprised. Emin waited a moment. His hands were clasped behind his back and Jephson saw them whiten as he clasped them harder. Then he resumed speaking.

And it happened again. The same two Arabic words, spat out insolently. This time Jephson thought he spotted who it was. In any case he saw soldiers in the front ranks turn around, look back, break the symmetry of their formation, begin whispering to each other. And this time Hawashi Effendi couldn't help but acknowledge it, and he looked around as well.

"What was that, Robbie?" Jephson asked in an undertone. "What did the chap say?"

But whatever Nelson replied was drowned out by yet another shout, a longer one this time, not only of those two words but including them among a torrent of others, a sudden angry speech. And the man making it did not try to conceal himself. He stepped out of the ranks, a rough-looking corporal or sergeant as best as Jephson could make out by the flashes on his sleeve, brandishing his rifle, pumping it in the air to punctuate his words, angry, insulting words whatever they might actually mean, mutinous words; and the restless movement among the soldiers, the turning of heads, the breaking of formation, the agitated whispering swiftly spread, grew to a menacing rumble.

"Seize that man. Seize him and put him in irons."

Emin's shrill command sliced through the mounting noise and momentarily silenced it. But when neither the Egyptian nor any of his officers made a move to obey their pasha, it renewed with increased force, with restless, explosive energy.

"Do you hear what I say, Hawashi Effendi? I want that man arrested at once. He speaks lies and treason."

And again there was an instant of quiet, of bated breaths.

And then Hawashi Effendi replied, "No, Pasha. He speaks the truth. It is you who speak lies."

Emin went white.

"These things that you tell us, they are nothing but lies. They are nothing but false promises. We have heard them many times before. How many times have we heard of a relief expedition on the way to save us? Too many times. But we see no relief expedition. We *still* see no relief expedition. The dervish is now at our gates, and we see only these few ragged men." He pointed to the askaris and *pagazis* aboard the *Khedive*. "They cannot save us."

"But I tell you, this is but a portion of the advance column. The relief column–"

"Lies."

"Be silent!" Emin was trembling with rage. "Be silent, I say. I am your mudir, and you will listen to me. In the forests of the Ituri–"

"No, I will not listen to you. I will not listen to any more of your lies. I will speak the truth. We have been abandoned as the people of Khartoum were abandoned. No one comes to save us as no one came to save the people of Dafur or the people of Bahr al-Ghazal. We must save ourselves. We must either submit to the will of the Mahdi or we must flee."

"This is treason, Hawashi Effendi. This is treason and mutiny."

"Call it what you wish, Pasha, but it is the only way we can avoid the fate of Khartoum and Dafur and Bahr al-Ghazal. When the dervish comes, we must either surrender or flee."

And at that there was an uproar, a terrible outcry, a deafening shout of jubilant defiance.

"Captain Nelson, get the Maxim down here," Stanley shouted.

"Sir?"

"Damnit, man, get it down here now. Go with him, Arthur."

"Come on, Robbie." Jephson started back up the gangway on the run, brushing past Casati.

"Oh, Jesus Maria." The Italian stopped dead in his tracks.

Jephson glanced back and saw an incredible scene: Emin had lunged at Hawashi Effendi and seized him by the throat. Despite his small size, his advanced age, his usually mild manner, he was showing himself to be an astonishing tough and tenacious scrapper. Stanley had immediately moved to restrain him, but was having a hard time pulling him off. The Egyptian went down on a knee screaming obscenities, clawing at Emin's hands. Emin hung on like a maddened ferret. The noise all around had exploded into pandemonium.

Jephson dashed onto the *Khedive*'s deck, adding his voice to the racket, barking orders at the Maxim gun crew, pushing and shoving the askaris this way and that, getting them to unlimber the weapon and manhandle it down the gangway. By the time they had it down on the wharf, Stanley had managed to separate Emin and the Egyptian, but the situation was still one of threatening disorder. The noise was still deafening, and there was still the very real danger that one of the rifles in the hands of the wrought-up soldiers would be fired, even if only accidentally, and set off a massacre. The Egyptian was still on the ground, his officers helping him to his feet. Emin was a few steps away, shoved there by Stanley, bareheaded, his spectacles half off his face, his face white with rage. Stanley was between them, one arm extended toward Emin, holding him off while he shouted at Hawashi Effendi in a garble of Swahili, Arabic, and English.

"Get those men back on parade. Order them to fall in. What are they? Savages or soldiers? Fall them in, goddamnit. Fall them in."

The Egyptian, however, ignored him. Scrambling to his feet, pulling free of the helping hands of his officers, he made for Emin. Stanley immediately blocked his way. Hawashi tried to push past him, but Stanley grabbed his arm and jerked him back. At the same moment he caught sight of the Maxim being trundled off the gangway.

"Set that gun up, Captain. Run a belt into the magazine."

Nelson was holding Emin's fez. He had picked it up when it came sailing off during the scuffle and now didn't know what to do with it.

"For Christ sake, get over here, Robbie," Jephson shouted at him.

Nelson hesitated. Then, idiotically, he handed the fez to Emin before hurrying over to the automatic gun.

This diverted Hawashi Effendi's attention. Clearly, he had never seen a weapon like this before and watched in dumbstruck fascination as the gun crew swung it on the crowd and scrambled into firing position.

"Do you want to see how it works?" Stanley still had hold of the Egyptian's arm. "Do you want to see how it kills? Or are you going to order your men back into formation?"

These words, shouted full in his face, awakened the Egyptian from his momentary reverie; and with a sudden furious wrench, he broke Stanley's grip. Stanley immediately grabbed for him again but missed. There was too much of a wild melee now, too many soldiers crushing in, circling around, pointing loaded rifles.

"Fire in the air, Captain. Give 'em a burst in the air."

"In the air, for God's sake!" Jephson leaped forward and slapped up the gun barrel in the nick of time.

And everyone ducked. The garrison officers and the soldiers and civilians flung themselves to the ground. Women and children began screaming as the sudden thunderous rattle of hundreds of bullets ripped through the dusk, as the gun barrel spat jagged white flames into the gloom.

"*Tena*," Stanley commanded. "*Na tena*." Three murderous bursts in no more than three minutes, a thousand rounds expended. Then he raised his hand and the firing ceased and there was silence again, a profound silence. "Have you seen enough, effendi?" Stanley asked, his voice harsh in the silence. "Have you seen enough?"

Hawashi Effendi looked up at Stanley, looked at the Maxim, looked around to assess what damage had been done by this monstrous machine. The others also looked up, raised their heads, got to their feet, and looked at one another to see who had lived and who had died in those unimaginable killing volleys.

"Right, then. Fall these soldiers in. Re-form the parade."

For a moment Hawashi Effendi hesitated and glared at Stanley with his odd cocked eyes, as if contemplating some further insolence, some further mutinous defiance. But only for a moment. The Maxim had made the predictable impression, and he turned away, muttered a few words to his officers, and gestured at his soldiers. It was hardly necessary; the men had gotten the message well enough on their own and were drawing back, re-forming their ranks.

Stanley turned to Emin. "Pasha."

Emin had replaced his fez and readjusted his spectacles, but he obviously was still in a violently agitated state, pale as a ghost, deeply shaken, his rage just barely under control. He came forward now with his hands clenched into fists at his sides and stared at Hawashi Effendi with a terrible intensity. Then he began shaking his head, shaking it slowly back and forth in disgust, anger, dismay. It was obvious he couldn't speak. Whatever words he might have found to express his turbulent feelings choked in his throat, and he turned his back on the Egyptian and walked away.

Stanley called to him again.

"What do you want of me, Mr. Stanley? What would you have me do? If they will mutiny, if they will run away when the dervish comes, if they will go over to the Mahdi to save their skins, what can I do to prevent them? Shoot them with your machine gun? Shoot them in order to save them?" He started toward Hawashi Effendi again, blotches of color like virulent rashes erupting on his cheeks as words suddenly came to him, burst out of him. "No. By God, no. Let them save themselves. Let them mutiny. Let them flee when the dervish comes. Let them surrender to his tender mercies. Let them be taken into slavery. Let them have their throats cut like the worthless sheep that they are. It is all the same to me. They are fools and worse. Insolent dogs. Jackals. For two years they have remained faithful to me. For two years they have remained at their posts with iron courage and put their trust in me as children put their trust in their father. And now, when the help I promised them at last is at hand, *now* they will mutiny. Now they will run away. Now they will surrender. Oh, yes, they are fools, fools and worse. I wash my hands of them." He turned away again.

It was difficult to judge from the Egyptian's expression what effect Emin's words had on him; the vague unfocused, almost comical gaze of his walleyes revealed little as they wandered from Emin to Stanley to Jephson and Casati, to Nelson and the gun crew and the still smoking Maxim. Then unexpectedly he heaved a sigh, the deep, weary sigh of a man who has been sorely and unfairly tried, and said a few words in Arabic to one of his officers. The man nodded and hurried back toward one of the warehouses that enclosed the waterfront's landing stage. He disappeared into the shadows back there. A minute or two elapsed. Then a lantern went on in a window of the warehouse. It moved from window to window down the length of the building. Then it returned and appeared in the doorway. By its light, Jephson saw the officer come out again. Two men, no, three, came out after him.

Hawashi Effendi said something in Arabic. Jephson looked at him. He had spoken to Emin but was half turned away, watching the officer returning now followed by the three men. Emin did not respond to whatever he had said, for he was also watching the officer and three men, watching them with rapt attention. And then Jephson, with a shiver of horrified recognition, saw what they were watching.

It was the scene on the Wadelai jetty all over again: A peacock dervish—wild hair, patched jubbah—was being dragged along by two soldiers. As way was made for him through the ranks, a restless murmuring swelled and, like a moaning wave, followed him. He was in far worse shape than the one at Wadelai, far more brutally tortured, his multicolored jubbah torn to shreds, his face beaten into a mass of blood-caked bruises, his legs and arms twisted and probably broken, shackled in irons. He was dumped face down at Emin's feet. He might as well have been dead.

"Have you seen him before, Pasha?" Hawashi Effendi asked.

Emin stared down at the creature.

"Has he been to Wadelai?"

Emin nodded.

"Yes, and he has been to Chor Ayu and to Labore. And to Muggi. And to Kirri. And to Bedden. And to Rejaf. He has been to all the forts and stations along the river, appearing at dawn out of the river's mists, a messenger who delivers no message, a messenger of the Mahdi, the messenger of God."

Emin dropped to his knees beside the dervish and rolled him over on his back. Stanley and Jephson moved closer. Nelson came over from the Maxim. Casati, however, hung back speaking in an undertone in Italian, speaking to himself. Gingerly Emin forced open the dervish's mouth and probed into it for the tongue. But here too there was no tongue.

"All is lost, Pasha. All is lost. Already the garrison at Rejaf has decided to go over to the Mahdi."

"What?" Emin looked up.

"Hamad Aga, commander at Rejaf, has sent a delegation under a flag of truce to the dervishes at Lado. He means to bow to the Mahdi's will and surrender Rejaf to them in exchange for a pledge that the lives of his people will be spared."

"When was this?"

"Three days ago, four. The delegation has not yet returned."

"And it will never return. Oh, the fools, the poor fools. They are dead by now or enslaved." Emin stood up. "And what of the other garrisons? What of Bedden, Muggi, and Kirri?"

Hawashi Effendi shrugged. "It is much the same there as it is here, Pasha. They too have heard of the relief expedition. They too have heard that Bula Matari comes. They too are waiting to see what he brings. And when they see, when they see . . . *Inshallah*." He did not bother completing the thought, merely shrugged again. "It is in Allah's hands."

"I'll be damned if it is," Stanley said.

All eyes turned to him.

"I'll be damned if I've come all this way and put my people through all this hell in order to see the whole thing come to nothing at the final hour. I'll be damned if I go back to England with nothing to show for it. Arthur, disembark the askaris and the *pagazis*. Disembark the weapons and ammunition. I'm not giving this up without a fight. By Christ, I'm not. I'm not giving this up without making a goddamn good bloody fight of it right here in Duffile."

"In Duffile?"

"Yes, in Duffile. Listen to me, Pasha. This is what you must do. Evacuate all your northern garrisons and withdraw them here to Duffile. Go to Rejaf. Go to Bedden and Kirri. Go to Muggi and Labore and Chor Ayu. Go to all the stations and the forts. Go with Mr. Jephson and Captain Nelson. Go with my askaris and the Maxim and find out what has happened there, which have been lost and which have not. But it doesn't matter. The thing you must do is round up whatever troops still remain loyal to you and bring them here to Duffile. Concentrate all the forces you still command here in Duffile. And hold Duffile. Hold it at all cost. Hold it until I return."

"Until you return? Until you return from where?"

"I am going back for the rear column."

"But–"

"No, Pasha, listen to me. Hawashi Effendi, listen to me. All of you, listen to me. I have an army coming, an army strong enough to drive the dervish out of Equatoria forever, an army of a thousand men bringing hundreds of tons of weapons and ammunition. They are following the trail I blazed for them through the Ituri. They are emerging into the grasslands of the Watusi. They are approaching Nsabe on the Albert shore. They are my rear column and I am going back for them. Six weeks, Hawashi Effendi. Keep your courage for six weeks. Hold Duffile for six weeks and by then I will be here with my rear column and we shall drive the dervish from Equatoria forever."

PART FIVE

The Rear Column

· ONE ·

"DAMN THOSE NIGGERS. Damn them to hell."

Jack Troup made no reply. He and Ted Barttelot were standing at the river gate of the fortified encampment at Yambuya looking out across the Aruwimi, listening to the drums of the Basoko in the jungle on the other side. These had started up, as usual, at sunset and could now be counted on to go on through most of the night, a relentless monotonous beating blending into the relentless monotonous rumbling of the river's rapids, grating on the nerves.

"If they'd just come out and fight. If they'd just once give me a chance to get at them."

"Oh, they ain't likely to do that, Major. They've got more sense than to do anything like that."

"Yes, I know." Barttelot slapped his riding crop hard against his thigh. "They'll just keep sneaking about in the woods, thumping on those infernal tom-toms, and wait for us to starve."

This was July 28, 1887, a month to the day after Stanley and the advance column had set off into the Ituri, and although there wasn't any real danger of starvation, the fact of the matter was that during that month no headway had been made in winning over the local Basoko tribesmen and inducing them to trade. After the brief palaver with Baruti when the expedition first arrived, they had cleared out; and except for these nightly demonstrations of drumming, no contact had been had with them since.

The goats and fowls they had left behind in their haste to be gone had all been pretty much eaten up by now, and the only food readily available to the encampment in any abundance was the manioc in the outlying plantations that they hadn't been able to carry off. Even supplemented by plantains and beans foraged from the forest and by carefully doled out rations of rice and biscuits from the expedition's own stores—and as these latter would be needed on the march once the rear column set off on Stanley's track, Barttelot doled them out exceedingly carefully—it made for a dreary, unsatisfactory diet. And it was a diet that would have to be suffered for at least two more weeks, since neither the steamer bringing up Herbert Ward and Billy Bonny and the rest of the rear column from Equator Station nor the porters Tippoo-Tib had promised to send down from his settlement of Singatini at Stanley Falls could be expected to reach Yambuya much before then.

"Mr. Stanley should never have let Baruti skip off like that. That was a mistake. We could have used the little nigger as a go-between."

"Well, I don't see what he could have done about it, short of tying the boy up."

"That's what he should have done then, tied him up. I would have tied him up."

"I'm sure you would have, Major."

Barttelot looked at Troup. "That's right," he said. "I would have."

The two white men stared at each other with a barely concealed antipathy. Barttelot's beard, which he had started on first arriving at Yambuya, was fully grown now, a dark honey color, silky in texture but close-cropped and neatly trimmed so that it did not conceal his astonishing good looks, the chiseled line of his jaw, the firm, shapely mouth, the straight perfect nose. Everything about him was straight, perfect, neatly trimmed: the sun-bleached golden hair beneath his freshly chalked pith helmet, the knife-edge creases in the sleeves of his khaki tunic rolled up just so above his elbows, the angle that the bandolier across his chest made with the heavy holstered Webley revolver on his hip, the high polish of his riding boots, the blue kerchief knotted around his neck. By contrast, Troup looked bearish, unkempt, straight out of the woods with his huge orange beard and ragged-brimmed straw hat and collarless blue work shirt and dark serge trousers held up by red braces and stuffed down into nail-studded woodsman's boots, a Bulldog pistol jammed into the waistband at the back. Nevertheless he held the hard gaze of Barttelot's gem-bright blue eyes; he refused to be intimidated by this high-born Fusilier officer. And it was Barttelot who finally looked away.

"Yes, it was a mistake all right, letting that little nigger skip off like that. Another of Mr. Stanley's mistakes. . . . I say, you up there! Are you asleep?"

Directly to the left of the river gate was a twelve-foot watch tower. Two men were on it, barefoot askaris in turbans, tunics, and brightly patterned *kangas,* armed with Winchester repeaters; and if they had been sleeping when Barttelot shouted up at them, they weren't now.

"You'd best keep on the alert, boys. You hear those drums, don't you? Tonight may be the night the Washenzi come for us. We don't want to end up in their cooking pots." And snapping his riding crop, Barttelot continued on his round of the encampment's sentry posts, Troup ambling along at his side.

The encampment occupied only about a quarter of the original Basoko village of Yambuya and was laid out roughly as an irregular triangle, the three sides formed by ten-foot-high stockades of closely set poles cut from the iroko trees of the surrounding forest. The north side, running about 150 yards along the Aruwimi, was further protected by the fifty-foot-high bluff that dropped down steeply to the river's muddy embankment. A ditch ten feet from the stockade, seven feet wide, five feet deep, and spiked with bamboo skewers, served a similar function along the seventy-five-yard length of the east side (the base of the triangle) and along about half the 250 yards of the south side (the triangle's hypotenuse), with the remaining 125 yards or so of that side protected by a natural ravine through which a stream ran.

In addition to the river gate, there were two others, one in the east stockade opening out to the path along the Aruwimi's left bank, which the advance column had followed into the Ituri, the other letting out through the south side to the creek in the ravine from which the encampment drew its water. Next to each of these gates, as at the river gate, twelve-foot-high watchtowers had also been erected. Beyond them, for several hundred yards to the east and south, the land had been cleared. That was the area that had comprised the other three-quarters of the original Basoko village; but in order to provide a field of fire from the fortified encampment, the dwellings there had been burned to the ground all the way back to the surrounding manioc fields. Beyond the manioc fields, the Ituri began.

At present, two hundred men (apart from Barttelot and Troup), half askaris, half *pagazis,* plus thirty-six Wanyamwezi women and boys, were in the encampment, garrisoned in the Basoko huts that had been left standing. These tall conical structures with roofs shingled with overlapping palm leaves stood in orderly rows around what had been Yambuya's main marketplace and which Barttelot had since converted into the fort's parade ground. There were a sufficient number of them not only to comfortably house that portion of the rear column already there but also the 309 *pagazis*, women and boys, who were coming upriver on the steamer from Equator Station with Ward and Bonny. Troup occupied one of the larger ones near the south gate. Barttelot, however, regarded them as unsuitable for a white man and had had a house of mud-plastered wattle and bamboo with rough plank flooring and a canted thatch roof built for him in the corner just beyond the river gate where the east and south stockades joined to form the apex of the triangle. And as there was little else to do while waiting for the steamer and Tippoo-Tib's porters, he also had had a kitchen built there, storehouses for the expedition's supplies, a latrine for the Europeans, and a long open shed covered by a thatch roof and containing the expedition's canvas folding chairs, a newly made plank dining table, and some empty crates to serve as side tables, which he referred to not entirely jokingly as the officers' mess. It was to this that he and Troup made their way after completing the round of the sentries.

Night had fallen by then, the quick jungle night, the last of the pastel streaks of sunset over the river suddenly winking out and the inky blackness of the surrounding trees just as suddenly rushing in. The air was still thick and oppressive with the heat and humidity of the day, and with the whining hordes of insects that came out with the night. A half-moon had risen, and there were countless stars; but in the east above the black canopy of the Ituri, the clouds that would bring the nightly rain were massing, and there were flickers of lightning and the faint growl of thunder. Everywhere in the encampment cooking fires were burning.

"Let's have some light in here, Bartholomew," Barttelot shouted, ducking in under the low eave of the mess. "For God's sake, boy, get a lantern in here."

"Yes, sah." Bartholomew, a mission-educated Wanyamwezi cookboy dressed in a short white jacket and short trousers like a Zanzibari steward, hurried over from the kitchen with a bullshot lantern.

"Put it here. Here, for God's sake. Not there. Are you blind? What use is it going to do us there? All right. Now get the chop. *Upesi-upesi.*"

"Yes, sah."

"Stupid goddamn nigger." Barttelot dropped his riding crop on the dining table, removed his helmet, unbuckled his bandolier and holster, and dropped them beside it, then dropped himself into one of the camp chairs, stretching out his booted legs, crossing them at the ankles. Troup drew up another of the camp chairs, but no sooner was he seated than Barttelot was back on his feet.

"Chop, boy. We're wating for our chop."

"Yes, sah. *Kwa hivi karibu*, sah."

"Christ." Barttelot untied the blue kerchief around his neck, unfastened the top clasps of his tunic collar, and began pacing back and forth. "Christ, I hate all this endless waiting about. I signed up for a campaign, a grand dash through the heart of Africa, and all I've been doing is this endless waiting about."

"Just another fortnight, Major, and we'll be on our way."

"Yes, another fortnight. And it won't be a moment too soon, I can tell you. Not a moment too soon to get away from this stinking hole." Barttelot threw himself back into the camp chair. "Where's that chop, boy? I'm warning you, if that chop ain't here—"

"Chop here, sah. Chop here." Bartholomew came scurrying back from the kitchen with a large wooden tray laden with a steaming bowl, enameled tin plates, tinware cutlery, a kettle of tea, and enameled tin cups; but because of Barttelot's things on the table, he could find no place to set it.

"Oh, for God's sake." Barttelot swept his helmet, revolver and bandolier from the table. "Put it down, will you? Just put it down anywhere."

The boy slid the tray onto the edge of the table and quickly set out the plates and knives and forks, the bowl and kettle and cups, arranging them as he had been taught.

"What's this?" Barttelot poked his fork into the bowl.

"*Posho*, sah."

"*Posho*, eh?" Barttelot stirred his fork through the grayish glutinous mass, uncovering some pieces of pigeon meat. "You mean manioc, don't you?"

"Yes, sah, manioc."

"How did you prepare it? Did you prepare it properly? Did you soak it first?"

"Oh, yes, sah, I soak it first."

"How long did you soak it?"

The boy glanced at Troup, uncertain what to reply, as if he were being tested or tricked.

"I'm sure he soaked it long enough, Major," Troup said. "He knows it's poisonous if it's not soaked long enough. I've explained it to him often enough."

"Sure, and you've explained it to all the others often enough as well; and we've already got a dozen of them down sick because they ate the stuff without properly soaking it. Stupid damn niggers. Poisoned themselves." Barttelot suddenly grabbed hold of Bartholomew's arm. "You don't want to poison me, do you, boy? Or do you?"

"Oh, no, sah, no."

"Hah! I bet you don't. You love me too much, don't you?"

"Yes, sah."

"Sure you do. All right. Now get out of here." Barttelot shoved the boy away and began ladling a portion of the *posho* and pigeon onto his plate, then pushed the bowl over to Troup, poured himself a cup of tea, and started eating. "What god-awful stuff."

Troup watched him for a moment, then served himself, and they ate in silence for a while. It was their nightly ritual, this dining together in the "officers' mess." Barttelot had instituted it on the first day after Stanley and the advance column had departed. Troup could easily have done without it. He was never at ease around Barttelot, certainly had no small talk to make with him; Barttelot was too far above him socially, too much the British officer, the privileged gentleman, the arrogant aristocrat for that. Barttelot, however, insisted on it. Not that he enjoyed Troup's company any more than Troup enjoyed his, but because it was correct form. In his view, officers in the field, white men among natives, no matter that the class distinctions between them might make it impossible for them to meet as equals in London, were duty-bound to stand together and together to stand apart in order to establish their superiority and enforce their authority on the men under them.

"And to think how those sons of bitches are eating right now."

Troup looked up from his plate. "Which sons of bitches are those, Major?"

"The slavers—Tippoo-Tib and his gang. Christ, what a feast they laid on for us when we were there: pilaf, curries, kabobs, fruits, sherbet, cheese, breads, wine. It makes my mouth water thinking of it. You've been to the Falls, haven't you, Troup?"

"A couple of years ago."

"That's quite the little paradise he's built for himself there, isn't it? Gardens, orchards, villas, silks and jewels, hashish and harem girls—every imaginable delicacy, every imaginable pleasure." Barttelot pushed his plate away, the *posho* barely half eaten, and fished a packet of cigarettes and his ivory cigarette holder from his tunic's breast pocket. "Quite the little paradise all right," he said, fitting a cigarette into the holder. "While we're stuck in this stink hole." He lit the cigarette, drew deeply on it, and blew the smoke out into the night.

Troup resumed eating. The food didn't bother him in the way it did Barttelot. He was used to it. He had lived on this sort of fare more often than not in his years in Africa and had learned not to expect anything much better. As long as it stuck to the ribs, he was satisfied; and besides, he suspected that once they were under way in the Ituri, he and Barttelot and everyone else would look back on meals like this with longing. And so he went on eating.

"How far do you suppose it is?"

"The Falls?" Troup shrugged. "Three, four days by canoe. Two down the Congo to the mouth of the Aruwimi. Then another day or two up the Aruwimi to here."

"And overland? Straight across the neck between the rivers?"

"Oh, I don't think Tippoo-Tib'll send the porters down here overland, Major. It's far easier and faster by water."

"I wasn't thinking of the porters coming down here. I was thinking of my going up there."

Troup stopped eating, his forkful of *posho* arrested at his mouth. "Mr. Stanley was quite specific about that, Major, about not going up to the Falls."

"Mr. Stanley isn't here."

"Even so, sir, the orders he left—"

"I'm perfectly aware of the orders he left. But there are occasions when the officer on the scene must use his own judgment about following orders. And this strikes me as such an occasion. Mr. Stanley assumed we'd be able to keep this camp well victualed while waiting for the rest of our men and for Tippoo-Tib's porters by trading with the local niggers. Well, that's not turned out to be the case. We can't even find those bloody bastards, let alone get so much as a bean out of them. We've got to feed ourselves on this poisonous mush while up at the Falls Tippoo-Tib and his cutthroats are rolling around in the lap of luxury with more food than they know what to do with. Well, hell, why not go up there and see if I can't get some of that food for ourselves?"

"I can't agree with that, Major. There ain't nothing all that much wrong with this chop. It'll hold us well enough for another two weeks. And Mr. Stanley—"

"I think you've misunderstood me, Troup. I didn't ask you whether you agreed with me or not. All I asked you is how far you reckon it is to the Falls by land. Would you do me the courtesy of answering that?"

Slowly, very deliberately Troup replaced his fork on his plate. Then, keeping his voice steady and calm, he said, "At least six days. More likely seven."

"Thank you."

"I mean, each way, Major."

"I realize that."

"So by the time you got there and back, you can figure Ward and Bonny and the rest will have just about got here and we'll be ready to move out. So it wouldn't make too much sense, would it?"

"I'll decide that," Barttelot said and squashed out his cigarette in his uneaten *posho*. He stood up from the table and resumed his restless pacing.

The flashes of lightning were coming more frequently now, and the crack and rumble of thunder sounded always a bit closer, momentarily drowning out the sounds of the river and the sounds of the drums. A breeze had sprung up, scattering the swarms of mosquitoes and moths that gathered around the lantern, setting the flame flickering. Troup returned to his meal. He wanted to be done with it before the rain came.

"I'll make the round of sentries tonight, if you like, Major," he said after he had cleaned his plate and poured himself a final cup of tea.

"No, that's all right. I'll do it."

"You've done it every night so far. It don't seem quite fair. You're entitled to a full night's sleep once in a while, like everyone else. Why don't you let me do it for you? I can do it just as well."

"No you can't." Barttelot stopped his pacing. "I wish you could, but as a matter of fact you can't."

"And why's that, Major?"

"Because you're too easy on these niggers, Troup." Barttelot returned to his place at the table and went through the business of lighting another cigarette. "Far too easy. You'd let them get away with murder."

"Murder, Major?"

"Well, maybe not murder. But you sure as hell wouldn't give much of a damn if you caught one of them eating on guard or leaving his post to piss. You'd give him a slap on the wrist and let it go at that."

"You're probably right."

"I know I'm right."

"I guess I just don't see it the same way you do, sir."

"That's because you're not a soldier, Troup."

"No, that's right. I'm not a soldier." Troup drank off his tea. "Well, I guess I'll turn in now. Unless there was something else."

"No, there's nothing else."

Troup stood up, then hesitated. Barttelot looked up at him.

"When exactly was it that you were planning to go up to the Falls?"

"I haven't made up my mind yet. I'll let you know when I have."

"Well, you know how I feel about it."

"Yes, I know."

"Right then. I'll say goodnight, Major."

"Goodnight, Troup."

Troup went to his hut, leaving Barttelot alone in the mess, smoking by the flickering lantern light.

The next day began with a flogging. Most days at Yambuya began with a flogging of one poor wretch or another for some infraction of Major Barttelot's rules. Today it was an askari Barttelot caught sleeping on guard during the 2 A.M. sentry round. That would have been bad enough—the punishment was twenty-five lashes—but the damn fool had claimed he hadn't been asleep even though he had been sleeping so soundly when Barttelot came upon him that Barttelot had been able to take away his rifle before awakening him. The lie earned him an additional ten cuts.

Troup watched from the entryway of his hut as the fellow, a feisty bloke, stripped to the waist and looking around cockily, was tied to a rude wooden triangle at the center of the parade ground that Barttelot had had erected for this purpose even before the stockade around the encampment had been completed. It was 5 A.M., the air was still fresh and cool from the previous night's rain, and the birds of the forest were out in force shrilling away in the pearly blue light of the slowly brightening dawn. The two companies of askaris of about fifty each (only those on guard duty were exempted) were paraded in double file on either side of the whipping post. The Wanyamwezis—men, women, and boys—were also required to watch for instructional purposes, but as Barttelot did not insist that they fall in in any formal order, they hung back around their cooking fires finishing breakfast, looking on like spectators at a fair. Barttelot, in a sharp clean uniform, bandoliered and pistoled, his sun helmet pulled low over his eyes, his hands clasped behind his back holding the ever-present riding crop, oversaw the punishment; but it was the Sudanese corporal on whose watch the fellow had slept who was obliged to administer it. He also was stripped to the waist. His instrument was the *chicotte*, a cured hippo-hide whip with edges like knife blades and as hard as wood.

The askari took the first few strokes with a bravura defiance, twisting around after each to sneer at his tormentor. But after a half-dozen or so he quit doing this and pressed his forehead against the whipping post and closed his eyes. Then his legs gave out from under him and he sank to his knees, his wrists pulling against the thongs that bound them, his arms pulling out of their sockets. By the time the awful welts raised on his back began to bleed, he was crying out like a child, the muscles and sinews and limbs of his body twitching and quivering uncontrollably. Before all thirty-five cuts would be administered, he'd be unconscious.

Then the next phase of the fort's daily routine would commence. Details would be counted off for general housekeeping chores, policing the grounds, sweeping the streets, emptying the latrines, repairing breaks in the stockade, replacing the sharpened spikes in the ditch. Others would be sent out to chop wood, harvest manioc, draw water from the creek, forage for food. The askaris would be drilled, marching and countermarching around the parade ground in the rising dusty heat of the morning, performing the manual of arms, breaking down and cleaning their weapons, taking target practice, standing inspection, going out on scouting patrols. It was mostly unnecessary activity, a reflection of Barttelot's abhorrence of idleness of any kind, in himself or in those around him, and Troup didn't bother to stick around for it. He fetched his eight-bore Reilly hunting rifle and a box of cartridges; and even before the flogging was over, while the poor bastard was still conscious and screaming, he left his hut.

Barttelot called to him. "Where are you going, Troup?"

"To check the nets, Major."

"Check the nets? For God's sake, there's nothing in those nets. There's never anything in those nets."

"Maybe there will be this time."

"Well, don't be too long about it. Don't just wander off on one of your rambles."

Troup made a vague noncommittal reply and kept going. He rounded up three Wanyamwezi trackers armed with muskets and spears, and the ranking headman in the camp, a corpulent, somewhat sleepy-looking fellow by the name of Munichandi, a relative by marriage of Uledi's who was expert with a Sharps carbine, and led them out of the fort by the river gate.

Checking the nets was a figure of speech, a catchall phrase covering a multitude of sins. To be sure, once it became clear that the Basoko wouldn't trade, Troup had tried his hand at fishing to supplement the fort's rations, rigging up wicker baskets and traps of mosquito netting in the river's rapids, a technique used on the Congo. But for some reason it didn't work particularly well in the Aruwimi. From time to time, a peculiar carplike fish with teeth outside the jaws (no one knew its name) would turn up flopping around in a net and be made into soup or stew; but if schools of these creatures or any other species of fish ran in the river, they apparently were too cunning to be caught in this way. Even so, he kept at it, devising new contraptions, setting them at different, more distant locations. It gave him an excuse to get out of the fort, get away from Barttelot, as did his hunting forays each dusk. And so now, with Munichandi leading the way and the trackers strung out behind him, he set off upstream along the Aruwimi's muddy bank. He had rigged the latest of his traps in the river's next reach, above where it made a sharp bend from the northeast, well out of sight and hearing of the fort on the off-chance that it was the noise and activity of the fort that spoiled the fishing.

A Basoko canoe was beached on the shore there.

Munichandi saw it when he stepped around the river's bend; and he immediately stepped back, raising his hand in an urgent signal to those behind him. Troup and the trackers came up quickly. The canoe was about a quarter-mile farther upriver, pulled in prow-first among the reeds and ferns and mossy driftwood of a swampy backwater. It was a fair size canoe, but only one person was in it, a boy lazing in the stern, a paddle across his lap. The early-morning sun, still huge and orange and benign, was just showing itself above the treetops; and its slanting rays filtering through the canopy of leaves and branches dappled the boy's dozing figure.

Even at that distance, Troup recognized who he was. "I don't believe it," he said with a big grin. "Christ, what luck. What fantastic luck."

Munichandi and the trackers crouched around him, puzzled by his sudden show of delight.

"*Iko* Baruti," he said to them.

The name didn't immediately register, but when Troup explained it was Bula Matari's *toto*, Munichandi remembered the lively little blackamoor from the trip up the Congo and was all for going and getting him at once.

"*Ngoja kidogo.*" Troup grabbed the headman's wrist. "Not so quickly. We must consider this."

Troup wasn't at all sure how Baruti would react on seeing them. After all, he had been shamelessly eager to quit the expedition and get back to his own people when they first reached Yambuya, and he might misinterpret Troup's sudden coming for him now as an attempt to separate him from them again. And, besides, he almost certainly wasn't alone. He must have come with others in a canoe of that size and, probably being the youngest, had been left behind to guard the craft while they went about their business.

"They are stealing the manioc," Troup said. "My guess is they're stealing the manioc from the fields around Yambuya."

It was their basic food, after all, the staple of their diet. To be sure, they had goats and fowls, most of which they had managed to carry away when the expedition arrived, and they gathered the wild fruits and legumes of the forest and hunted its game and doubtless had better luck fishing the river than Troup had had. But the manioc was their bread, their rice, their flour. They baked it and boiled it into dozens of dishes. They would not willingly go long without it.

And so, tentatively at first, then always a bit more brazenly, they probably had been coming over in small bands like this during the night; and while the fort slept, while the sentries slept, while their drums distracted attention, they had been harvesting the succulent root to replenish their supply. It was a stroke of pure luck that Troup and Munichandi and the trackers had chanced to be abroad early enough and far enough upriver to catch them at it. Or perhaps they had grown lax and overconfident as a result of the ease with which they had gotten away with these raids until now.

"Go and find them, Munichandi. By now they must be making their way back here from the fields. Go and find them. And capture them."

Munichandi nodded and started away, but again Troup took hold of his wrist. "But do not harm them. There cannot be more than ten of them, if even so many, and they will be burdened by the manioc they carry and will not be able to make use of their bows. So it should not be difficult to capture them without harming them."

"*Ndiyo,* Bwana."

"*Vizuri.*" Troup released his wrist. "I will wait here. Bring them to me."

Munichandi and the trackers hurried back downriver a few hundred feet before scrambling up the embankment's bluff and slipping into the forest. When they were gone, Troup again peered around the river's bend. Baruti must have heard something, because he was up on his knees now, looking downriver through the foliage almost directly at Troup. Troup ducked back. How bizarre, he thought, playing hide-and-seek with his little friend as they had played it together in London so many times before. But now his little friend was a little savage, his eyes circled with white paint, a yellow stripe down his nose, a necklace of crocodile teeth around his neck, a skirt of shredded leaves covering his loins, not a trace of his years in civilization on him.

Troup sat down and started to pull out his tobacco pouch but then thought better of it—Baruti would smell the smoke—and leaned back against the bluff. In the branch of a palm tree above his head a black weaverbird was building a nest. He watched it for a while, admiring its skill and patience, enjoying its busy chirping, then stole another peek at Baruti. The boy had gotten out of the canoe and come ashore with the paddle (as a weapon perhaps; he had no other) and was scanning the forest atop the bluff.

And then he heard the commotion: the shouts, the crashing through the brush, a woman's trilling ululation, a rifle shot, birds breaking from the trees, monkeys shrieking. He leaped back into the canoe.

"Damn." Troup jumped up and went dashing up the bank shouting the boy's name.

Baruti hesitated an instant to look at the red-bearded white man racing toward him; and doubtless in that instant he recognized Troup, but it didn't influence him. Digging hard with his paddle into the river bottom, he shoved off and backpaddled furiously away from the shore.

"No, Baruti. *Njoo hapa.*" Troup splashed into the river after him. "*Hakuna kitu, toto. Njoo hapa.*" But he had no hope of catching him. In four steps he was waist deep. In another two steps he'd be in over his head. He backed up to where the water only reached his knees and went on shouting.

And then Baruti suddenly ceased his frenzied flight. About fifty yards from shore he reached over the side and grabbed the gnarled branch of a log that was snagged on some rocks and brought the canoe to a halt in the fast-rushing stream. It wasn't because of Troup's imprecations, however. It was because just then Munichandi and the trackers emerged from the forest with their captives. Troup glanced around. There were only six of them; but they made an even less formidable force than he had expected, since three were women and the other three boys not much older than Baruti. One of the women was still clutching a basket filled with manioc tubers; the others apparently had thrown theirs away during their attempt to escape. The boys had bows and quivers of arrows, but these were still slung.

As the trackers prodded them forward with their muskets and spears, forcing them down the bluff to the riverbank, the women made pathetic whimpering sounds, but the boys kept silent, walking stiffly, staring straight ahead. They were painted and dressed much like Baruti; but being slightly older, having passed their childhood with their tribe, they had crimson parrot feathers in their hair and the cicatrices of manhood tattooed on their chests. Troup looked back at Baruti. The boy was in an agony of confusion and indecision, wanting to flee but unable to bring himself to abandon his people.

"Come back, Baruti. I mean you no harm. You know that, *toto*. I am your friend." As he spoke, Troup backed out of the river. The water was cold and uncomfortable and playing havoc on his boots. "At least come a little closer so that we may palaver."

After a moment's consideration, his eyes glancing back and forth between Troup and the Basoko, Baruti let go of the snagged log and paddled toward shore. He did not come all the way in, however. About ten yards out he caught hold of a clump of reeds and swung broadside to the bank. It was close enough.

"*Vizuri*, Baruti," Troup said and, in order to make his appearance less threatening, squatted on his haunches.

Baruti studied him carefully—as if to make certain who he was. Then he said, "Why are you still here, Bwana Troup?" He said it in Swahili, and his voice startled Troup. It wasn't quite the childish soprano he remembered. "Why haven't you gone on with Bula Matari?"

"But you know why, Baruti. We are awaiting the remainder of our people. You know we left them at Equator Station because the steamers were not strong enough to bring them here all at once. We will go after Bula Matari once they get here."

"No, you should go now. You should go this very day. You

should go so that we may return to our homes and fields. You should go before you bring the slavers down on our heads."

Troup stood up. Hearing Baruti talk like this disconcerted him. A month back in the jungle with his own people and the silly little blackamoor boy of London had become a man. "No, Baruti, I am sorry but we must wait here for the rest of our people. We shall go when they join us."

Baruti pulled a sour face and looked at the Basoko captives. They were now down on the riverbank, herded together under the trackers' weapons a few yards behind Troup. The woman with the manioc hugged the basket to her breasts as if it were a baby. Baruti called something to her in the Basoko vernacular.

"No harm will come to her, *toto*. I promise you. No harm will come to any of them."

"Well, why do you hold them then? What do you want of them?"

"They have been stealing the manioc."

"They have not been *stealing* the manioc, Bwana Troup. It is *their* manioc. It is the manioc they themselves planted. You are the ones who have stolen it."

"Yes, that is true but—" Troup cut himself off. Munichandi had come to stand beside him, and he felt foolish getting into an argument with a ten-year-old boy. So he said, "Listen to me, Baruti. I want to speak with your chief. It is best that I speak with him about these things. Take me to him."

"Bwana." This was Munichandi, a note of warning in his voice.

Troup ignored him. "Do you hear what I say, Baruti? I want you to take me to your chief. I want to speak with him about these things. I want to settle these things with him. I want to make peace with him. There is no need for trouble between us. We have not come here to do harm. You know that. And soon we will be gone. But until then there should be peace between us. There should be friendship. There should be trade. I want to speak of these things with your chief, Baruti. Take me to him."

Baruti made no reply to this.

"Listen to me, *toto*. Look at me. This is Troup. This is your old friend Bwana Troup. You know you can trust me. Have I ever given you reason not to trust what I say? Take me to your chief. We will settle everything between us."

Baruti fidgeted in the canoe, shifting his paddle from one side to the other, shifting his grip on the clump of reeds from one hand to the other. Then at long last he said, "Only you?"

"Yes, only me, *toto*."

"Bwana," Munichandi warned again.

"Keep out of this, Munichandi. It is all right. Yes, *toto*, only me."

"And you will leave your gun?"

Troup hesitated at this for a moment. Then he said, "Yes, all right, I will leave my gun." He handed the heavy eight-bore Reilly to Munichandi.

"And also your little gun?"

Troup smiled wryly. "You should be able to trust me better than that, *toto*. But all right, I will also leave my little gun." He removed the Bulldog pistol from the back of his waistband.

"Bwana," Munichandi said, taking it. "These Washenzi are cannibals. They feast on the flesh of men. How can you think to go to them unarmed?"

"Because this boy is my friend. In his company I have nothing to fear." Troup said this loud enough for Baruti to hear. Then he said, "*Haya, toto? Vyema?* All right then, bring the canoe to me."

"No, you must come to me."

Troup shook his head in exasperation. But he didn't really blame the boy; he understood his mistrust. Thinking that he'd probably have to swim a few strokes to reach the canoe, he bent over and began unlacing his boots.

"But first my people must come to me."

Troup straightened up.

"Have them released, Bwana Troup. Have them come to the canoe."

"No, Baruti. *Ninasikitika*. I am sorry, but they must remain here. They must remain here until my safe return."

The boy probably had expected that. He probably felt he had to at least make the attempt but was realistic enough to know that it really couldn't be any other way. In any case, he made no protest. He again looked at the three Basoko boys and three Basoko women and again called something to them. The woman hugging the basket of manioc called something back.

And again Troup said, "No harm will come to them, Baruti. I promise you. They will be treated well until my safe return." Then he completed unlacing his boots, removed them, tied them together and slung them over a shoulder. "Take these people back to camp, Munichandi. Explain to the major who they are and where I've gone. And see to it that no harm comes to them."

"You are foolish, Bwana. You are very foolish."

"We shall see," Troup replied and waded into the river.

· TWO ·

THAT DAY PASSED and then the next, and Troup did not return. And during the nights of those days, for the first time, the Basoko drums were silent and only the rumble of the rapids was heard. It worried Barttelot. And at the same time it also elated him. It worried him because he knew (although he'd be the last to admit it) that he couldn't afford to lose Troup, that he relied on the old Africa hand's knowledge of the country and the ways of its inhabitants, knowledge that would be crucial once they set off on Stanley's track into the Ituri. But even so, as one day of Troup's absence was succeeded by another, he experienced a mounting sense of excitement. For now at last something was happening, now at last he could take some real action and put an end to the deadly boredom of all these weeks of dreary waiting. His plan was to give Troup one more day to get back and then take out a war party in search of him.

The problem, of course, was where to search for him. Munichandi and the trackers were no help on that score. Barttelot had questioned them closely when they returned with the Basoko hostages, but all they could tell him was that Baruti had taken Troup upriver and had vanished with him into the jungle around the next higher bend. Barttelot did not altogether believe them. Their story of what had happened, their stumbling on Baruti by chance like that, struck him as too pat. It had the smell of conspiracy about it. He suspected they were concealing something from him, as he always suspected they were concealing something from him. Although he felt sure enough about the Sudanese askaris, men he himself had recruited in Aden and who were used to his sort of military discipline, he was well aware of the Wanyamwezis' dislike of him—their resentment of his methods, the deliberately stupid faces they always showed him—and he kept at them, badgering and threatening them. But in truth there was nothing they could add: Bwana Troup had persuaded Bula Matari's *toto* to take him to the Basoko chief; but where that might be, how far upriver, how far and in which direction from the river, they had no way of knowing. When the time came, Barttelot realized, it would have to be one of the Basoko captives who would serve as the search party's guide.

He had them separated. The three women were left pretty much to their own devices, free to roam about the fort as they wished; but the three boys, despite Munichandi's protest that Troup had promised they would be well treated, were imprisoned in a small hut that faced the parade ground and placed under twenty-four hour guard with a goatskin of water as their only nourishment. But Barttelot didn't have any illusions about them. They wouldn't break easily. He saw it in their eyes. They were young and full of pride and probably welcomed a trial of this sort as a test of their manhood. It was the women he was counting on.

They stayed close together and, despite their relative freedom, stayed close to the hut where the boys were held. To the Wanyamwezis and Sudanese, they were objects of uneasy curiosity. They believed them to be cannibals and were afraid to get too near them; and when Munichandi, trying to honor Troup's word, ordered his own women to feed them, they shoved the bowls of manioc porridge at them and quickly scampered away and watched them eat from a safe distance as they might a trio of wild animals.

It was difficult to judge their ages. They were older than the boys but still young, indeed probably had not yet borne children by the look of their bodies, their small, firm, upstanding breasts, their smooth round bellies, the chunky thighs that emerged from their short skirts of shredded palm leaves. Their woolly hair was cropped close to their small skulls, and their features were broad and flat but pretty in their own way. Their skin color was a shade lighter than that of the people on the Congo and shiny from coatings of camwood grease. They hesitated to eat what was given them at first; but when hunger finally overcame them, they ate with a furtive intensity, revealing tiny sharply filed teeth. Barttelot kept an eye on them while he made his restless rounds of the fort; and he often made it a point of being there when they ate, standing over them, walking slowly around them, inspecting them. And then at sunset of the third day of Troup's absence he made his choice.

There had been no floggings that day. No askari had been caught asleep at his post, no *pagazi* malingering on his job. An anxious watchfulness pervaded the camp, although for what or against whom no one really knew. Twice that day Barttelot had gone with Munichandi and a squad of askaris to the place on the riverbank from which Troup had paddled away with Baruti, and had peered upstream through his field glasses into the thick tangles of overhanging vegetation into which he had disappeared.

The drumming of the Basoko had come from back in the jungle on the opposite side of the Aruwimi, but Barttelot was convinced they weren't there any longer. Indeed, he was convinced that, apart from the drummers, the Basoko had never been there, that the drumming had been a cunning diversion, that when the Basoko had fled Yambuya they had fled into the jungle on this side of the river and therefore it was on this side of the river that he would have to go in search of them. He didn't really have any hard evidence in support of this. It was little more than a hunch or, perhaps more accurately, a hope. For the idea of crossing the river in search of the Basoko was not appealing. He let the field glasses drop on his chest and took a last look around with his naked eyes; then he signaled Munichandi and the askaris and they headed back to the fort. He had as yet told no one what he planned.

The sun was low on the river in the west and rain clouds were beginning to stack up over the forest in the east by the time they got back. Barttelot immediately went off to make the rounds of the sentries. Each of the lookout towers and shooting platforms contained a full complement of riflemen, and extra pickets had been posted at the fort's three gates. All the work details were back within the stockade; and now that Barttelot and his squad had also returned, the gates were shut and bolted. Munichandi mustered and counted the Wanyamwezis to make sure none had been left outside. Then the cooking fires were lit. Crossing the parade ground to the officers' mess, Barttelot stopped at the hostages' hut.

The askari on guard snapped to attention and saluted. The three Basoko women, who had been hunkered down in the dust there, got to their feet. Barttelot ignored them and ducked into the hut. The three Basoko boys were crouched at as widely separated intervals as they could get in the small enclosure. They had probably been seated close together, like the women, and had sprung into this formation on hearing Barttelot approach, their eyes wide and bright and as watchful as wild animals'. They'd been nearly three days without food, but that didn't seem to have sapped their youthful strength. Their muscles were hard and toned and tightly coiled; they looked keenly alert, full of hate and ready to spring. Barttelot remained at the hut's entry. These savage little niggers might just be crazy enough to try and jump him if he stepped into their midst. Idly slapping his riding crop against his thigh, he studied them. They were as alike as three peas in a pod; he couldn't see any difference among them. Maybe they were brothers.

"*Mbali gani? Mambo yanaendeleaje?*"

They didn't reply. They went on watching him fiercely, nostrils flared, breath bated. He ducked back out of the hut. The askari still stood stiffly at attention. The three women had inched around to the other side of the hut and squatted on their heels there. Now they got up again and moved farther away. Barttelot went over to them. These he could tell apart. One was smaller than the others. One had bigger breasts. One had an intricate pattern of cicatrices tattooed across her cheekbones and was probably the oldest.

"Munichandi."

The headman was standing at the cook fire in front of his hut, watching his women preparing manioc. He came over when Barttelot called.

"Those boys in there, it is time they were fed. Let them have some of that *posho*."

Munichandi responded enthusiastically to this. "Oh, yes, Bwana. It is time. I fetch it myself."

"But don't go in there with it, you hear? Just shove it in through the door. Those little cannibals are hot. They might eat you instead."

Munichandi grinned. "No, no, Bwana. It will be all right. I will take care. This is a good thing you do. A good thing." He started back to the cook fire.

"Wait a minute. There's something else."

"Yes, Bwana?"

"I want this girl washed."

"Washed?"

"Yes. This one." Barttelot indicated one of the Basoko women. "I want her washed, bathed, scrubbed, boiled if necessary, but I want all that foul-smelling grease off her. And then I want her brought to my quarters."

Munichandi looked at Barttelot queerly. Then he looked at the woman Barttelot had selected. She was the one with the largest breasts. Although she didn't understand what was being said, she was keenly aware that she had been singled out, and she drew away. "Washed?" Munichandi asked again.

"Yes, washed. Damnit, man, what's so hard to grasp about that? Take her to your women. Have them do it. And then bring her to my quarters. *Unanifahamu?* Do you understand?"

Munichandi nodded.

"Well, get on with it then."

Munichandi kept nodding dumbly for a moment, then finally went over to the Basoko girl. And she started to scream. And the other two also started to scream. And the three Basoko boys came flying to the hut's entryway at the sound of this screaming, screaming themselves.

"Jesus Christ, get them back in there. Don't let them out of there. And shut those bitches up."

"They believe we are taking her to be killed, Bwana."

"I don't care what they believe. Just stop their bloody racketing. And get those boys back in the huts. Goddamnit, askari, don't you hear what I say? Get them back in there."

Striding over to the hut's entry himself, Barttelot slashed at the three boys with his riding crop, slashed at their faces so that they threw up their hands and fell back. And then, with a crowd swiftly gathering from all over the fort to see what all the noise was about, Barttelot turned on his heels and walked across the parade ground to the officers' mess and raised a racket of his own there, shouting for the kitchen boy Bartholomew.

"What is happening, sah? Why do the Washenzi scream so?"

"How's that any of your business, boy? Your business is to have my chop on the table. Where is it? I don't see it."

"I fetch it, sah. But, oh listen, how that *bibi* screams. Yes, sah. I fetch chop, sah. *Upesi-upesi.*"

Barttelot removed his helmet, bandolier, and pistol and dropped them on the mess table beside his riding crop and looked back across the parade ground. It didn't take long for order to be restored there. Once Munichandi dragged off the girl Barttelot had chosen, the howls of the other two subsided; and the boys retreated into the hut to nurse the cuts and bruises they had sustained from the askari's rifle butt. Barttelot sat down at the mess table and again shouted impatiently for his food. It was the usual dreary fare, manioc gruel with, tonight, pieces of some unidentifiable fish in it, a pot of weak tea, and some plantains a foraging party had brought in. There was enough for two. Bartholomew had continued cooking for Troup throughout his absence, as if by doing so, he was working a charm that would guarantee Troup's return. It was a waste, of course, the sort of foolishness Barttelot ordinarily wouldn't tolerate. But out of his own anxiety over Troup's absence, he chose not to notice it.

He was still eating when the girl was brought to him. Munichandi and a Wanyamwezi woman brought her and stood on either side of her just outside the officer's mess. Presumably she was now clean, but it was too dark beyond the glow of the mess lantern to tell; and besides, somebody had put a *kanzu* on her, the long loose nightgownlike garment of white muslin some of the Wanyamwezi men wore. That at least looked clean. Barttelot pushed away his plate.

"What've you put that damn thing on her for? Christ, she looks like a ghost. Take it off her."

"But, Bwana, her *skati* was also filthy with the grease and she has nothing else."

"Just take it off her, will you? I want to see how well you've washed her up."

Munichandi shrugged and passed the order to the Wanyamwezi woman, who, steeling herself against her fear of contact with this savage creature, snatched up the robe's hem and pulled the garment over the girl's head. She was totally naked beneath it. Barttelot had to laugh. The girl, in a flush of mortification, instantly struck that most classical of all poses of naked women the world around, knees pressed together, one slightly bent over the other, both hands covering her private parts, eyes lowered in shame.

"Bring her closer. Bring her into the light. Take your hands away, girl. Let me see what you have there." Barttelot picked up his riding crop and flicked it at the girl's hands. "Take them away, do you hear?"And when, closing her eyes, she did take her hands away, he forced the riding crop between her thighs. "Stand up, girl. Stand up straight. Separate your legs."

Munichandi and the Wanyamwezi woman looked away.

Once he had gotten the girl to stand erect, to unbend and separate her knees, Barttelot withdrew the riding crop and placed his hand on her flank and ran it up the curve of her buttock to her waist. Her flesh quivered beneath it. "Well, you've got the grease off her anyway," he said. He sat back and produced a cigarette from his tunic pocket, fitted it into his ivory holder, and, lighting it, let his eyes roam over her body. Then he said, "Take her to my quarters."

Eyes still averted, Munichandi took the girl's wrist.

"Not you, Munichandi. You stay here. Have your woman take

her and remain with her there until I come." Smoking contentedly, Barttelot waited for the Wanyamwezi woman to lead the naked girl away. When they were out of earshot, he said, "I am going to let her go, Munichandi."

Munichandi turned to him in surprise.

"Listen to me, Munichandi. This is my plan. Later tonight, after the moon is down, I will free the girl. I will tell her she has pleased me and for this reason I am freeing her. I will let her go through the south gate. And you will follow her."

Munichandi made no reply to this.

"Select the best of your trackers and lie in wait outside the south gate. When the girl appears, follow her. Follow her cleverly. She will go to her people. Of that we can be certain. She will show us the way to the Basoko village where they hold Bwana Troup. Mark the way well. Blaze a clear trail. At first light in the morning I will come after you with a troop of askaris."

Still Munichandi said nothing.

"*Unanifahamu?*" Barttelot asked with some annoyance. He always found himself asking this question of these damn niggers. "Do you understand?"

Munichandi nodded.

"Right then. Go on, select your trackers. Instruct them. Be ready for the girl at the south gate when the moon is down." Barttelot gathered up his things, the helmet and bandolier, pistol and riding crop, and stood up from the table. "Do you have any questions?"

Munichandi shook his head.

"Well, go on then. What are you waiting for?"

"There are thousands of Basoko, Bwana. And they are cannibals."

"You need not concern yourself with that. Just follow the girl. Find the way to her village. After that you can come back. I will see to the rest." Barttelot went to his quarters, unfastening the clasps and buttons of his tunic.

The Wanyamwezi woman and the naked girl were waiting outside his house. They hadn't dared go in. They stepped aside when he arrived, the girl pulling back behind the woman.

"*Basi,*" he said to the woman. "*Nenda zako.*"

She exhaled a sigh of relief and hurried away.

"All right, my lovely. It's just the two of us now. Come along." Barttelot took the girl by her slender upper arm and felt it tense under his grip. He was surprised to discover how muscular it was. "There's nothing to be afraid of," he said. "I'll warrant you've done this a thousand times." And he propelled her firmly ahead of him into his house.

It was a pleasant enough habitation. During the hardest rains the roof tended to spring leaks and, no matter how often he put men to repairing the thatch, it could be counted on to go on leaking in one spot or another; but apart from that it was, considering the circumstances, a remarkably comfortable place: a single large room furnished with his field cot and air mattress and mosquito netting, a washstand with an enameled basin and pitcher and polished metal mirror, a field desk, two canvas folding chairs, the boxes and crates of his personal baggage serving as tables, rough planking over the packed earth for flooring, and a rough plank door hung on leather hinges for privacy.

He closed the door behind them now and lit a lantern suspended from the roof beam. In its soft orange glow, swaying from his touch, and the shifting shadows it cast, the naked girl with her full breasts and meaty thighs and round belly, cannibal that she might be, looked positively alluring. He dumped his helmet and pistol and bandolier and riding crop on one of the canvas chairs, removed his tunic, hung it on the back, and sat down on his cot.

"Right then. We'll start by taking off these boots." He stuck out his right leg. "Come here, girl. Get down here. Take these damn things off me. This one first." He pulled her down between his knees; and when, after a moment of hapless bewilderment, she finally got the idea what he wanted her to do, he leaned back a little and braced himself on the edge of the cot and placed his other boot on her naked shoulder. "Pull hard, my lovely. You've got to pull hard." And with the foot on her shoulder, he kicked her away. She went sprawling on her backside with the right boot in her hands. "*Vizuri*. Well done. Nothing to it, eh? Now the other."

She did not look up at him. She did not make a sound. And when he sent her sprawling with the second boot, she remained seated on the rough flooring, her legs splayed out in front of her, the boot clutched between them, shielding her sex. It annoyed Barttelot; for this sort of thing, he'd prefer her in a livelier mood.

"All right. Now the trousers." He unbuckled his belt and began unbuttoning the flies. "Come back here, my lovely. The trousers go next."

She set the boot aside and dutifully got back on her knees.

"Take hold of both cuffs. You can do this at one go." Barttelot raised himself an inch or two off the cot so that the seat of his trousers could freely slide down over his hips when she pulled.

And that was when he heard the drumming.

He wasn't immediately certain what it was. The sound was faint, distant, and not coming as it had in the past from directly across the river. It might have been thunder rumbling down from the rain clouds in the east. But whatever momentary question he might have had about it was dispelled by the girl. She recognized what it was right away and, letting go of his cuffs, turned toward the door, head cocked expectantly, lower lip caught between her tiny filed teeth. And then there was a shout. It came from a sentry at the far end of the fort, probably on the shooting platform at the east gate. Barttelot jumped up and quickly redid his flies. In stocking feet, stripped to the waist, belt buckle flapping, he dashed to the door and flung it open. The sound was immediately louder, and there could be no question then that it was drumming. He glanced back at the girl. She was on all fours, staring at him with wild eyes.

"You stay there. Don't you dare try to come out." He slammed the door shut behind him and ran toward the river gate.

Everywhere people were running, and all along the riverside and eastern stockades the sentries were shouting the alarm. Bartholomew came bounding out of the kitchen in a panic and collided with Barttelot.

"Christ." Barttelot yanked the boy back on his feet. "Get over to my house and guard the *bibi*. Don't let her get out." Shoving the boy out of his way, he made for the watchtower at the river gate and scrambled up. The askaris there moved aside to make room for him, jabbering excitedly, fitting rounds into the chambers of their rifles, snapping the bolts, pointing out to the river, taking no notice of his half-dressed state. He instantly regretted not having had the presence of mind to bring his field glasses with him.

Dozens of torches were burning on the river, floating down the river out of the jungle in the east, probably as much for ceremonial reasons as to light the way of the flotilla of canoes that carried them. They were big canoes with high carved prows, silvered by the newly risen moon. Besides the torchbearers in each, each canoe carried warriors armed with bows and arrows, painted fearsomely, feathers in their hair, and upstanding oarsmen wielding long ivory-topped paddles, and drummers drumming with passion. They came downriver slowly, skillfully holding themselves against the rush of the current, skillfully maneuvering through the moon-glistening rapids, advancing to the hypnotic beat of the drums in rather impressive formation, a lone canoe in the lead, two abreast behind it, then three abreast behind those, and then another three abreast, and another three, and another three, appearing from around the bend at the head of the reach. There was no telling how many there would be in all, how many more were still out of sight around the bend. They just kept coming. While he watched, Barttelot counted more than twenty.

"Jesus Christ. Now we'll have a bit of fun at last. Hold your fire, askaris. Hold your fire until I give the order. I don't want to hear a shot fired until I give the order." He clambered back down from the tower.

"*Lini*, Bwana?" one of the askaris called after him.

Barttelot jumped to the ground and looked back up. "Soon, boy. Soon enough. Don't you worry. You'll have your chance soon enough." He raced back to his quarters.

Bartholomew flung open the door for him. The girl was in there much as he had left her, on all fours, her nostrils flared, her eyes dilated, her mouth open as if she were straining all her senses to discover what was going on outside. He grabbed up his boots and while stomping his feet into them slung his bandolier over one bare shoulder and unholstered his pistol.

"It's going to be a duck shoot," he said. And suddenly he was grinning. "A regular duck shoot, by God. We're going to blow every one of those goddamn niggers right out of the water." And he dashed out again. "Munichandi."

The headman was racing about organizing the Wanyamwezis, sending the men with firearms to reinforce the askaris along the stockade, chasing the women and boys into the huts to keep them from getting underfoot.

"Lock up the two Basoko girls. Lock them up in the hut with the boys. I don't want them running around loose. I don't want them getting away."

"*Ndiyo*, Bwana."

"Hold your fire. Hold your fire." Barttelot ran down the full length of the riverside stockade shouting up at the askaris on the shooting platforms and at those at the loopholes and on the fire steps beneath them. The drumming on the river was growing more frenzied, and he had to shout louder and louder to make sure he was heard. "Not a shot. I don't want to hear a shot until I give the order. . . . Hey, you there. Where the devil do you think you're going? Get back to your posts." This to a handful of askaris who were picketed along the southern stockade but who were rushing over to get a look at the Basoko from the riverside. "All of you, get back to your posts. Where's your corporal? Corporal, get those men back to their posts."

There were at least thirty canoes visible on the river and still more were coming, but they were staying close to the far shore, well out of range of even the Winchesters, bunching up there in a blaze of torchlight. Only the lead canoe and the two following it had turned toward the fort. And someone in the prow of the lead canoe was shouting up at them.

"Keep sharp, boys. Keep sharp. It's some kind of fool trick." He cocked the hammer of his Webley.

About halfway across and still out of range, the two accompanying canoes fell back, leaving the lead canoe to come on alone, the man in its prow still shouting. It was impossible to make out what he was shouting, what with all the drumming and the steady rush of the rapids—and now also the rumble of thunder from the rain clouds lowering over the forest in the east.

And then one of the askaris said, "*Iko* Bwana Troup."

"What?"

"*Ndiyo. Kule.* It is Bwana Troup."

Barttelot squinted hard at the canoe and again cursed himself for not having sense enough to bring his binoculars. But he didn't really need them. The canoe now was close enough. It was Troup, all right. You couldn't mistake the big red beard, the floppy straw hat. He stood in the canoe's prow, one foot up on the gunwale, shouting through cupped hands. An old savage in a headdress of gray and green parrot feathers and wearing a monkey-skin cape stood beside him leaning on a carved walking staff. Behind them were warriors, flanked by standing oarsmen and torchbearers, but there didn't seem to be any drummers in this canoe.

Barttelot scrambled down from the tower. "Open the gate. That's enough. Hold it there. And stand sharp." He stepped through the partially opened gate and went to the edge of the bluff, fifty feet above the riverbank.

The canoe was now only ten or fifteen yards offshore; and seeing Barttelot appear on the bluff, Troup took off his hat and waved.

"I can't hear a word you're saying, Troup. I can't hear a bloody word of it."

But then he did hear. "Have them hold their fire, Major. All is well. Have them hold their fire."

"They're holding their fire," Barttelot called back testily. "You don't hear anyone firing, do you?"

But Troup went on shouting. "All is well. Have them hold their fire. We're going to beach now, Major. Don't do anything sudden. Don't let anyone do anything sudden. These kaffirs are jumpy as hell."

As the canoe ran up on the beach, Troup leaped out. Six warriors leaped out after him and formed a ring around him. The old savage in the monkey-skin cape and feather headdress, however, remained in the canoe, holding his walking staff, looking up at Barttelot on the bluff, studying the stockade that had been built around this portion of his village, peering at the askaris and Wanyamwezis along it. He himself was unarmed. The wrinkled, sagging skin of his chest beneath the cape was painted red with camwood; there was a white stripe across his forehead, a small white patch beneath each eye, and a piece of wood or bone pierced through his nostrils. Troup said something to him, but whatever it was, it didn't seem to make much of an impression. Then Barttelot saw Baruti making his way from the canoe's stern. He took Troup's place in the canoe's prow next to the old cannibal. Evidently he was the interpreter.

"Would you come down here, Major."

"What the devil is this all about, Troup? Where have you been? You've been absent without a word to me for three days, and now you turn up with a whole goddamn army of niggers on your heels."

"It's all right, Major. All is well if you'd just come down here."

"I think it'd be a hell of a lot wiser if you came up here."

"Please, Major. We've got a fair chance of getting some trade going with these folk. You know—goats, fowls, fish—just the sort of thing we need. So just come down here nice and friendly. They're jumpy enough as it is."

Barttelot studied the situation. The two canoes that had escorted the lead canoe were holding their position in midriver. Behind them the last three of the flotilla to appear from out of the forest were slipping into place with the others anchored along the opposite bank. That brought the total to more than fifty, as best as Barttelot could judge.

"You two," Barttelot said to the askaris peering out through the partially open gate behind him. "Come with me."

They stepped out hesitantly.

"Oh, no, Major. Just you. No one else. They don't want anyone else. And leave your pistol."

Again Barttelot had a look around. What the hell, two askaris and a pistol weren't going to be much of a help if there was trouble. And if there was, he could give the order to the riflemen to fire just as easily from the bank as up on the bluff. So he handed his pistol to one of the askaris and, signaling them both to get back behind the gate, started down the stepped path that had been cut into the face of the bluff. Absentmindedly he had held on to his bandolier, slung from one shoulder, and hooked a thumb in it now as he descended. When he reached the beach, the drumming stopped.

"You remember Baruti, don't you, Major?"

Barttelot nodded, but the boy didn't look at him.

"And this is Ngungu, chief of the Yambuya Basoko. He's as suspicious a bugger as I've ever come across, I can tell you. But I've been working on him these last few days, and I think we can bring him around. They've got plenty of livestock and fowls, and they're interested in getting back their manioc. Baruti, make the introductions. Tell him this is the chief of our people, the brave and famous soldier of the great Queen across the sea, of whom I have spoken to him." This last Troup said in Swahili.

As Baruti began translating into the vernacular, the remaining warriors in the canoe also got out and, with the six already on the beach, arranged themselves into a circle around the two white men. Barttelot glanced at them and then at Troup. Troup, however, was keeping his eyes fixed on the chief, trying to read in the old man's expression his reaction to what Baruti was saying.

"I don't much care for the look of this, Troup."

"It's all right, Major. They're more scared of us than we are of them. Go on, Baruti. Tell him that our chief is eager for peace and trade between our peoples and invites him to come into our camp and make blood brotherhood with him."

But before Baruti could translate this, the chief spoke. It was in a high-pitched tone, sharp and angry, and it drew a growling murmur of approval from the warriors on the beach and the oarsmen and torchbearers in the canoe.

"What does he say, Baruti?"

"He say he wants his children. He say he is here to have the three *msichana* and the three *mvulana* you stole returned to him."

"Yes, of course. They will be returned to him. Tell him to come into our camp and sit by our fire and make blood brotherhood with our chief and peace between our peoples. Tell him we wish to feast with him and exchange gifts with him and return his children to him."

Baruti shook his head."No, Bwana Troup. He will have the *msichana* and *mvulana* returned to him now. Before anything else."

Troup studied Baruti critically. It was a constant amazement to him how the little silly blackamoor of London had matured into this sober, authoritative adult. "Don't you tell me no, Baruti. I do not speak to you. I speak to Ngungu. Put to him what I say. And tell me what *he* answers."

Baruti shrugged and spoke with the chief at somewhat greater length than Troup thought warranted, perhaps interpolating his own advice into the translation. In any case, the chief's reply was brief. "It is as I have told you, Bwana Troup. Ngungu will have his children returned to him first. They have been held as hostage for your safe return, and now that you have returned safe and unharmed he will have them brought to him. That was your promise."

Troup exhaled a weary sigh and nodded. "Yes, it was," he said in English. "Yes, all right, I suppose it's only fair." He turned to Barttelot. "I guess we had best bring them down here, Major. I don't think we're going to get any closer to a trade arrangement with this bugger until we do. Where are they?"

"Munichandi's holding them," Barttelot replied. "But he's not going to bring them down here. We're not just going to turn them loose. We're going to get something for them. If this old nigger wants them back, he's going to have to give us something for them. He's going to have to trade for them."

"Now wait a minute, Major. That ain't the bargain I struck."

"I don't know anything about what bargain you struck, Troup. Frankly I don't know why you struck any bargain with them. And I don't know why you're babying them like this now. Blood brotherhood, peace parleys—"

"That's how it's done in this country, Major. It's the only way to get this sort of thing done in this country."

"Maybe by you, Troup, maybe by Mr. Stanley. But I've my own ideas how to handle niggers. Baruti, tell your chief we are in need of goats. Tell him we are in need of fowls and fish. Tell him if he wants his children back, he must—"

"No, Baruti. Don't tell him that. Don't say anything."

But Baruti hadn't been planning to say anything. Barttelot had spoken in English, all the exchange between Troup and Barttelot had taken place in English, and he hadn't understood much of it. He was aware, however, that a dispute of some sort was developing between the two white men, and he eyed them suspiciously. So did the chief and the warriors.

"Listen to me, Major." Troup took hold of Barttelot's arm as if wishing he could draw him away and speak to him privately. "You're going to wreck this whole goddamn thing."

"Take your hand off me, Troup."

"Oh, Jesus." Troup rolled his eyes in exasperation, but he let go of Barttelot. "You're not looking past your own nose, Major. It ain't going to work this way. These blokes ain't going to pay ransom."

"Let's just see if they won't. Let's just see if I don't have the means to persuade them to. Baruti."

But Baruti had turned away. The chief was speaking again in that sharp, angry high-pitched voice; and whatever he was saying was causing a stir among the warriors on the beach. They tightened their circle around Troup and Barttelot.

"*Kile ni nini*, Baruti?"

Baruti turned to Troup. "They are dead. Ngungu say they are dead."

"What? Who's dead?"

"The three *msichana*. The three *mvulana*. Ngungu say they are dead. He say the major killed them while you were with us and that is why you quarrel with him now."

"No, that's not so. Tell him it's not so," Troup shot back. But then his face suddenly went white and he turned to Barttelot. "It isn't, is it, Major? You haven't had them killed, have you?"

"Now look here—"

"Answer me. Just answer me. Because if they're dead—"

"Nobody's dead. They're all safe and sound, don't you worry."

"Well, we better let these blokes see that for themselves. Because if they get it into their heads that we've killed them . . . Munichandi."

"You just hold on there, Troup. I'm in command here. I give the orders here."

"Well, give it then. Have Munichandi bring them to the river gate. You can haggle about what you want to do with them afterward. But at least let these buggers have a look at them. Let them see that they're still alive and kicking. Or you're not going to have a chance to haggle about much of anything. Don't you see what's happening? Take a look out there."

The two canoes that had remained in midriver were now on the move again, coming toward shore. And Barttelot saw why: A torchbearer in the chief's canoe was waving his torch at them. In a moment perhaps all the canoes waiting along the far bank would see the signal and also start coming across.

"I keep telling you, Major. These buggers are jumpy as hell. Anything could set them off."

"Yes, well, I think it's time then that we got the hell out of here. Come along." Barttelot turned toward the path leading up the face of the bluff.

The warriors, however, were blocking his way.

"Tell them to get out of my way, Baruti. Tell them I'm going up to the fort to fetch the children, to show them they are not dead."

Baruti relayed this information to the chief. The chief considered it for a moment, squinting at Barttelot appraisingly. Then he gestured with his carved walking staff and the warriors stepped aside.

"Come on, Troup."

Troup shook his head.

"Don't be a fool, man. This is going to get rather sticky in a minute. It won't be a healthy place to be."

"They won't let me go, Major."

"What do you mean they won't let you go?"

"I told you. I struck a bargain with them. That was the bargain I struck. They won't let me go until they get their children back."

It took a moment for this to register. Then Barttelot said, "Oh, Christ, that's fine. That's just fine."

"So do me a favor. No tricks. Just go on up there and get them. All right?"

"Well, I don't see that you've left me much choice. You've pretty well tied my hands, haven't you?" Barttelot looked around. The two canoes were now running up on the beach, one on either side of the chief's canoe, and a dozen or more warriors from each were jumping out and wading ashore. "And I can't say that I appreciate it. I can't say I appreciate it at all." And with a thumb hooked in the bandolier slung from his naked shoulder he went up the path to the fort.

Several minutes passed. No one spoke. The askaris on the shooting platforms and at the loopholes in the stockade peered down their rifle barrels at the Basoko warriors on the beach. The Basoko warriors on the beach, now numbering nearly forty from the three canoes, peered back up at the river gate through which Barttelot had disappeared. The chief, Ngungu—motionless except for his hand clasping and unclasping his walking staff, Baruti at his side in the prow of the main canoe—also watched the river gate. The torchbearer in the stern had quit his signaling, and the canoes clustered against the opposite bank remained where they were. Troup removed his straw hat and wiped his brow with his sleeve. The air was thick and muggy and still, the stillness before the rain, the mass of clouds from the east now lowering over the water, rumbling with thunder, shimmering with flashes of sheet lightning, obscuring and revealing a racing moon. The mosquitoes and flies were out in force, whining in the stillness.

"*Kule*, Baruti. *Tazama kule*. Look there. There they are."

Troup shouted this before he actually saw them when some figures suddenly appeared at the partially opened gate. But it was them all right. The three boys came first, then the two women who had been with them in the prison hut. Munichandi and the askari who had guarded the hut herded them out. They came forward hesitantly, glancing from side to side and to the rear, until they reached the edge of the high bluff, where they stopped in plain view, unsure what to do. Munichandi and the askari remained behind them, not wanting to expose themselves unnecessarily to the warriors below.

"There, Baruti, you see. They are not dead. They are alive and well. No harm has come to them, as I promised none would."

"There is only five, Bwana Troup. There were six who you stole. There is a *msichana* missing who was with the others but who I do not see."

In truth, Troup didn't remember exactly how many hostages had been taken, but he did not doubt the boy. "Munichandi, there is another woman. Where is she?"

"Here. Don't worry, Troup. She's here." That was Barttelot. He came through the river gate with the girl who'd been held in his quarters. He held her by the upper arm and in his other hand once again gripped his pistol; and as he brought her forward to the edge of the bluff, a soft groan arose from Baruti and Ngungu and the warriors on the beach. It took Troup a moment to understand what elicited it. He hadn't immediately realized that the girl was stark naked. After all, these Basoko were so very nearly naked anyway, the women as unmindful of their bare chests as the men. But then he noticed the girl's posture, the way her hands were pressed between her thighs and her knees bent one over the other.

"Oh, Christ."

"Go on. Get along." Barttelot released the girl's arm with a shove. "I'm giving them back, Troup. I'm giving them all back to save your hide. Go on, all of you. Get out of here."

The three boys took only a moment to grasp what was happening and dashed down the bluff to the beach. And the two other women, seeing that, came after them quickly enough. But the naked girl remained where she was.

"Go on, girl. Get along with you." Barttelot prodded her with his pistol. "I'm done with you."

She stumbled a few steps forward, then stopped again, turning away from her people on the beach, crouching deeper, covering herself further. And then Baruti jumped out of the canoe and ran across the beach toward her. All along the stockade, the askaris immediately tensed over their rifles.

"Baruti," Troup cried out.

The boy stopped at the foot of the bluff and called up to her. She turned slightly, looking over her shoulder down at him. He extended his hand and called again, and then started up the path toward her. Again Troup shouted a warning, but now the girl realized that the boy was putting himself in jeopardy for her sake and, reaching out her own hand, ran down the path to him. He flung an arm around her waist, and together they ran across the beach to the chief's canoe. The other five had already jumped in and were being hurried back to safety in the stern.

"All right. That's all of them. They've got all of them back. So you're free, Troup. You can come up here now."

"Yes," Troup said but he turned to Ngungu.

The chief was watching Baruti bring the naked girl into the canoe. When she was aboard, he removed his monkey-skin cape and thrust it at her. She took it without looking at him and quickly tied it around her waist like an apron, then hurried back into the stern, in her humiliation not looking at the oarsmen and torchbearers she passed.

"Baruti, tell Ngungu–"

"I said you can come up here now, Troup."

"I hear you, Major."

"Well then?"

"I want to see if I can salvage anything from this, Major. I want to see if we can still deal with these chaps now that we've returned their people."

"I'm not interested in dealing with them, Troup. Just get up here."

"For Christ sake, Major, if we can get a hold of some goats–"

"Get up here, Troup. I'm ordering you to get up here. I'm having this gate closed in a minute and I want you up here before I do." Barttelot walked back to the river gate.

Troup studied him for a moment, standing in the gate's opening, stripped to the waist, the bandolier slung from one shoulder, the pistol in his hand. He couldn't make out the expression on his face. But he saw that Munichandi and the other Wanyamwezis had cleared off, leaving only askaris at the gate. Then it dawned on him what was happening, and he turned to Baruti.

"*Nenda zako, toto.* Go away from here. Go away quickly. Tell Ngungu. Gather up your people and go away."

"Troup, I'm waiting for you."

"Right away, Major. Listen to me, Baruti. Tell Ngungu, he must get his people away from here. There will be trouble."

Baruti stared at him for a moment, uncomprehending. Then he suddenly understood and began shouting at the warriors on the beach. They whirled around toward him.

"What are you doing, Troup? Goddamn you, man."

"Get them out of here, Baruti. Get them out of here." And dropping into a deep crouch, hanging on to his straw hat, Troup made a dash for the path leading up the bluff.

The first shot was fired while the warriors were still on the beach. They hadn't responded to Baruti's warning. They had been waiting to hear from their chief. But when the first shot was fired, they ran for the canoes.

"You bastard," Troup shouted as he went hurtling through the river gate. "You crazy goddamn bastard. Why did you do that?"

But Barttelot wasn't there to answer. He had scrambled up to the watchtower beside the gate and was standing there with his pistol braced in both hands firing down at the beach.

Only two Basoko were killed. A few others may have been hit, but if so, their mates managed to drag them away. They hadn't tried to make a fight of it. Perhaps Baruti had warned them about the guns. Perhaps they already knew what guns could do from their experience with Tippoo-Tib's slavers. Or perhaps they had never intended to fight at all, had only come to recover their stolen children and entertain the white man's offer of peace and trade. But whichever the case, they cleared out as quickly as they could once the firing started, the warriors on the beach scrambling back into the canoes, the drummers starting up again, the torchbearers frantically waving their torches, the oarsmen pushing off and paddling like demons. And then the rain came.

Barttelot kept every askari and every Wanyamwezi at a firing position along the riverside and eastern stockades all through the night, expecting the Basoko to regroup and attack, and hoping they would. But when morning came, fresh and clear from the rain, there were only the two dead warriors lying facedown on the beach. Buzzards had gathered around them. A detail of askaris went down and threw the bodies to the crocodiles.

· THREE ·

ON AUGUST 14, the paddle-wheel steamer *Stanley* returned to Yambuya bringing up Herbert Ward, Sergeant Billy Bonny, and the remaining contingent of the rear column—three hundred *pagazis*, nine women and boys, twenty-three riding and pack animals, and some eighty tons of stores and equipment—from Equator Station.

It was eleven-thirty in the morning, a Sunday, and the sodden, suffocating heat of the day was nearing its zenith. Barttelot and Troup were down on the beach beneath the fort's river gate, the rest of the encampment was gathered atop the bluff behind them, watching in sunstruck silence as Shagerstrom, the *Stanley*'s captain, his shaggy head stuck out of the wheelhouse, a yellow meerschaum pipe clasped between his teeth, gingerly picked his way through a channel along the opposite bank (the Aruwimi's single safe channel for a vessel this size) until he reached the first of the rapids. Then he began the tricky business of maneuvering her across, with the Bangala crewmen hanging over the side sounding the fathoms; Walker, the engineer, periodically popping out of the engine room to shout instructions at them; the Wanyamwezi passengers, packed like sardines along the lower deck rail, waving to their mates on shore.

A half-mile or so farther upriver, skulking in the orchilla weed overhanging backwater, a lone Basoko in a canoe also watched the steamer's arrival. Troup had noticed it on coming out of the fort, but apparently Barttelot hadn't and he had chosen not to mention it to him. Nothing had been seen of the Basoko since the trouble two weeks before. When they had cleared out that morning after the shooting, they had cleared out for good. Their nightly drumming never resumed. And when Troup, on the off-chance that he might be able to repair the damage Barttelot had done, made a secret reconnaissance of the village where Baruti had taken him, he found the village abandoned. So the Basoko reappearance now was something of a surprise.

Troup guessed it was Baruti's doing. After all, the boy understood the significance of the steamer's return and probably had advised Ngungu to keep a watch on the fort to see when the now reunited rear column would at last depart. No harm in that—let them watch and see whatever they liked—but Troup decided it was just as well not to call Barttelot's attention to it. There was no knowing what *he* would make of it and try to do about it. With every passing day, his behavior was becoming more erratic.

"Ahoy there, lads. Ahoy, you buckos."

That was Bertie Ward, having a bit of fun playing at being a sailor. He elbowed his way through the crush of Wanyamwezis at the lower deck rail; and when the steamer edged in as close as she could get, swinging starboard in the shallows with a great churning of muddy water as her paddle wheels reversed, he ordered the gangway lowered and came down it with the jaunty rolling gait of a buccaneer. Troup smiled at the sight of him, wearing a battered Aussie campaign hat, one side of its wide brim tacked up against the crown, a canvas shooting jacket with a profusion of cartridge loops, dark green corduroy knickerbockers, and a Sharps carbine casually slung upside down across his back.

"Major. Jack, old boy." He shook hands with Barttelot and gave Troup an exuberant hug. "How have you chaps been faring? Any trouble? Have the natives been friendly?" He asked this lightheartedly, not really expecting an answer.

But he got one, quick and sharp. "Not half as friendly as Mr. Stanley led us to expect," Barttelot said. "Nor, for that matter has his great chum Tippoo-Tib been half as forthcoming."

"Oh?"

"The bloody niggers have been trying to starve us out. And as for Tippoo-Tib, we haven't seen hide nor hair of the porters he promised."

"You haven't? I say, that doesn't seem right. It's been six weeks."

"I'm perfectly aware how long it's been," Barttelot replied and, brusquely brushing past Ward, went up the gangway.

Ward looked at Troup. "What's eating him?"

Troup shrugged. "I'll tell you about it later," he said and followed Barttelot onto the steamer.

"My congratulations, Captain," Barttelot said. "You made excellent time. You're practically dead on schedule. I confess, I didn't expect it, what with the way everything else around here has been buggered up. I take it you had no further problems with this tub."

"None to speak of, Major," Shagerstrom replied, coming down from the bridge.

"And you've managed to bring everything up? All the men and loads? You haven't had to leave anything behind this time?"

"No, it's all here. You can check everything against the manifest when you offload."

"That's fine. And with your permission, I'd like to offload now."

"Now? Oh, surely not now, Major. Not at this time of day. It's too beastly hot for that. Give it a couple of hours, when it's cooled off a bit. In the meantime, we can have a spot of lunch. I rather thought you and Mr. Troup might like to eat on board, so I've had my cookboy put up some chop. Nothing fancy, but I suspect it'd make a welcome change from what the two of you have been having."

"I'm sure it would, Captain. Because what we've been having has been pretty damn awful, manioc mostly. Manioc mush. Hardly ever even a scrap of meat. The damn niggers hereabouts refuse to trade with us. They—" Barttelot cut himself off, hearing a peevish whine creep into his voice. "But I'm afraid we're going to have to pass it up. I'm anxious to get the stores and equipment offloaded and the new men organized and assigned to billets."

Shagerstrom looked at Barttelot quizzically for a moment, then said, "As you wish, Major."

"Mr. Troup."

Troup and Ward had stopped to talk with some of the newly arrived Wayamwezis. They came over.

"Have Munichandi bring his *pagazis* on board, will you, Mr. Troup? And Mr. Ward, round up your people. We're going to start offloading."

"But what about lunch?" Ward asked. "I thought we were going to have lunch. Captain Shagerstrom's boy has laid on a grand meal for us, Major, a sort of farewell meal."

"We're passing it up."

"But why?"

"Because we've got to get on our way, Mr. Ward." And again that strained, grating note of irritation invaded Barttelot's voice. "Because we've got to get the hell out of this pest-hole and on the march after Mr. Stanley as soon as we bloody well can. That's why."

"Yes, I realize that. But we can't get on our way yet. We don't have enough porters. You said so yourself. You said Tippo-Tib's porters haven't turned up yet."

"That's right, Mr. Ward. I said that. They haven't. And that's precisely why I want this vessel offloaded as quickly as possible. So that I can go up on her to the Falls and see what in God's name is holding them up."

"So you can do what, Major?" This was Shagerstrom.

"I have to ask you to do me this favor, Captain. The porters Tippoo-Tib promised us are overdue. They should have been here before this. I've been meaning to go up to the Falls for some time now to see what's happened to them. But as Mr. Troup has been kind enough to remind me, Mr. Stanley was quite specific about none of us going up there. He was confident there'd be no need, that Tippoo-Tib would get the porters to us in plenty of time, certainly by the time you returned from Equator Station with the rest of our men and loads. Well, he was wrong, Captain. He was as wrong about that as he has been about any number of things. They're still not here. And we can't move out until they get here. We're stuck in this place until they get here."

"I don't know, Major. I really ought to be getting back to Leopoldville. There's going to be enough of a fuss about the steamers as it is, what with the way Bula Matari commandeered them."

"It'll only delay you a day or two, Captain. A day or two won't make any difference. And it'll save me a week of hard slogging through the forest."

"I really don't know, Major," Shagerstrom said again and looked at Troup.

Barttelot also looked at Troup, as if expecting him, indeed challenging him, to raise an objection. But Troup raised no objection. There was no objection he could raise. What Barttelot said was true. They had to get on the march into the Ituri as soon as possible. Stanley was counting on them being no more than six or seven weeks behind him. But the reunited rear column, adding those Shagerstrom had brought up from Equator Station to those Stanley had left behind at Yambuya, had well in excess of a thousand loads to carry to Lake Albert and barely 400 of its own *pagazis* and a score of pack mules to carry them. Clearly they couldn't get on the march until the 600 porters contracted from Tippoo-Tib arrived. The only real question was why they still hadn't arrived.

"Do you want me to go with you, Major?"

"No, I'll handle it."

"He's a tricky customer, Major. A bazaar Arab to his marrow."

"I can manage him. Don't you worry. I've managed his sort before. You just have the column ready to move out when I get back. Well, Captain, what do you say?"

"How long were you planning to stay at the Falls?"

"That doesn't matter. I'm not asking you to wait for me. Just drop me off and be on your way. I'll come back with the porters."

They departed Yambuya at two that same afternoon, sailing westward down the Aruwimi into the Congo, then southward up the Congo to Stanley Falls. Altogether it was a voyage of about 185 miles—sixty to the mouth of the Aruwimi, another 125 up the Congo but with the steamer now lightly loaded—the only passengers and cargo aboard were five askaris Barttelot brought along as a bodyguard, a riding donkey, a pack mule, twenty *pagazis*, plus the kit and supplies needed for the return trip overland—they made good time. They reached the confluence of the two rivers before sunset; and by two the following afternoon, they were within sound if not yet quite sight of the Wagenia cataract, the last of the series of seven falls.

As they steamed toward it, canoes came down to meet them. These were Arab canoes, for this now was Arab country, the northern frontier of the vast realm that Tippoo-Tib had overrun and ravaged and conquered and now ruled with the imperiousness of an absolute monarch.

Seeing its major settlement, Singatini, from the bridge of the steamer, as he had seen it in late June when he had come up with Stanley and Jephson, Barttelot was again struck by the utter improbability of the place, its luxuriousness, its air of cosmopolitan civilization, the handsome, palm-lined promenade along the riverfront, the tents and kiosks of the souks and bazaars on the beach, and beyond that, where the jungle itself began, the skyline of minarets and domes and flat-roofed white-washed palaces and villas with ornamentally carved balconies and heavily timbered, brass-studded doors surrounded by lush gardens of bougainvillea and frangipani and orchards of flowering fruit trees. It was a miniature Zanzibar cut out of the blackest forest, an Arabian nights fantasy set down in the heart of a savage wilderness. But unlike that first time, he did not see the sultan of the place, Tippoo-Tib himself, among the colorful crowds of robed Arabs and loincloth-clad Zanzibaris, musket-bearing Manyema gunmen, and half-naked slaves who gathered along the riverfront as the steamer approached. Indeed, scanning their faces through his binoculars, he saw only one that he recognized from the previous visit: a dark-skinned, hawk-nosed fellow with coal-black eyes and a pointed coal-black beard, wearing a golden hoop in one ear, a short silver-embroidered maroon vest over his white djellaba, a similarly embroidered maroon skullcap, soft leather boots with curled toes, and a jeweled ceremonial Shirazi dagger in his belt.

"Well, I don't suppose we could expect the old boy to put in a personal appearance for anyone but Mr. Stanley," Barttelot remarked, lowering his field glasses.

Shagerstrom didn't reply. He probably hadn't heard him. He was busy bringing the steamer portside along the riverbank, shouting instructions down at Walker in the engine room and to the crewmen on the lower deck making ready to fling their lines and hawsers to those ashore. When at last he had her safely moored, he stepped out of the wheelhouse. "What was that you said, Major?"

"Who's that chap down there? I met him the last time I was here but I can't think of his name."

"Which one? Oh, that's Tippoo-Tib's brother, Selim–Sheik Selim bin Mohammed."

"Yes, that's it. Selim bin Mohammed."

The Arab had come all the way down to the water's edge to watch as the deckhands lowered the gangway and Barttelot's party disembarked: first the five Winchester-armed askaris, then Bartholomew the cookboy leading Barttelot's riding donkey, another boy leading the pack mule loaded with Barttelot's personal baggage, and then the twenty *pagazis* carrying the bundles and boxes of supplies needed for the return journey. When all were ashore, he looked up at Barttelot and Shagerstrom on the bridge and salaamed. Two other Arabs in sheikly dress stood a step or two behind him; and a squad of Manyema gunmen formed a semicircle around them, keeping the rest of the people on the beach at a respectful distance. Barttelot returned the salaam.

"Well, I'll say goodbye to you now, Major."

"Aren't you coming ashore?"

"No, I think not. There's still plenty of daylight left. I'm anxious to get back to Leo as soon as I can. I can make some good headway before dark."

"These buggers set an awfully good table, Captain. It'd be a pity to miss out on one of their feasts now that you're already here. Why not start back first thing tomorrow?"

"It's tempting, I'll say that, Major." Shagerstrom looked out to the houses and flowering gardens of Singatini, then shook his head ruefully. "But I think not. I think I'd best be on my way. I'm long overdue."

"Very well. Thanks for the passage."

"*Si kitu.*" Shagerstrom shook Barttelot's hand. "Good luck."

"Thanks." Barttelot turned away and headed for the ladder leading down from the bridge.

"And be careful."

Barttelot looked back.

"He's a tricky customer, Major. Like Jack said, he's a bloody fox. So be careful. Be on your guard."

Barttelot hesitated a moment as if he intended to reply to this, but then merely nodded and went down the ladder.

The *pagazis*, waiting on the beach, had downed their loads and stood around gawking at their extraordinary surroundings. But the five askaris had paraded at the foot of the gangway and, when Barttelot came down it, snapped sharply to attention and presented arms. It was a crisp performance after all the drilling Barttelot had put them through, smart and impressive, as Barttelot intended it to be. He touched his helmet with his riding crop and strode over to the Arab.

"*Salaam aleikum*, Selim bin Mohammed."

"*Salaam aleikum*, Major Barttelot. It is Major Barttelot, is it not?"

"It is. Major Edmund Musgrave Barttelot, Seventh Royal Fusiliers, commanding the rear column of Mr. Stanley's Emin Pasha relief expedition."

"Welcome to Singatini, Major Barttelot. To what do we owe the honor of this unexpected visit?"

"Unexpected, Selim? No, I shouldn't think it is unexpected."

"No?"

"It is now more than six weeks since I was here with Mr. Stanley. It is now more than six weeks since Mr. Stanley contracted with your brother to provide my rear column with six hundred porters. It is now more than six weeks that I have been waiting in Yambuya for those porters. Surely it is not unexpected that after all this time I have finally come to Singatini to ask your brother, Hamed bin Mohammed, what has become of those porters."

"Ah, the porters. Yes, of course, the porters."

"So please be so good as to take me to him, Selim. My column is ready to march. I have no time to waste."

But before the Arab could respond to this, the steamer's whistle sounded a shrill blast and everyone turned to watch her put off from shore.

Selim turned back to Barttelot. "When does the steamer return for you, Major?"

"She doesn't. She goes now to Leopoldville."

"Oh?" Selim cocked an eyebrow quizzically. Then, smiling, he said, "Ah, yes, I see. Of course. That is why you have brought this little caravan with you." He pointed to the *pagazis* and animals. "You intend to make the journey back to Yambuya overland."

"That's right. And I intend to make it with the porters your brother promised to provide me. So if you please, Selim, let us go to him. I wish to settle this matter quickly and be on my way."

"Ah, but I am afraid it cannot be settled quite so quickly as that, Major."

"Why not? Oh, for God's sake, don't tell me he isn't here."

"No, it is not that, Major. He is here, but at the moment . . . How shall I put this? Well, let me just say that at the moment he is otherwise engaged. A man like my brother, as you surely will understand, has many matters to engage him." Selim made a vague fluttering gesture with his hand and smiled knowingly. "But I shall have him informed that you have come, and I am certain he will be eager to see you as soon as he is free." Selim said a few words in Arabic to one of the two Arabs standing behind him, and the fellow hurried off. "In the meantime, allow me to offer you and your men the hospitality of Singatini in his stead. Come." He reached to take Barttelot's hand in the Arabian fashion, as Tippoo-Tib had done on the previous visit, but Barttelot withheld it.

On that previous visit a gaudily striped marquee had been set up on the waterfront promenade to receive the visitors; and Barttelot now looked for something similar among the tents and kiosks of the bustling bazaars and souks, expecting to be taken there. However, this time there was no such marquee. This time he was taken into Singatini itself.

On entering into its humid shadows from the blaze of the beach, Barttelot saw how much there was to it, how much more than a settlement or trading station; it was truly a town, a jumble of structures of every description covering several acres of ground—stables, smithies, shops, storehouses, sheds, barracks for the gunmen, tembes for the servants, besides the mosques and villas seen from the river—all closely packed around flagged plazas and along high-walled cobblestoned alleyways, a town in which a man could get lost. He looked back. His askaris in single file had been following him and Selim, and behind them in a column of twos with their loads were the *pagazis* and mule and donkey. Now, however, the second of the two Arabs who had been with Selim on the beach turned them off into a side street. It was the cookboy Bartholomew's cry of surprise at this development that had caused Barttelot to look back.

"They will be made comfortable, Major," Selim said, also stopping to look back. "They will be well looked after."

"I am sure they will," Barttelot replied, but he didn't like it. He didn't so much mind about the *pagazis*, but he had planned to have his soldiers with him when he met Tippoo-Tib, for the impression they would make, for the status they would bestow.

"They will not be far," Selim went on, as if divining Barttelot's thought. "You can call them to your side whenever you wish."

Barttelot nodded but remained where he was, watching his little caravan disappear up the narrow crooked street. Then he went on with Selim alone.

They came to a small enclosed square, entered through a low archway, partially paved with flagstones, newly planted around with mango and lime trees and with a rock-rimmed fountain at its center. It was a cul-de-sac. On the left was a ten-foot-high wall of baked brick with smoothly rounded tops. A stone bench facing the fountain and shaded by an arbor of flowering lianas stood against the wall directly ahead. The wall on the left seemed to close off a garden; branches of crimson flamboyants, pink and white bougainvillea, blue jasmine, and purple mimosa showed over the top, their fragrance hanging heavy in the still, humid air. An ornately carved brass-studded door, at the moment shut, provided access through it. On the right was a single-story, flat-roofed whitewashed house with a door exactly mirroring the one in the wall opposite, with small windows on either side covered by Moorish grillwork to filter out the sunlight.

"Your quarters, Major," Selim said, directing Barttelot to the house. "I hope you find it to your liking." He clapped his hands.

The door was opened from the inside by a servant in white caftan and skullcap. Barttelot, however, did not enter. He looked around the little square. Sunlight slanting through the delicate leaves of the young fruit trees dappled the irregularly cut flagstones. The tinkling of water in the fountain echoed musically from the enclosing walls.

"We are here within my brother's compound," Selim said, following Barttelot's gaze. "His own house stands just there, in that garden."

"It is quite lovely."

Selim bowed.

"Tell me something, Selim."

"Whatever you wish."

"I've been wondering about this since I last was here. I've been wondering about it during all these weeks of waiting for the porters in Yambuya. Mr. Stanley took your brother's word about the porters, Selim. He wagered the success of his expedition on the strength of your brother's promise to him in that regard. What I have been wondering, Selim, is whether he was mistaken to do so."

Selim's expression stiffened. "My brother is a man of his word, Major. He does not break his promises."

"Yes? Then tell me, Selim, why has he not yet sent the porters?"

"There have been difficulties, Major. As you know—you yourself were there when my brother explained it to Bula Matari—we do not have a sufficient number of men here in Singatini to spare six hundred for you. We have had to send to Kasongo for them. And Kasongo is far. But it is not my place to discuss this with you, Major. You must discuss it with my brother. I will go to him now and see when he will be free to receive you. I will return for you directly that he is. In the meantime, I think you will find everything you require in the house."

Barttelot watched Selim stride across the square, open the door in the wall opposite, and pass through into the garden beyond. It surprised him that the door was neither locked nor guarded. Selim hadn't needed a key; no one had appeared to be on the other side. Evidently Tippoo-Tib felt himself secure in his lair. Barttelot glanced at the servant standing in the doorway of the house, but he still didn't go in. He walked back to the archway through which he and Selim had entered the square and looked up the winding cobbled alleyway they had come down. He could see the side street where his caravan had turned off but not much farther. The high walls, the closely packed buildings with their overlooking balconies, the trees and foliage of the gardens, and the twist of the alleyway itself cut off his line of sight back to the river.

Absently slapping his riding crop against his leg, he studied the scene, meaning to fix certain landmarks in his memory so that he'd be able to find his way through the jumble back to the river on his own. While he looked, people came and went: a man riding a donkey, a woman passing from one street into another with an earthenware jug on her head, children scampering over the rooftops, Manyema gunmen leading a yoked column of slaves. They threw him a curious glance but did not approach, did not dare come near, let alone enter this square within their sultan's compound. Here all was quiet; here a pleasant, peaceful stillness reigned. He went into the house, selected a mango from a variety of refreshments set out for him in there, and, polishing it in his hands, his riding crop tucked under an arm, went back out into the square.

He waited two hours. He sat on the stone bench facing the fountain and ate the mango, then went over to the fountain and washed the juice from his hands in the pool. There were carp and frogs in the pool, but his splashing in the water didn't frighten them. The fish came over to see if he had food for them, and the frogs, seated on lily pads, croaked contentedly. Drying his hands, he walked around the square, taking another look through the archway up the alley, then sat down on the stone bench again and smoked a cigarette. Twice he went back into the house for refreshments, some bread and cheese, a glass of milk, another mango.

He was restless of course, annoyed by the need to wait, impatient to get this matter settled and be on his way, rehearsing in his mind as he paced around the square what he would say to Tippoo-Tib and what tone he'd use to say it: firm without being impolite. He must not risk offending the bugger and give him an excuse not to supply the porters. He was at his mercy in this—Stanley had left him at his mercy—but oddly he was not quite as restless or impatient, the waiting didn't annoy him quite as much as it ordinarily would have. There was something about the quiet of the square, the pleasant stillness, the tinkling of the fountain that had a peculiarly lulling effect; he found himself relaxing in a way that he himself vaguely realized might not be such a good thing.

The sun passed over the square, and the sharp black shadows cast by the fruit trees were swallowed up in the soft blue shadows cast by the walls. The birdsong and the frogs' croaking seemed to grow livelier, and the fragrance of the flamboyants and jasmine richer and more intense with the lessening of the day's heat. He looked at his pocket watch; it was coming on to five. He smoked another cigarette, then continued on yet another aimless round of the square, idly flicking at his boots with his riding crop, counting the flagstones he crossed.

When he came to the door in the wall to Tippoo-Tib's garden, he pushed at it experimentally. It swung open easily and as easily swung shut. After a moment he pushed it again and held it open with his foot and looked in. It was a lush, gorgeously disordered garden with no sign of formal design, more nearly a walled-off section of jungle than a garden in the usual sense, so wildly overgrown with shrubs and plants and flowering trees that all that could be seen of Tippoo-Tib's house, a hundred or so yards away, was a fuzzy patch of white, shimmering like a mist within the riot of brilliant greens and reds and yellows of the foliage. A lane of white-washed gravel led toward it from the door. Letting the door swing closed behind him, he took a few cautious steps down this lane. When Selim had passed through, no one had appeared, but Barttelot suspected that in his case guards would materialize soon enough. They didn't. He went on tentatively, clasping his riding crop in both hands behind his back. He wasn't really going anywhere; he expected at every step to be stopped; he was just looking around. The perfume of the flowers was incredibly sweet, intoxicating, and the singing of the birds in the trees exuberantly beautiful.

About a quarter of the way along, the gravel lane divided. Bearing to the right it continued on toward the patch of white of Tippoo-Tib's house, still thickly obscured by the riot of intervening vegetation. To the left, however, it curved off into a small circular clearing of neatly cropped grass glowing orange in the rays of the lowering sun. Barttelot stopped. A child was there, a little Arab boy dressed only in a shirt, his thumb in his mouth. He stared at Barttelot seemingly unafraid; but when Barttelot started toward him, the child scampered away. Barttelot stopped and waited, thinking that his presence must have been noted now, and someone surely would come. But still no one came. He looked up at the sky over the clearing—pale blue but already streaked with the dark clouds that would bring the nightly rain—and saw a flock of cranes flying west toward the river. And an odd idea occurred to him: perhaps Tippoo-Tib had expected him to do this, had expected that in his restlessness he would not be content to wait and would come on his own before anyone sent for him, and therefore had left the garden door unlocked for him and the garden unguarded. An odd idea; he shook it off and continued strolling toward the house.

And then quite suddenly he was there. It had seemed to be still some distance away, but the light in the garden at this hour was deceptive; and before he quite realized it or was prepared for it he found that he had passed through the last of the trees and flowering bushes and had emerged into yet another clearing, this a large grassy park where bulking over him stood a sprawling structure two stories high topped by a fretted turret, something like a widow's walk, from where doubtless one could see out to the Congo. If not a palace exactly, it was certainly a villa, star-shaped in design, its whitewashed walls now glowing a brassy gold in the sunset.

The gravel lane had brought him to its southwest corner; a stoop of two stone steps there led up to a door. This was surely not the main entrance; it was too nondescript. The main entrance of a building of these grand proportions must be something quite grand itself, giving out onto a grand veranda, giving out onto a grand prospect of the river. This was a back door. It probably led into kitchens or storerooms or servant quarters. The first story on this side of the building had no windows, but there were a few on the second: narrow embrasures, arched, screened with grillwork, with small wooden balconies. He looked up to see if anyone was looking down at him from these or from the roof or from the turret. No one was. So he went on. He climbed the two stone steps and tried the door. It too was unlocked.

It was dark inside because of the absence of windows, but after a moment his eyes adjusted well enough to make out a small foyer or antechamber with stone floor and tiled walls. A corridor led off it at an angle into what must be the center of the building; and at the far end he saw light, the last rays of sunlight streaming through a window, or perhaps lantern light. He started toward it. His boot heels, striking the stone of the floor, echoing from the tile of the walls, sounded very loud, and he immediately stopped. Now surely he must be discovered. He realized he was holding his breath. And then he heard music, the music of stringed instruments whining plaintively, the jangle of metal castanets, the throb of a drum, the trilling notes of a flute. He took off his helmet and smoothed his hair, straightened his tunic, adjusted his pistol belt, and tucked the riding crop firmly under an arm. He strode down the corridor purposefully.

The corridor brought him into a large circular room with an immensely high domed ceiling supported by calcimined pillars. The floor of highly polished pink granite was scattered about with Persian carpets, and the tiles in the ceiling had been arranged into a mosaic of Arabian script. The place had the look of a mosque. He had entered it from the south. In the west wall, through which streamed the sunlight, were two arched windows on either side of heavily timbered double doors standing open on a porticoed veranda, which in turn looked out across a formal garden of palms and fruit trees, mimosa bushes, fountains, and benches. To his right in the east wall was an archway, lower than the opposite windows and doors and covered by an embroidered hanging. It was from behind this hanging that the music emanated. On either side of it guards were posted, ebony-black Manyema in long belted white shirts, barefoot and armed with spears. They were lounging on their spears, listening to the music as if captivated by it; but as soon as Barttelot appeared, they drew themselves to attention. He expected them to challenge him and waited for this, preparing a sharp reply in Swahili. But they said nothing. Perhaps he was expected after all. Yes, perhaps he was. He went to the archway and drew the hanging aside.

"Ah, the beautiful soldier."

Barttelot immediately recognized the voice, remembered this insinuating appellation the Arab had coined for him on the last visit, but did not at once see him. He saw the dancer. She was no longer dancing. She had stopped, as had the music, when he stepped through the archway. She was now momentarily frozen in the pose of her last step, in the attitude of her last movement, her arms raised above her head, her hands joined at the wrist mimicking the form of a blossom, her body turned away from him, one leg extended, one hip swayed; but she was looking back at him over her shoulder, through her raised encircling arms. The lower part of her face was masked by a short silver-spangled veil. Her eyes above it, deeply shadowed, kohl-rimmed, seemed blank and unseeing, distracted from the rapture of the dance. She appeared to be naked to the waist. She wore the yellow silk Turkish-style pantaloons of an odalisque, tightly fitted over her hips and buttocks, loose as a skirt down her long legs, then tightly gathered again around the ankles. There were bangles and bracelets on her arms and rings and gemstones on her fingers and flowers in her hair, rust-colored hair, possibly hennaed, reaching below her shoulders down her back; but her shoulders and back were bare, and no string or strap crossed them to indicate that any garment covered her front. Her bare back and shoulders were as white as a European's. She lowered her arms and turned away.

"Major Barttelot. Bula Matari's beautiful soldier. Come in."

And now, shifting his eyes from the girl, Barttelot saw him.

He was lounging at full length among a profusion of silk and embroidered pillows on a low divan in a loose white caftan, plain as a nightgown and casually unbuttoned at the throat, a small, knitted white skullcap on his head instead of a turban, showing his hair to be as curly and snow-white as his beard. He had raised himself on an elbow upon Barttelot's entry, and a cordial smile played on his expressive, cultured, dark mahogany face; his eyes were heavily hooded.

Seated cross-legged around him on the floor or reclining on pillows and bolsters of their own were his sheiks. There was Selim; there was Sefu, the son; and Rashid, the nephew; and several others Barttelot recognized from his previous visit. Each had a water pipe in front of him, tall, marvelously intricate devices, gurgling softly, and the air of the room was hazy and sweet from their smoke. The room was a smaller replica of the one on the other side of the archway—polished pink stone, multicolored tiles, pillars holding up a high domed ceiling—but it had no windows. Brass lamps suspended from gilded chains and flickering candlesticks in ornamental holders provided the light in the room—soft mysterious light casting a confusion of shadows—and added their oily pungent odor to the sweet smoke of the hookahs.

In each of the walls was a tapestry-hung archway similar to the one through which Barttelot had just stepped, presumably leading to other similar rooms deeper in the building's interior. A spear-bearing Manyema guarded each; and along the walls between them clusters of serving women and slaves stood holding trays and platters, arrested in what they had been doing by Barttelot's entry. The musicians, an orchestra of several Arabic and native instruments as lovely and jewellike as the hookahs, sat on the floor in a circle behind the group of sheiks lounging around Tippoo-Tib's divan. The dancing girl stood in front of them, facing them, her left hand now resting on her hip, her right hand on her left shoulder so that her arm crossed the front of her torso and at least partially concealed what Barttelot presumed were her bare breasts, her white breasts.

"Come in, Major Barttelot. Come in. You are in time for a special entertainment. It has only just begun."

· FOUR ·

"*Bimbashi. Bimbashi rudi.* The major returns."

The news was shouted by the sentry on the watchtower at the south gate, and Bonny brought it on the run to Troup and Ward in the officers' mess. It was the first of September. Counting two days for the trip there by steamer and six or seven days back overland, Barttelot had been up at the Falls with Tippoo-Tib for more than a week.

"It's about time," Troup said, getting up from the mess table.

It was midmorning, and he and Ward had been whiling away the time lounging over their breakfast. There was little else to do. The rear column was ready to march. The arms and equipment and provisions offloaded from the *Stanley* had been inventoried and repacked for the trail, the mules and donkeys groomed and reshod, and the newly arrived Wanyamwezis assigned to companies—there'd be twelve in all once Tippoo-Tib's porters got there, a caravan of more than a thousand people and thirty animals transporting nearly two hundred tons of goods—and with that done, Troup had put Yambuya on a relaxed footing. He had done away with Barttelot's ritual drills and fatigues. He still kept sentries posted on the stockades but far fewer in number than Barttelot had, and he didn't bother getting up or having anyone else get up in the middle of the night to check on them. (He was perfectly satisfied that the Basoko posed no threat, no matter what, in his lust for action, Barttlelot had fantasized.) And he had stopped the floggings.

Bonny wasn't happy about any of this. He was Barttelot's man; his ideas on how the fortified encampment should be run were as rigid as Barttelot's, and he was constantly coming to Troup to express his disapproval of what was going on. And Troup constantly brushed him off. The stiff-necked fireplug of a man half irritated and half amused him with all his saluting and stomping of boots, his parade-ground barks of "yes, sir" and "no, sir," and he derived a certain satisfaction out of frustrating him, as if by doing so he was frustrating Barttelot as well.

"Has he got the Manyema porters with him, Sergeant?"

"I couldn't tell, sir."

"Well, let's go and have a look."

The journey from Singatini across the neck of land between the Congo and Aruwimi rivers brought Barttelot back to Yambuya from the southeast. When the sentry on the south-gate tower first spotted him, he was just emerging from the trees of the forest that surrounded the fort on that side; and now, as Troup had the south gate swung open for him, he was passing through the bright green scrub of the manioc fields. He was riding his donkey with the cookboy Bartholomew walking at its head holding the halter; and behind them in single file, following the rough, twisting lanes through the plantings, came the rest of his little caravan. Troup counted them: the five askaris, the twenty *pagazis* with the loads on their heads, the pack mule being pulled along by the muleteer. There were no Manyema porters.

"What's the matter with him?" Ward suddenly asked.

"Why? What?"

"Look at him, Jack. Look at the way he's seated on that animal."

Troup had been watching the forest to the south, hoping to see Tippoo-Tib's porters in a caravan of their own emerge from the trees there and follow Barttelot's men into the manioc field. Now he looked back at Barttelot. Ward was right. There was something peculiar about the way Barttelot was riding. His body was slumped too far forward, his shoulders were hunched, his head was hanging.

"I think he's hurt."

And just at that moment, as if he had heard, Barttelot jerked up his head, and by that movement he accidentally threw off his helmet. But he didn't seem to notice. He stared straight ahead. Then, quite as abruptly, his chin dropped back on his chest.

"Come on."

All three of them dashed out through the gate, their boots clattering on the plank bridge that spanned the ravine and creek on this side of the fort, and on into the spongy scrub of the manioc. Troup reached him first.

"Major, are you all right?"

Bartholomew had stopped the donkey. He had been leading it; Barttelot was only seated on it, being carried by it, not riding it. At the unaccustomed cessation of motion rather than Troup's words, Barttelot raised his head again. He looked at Troup but didn't seem to see him. His eyes were glazed; his face dripped with sweat; his once neatly trimmed beard was wildly ragged.

"What's wrong with him, Bartholomew? Has he been hurt?"

The cookboy shook his head.

"What then? What happened?"

Bartholomew kept shaking his head stupidly. The rest of the caravan bunched up around Troup.

"For Christ sake, what happened? Doesn't anyone know what happened?"

No one replied. Bonny fetched Barttelot's helmet from where it had fallen; and now, throwing an arm around Barttelot's waist to hold him steady in the saddle, he reached up and placed it on his head. And at that, Barttelot again raised his head, and made a growling sound.

"Can you make out what he's saying, Sergeant?"

"No, sir."

"It's fever, Jack. The poor fucker's come down with a bad case of some sort of fever."

"Yes, you're probably right. We'd best get him into camp. Best get him into bed. Sergeant."

"Yes, sir."

With an arm still around Barttelot's waist and taking the reins with his free hand, Bonny set the donkey off at a trot toward the south gate. But when Bartholomew, still holding the animal's halter, started to go along, Troup pulled him away.

"Are the porters coming, Bartholomew? Did the major get the porters?"

"Porters, sah?"

"Tippoo-Tib's porters. The Manyema. Are they coming?"

"I do not know, sah."

Troup looked around in exasperation. The caravan was filing through the south gate; and the Wanyamwezis and Sudanese there were crowding around, eager for news of the journey, baffled by Barttelot's condition. Troup looked back at the cookboy. "Now listen to me, Bartholomew. I want you to tell me everything that happened. Just tell me exactly everything that happened from the time you arrived in Singatini."

But there was little the boy could tell. They had arrived in Singatini. They had been met on the beach by an Arab. After a brief palaver on the beach, they had been taken into the town. And there they had been separated. The major had gone one way, the rest of them another. They had been provided with quarters and told to wait there. They waited for several days. They did not see the major during those days. They ate and drank and rested and waited. Then the major returned and they started back to Yambuya.

"And when the major returned, what did he say?"

"Say, sah? He did not say anything, sah. He was like this, sah, like he is now."

If it was fever, it was a kind of fever Troup had never before encountered in Africa. For a day and a half after he got back, Barttelot lay unconscious on his cot under the mosquito netting in his house near the river gate, as still and cold as a corpse. Then he began to rave, go into dreadful spasms, erupt in torrents of perspiration, and rave incomprehensibly. Bonny remained with him day and night. He slept more often than not in full uniform on a pallet beside Barttelot's cot, awakening again and again in the middle of the night to the man's animal grunts and lunatic shouts, trying to calm him and keep him from injuring himself in his frantic thrashings, dosing him with quinine and calomel, bathing his face, sponging his lips, covering him in his blanket, changing his sweat-soaked clothes.

Troup, bewildered by this development, came in to see him a dozen times a day, each time with greater impatience and less sympathy. In those periods, when Barttelot lay quiet, exhausted by his tormented exertions, eyes open but unseeing, Troup tried to talk to him, question him about what had happened at the Falls, what arrangements he had made with Tippoo-Tib about the porters, when they were coming. And when the major was again seized by one of his fits and transported into a delirium, Bonny kneeling by the cot and holding him, Troup listened to his wild exclamations and tried to make head or tail of them.

"Poisoned? Is that it? Is that what he's saying?"

"Yes, sir. I think so, sir. I think he says he was poisoned."

"But poisoned by whom?"

"The niggers, sir. The niggers at the Falls."

"But why, for Christ sake? Why in God's name would they want to poison him?"

"I don't know, sir."

Troup exhaled a sigh of utter vexation and slumped back in the canvas camp chair at the foot of Barttelot's cot. Behind him, leaning against the doorjamb of the house, Ward was looking in. And behind him, Troup knew, in every part of the encampment, the Sudanese and Wanyamwezis were standing stock-still, turned toward the house, listening. Barttelot's ravings frightened them; his senseless shouts worked on their nerves. They regarded it as an evil omen; and whenever it began, they stopped whatever they were doing and listened as they might listen to the howling of a demon.

"That's crazy," Troup said and stood up. "That's just plain crazy. He ain't been poisoned. No one's poisoned him. Who the hell would want to poison him?"

"It's fever," Ward said from the doorway. "Some kind of brain fever."

"It ain't even that," Troup snapped.

The sudden anger in Troup's voice took Ward aback. "What is it then? What do you think it is?"

"How the hell should I know? How the hell should I know what he was doing up there at the Falls all this time? He could've been doing anything." Troup walked over to the cot.

Barttelot had fallen back on the soiled pillow, quiet again for the moment, his mouth open, breathing wheezingly, his untrimmed beard matted with perspiration. Troup got down on his knees beside him across from Bonny.

"Can you hear me, Major?"

"I think you should let him rest, Mr. Troup. I think you should just let him sleep now," Bonny said.

"Let him sleep? For Christ sake, how can I let him sleep? I've got to find out about the porters. . . . Major. Wake up, Major."

"Mr. Troup, please, sir. Don't do that."

"Jack."

Troup jumped to his feet and went out of the house.

Ward followed him. "Take it easy, Jack. There's no sense riling yourself up. You're just going to make yourself sick too."

"Bert, listen. We're already more than eight weeks behind Bula Matari. We're never going to catch him up if we don't get going soon. We've got to get hold of those porters and get going. I don't know what happened to him up there at the Falls. I don't know what he did to himself up there, but we can't just hang around here waiting for him to wake up and tell us. We've got to get hold of the porters and get going. Otherwise this whole thing is for nothing."

"Do you want me to go up there? I could go up there and find out where they are."

Troup looked around indecisively. "That'd be another two weeks lost."

"Maybe I can do it faster. You know, travel light."

Troup didn't reply. He didn't know what to reply. He took off his straw hat and ran a hand irritatedly through his thick red hair.

"Mr. Troup." Bonny had come to the doorway of the house. "He wants to speak to you, sir."

"What? Is he conscious?" Troup hurried back into the house.

Barttelot was up on an elbow straining to see down the length of the cot. The bedclothes were wrapped in a filthy tangle around his bare legs, his beard splattered with spittle, his mouth cracked and dry. "Is that you, Troup?"

"Yes, Major, it's me, Troup."

"I'm dying, Troup. I've been poisoned."

"You haven't been poisoned, Major. Don't talk nonsense. Who'd want to poison you? It's some kind of fever."

"Oh no, it's poison, Troup. I know it is. It was put into my food. Into my wine. Into my pipe."

"By who?"

"Tippoo-Tib."

"Why in God's name would he do something like that?"

"Oh, he didn't do it himself. Oh, no, he's far too cunning for that. He was all guile and friendliness. All guile and friendliness. He had her do it."

"Her?"

"Yes, she did it. I saw her do it. I only realized too late what she was doing."

"And who is she?"

"I don't know. I don't know who she is." Barttelot slipped off his elbow and let his head drop back on the pillow.

Troup glanced at Ward and Bonny. Bonny kept a straight face as if he hadn't heard this or had heard it before. Ward, however, couldn't restrain a lascivious smile. Troup looked back at Barttelot. "And the porters, Major? What about the porters?"

But Barttelot didn't answer. He was breathing deeply.

"Don't go to sleep on me, Major. I've got to know about the porters. I've got to know what arrangement you made."

Barttelot opened his eyes.

"The porters, Major. Tippoo-Tib's Manyema. Are they coming?"

"Yes, they're coming."

"When?"

"He sent to Kasongo for them. He told Mr. Stanley he would have to do that. He told him he didn't have sufficient men at Singatini to spare six hundred for us and would have to send to Kasongo for them. It's true. I was there when he told him that. It was the first time I was there. I heard him tell that to Mr. Stanley then."

"And?"

Barttelot's eyelids, fluttering, had begun to close again. He opened them with effort. "And? And he sent to Kasongo for them. There were some difficulties. And Kasongo is far. But he sent for them and they are coming. They are on the way. He expects them at Singatini any day."

"Then why didn't you wait for them? I mean, you were there for more than a week as it was. Why didn't you wait another few days and bring them back with you?"

"But she was poisoning me, Troup. Didn't I tell you that? I discovered she was poisoning me." Barttelot suddenly pushed up on his elbow again. "I had to get away. I couldn't stay." And growing agitated again, going into one of his seizures again, he reared up off the cot and clutched at Troup's shirt. "I didn't dare stay. Not even for another day. She was poisoning me."

Bonny immediately came to his side.

"Yes, all right. Calm yourself." Troup took hold of Barttelot's hand and forcibly pried his clawing fingers from his shirt and in a kind of revulsion backed away from the cot, leaving Bonny to minister to the thrashing man.

· FIVE ·

A SHARP CRACK, then a rattle as if an avalanche had been set loose somewhere far away. But even in his sleep Troup recognized what it was. He sat up, tangling his hair in the mosquito netting.

"Bert."

Ward was rolled over on his stomach in the other cot in the big hut they shared, his face buried in his pillow. He pushed up on his hands and looked over at Troup. "What?"

"Listen."

But just at that moment there was nothing to hear, and Troup thought he might have dreamed it. He went to the doorway of the hut and looked out. Ward pulled his mosquito netting aside and swung his legs over the edge of his cot, watching Troup quizzically. And then there it was again, the distinctive crack and rattle of a volley of musket fire. Ward grabbed for his trousers.

It was still night, a good hour yet before first light; and except for the sentries on the stockade, the encampment was asleep. Only a few people had been awakened by the shooting; and these, peering out of their huts, not knowing quite what to make of it, watched as Troup and Ward hurried to the east gate and scrambled up the watchtower. The two askaris on sentry duty there turned with a start when they clattered up on the platform.

"*Kile ni nini?*"

"*Sijui*, Bwana."

"But you heard it? It was musket fire?"

"*Ndiyo.*"

Troup and Ward went to the front railing and looked eastward over the spiked ditch that protected this side of the fort, across the ravaged ground where the rest of Yambuya had stood and had been leveled to provide the encampment with a clear field of fire, to the black wall of forest from which the Aruwimi emerged in a cascading rush of rapids. It had rained during the night, and everything was dripping and puddled and steamy; but the clouds rolling downriver were breaking up, and the fading stars could be seen racing among them against patches of dark blue sky. The shooting had stopped again, and for the moment anyway there was nothing to hear but the whir of cicadas and the chirping of birds anticipating the dawn.

And then the sky to the east burst into flames.

"Jesus!" Ward exclaimed and involuntarily stepped back.

It was unnecessary of course. The fire was some miles away, deep in the forest; but its sudden explosion, the tongues of flame and showers of sparks whirling up through the trees, were as shocking as if a volcano had erupted. And then the crack and rattle of gunfire resumed.

"Slavers," Troup said.

"Right," Ward replied. "Probably our Manyema porters. Tippoo-Tib probably finally got around to sending them, and the bloodthirsty fuckers couldn't resist taking a little plunder on the way."

Troup nodded and leaned his elbow on the railing.

"We're going to have trouble with them, Jack. I've always thought that. We're going to have trouble driving a bloodthirsty lot like that through the Ituri."

Troup nodded again, staring at the flames slashing up through the forest, listening to the crackle of gunfire deep down within it, imagining the destruction these signified and wondering which village was suffering that destruction, whether it was the village to which Baruti and his people had fled for safety from the white man's column. Meanwhile, below him, the encampment was awakening and Wanyamwezis and Sudanese were gathering excitedly at the gates and loopholes in the stockade to witness the spectacle.

"The major's up."

Troup looked around. "Where?"

"Down there."

Barttelot was walking upriver along the beach at a leisurely pace, apparently unsurprised, or at least unperturbed by the conflagration, fully clothed in helmet, uniform, and boots, his pistol and bandolier strapped in place, his riding crop in hand. He was pretty much recovered from the fever or whatever it had been; but as far as Troup was concerned, there was still something definitely wrong with him. It wasn't anything Troup could put his finger on and so he made no mention of it; but he suspected Ward also noticed it, a certain distracted air, an unnatural indifference to what was going on around him.

Since his return from the Falls the severe military regimen that Troup had relaxed while he was away had been reimposed. But this was less Barttelot's doing than Bonny's. Barttelot gave Bonny a free hand in these matters, and Bonny went at them with a will: the drills and inspections, the scouting patrols, the obsessive repair and reinforcement of the stockade as if an attack were imminent, the nightly round of the sentries, the floggings. Three people had died: an askari from an incredibly harsh flogging of a hundred strokes, a *pagazi* from heat exhaustion, a woman from manioc poisoning. There was also an alarming rise in the number of sick and injured: malaria, blackwater, dysentery, accidents on the work details, an axe slipping, a pickhead flying, a man falling and breaking bones. And the injuries and illnesses, no matter how minor, quickly festered in the swampy climate. Troup worried that even if the men didn't actually mutiny under these conditions, they'd fall prey to a fatal apathy that could destroy the column before it finally got under way into the Ituri as surely as any outright mutiny would. But his warnings to Barttelot about this fell on deaf ears. Barttelot didn't seem to hear or care; he was caught up in some queer private world of his own.

Now he stopped at the head of the reach where the Aruwimi emerged from the forest and, with his riding crop tucked under an arm, gazed upriver through his field glasses toward the spot where the slavers had struck. The shooting had ceased, and as the dawn came up the flames died down, leaving only a plume of thick black smoke rising into the slowly brightening sky. Bonny too was awake by now, scurrying about the encampment, his rasping voice barking commands, chasing people away from the gates and loopholes, parading the askaris, mustering the work details.

"I'm going to get dressed," Ward said and started down from the tower. But seeing that Troup did not follow him, he went back to the railing.

"He's waiting for something," Troup said after a moment. "Look at him, Bert. He's waiting for something."

"The Manyema most likely. If they are the porters Tippoo-Tib sent, I expect they'll turn up here once they're done with their dirty work at that village."

"Most likely," Troup said, but he went on watching Barttelot. Ward remained at his side.

And then the first Basoko appeared. He was almost certainly dead; in any case he made no move and was merely a black shape being rushed along by the river's current, bobbing senselessly, rolling over in the rapids, slamming into rocks, snagging on driftwood, and then swirling away downstream like so much rubbish. The next two were alive, swimming frantically. One made it to the opposite shore and scrambled out through the reeds of the swamp there, then looked back to see how his mate was faring. That one also seemed to have a chance of making it, but at the last moment an eddy caught him and sucked him under. He didn't resurface. The fellow on shore dashed into the forest and disappeared. A canoe came by almost immediately after that, turning end around end, apparently empty. But one turn swung it close to the near bank, almost to Barttelot's feet, and Troup and Ward from their elevation on the tower could see several bodies lying rigid in its bottom.

"The fuckers," Ward said. "The filthy fuckers." And now he did go down from the tower.

In the next half-hour more such human debris of the slavers' raid passed down the river, a few alive and making it to shore safely (although none to the Yambuya shore, as afraid of the white men as of the slavers), most not making it to either shore. And then it was over. Troup waited a while longer in morbid fascination. Perhaps some of the villagers had also gotten away upstream, but the odds were that most by now were either dead or in chains. In the sky above the village, circling in the smoke, buzzards and kites began gathering. Then Troup also went down from the tower.

He was in his hut getting dressed when Ward looked in. "Selim's here, Jack–Selim bin Mohammed, Tippoo-Tib's brother. He's down on the beach talking to the major."

"Has he got the Manyema with him?"

"Yes, but–"

"What?"

"I don't know." Ward shook his head as he and Troup crossed the parade ground to the river gate. "I've got a funny feeling. There's something queer about it. In any case, the Manyema he's brought don't add up to anywhere near the six hundred we were promised."

"I'll take how many he's got. Anything's better than nothing at this stage, Bert. We've been waiting around too long as it is anyway. In fact, I was just thinking maybe we ought to start a caravan off into the Ituri right now with as many of the loads as we've got men of our own to carry them. So however many Selim's brought, that'll mean just that many more loads we can get started on the way."

"If they'll carry loads."

"What do you mean?"

"Have a look for yourself."

Troup pushed through the crowd of Wanyamwezis and Sudanese gathered at the river gate and looked down from the embankment's high bluff to the beach below. It was aswarm with Manyema, armed with muskets and spears. They had arrived in a fleet of about twenty Arab canoes, and there were probably 300 of them, ebony-black brutes wearing breechclouts, their heavily muscled bodies gleaming with sweat, their heads shaved, brass rings in their noses, their cheeks tattooed with cicatrices, their thick upper lips ornamentally cut into grotesque fringes. They squatted in menacing clusters everywhere up and down the bank, leaning on their weapons; and from time to time they glanced up at the sentries on the fort's stockade as if appraising their strength. Selim, in a white turban and belted white djellaba, both badly soiled from his morning's work, and Barttelot, swatting himself absently with his riding crop, stood in their midst talking animatedly, like old friends. Bonny was also down there, standing a bit to the side and pretending not to listen.

"What do you think?"

"You're right. That lot ain't porters. They're gunmen. There's no way we'd get them to carry loads through the Ituri."

"Then what the hell are they doing here? What did he bring them here for?"

"Come on. Let's find out."

Bonny was the first to notice Troup and Ward coming down the stepped path in the bluff, and he hurried over to intercept them.

"What is it, Sergeant?" Troup asked with some impatience.

"I'd like to talk to you, sir."

"Yes? Go on."

But Bonny hesitated. He looked acutely uncomfortable.

"Is this some kind of delaying tactic, Sergeant? Are you trying to keep me from going over there and hearing what the major and Selim are talking about?"

"Oh, no, sir. Nothing like that, sir. I hope you hear what they're talking about."

"What then? I was just on my way over there."

"I wanted to ask you something."

"Well, go ahead."

But now Bonny glanced at Ward. "It's sort of private, sir."

"I didn't know you had any secrets from me, Billy," Ward remarked lightly and continued on his way over to Selim and Barttelot, leaving Troup and Bonny alone.

"All right now, Sergeant. What the devil is it?"

"Don't let him go, sir."

"Go? Don't let who go? Where?"

"Major Barttelot, sir. He means to go back to the Falls."

Instinctively Troup looked over at Barttelot.

Barttelot looked back. With Ward coming over, he realized Troup must also be down on the beach. Now he called to him. "Would you join us over here, Troup. This concerns you."

"Right away, Major." Troup turned back to Bonny. "Where did you get that idea, Sergeant?"

"I heard him talking about it with the Arab, sir. That's why the Arab's come—to take him back to the Falls."

"Troup."

"I'm coming, Major."

"Don't let him go, sir. I know him, sir. I've served with him a long time. It would be a mistake to let him go."

Troup peered closely into Bonny's flushed, perspiring face. "There's something you're not telling me, Sergeant. There's something you know that I don't know. What is it?"

Bonny looked away.

"Did he tell you what happened to him at the Falls? Is that it?"

"No, sir. He didn't tell me anything, sir."

"But something did happen to him at the Falls, and you know what it is. Or at least you've got a pretty good idea what it is. Look at me, Sergeant. Tell me what you think it is."

"I don't know, sir. I swear I don't. I only know he mustn't go back there."

"Troup, will you get over here. We've arrangements to make that concern you."

"You mustn't let him go, sir. I'm saying it for his own good. For the expedition's good. You must stop him."

"And how do you propose I do that? What should I say to him? Should I say, 'Sergeant Bonny told me not to let you go'?"

"Oh, no, sir. Don't say anything like that."

"What then?"

Bonny didn't reply. And then Barttelot called again with rising impatience, and Troup, giving Bonny a last searching look, went over.

"You know Selim bin Mohammed, don't you, Troup? Sheik Selim, this is John Rose Troup, one of Mr. Stanley's most trusted lieutenants from his earliest days on the Congo."

"Ah, yes, of course. Mr. Troup. We have met before."

"We have, Sheik, some years ago, in Bula Matari's company. I am flattered that you remember."

"Ah, but one does not easily forget the brave men of Bula Matari's company."

Troup bobbed his head in acknowledgment of the compliment.

"Selim will be accompanying us on the march to Albert Nyanza, Troup. Tippoo-Tib has seconded him to our expedition as chief of the porters he is providing us and also to have him learn the way through the Ituri that Mr. Stanley has pioneered."

"It will be an honor having the brother of the great Hamed bin Mohammed accompanying us."

And now it was Selim's turn to bow.

"But if you permit me to ask, Where are these porters of whom you are to be chief? These men you've brought with you today"—he indicated the Manyema hunkered on their haunches all around them—"they surely are not porters."

"Oh, no, they surely are not porters." Selim smiled at the very ludicrousness of the idea.

"Then who are they?"

"They are soldiers, Mr. Troup."

"Soldiers, Sheik?"

"Yes, soldiers, Mr. Troup, soldiers to reinforce your escort of askaris. For, I will confess I am not as brave as you. I fear the terrible Ituri more than you and so desire more protection against its perils than that which your few askaris can provide."

"I see." Troup looked around at the ugly mob of gunmen. And he thought, The Ituri has far more to fear from them than they from the Ituri. For they were the spearhead of the slaving army that would now follow Stanley's trail into the Ituri, as other slaving armies had followed his trail down the Congo. The raid this morning was only the start of it. But he kept the thought to himself. This was, after all, the bargain Stanley had struck. Aloud he said, "And the porters, Sheik? Where are they?"

"They come from Kasongo, Mr. Troup. As no doubt Major

Barttelot told you, my brother had to send to Kasongo for them."

"Yes, Major Barttelot told me that. And he also told me that they were expected at Singatini any day. And he told me that nearly a fortnight ago."

"Ah, yes, I understand your annoyance. The delay has been most unfortunate. But Kasongo is far and there have been difficulties. But I assure you, the porters are now at last on their way. In fact, I am going back to Singatini now to bring them to you."

"And I am going with him," Barttelot said.

Troup had expected this–he had been forewarned–but it startled Ward. He hadn't been in on the conversation with Bonny.

"You're going back with him to Singatini, Major?"

"That's what I said, Mr. Ward. In the meantime, I want you and–"

"But I don't see why that's necessary. Selim knows the way. It seems to me he can bring those porters down here perfectly well on his own."

"I know he knows the way. Of course he knows the way. Are you trying to make me out to be a fool, Mr. Ward? It's not a question of his knowing the way. That's not why I'm going back with him."

"It's not? Then why are you?"

"Yes, Major, I'd like to know that too," Troup put in. "Why are you?"

But it wasn't Barttelot who answered. It was Selim. "My brother requested it, Mr. Troup. There are some matters he wishes to discuss with the Major."

"And what are those?"

"Well, for one thing, there is the matter of the payment of the porters."

"The payment of the porters? What are you talking about? That was all settled with Mr. Stanley long before he ever left here."

"Ah, but perhaps not quite in the detail my brother would wish."

"In what detail? What is this, Selim? This is pretty late in the day to be bringing something like this up. Tippoo-Tib agreed with Mr. Stanley to six pounds sterling the head plus the chance to follow his trail through the Ituri. If he had any questions, why didn't he bring it up with Major Barttelot when he was in Singatini this last time? Christ knows, he was there long enough."

"Now just hold on, Troup. If Tippoo-Tib wants to discuss

the payment of the porters with me or any other matter Mr. Stanley failed to make clear, then I consider it my responsibility to go back up there and sort it out with him."

"That's rubbish, Major, and you know it. That's not why you're going back up there. Sergeant Bonny!"

"You leave Sergeant Bonny out of this, Troup. This doesn't concern him."

"Oh, yes it does, Major. It concerns all of us. It concerns the outcome of this expedition. I don't know what you got yourself into up there at the Falls, but we can't afford to risk any more delays. We've got to get on the march to Lake Albert right now. We've got to form up a column of all our own *pagazis* and pack animals and as many of these Manyema here as will carry loads, and you and Sergeant Bonny get them on the march into the Ituri. Bert and I will wait here for Selim to bring down the rest of the Manyema, and we'll follow after you with the remaining loads."

"Jack's right, Major. It's the only sensible scheme. We've got to get going with at least some of the stuff."

"Ah, but effendis, effendis, one moment please," Selim intervened. "I fear I have not made myself understood. Major Barttelot *must* come back with me to Singatini. For, you see, the Manyema will not march into the forest with you until he has. Not these Manyema who I have brought with me today. Not those Manyema who I am going back to Singatini to fetch. My brother will not allow them. So it is pointless to quarrel about it."

There was a moment of silence after this, a moment in which Selim's words sank in.

And then Barttelot said, "Well, there you have it, Troup. There you have it. There's nothing more to say."

Troup looked at him. Slapping his riding crop against his thigh, the major looked away.

The Manyema Selim left behind at Yambuya, the gunmen, his "soldiers"—there were 220 of them; nearly one hundred of the original mob, in five of the canoes provided an escort for his return journey to Singatini with Barttelot—made camp in the cleared ground outside the fort's eastern stockade where the larger portion of the Basoko village once had stood. It was a sprawling makeshift camp, noisy and dirty and, in Troup's opinion, much too close. The dwellings for the most part (although a *tembe* of sun-baked mud bricks with a conical thatch roof was also erected) were of the crudest kind, of sticks and leaves, little more than shelters against the worst of the midday sun and of hardly any use against the torrential nightly rains. They were haphazardly thrown up on no discernible plan, some thrown up against the wall of the stockade itself. There were no sanitary arrangements. Cooking fires were built anywhere. Garbage and ordure were dumped everywhere. Greasy burlap sacks of provender and provisions were piled helter-skelter out in the open. A flock of goats and innumerable fowls (no doubt taken in the raid on the Basoko village upriver; but where were the Basoko who also must have been taken in the raid?) roamed around loose, adding to the general filth of the place. The Manyema themselves kept up a constant hullabaloo, coming and going, disappearing into the forest and returning, hauling their canoes up from the river and down again, pressing against the stockade and peering in through the loopholes, shouting at one another and firing off their muskets, getting drunk on palm wine and getting into fights, gambling with bones, beating on drums, staging raucous dances around their fires at night.

They were a jungle people, from far up the Congo to the west of Lake Tanganyika. When Tippoo-Tib first struck into those regions some fifteen years before, he had made war on them as he had on all the other tribes he encountered. But he soon learned they were different from and more formidable than those other tribes, exceptional in their physical strength, heedless in their courage, heartless in their ferociousness—qualities he admired and prized—and so he made alliances with their chiefs and hired them into his slaving armies as gunmen and porters to prey on their neighbors. Big, mean, ugly brutes with shaved heads and tattooed faces and mutilated lips, man-eaters out of the darkest forests, they swarmed around their camp, surging against the walls of the fort, with a restless, savage exuberance.

The Wanyamwezis and Sudanese were terrified of them. They watched them from behind the stockade; and although they envied their food and the freebooting anarchy of their camp, they found every excuse to avoid going out among them. They did go out, of course. Bonny, in his single-minded devotion to the fort's regimen, saw to that. But he had a battle on his hands each time he rounded up the work details; and when at last he had them rounded up—the wood choppers, the manioc harvesters, the water bearers, the foraging and hunting parties, the stockade and ditch patrols—and the gates were swung open for them, there was always a moment of tremulous expectation pregnant with ominous possibilities. The Manyema stopped what they were doing, stopped their infernal racketing to watch with menacing dog-yellow eyes. In the unaccustomed quiet, Bonny's commands rang out with a hysterical insistence; and when the last of them had filed out, dragging their feet, glancing around uneasily as if being taken to their deaths, the gates were quickly swung shut and bolted behind them. No one wanted the Manyema to get in.

And then more Manyema arrived.

It was in the early morning of the sixth day after Barttelot's departure. Selim had said that the journey to Singatini would take three days, so theoretically at least the canoes that were spotted making their way upriver from the Congo confluence that morning could have been Barttelot and Selim returning with the porters. There were about thirty of them strung out in a line a good half-mile long, each packed to the gunwales with men. An Arab in a billowing blue djellaba and white turban stood in the lead canoe, one foot on the prow, cradling a long musket in his arms. Peering at him through his field glasses from atop the embankment outside the river gate, Troup immediately saw that he wasn't Selim. He was younger, beardless, chubby; he was Tippoo-Tib's son Sefu. Barttelot wasn't with him. Even so, he might have been sent ahead with these men as a first contingent, with Barttelot and Selim to follow with the rest in the next day or two.

Troup hailed him. He gave no sign of having heard and kept on going, his canoe and those in his wake passing the fort, the paddlers stroking hard against the current. Their chanting with each stroke sounded like the beating of drums across the water. When they came abreast of the Manyema encampment beyond the eastern stockade, Sefu fired his musket into the air. Instantly the Manyema on shore responded with a salvo of their own; and with savage shouts and ululations, most of them charged down to the riverbank and shoved off in their canoes. Troup let his field glasses drop on his chest. Ward was standing next to him, but neither man said anything. They simply watched as the canoes, one by one, rounded the bend at the head of the reach and were swallowed up in the overhanging foliage of the jungle.

They didn't hear the shooting this time. They listened for it throughout the day, pausing in their round of activities at any unusual sound; and on several occasions Troup climbed up the east-gate watchtower to scan the jungle's canopy for signs of fire. He hadn't the least bit of doubt as to what the Manyema were up to, but apparently they had gone much farther upriver this time, much deeper into the jungle than had the first gang of slavers the week before.

They began returning toward sunset. Not all returned, and most of those who did were from the original Manyema camp. Evidently the others were remaining in the jungle, building yet another camp, or perhaps pushing on still farther in their invasion of the Ituri, while those who returned returned only to bring back the loot of the day's work.

Troup and Ward went down to the beach as the canoes drifted in on the current. The Manyema in them, growling and snapping in their native vernacular, freely using their muskets and spears as clubs and prods, manhandled their captives out of the canoes. There were old men and young warriors among the captives, boys and women, girls and children. They were naked as the day they were born and fettered one to the other by their necks with big Y-shaped yokes cut from the limbs of ebony trees, their heads bowed by the weight of these cruel devices, their hands bound behind their backs. Troup scrutinized them in a grim silence; but as each new coffle trudged by and stumbled up the crumbling clay of the steep bluff of the embankment into the Manyema camp, Ward would shake his head mournfully and mutter an obscenity. It wasn't that this was an unfamiliar sight. He and Troup had often enough been in country where slavers plied their bloody trade and so had seen its like before. But as familiar as it was, it was never anything less than appalling, the brutality of the captors, the hopeless resignation of the captured.

And then all of a sudden Troup emitted a soft strangled groan.

"What's the matter?" Ward asked.

It was fast falling dark by now. Bonny had brought the work details back into the fort, and cooking fires were burning up there and in the Manyema camp as well; and what would prove to be the last of the canoes to return that night had just run up on the riverbank.

"It's just what I was most afraid would happen one of these days."

"What is?"

"That's Ngungu."

Ward looked at the Basoko coming ashore from this last canoe. There were five of them yoked together in a line: two women, two boys, and at the end of the line an old man. "Who?"

Troup turned to Ward and only then did he realize that Ward

of course couldn't make the connection. All contact with the Basoko had been broken off before he had come up to Yambuya from Equator Station.

"These are Baruti's people, Bert. That old bloke there, Ngungu, he's their chief."

"Oh, Jesus." Ward's eyes immediately darted to the two boys in the coffle and then up to the Manyema camp where the Basoko who had been brought in earlier had been taken. "And Baruti?"

"I didn't see him. Did you?"

"No."

"Maybe he got away. Some of them must have gotten away."

And now Troup also recognized one of the two women in the coffle. She had been one of the hostages in Yambuya, the last one Barttelot had released, as naked now as she had been then, but with her hands bound behind her back, unable to cover herself. Coming nearer, she made an effort under the weight of her yoke to look sideways at the two white men. Because of that she stumbled; and with her hands useless to her, she couldn't catch herself and fell, dragging down the woman behind her and then the two boys behind *her* in a helpless heap. But the old man, Ngungu, kept to his feet and, bracing his legs, leaning backwards with all his strength, tried to pull his children up again. He too was naked. Stripped of his cape and feathers and all the finery of his office, he was now just a frail old monkey of a man but a fiercely defiant one for all that.

"Easy, Jack!"

Troup had started forward instinctively when the Manyema began kicking the fallen Basoko to get them to their feet. Ward immediately grabbed his arm. "Easy, man, easy."

"Let go of me."

"Just take it easy, will you? We can't afford to start anything with these fuckers. They're supposed to be on our side, you know."

"Yes, I know. But just let go of me. All I want to do is talk to him," Troup said and scrambled up the bluff after Ngungu.

The captive Basoko had been herded behind the solitary tembe in the Manyema camp, not far from where a cooking fire was burning. They were seated on the ground, their heads bowed down to their drawn-up knees by the weight of their yokes, their hands still tied behind their backs. There were about seventy of them; and now Ngungu, the two women, and the two boys were added to their number. The Manyema didn't bother to guard them—in their hobbled condition there was little chance of their getting away—and went over to the cooking fire. A battered iron kettle simmered over it, giving off a pungent odor, and a score of other Manyema squatted around it eating with a savage concentration. As Troup and Ward came up over the bluff into the camp, they looked up with the lazy indolence of well-fed beasts, their hands and faces smeared with the grease of what they were eating. It was meat, dripping chunks of it boiled on the bone in the kettle. But what kind of meat? By the size of the bones, it was meat from an animal much larger than a goat. Its sweet, tangy smell made Troup and Ward's stomachs turn over.

"Who is chief here?" Troup asked in Swahili.

None of them replied. They remained hunkered on their muscular haunches like feeding dogs and studied Troup with their dull yellow eyes. Troup and Ward passed them by and went on to where the Basoko were huddled behind the tembe. Knowing now who they were, Troup realized that he recognized many of them: another of the women who had been held hostage in Yambuya and one of the boys, several men who had been among the warriors and torchbearers in the canoe that had brought him back to Yambuya with Ngungu, an old woman who had been introduced to him as Ngungu's principal wife when he had visited their village. But he didn't see Baruti.

"Ngungu."

The old chief raised his eyes. He couldn't raise his head. Troup got down on his knees in front of him.

"Jack."

Troup looked around. Manyema were coming over. Apparently, the mere presence of the two white men in their camp had caused them no particular concern. That they had chosen to interest themselves in these newly acquired slaves was, however, something else. Those at the cooking fire who had watched them pass by with indifference now stood up. Others came out of their ramshackle huts carrying muskets and spears.

"Don't do anything dumb, old boy."

Troup nodded and turned back to Ngungu. He couldn't tell if the old man recognized him. His eyes were blind with hatred and defiance. Everyone must seem an enemy to him now.

"Baruti?" Troup said. "Where is Baruti?" He said this in English. There was no point using Swahili. Ngungu didn't understand Swahili, and Troup couldn't speak Kisoko. He could only hope that the old man would realize what he was getting at by hearing him say Baruti's name. And so he said it again. "Where is Baruti?"

"Jack."

"What?"

"Look at her."

"Who?"

"That one over there."

It was one of the women who had been held hostage in Yambuya, the one who had stumbled trying to see who they were. She had lifted her head. All the others remained downcast, slumped in a despairing, defeated stupor; but she had managed to lift her head and was looking at Troup.

And so Troup said it to her. "Baruti? Where is Baruti? What has become of Baruti?"

Holding her head up with great effort, straining against the terrible weight of the yoke, she closed her eyes.

· SIX ·

"My beautiful soldier. Oh, my beautiful soldier."

She turns him on his side, to the very edge of the narrow divan so that he is in danger of falling, and kneels behind him on the cool slate tiles of the seraglio floor. In front of him a sad-eyed little slave boy in a short white shirt comes forward in slow motion, as if moving through an invisible but viscid fluid, holding out the amber mouthpiece of a hookah's curling hose. Dreamily, he takes it into his mouth, lets it slide along his tongue, and draws deeply into his lungs the harsh pungent smoke that bubbles through the milky water. Music is playing, the thrilling, irritating whine of catgut strings, the pure sustained note of a wooden flute, the hollow thump of a drum, the jangle of brass finger cymbals running along his nerves like angry insects' feet.

"Oh, my beautiful soldier," she says again.

And he feels her face press closer and her unpinned hair, long and silken and hennaed, fall across the back of his naked thighs; and again drawing deeply on the pipe, he closes his eyes and awaits the rush of all the sensations.

"You will take me with you," she whispers. "You will buy me and take me with you to the shining sea."

It is ridiculous. Of course he will not buy her. Of course he will not take her with him. She has no name. Or rather she has many names, fanciful names, names she imagines will please him—Florinda, Giaconda, Verbena, Beryl, and Amethyst—names invented by a girl dreaming of escape to the sea. She claims to come from the Balkans, from the mountains of Albania or the plains of Romany, where the janissaries of the Ottoman Turks steal the prettiest children and sell them down the caravan routes into the harems of the agas and mudirs and emirs of the Orient and Africa. She claims to be one of those children pleading to be returned to her European home. But is she? Or is she Circassian, just another Circassian whore?

"Show me your face." Twisting to look back over his shoulder, he means to reach down and take a handful of her hair and lift her face away from his thighs but then remembers his wrists are tied. Although it renders him helpless, it does not worry him. What more harm can she do him? She already has poisoned him. "Show me your face. Let me look at you."

She raises her head and looks up at him from a very great distance. Her face is white.

"Verbena! Hah! What nonsense."

"Beryl. Beryl and Amethyst," she replies and slowly slides up that seemingly great distance, pressing hard against him, skin against skin slippery with sweat, until she brings her chin to the crook of his shoulder and wedges it there and says softly but with utter confidence, "You will buy me and take me to the shining sea, yes?"

"Yes."

She laughs and turns him on his back, onto the profusion of pillows on the narrow divan, so she can crawl on him and adjust him between her legs and then let her full weight, stretched out at full length, fall on him, pinning him as he pins her.

He doesn't move. He doesn't dare move. It would be catastrophic to move. And so, holding his breath, tightening the muscles of his thighs, trembling with the excruciating tension of it, he gazes besotted through the fall of her hair, past the curve of her cheek, down the slope of her back, over the rise of her white buttocks, and there the little slave boy holding the pipe solemnly gazes back, a little erection poking out from the under the hem of his shirt.

"What is it?"

The sheiks are entering the room. This is a room within the labyrinth of rooms that make up Tippoo-Tib's seraglio, domed and columned and tiled and decorated with hanging tapestries, and the sheiks enter it from a walled courtyard overgrown with flowers. They are accompanied by an entourage of slaves and dancing girls. Moonlight bathes the courtyard from which they enter.

"What is it? Has Tippoo-Tib returned?"

They ignore him and arrange themselves on the bolsters and carpets scattered around the room. Pipes of hashish are brought to them. Platters of sweetmeats, bowls of fruit, earthenware ewers of palm wine are handed around. Tippoo-Tib isn't among them. Evidently he hasn't returned. Returned from where? Kasongo. He went to Kasongo to supervise the dispatch of the porters for the rear column. At least that is what they tell him each time he asks. When was that? He has lost track of the days in Singatini awaiting Tippoo-Tib's return. Hundreds of Manyema have passed down the river in those days, fleets of canoes, armies of slavers making for the Aruwimi and Yambuya. Tippoo-Tib will return with the last of them and then he and Selim will go back to Yambuya and get the rear column under way. At least that is what they tell him each time he asks. Are they lying? He suspects they are lying. He suspects they are always lying. Look at them. Look at how they lounge on their pillows smoking their hookahs and whisper to each other with knowing smiles. Oh, yes, they are lying. They are always lying. But what is he to do? There is nothing he can do. He is at their mercy. Stanley has left him at their mercy.

The music has changed. The drumbeat has quickened. And two of the dancing girls have started dancing. No, they are making love. One stands with arms above her head, legs apart. The other kneels in front of her and pulls her silken pantaloons halfway down her thighs and embraces her hips. He sits up. He is wearing a loose caftan. His wrists are untied and he is holding the hookah himself, cradling it in his arms, sucking its amber tip like a woman's teat. And it is raining, smashing down the flowers in the courtyard, overflowing the fountain, flooding the flagstones, blotting out the moon. Candles tucked away in niches among the columns provide the only light; and in their pools of flickering orange glow the sheiks nibble pieces of fruit fed to them by their slaves, their heavily lidded eyes fixed on the two dancing girls. The one standing—the one being loved, throwing her head back and forth in ecstasy—is the white girl: Verbena, Amethyst, Beryl. This dawns on him slowly and slowly fills him with rage.

"Whore," he cries out. "Whore."

No one takes notice. Lightning flashes, thunder cracks, the rain smashes down, the music rises to a din, drowning out the word. Or perhaps he didn't actually cry it out. Perhaps the word only rattles around in his head. Whore. Whore. He gets up and, getting up, falls and, falling, is noticed and, noticed, becomes the object of derisive laughter. Selim comes over and helps him to his feet.

"She shouldn't do that, Selim."

"No."

"She's mine. Didn't you give her to me?"

"Yes, yes, of course."

She has lowered her arms, placed her hands on her hips. Her legs are still parted, her pantaloons still pulled down. The other girl is still on her knees, but she has looked around. When Selim speaks, she starts to get up, but the white girl grabs her shoulder and forces her to stay.

Selim shrugs. "She wants to be finished," he says. "Will you allow her to be finished?"

"Finished?"

Selim takes hold of himself between his legs and gives himself an obscene shake.

"Oh, all right, let her be finished."

He sits down among some cushions stacked at the base of a column and leans against the column. His hashish pipe, which he dropped when he fell, is restored to him. Sugar cakes and wine are brought to him. The little slave boy fans him with a branch of palm. The music resumes. Selim stretches out beside him and rests a hand indolently on his thigh. He pushes it away. Selim laughs softly and also leans back against the column so that, although their bodies angle off in opposite directions, their heads are close together.

He shouldn't be here. He isn't so besotted that he doesn't know this. He should go back to Yambuya. Indeed, he should have gone back long before this. They are waiting for him in Yambuya. He has already been away too long. But he doesn't want to go back. He sucks on his pipe and, letting the acrid smoke curl slowly from his nostrils, looks at Selim. Selim is looking at the girls making love.

"You are lying," he says blandly.

Selim turns to him.

"I know you are lying. I only don't know why."

Selim gazes at him, then looks back at the girls and says, "She will be finished soon."

Yes, she will be finished soon. He can see that for himself. It is still raining, but now only lightly; the thunder and lightning have ceased and so has the music. The musicians too are waiting for her to be finished. And when she is, she sprawls on her back, a forearm flung across her eyes as if to shield them from the candlelight, her hair fanned out on the tiles. The other girl sits up. She is brown, Abyssinian or Nubian, with kinky black hair. Compared to her the white girl truly seems white.

"Is she white?"

Selim nods.

"Where does she come from?"

Selim shrugs. "They bring them down the Red Sea, but from where exactly . . ." He shrugs again. "From everywhere—from Ethiopia, from the Sudan, from Egypt and Turkey and Palestine, from Syria and Persia and the Lebanon—"

"And also from Europe?"

"Oh, yes, and also from Europe."

"She wants me to take her there."

Selim laughs. "By all means, take her there."

As if she has heard this exchange, the white girl pushes up on an elbow and looks around. Then she stands up and comes over and stretches out beside him. Drawing up her knees like a little girl going to sleep, she takes his hand and places it between her thighs. The other girl, the brown one, also comes over, and she crawls into Selim's arms. The music resumes, more quietly. The slaves carry around the fruits and the wine. The sheiks smoke their pipes. The white girl falls asleep.

"Our time in Africa draws to a close, effendi. The Arab rule here is now very nearly done. We know that. We know that you will take our place. You, the white man, will drive us out of Africa and rule where we once ruled with a far greater efficiency than that which we could ever bring to bear. Oh, yes, we know that. But you cannot expect us to assist you in this process. You cannot expect us to hasten our own demise."

Is this in reply to the question he asked? But he no longer remembers the question he asked. The girl stirs in his arms, gropes sleepily for the mouthpiece of the hookah, sucks on it, then settles down into sleep again. He cups the back of her head in his hand. How small the skull seems beneath the great mass of hennaed silken hair.

"You will build forts in the forest. You will build forts and trading stations once the spell of the forest is broken just as you built forts and trading stations on the Congo once the spell of the Congo was broken. Once Bula Matari broke the spell. And that will be the end of it for us. Then our day will truly be done."

He has heard this before. Somewhere someone spoke precisely these words before. The spell of the forest.

"Therefore, would it not be the height of folly for us to assist him in breaking the spell of the forest? Would we not be merely assisting him in hastening our own demise?"

"But why then did you say you would? And, by saying this, keep us waiting for so long in Yambuya?"

There is no answer. Selim is no longer there. No one is there. Only the white girl asleep in his arms is there. The rain has stopped. A soft breeze has sprung up, blowing in from the river, shaking the raindrops from the flowers in the courtyard, clearing away the smoke of the hookahs. The candles gutter and a pearly gray light creeps into the room like a mist upon the tiles.

Troup, standing in the doorway of his hut, peered out into the pearly gray light of the dawn. Something peculiar was going on out there, figures darting about furtively, a half-dozen, maybe more. He couldn't tell how many exactly; he could only catch fleeting glimpses of them in the misty silvery dimness—stooped figures appearing and disappearing in the streets between the rows of huts where the Wanyamwezis were billeted. Who were they? If they were Wanyamwezis or, for that matter, Sudanese, they obviously were up to no good. But he didn't think they were. They didn't look familiar. They might be Manyema.

There were by now several hundred Manyema in the vicinity of Yambuya. They had been arriving almost without letup since Barttelot had gone to the Falls with Selim, pushing upriver in fleets of canoes, coming down overland in caravans, raiding the Basoko villages along the way. In addition to their camp outside the fort's eastern stockade they had built a second one, as noisy and noisome as the first, across the river; and a third, of the same sort of primitive lean-tos and baked-mud tembes and rubbish heaps, was sprouting like a field of noxious mushrooms after a rain about a quarter of a mile downriver as well. So in effect they surrounded the fort, pressed in on it on all sides. But this was something new: Manyema *inside* the fort. That hadn't happened before—not, at least, as far as Troup knew. He went back into the hut and got his Bulldog pistol.

This woke up Ward. "What is it?"

"I'm not sure," Troup replied as he loaded the pistol and returned to the hut's doorway.

Seeing this, Ward fetched his Sharps carbine down from the rack above his cot and went to the doorway as well. It was 4:30 A.M.

"There. Do you see 'em?"

"Manyema?"

"I think so."

"But what are they doing here? How'd they get in?"

Troup shook his head. Two of the figures, then two more, had crept up between the Wanyamwezis' huts to the edge of the parade ground, paused there for an instant in a crouch, looked around warily, then dashed across the parade ground toward the river gate, where they were swallowed up in the shadows cast by the buildings of what was regarded as Barttelot's compound—his house, the officers' mess and kitchen, the officers' latrine, and the two large storehouses he had had built in the corner formed by the fort's south and riverside stockades.

"They're after the guns, Jack."

"What?"

"I knew it had to be something like that. I never for a moment believed Tippoo-Tib was sending them here to help us."

"What the devil are you talking about?"

"The guns, Jack. Those buggers are after the guns and ammunition. That's what this is all about. That's why Tippoo-Tib's been sending them here. To get hold of the guns and ammunition. Not to help us."

In fact, that was where the guns and ammunition were, the guns and ammunition for Emin Pasha's relief, in the storehouses in Barttelot's compound, precisely where the four prowlers had disappeared. Troup pulled back the hammer of his pistol.

Both barefoot and in their underwear—Troup in singlet and long woolens, Ward in khaki shorts—they started out of the hut. But just then two more figures stepped into the open of the parade ground. These two, however, had made their way to it from the south side of the fort and therefore were much closer to Troup and Ward's hut than the first four had been. They immediately spotted the two white men coming out its doorway, and they immediately turned and ran. Ward ran after them; but Troup's concern was for Emin's guns and ammunition, and he made for Barttelot's compound. As he raced by Bonny's tent—Bonny had pitched it beside Barttelot's house when Barttelot was sick, and it was still there—Bonny looked out, his face smeared with shaving soap.

"Did you see where they went?"

"Who?"

Troup didn't bother replying and kept going, past Barttelot's house, around the officers' mess and kitchen, and back to the storehouses. No one was there. Cautiously he tried the door of one and then the other. Both were locked, as they were supposed to be. Clutching his pistol with both hands, he circled around to the other side. And when Bonny came running around after him, he almost shot him.

"Holy Christ."

"There are Manyema in this fort, Sergeant. Four of them came back here. They passed right by your tent. Didn't you see them?"

"Manyema, sir? No, sir, I didn't see any Manyema."

Troup went over to the river gate and tried it, but it too was secure, the heavy rough-hewn beam that served as its bolt jammed solidly into place.

The fort was awake now, partly as a result of the ruckus Troup and Ward had caused but also because it was nearly 5 A.M., when Bonny would have rousted them anyway. They came out of their huts, unsure what was happening. Bonny followed Troup back to the parade ground.

"Did you catch them, Bert?"

Ward, returning to the parade ground from the opposite direction, shook his head. "No, they got away."

"Through the south gate?"

"No, it's shut."

"Then they must still be in here. The river gate's shut too. Sergeant, I want a search made. There are at least six Manyema somewhere in this fort. I want you to find them."

"Yes, sir."

But he didn't. The search was certainly thorough enough; and once they were dressed, Troup and Ward participated in it, combing over every inch, going through every structure inside the stockades, rooting around in the storehouses, turning everyone out of the huts, examining the latrines and cookhouses and granaries. But there was no trace of any Manyema. They had gotten clean away. But how? They couldn't have scaled the stockades—ten feet high and with sentries posted at frequent enough intervals along them (at least some of the sentries must have been awake)—without being seen. And even supposing they had opened one or another or all three of the gates and got out that way, how could they have arranged to have the gates bolted behind them? Unless, of course, they had accomplices; unless there were people inside the fort willing to help them. But who? The Wanyamwezis? The Sudanese? They stood around now in anxious groups, muttering to each other, buzzing with apprehension. They hated the Manyema, were terrified of them, wouldn't go anywhere near them if they possibly could avoid it.

"I don't like this, Jack. Truth is, I never liked it. Bula Matari's made a mistake."

"Oh, Christ, you're not going to start on that too, are you? You're getting to sound more like Barttelot every day."

"Yes, maybe, but there's no getting away from it, Jack. The fact is we still haven't seen hide nor hair of the porters Tippoo-Tib promised. All we've seen are these bloody gunmen. There must be damn near a thousand Manyema all around us by now, and not one of them's a porter. Every last one of them's a gunman."

Troup didn't make any response to this. There was none he could make. He had left his pistol in his hut when he had dressed, and now he went back there to get it.

Ward went with him. "It's a fact, Jack. Face it. Tippoo-Tib's not sending the porters."

Still without replying, Troup stuck the pistol into his waistband and started back out of the hut.

Ward grabbed his arm. "Jack, listen, will you? You don't have to defend Bula Matari to me. I'm not Barttelot. You know what I think of the man. I've served with him almost as long as you have. I've been through a lot of the good and bad with him too, you know."

"Then don't sell him short."

"I'm not selling him short. But he's human, Jack. He can make a mistake. And he's made one this time, and a bad one. Tippoo-Tib's not sending those porters. All this back and forth. All these delays. All these excuses. He's just throwing dust in our eyes. He never had any intention of sending us those porters."

"Then why did he say he would? Why didn't he just say no when Bula Matari put it to him in the first place? Why didn't he say straight away he didn't have men enough to spare or the price wasn't right or any other goddamn thing?"

"Because he wants the guns. What I said before. The guns and ammo we've got here, the stuff for Emin, they're a treasure to Tippoo-Tib. They're gold to a slaver. He'd do anything to lay his hands on them."

"And how do you imagine he expects to lay his hands on them?"

Ward didn't answer.

"You don't know."

"No, that's right, I don't. But he's got a scheme. I'm sure of that. He's a wily bastard. You know that better than anybody. He's bound to have something up his sleeve. I mean, just look at it. He's kept us stuck here with all his promises and excuses. He's sent a bloody army of gunmen here, and more are coming every day. He's managed to get Barttelot out of the way up at the Falls, and you can pretty well guess what's going on with him up there. And now we discover half a dozen of his gunmen prowling around inside the fort and we don't know how they got in or out. So? What the devil are we supposed to make of it?"

"That he plans to attack us?"

"Maybe."

"Oh, come off it, Bert. The sun's getting to you." And again Troup started out of the hut.

But again Ward grabbed him and held him back. "Jack, you're deliberately blinding yourself. You're deliberately refusing to look at what's going on out of some kind of skewed loyalty to Bula Matari. You don't want him to be wrong. You don't want to admit he could've made a mistake. But he has, Jack. I don't know how. I don't know why. Maybe he's getting old. Maybe he was in too much of a hurry. Maybe all he had on his mind was getting through the Ituri, being the first ever to get through it. But he figured this one wrong, Jack. We're never going to get those porters. I'm dead sure of it now. Tippoo-Tib's never going to send them."

"You're forgetting one thing, Bert, the one thing Bula Matari counted on when he made this arrangement, the one thing that nailed it down for certain."

"What?"

"Tippoo-Tib's greed. His greed to extend his raiding circle through the Ituri. He knows there's only one man who can show him the way through the Ituri, just as there was only one man who could show him the way down the Congo. So he's not going to do anything to cross that man."

"Oh, for God's sake, Jack. You don't really believe that?"

"You're damn right I do," Troup replied and walked out of the hut.

He remained awake that night. He told Bonny not to bother with his usual nightly rounds of the sentries, that he'd see to it. Ward stayed up to make the eleven o'clock round with him and then went to bed. Since the next round wouldn't occur until 2 A.M., he expected Troup to turn in as well. He didn't. He left the hut with his pistol. A moment later the lantern came on in the officers' mess, and Ward saw him sit down in one of the canvas-back camp chairs there, throw his feet up on the mess table, and settle back to the business of rolling a cigarette. Once he had it lit, he turned off the lantern, so all Ward could see of him was a circle of his shaggy red beard intermittently illuminated by the glow of the cigarette's coal as he puffed. He evidently intended to sit up until the next sentry round, and Ward considered going over there and sitting up with him, but he suspected that Troup preferred to be alone.

Ward woke around two, when the nightly storm was at its height. Troup's cot was still empty, but there was no way of seeing through the sheets of rain whether he was in the officers' mess or had started on the sentry round. Around four, Ward woke up again, this time because of some sort of commotion outside the hut. He dashed to the doorway. The commotion was coming from the Wanyamwezi lines, where the Manyema had been first spotted the night before. Troup was there manhandling someone, shoving him along, jabbing him in the back with his pistol. He flung him facedown in front of Munichandi's hut.

"Get out here, Munichandi."

The headman popped out of his hut.

"Where are the others? What did you do with them? There were at least six altogether. I saw you let them in."

Munichandi glanced around haplessly. Heads were popping out of huts. Sentries were scrambling down from the watchtowers. Bonny dashed out of his tent. Ward hurried over, certain that Troup had caught a Manyema sneaking into the fort.

But it wasn't a Manyema. It was a Wanyamwezi.

"You've got them stashed away in here somewhere, and I want to know where. I'm warning you, Munichandi. Don't make me hunt them up myself."

Ward bent down to get a closer look at the fellow. He was a Wanyamwezi all right, but Ward didn't recognize him. He wasn't one of the Wanyamwezis Ward and Bonny had brought up from Equator Station or one of the Wanyamwezis who'd been waiting in Yambuya when they had come up.

"Who the hell is this, Jack?"

"A deserter."

"What do you mean, a deserter? A deserter from what?"

"From the advance column. One of Bula Matari's *pagazis.* He quit the march somewhere in the Ituri and came back. And there are at least five more of the cowardly bastards somewhere in the fort. Munichandi's been hiding them. He's been stashing them away right under our noses as they came back. Eh, Munichandi? Well, the game's up, boy. The game's up."

A crowd had gathered. If what Troup was saying was true, they all must have been in on it. Munichandi couldn't have done it on his own, covering up the deserters' presence, letting them in and out of the fort at night, feeding them. They all must have been in on it, so their agitation now was not that there were deserters but that they had been discovered. For there was no more serious crime on an expedition of this sort than desertion. And they knew it.

"I'm giving you five minutes, Munichandi. I'm going over to the officers' mess, and in just five minutes I want to see every last one of these deserters paraded in front of me."

There were eight of them. Five were Wanyamwezis—a tracker, a tent boy, a muleteer, and two *pagazis*—the other three were Sudanese askaris, one a sharpshooter from Stanley's bodyguard. They had not all deserted and returned to Yambuya at the same time, nor had they been the only ones to desert. The tent boy, for example, had quit the march not much more than a week from Yambuya, when the advance column had lost the trail after the last Basoko village and was wandering aimlessly in the forest; and he had done so in the company of two older Wanyamwezis. Those two, however, hadn't made it back; one had been killed by tribesmen, the other had drowned in a swamp. The tracker, muleteer, and one of the *pagazis* had kept on until the advance column found its way back to the Aruwimi again and were involved in the fight at the village where a number of canoes had been captured and Stanley had divided the column into a land and river party. It took them nearly two months to return to Yambuya. On the way they ran into four others, who, fearing the punishment that awaited them for desertion, decided to bypass Yambuya and try to get down the Congo to Equator Station. What became of them no one would ever know. Two of the Sudanese told of going as far as a great cataract on the Aruwimi and participating in the portage around it, then remaining there under Will Hoffman's command to guard part of the stores while the rest of the column pushed on upriver—straight into an ambush. Thousands and thousands of Washenzi had fallen on the column, they said. They had heard the noise of the terrible battle and panicked and run away, convinced that the column had been wiped out to the last man. The third Sudanese knew better. He knew the column had survived the fight, although he believed Captain Nelson had been killed in it. His story, though, was that he had been knocked unconscious in a tremendous hand-to-hand engagement with dozens of howling savages and, when he woke up, had discovered that the column had moved on, leaving him behind for dead.

It was difficult to judge which or how much of these stories could be believed. After all, they were being told by men eager to cast their actions in the most favorable light and who undoubtedly exaggerated the difficulties of the march in hope of providing mitigating circumstances for their crime. But the story that was most difficult to believe was told by the *pagazi* who had been the last to return to Yambuya. He had returned only three days before. Of the eight, he had stuck with the march the longest, had traveled the farthest. He had reached the slave camp at Ipoto.

"The slave camp at Ipoto?"

Troup and Ward were seated behind the table in the officers' mess like judges of a tribunal. Bonny stood behind them at strict attention, and the deserters were paraded in front of them in a single rank just under the overhanging eave of the mess's thatched roof. They were a pitiable lot, little more than bags of bones clad in rags, with festering sores on their arms and legs, one shivering with fever, another with a broken arm that had gone septic. Formally, they were prisoners, but Troup hadn't bothered to have them fettered. How would they escape? Where would they run? The entire population of the fort was gathered around them. A detachment of Winchester-armed askaris guarded them. Munichandi and the other headmen stood with them. And morning had come.

"What slave camp at Ipoto?"

"The slave camp of Kilonga-longa."

"An Arab slave camp?"

"Yes, Bwana, a great Arab slave camp."

Troup leaned forward. "What are you talking about, boy? An Arab slave camp? There are no Arab slave camps in the forest. The Arabs do not go into the forest. They dare not go into the forest. So why do you speak such a lie?"

"I do not speak a lie, Bwana. I speak the truth. At Ipoto there was a great Arab settlement, the slave camp of Kilonga-longa. I swear it."

"You swear it? Now you swear to such a lie? You swear that you went with Bula Matari farther than this cowardly tent boy went, farther than this woman of a tracker and this weakling *pagazi* and muleteer went, farther than the great cataract and the terrible ambush these miserable excuses for askaris tell about, farther than where the Aruwimi narrowed and turned to stone, so that Bula Matari had to give up on the river and strike into the forest without trails or villages, and there, in this place of horror and starvation and death, hundreds of marches from here where no one has ever gone before, you swear to me that you came upon a great Arab settlement, a great slave camp? You swear such a lie to me?"

"It is no lie, Bwana. I swear it because it is the truth."

Troup sat back in his chair.

"It was in a valley, Bwana, a valley deep in the forest through which a quiet river ran. There were plantations of maize and rice there and orchards of limes and mango along the riverbank. There were herds of livestock and many houses and people–Arabs and Manyema and hundreds of Washenzi slaves they had captured in the forest. We came to it when we thought all was lost, when we were starving and dying and thought we could not go even one more step farther. It is true, Bwana. I do not lie. *Tafadhali.* Please believe me."

Troup said nothing. He took out his tobacco pouch and packet of papers and slowly rolled himself a cigarette. Ward watched him, admiring the calm steadiness with which he did this, as if what he had just heard wasn't catastrophic, as if it wasn't the smashup of his last best hope that Bula Matari hadn't made a dreadful mistake. But perhaps that was because he didn't believe it. Yet there was no reason for this *pagazi* to lie.

"And who is this Kilonga-longa?" Ward asked, himself now leaning across the mess table. "An Arab for certain?"

"Oh, yes, Bwana. An Arab for certain. A sheik. Abed bin Salim. Known to all as Kilonga-longa."

"And from where does he come, this Abed bin Salim? What sultan does he serve?"

The *pagazi* looked puzzled. He didn't seem to understand the question. Then he said, "But what other sultan is there to serve, Bwana? Is there not only one sultan?"

"Hamed bin Mohammed? Tippoo-Tib?"

"Yes, Bwana. Hamed bin Mohammed. Tippoo-Tib."

"And it was for Hamed bin Mohammed that he went into the forest? It is for Tippoo-Tib that he catches slaves from his camp at Ipoto?"

"Yes, Bwana. For Tippoo-Tib. For none other."

"And how long has he been there? How long has he had this camp at Ipoto?"

"That I could not say, Bwana. But it is a great camp. It surely has been there for many moons."

"*Nafahamu*," Ward said and turned to Troup.

Troup was smoking. The cigarette was stuck in the corner of his mouth, the glowing coal burning perilously close to the hairs of his shaggy red beard. Squinting through the smoke, he appraised the *pagazi* for a moment, then turned to Ward. He didn't say anything, and the look in his eyes forestalled Ward from saying anything either.

"Do you want them shot or hanged, Mr. Troup?"

Troup glanced over his shoulder at Bonny.

As far as Bonny was concerned, the interrogation was over, the crime proved, and all that remained was for the punishment to be pronounced and executed. He had entirely missed the devastating significance of the fact that Tippoo-Tib's slavers were already in the Ituri, that Tippoo-Tib did not need Bula Matari's expedition to show him the way there. "A firing squad would be the simplest, sir. But if you prefer, it ain't all that much trouble to build a gallows."

"No, I don't suppose it is." Troup flicked away his cigarette and stood up. "But it'd be a waste of energy and time. Just shoot 'em."

· SEVEN ·

THE NEXT DAY Troup set off for the Falls.

He traveled light—just with a tracker, a pack mule, and the cookboy Bartholomew as muleteer—and headed south by southwest across the neck of land formed by the confluence of the Aruwimi and Congo rivers. This was thickly forested land but not so killingly forested as the Ituri. There were creeks to ford and swamps to swim, deadfalls of immense trees to climb over, and acres of canebrake to hack through. But there also were long stretches of grassy country where the trees grew wide apart and the road between was mossy and easy on the feet, where sunbeams pierced the canopy of leaves in brilliant patches, aswarm with butterflies, and birds sang out in a million competing songs. It was the kind of traveling Troup ordinarily loved; and under other circumstances he would have had a good time of it and made good time at it, pushing his little caravan along at a rate of twenty or twenty-five miles a day, completing the journey in less than five days. But he didn't, and the reason he didn't was the slavers.

For this was slaver-held country, and he was anxious to avoid them. All the villages here were under Tippoo-Tib's rule, and Troup no longer trusted him. He didn't know what the Arab was up to. He didn't know what game he was playing. Perhaps Ward was right. Perhaps he was planning to attack them. Perhaps he had kept them waiting in Yambuya with his false promises and elaborate excuses until he was ready to fall on them and take their guns. But whatever his game, whatever he was planning, it was no longer possible to believe he was planning to help them. He had found his own way into the Ituri; he already had a slave camp there. He didn't need Bula Matari or Bula Matari's men for that. So Troup traveled circuitously, staying clear of the most used trails, skirting the Arab-occupied villages, keeping a sharp eye out for roving slaving gangs. He bedded down in hollows and ravines at night and made a cold meal of biscuits and foraged beans so as not to give away their presence with a fire.

Toward dusk of the seventh day they reached the right bank of the Congo at about one degree of latitude north of the equator, some five or six miles below Stanley Falls. Uneasy about entering Singatini in darkness, unsure of the reception he'd get there, Troup decided to hole up where he was and make the last leg of the journey in the morning. He set up camp in the bush near the riverbank where a bamboo thicket provided good cover and a grove of wild plantains provided supper. From there he could hear the rumble of the Falls and see the flickering orange specks that were the lanterns and fires of Singatini. He wasn't sure exactly what he was going to do when he got there. The only thing he knew for sure was that he was going to get Barttelot out of there. Whether he'd say anything to Tippoo-Tib about the slave camp at Ipoto, whether he'd confront the Arab with this evidence of his duplicity, or whether he'd keep his mouth shut and let Tippoo-Tib believe they still counted on him for the porters—that he'd decide on the spot. The main thing was to get Barttelot back to Yambuya.

He crawled into his tent. He didn't bother to undress. He smoked a cigarette, then wrapped the Winchester he had brought with him in oilskin to protect it from the rain that would come in a couple of hours; but his little Bulldog pistol he took under the blanket with him.

And then suddenly he came awake. It was only for a split second. He had heard a shout. And somehow in that split second he knew that it was Bartholomew who had shouted. He also knew that it was raining, so it was at least two hours since he had turned in. As he hurriedly flung off his blanket, knowing that Bartholomew had shouted, knowing that it was raining, trying to shake off his sleep and put these two facts together, he was clubbed across the head.

"How can I tell you how sorry I am, Mr. Troup? How can I ever expect you to forgive so dreadful a mistake? But still, effendi, sneaking up on us like that in the dark . . ."

Troup opened his eyes. And immediately shut them. It was daylight and the light stabbed through his eyes, setting fire to the excruciating pain in his brain.

"I mean, how were they to know? I am not excusing them. By

no means would I try to find excuses for them. They will be punished, I assure you, effendi. They will be punished severely for this terrible deed. But still, sneaking up on us like that in the dark. I of course came as soon as I heard it was a *wasungu*. I didn't waste a minute."

Troup was lying on his back and thought he might still be lying in the tent. But warily letting his eyes open again, he saw he wasn't. He was in a cage. It was the sort of cage, made of bamboo stakes, that the Arabs in Singatini used as holding pens for the slaves they intended to transport upriver. The gate of the cage was open; and squatting in the opening, dressed in a richly embroidered aba, wearing a maroon skullcap, stroking his cutthroat's beard, was Selim, talking and talking.

But Troup knew that all of it—the apologies, the concern, the assurances that those responsible would be punished, the repeated refrain "but still, effendi, still, sneaking up on us like that . . ."—was shit. Even if a gang of Manyema gunmen on coming upon the campsite in the forest had actually believed it represented a threat, that unknown enemies were sneaking up on Singatini in the night, even so there was no excuse for what they'd done. They would have seen right away that there were only three of them and that one was a white man and one a mere boy. Whatever their suspicions, they could just as easily have taken the three under guard to their sheik. There was no excuse for a sudden brutal attack; there certainly was no excuse for throwing a white man in a cage. Gingerly Troup touched the crown of his head. A thick cotton bandage covered it. It was stickily damp, but he couldn't tell whether from sweat or blood.

"You have been looked after, effendi. Our best physician has looked after you. He tells me it is a serious wound but that a strong man like you, with proper rest and care, will heal quickly."

Troup pushed up on an elbow and, wincing from the awful pain, had a look around. A jumble of tembes and huts and cages and dusty bazaars—this was the backside of Singatini, where the slaves were held and the Manyema were billeted, some distance down river from the villas and gardens of the Arabs themselves. It had the same fetid stink as the Manyema encampment at Yambuya. Behind Selim, a few turbaned Arabs and a mob of half-naked blacks peered into the cage.

"Where are my boys, Selim?"

"Your boys?"

"I had a tracker and a cookboy with me."

"Oh, yes. They ran away. Slippery as eels, the Manyema tell me. They ran away."

"And the mule?"

"The mule?"

"I had a pack mule with me."

"I heard nothing of a pack mule. It must have run away as well."

It was shit all right. Maybe, just possibly, Bartholomew and the tracker had run away, had managed to slip off into the rain and darkness of the forest. But the mule? No, the mule had been staked on a short lead.

"Am I a prisoner, Selim?"

"A prisoner? Oh, my dear Mr. Troup, haven't you been listening to what I've been saying? Of course you are not a prisoner. It's all been a dreadful mistake."

"Then it isn't necessary for me to remain in here."

"No, of course not. If you feel well enough to move." Selim backed out of the cage and stood up. "I would have had you moved before this, but I was fearful it might cause you further injury."

Troup got on his knees. The cage was too low for him to stand erect inside it, so he was obliged to crawl to the opening. There Selim extended him a hand but he didn't take it; he stood up on his own. And closed his eyes again to suppress the sudden rush of nausea and dizziness. When he opened them, he realized that one of the Arabs who had been peering into the cage was Tippoo-Tib.

"Mr. Troup, *salaam aleikum.*" The sultan bowed, touching his heart, lips, and forehead. "It is a long time since we last met. How unfortunate that we should meet again under these circumstances."

Troup nodded noncommittally. Compared to Selim, Tippoo-Tib was plainly dressed in a simple caftan, a white turban, and leather slippers. But there was no mistaking the woolly white beard, the hooded eyes. His words were courteous, his tone friendly, his elegantly intelligent features composed in an expression of concern; but there was no way of knowing what was going on behind those hooded eyes.

"I've come for Major Barttelot. I take it he's still here."

"Oh, yes, he is still here," Tippoo-Tib replied. "He is our honored guest. The beautiful soldier."

Beautiful soldier? The phrase startled Troup. "I'd like to see him."

"Of course."

"I'd like to see him now."

"Now? You would not prefer first to eat? Or to bathe perhaps? To refresh yourself a bit and regain your strength, have our physician examine your injury and change the dressing?"

"No."

"But what is the urgency? Major Barttelot will not go away."

"Nevertheless, I would like to see him now."

The Arab shrugged. "Very well. You shall see him now. Come." He took Troup's hand in the Arab fashion.

They proceeded in procession, Troup with Tippoo-Tib, Selim and a few other Arabs behind them, a troop of Manyema gunmen behind them, a gaggle of curiosity seekers—native men and boys and women—behind them. It was some distance they had to go, and Troup realized that he really wasn't up to it; every step jarred the splintering pain in his head and brought the slime of nausea to his throat. They passed through a labyrinth of dirt streets and walled alleys, narrow archways and cobbled courtyards, overgrown gardens and noisy bazaars, passing in and out of the blinding sunlight. Troup couldn't keep track; he lost all sense of direction. Maybe he should have bathed and eaten and refreshed himself first; maybe he should have let the physician see to his wound; maybe it was a mistake to let the Arab take him into this bewildering maze in his weakened state.

The farther they went, the more the procession behind them diminished, because the deeper they penetrated into the Arabs' own quarter, the fewer were the people who were permitted to enter there, until finally only Tippoo-Tib and Selim were with him. They stepped through an archway into a walled courtyard with a small fountain, then through a doorway in one wall of the courtyard into a fantastic garden, then through this garden down a winding path strewn with whitewashed gravel.

At the end of the gravel path they came to a grand villa standing in a park. Its double doors at the back of a grand veranda were opened for them by slaves in spotless linen. They entered a large reception room with stone floor, domed ceiling, and mosaics of tile on the walls. They passed through this room down a long dim corridor only to emerge again into the bright sunlight of a courtyard with a fountain and benches and flowering trees. They passed from there into yet another room and down yet another corridor and out again into yet another courtyard. As they went, there were slaves and serving girls and guards along the way who scurried to the side as they approached and watched them silently as they passed. Troup was aware of them but only from the corner of his eyes. He was concentrating on keeping his pain and nausea and dizziness at bay. He now no longer had any idea where he was. And now he was in yet another enclosed courtyard. A slave boy dozed on a stone bench there. He jumped up when Tippoo-Tib clapped. An intricately carved, wooden door, studded with brass fittings, opened on the courtyard. The slave boy ran to it. It opened inward.

"As you requested, I have brought you to Major Barttelot, effendi," Tippoo-Tib said, indicating the room behind the door. "You will find the beautiful soldier in there."

Troup looked in. After the bright sunlight it took a moment for his eyes to adjust to the dimness. Then he said, "Oh, good God."

Tippoo-Tib and Selim smiled.

Barttelot was half naked. He was naked from the waist down. He was lying facedown on a sofa. His wrists were tied above his head. A harem girl was kneeling beside him. She was entirely naked. When the slave boy had opened the door, she had stopped whatever she had been doing and looked up, showing a pale oval face surrounded by a wild mass of auburn hair. Barttelot raised his head and looked back over his shoulder. The pupils of his gemlike blue eyes were mere pinpoints. His blond beard was untrimmed and knotted. His handsome features were slack and loathsome.

"Is that you, Troup?" he asked.

Troup started toward him. But when he realized that Tippoo-Tib and Selim were also coming into the room, he stopped. "Would you leave us alone. I'd like to speak to the major alone."

"As you wish," Tippoo-Tib replied. "Send the boy if you have any need of us."

"Thank you. I will."

Troup watched the two Arabs return to the courtyard and disappear down a walled alleyway in the opposite direction from which they had come. He had no idea where they'd gone or, for that matter, whether they really had gone. He turned back to Barttelot. Barttelot had let his face drop on the pillows on the sofa between his tied wrists. The girl was still kneeling beside him, waiting to see what would happen, brazenly unashamed of her nakedness. The slave boy hovered uncertainly by the door.

"*Nifunge mlango*."

Whether or not the boy understood Swahili, he understood Troup's gesture and closed the door. Without the shaft of sunlight the door had admitted, the only light in the room was that which filtered through the stone grillwork of two small circular windows high on the wall opposite the door. It was a milky light in which motes of dust swirled. Perhaps there was another courtyard on that side, but there didn't seem any way out of the room into it. On a third wall, however, a tapestried hanging, Troup discovered when he pulled it aside, covered an arched egress into a corridor. The corridor was dark; he couldn't see where it led. He went over to Barttelot.

The girl stood up then and moved a few steps away. A real whore, Troup thought. She allowed him to look at her, doing nothing to cover her nakedness. She was used to men looking at her nakedness. He got down in her place beside Barttelot and realized that Barttelot was wearing a caftan and his half-nakedness was a result of its having been pushed up above his waist. Roughly, disgustedly, Troup yanked it down, then untied Barttelot's wrists and as roughly and disgustedly rolled him over on his back. Barttelot lay amid the pillows on the sofa for a moment with his eyes closed. Then he opened them and smiled.

The smile infuriated Troup. "You dumb bastard. What in Christ's name are you doing here?"

"Doing here?" Barttelot raised his head from the pillows. He spoke with an unreal lucid calm. "Why, I'm waiting for Tippoo-Tib to return from Kasongo with the porters."

Troup's anger erupted at this. All his anxieties and frustration burst loose. And he slapped Barttelot across the face.

The girl emitted a startled cry and protectively stepped forward. The slave boy turned away and cringed against the door. Barttelot himself fell back on the pillows.

"Why did you do that?" he asked in eerily mild surprise. It was as if he hadn't felt the impact of the blow.

"Because Tippoo-Tib's not in Kasongo. He's here in Singatini. He's right outside."

"He is? Really? Well, then we can go, can't we? We can at last be on our way to the shining sea." And saying this, Barttelot closed his eyes contentedly and let his head roll to the side.

"Get some water, girl. And some cloths and loofahs. And tea. Hot tea."

The harem girl, in all her insolent, provocative nakedness, hands on hips, her full breasts rising and falling with her breath, didn't respond. It was difficult to judge in the milky light, but all the alluring flesh she displayed seemed very nearly white. Probably a Circassian, Troup thought.

"Do you understand English?"

"Yes."

"Then do what I say. And get some chop too. Some *posho*."

"Are you going to hit him again?"

The question took Troup aback. What did this harem girl care whether he hit Barttelot again? "No, I'm not going to hit him again."

The girl said something in Arabic, and she and the slave boy left the room through the archway covered by the tapestried hanging. Troup took hold of Barttelot's dirty bearded face and shook it back and forth, seeing if he could rouse him from his stupor in this way. He couldn't, of course. Barttelot was out, lost in a drugged dream. Troup sat back on his heels and touched the bandage on his head. It was crusted; whatever had been seeping through had dried. But his head still ached murderously.

When the slave boy and girl came back, the girl was dressed. Her hair was still an unpinned unruly mass, and she was still barefoot; but she had at least pulled on the sort of hooded rough linen ankle-length robe that the Arabs' serving women wore. And like a strong, skilled serving woman, she deftly carried a large earthenware ewer of steaming water on her head and a shallow basin of beaten pewter containing rags and sponges in her hand.

The boy followed her, struggling with a heavy brass platter laden with food and drink. They set these down on the tile floor beside the sofa. Troup reached for the earthenware ewer, but the girl was quicker. She slithered on her knees between Barttelot and Troup and poured water from the ewer into the basin and with one of the loofahs began sponging Barttelot's face. She understood what was wanted. So Troup let her do it, sitting back on his heels, watching her vigorous yet surprisingly careful ministrations.

Who was she? Was she the one Barttelot had fancied had poisoned him? Her face was in profile to Troup, a pretty enough face with small sharp features. The auburn color of her hair was plainly artificial, but even so she could be white. The Arabs had white odalisques in their seraglios. They bought them from the Ottoman Turks, whose empire stretched deep into the Balkans. Perhaps she was from the Balkans.

She worked on Barttelot with earnest concentration, repeatedly having the slave boy freshen the water in the basin. And after a while she also tried to make him swallow some tea and eat some rice. But it was a futile exercise. From time to time Barttelot would come awake to protest these activities and then slip back into the mists of his doped mind, the tea dribbling down his chin, the rice spattering in his beard.

"What is your name?" Troup asked after some time.

"Verbena," the girl replied, not looking at him, continuing her work.

"Leave it off, Verbena. It's hopeless. We'll just have to let the son of a bitch sleep for a while."

The girl looked at Troup. "Have you come to take him away?"

"Yes," Troup replied and waited with some curiosity for what she'd say to that.

But she didn't say anything. She took a clean cloth and wiped the rice and spilled tea from Barttelot's face, then sat back on her heels, leaving the hand that held the cloth resting gently on Barttelot's chest.

"Let me have some of that chop. I haven't eaten since last night."

The slave boy brought over the food. It wasn't only rice; there were thick chunks of broiled meat on kabobs, cheeses and fruits and bread as well. Troup knew that after the miserable diet on which he'd been living these past months this fare was too rich for his shriveled stomach, so he restrained himself from wolfing it down. But God, it was good. He looked at the unconscious Barttelot. Food like this, hashish, women, gardens in luxuriant bloom, courtyards with tinkling fountains, nights and days spinning away undifferentiated except by dreams–Stanley knew about such Arabian seductions and had warned against them. But Barttelot had paid no heed. The beautiful soldier. Oh, yes, the beautiful soldier. Tippoo-Tib must have realized that he wouldn't be able to resist such seductions; he must have seen something in Barttelot that had told him that this beautiful soldier could be made to forget his duty by them. And that must have played a part in his game.

When Troup finished eating, he had the slave boy pour out a fresh basin of water and he washed his face and hands. Then he again explored the bandage on his head with his fingertips. His nausea and dizziness had abated somewhat. But his head still ached brutally. It worried him. Perhaps he should have the girl change the bandage. She looked at him as if she knew what he was thinking.

"Is his kit anywhere around here, Verbena? His uniform, boots, pistol?"

"Yes."

"And what about mine? Do you have any idea where my kit is?"

"Yes," the girl said again.

"Well, fetch them then, will you?"

Again the girl spoke in Arabic to the slave boy, and the boy slipped out of the room behind the tapestried hanging. The girl, however, remained beside Barttelot. Tippoo-Tib had made a cunning choice in her, a white girl or one at least who could be mistaken for white. Doubtless that too was part of his game. Troup got up and went to the door, opened it partially, and looked out into the courtyard. No one was about, neither Tippoo-Tib nor any spy sent in their place. Troup had a look around, first up the alleyway from which he and Tippoo-Tib and Selim had come, then down the alleyway where Tippoo-Tib and Selim had gone. He could see no one. He wondered how much longer it would be before someone came. He went back into the room.

The slave boy had returned with his and Barttelot's kit. Everything seemed to be there; or at least everything of his seemed to be there: his rucksack and blanket roll, the oilskin-wrapped Winchester, the Bulldog pistol, the dismantled tent packed in its canvas bag, even his battered straw hat. He assumed all Barttelot's gear must be there as well. In any case, the holstered Webley revolver and bandolier were there, which was what counted. The boy couldn't have carried it all on his own, but whoever had helped him was gone. The stuff was piled neatly in a corner. Troup picked up the Bulldog pistol and stuffed it into his waistband and gingerly put on his straw hat. The girl was still at Barttelot's side.

"How is he?"

The girl shrugged. Barttelot's mouth had fallen open and he was snoring.

"Let's get him dressed."

The girl did this too, as she had done the washing and feeding, with dexterity and care, pulling the caftan off over Barttelot's head, maneuvering his limp limbs into his underwear, his trousers, his shirt and tunic. Troup needed only to stand by and admire her proficiency—How many times had she done this before and for how many men?—until it came to getting him into his boots. There Troup had to lend a hand.

"All right. Now let's see if we can get him on his feet."

With the girl taking one arm over her shoulder and Troup taking the other, they stood him up. His knees were like jelly.

"We're going for a walk, Major. Come on. You can do it. Here we go. Step out now. Step lively."

Maybe it did some good; maybe the exertion pumped some blood to his brain. But it didn't seem like it. He in no way seemed to come alive. He just let Troup and the girl drag him around.

"The hell with it."

They let Barttelot collapse back on the sofa. Troup stood over him looking down at him. The sight filled him with revulsion and contempt. The aristocratic gentleman, the arrogant Imperial Army officer, so sure of himself—and so cheaply brought low. He had never liked him. Now he hated him. Why should he bother with him? Why shouldn't he just go back to Yambuya on his own and leave him here, leave him here to rot in the depravity he had so eagerly embraced? He'd only have himself to blame. He had brought it on himself. Troup took out his tobacco pouch and rolled himself a cigarette. With the approach of dusk, the room, never bright, had grown increasingly glum, so the striking of his match was startling. The girl, seated on the floor beside Barttelot, shielded her eyes.

"Do you know the way out of here, Verbena?"

The girl lowered her hand.

"Can you show me the way to the river?"

"Yes."

Troup went back to the door, leaned in the doorway, and looked out into the courtyard. It was still light, the bluish light of early evening, but it would not be long before it was dark. In two hours or less night would fall. That would be the time to go. If Barttelot had roused himself by then, he'd take him along; if not, he'd go alone. Actually he'd prefer to go alone. It's be easier, safer. The Arabs probably thought of Barttelot as their hostage—albeit a most willing hostage, to be sure—and believed that as long as he was in Singatini the rear column would remain in Yambuya waiting for him to return. They probably wouldn't trouble themselves about Troup's departure; but if he tried to take Barttelot along, there was no telling what they might do.

"Is that you, Troup?"

Troup flicked away his cigarette and turned around. Barttelot was still sprawled on the sofa, his arms hanging lifelessly over its sides, his head lolling on the pillows the girl had pushed under it; but at least his eyes were open and seemed focused. Troup went to him, all his anger and loathing returning in a rush.

"Get up. Get on your feet, Major."

"I'm sick, Troup. Can't you see? I've been poisoned."

"You've not been poisoned. You dumb bastard, you've poisoned yourself. Get up, I say."

"What are you doing?"

Troup had grabbed hold of the lapels of Barttelot's tunic and jerked him up into a sitting position. But Barttelot was dead weight. He fell forward against Troup, toppled to the side, slipped to the floor, half on the sofa, half off, his legs twisted under him. He thought it funny and giggled.

"Jesus Christ. Look at you. Look at what you've done to yourself. Major Barttelot, Seventh Royal Fusiliers. Just look at you now. Give him some tea, Verbena. Get some chop in him."

The girl, steadying Barttelot's head with one hand, brought a cup of tea to his lips with the other. Barttelot turned his face away from it.

"Drink it, damn you. Drink it."

"Don't give me orders, Troup. I don't take orders from you. I'm in command here. I'm the one who gives the orders."

"You give the orders? Don't make me laugh. Who'd obey orders from the likes of you? Look at yourself. A mule wouldn't obey orders from you."

The fury in Troup's voice—the disgraceful condition in which Troup had found him—was beginning to penetrate Barttelot's fogged brain. He changed his tone. "This isn't my fault, Troup. You don't understand. I tell you, I've been poisoned."

"By what? By hashish? By fucking a harem girl?"

Barttelot didn't reply. The girl offered him the tea again, and this time he took a sip. Their faces were close together. He looked into her eyes. "Beryl," he said. "Beryl and Amethyst." She gave him more to drink, slipping the tips of her fingers into his mouth. "She's white, you know. She's from the steppes of Romany."

"Give him something to eat."

Barttelot let the girl feed him. He sat on the floor, his back against the sofa, his mouth open. She fed him like a baby or an invalid, from time to time wiping his mouth with a clean cloth. Troup watched them. There was something he didn't quite understand going on between them. It was now almost totally dark in the room, and he had the slave boy light a candle.

"All right. Now stand up."

The girl helped Barttelot to his feet.

"Now put these on." Troup handed Barttelot his pith helmet, the holstered Webley revolver, the bandolier.

Again the girl helped him; but as soon as he had the revolver and bandolier on, before she could put the helmet on his head, it was as if their weight was too much for him, and he sat down on the edge of the sofa.

"Stand up, damn you. Will you stand up? We've got to get out of here."

"Get out of here? But what about the porters? We've got to wait for the porters. Tippoo-Tib's bringing them from Kasongo."

"Forget about the porters. There are no porters. Tippoo-Tib's not bringing them from Kasongo or anywhere else."

"But Mr. Stanley—"

"Mr. Stanley was wrong."

Barttelot's slack expression changed at this. A flicker of intelligent interest came into his glazed eyes. He became perceptibly more alert. "Mr. Stanley was wrong? *You* say that, Troup? You say Mr. Stanley was wrong?"

"Stand up, Major."

Barttelot stood up with sudden surprising alacrity. "Mr. Stanley was wrong. Yes, I knew it. By God, I knew it. I was the first to say it. Wasn't I the first to say it?"

"That isn't the point."

"But I was the first. He was taken in. Our hero, our great leader, Bula Matari was taken in. Tippoo-Tib lied to him, and he was taken in just like he was taken in by King Leopold. Isn't that what I've been saying? Isn't that what I've been saying all along?"

"All right, that's what you've been saying. But that isn't what matters now. What matters now is to get back to Yambuya."

Barttelot, however, as suddenly as he had stood up, sat down again. Clearly the effort had been too much. His face drained of all color, and for a moment he rested it in his hands. But then, again with a sudden rush of animation, he looked up. "How do you know?"

"How do I know what?"

"That Mr. Stanley was wrong. That Tippoo-Tib lied to him."

It was then that Troup told Barttelot about the deserters from the advance column and what had been learned from them about an Arab settlement deep in the Ituri. Barttelot listened to this with a steadily brightening expression, a steadily broadening smile, nodding his head and repeating, "I knew it; I knew it all along." But Troup wasn't at all sure that he really comprehended what he was being told, that he fully grasped the significance of it. His mind was still too sluggish. All he seemed able to focus on, all he seemed to get out of what Troup was saying was that Stanley had been wrong, that Stanley had made a mistake. The smile was the smile of one feeling himself vindicated, the bright expression an expression of gloating.

"Tippoo-Tib doesn't know we know this. At least, I don't think he does. I can't imagine how he could. He's not likely to know that some deserters made it back to Yambuya. And I haven't said anything to him. I think it's best that way. I think it's best to let him believe we still trust him, that we're still counting on him for the porters. It might hold him off for a while, give us more time. He's got something up his sleeve. I don't know what it is, but he must have had some reason for keeping us stuck in Yambuya. Ward thinks he's after our guns. He thinks he's just waiting for the right time to attack us. Christ knows, he's assembled enough gunmen at Yambuya to do the job if that's his game."

Smiling, gloating, Barttelot went on nodding.

"Are you listening to me, Major? For God's sake, do you understand what I'm saying?"

"Oh, I understand what you're saying all right, Troup. It's not that difficult to understand, you know. The game's up. The expedition's a bust. Mr. Stanley's made a thorough botch of it. We'll just have to pack it in and go home."

"No, that's not what I'm saying."

"It's not?"

"No, damnit, we're not going to pack it in and go home. We're not going to give up that easily. We've got a job to do and we're going to do it. We're going to go through the Ituri. We're going to get the relief to Emin."

"Without porters, Troup? Without porters?"

"We'll get porters. We'll get them from somewhere else. Or if it comes to that, we'll make double marches, triple marches."

"Oh, Troup, Troup. You know, I admire you. Mr. Stanley's left you in the soup. He hasn't cared a fig what happens to you or to anyone else. He just rushed off to snatch the crown of glory for himself. And you're still willing to follow him. You're still willing to go into the Ituri after him. Does your loyalty know no bounds?"

Troup turned away in exasperation and looked at the harem girl. She was still holding Barttelot's helmet. Doubtless she had understood every word of the exchange between the two white men, but she only had eyes for the one, the beautiful soldier.

"Listen to me, Major. I'm going back to Yambuya. To tell the truth, I don't give a damn whether you come back with me or not. If you want it that way, I'll go back alone and take command of the rear column myself."

"Is that a threat, Troup? Are you threatening me with mutiny?"

"I'm not threatening you with anything, Major. I'm just telling you where I consider our duty lies. No matter what the obstacles, no matter what's gone wrong with Mr. Stanley's plan, we've got to try to get through the Ituri. We've got to try to get the relief to Emin. That's why we signed on for this expedition."

"You're a fool, Troup, a fool on a fool's errand. You're Stanley's fool. It can't be done. You'd never make it. You'd be marching to a certain death."

"Maybe. Maybe not. But I intend to try it. And then whatever happens there will always be the question: Where was Major Barttelot in all this? Where was Edmund Musgrave Barttelot, Major, Seventh Royal Fusiliers, commanding Stanley's rear column? Where was he when the rear column marched into the Ituri? In the seraglio of Tippoo-Tib? In the arms of a whore?"

Barttelot was still sitting on the edge of the sofa looking up at Troup. He held Troup's eyes for a moment, then looked down at himself as if only now realizing he was wearing his field uniform, his revolver, his bandolier. He adjusted the buckle of his belt and pulled down on his tunic to straighten it. Then he extended his hand to the girl. She gave him his helmet and he put it on.

"Where's Tippoo-Tib? Is he back from Kasongo yet?"

"He's back from Kasongo. If he ever went."

"Send for him."

"What for?"

"I want to thank him for his hospitality. And tell him to his greasy face what I think of his duplicity."

"No. I tell you, I don't think he knows we're onto him yet. And it's best we leave it that way." As he spoke, Troup went over to the pile of his and Barttelot's kit and began rummaging through it. "I'm not sure what he's got up his sleeve, but whatever it is he's been taking his own sweet time about it. And I want him to keep on taking his own sweet time about it. We need all the time we can get. I don't want to give him any reason to feel he's got to take whatever action he has in mind any more quickly than he originally planned to take it." Troup pulled his rucksack with the blanket roll tied to it out of the pile and slung it over a shoulder, then unwrapped the Winchester and stuffed his pockets with cartridges. The tent and his other stuff he'd have to leave; without the mule and Bartholomew and the tracker, it'd be too much to carry. He picked up Barttelot's rucksack and blanket roll. "Here."

"You really are a fool, Troup. You think we can get out of here without Tippoo-Tip's knowing?"

"We've got to try. That's all we can do about anything now—try. Put this on." Troup handed the rucksack and blanket roll to Barttelot. "The girl will show us the way. Our best bet is to make for the river a mile or so downstream. With a bit of luck we'll be able to get hold of a canoe and be back in Yambuya in three days."

The girl, barefoot, wearing only the long hooded robe, slipped out into the dark corridor behind the tapestried hanging. Barttelot followed her, unsteady on his feet under the added weight of his rucksack, stretching out a hand in front of him to keep in touch with the girl in the darkness; then Troup, his head cracking with pain, the nausea returning, clearly more seriously hurt than he allowed himself to believe; then the little slave boy, obviously not knowing what else to do, possibly thinking it was his fate to follow the white man to whom he had been assigned and, indeed, lugging along, without being asked, some of the kit Troup had chosen to leave behind.

Troup was under no illusion; it was a harebrained gamble. He was sure the girl understood what they were trying to do; but whether she'd do it, whether there even was a way to do it, or whether she was in on Tippoo-Tib's game and would now lead them straight into the Arab's arms, he had no way of knowing. But he also was sure that neither he nor Barttelot could find the way out of this maze of corridors and courtyards on their own. So he had to take the gamble; he had to put his trust in her. And besides there was that something inexplicable between her and Barttelot, that peculiar protectiveness she exhibited toward the beautiful soldier that gave him hope that his trust wasn't entirely farfetched.

The corridor led to a door. The girl opened it, looked out, looked around warily, then pulling on the hood of her robe over her mass of unpinned hennaed hair and covering the lower part of her face with a piece of the cloth, she stepped out and signaled the others to follow. Troup expected to find himself in another of those myriad rooms or courtyards through which he had passed on the way in. But this wasn't a room or a courtyard. It was a large wildly overgrown garden. From the door through which they stepped a path of whitewashed gravel provided a serpentine way through its flowering bushes and trees. It looked familiar. It was nearly night now; the sky was still a pale blue, tinted with the pinks and greens of the recently set sun, but on the ground it was already dark, so he couldn't be sure.

About a hundred yards along, the winding path divided, one branch continuing on southward through the trees, the other curving away to the right into a grassy clearing. This too struck Troup as familiar. There was a cistern well at the center of the clearing; and a serving woman, robed, hooded, and veiled like the harem girl, was drawing water from it. She glanced around at the two white men sneaking past but showed no special interest in them. They went on and eventually came to another door, this one set in a mud-brick wall that evidently marked off one end of the garden, and the girl again went through the business of opening it, looking out cautiously, then signaling them to follow. And this time they did step into a courtyard. And this time Troup was certain that he recognized it: the facade of the house directly in front of them with its grilled Moorish windows, the fountain at the center with its frogs and goldfish, the stone bench against the wall to the left under the lime saplings, the archway leading out into a cobbled alley on the right. No, he had no doubt about this courtyard; he remembered coming into it with Tippoo-Tib and Selim.

The girl would now lead them through the archway into the cobbled alley. And when she did, he realized what a fool the Arabs had made of him, taking him to Barttelot by the most convoluted route they could devise in order to deliberately confuse him. But that didn't matter now. He knew where he was. The Congo was straight ahead, down the cobbled alley, no more than a half-mile away. But the girl didn't go in that direction. No sooner had they passed under the arch than she darted around a corner to the right into a narrow dirt street, hemmed in on one side by the flaking whitewashed walls of single-story flat-roofed buildings and on the other by the foliage overhanging the wall of the garden through which they just had passed.

"Hold on!"

The girl looked back.

"The river's that way, isn't it?"

The girl nodded.

"Then why aren't we going that way? I want to go to the river."

"It is not safe that way," the girl replied with some impatience and continued up the dirt street.

Barttelot started after her; but when he realized Troup was hesitating, he stopped. The slave boy hadn't moved. With Troup standing indecisively at the corner, looking first down the cobbled alley that led to the river, then up the dirt street the girl proposed to take them, the boy's way was blocked. After a few steps, the girl stopped and looked back again.

"Come," she said. "You want to go home. I take you home." She was still holding that bit of cloth of her hood across her face as a veil so that only her eyes showed. And there was nothing to be told from her eyes.

"What do you think, Major?"

"I think the whole thing's crazy."

"Do you trust her?"

Barttelot looked at the girl. They looked at each other. Perhaps he could tell something from her eyes. Then he said, "Come on. What's the difference? Either way it's crazy."

Of course it was crazy. The street, going north parallel to the river, was empty; but it was crazy to believe they were unobserved. Anyone could be watching them from the rooftops and windows of the buildings on their left. And then a man on a donkey rode into the street from a crossroad up ahead. They pressed against the garden wall to let him pass. He was a half-caste of some sort, wearing a turban and beard and dirty caftan, his donkey loaded with pots and pans. Like the woman at the well, he showed no interest in them and passed on with an absentminded bow.

At the crossroad from which he had appeared, the girl turned left. This was another alley leading west toward the river. But after a second's indecision she chose not to go that way. Halfway down the alley a fire was burning in a brazier and a group of men were standing around it. They could be Manyema; in any case, they had rifles, and that was what put her off. Troup's confidence in her rose a notch. After another moment of assessing the situation, she gathered up the skirt of her robe and dashed across the crossroad; and then one by one Barttelot, Troup, and the slave boy dashed across after her. On the other side they waited a moment in a bunch, but evidently the men at the brazier hadn't noticed them, and they continued up the dirt street.

And then they saw firelight up ahead here too. The girl ducked under the veranda of one of the buildings on their left. The two white men and the boy ducked in after her. They were all breathing hard. They hadn't actually been running; it was a result of the idiotic holding of their breath as if by that they could prevent themselves from being seen or heard. Barttelot's face was bathed in sweat. The girl took his arm and pulled him against her to rest. Troup's head was pounding, and he had the distinct feeling that his wound had split open under its bandage and was again oozing blood. But he didn't take off his straw hat to check; he didn't want to know. He peered up the street at the firelight and saw that the garden wall on the right and the increasingly ramshackle buildings on the left ended there. The firelight came from dozens of small fires scattered about an open square.

"What is it—a souk?"

The girl nodded.

Troup looked again. It was now at last fully night; the sky was black, the stars were out, so he could see only that which was lighted by the many small fires: a kiosk, a stall, blankets spread on the ground displaying wares, a sheet of canvas held up by bamboo poles, people milling about buying and selling. Their voices carried only faintly into the darkness of the narrow dirt street.

"It is the souk of the slaves," the girl said. "Their quarter is just beyond it. We will be safe once we get to their quarter."

"But how do we get across the souk? Aren't there Manyema there?"

"Sometimes. And sometimes the Arabs as well. But not always. They come and go. I do not think they will be there now. I will send the boy to see."

"And if they are there?"

"Then we will find another way," she replied confidently; and still clinging to Barttelot's arm, she spoke to the slave boy in Arabic.

He was a bright little fellow. Whatever she told him to do, he seemed immediately to understand and without complaint set off to do it. He handed the girl the load he had been lugging—it was Troup's dismantled tent plus a box of biscuits, all he could manage—and raced up the street into the souk.

Of course it had been a crazy gamble from the start. The boy didn't betray them. If anything, unthinkingly, they had betrayed themselves. They should have realized that as soon as the boy set foot in the souk, any Arab who might by chance be there would immediately recognize him as Barttelot's boy. And so it was. The next time they saw him, hardly five minutes later, an Arab was bringing him back by the scruff of the neck. Another walked behind him with an escort of four Manyema gunmen. Troup's heart leaped at the sight, and his first reaction was to make a run for it.

He looked back down the street from where they had come, to the crossroad they had dashed across, to the alley that led out under the arch from the courtyard, each of which would take him to the river. Which should he try? How far did he suppose he would get? That would be an even crazier gamble. He'd never make it. He'd just set off a mad hue and cry and be brought down with violence, and his aching head couldn't deal with any more violence. The only thing to do was brazen it out. Seeing the boy returning with the Arabs and Manyema, the girl pulled Barttelot deeper into the shadows of the veranda. But Troup stepped out into the street to meet them.

"Ah, Mr. Troup. What can this mean? First we discover you stealing up on us in the dark. Now we discover you stealing away from us in the dark."

It was Tippoo-Tib. The other Arab, the one with the gunmen, of course was Selim. What a perfectly wonderful coincidence that they both should just happen to be in this particular souk where Arabs seldom went, and to be there at just this particular time.

"And here is Major Barttelot as well."

"And here is Tippoo-Tib," Barttelot retorted and, pushing aside the girl who ludicrously had been trying to hide him with her body, stepped out of the veranda's shadows. "So you're back, Tippoo-Tib. You're back from Kasongo at last."

"Yes, Major, I am back."

"I've been waiting for you to get back for some time, you know. How is it that neither you nor Selim bothered to inform me that you were?"

"Ah, but we did, effendi, or I should say we tried. I only got back last night, and I immediately went to you then, and then I went again this morning, twice this morning as a matter of fact, once with Mr. Troup, as he can confirm. But unfortunately each time I went, you were—How shall I put it?—otherwise engaged."

"I see. Otherwise engaged, was I? And the porters, Tippoo-Tib? The porters you went to Kasongo for? Are you also going to tell me that you brought them back as you promised?"

"Yes, Major, I am also going to tell you that. Why?"

"Why? Because I don't believe you. That's why. Because I know you're lying."

"Major!" Troup grabbed Barttelot's arm.

But Barttelot shook him off. "You've been lying all along. You lied to Mr. Stanley. You've been lying to me. You never had any intention of helping us. You've been playing a double game. I must say, I suspected it, even if Mr. Stanley didn't. I suspected it from the first time I set eyes on you. But now I know it for certain. For you see, Tippoo-Tib, we've discovered—"

"Shut up. Damn you, just shut up, will you? You must excuse him, Tippoo-Tib. He is overwrought."

"No, let him speak, Mr. Troup. I would like to hear what he has to say. He insults me. He impugns my honor. He calls me a liar to my face. I would like to know what entitles him to speak to me so. Tell me, Major, what is it that you've discovered that entitles you to speak to me so?"

Barttelot hesitated for a moment, as if suddenly realizing he was making a mistake, as if suddenly remembering Troup's warning. But then, in a rush of self-induced self-righteous fury, he let it burst out. "Your settlement at Ipoto, Tippoo-Tib. That's what we've discovered. The slave camp of your sheik Kilonga-longa deep in the Ituri, hundreds of marches from here."

It surprised Tippoo-Tib. Troup saw that immediately in the change in the Arab's usually serene expression, in the quick glance he exchanged with Selim. As Troup had suspected, he hadn't had any idea that they knew about this, hadn't imagined there was any way they could. But he said nothing. He let Barttelot go on.

And Barttelot went on. "So it's all been lies. All your promises of porters have been nothing but lies. Because you already know the way into the Ituri. You've already broken the forest's spell. You've no need of Mr. Stanley for that. So why should you provide us with porters? Why should you help white men invade your realm? Why—"

Barttelot broke off. Although Tippoo-Tib, studying him with those malevolently hooded eyes, still had said nothing, it was finally becoming clear to him the danger his imprudence was putting them in. For more and more Manyema were coming into the dark narrow street. They came into it from the souk ahead; they came into it from the crossroad behind, dozens of them, armed to the teeth, filling the street so thoroughly that soon there'd be no way out of it.

Then at last Tippoo-Tib spoke, and despite the bite of his words he spoke with his usual courteous calm. "You are an ignorant man, Major Barttelot. An ignorant and arrogant man. For you, as for so many of your countrymen, I am just another nigger in the bush, just another smelly wog capable of any sort of villainy. But I forgive you. I choose not to take offense. I am sure Mr. Troup does not share your low opinion of me. Am I not correct in this, Mr. Troup?"

Troup didn't answer.

"Mr. Troup, surely you do not hold me to be the liar and scoundrel Major Barttelot makes me out to be. Surely you do not believe that I have been playing a villainous double game."

"I would have hoped not, Tippoo-Tib. For the sake of your friendship with Bula Matari, for all our sakes. But you will agree we have been waiting a very long time for the porters you promised."

"Yes, I do agree. But as I forewarned Bula Matari and have said many times since, I have had great difficulty finding men enough to spare. But I *have* found them. For the sake of my friendship with Bula Matari, for all your sakes, I went to the great trouble of finding them. As you have seen with your own eyes, I have sent nearly a thousand men to you in Yambuya."

"The men you have sent to us in Yambuya are gunmen, Tippoo-Tib, not porters."

"They are my men, Mr. Troup, and will do what I tell them to do."

"Oh, of that I am sure, Tippoo-Tib. But I am not so sure what you will tell them to do."

"So." Tippoo-Tib emitted a sharp, bitter laugh. "So you do share Major Barttelot's low opinion of me."

"My opinion is of no consequence, Tippoo-Tib. It is in your hands to prove me right or wrong. But whichever it is to be, we must now return to Yambuya and get our column on the march. We have delayed far too long as it is. I take it we are not your prisoners. We are free to return to Yambuya?"

"Don't make me out a worse villain than you already have, Mr. Troup. Of course you are not my prisoners. Of course you are free to return to Yambuya."

"Then please have these men stand aside."

Tippoo-Tib looked around at the Manyema blocking the street. He gestured to them and they opened a path to the souk ahead.

"A final word, Tippoo-Tib."

Tippoo-Tib looked at Troup. "Yes?"

"Don't do anything stupid."

"Stupid, Mr. Troup?"

"As I say, we intend now to march into the Ituri. We intend to bring the relief supplies to the Pasha on the lake. If you choose to help us, if you choose to keep your word to Bula Matari, he and we and all England will be most grateful to you. But if it is your intention to interfere with us in any way, if you have any designs on us or on the supplies we mean to bring to Emin Pasha, I warn you, Tippoo-Tib, you will bring the wrath of Bula Matari and that of all of England down on your head. And you will be destroyed."

"Oh, Mr. Troup, sooner or later England will destroy me anyway. I am under no illusion about that. My days here are numbered. Sooner or later the white man will drive me and all my kind out of Africa and rule in our place."

"Well, let it be later than sooner."

The two men looked at each other for a long moment. Then Troup hitched his rucksack and blanket roll higher on his back, tucked the stock of his Winchester under his arm, and started up the path the Manyema had opened for him. His head cracked with a truly nauseating pain, but he looked neither to the left nor the right at the armed Manyema who lined his way. He kept his eyes fixed on the firelight in the souk up ahead, wondering whether he would get that far.

"Are you taking the girl with you?"

"What?"

The slave boy, after having been brought back from the souk by Tippoo-Tib, had prudently vanished. But the harem girl was still there. The box of biscuits the boy had handed her she now had balanced on her head. The dismantled tent in its canvas sack she carried under one arm, and the other she had hooked through Barttelot's. Tippoo-Tib was smiling at the pair.

"You can take her," he said genially. "I have no objection. I gave her to the beautiful soldier. Take her, Major Barttelot. Take her with you if you wish."

Barttelot looked at the Arab, then at the girl in surprise. The girl gripped his arm more firmly, said something to him. Troup couldn't hear what it was.

"Major."

Barttelot looked at Troup. Surprise, confusion, indecision, temptation were in his expression. He looked at the girl again, and again she said something to him. Was she pleading with him? In any case, she clung to him with all her might. Wavering, he once again looked at Tippoo-Tib. And perhaps it was the Arab's leering grin that decided him. For then, with such sudden and cruel force as to knock the biscuit box from her head, he shoved the girl away and said, "Let's go, Troup. Let's get the hell out of here."

But it wasn't to be as simple as that. Later Troup would wonder whether the girl had been put up to it, whether he had heard Tippoo-Tib say something to egg her on. He'd never be sure. It all happened too fast. As he was turning toward the souk again, as Barttelot was starting to follow him, the girl dropped the tent and jumped on Barttelot. She jumped on his back. It was so unexpected and Barttelot was so unsteady on his feet anyway, that she brought him to his knees. Delighted prurient laughter erupted from Tippoo-Tib and Selim and the mob of watching Manyema.

Barttelot whirled around, flailing his arms in a fury, and leaped up. Still on the ground, the girl grabbed at his feet, wrapped her arms around his ankles, and cried out. But what she cried was incoherent. The laughter and gleeful shouts of those watching this ridiculous scene had surged to a raucous uproar and drowned out her words. His face burning with rage and embarrassment, in danger of being toppled by her hold on his legs, Barttelot kicked the girl away. It was vicious; his boot repeatedly struck her in the stomach, the breasts, the side of her head. It was too much.

Troup rushed back to put a stop to it. But by the time he got to them, Barttelot had driven her off. She lay sprawled in the dirt, propping herself up on an elbow, clutching at her breasts with her other hand. The hood of her robe had fallen back, revealing her mass of auburn hair, and the skirt of her robe had hiked up above her knees, revealing a beautiful length of naked white leg.

"Let's go, Troup."

Troup, however, continued looking at the girl, watched as she struggled to her feet. The laughter of the Arabs and Manyema had subsided somewhat. The way she clutched her breasts, even now that she was standing, seemed to suggest she had suffered a serious injury from Barttelot's unwarranted brutality.

"Are we going or aren't we? You were the one who was in such a bloody hurry to get back to Yambuya."

"I go with you," the girl said. Although her voice was low, she could be heard now. The laughter had ceased altogether. She took a step toward Barttelot, still clutching herself. "I go with you. You take me with you. You promised that to me. You promised you would take me with you. You promised you would take me home to the shining sea." She came nearer as she spoke.

Barttelot turned away from her.

"Take her, Major Barttelot," Tippoo-Tib said. "Why don't you take her?"

And it was what happened at this point that Troup would never be sure of. He was sure Tippoo-Tib had said at least that much, that Barttelot should take the girl with him, and he remembered thinking at the time that even though there were women in the rear column at Yambuya and this was a strong woman and possibly even a white woman and one who had seemed sincere in her attempt to help them, her effect on Barttelot in the days and weeks ahead would surely be ruinous, that it had already very nearly ruined him.

But then she cried out, "My beautiful soldier. Oh, my beautiful soldier." And threw herself on Barttelot again.

Troup immediately sought to intervene, determined to avoid entertaining the Arabs and Manyema with another demeaning ugly scuffle between the two. But just as he did, just as he grabbed at the girl's hair to pull her away from Barttelot, Barttelot looked at him, looked at him over the girl's shoulder. Oddly, this time he made no effort to fend her off. He simply looked at Troup. The expression on his face was unfathomable.

Then the girl stepped away on her own. She was no longer clutching her breasts. Her hands hung at her sides. And the haft of a dagger protruded from Barttelot's stomach. The blade couldn't be seen; it was buried deep in his gut. He continued looking at Troup with that unfathomable expression until he fell forward on his face.

· EIGHT ·

IT WAS THE QUIET that roused Troup from his trance.

Robotlike, hour after hour since daybreak, he had been paddling against the current, automatically feathering on every stroke, instinctively shifting from one side of the canoe to the other to keep the prow headed upstream, thinking of nothing, mesmerized by the blinding glare of the sun reflecting off the quicksilver surface of the Aruwimi, his head cracking with pain, his body shivering from fever.

Barttelot lay stretched out at his feet in the canoe's bottom, sewn into his own blankets and packed with salt, stinking in the midday heat and crawling with flies. Troup had come to imagine half deliriously that the flies were flies from Singatini, that the same flies, like hired mourners, had been accompanying the corpse throughout the four days of the journey down the Congo and up the Aruwimi. And now all of a sudden it seemed as if their ugly voracious buzzing was the only sound to be heard. He looked up, startled out of his trance by this unnatural quiet, and saw that he had made it back to Yambuya at last.

Less than a quarter of a mile ahead on his right, atop the high bluff of the river's embankment, stood the fort's riverfront stockade. On the sun-dazzled beach beneath it a solitary figure was waiting. Troup stopped paddling and studied the scene. The quiet was uncanny. And then he realized what accounted for it. The Manyema were gone. Their encampments above and below the fort and across the river from it were empty. The hundreds of cannibal gunmen who had inhabited them with so much raucous, threatening activity were nowhere to be seen. They had cleared out. Troup resumed paddling with a sudden surge of energy brought on by a rush of panic, not daring to let himself think what might have happened while he'd been away.

It was Ward who was waiting on the beach. He waded out into the river to catch hold of the canoe's prow and pull the craft ashore. Troup, however, remained seated in the stern, the paddle across his knees. His head was splitting; he needed a moment to catch his breath. And then, surprising himself and shocking Ward and revealing to both how sick he was, he leaned over the side of the canoe and vomited into the river. Ward immediately waded back into the water to help his friend, and it was then that he noticed the putrid smell and swarms of flies emanating from the bottom of the canoe. He looked in and saw the lumpy blanket-sewn bundle lying in the slimy green salt-stained seepage of the canoe's bottom.

"Jesus. Who is it?"

Troup still hadn't tried to get out of the canoe. He sat there now waiting for his head to clear of the dizziness that had come with the attack of nausea.

"It's not the major, is it, Jack?"

Troup nodded.

"What happened?"

"He got himself killed. He fell for the oldest trick in the world and got himself killed." Now Troup did climb out of the canoe. His knees gave way as soon as he stepped into the calf-deep shallows, and he had to grab the canoe's gunwale to keep himself from falling, rocking the canoe as a result and scattering the flies and sloshing the water in the bottom over the corpse. He looked down at it. "Major Barttelot, Seventh Royal Fusiliers, Queen's officer and gentleman, hero of the second Afghan war and the battle for Tell el-Kebir, repeatedly mentioned in dispatches. He fell for the oldest trick in the world and got himself killed. All it took was some hashish and a harem girl. Nothing more complicated than that."

Troup turned away from the canoe and started wading ashore. "You know how he was always harping on Bula Matari's mistakes. Well, I'll tell you, Bert, he was Bula Matari's worst mistake—picking him for second-in-command, leaving him in charge of the rear column. There was nothing to him. Nothing inside of him. Nothing at all. He was all show. Christ, we'd have been long gone from here if it'd been either of us in charge. If it'd been either one of us who'd been dealing with Tippoo-Tib all this time up at the Falls, we'd have figured out his game and gotten the hell out of here long before this. But, no, it was him. Major Edmund Musgrave Barttelot, the beautiful soldier. Bula Matari picked him. And why?

Because he was a gentleman. Bula Matari always was a sucker for a gentleman, like he himself never was."

Ward walked beside Troup, watching him intently, not listening too closely to what he was saying. He didn't know about Troup's head wound because he couldn't see the bandage under his straw hat; but from the rambling way Troup spoke, from his unsteady gait, from the vomiting and shivering, he realized Troup was in terrible shape. When they reached the beach, Ward shouted up to the fort for help. Munichandi and a half-dozen Wanyamwezis appeared at the river gate and came hurrying down the stepped path in the embankment's high bluff.

"What's happened to the Manyema, Bert? Where are they?"

"I don't know. They just pulled out one night. I thought they'd gone off on one of their slaving raids, but that was more than a week ago and they haven't come back yet."

Troup didn't comment on this. He closed his eyes, fighting back another wave of nausea.

"Munichandi, Major Barttelot's in the canoe. Have the boys bring him up to the fort along with his and Mr. Troup's kit. Come on, Jack. Let's get you to bed. You look awful."

Troup opened his eyes in time to see the Wanyamwezis wade into the river and gather around the canoe. Ward's instructions to them had been far too inexplicit. They hadn't expected to find Barttelot lying in the canoe's bottom, sewn into his blankets. They stepped back in surprise, covering their faces against the smell.

"And bring the canoe up too," Troup called to them. "I don't want to risk losing it. We're going to need it."

Nothing seemed changed in the fort since Troup had been gone. The only change was the quiet, a quiet that seemed to seep in through the stockades from the abandoned Manyema camps outside, like the lingering stench of the ordure and garbage left behind in those camps. No one spoke. No one greeted Troup's return. The Wanyamwezis and Sudanese, the men, women and boys of the rear column, stood around in small groups watching in silence as he and Ward entered through the river gate. A minute or two later Munichandi and the Wanyamwezis entered after them carrying the canoe. They had chosen to leave Barttelot and the kit in the canoe and bring the whole lot up in one trip, so they entered like pallbearers in a cloud of flies, carrying the canoe between them like a bier. They set it down in the center of the parade ground near the flogging post Barttelot had erected. As they did, Bonny stepped out of his tent.

"Mr. Troup, welcome back, sir." He came over briskly. When he reached Troup, he saluted. "Has the major returned with you, sir?"

"Yes," Troup replied. He pointed at the canoe. "The major has returned with me."

The men who had brought the canoe up had moved away from it to get clear of the stench and flies. Bonny looked into it. He obviously didn't immediately make out what he was looking at, what the damp bundle of blankets in the bottom signified.

"That's the major, Sergeant. He's dead."

"Dead?"

"That's right, Sergeant, dead. You remember him talking about a harem girl poisoning him? Well, in the end she didn't poison him. She stabbed him."

Bonny again looked into the canoe.

"It doesn't surprise you, does it, Sergeant? You always had the idea that sooner or later this is how he'd finish up. You even tried to warn me."

Bonny got down on his knees beside the canoe and, chasing off the flies, began feeling around the damp blankets, trying to determine which end of the corpse was up. It wasn't a simple matter; the salt in which it was packed and the bloating that had occurred in the past week had grotesquely misshaped it. But when he did, he proceeded to tear apart the threads that held the blankets together.

"Come on, Jack." Ward took Troup's arm.

But Troup remained long enough to see Bonny uncover Barttelot's face. Against the heat and the humidity, the salt hadn't done much good as a preservative. The face was dreadful.

"The beautiful soldier," Troup said and went with Ward to their hut at the other end of the parade ground.

"Right now, out of these clothes and into bed. What you need is a good dose of quinine and a long sleep."

But Troup merely sat down on the edge of his cot and rested his shaggy bearded head in his hands. "We're in the soup, Bert," he said. "You were right, you know. We're really in the soup."

"We'll talk about it later when you're feeling better."

"Did you see which way they went?"

"Who?"

"The Manyema."

"No, they pulled out during the night, but I reckon they

headed upriver, you know, following Bula Matari's trail into the Ituri. They're probably halfway to Kilonga-longa's slave camp at Ipoto by now."

Troup shook his head. "No, I don't think so. I think they're waiting for us, Bert. I think they're waiting for us somewhere in the forest." He removed his ragged straw hat and let himself collapse on the cot.

And then Ward saw the filthy blood-encrusted bandage that covered the crown of Troup's head. "Jesus Christ, Jack, what's that? What happened to you?"

"I got jumped on the way to Singatini. A gang of Tippoo-Tib's gunmen jumped me. And I think they killed Bartholomew and the tracker I had with me. They didn't get back, did they?"

"No." Ward got down on his knees beside Troup's cot in order to make a closer examination of the wound.

"I didn't think so. They killed them or put 'em in chains." Troup winced as Ward peeled back the sticking plaster.

"This is a mess, Jack, a bloody awful mess."

"Where are you going?"

"To fetch the medicine chest. That thing's infected."

"No, wait a minute." Troup pushed up on an elbow. "Listen to me, Bert. I think you were right. I think Tippoo-Tib's after the guns. But I don't think he's going to attack us. Not straight out. The son of a bitch's too cunning for that. He knows better than to do anything that'll put the responsibility for wrecking the column directly on his shoulders. He doesn't want to be in the position where anyone can point a finger at him and blame him for destroying us. So he's just going to wait, Bert. He's just going to go on biding his time like he's been doing, figuring all he has to do is wait long enough and he won't have to destroy us to get the guns. We'll destroy ourselves. One by one, we'll destroy ourselves like Barttelot destroyed himself."

Ward was standing in the doorway of the hut, and he heard Bonny shout a command concerning the disposition of Barttelot's body.

"We can't let it happen, Bert." Troup suddenly sat up, swinging his legs over the side of the cot. "We mustn't let it happen."

Ward went back to him. "We won't, Jack. *You* won't. You're in command now and you're not Barttelot. But you've got to be alive and well. You're no good to us dead. So lie down and let me see to that wound of yours."

Troup lay back down on the cot, expelling a terrible sigh of exhaustion. "We've got to work out a plan, Bert," he said more quietly. "We've got to figure out what we're going to do."

"We will. Just as soon as I've fetched the medicine chest."

But they didn't. By the time Ward returned with the medicine chest, Troup was asleep. He had held himself together long enough to get back to Yambuya with Barttelot, but it had cost him dear, the very last drop of his strength; and when he fell asleep, it was into a profound fevered sleep, all of a sudden, like a lamp being snuffed out. Ward did his doctoring on an unconscious man, scissoring away a large patch of the rough red hair, cleaning out the wound with carbolic, dressing it with a huge wad of cotton and sticking plaster, injecting him with a half-grain of morphine for the pain. Then he pulled the mosquito netting down around the cot and went out to Barttelot's funeral. In that climate there was every reason to hurry up the affair. As it was, the corpse had swollen to almost twice its size.

Bonny had had the grave dug outside the fort's south gate and had had it cushioned with a bed of palm leaves and the body (the blankets resewn around it and still packed with salt) placed on these and covered with more palm leaves. An honor guard of askaris, their Winchesters at the trail, paraded on either side of it. Except for Munichandi and the gravediggers, however, none of the Wanyamwezis attended.

"Let's get on with it, Billy."

"Isn't Mr. Troup coming, sir?"

Ward shook his head.

"I would have thought Mr. Troup would want to be here, sir, seeing how he's now in command."

"Mr. Troup's in no shape to be here, Billy. Let's just hope his won't be the next grave we have to dig here."

"It's as bad as that, is it, sir?"

"Yes, thanks to Major Barttelot, it's as bad as that. If he hadn't had to go after him to the Falls– Oh, what's the difference. Just get on with it, will you? Have them close the grave."

"But what about the service, sir? What about ashes to ashes and dust to dust? What about that part?"

"I don't know it. I'm sorry."

"Well, a eulogy then. What about a eulogy? He should at least have a eulogy."

"You speak it, Billy. You knew him better than I did."

"I'm not a speaker, sir. I'm not an educated man. It's not my place to speak the eulogy over the major's grave. I wouldn't know what to say."

"Just say whatever's in your heart."

Bonny looked down into the grave, at the palm leaves that covered the lumpy, misshapen bundle, at the swarms of flies that crawled over the palm leaves. Then he looked up at Ward again. Rivulets of sweat were streaming down his ruddy face, but there also might have been tears.

"Well, Billy, why don't we just say he was a beautiful soldier."

"He was, sir. Yes, sir. He was that. A beautiful soldier. He never had a chance to show it here in this accursed place, in this Congo. But at Kabul—you should have seen him on the ramparts at Kabul, sir, and at the gates of Tell el-Kebir and on the march from the Red Sea to Kenneh. Oh, he was beautiful, sir. A brave and beautiful soldier."

"I'm sure he was, Billy. I'm sure he was. Now let's let him rest in peace."

When Ward looked in on him again, Troup was still sleeping; and he went on sleeping through the rest of that day, a disturbed, nightmare-ridden sleep. He was still sleeping, emitting guttural grunts and half-intelligible phrases, his breathing labored, his limbs twitching, his bedclothes soaked with sweat, when Ward came in after making the sentry round at eleven that night. He hung up his carbine and performed his toilet in the dark and was just untying the bundle of mosquito netting over his cot when he realized Troup had fallen still. Suddenly there was none of the restless movement in the neighboring cot, none of the feverish sounds. For a heart-stopping moment he didn't even hear Troup's breathing and thought the man had expired. But in fact all that had happened was that Troup had awakened.

"Bert."

With a grateful sigh of relief, Ward went over to him. "How's the head, old boy? Feeling any better?"

"Yes. Hundred percent better." Troup's mouth was so dry that his tongue stuck to the roof and his words came out slurred like a drunk's. He pulled himself up into a sitting position.

"What can I get for you?"

"Nothing. I'm fine."

Nevertheless Ward fetched a canteen of water and, pulling aside Troup's mosquito netting, handed it into him; and while he drank thirstily from it, he examined the wound. A fresh ooze of yellow-green pus had stained the new bandage. "Go on back to sleep, Jack," he said taking the canteen from him. "That's the best medicine for you. Do you want another shot of morphine?"

Troup shook his head. "What's our strength, Bert?"

"Our strength?"

"You know, the muster. How many people do we have?"

"Oh, I'd say about four hundred and fifty."

"And how many are fit to carry loads?"

Ward shrugged. "They're all in pretty poor shape, Jack, one way or another; but I suppose we've got twenty or twenty-five who're really on their last legs. And four or five of the mules aren't looking any too good either."

"And how many loads have we got?"

This too was a matter of conjecture. There had been pilferage, there had been the necessary consumption of provisions, but under Barttelot's strict discipline and niggardly rationing regimen, not that much. "Nine hundred fifty, nine sixty."

"We can do it in double marches then."

"Double marches? Come on, Jack. Don't talk nonsense."

"No. Listen, I've been thinking about this. What we've got to do first off is sort out the loads and decide what's absolutely essential and what we can afford to dump. I figure we can get the number down to eight hundred, maybe seven fifty. All right. Then I figure we can put half the askaris to work as *pagazis*. What does that give us? Leave out the sick, the trackers, the mule boys, the front and rear guards. Three ten, three twenty? Plus the animals. That's four hundred loads for sure. With Bula Matari's trail to follow, we can do fifteen, twenty miles on each march, make camp, come back for the other four hundred loads and bring them up the next day."

"Jack, for Christ's sake, be sensible. That'd take forever. By the time we got through to Emin, we might just as well not have bothered."

"No, you don't understand me. I'm not proposing to go *all* the way through the Ituri double marching like that. Of course that's not reasonable. But as a start, Bert. To get away from here. Until we get more porters."

"But where are we going to get more porters from?"

"You're going to get them. From Equator Station."

Ward didn't say anything to this. It occurred to him that the head wound and fever might have made Troup delirious.

"I want you to go back downriver to Equator Station, Bert.

That's why I saved the canoe. I want you to go to Van Gele at the station and tell him what's happened here and have him round up as many porters as he can. He's got Houssas and Bolobo around there. They make good porters. Tell him we'll pay them whatever they want."

Ward began shaking his head.

"Don't shake your head, Bert. You can do it. You can make it in a fortnight, three weeks at the most, traveling light, with just a few good men. You can catch us up before the next month is out."

"No, Jack, I won't do it. It's out of the question. I'm not going to leave you."

"It's our only chance, Bert. What else can we do? I've been thinking about it. It's either that or give it up altogether, pack the whole thing in. That's what Barttelot wanted to do. Is that what you want to do? I'll be damned if I do. We've come too far, Bert. We can't give it up now. Bula Matari's counting on us."

"Send Bonny then."

"He'd never make it. You know that. He doesn't know this country the way you do. He'll be of more use to me on the march. He'll keep the men going. He's good at that. That's about all he's good at, but at least he's good at that, driving men on."

Again Ward remained silent, scrutinizing his friend. Maybe Troup wasn't delirious; but he was sick, very sick, not only with fever and pain but also with desperation. There was no sense arguing with him. Whatever they decided to do, no matter how hopelessly fantastic, it would be some time before Troup would be in any condition to do it anyway.

"You know I'm right, Bert. You know there's no other way. Say you'll do it."

"Go back to sleep, Jack. We'll talk about it in the morning."

"No. I want you to tell me now that you'll do it."

"I hate the idea of leaving you, the shape you're in."

"Don't worry about that. I'll be all right. You'll see. I'll be up and about by morning."

He wasn't, of course. If anything, he was sicker. He got dressed, but the effort was enormous; and when he went with Ward to the officers' mess for breakfast, he discovered he couldn't keep food down. He vomited up the first bite and went on vomiting in dreadful spasms of dry heaves until he very nearly passed out. Ward got him back to the hut without protest. Another day or two of rest, he agreed, wouldn't matter all that much, and he fell asleep or fainted while Ward was doctoring his wound. It looked uglier, angrier than the day before. Because of the thickness of Troup's hair, Ward couldn't tell how far the infection had spread. But it had spread; in this awful moldering climate it was spreading quickly. Flies and gnats and ticks were getting into it. Ward cleaned it out as best he could and covered it as thoroughly as possible with a new bandage.

Bonny was waiting for him on the parade ground. While Barttelot and Troup had been away at the Falls, he had accepted Ward as his commanding officer; and now that Barttelot was dead and buried and Troup incapacitated, he was perfectly prepared to go on taking his orders from him. As ever the dutiful sergeant major, he had seen to the changing of the guard on the stockades and had mustered the work details on the parade ground. He saluted when Ward came over. Troup was right, Ward thought. Bonny would be more useful on the march taking orders. He'd be lost trying to make his way downriver to Equator Station with no one to tell him what to do.

"Let's get the column ready to march, Billy. We're going into the Ituri at last."

"Yes, sir."

That was all. Yes, sir. Ward had to smile. Bonny did not have a single question to ask about an order so improbable, so outlandish, so certainly hopeless as that.

The preparations for the march took ten days. Troup got up a few times during those days to consult with Ward on the selection of the loads and help him work out how to reduce their number, but each of those times he was up for only an hour or so. Then pain or fatigue or nausea or fever would overwhelm him and he'd retreat to his hut. He wasn't recovering or was recovering very slowly. The main trouble was the nausea, his inability to eat; and not eating, he was steadily losing strength. The bandage swathed his head like a turban; his eyes sank deep into the bruised shadows of their sockets; his cheeks turned as yellow as parchment and caved in. His body grew noticeably thinner from loss of weight. He looked terrible. Even his big orange buccaneer's beard seemed diminished, sparser, mangier.

On the morning of the eleventh day after the preparations for the march had begun, on the day after all the sorting out and repacking of loads had been completed—they had been winnowed down to 787 and arrayed in march order at the fort's east gate, while those being jettisoned were locked in the fort's storehouses—on that morning Troup got up and dressed before Ward. Surprised, hurriedly pulling on his trousers, Ward followed him out of the hut into the gray mist of the dawn. Birds were singing, the ground was puddled from the night's rain, stars were still out in the sky, and here and there women were starting cooking fires; but except for the sentries on the watchtowers, only a few of the men were yet awake. Troup's presence startled them. They hadn't seen him up this early in some time. Bonny was still in his tent shaving.

"Munichandi."

The headman came out of his hut. He too was startled by the sight of Troup looking so gaunt, his clothes hanging so loosely from his frame, the thick bandage showing beneath the brim of his ragged straw hat.

"The canoe, Munichandi." Troup indicated the canoe in which he had returned from the Falls, which had served as Barttelot's bier. Overturned to keep out the rain, it still lay by the whipping post at the head of the parade ground. "Have it taken down to the river."

"Jack."

"It's time, Bert. It's long past time. Get your gear together. Sergeant Bonny."

Toweling his face, Bonny looked out of his tent, saw Troup, tossed the towel aside, and dashed over.

"Double rations for everyone this morning, Sergeant. I want everyone to eat well and hearty this morning. Because this morning we start the march."

"Yes, sir."

"Jack, you can't do it. For God's sake, man, look at you."

Troup turned to Ward, fixed him with his bloodshot, feverish eyes. "What do you want from me, Bert? Tell me. What do you want me to do? Do you want me to pack it in?" There was a pathetic desperation in those eyes.

Ward looked away. There was a growing bustle and stirring all around now, Munichandi rousting out *pagazis* to carry the canoe down to the river, Bonny gathering the headmen and the corporals of the guard for the distribution of the extra rations, people emerging from the huts, having heard Troup's statement that this was the day they would begin the march. Looking at them, unable to look at Troup when he said it, Ward said, "Yes, that's right. I want you to pack it in, Jack."

Troup made no reply to this. Perhaps he hadn't heard it.

Ward looked back at him. "It's hopeless, Jack. You'll never make it."

"I intend to try. I owe it to Bula Matari."

"Well, at least wait a few more days. At least wait until you get some of your strength back."

"We've waited too long already. We can't afford to wait any longer. Get your gear together, Bert. That's an order."

It took Ward less than an hour to get his gear together. When he came back out of the hut, the sun hadn't yet put in its appearance; but the sky was blue, the stars gone, the mist dispersed, and the first of the day's sticky heat could already be felt in the air. It was 5 A.M.

"I'm set, Jack."

"Munichandi, get some boys to take Mr. Ward's kit down to the canoe. Have you decided who you're taking with you?"

"I'm not taking anyone. You'll need every able body you can get. I'll manage well enough on my own."

"No, Bert, you've got to have a few men with you. At least a tracker. Just to have someone back you up in case something happens."

"Nothing's going to happen."

The two men crossed the parade ground to the river gate.

Bonny, seeing them, broke off what he was doing and came over. "Good luck, sir."

"Thank you, Billy. Same to you."

"Thank you, sir." Bonny saluted.

The river gate had been left open by the men who had carried the canoe and Ward's gear down to the beach. The canoe was in the water, the gear was in the canoe, and the men were standing around it calf-deep in the river.

"I'll get back as soon as I can, Jack. You can count on it. I'll catch you up in the forest as soon as I can with as many porters I can lay hands on."

"I know you will. But, Bert, listen."

"What?"

"The main thing is to get word out. The porters, your getting back to us with porters, if you can do it . . . I'm not fooling myself, Bert. I'm not completely out of my head with fever, you know. I know what the chances are. I know it's a long shot. But whether or not you can do it, the main thing is to get word out.

Get word to London what's happened here. I don't want the world not to know what happened to us. I don't want us just to vanish into the forest without the world ever knowing what happened."

"I'll get the word out, Jack. Don't you worry. *And* I'll catch you up with the porters."

"Good man. Now come on."

"No, don't come down with me. Save your strength. You're going to need it. Every last bit of it."

"All right. Safe journey, Bert."

"You too, Jack. *Kwa heri.*"

The two men shook hands, and then Ward went down to the beach. Troup watched as he climbed into the canoe, took his seat in the stern, and the men shoved him off. He turned the craft downstream and the current caught him quickly. He looked back once, raising his paddle. Troup raised his arm. The sun was beginning to show itself now in stripes of crimson and orange on the horizon. Ward paddled away from the sunrise. When he disappeared around the first bend, the men on the beach came up the embankment's bluff and Troup went back into the fort.

"Sergeant Bonny." In the disorderly crowd milling about the fort, hurrying with the last-minute preparations, Troup could not locate the sergeant. "Munichandi. *Iko wapi* Sergeant Bonny?"

"*Yeye nende kule*, Bwana." The headman pointed at the south gate.

It too had been left open. Stepping through it, Troup saw Bonny on the other side of the bridge that crossed the creek in the ravine, in the manioc field beyond where the grave was. Bareheaded, his head bowed in a posture of prayer, Bonny was standing by Barttelot's grave. A wooden cross had been erected at its head and a mound of rocks covered the rest to keep animals out. Troup had never visited it, and he didn't go there now. He waited on this side of the bridge, willing to give Bonny a decent amount of time to make his last farewell to the man he had served so long. But almost immediately, sensing he was being watched, Bonny turned around and, seeing Troup, put on his helmet and came back to the fort. But it wasn't *his* helmet. As he crossed the bridge, Troup saw that Bonny was wearing Barttelot's helmet. And he had Barttelot's Webley revolver strapped to his waist and Barttelot's riding crop tucked under his arm. He realized that Troup noticed this.

"Sir, I mean to carry these things through the forest for the major. I mean to carry them in his place to Albert Nyanza. I hope you have no objection."

"No, Sergeant, I have no objection. Now go and parade the column for the march."

· NINE ·

IT TOOK STANLEY just under nine weeks to get back to the rear column. Having his own trail to follow, knowing the way and the shortcuts and what trouble to look out for, the current in his favor when he again reached and re-embarked on the Aruwimi, and traveling only with his paramount chief Uledi and fifty well-provisioned hand-picked men, he was able to cover the ground more than twice as quickly as he had on the outbound journey. But he never believed he would have to cover as much of the ground as he did. Each day, along every mile of the road, at every bend in the river, he expected to meet the rear column of more than 1,000 people—more than 400 of his own and 600 of Tippoo-Tib's with Major Barttelot at their head—marching toward him. And each day, on every mile, around every bend, his anxiety and anger grew when he didn't.

"Bula Matari. *Tazama kule.*"

This was on the fifty-ninth day of the return trek when they were on the last navigable stretch of the Aruwimi, not more than 200, perhaps not even 150 miles from Yambuya, where rapids and cataracts would once again make the river unusable and they'd have to take once more to the forest path. They were descending on the current in five of the canoes that had been sunk with stones where the advance column had had to abandon the river on the outward march. Stanley was seated in the stern of the lead canoe, grubby, heavily bearded, his hair shoulder-length, an Express hunting rifle across his knees. Uledi, wearing a filthy turban and an equally filthy long white shirt, his tattered embroidered vest crisscrossed by bandoliers, stood in the prow, leaning on a tall musket.

"Look there," he said again, pointing to the river's left bank.

Stanley stood up. Four or five men were crouched in a huddle at the water's edge. They were black men but not natives. They wore shorts or shirts or skirts of cotton cloth. On the higher ground behind them at the edge of the jungle was a village. Stanley remembered it. This was where the advance column had acquired the first of its canoes and split into a river and land party. It was burned to the ground. He raised his field glasses, but by then the men on the bank had spotted the canoes and were running away.

"Pull for shore."

Stanley and Uledi jumped out of the canoe before it beached, and Stanley, shouting in Swahili, started after the running men. Uledi, however, remained at the water's edge staring down at something those men had left behind. There was a look of horror on his face. Stanley went back to see what he was looking at. It was a corpse, the emaciated body of a naked boy. Stanley's first thought was that the men who had run away had been in the process of burying it or anyway casting it into the river by way of burying it. Except that it was dismembered. One arm was off, there was a deep incision from the breastbone to the stomach, and some of the entrails had been pulled out.

"Cannibals." Stanley looked up to the forest where the men who had done this had disappeared. "You remember, Uledi. The Washenzi in these parts are cannibals."

"Those men were not Washenzi, Bula Matari. You saw how they were dressed."

"Manyema then?"

"Maybe Manyema. But this boy is not Manyema. And he is not Washenzi either. I know this boy. This boy is Wanyamwezi."

The other canoes were beaching now, and one by one the men in them came over to see what was going on. Ten of them were Sudanese, the best of the askari sharpshooters, but the rest were Wanyamwezis, *pagazis* and trackers, and they too immediately recognized the dismembered boy and drew back in horror.

"He was one of those we left behind in Yambuya, Bula Matari. He was one of the rear column."

Stanley again looked up at the dark wall of the forest and at the village in front of it. In the fight for the canoes so many months ago, he had had the village's huts put to the torch and now could see no sign or hear any sound of life among its rubble. There wasn't even birdsong. It was high noon; and in the blinding light and blazing heat of that time of day, all he could hear was the swarming hum of flies and mosquitoes. And the forest was also still. He didn't know what to think. Were the Manyema about? Was the rear column near? Were the Manyema preying on the rear column? Was the rear column preying on itself? Levering a round into his rifle, he started up through the village toward the forest. Uledi, giving orders to the Wanyamwezis to bury the boy, fell into step beside him. The ten askaris followed.

They pushed into the trees, forced aside the tangles of vines and curtains of orchilla weed, the spiky secondary growth and underbrush of giant fern, and came to a trail. This was the trail the land party of the advance column had hacked out along the river while the river party had proceeded in the canoes that had been captured at the village. There was no sign of the men who had run away from the beach; but on the side of the trail, directly in front of them, was a wooden box, a box of biscuits splintered and broken open, either deliberately or from a fall. About half the biscuits were still in it, green with mold and crawling with insects and butterflies. There was no mystery as to what it signified. It was someone's load or part of it anyway, and that someone had thrown it away to lighten his burden or had broken it open and deserted the march. That sort of thing had happened often enough during the advance column's march (although much farther on into the forest) and certainly could be expected to have happened during the rear column's.

Stanley peered west down the trail through the forest's aqueous gloom toward Yambuya. Doubtless more such litter would be found in that direction. But there was no point going in that direction. This smashed and pilfered box of biscuits said clearly that the rear column had made it at least this far. The only question was, How much farther had it made it? It couldn't be much farther. They would have spotted some sign of it during the journey downriver long before this if it had. Stanley had kept a sharp lookout during every mile of the way. They couldn't have missed catching at least a glimpse of a column of so many people and animals, couldn't have been deaf to at least some sound of them. So he turned left and started up the trail to the east, away from Yambuya.

A few steps farther along was another load, this one a barrel of trading beads. It was intact; it hadn't been discarded. Its carrier sat beside it, one hand resting on it protectively, his back leaning against the bole of a palm tree. He too was a Wanyamwezi, as emaciated as the boy on the beach. His eyes were open, watching Stanley and Uledi approach, but Stanley knew he was dead by the flies and maggots that covered his face. Uledi kneeled down next to him, but as soon as he touched him, he toppled over on his side.

"How long has he been dead?"

Uledi rolled the fellow onto his back and straightened out his limbs. "A few days," he said, feeling the limbs.

"What killed him?"

Uledi shrugged and stood up. "Hunger? Exhaustion? Fever?"

They went on, leaving the body stretched out beside its load at the side of the trail. No doubt Uledi had recognized it too, but there was no mention made of burying it. They knew now that they'd find more bodies, so it would make more sense to wait and bury them all at once. And they did find more. In the course of less than 200 yards, they found eight more in various grotesque and likelike postures. Some had dropped in the middle of the trail, others had gone off into the woods on the right, still others appeared to have been trying to make their way down to the river on the left when they had died. Two were women, one with a cooking kettle; one was an askari without his rifle; there was a tracker lying on his spear; there were four Wanyamwezis grouped together as if chatting, two with their loads intact beside them, one with his load of cloth torn open, one with no load at all. And there were also more loads with no bodies attached to them, and partial loads and scraps of cloth and lengths of rope and bits of hardware, an axe head, the shattered haft of a billhook, a dented paraffin tin lying in the greasy puddle of its own contents, a sheet of paper trodden into the spongy earth of the trail. And there was the carcass of a mule, stripped of its flesh by animals or vultures or men. But where were the living?

And then they saw smoke.

They all saw it at the same time. They had been proceeding slowly, taking each step with caution, Stanley and Uledi together, the ten askaris two-by-two behind them, holding their weapons low and away from their bodies at the ready, glancing at this piece of litter or that, at each body as they came to it in turn, stopping at none to examine it more closely, just pressing on to find the rear column, which surely must be near. From time to time a parrot would squawk or a fish eagle cry as they passed, and monkeys would scramble away chattering in the treetops; but at high noon in the humid, stinking twilit gloom, the jungle was essentially asleep. And then they saw the smoke. It was a mere wisp, discontinuous gray-white puffs from a fire either just getting started or just dying down, off into the forest to the south. They might have passed it by except that there was a natural widening in the trail here, a clearing of deadfall and lightning-blasted trees, of boulders and trampled elephant grass.

Stanley raised his field glasses to scan the clearing and immediately saw a figure. Another dead body? No, it darted away. He lowered the glasses to see where it had gone. He couldn't. He stepped off the trail into the clearing and brought the glasses to his eyes again looking for the source of the smoke. And he saw a tent. It was pitched in the lee of a huge slab of split granite like a giant tombstone, perhaps a quarter of a mile away on the far side of the clearing. The source of the smoke, a small fire of twigs and grass, both green or damp by the look of the smoke, was burning in front of it. And someone was squatting beside that.

"Have a look, Uledi." Stanley handed the glasses to the chief and, turning him by the shoulder, directed him toward the place he had seen the tent. "What do you make of it?"

Uledi refocused the eyepieces and studied the spot Stanley had directed him toward, then scanned the entire clearing from left to right before handing the glasses back to Stanley. "It is the sergeant major, Bula Matari. And he has many of our people with him."

Stanley looked again. Uledi was right. The old chieftain's eyesight was amazing. Now that he had identified the figure squatting at the fire as Bonny, Stanley saw that it was Bonny. He could make out the uniform, the helmet, the bull-necked fireplug shape. And there were Wanyamwezis and Sudanese there as well. But unlike Bonny, they had realized they were being watched and had scattered out of the clearing into the surrounding bush while Bonny remained at the fire eating. Was this the rear column? Had they come upon the rear column at last? But where was Barttelot then? And Troup and Ward? And why did the men run away from them?

"Come on."

They were more than halfway across the clearing before Bonny became aware of their presence. He looked up from what he was eating. Then he dropped it, jumped up and also ran away.

"Bonny! Sergeant Bonny, what's the matter with you? It's Mr. Stanley."

Bonny dashed around to the other side of the huge granite slab against which the tent had been pitched, and a terrible thought occurred to Stanley: Bonny had deserted. That would explain it. Bringing up the rear of the column, Bonny had deserted the march with the men they had seen here. That was why there was no sign of Barttelot or Troup or Ward. That was why these men ran away.

"Come back here, Sergeant. It's Mr. Stanley, I tell you."

There was no response. But there also was no sound of further movement. Bonny was still behind the rock. Uledi kneeled down by the fire and picked up the piece of food Bonny had been eating. The askaris gathered around to see what it was. Stanley signaled them to circle around the granite slab in the other direction in order to cut Bonny off if he attempted to escape that way.

"You're surrounded, Sergeant. There's no way you can get away from here. If you try, you'll be shot as a deserter. So just come out of there."

He didn't. Stanley realized he would have to go get him. He checked that the askaris were in position, then, not knowing what to expect, went around the rock. On that side the rock cast a dark shadow and it took his eyes a moment to adjust to it. Then he saw Bonny.

Bonny was standing rigidly at attention. His uniform tunic was buttoned all the way up to his throat. His helmet was set squarely on his head. He wore his holstered revolver in the regulation manner. He had a riding crop tucked under his arm. He was the very picture of the sergeant major presenting himself for duty to his commanding officer, the picture he had always made whenever in Stanley's presence.

But there was something wrong with the picture. It wasn't merely that his usually well-kept uniform was in shreds. It wasn't merely that his body was shriveled to half its bulk and gave off a disgusting odor and his once clean-shaven face was overgrown by a wild greasy beard and that his mouth hung open stupidly and dribbled drool and that his eyes seemed mad and empty and did not look at Stanley but past him, off at some unseen sight in some unknown distance. Such things as these, in and of themselves, wouldn't necessarily have shocked Stanley as he now was shocked. After all, the jungle was the jungle, and there was no way of knowing what the man had experienced in it since Stanley had seen him last. No, what was wrong, what struck Stanley as eerily wrong, was the riding crop. It wasn't Bonny's. Bonny had never carried a riding crop. It was Barttelot's. And so was the helmet. And so was the revolver.

"Where'd you get those things, Sergeant?"

"Sir?"

"Those are Major Barttelot's things. The helmet, the pistol, that riding crop—those belong to Major Barttelot."

"Yes, sir."

"Well, what the hell are you going with them? Where is he?"

"He rests in peace, sir. The beautiful soldier rests in peace."

"He's dead?"

"Ashes to ashes, sir. Dust to dust."

"How did he die? Where did he die?"

"In the arms of a woman, sir. By a woman's hand. As I always knew he would."

Bonny spoke in a flat monotone, in the voice of a madman. By now the askaris had circled around to this side of the rock, but Bonny didn't see them. He continued staring blankly off into space. The others, however—the Wanyamwezis and Sudanese who had scattered out of the clearing when Stanley and his men had approached—did, and tentatively now, still half fearfully, they began emerging from the surrounding trees and brush, from behind boulders and the wreckage of deadfall, a desperate, pathetic-looking lot, clad in tatters or not clad at all, covered with bruises and sores, shivering with fever, as emaciated as the dead found along the trail, peering with huge hollow eyes at Stanley and the askaris and slowly, dimly beginning to realize who they were.

"Bula Matari, look at this." Uledi, now also coming around to this side of the rock, carried the piece of food Bonny had been eating and had dropped when he had run away. "See what this is." Uledi held it out for Stanley's inspection. It was a chunk of meat. It hadn't been properly cooked. It was more than half raw. It had only been singed in the flames of the fire. "Do you know what this is?"

Stanley shook his head.

"It is a buttock, Bula Matari, the buttock of a man. Look." Uledi turned the chunk of meat over.

Stanley quickly averted his eyes from what was revealed. "For God's sake, throw it away."

Uledi threw it away.

Stanley looked back at Bonny. Bonny hadn't changed his posture. He still stood stiffly at attention, the riding crop under his arm, his eyes fixed on God knew what in the distance.

"Sergeant."

"Sir."

"Do you know who I am, Sergeant?"

"Yes, sir."

"Who am I?"

Bonny didn't reply.

"Look at me, Sergeant. Tell me. Who am I?"

And now Bonny did at last look at Stanley. And he looked at him. And he looked at him. And then he began to cry.

"Oh, dear God." Shaking his head, Stanley turned away. "Round up all these men, Uledi. Round up as many as you can find and see what you can learn about what happened here. Come along, Sergeant."

"Yes, sir."

They returned to the tent on the sunny side of the granite slab. It was safely sheltered by the rock and correctly pitched. The canvas was smooth, the guy ropes taut. There was even a gutter dug around it to keep out the rain. By the look of the gutter, Stanley reckoned it had been there several days, probably more than a week. A number of crates and barrels and bales were neatly stacked next to it and carefully covered with canvas tarpaulin, and the fire in front of it was obviously just the most recent of many fires that had burned there during those several days. The place had the look of a well-made camp, not of some haphazard hiding place of deserters on the run.

And then looking up and around, it dawned on Stanley that it was a camp, that the entire clearing was a campground of the sort a column on the march would make for a break of a few days. It was a natural clearing to begin with (that was what its attraction would have been in the first place), but he could see that efforts had been made to clear it further and that something of a zareba of brush and rocks had been erected around its periphery and that there were other fire pits and that shelters had been built of the kind the Wanyamwezis built on the march and that here and there were piles of the loads they had carried.

As Uledi and the askaris rounded them up, as word passed back into the forest that it was Bula Matari who had come and the Wanyamwezis and Sudanese, first by the tens and then by the scores, began returning to and assembling in the clearing, it became clearer to Stanley that this could very well be the campground of the rear column or what was left of it. Perhaps 250 men, women, and boys; perhaps 300 loads. There were no donkeys or mules. Undoubtedly they had been eaten.

"What happened to Mr. Troup and Mr. Ward, Sergeant?"

"Oh, we expect Mr. Ward any day now, sir. He's bringing up porters from Equator Station. We expect him to catch us up any day now."

"From Equator Station? He went to Equator Station?"

"Yes, sir. Mr. Troup sent him to Equator Station when he discovered that the nigger Arab was lying. You know, that nigger Arab at the Falls, sir, the one who killed the major. That shit bastard nigger Arab was lying. He was lying all along." Bonny's flat monotone voice suddenly turned shrill, his impassive expression became animated. Spittle began flying from his mouth. "Lying and lying, lying all the time, sir. We waited and waited, sir. We waited and waited and waited. But he was lying, sir. Lying and lying. But the major wasn't fooled. The major always knew he was lying. Lying and lying . . ."

"All right, Sergeant. Calm yourself." Stanley put a hand on Bonny's shoulder.

"Yes, sir."

"And where is Mr. Troup, Sergeant?"

"Mr. Troup, sir? He is sleeping."

"Sleeping?"

"He is very sick, sir. He must rest. He suffers very much in the litter. We have been carrying him in the litter since the desertions began, since the day he went back to try and catch the first of them and the Manyema began attacking the column. But the litter is very hard on him, sir. He needs to rest. As soon as he can be carried again, we will go on."

"And where is he sleeping, Sergeant?"

"Why, there, sir, in his house." Bonny pointed to the tent.

Ducking into the tent, Stanley was immediately assailed by the atrocious smell and was sure that Troup was dead, that Bonny in his madness had been keeping watch over and awaiting the revival of a man who was dead. Sleeping? Resting in peace?

But the corpse stirred. The skeleton breathed.

"Jack."

Troup was stretched out on a bed of palm leaves. Mercifully, a blanket, soiled and sodden, covered his starved body from the chin down; but his arms lay above it, and they were nothing but bones sheathed in brittle parchmentlike skin erupting with boils. His shrunken caved-in face was lost in the wild mane of his lice-infested hair and beard. At the sound of his name, he opened his eyes, bloody eyes.

"It's Bula Matari, Jack."

"Bula Matari?"

Stanley went to his side, took hold of his hand.

"Is it really you, Bula Matari? I'm not dreaming?"

"No, you're not dreaming, Jack. It's me."

"Oh, thank God. We've caught you up at last. Are we at Albert Nyanza?"

"Yes, Jack, you're at Albert Nyanza."

"Oh, thank God. Are we in time? Does Emin Pasha still hold his forts on the Nile?"

"Yes, Jack, you're in time. Emin Pasha still holds his forts on the Nile."

"Oh, thank God." Troup squeezed Stanley's hand. "Well, we showed them, didn't we, Bula Matari? Just like you said we would. We've made them sit up and take notice again. We've amazed them one more time."

"Yes, Jack, we have. We've amazed them one more time."

A ghost of a smile flickered across Troup's face, and he closed his eyes and relaxed his grip on Stanley's hand. And that night he died.

PART SIX
Flight

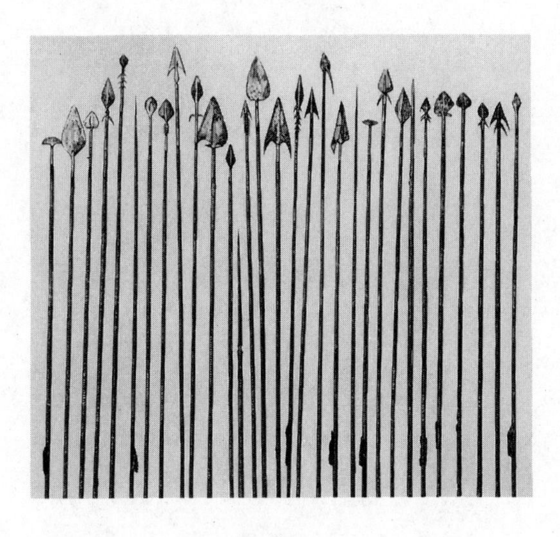

· ONE ·

THE FIRMAN READ:

> The whole of the Sudan and all its dependencies, excepting only this one of Equatoria, have acceded to the rule of the Mahdi, the Messenger of God, and have submitted to this holiest of all God's Imams and have given themselves over to him along with all their children and possessions and have become his followers, and whosoever opposed him was killed. And so we now come to this single exception of Equatoria, to the seat of its Government at Lado, in three steamers and nine nuggars with ten thousand Ansars, faithful soldiers of God, and we bring with us such news as will ensure to you your welfare and the welfare of all your people in this world and in the next, and to tell you what God and His Prophet wish of you and to assure you a free pardon, to you and to whomsoever is with you, and the protection of God and His Prophet for all your children and all your property on the condition that you too submit to God and His Messenger, as have the whole of the Sudan and all its dependencies. Otherwise you shall die.

It was found nailed to the postern gate in the northern battlement of Duffile. It was written in Arabic in a beautiful hand. It was addressed to Mohammed Emin Effendi, Pasha of Equatoria. It was signed by Emir Omar Saleh, faithful servant of the Mahdi's successor, the Khalifa Abdullah. And it was dated February 15, 1888. Pretty much as Emin had predicted, the main body of the dervish army from Khartoum had forced its way through the swamps of the Sudd and reached Lado just a little more than six weeks after Stanley had started back for the rear column.

Those had been hectic weeks. Emin, along with Jephson and

Nelson, the thirty *pagazis* and twenty askaris, the Maxim gun and crew, had visited each of the forts and river stations north of Duffile. As the Nile in this stretch—the hundred-mile stretch between Duffile and Lado, beginning with Fola Falls downriver from Duffile—was much broken up by rapids and cataracts and thus unnavigable for the *Khedive*, they had made the journey to each station overland through a terrain of increasingly arid and desertlike plains, of always more sparsely vegetated and rocky hills. And to each they had brought the same message and the same command, the message of the coming of Bula Matari's great caravan of hundreds of tons of arms and ammunition and relief supplies, the command to withdraw to and concentrate their forces in Duffile, there to hold off the dervishes until this great caravan's arrival.

In this, Rejaf, the northernmost of the river stations since Lado had been abandoned, was a dead loss. The garrison there had mutinied, and its commander, Hamad Aga, had sent a delegation under a flag of truce to Lado to make his submission to the Mahdi. Although the delegation hadn't yet returned—and, in Emin's view, would never return—Hamad Aga and his 200 soldiers were content to wait, believing that the only sane course in the face of so terrible an enemy was to lay down their arms and put their trust in Allah that they would be spared. And no amount of argument could dissuade them. Each of the others, however—Bedden, Kirri, Muggi, Labore, and Chor Ayu—each with a varying degree of enthusiasm, some reluctantly, some sorrowfully, some fatefully, some with an eagerness bordering on panic, had agreed. And they had dismantled their mountain guns, emptied their arsenals, cleared out their granaries and storehouses, loaded their mules and mule-drawn carts, herded together their cattle and goats and sheep, set fire to whatever they had to leave behind, and retreated south along the dusty left bank of the Nile to Duffile.

There, the twelve-foot-high, twelve-foot-thick earthwork battlements that enclosed the station on the north, west, and south were shored up and additional shooting platforms and firing positions built. The twelve-foot-wide, twelve-foot-deep moats around the base of these battlements were spiked with bamboo, and the newly acquired mountain guns from the northern forts were emplaced and sandbagged in support of the two already there (one on the wharf in case the dervishes tried to come at them from the other side of the river). The Maxim was entrenched atop the rampart at the west gate, where it would have a clear field of fire north to south across the cultivated fields that lay on the plain outside the walls. The produce of those fields—maize and millet, ground nuts and *m'tama*—was harvested and stored. While the danger was not imminent, the cattle and sheep were allowed to continue grazing out in those fields, and the people of the surrounding tribes, mainly Bari to the west of the Nile and Shuli to the east, were allowed to continue coming into the station to trade; but they had been warned that a time would come when the gates would be closed to them.

And now that time had come.

The soldier who had opened the north gate for the herdsmen to take their cattle out to graze and to let the tribesmen in to trade discovered the firman nailed to the postern on the morning of February 18. It had taken only three days for the ultimatum to be delivered from Omar Saleh in Lado, one hundred miles to the north. The soldier who found it couldn't read and turned it over to the corporal of his guard, who, also being illiterate, brought it to Hawashi Effendi, the garrison commander, who, upon reading it, immediately took it to Emin Pasha without saying anything about it to anyone.

Emin was at breakfast with Jephson, Nelson, and the Italian steamboat captain, Casati, in the garden of his compound in the northeast corner of the station. From where they sat in wicker chairs around a folding table under flowering jasmine trees they could hear the rumble of Fola Falls a quarter of a mile downstream and could see the boat sheds and engineering shops and warehouses of the landing stage, and beyond these the paddle-wheel steamer *Khedive* tied up to the wharf.

Since originally bringing Jephson, Nelson, and the others up to Duffile more than six weeks before, Casati had made two round-trip voyages south. The first took Stanley back to the advance column's camp at Nsabe on the lakeshore from where he started his return trek through the Ituri. The second trip ferried refugees from the northern forts and Duffile to Wadelai. This morning he was to make a third trip upriver carrying more refugees to Wadelai and then to continue on into Albert Nyanza to Nsabe to see if Stanley had yet returned with the rear column and, if so, to start ferrying them and the relief supplies to Duffile. The refugees bound for Wadelai on this trip were already gathered on the landing stage with their motley collection of household goods, and had been gathered there since well before first light.

"Where is the man who brought this, Hawashi Effendi?"

"He is gone, Pasha. Whover he was, no one saw him. He nailed it to the gate but no one saw him either come or go."

Emin unfurled the firman. "Sit down, Hawashi Effendi. Have coffee with us."

But the Egyptian remained standing while Emin read the firman. Jephson had a peek at it over Emin's shoulder. It was a beautiful piece of work; the flowing Arabic script with its curls and curlicues and surprising dots and dashes in jet black ink on translucent paper was less a missive than an elaborate design. Emin passed it across the table to Casati, the only other one there who could read Arabic.

"What does it say?" Jephson asked.

Emin made a dismissive gesture and removed his wire-rimmed spectacles from his beak of a nose and polished them on the edge of the tablecloth. He was dressed in his immaculate white linen suit, the ever-present tasseled maroon fez on his head. "It is the same old business, my boy. Surrender or die. We have heard it many times before."

"But this is the last time we shall hear it, Pasha," Casati said grimly, dropping the paper on the table amid the remains of the breakfast; and Jephson braced for one of the Italian's emotional outbursts. But it didn't come. This was Casati's other mood, bleak despair. He said nothing further.

"Where is Bula Matari, Pasha?" Hawashi Effendi asked. "Is it not time that he returned? Did he not promise us that he would return by this time?"

"Captain Casati goes to Nsabe today, Hawashi Effendi. Allah willing, he will find Bula Matari there and already on the way to our aid."

"And if he does not?"

At this Nelson stood up. He still seemed a frail shadow of his former self, if for no other reason than the loss of his teeth and the whitening of his hair. That made him look old and horrible. But actually he was much improved. He had gained back most of his weight and strength and also a semblance of his former quiet competence. His eyes no longer looked quite so desperate. "Come along, Hawashi Effendi," he said, taking the Egyptian by the arm fraternally. "Let's have a look at our fortifications. I take it it will not be long now before we have the chance to see how well we have made them."

"And you too, Gaetano, come along," Emin said, also standing up from the table. "It is time you were under way. We want to have Bula Matari and his men back here as soon as we can."

Jephson watched the two pairs walk off in opposite directions,

Nelson and the Egyptian toward the bandstandlike *barazan* under the three giant fig trees at the center of the station, Emin and the Italian down to the landing stage. He took a last sip of his coffee, a last bite of the honey-dipped white bread of breakfast, and also stood up. He, like all the others, now also had a beard, and it made him look older, no longer quite the callow youth who had started out on this expedition more than a year before. He was leaner, harder, stronger, less trusting, his skin weathered by the African sun, his eyes set deeper in their sockets and surrounded by myriad wrinkles and minor scars, having seen so much. But he still felt himself to be that callow youth. The dervishes were coming, and he was afraid.

A cloud of dust on the horizon. A single spiral of red dust rising from a jagged cleft in the rocky brown hills that formed the northwestern horizon under the blaze of the desert-white sky. And a speck of black within that cloud of dust. Seen through Jephson's field glasses, the speck of black became a horseman, and the cloud of dust was that raised by his galloping advance. Jephson could tell that the horseman's advance out of those hills down into the treeless plain was at a gallop of terrific speed by the way his jubbah billowed out behind him. But he didn't seem to get closer. In the delusive undulating, almost liquid waves of heat that shimmered on the arid, windless plain he seemed to advance for hours but never come nearer, only grow larger and more clearly defined in the field glasses' lenses. A lone horseman, riding hunched high up on his horse's neck, holding aloft a knobbed lance, his head wrapped in a multicolored turban, his flying jubbah speckled with patches of red and black and green: a peacock dervish. Jephson lowered his field glasses in order to see the fearsome figure with his naked eyes.

This was ten days after the firman had been received, ten days in which they had been keeping watch on the northern and western horizons for something of this sort to happen. Jephson was on the rampart above the west gate with Nelson, the askaris, the Maxim gun and crew. Hawashi Effendi was with them. His officers and the bulk of his troops, the commanders of the five forts to the north who had withdrawn to Duffile and the bulk of *their* troops, standing, kneeling, lying prone behind sandbags, about 900 in all—plus four of the Krupp mountain guns—were positioned along the north and west battlements. Except for the mountain gun at the corner of the west and south battlements and one above the south gate, the southern approach to the station was being left uncovered for the time being. After all, the first attack must surely come from the north and west. Two hundred men, however, were dug in along the riverbank with the seventh mountain gun to defend the station's east side just in case the dervishes tried something tricky, and 300 men were being held in reserve at their barracks within the station itself. All semblance of normal life within the station had ended with the arrival of the firman. The gates had been closed, a rationing system imposed, and all the problems that a siege would bring were already beginning to be felt. Emin came up on the rampart, carrying his walking stick.

"A peacock dervish, Dr. Emin," Jephson said and offered the wiry little man a look through his binoculars.

But Emin waved them aside—his eyesight was too poor to be much helped by them—and peered out blindly in the general direction of the cloud of dust on the plain. "Only one, my boy?"

"Yes, sir. Only one."

"How odd. Why only one?"

Jephson raised his glasses again and the horse and rider sprang to almost life size in the lenses. They were now about halfway between the hills from which they had appeared and Duffile's north battlement, halfway across the plain and headed toward the station's north gate. They had broken through that mirage of immobility and could be seen now to be in full motion, in furious, thundering motion, the rider hanging on to the horse's mane for what seemed like dear life, still brandishing high his knobbed lance or spear—lance or spear with a knob on the end—anyway something round on the end. Jephson began adjusting the eyepieces of the binoculars to keep them in focus on the rapidly advancing figure, to focus them on whatever that round melonlike thing was at the end of his spear.

"What the devil's that, Robbie? He's got something stuck on the end of his spear."

"Yes."

"Can you make out what it is?"

There was a pause. Nelson, Jephson, and Hawashi Effendi stood in the burning blaze of the midday sun, each with his field glasses at his eyes; Emin stood beside them clutching his cane behind his back, waiting to hear what one of them would reply.

Then Nelson said, "A head."

Jesus, yes, a head. Jephson had realized it was a head even before Nelson said it. It suddenly jumped out at him in the binoculars' lenses, a bearded head with grinning mouth and open eyes, a head with only the slender shaft of the spear for a body, riding high above the horseman's own head, bobbing dementedly with the horse's pounding gallop, grinning and staring in the clouds of dust as if both amused and terrified to be taken on such a breakneck ride. Jephson lowered his glasses in order to better judge how close it had come. Almost simultaneously so did Nelson. But Hawashi Effendi kept peering at it through his.

And then he said, "It is Hamad Aga's head."

"Hold your fire. Don't let anyone fire."

Now the Egyptian also lowered his glasses and turned to Emin. "I tell you it is Hamad Aga's head, Pasha."

"Nonetheless, no one is to fire."

The peacock dervish was in fact within firing range now, certainly well within the firing range of the Maxim and mountain guns, no more than 400, 350 yards from the north gate. And yet he kept thundering toward them, bearing down on them with his grotesque burden at full galloping speed. All along the battlements the soldiers tensed and their officers looked around at Hawashi Effendi, awaiting his order to fire.

"There is no point killing one," Emin went on hurriedly. "There is no point wasting precious ammunition killing only one. Am I not right, Captain Nelson? We must conserve our ammunition. We must put it to the best possible use."

"That's right, Pasha."

"Of course that's right. And this is not its best possible use. Killing one dervish. No, no, there is no use in that at all. Let us see what he'll do. Where is he now?"

Three hundred yards away, two hundred fifty, two hundred, the dervish rode on as if meaning to smash himself through the north gate and explode. Maybe that was it. Maybe beneath his robes he was taped with dynamite sticks and the fuses were already burning and the head was only a diversion. The soldiers on the battlements tracked him with their rifles; the Maxim gunner swung the gun barrel always more to the north to keep the horseman in the hairlines of his sight.

But then, when less than 150 yards from the gate, the dervish performed a stunning feat of horsemanship. In one fluid motion he spiked the spear into the ground and wheeled his horse around it in an impossibly tight turn and, never once breaking stride, risking breaking his horse's legs, went galloping back toward the hills from where he'd come. The maneuver caused such an explosion of dust that everything was obscured for a moment and Jephson wasn't sure what had happened. But then as the dust settled, he saw what the dervish had left behind: the head on the spear, still trembling from the force with which the spear had been thrust in the ground, the head of Hamad Aga, commander of the garrison at Rejaf that had mutinied, the head of the man who had believed that by surrendering to the Mahdi his garrison would be spared. And in this too the dervish's horsemanship had been remarkable, for the head of Hamad Aga directly faced the station's north gate, less than a hundred yards from it, grinning and staring at it, half amused, half frightened, as if asking to be let in to tell the terrible story of the massacre at Rejaf.

"The poor devil," Nelson said.

"Yes, the poor devil," Emin replied. "The poor foolish devil. But we owe him a debt of gratitude, Captain. He has done us a valuable service. Yes, in the end, by the very nature of his end, he has done us a most valuable service. Come, Hawashi Effendi, let us fetch our poor foolish friend and show him to the people so that they may know what comes of putting faith in the Mahdi's word, so that they may see what befalls those who would surrender to him."

Jephson and Nelson remained on the rampart when Emin and the Egyptian went down. A few minutes later they saw the north gate open and Emin and Hawashi Effendi come out. Several soldiers and two officers accompanied them. Emin strode out purposefully; but although the peacock dervish by then was once again a mere speck of black in a cloud of dust vanishing into the shimmering mirage of the empty plain, the others followed hesitantly, uncomfortable about being in the open. They gathered around the head on the spear, and almost immediately an argument about what to do with it erupted. Emin argued with Hawashi Effendi; the two other officers argued with Emin. That was Emin's style: to argue, reason, cajole, scold, flatter, persuade. He never issued a direct command.

"You know, Robbie, Dr. Emin might be right about that head. It just might give the people here second thoughts about surrendering to the dervishes. But I'm not so sure it won't also terrify them enough to make them try a run for it to the south before the dervishes have a chance to do the same to them."

"Yes, it might. But even if it does, it's too late for that now. It's too late for anyone to try and make a run for it anywhere now. Look."

Nelson had his field glasses at his eyes again. Jephson raised his.

"Jesus!"

It was an awesome sight. Clouds of dust, hundreds of clouds of dust, thousands of clouds of dust—each enveloping a black speck, each containing a horse and rider—were appearing on the rocky ridges of the shimmering horizon where the peacock dervish had disappeared and were slowly moving down into the treeless plain. It was impossible at this distance to see how they were armed. But Jephson knew well enough that unlike the lone peacock dervish they would not be armed only with spears. In their conquest of the Sudan, in their victories at El Obeid and Suakin, at Darfur and Bahr al-Ghazal and Khartoum, in their defeats of the armies of Hicks and Baker and Wolseley and Chinese Gordon, they had acquired armories of the most modern weapons and munitions.

"What do you think, Robbie?" Jephson asked. "Will they attack in the middle of the day like this?"

"Not if they're smart soldiers. And on the basis of their past performance, I think we've got to grant they're bloody smart soldiers. No, my guess is they'll wait until late afternoon, when we have the sun in our eyes."

Now something else was happening. Following those thousands of horsemen out of the hills, streaming down among them into the plain, came thousands of men on foot, infantrymen. Omar Saleh's boast in the firman that he had an army of ten thousand with him looked as if it might very nearly be true. But Nelson was right. They were not coming to attack, at least not now. Once out of the hills, they spread out like a swarm of ants upon the plain, the horsemen dismounting, the infantrymen pitching tents, raising a veritable tornado of dust. They were going into camp, perhaps two miles north and west of the battlements of Duffile. By now the officers and soldiers on the battlements had seen them, and a low murmuring groan passed through their ranks. Perhaps it was this that alerted Hawashi Effendi. In any case, he too became aware of the arrival of the dervish army, and whatever argument he and the others were having with Emin ceased. They unstuck the spear with Hamad Aga's head and beat a hasty retreat back into the station.

It started four hours later, two hours before sunset when, as Nelson had predicted, the sun had lowered to just above the jagged barren peaks of the hills on the horizon and shone directly in their eyes. And it was the same as it had been with the peacock dervish: They kept coming and coming for what seemed forever without ever appearing to get nearer, just growing larger and larger in their overwhelming number, troops of cavalry in the forefront, holding rifles high, platoons of infantry running like madmen between them, armed with rifles and spears and shields and bows and arrows. But there was one thing different this time. There wasn't the silence. When they were about halfway across the plain, still about a mile from the north battlement, Jephson heard the sound. It took him a moment to realize what it was. It was the dervishes screaming.

He was on the rampart above the west gate with the askaris and the Maxim. But neither Nelson nor Hawashi Effendi was with him now. They had gone to the command post set up at the mountain gun at the corner of the north and west battlements. Emin had been with them there when the dervish army started on the move, but soon after he had gone down to be among the civilians of the station.

Nelson looked down the line of men positioned along the west battlement toward Jephson at the west gate, shouted something to him that Jephson couldn't hear, and gave a good-luck sign. Jephson returned it with more enthusiasm than he actually felt and looked the rest of the way down the line of men on the west battlement to the mountain gun at the corner of the south battlement. They were in good position thanks to Nelson. Hawashi Effendi had come to defer to and rely on Nelson's judgment in these matters, reassured by that quiet, calm competence in him, and Nelson had dug them into a damn good defensive position. The dervishes would have the harder job; they were the ones in the open, the ones under the gun. But their overwhelming numbers, their horrible screams, their holy madness, and their suicidal charges had in the past repeatedly overcome defenses every bit as good as these.

They were coming fast, Jephson saw now as they broke through the undulating mirage of the plain, but not as fast as the peacock dervish had come and with none of his bravura recklessness. The horsemen seemed deliberately to be reining in, prancing their horses so that the infantry could keep pace with them. And not all of their forces had been committed yet. Back on the plain the tents were still pitched and thousands of horsemen and infantry men were milling about there, waiting their turn. Omar Saleh probably was holding them in reserve for a second and perhaps even third wave of assault; but if he truly had 10,000 men with him, that still meant nearly 5,000 screaming dervishes were coming at them now.

"Steady, boys," Jephson said to his askaris and the Maxim

crew. "Keep steady." That was the idea, he said to himself. Just keep steady, and don't let these screaming bastards rattle you.

But someone did let the screaming rattle him. A shot was fired. A soldier on the north battlement opened up with his Remington, and instantly a score or more followed suit. A ragged volley. It was stupid. Even the foremost of the charging horsemen were still out of range of the Remingtons. Jephson could see the shots thud uselessly into the ground at least a hundred yards short, kicking up spurts of dust, wasting ammunition. Soon enough a platoon commander or sergeant got them to quit it. But then, no more than five minutes later, four of the mountain guns fired.

Jephson would never know whether this had been on someone's command or whether the gunners too had lost their nerve, but it didn't matter. The dervishes *were* in range of the mountain guns; and as soon as they opened up, the battle was joined. All down the line of the north and west battlements, the back rank of soldiers, those standing, fired, and then the kneeling second rank in front of them fired, while the first reloaded, and then those lying prone behind the sandbags fired. And the dervishes replied, the horsemen firing from their thundering steeds, running men on foot hurling spears, riflemen and bowmen dropping to their knees, firing and then leaping up and coming on, screaming. The noise was terrific, the explosions of shot and shell deafening. The screaming of bullets and arrows and spears and men was a sound from hell; and the smoke and dust and cyclones of dirt torn from the earth and flung into the sky created a sudden darkness. Immediately bodies were falling everywhere; horsemen were blown from their horses, horses blown to pieces, infantrymen blown into the air; and on the battlements as well, especially among the standing ranks, bodies were falling backwards and forward, falling where they stood, crumpling into twisted attitudes, also screaming.

"Steady, boys, steady," Jephson said again and placed his hand on the Maxim gunner's shoulder.

It was soaked with sweat. They were all soaked with sweat. The heat was as terrific as the noise, infernal heat, the heat of the sun, the heat of the earth, the heat of the smoke and dust, the heat of the explosions, the heat of blood and guts, the heat of nerve-wrenching tension, the heat of excitement, the heat of battle. But they were good boys these askaris, good soldiers, veterans of Gordon's and Wolseley's campaigns, drilled to a fighting edge by Barttelot. They held steady despite the noise and heat. They awaited Jephson's command. With his hand resting on the gunner's shoulder, he kept his eyes fixed on the spot where the spear with Hamad Aga's head had been stuck into the ground, trying desperately to ignore all the hell that was breaking loose around him. He calculated that the spot where Hamad Aga's head had been was just under a hundred yards from the north gate; and in his mind he drew an imaginary line from it around to the west gate and decided that when the first dervish crossed that line . . .

"*Sasa, rafiki! Sasa!*" He pounded the gunner's shoulder. "Now, man! By God, now!"

And the gunner squeezed the Maxim's trigger.

It was the Maxim that did it. More than the shrapnel-whistling explosions of the mountain guns' shells, more than the volley upon volley from the flaming barrels of the Remingtons and Winchesters, it was the Maxim that did it. It was a killing machine, an unrelenting killing machine, producing a sweeping curtain of death. But it wasn't merely its terrible killing power that did it. The dervishes were accustomed to killing and killing machines. The mountain guns and the Remingtons and Winchesters were killing machines. And against these they would keep coming. Despite the havoc these wreaked and the blood they spilled and the brains they burst, against these they *did* keep coming—fearless, undaunted, screaming, seeking paradise in a holy death. No, it was the *surprise* of the Maxim that did it. It was the newness, the strangeness, the relentlessness of this terrible unknown killing machine that broke their charge. They had never experienced anything of its like before. They were stunned by its ceaseless spitting death. Their horses shied and reared in the teeth of it. The men on foot stopped dead in the face of it; and then they wheeled and broke and ran, horseless riders, riderless horses, panicked infantrymen, leaving the field littered with their wounded and dead and dying.

And a great roar of huzzah went up from the battlements.

Jephson couldn't believe it. It happened so fast. One moment all the legions of hell were bearing down on them. The next moment they were in full flight back across the plain. The great huzzah roared along the battlements like thunder. Jephson looked over to the command post at the corner of the north and west battlements. Emin was scampering up there from the station below to see what had happened. Hawashi Effendi was waving his saber jubilantly. Nelson was racing toward Jephson with a crazy toothless grin. Jephson tingled with delight, shivered with pleasure, hot with the mindless lust of killing, reeling with the heady wine of this quick astonishing victory. He slapped the Maxim gunner's back fiercely, and the man whirled around with a demented smile. The askaris leaped up and brandished their weapons and shouted derision at the fleeing dervishes.

"Good show, Arthur, bloody good show. Now let's get this gun out of here."

Nelson began issuing orders to the Maxim crew to limber the weapon and drag it down from the rampart. He wanted it repositioned farther south along the west battlement. Jephson saw why. A second wave of dervishes had been launched, not quite all those in reserve—Omar Saleh was still holding enough back for a substantial third wave—but a couple of thousand anyway; and when their charge collided with the flight of the first wave in the opposite direction, the impact brought both to a halt in a storm of dust. This was about a mile away; and now the first wave was regrouping, horseless riders chasing riderless horses, mounted horsemen wheeling and prancing and quieting their steeds, infantrymen re-forming ranks and falling in with those of the second wave, catching their breath, checking their weapons.

They weren't done yet. They were readying themselves for another assault. But obviously this assault wasn't going to come at the north and west sides of Duffile. It was going to come at the west and south sides. The regrouping army was moving south, so Nelson wanted the Maxim moved south in order to do its killing there and also in order to give the dervishes the impression there was more than one. Jephson scrambled down from the rampart after it.

The station was in chaos, the streets mobbed with excited, exhilarated humanity. Civilians were rushing up on the battlements to bring down the dead and wounded, to repair the defenses, and refill the sandbags. The soldiers who had been held in reserve in the barracks were hurrying out to take positions on the undefended south battlement and to replace the fallen on the north and west battlements, and the soldiers on the north and west battlements were being resupplied with shot and shell. Rations were being distributed. Water was being drawn from the river. Livestock that had broken loose in panic at the noise of the battle were being rounded up and driven back into their kraals. And chickens were flying around everywhere, being chased by boys and yapping dogs. The Maxim crew had to beat and bully its way through these crowds to drag the gun far enough south along the base of the west battlement to haul it up and sandbag it into position just to the right of the mountain gun emplacement at the corner of the west and south battlements.

Hardly an hour had passed since the attack had been launched, so there was still an hour of daylight left and something close to an hour of twilight after the sun would set. But the dervishes didn't seem to be in any particular hurry. They were keeping their distance of about a mile and were moving to the south at nothing much quicker than a trot.

"Do they fight at night?"

"I don't know, Arthur. I've never been up against these chaps before. They might."

But they didn't, not in the last hour of daylight, not in the hour of twilight, and at no time during the night. Jephson could see that this rather surprised Nelson, that he couldn't quite understand why they didn't, if for no other reason than to force the defenders to expend precious ammunition. That was the whole crux of this engagement, the life-and-death issue on which Duffile would either stand or fall: ammunition.

Nelson had taken a careful inventory of the station's arsenal before the attack; and after the sun set, he and Hawashi Effendi and Jephson–Emin was in the hospital looking after the wounded–made a tour of the defenses to see how much had been spent. Twelve men (including one officer, the commander from Labore) had been killed, twelve others had been critically wounded and probably would die, while twenty-one wounded had a fair chance of recovering and returning to the lines. Against that, by a rough estimate of the bodies strewn across the field of battle, about two hundred dervishes had been killed (there was, of course, no way of telling how many had been wounded and had made it back to their lines and, having made it back, would die there); but how much ammunition had been spent to accomplish this, Jephson did not know. He knew the situation with the Maxim; he knew there were enough rounds for it to put on the kind of show that it had in the first attack at least another twenty times. But how many more times could the mountain guns and the riflemen put on that kind of show? Nelson didn't say.

Jephson spent the night on the rampart with his askaris and the Maxim, a blanket wrapped around his shoulders against the chill, watching out for some kind of maneuver on the part of the dervishes. It was a moonless night but so crisp and clear that the countless stars in the desert sky cast shadows on the surrounding plain and illuminated those thousands of horses and men massed about a mile away. They didn't seem to be doing anything. To the north, where the dervish tents were pitched, where the third wave of cavalry and infantry camped, where Omar Saleh and his generals could be supposed to be, the orange specks of cooking fires could be seen; but if the army facing Duffile on the west had had supper, it had had it cold. Jephson and his men had it hot. Women brought it up from the station below, steaming and savory, maize *posho* and beans, yams and kabobs of mutton, and *m'tama* beer to wash it down. Unlike ammunition, food wasn't a problem. Thanks to Emin's foresight and planning, the station's provisions were more than sufficient to see it through even the most protracted siege. And that was what made the quiescence of the dervish army so much more surprising.

Omar Saleh surely must know that for all practical purposes the garrison couldn't be starved out, that his best tactic for taking Duffile was to hit it and keep hitting it until the defenders ran out of ammunition, that to sit back and wait was only to give Stanley and the rear column that much more time to get there with a massive resupply of guns and ammunition. Why he didn't act on this knowledge, what trick he might have up his sleeve, worried Jephson, and he would have liked to discuss it with Nelson. But Nelson spent the night patrolling the battlements and shoring up the defense on the riverside in case that was the trick Omar Saleh had up his sleeve.

Sometime after midnight Emin broke off his labors in the hospital and came up on the battlement to pay Jephson a visit. He was wearing a surgical apron smeared with blood, a surgical cap in place of his ever-present fez, and a surgical mask, unfastened and hanging down loosely on his chest beneath his beard. He looked bone weary, his cheeks pinched and drawn, his eyes behind the lenses of his spectacles blearier than ever. But he was cheerful for all that, in high spirits, full of his usual nervous energy.

"We gave them a good sock today, didn't we, my boy? We gave them something to think about. We're not going to be such easy game as they thought. No, no, not easy game at all. They know that now, eh? And we've got Bula Matari to thank for it." He went over to the Maxim and patted the barrel appreciatively. "This is what did it, all right, this wonderful, terrible gun of his. And the way you handled it my boy." He turned back to Jephson and took hold of both his hands. "It was brilliant, my boy, brilliant, the way you handled it. And the way you handled your askaris. They were brilliant too, steady as steel, brave as lions." And he went over to them and told them this in Swahili, also taking each by the hand.

And as he came over to them and took their hands, the askaris, who had been lounging against the sandbags, stood up beaming with delight, flattered to receive the personal congratulations of the Pasha himself, the Mudir of all Equatoria. It was clear that they didn't quite know what to make of this odd little man, would never know what to make of so utterly incongruous a hero of the war against the dervishes; but it was equally clear that they liked him, that they were drawn to his enthusiasm and kindliness.

"And so were all the others, all of them, every last soldier in the line, they were brilliant too. Wouldn't you say so, my boy? Not one of them flinched. Not one of them gave an inch. They fought like lions too. Isn't that so?"

"Yes, sir, it's so."

"Yes, it is so. I never doubted for a moment that it would be so. And they'll go on fighting like this, my boy, you'll see. Just give them the means. Just give them the weapons and ammunition and they'll go on fighting like lions. This is their home, and they will fight for it like lions. And now, thank God, they will have the means. They will have the weapons and ammunition. Bula Matari is bringing them, just as he brought this terrible gun. Oh, it's all over for Omar Saleh now. He'll never take Equatoria now. Once Bula Matari gets here, we'll see the last of him and his dervishes once and for all." Emin went to the edge of the battlement and looked out over the waist-high stack of sandbags toward the starlit forms and figures of the dervish army in the west. "What are they doing now, my boy?" he asked.

"They don't seem to be doing anything," Jephson replied and went over to stand by him.

"Licking their wounds, I'd say. Yes, that's what they're doing. Licking their wounds. We gave them a terrific sock. They never expected it."

Jephson would have liked to believe that, would have liked to be infused with a bit of Emin's optimism. But it was just too damn quiet out there under that ghostly starshine. There wasn't a sound, not even from the bodies of the fallen dervishes beneath the battlement. They couldn't all be dead. Surely some must still be alive, if dying, and some sound, no matter how faint, no matter how inhuman, ought to be heard from them. But there was no sound at all in the crisp windless night. From time to time a shot rang out, a sporadic volley of rifle fire, a shout of warning from one redoubt to another; but this always turned out to be a measure of the jumpiness of the soldiers on the battlements. There was nothing to shoot at, nothing to warn about. Even the carrion eaters—the vultures and jackals, the buzzards and hyena—hadn't put in an appearance yet. They were cautious, cowardly creatures. The extraordinary noise of the battle had scared them away. And despite the profusion of dead and dying meat on the battlefield, they still kept away. They were unimpressed by the quiet. They weren't deceived by it. They sensed something false and dangerous in it. So did Jephson.

"It is my home as well."

"Sir?"

Emin had clasped his hands behind his back as he continued to look across the sandbags out to the vast barren plain and the rocky jagged crags and ridges and arid hills that formed the horizon. The stars seemed very close on those hills, seemingly falling out of the infinite expanse of the velvet-black sky onto those hills.

"I too will fight for it like a lion."

He said this softly, almost dreamily, more to himself than to Jephson, staring off into the boundless space of the plain and hills and sky, probably actually seeing very little with his myopic eyes and yet probably seeing everything he wished to see. In this moment of private, dreamy contemplation, his high spirits and cheerful energy ebbed; and his immense fatigue, the terrible toll of the huge effort he had made and had made for so long to hold his garrisons against the dervishes showed clearly, in his long, narrow, bearded fatherly face.

Jephson felt a sudden rush of affection for him. They had been together now for more than two months; and in everything—in his generosity and gentleness, in his intelligence and innate courtesy, in his endearing eccentricities, in his courage and inventiveness—Jephson's original opinion of him had been confirmed and doubly confirmed. But in those two months he had learned very little more than he had learned in the first few days about his mysterious history.

"I love this place," Emin went on and unclasped his hands and made a sweeping gesture across the open desert land he almost certainly could not see. "There is something so beautiful here, something so pure."

Jephson made no reply to this. He felt it was not addressed to him but to someone or something only Emin could see.

"I was a long time finding it, a very long time. And it is now my home as well." Emin reclasped his hands behind his back. "I will never leave it. I will fight for it like a lion. I will never let anything in the world drive me from it."

There was a pause. Jephson waited for Emin to go on, but Emin didn't go on. He seemed to have slipped into his dream.

"Dr. Emin?"

"Yes?"

Jephson hesitated. What he wanted to ask him was indiscreet, perhaps even rude. So he hesitated. But what he wanted to ask him, he had wanted to ask so many times, on so many different occasions during these past two months and, somehow he felt that if he was ever going to ask him this was the time, in this moment of quiet contemplation, here under the cold shine of the desert stars, when it might seem less indiscreet, less rude. And so he finally did ask him.

"Who are you, Dr. Emin?"

Emin turned to him and smiled, a gentle, kindly smile. "My boy, what a question. Why do you ask it? Who do you think I am?"

"I don't know, sir. I only know that you are not who the world believes you are. I only know that you are not a Turk. I only know that you are not Mohammed Emin Effendi."

"No?"

"No."

Emin turned away again. The smile was still on his face. "No," he said softly, looking toward the distant horizon. "You are right, my boy. I am not a Turk. I am a Jew. My name is Eduard Schnitzer. I am a Jew from Silesia, a wandering Jew."

· TWO ·

DUFFILE NOW CAME under siege.

Despite all logic arguing against such a tactic, despite all commonsense calling for a strategy of unremitting attack, Omar Saleh sent his army against the battlements of the station only intermittently in the next few weeks. There were isolated skirmishes and incidents of sniping during that time, occasional bombardments and hit-and-run raids; but as for full-scale assaults like the first, there were only four. It was as if Omar Saleh believed he had all the time in the world to bring Duffile to its knees, as if he weren't in the least bit concerned about Stanley getting back with the rear column and the relief, as if he knew something Duffile's defenders didn't know.

To be sure, when he did attack, the attacks were awful—wave upon wave of screaming dervishes, the earth trembling under the pounding of their thousands of horses' hooves, the day turning to night in the smoke of the explosions—and resulted in awful losses in men and munitions. But as each attack was beaten off and afterwards there always was a week or more of respite in which to repair the defenses and reorganize the troops and patch up the wounded and bury the dead, morale remained fairly high. The victories instilled confidence. The even greater losses each attack inflicted on the dervishes were evident in the rotting, bloating corpses strewn across the plain. And although there was reason to worry about the steadily diminishing stocks of ordnance in the arsenals (Nelson kept the exact tally secret in order to avoid exacerbating the worry), the expectation of the *Khedive*'s imminent return with Stanley still ran strong.

All this changed on April 9.

From first light that day, before the mists of morning had burned off and the last stars on the western horizon had winked out and the sun had shown itself above the Nile, the dervishes were seen once again to be on the move, working themselves into a holy frenzy for another attack. And by the look of it, this was to be the most ferocious attack yet. Omar Saleh was committing all his troops this time and, moreover, was maneuvering them into position to hit all three landward sides of the station at once.

"Something's happened," Nelson said, studying the movement through his field glasses. "Something or someone's built a fire under that bugger. He means business this time."

"It's Mr. Stanley," Jephson replied. "I'll wager you anything that's what it is, Robbie. Mr. Stanley's finally back. The *Khedive*'s probably no more than a day or two upriver, and Omar Saleh's got wind of it and reckons he's got to take us now or he never will."

And he very nearly did. The sheer weight of this assault, the thundering impact of almost 10,000 warriors stretched the defenders to their limit; and to make matters worse, the dervishes came at them not only on all three landward sides but from across the Nile as well. No sooner had the attack been launched than thousands emerged from the bulrushes of the opposite bank and, screaming their terrifying screams, pushed out into the river in hundreds of canoes and rafts. It was suicidal. They were sitting ducks on the open water; the current rushing over Fola Falls was far too swift for them to have a realistic chance of making a landing, let alone securing a bridgehead, but it also was dangerous and frightening and it forced Nelson to pull soldiers out of the lines on the battlements and thus weaken his landward defenses in order to repel them. And to keep repelling them. For despite the carnage, they kept coming on all sides, in full cry and fanatic fury.

They were familiar with the Maxim now; they weren't astonished by its killing power anymore, and so they kept coming, savagely, fearlessly, into its sweeping curtain of death, into the relentless volleys of rifle fire from the barricades, into the flashing, deafening explosions of the mountain guns' shells, into the smoke and dirt and cyclones of shrapnel these threw up. And they got closer this time, closer than they had ever gotten before. They got to the edge of the moat beneath the battlements, and their shot-up bodies and blown-apart horses fell into the moat and were impaled on the spikes there like so much butchered meat. And still they kept coming. They came up out of the moat like ghouls, bloody and torn, and clawed their way up the slopes of the earthwork ramparts and leaped the moat on their horses and crashed against the gates and scrambled from their rafts and canoes onto the wharfs of the riverfront and had to be beaten back with rifle stocks and bayonets and sabers and knives and billhooks and clubs, hand to hand.

A mountain gun exploded. Hastily and improperly charged by its sorely tried crew, it blew up in a shower of blood and steel and its crew's dismembered limbs. A granary caught fire, and the flames spread quickly to the central bazaar. A band of dervishes breached the south gate and managed to hack to pieces a dozen civilians before being hacked to pieces themselves. Sandbags split like soft bellies, knifed open by arrows and spears. Whole sections of the earthworks crumpled under the hammering of shot and shell. The minaret of the mosque toppled onto the roof of the *barazan*, and cattle stampeded. The Maxim gunner was shot through the throat, and Jephson took over the gun. It was sizzling; the cartridge belt kept jamming after every dozen rounds; the sting of gunpowder burned his eyes. Four more askaris went down, and then a fifth began shrieking, his right arm blown away at the shoulder. It couldn't go on. There was no way this hell could go on. But it did go on. It started at ten in the morning and went on through the worst heat of the day, three hours, four, of searing heat and deafening noise, of blinding smoke and storms of dust, of suffocating stench and unslakable thirst, of steaming blood and rivers of spilled guts, of ceaseless pain and death and dying.

And then at last it stopped. By some miracle of courage, this attack too was beaten back. By some insane rule of battle, the dervishes broke it off just at the moment it might have succeeded. But no great huzzah went up from the battlements this time. The only sounds to be heard this time were the cries of the wounded, the groans of the exhausted, the weeping of the deranged.

Jephson rolled off the gun—his face black with grease, his eyes red with tears, his lungs burning in his chest—and slumped like a rag doll against the shattered barricade. The Maxim gunner was stretched out beside him, but he wasn't dead. The four askaris were dead, and the one who had lost an arm was dead also. They were twisted in rigid tormented poses in the dirt of the disgorged sandbags, but the gunner was still alive. Jephson saw that the blood oozing out of the hole in his throat gurgled and bubbled with breathing. And he thought, Someone better come up here and take him down to Dr. Emin in the hospital. But no one came up to take him down. The stretcher bearers and water carriers who had rushed up on the ramparts after each of the previous attacks to succor the defenders and repair the defenses did not rush up this time.

A stunned silence had descended on the station. The smoke

from the explosions and still-burning fires hung over it like a pall. Jephson went on staring at the wounded gunner in a numbed silence of his own, watching in dumb fascination as the gurgling in the blood grew fainter, the bubbles smaller. He knew very well that it was up to him to take the gunner down to Dr. Emin in the hospital, or at least to order one of the still living askaris to take him down, but he didn't have the energy to do either. All he wanted to do was sleep.

And then he heard the blast of the steamer's whistle.

Perhaps he had slept. In any case his eyes were closed. He opened them. If he had slept, he hadn't moved an inch while he slept, for when he opened his eyes, the gunner was still lying directly in front of him. Only now the gunner was dead. The blood no longer bubbled in the hole in his throat; the blood was black. He had let the gunner die. It didn't bother him particularly; it didn't seem such a terrible thing amid all this death and dying. The steamer's whistle sounded again, and he shifted his eyes away from the gunner.

There was a stirring along the battlements. The station below was awakening from its stupor. He didn't quite comprehend it. His brain wasn't fully functioning yet. His ears still rang with the noise of the battle; and the blast of the steamer's whistle was nothing in comparison to it. He stood up slowly, arthritically. It was incredible how tired he was, how much pain he felt in his bones. All along the battlements, soldiers were standing up in this creaky old man's way and turning toward the east, looking out across the station toward the Nile. And he also turned toward the east to see what they were looking at; and he saw, in the still blazing mid-afternoon sky above the gray pall of smoke hanging over the station, the black puffs of smoke from the steamer's stack.

"The *Khedive?*"

He said it quietly, more as a question than a statement. But then someone also said it as if in answer to his question, and then someone else said it; and soon it was being said up and down the battlements with growing force and greater affirmation, turning into a grand huzzah after all.

"The *Khedive*. Yes, by God, it's the *Khedive.* I knew it. Didn't I just know it? Bula Matari is back. Boys, *warafiki*, Bula Matari is back." And he bolted down from the rampart.

The station was a wreck. Roofs were caved in, walls were shattered, fires were smoldering in the rubble, and livestock were loose in the streets. The streets were slippery with blood, and bodies lay everywhere, stinking in the heat. But it didn't matter. The *Khedive* was back; and the place, just moments before at death's door, was coming jubilantly alive at the news. People rushed out of their hiding places shouting the steamer's name, grinning dementedly, slapping each other's backs, congratulating themselves for being alive, thronging down to the waterfront. They had stood off the worst the dervishes could throw at them, and now relief had arrived. Jephson pushed through these wildly exuberant crowds, every bit as wildly exuberant as they, looking this way and that for Nelson or Emin. Passing the hospital, he spotted them. They were just stepping out the hospital's doorway, Emin in his blood-smeared surgical apron, Nelson without his helmet.

"Hey, Robbie, what did I tell you? What did I tell you, old boy?"

"You told me, Arthur. You told me."

They grasped each other's hands like schoolboys who had just won a rugger match. Nelson's horrible toothless smile was a joy to see.

"Bula Matari's back, Dr. Emin. Equatoria is saved."

"Yes, yes, my boy. It's wonderful. Just in the nick of time."

"Where's Hawashi Effendi?"

"Dead."

"Oh, Christ."

"Blown up when that mountain gun blew up."

"Jesus. Poor devil."

"Yes, poor devil. So many poor devils," Emin said, and the crowd made way for him as he hurried down to the waterfront.

The *Khedive* was not yet in sight; she was still a good mile upriver and around a bend, and the only signs of her were the puffs of smoke from her stack and the intermittent blasts of her whistle. Emin, Nelson, and Jephson went out to the end of the steamer jetty. Dervish dead—caught on snags, trapped between rocks, washed against pilings—bobbed in the river's fast current and swirled in the eddies above Fola Falls. Scores of corpses from both sides of the battle were scattered along the riverbank and on the landing stage. But the excited mobs gathering there surged by them heedlessly, surged over them unseeingly in their eagerness to get a glimpse of the returning steamer.

"Over there," Nelson suddenly said, pointing upriver. "What's that?"

Jephson raised his glasses.

"What is it?" Emin asked, squinting helplessly in the direction the two Englishmen were looking.

The steamer sounded her whistle again and at last hove into view, rounding the bend, glistening white in the blaze of the afternoon sunlight, riding high in the water, following a channel close under the hills of the Nile's western bank; and just as she did, Jephson saw what Nelson was pointing at.

"Dervishes!"

"Yes." Nelson dashed off the jetty and raced for the gun emplacements on the south battlement.

The dervishes were on foot, armed with rifles, at least 200 of them, and they were swarming up into the hills that overlooked the river. There was no question what they were about. They were setting an ambuscade. In another few minutes the *Khedive*, if she stayed on her course, would come directly under their guns. Behind the barricades of rocks and cuts and gorges in those hills, they would have a clear line of fire onto her open deck.

And she did stay on her course. She had no choice but to stay on that course. It was the river's only navigable channel in this final stretch before Duffile.

Seconds after the dervishes opened fire on the *Khedive*, the guns on the south battlement opened fire on the dervishes. The dervishes were out of range of the Maxim, the Winchesters, and the Remingtons. Only one mountain gun, the one emplaced above the station's south gate, could reach them; and at first its shells fell short and wide as Nelson and the gunner frantically adjusted the range. So for several crucial minutes, the dervishes enfiladed the *Khedive* undisturbed. Jephson watched helplessly through his field glasses, his heart in his mouth. The vessel was being raked from stem to stern. Casati or whoever was in the wheelhouse tried to take evasive action, putting on steam, swinging the vessel sharply away from the bank, running the risk of foundering on a rock or going aground on a mudflat. The puffs of smoke coughed out of her stack with a panicked rapidity and merged into a single black plume; the whistle blasts became an unending scream. She was steaming for Duffile at her maximum speed, riding high in the water, running for home as fast as her paddle wheels would drive her. And she was going to make it, Jephson suddenly realized. The mountain gun had found the range, and the shells were now falling in among the dervishes, disrupting their murderous fusillades. Yes, if her boiler didn't burst, she was going to make it, he realized. She was already nearly halfway clear of the worst of the ambush.

And then he realized something else: No one aboard her was returning the dervishes' fire. There was no one aboard her *to* return the dervishes' fire. She was riding that high in the water, she was making such good speed because there was no one aboard her except Casati and his crew.

"No, no, no," the Italian roared. "How many times must I tell you, Pasha? He wasn't at Nsabe. And no one at Nsabe knows where he is. Not the Surgeon Parke. Not that big brute Hoffman. No one. They haven't had word of him since he started back through the Ituri."

They were in the garden of Emin's compound. The place hadn't escaped the ravages of the day's battle. There were corpses here too, and fires were smoldering, and there was brick rubble from the caved-in wall of one of the administration buildings and a crater from a misfired mountain-gun shell. Emin was standing at the edge of it, still in his bloody surgical apron and cap. Casati walked around it, shouting at Emin first from one side, then another. Nelson was still up on the battlement tracking the dervishes' movements. Jephson sat in one of the breakfast chairs, his legs stretched out, the knees of his trousers gone, his thumbs hooked in his cartridge belt, his bearded, grease-smeared chin resting heavily on his chest. The folding breakfast table was tipped over on its side next to him in a pile of smashed crockery.

"What do you make of it, my boy? It's now more than three months since he left. What in God's name could have happened to him?"

Jephson shrugged, studying the toes of his boots through half-closed bloodshot eyes. He had been asking himself the same question from the moment he realized that Stanley and the rear column were not aboard the *Khedive;* and he still couldn't imagine what the answer might be or, perhaps more accurately, didn't want to imagine what it might be. So many things, so many dreadful things, all intolerable to imagine, could have happened in the Ituri. He blocked his mind from imagining them. Actually though, he did not imagine they had happened to Stanley. He knew Stanley well enough; he knew that in his single-minded bull-like determination, Stanley, by main force, by brutal will, simply wouldn't *let* any of those things happen to him. No, the question really was, What had happened to the rear column?

"Bula Matari wasn't on the steamer, Captain."

Jephson looked up. Nelson had come into the compound. He still wasn't wearing his helmet. He must have lost it somewhere during the battle.

"I know," he said. "I saw."

"And what do you make of it? Where can he be after so much time? Captain Casati says no one in Nsabe has the least idea. Isn't that what you said, Gaetano?"

"Yes, Pasha, that's what I said. Jesus Maria, it is what I have said a hundred times. Do you want me to say it again? I will say it again. No one in Nsabe knows where he is. For all anyone in Nsabe knows, he is dead, and all the men with him."

"He's not dead," Jephson snapped and stood up. "He'll be back."

"Yes, Signor Jephson? When?"

"I don't know when. But he'll be back. You can be damn sure of it. You can bet your life on it."

"And what do you suppose I am doing, Signor Jephson? That is precisely what I am doing. I am betting my life on it."

"Well, you just go on doing that and you'll be fine." Jephson turned his back on Casati.

But Casati wasn't to be dismissed so easily. He was cooking now, stewing up into one of his fits. He took off his straw hat and slammed it against his thigh. "Fine? I will be fine, signor? What kind of idiot do you take me for? How will I be fine? Betting my life that Bula Matari will return? And so what if he returns? How is that going to make me fine? The dervishes are at the gate, signor. Ten thousand screaming dervishes are at the gate right now."

"I know that. For Christ sake, do you think I don't know that? Do you think I haven't seen them? Do you think I haven't killed enough of them? I've killed hundreds of them. That's all I've been doing is killing them and getting killed by them."

"My boy, my boy."

Jephson walked away before Emin could take his hands, as he clearly meant to do, walked away kicking viciously at stones and pieces of rubble, walked around to the other side of the shell crater, all of a sudden trembling uncontrollably.

"It has been a hard day," Emin said. "It has been a very hard day for all of us. We all are on edge. It is perfectly understandable.

No, Gaetano. Not a word. Not another word. We must stay calm. We must all stay calm and think carefully what we shall do now."

From the other side of the crater, Jephson could see the *Khedive* tied up to the wharf. The hundreds of people who had gathered on the landing stage to await her were still there, crowding against each other and against the side of the vessel. There was no question why they were there. They wanted to board the vessel and flee on her to the safety of the south. They were kept off only by her crew.

"My guess is it's the rear column, Robbie," Jephson said, turning away from the chaos on the wharf. "Something happened to *them*, not to Mr. Stanley. They could have lost our trail or bogged down foraging for food or run into trouble with Kilonga-longa's slavers, you know, that sort of thing. Or maybe they didn't get away from Yambuya when they were supposed to. Maybe something delayed them and Mr. Stanley had to go much farther back through the forest than he expected before meeting up with them. Maybe he had to go damn near all the way back to Yambuya before meeting up with them."

"Yes, maybe," Nelson replied. "That's one possibility."

"And if it is the correct one, Captain?" Emin asked. "I mean, what if he did have to go all the way back to Yambuya? How long would it take him to get there and then return to us?"

Nelson pulled a face. It was a comic-horror face. He didn't mean it to be—he meant it only to express his uncertainty at answering Emin's question—but without his teeth, his face had acquired a grotesque mobility. "Well, he's traveling light and he knows the way and the Aruwimi's current is in his favor. . . . I suppose he could make it back to Yambuya in nine or ten weeks. But as for returning here, that's another story. With all the men and loads of the rear column, that'd take him at least twice as long."

"So, what does that make it, Captain? About six months altogether, would you say? And he's already been gone three, more than three. So it would not be entirely unreasonable to expect him back here in . . . What? Ten weeks? Eleven?"

"Jesus Maria! Eleven weeks!"

"I'm warning you, Gaetano. I don't want to hear another word out of you."

Casati jammed his straw hat back on and flung himself into the chair where Jephson had been sitting. And Jephson thought they'd not hear another word out of him now for a while. He was going into his other mood, into one of his bleak sulks.

"Isn't that how you would reckon it, Captain? God willing, we could expect Bula Matari to return in ten or eleven weeks?"

"Something like that, Pasha. God willing."

"Well, that's not so bad. Not so bad at all. We've held out this long. We can hold out ten or eleven weeks longer."

"Not here, Pasha. Not in Duffile."

This took Emin aback. It also startled Jephson. Even Casati looked up out of his funk.

"Duffile's finished, Pasha. One more attack like today's and the dervishes will have it. They damn near had it today. I think the time has come to let them have it and withdraw to Wadelai."

"I see," Emin said and removed his spectacles and began busily polishing them on a corner of his surgical apron.

"I'm sorry, Pasha."

"No, no, Captain. I am sure you are entirely correct in this. It's only that, foolish as I am, I never really believed Duffile would ever have to be given up. It is the oldest of our stations, you know, the first ever in Equatoria. Sir Samuel Baker built it."

"It's a temporary sacrifice, Pasha. Think of it that way. It will gain us what we are most in need of right now, time. It'll put another hundred miles between us and the dervishes, and there's no telling how much time they'll take to come those hundred miles. And we'll be in a far stronger position in Wadelai with the men and munitions there to fight with. We'll be able to hold out there far longer than we ever could here."

"Yes, of course. I quite understand. It is the only sensible thing to do." Emin replaced his spectacles. "And when would you propose to do it?"

"As soon as possible, and at night. It'll take a few nights to get ready, but with a little luck the dervishes won't catch on to what we're up to until after we're gone."

"And you propose to use the steamer for this, of course."

"Yes."

"Well, you know, Captain, we have very nearly three thousand people here in Duffile, besides the soldiers, and it is my intention that every last one of them be evacuated to Wadelai, along with the soldiers. I will not leave even one soul behind."

"No."

"But they can't all be evacuated on the steamer."

"No, Pasha, they can't. We must reserve the steamer for the

garrison. The soldiers must have first priority on her, the soldiers and the guns and what's left of the ammunition. We must get all of that to Wadelai as quickly as we can, where it will do us the most good. I'm afraid everyone else will have to make the journey overland."

"Yes, I expected that would be the case. It couldn't be otherwise. How could it be otherwise?" Emin looked toward the jetty, toward the anxious crowd milling about on the landing stage. Then he said, "Well, we must just do the best we can and pray that God is with us."

The preparations for the withdrawal from Duffile took place in the course of the next five nights. Initially everyone was eager to go, indeed in a panic to go, showing none of the nostalgia for Duffile that Emin had shown. They had had enough of the dervishes' screams, enough of the pounding of their guns, enough of the blood they had spilled and the destruction they had wrought. They greeted the decision to abandon the beleaguered station as the commutation of a sentence to certain death. And, as soon as they heard about it, they swarmed onto the waterfront with all their worldly possessions, with the most ridiculous variety of household goods, with bedsteads and milling stones and baking ovens and crosscut saws and feather dusters and beat-up kettles and wooden armoires and chairs and tables, with livestock and fowls and pet parrots and dogs and sacks of grain. And they fought with each other and fought with the *Khedive*'s crew in a hysterical attempt to find places for themselves aboard the vessel. But when they realized they would not be allowed to board the vessel, when they saw that nothing—not brawling, bullying, bribery, or special pleading—would secure them a place aboard her; when squads of soldiers drove them off at bayonet point, and they understood at last that they were expected to make the hundred-mile retreat to Wadelai on foot, they lost heart. It was as if their effort to get on the *Khedive* was the last effort they could be expected to make to save themselves, as if all the wit and courage and resourcefulness and energy they had displayed in holding out against the dervishes for almost three years had finally come to an end. In stupefied silence, they returned to their homes or to the ruins of their homes and, in morbid apathy, sat down there to await their fate.

And so, while Nelson and Jephson went about supervising the business of dismantling the mountain guns and spiking those that couldn't be taken and emptying the arsenal and parading the troops, and while Casati saw to the loading of the *Khedive*'s holds with the weapons and ammunition and assigning the soldiers to their berths on her deck, Emin spent the time arguing with his people, scolding and cajoling them, exhorting and organizing them and trying by the sheer force of his personality to infuse spirit enough in them for this one final exertion of will and daring. And so it wasn't until the third night of the preparations that the exodus of the civilians actually got under way.

Only a few hundred went out that night, but their departure triggered another wild swing in the mood of the place; and the number quickly swelled into a suddenly panicked rabble on the following nights, pouring out through the south gate from the first moment darkness fell, when the gate was opened for them, until the last moment before the crack of dawn, when it was again closed. They poured out in disorderly caravans four and five miles long, poured down the road along the Nile's rocky left bank, men leading mule-drawn carts piled high with goods and provisions; women riding donkeys, holding infants to their breasts; boys driving herds of cattle with pie dogs snapping at their heels; thousands of people on foot carrying bales and boxes and barrels on their backs, pouring southwards in frightened, desperate confusion, pouring away toward Wadelai in a seemingly endless flood.

Jephson, leaning against the Maxim's barrel, watched them from the rampart above the south gate. How far would they get? How far would the dervishes let them get? The poor devils—so cumbersomely burdened, traveling at a snail's pace, already stopping every half-mile, the children and old folk already falling behind—were sitting ducks for the dervish horsemen. Emin had arranged for an escort of soldiers to accompany each night's caravan ten miles down the road or until daybreak, whichever came first, and most of the men in the caravan were in some way armed—with flintlocks or cap-and-ball pistols, with sabers or knives or spears—but no one was fool enough to believe this would do much good if the dervishes chose to swoop down on them. But the dervishes didn't choose to swoop down on them; and why they didn't, why they allowed the caravans to depart night after night unmolested, was as much a mystery as why they had besieged Duffile instead of attacking it relentlessly. Perhaps the preparations for the garrison's evacuation and the exodus of its civilians had escaped their notice. But Jephson doubted it.

"We're ready, Arthur."

Jephson went down from the rampart. Nelson and Emin were waiting for him. Nelson had replaced his missing helmet with a turban, which gave him an even more wraithlike appearance. Emin was dressed in his best suit and fez.

"Pretty much everything's loaded," Nelson said. "I think we ought to push off tonight."

"I'll bring down the Maxim."

"No. Leave it."

"What do you mean, leave it? Aren't we taking it with us?"

"Not tonight," Nelson said. "I want to keep it here for another day or two with a few of the askaris. We'll bring it up in one of the station's small boats later on."

"When did you decide this? I didn't hear anything about it."

"Dr. Emin and I talked it over just now."

Jephson looked at Emin.

"Just in case, my boy," Emin said. "Just in case."

"Just in case what?"

"You can never tell what these dervishes will do, my boy. Probably they will do nothing. I must say, they seem willing enough to let us depart in peace. But just in case . . . If that terrible killing machine is still here, they will think twice about doing anything, and that will give the people a little extra time to get away. You realize not all the people have gotten away yet. You see people are still leaving, and they will still be leaving after the *Khedive* sails and the garrison is gone. It is only right that we give them a little protection until they can get away too."

"It's either that, Arthur, or delay the departure of the *Khedive*. Dr. Emin would prefer that we delay the *Khedive*, but I think that'd be a mistake. I think it's crucial we get the garrison to Wadelai as soon as we can. So we'll leave the Maxim here with a few of the askaris for a day or two."

"And you with them?"

"Yes."

"No. That's out of the question, Robbie. That's completely out of the question. I won't hear of it."

"It's only for a day or two."

"No. It's the stupidest goddamn thing I ever heard. First of all, these people have only themselves to blame. They've had plenty of time to get away. For God's sake, they've had five days. It's their own damn fault that they're still here."

"Now that's unfair, my boy. That's really very unfair. We're asking these people to leave their homes. We're asking them to leave the place where they've lived all their lives. It is not an easy thing to do. It is only natural that some could not bring themselves to do it as quickly as others. I am not sure how quickly I could bring myself to do it."

"That's nonsense, Dr. Emin, and you know it. That's not why these people haven't left. They would have left without so much as a backward glance if they had been able to secure passage on the steamer. They would have left like a goddamn bolt out of the blue. No, the only reason they haven't left is because they're plain lazy. That's all there is to it. They don't want to walk. They don't want to carry their things. And besides, we need Captain Nelson in Wadelai. He's got to prepare the defenses there. He's got to organize the troops. I can't do it. You can't do it. He's the only one who can do it, just as he did it here. No, the whole idea is ridiculous. I'm going to have the askaris bring the Maxim down." Jephson started onto the rampart.

"Well then, I will have to stay," Emin said.

Jephson turned back.

"I cannot abandon my people, my boy. As I explained to Captain Nelson, I will not leave while even one of them is still in danger."

Jephson loked at Nelson. Nelson shrugged. Obviously he had heard all this before.

"I must stay until the last of them safely depart. Or stay, if they cannot safely depart, and share their fate. I am their mudir."

Slowly Jephson began shaking his head. This would not do either. This was every bit as unacceptable. For as much as Nelson was needed in Wadelai to make ready that station's defenses, so was Emin needed there to rally the people to make the defense. "This sounds rather like blackmail, Pasha."

"Blackmail, my boy?"

"Either we leave the Maxim or we leave you."

"Yes, it must be one or the other, my boy. You may call it blackmail if you like. But these are my people. It is my duty to protect them, in one way or another, in the best way I can."

Jephson looked away. The south gate was open and people were crowding out through it, pushing wheelbarrows, pulling carts, leading mules loaded down with all the foolish and useless impedimenta of their lives. Others still hovered around their homes, picking through their rubbish, packing their belongings, debating what to take and what to leave behind.

"All right," Jephson said, turning back to Emin. "I'll stay."

"Now hang on, Arthur–"

"No, Robbie, it might as well be me. If someone has to stay, better me than you or Dr. Emin. You're both needed in Wadelai. And what the hell, I've had plenty of experience working the Maxim."

· THREE ·

BUZZARDS BEGAN GATHERING. As day broke, buzzards and kites and vultures began dropping out of the sky. Unable at first to see what they were in the ghostly dimness of the false dawn, jumpy from the long night's vigil on the battlement, hearing only the mysterious sound of beating wings and throaty cluckings, fearful that dervishes might be sneaking up to attack, the askaris on the rampart above the south gate opened fire on them. But the firing stopped with the coming of morning, when in the cool gray-blue light that slowly materialized objects on the surrounding desert plain, the big, ponderous carrion birds were revealed for what they actually were. As ugly as creatures out of a nightmare with their small bald heads and beady eyes and hooked yellow beaks and obscenely fleshy, pendulous wattles, as macabre as morticians in their garb of dusty black feathers with white ruffs at their stretched naked necks, they alit clumsily on the bloated corpses of the dervish dead strewn everywhere beneath the battlements on the surrounding desert plain. The sight of them horrified Jephson. There were hundreds of them, thousands of them, descending one by one out of black squadrons circling ominously overhead, descending with grasping razor-sharp talons to pluck at the eyes and tear at the mouths and feed in the rectums of the hundreds and thousands of corpses of the dervish dead below.

Where had they come from? Why had they come now? For more than a month they had stayed away, had resisted the feast of rotting flesh laid out for them by the battle for Duffile. What had changed? Why did they feel safe to come and feast now? Jephson scanned the horizon through his field glasses. Nothing seemed changed. Under the vast bowl of the steadily brightening cloudless sky the plain was still. Not so much as a plume of dust disturbed the arid expanse. For all he could see, the dervish army had remained in its camp a mile away. For all he could tell, the dervish army was still asleep. But something must have changed. Otherwise the carrion birds wouldn't have come.

He had been awake all night after the *Khedive*'s departure, overseeing the exodus from the station, doing his level best to hurry the motley caravans down the road to Wadelai so as to be able to get away himself. Now with daybreak the exodus ceased. The people wouldn't go out of the station in broad daylight. As dangerous as they regarded going out at night, they were sure that going out in broad daylight would be suicide. So the south gate was once again shut and bolted, and those who still hadn't managed to get away returned to their homes, dragging their pathetic loads and luggage with them. There were still about 300 of them. They were by and large the dregs of Duffile: servants, orphans, widows, the poor, the old, the infirm. Some had rickety carts they had hammered together out of lumber scraps, others had wheelbarrows for trundling bricks, and there were also a few mangy donkeys and oxen among them; but mainly these were people who would have to make the long, treacherous retreat to Wadelai on foot, carrying their belongings on their backs. It would be at least another night, possibly two, before the last of them would leave.

Jephson went down from the rampart. The buzzards and kites and vultures circled above the station too but they didn't come down into the station itself. There was no food for them in the station. After the last tremendous battle the week before, the place had been cleaned up at least to that extent, the dervish corpses thrown into the river, the dead of Duffile buried. But, even so, with the place half-wrecked and almost totally abandoned, with the soldiers gone and the battlements unmanned and the spiked mountain guns pointing at the sky and the mosque destroyed and the roofs of houses fire-charred and the brick walls of barracks caved in and every sort of junk littering the streets and the remaining inhabitants huddling in the rubble amid swarms of flies, staring at him with desperate, silent appeal as he passed, the eerie sense of foreboding, an icy feeling of impending disaster grew. Perhaps he was being foolish; perhaps his shivering unease was the result of being alone, of not having Nelson or Dr. Emin to talk to but he couldn't shake it. It gripped his heart as he made his way through the ruined station to the waterfront.

The small boat in which Jephson and the askaris and the Maxim were to follow the *Khedive* to Wadelai once the last of the people had cleared Duffile—a round-bottom dory of rough-hewn ambatch boards with four sets of oars and oarlocks, a squared-off stern, and a long pointed prow—was tied up to one of the pilings of the steamer jetty. Two askaris armed with Winchester repeaters guarded it. Altogether, ten askaris plus the three-man Maxim gun crew had been left behind with Jephson. It was a ridiculously small number with which to defend the station in the event of an attack, but Jephson was willing to do with even two fewer in order to keep the dory guarded. He knew perfectly well what would happen if he didn't. The dory would be stolen. Even now, twenty or thirty of the people remaining in the station milled about on the landing stage eyeing it covetously, doubtless scheming how to lay their hands on it and, in it, make their escape to the south.

"Get away from here. All of you, get the bloody hell away from here." Jephson pushed through the crowd with a sudden surge of anger. All of a sudden he hated them, hated their laziness, hated their hanging about, hated them for still being here. It was because they still were here that he still was here, and he hated still being here; he was afraid of being here. "For God's sake, don't you buggers have anything better to do?"

The people on the landing stage moved away. But they didn't move far away. They hovered along the riverfront. They stayed by the river. The river was their hope. The river was their dream. It provided such a direct and quick and easy way to the south; it provided so much safer a road to Wadelai than overland—if they could only find the means to travel on it. Would they try to seize the dory by force? There certainly were enough of them to overwhelm the two askaris. Many would be wounded and killed in any such attempt but enough would get past the askaris to seize the boat and make their escape in it. Maybe the smart thing to do was remove the oars and oarlocks. But that wouldn't stop them; they'd push off anyway and find some other means of propelling themselves. Well then, maybe he should post a few more askaris on the jetty or, even better, bring down the Maxim. But that was ridiculous. Jesus, what was he thinking? If he did that, then what was the point of staying here at all? The point of staying here was to protect the station, not the boat. And besides, these people would never attempt to seize it. How could he imagine such a thing? Just look at them. Dear God, what a pathetic lot they were: old men with canes, withered hags, lost children, a few big lads suffering from fever or wounds from the fighting. There was nothing to fear from them. He should feel sorry for them. He had to stop being so jumpy.

He went back to the Maxim on the rampart above the south gate. The askaris there were having breakfast. There was at least that. Whatever else was awful about this place, there was no lack of food. For all that the refugees had taken with them in their flight to Wadelai, they had been able to take only a small part of the station's provisions. The storehouses were still well stocked, and goats and fowls ran loose in the streets. The askaris looted with a clear conscience. They had a cooking fire going on the rampart with spits of goat meat roasting over it and a kettle boiling rice. The Maxim was unattended. There was no reason for it to be attended. Nothing was happening. But why wasn't anything happening? In God's name, why didn't the dervishes do something? It didn't make sense. None of it made sense. And it was this very senselessness that was so unnerving.

"Bwana."

Jephson whirled around. But it was only one of the askaris bringing him breakfast, a bowl of the rice and roasted meat, a cup of tea. He took them and then discovered that he couldn't manage both while standing up. He either had to sit down or set the cup or the bowl down, and for an idiotic moment he couldn't decide which to do. Come on, man, what's the matter with you? You'll be out of here by tomorrow, the day after at the latest. What does another day or two matter? He sat down on a sandbag and, balancing the bowl on his knees, began sipping the tea. Yes, another day or two. In another day or two he'd be on his way to Wadelai. But who could say what might happen in another day or two? Anything could happen. He could be killed in another day or two. And for what? To protect some lazy kaffirs who shouldn't be here anyway, who should have left long before this. It wasn't worth it. Jesus, it wasn't. And, besides, what good would it do anyway? It wouldn't do any good. Nothing would do any good now. Something was wrong. Something had gone terribly wrong. That was why the dervishes didn't attack. That was why the carrion birds had come.

And why Mr. Stanley hadn't.

He stood up abruptly at the sudden jolt of this thought and knocked over the bowl of food on his knees. Yes, that was why Mr. Stanley hadn't come. Because something had gone terribly wrong. The askari who had served him stooped down to pick up the bowl.

"Leave it."

"I fetch more, Bwana."

"No, forget it. We're getting out of here."

The askari straightened up in surprise. "*Kumbe? Sasa?*"

"*Ndiyo. Sasa.* Come on, let's go. All of you, on your feet. Let's get the gun down to the jetty."

The askaris were tough boys, hard cases, savage fighters. When Nelson had selected them to remain behind with Jephson, they hadn't raised a word of complaint. But they no more liked the idea of staying in Duffile than Jephson did, and they weren't about to argue with this order of his now. They broke off their breakfast and came to their feet with alacrity and set about limbering the Maxim and gathering up their gear and kicking out the cooking fire with enthusiasm. Jephson scrambled down from the rampart.

"Open the gate."

People looked up, looked around, came out of their houses.

"Open the gate, I say."

More people emerged from the station's rubble and gathered in its littered streets to see what the white man was shouting about. But none responded to his command. So he did it himself, hauled back the south gate's heavy timber bolt, pushed out its heavy double doors.

"The gate is open. And there is the road, the road to Wadelai. It is the road to safety. Fetch your belongings and take the road. Fetch your belongings and go to Wadelai."

They looked at him as if he were crazy. He felt himself that he was crazy. He knew they wouldn't go. He knew damn well that nothing in the world would get them to leave the station in broad daylight. But he also knew that this much he had to do before he abandoned them. For his own sake, for the peace of his sleep in the nights to come, he knew he had to be able to tell himself that he had tried to get them to leave the station before he ran out on them.

"Listen to me, effendis. I beg you to listen to me. You must go to Wadelai. You must go now. You can remain here no longer. You can remain here not another day, not another hour longer. There is danger on every side of you here. There is danger above you here. Look above you. Do you not see the buzzards in the sky? Do you not see how the vultures fly? You must make haste. There isn't a moment to lose. Fetch your belongings and go to Wadelai. Fetch your belongings and save yourselves."

He said these things in a garble of English and Swahili and the few words of Arabic he had picked up, so they understood him only imperfectly. But what they understood caused them to draw away from him as they would draw away from a raving lunatic. In desperation he grabbed the arm of one of those who was drawing away. It was no one in particular. It was only someone who was standing closest to him at the moment, someone to persuade, thinking that if he could persuade even one to go the others might follow. It was an old man. But as soon as he grabbed him, the old man started screaming.

"Stop it, *mzee*. For God's sake, keep still. I mean you no harm. I mean only to help you. I tell you, *mzee*, you must flee to Wadelai. You must gather up your people and flee to Wadelai while there still is time."

But the old man wouldn't stop screaming. And then an old hag started screaming too. She probably was his wife and wanted to get him out of the white man's clutches. But she didn't dare come near. She was afraid that she too would be grabbed and flung out of the station to the vultures and the kites. So she just went on screaming in chorus with the old man's screaming.

"Oh, Jesus."

Jephson released the old man's arm; and the old man dashed to his wife, and hugging each other, they both went on screaming hysterically. By now the askaris had hauled the Maxim down from the rampart, and they stopped to see what all the screaming was about.

"Go on. Get the gun into the boat. Effendis, please, listen to me. You must listen to what I say."

But no one was listening. Seeing the askaris wheeling the Maxim down to the waterfront, seeing them with their packs on their backs and their rifles slung and lugging the ammunition boxes and their blankets and provisions and other gear, the crowd caught on to what was happening and went rushing down to the waterfront too.

Jephson went rushing down after them. "Stay away from there. I'm warning you. They'll fire on you. I'll give them the order to fire on you."

But it was all part of his craziness, the panic that had suddenly seized him. There was no need to fire on these people. The poor devils represented no threat. Once on the landing stage, all they did was watch in stupefied disbelief as the askaris loaded the Maxim into the dory and jumped in after it with the rest of their kit and equipment. And then they began to moan.

"For God's sake, listen to me. Why don't you listen to me? I tell you, you must take the road to Wadelai. You must take it now while you still have the chance."

But they didn't take the road to Wadelai. Perhaps they would that night when darkness again had fallen. Now they simply moaned in despair.

"Suit yourselves, you bloody damn fools. Stay here if you want. Stay here and die here if you want. But I'll be damned if I will." Jephson untied the painter and got into the dory.

The Maxim, with its three-man gun crew, was positioned in the stern, where it could cover their retreat upriver. Two askaris were in the prow with Winchester repeaters. The remaining eight took the oars, their rifles beside them on the thwarts. It made for cramped quarters for a journey of at least six days, but the boat was sound. It bore the weight of the men and equipment without shipping water, and Jephson reckoned that after a day or two they'd be far enough clear of Duffile and the dervishes to risk spending the nights ashore.

"Push off. What are you waiting for? Push off."

The askaris of the gun crew pushed away from the wharf, and those on the thwarts dug in with their oars and the boat shot out into the Nile.

"Make for the east bank."

Jephson went up into the prow. They'd be safer along the east bank. It would be harder to find open channels along the east bank, but their chances of coming under the dervish guns would be less.

"Pull, you boys. Put your backs into it."

Planting his feet wide to brace himself against the surge and buck of the dory against the current, he raised his field glasses and studied both banks, the bulrushes and ambatch thickets on the east, the rocky hills and bluffs on the west. There were no signs of dervish guns on either. But who could tell? Anything was possible. Nothing made sense.

"Pull, *warafiki*. Pull for all you're worth."

He looked back. They were making good headway. Duffile's jetty was receding rapidly. And so were the people standing on it. They had stopped their moaning. Or at least he could no longer hear them. They simply stared after the departing dory. He turned away from them. He was aware of what he was doing. He didn't pretend to himself that it was anything different. He knew very well the phrases by which it was called: desertion of his post, disobedience to orders, dereliction of duty. He was ratting out on the poor devils he was meant to protect, like the meanest of cowards.

But he didn't care. At that moment all he cared about was getting away. For at that moment he knew that the expedition had come undone.

Wadelai was both an easier and more difficult place to defend, what with the fort on a hill about a quarter-mile to the west of the river and the station itself down by the riverside. Once in the fort, the defenders would be virtually unassailable; cavalry charges couldn't realistically be launched up the steep slopes of the hill—the horses would never make it—and even the most fanatic foot soldiers would have little chance of reaching the battlements alive. But it also was true that once in the fort the defenders would be in a box, cut off from the outside world, vulnerable to a protracted siege and with no way to escape when their ammunition ran out. Peering at the station from the dory's prow as the askaris rowed toward it, Jephson tried to see what arrangements Nelson had made to solve this dilemma. But he couldn't see that Nelson had made any arrangements. All seemed utter chaos in Wadelai.

This was a week after the departure from Duffile. That it had been an uneventful journey—that the dervishes hadn't attacked; that indeed they hadn't even been seen, that the caravans of refugees from Duffile, which had been seen making their weary way south along the Nile's west bank, were apparently being allowed to pass unmolested, that the people Jephson had abandoned in Duffile most probably would be allowed to do the same, and therefore there was no obvious reason for his panic—none of this had calmed Jephson's fears or eased his foreboding. Throughout those seven days toiling against the current through the swampy channels of the Nile, he had remained convinced that something terrible had gone wrong, and now what he saw in Wadelai only confirmed him in this.

The place was in an uproar. People streamed up and down the hillsides, jammed the station, overflowed the waterfront, mobbed the steamer jetty, swarmed on and off the steamer tied up at the jetty. But there seemed no sensible purpose to all this activity. Not only did it seem that no preparations had been made for the station's defense, but none of the frenzied hustle and bustle seemed directed at doing so even now. The battlements of the fort were unmanned. The crops in the fields were unharvested. Sheep and cattle grazed untended in those fields. But what was worse, the equipment and armaments that had been evacuated from Duffile, the kegs of gunpowder, the crates of cartridges, the boxes of percussion caps, the mountain guns themselves, which had been unloaded from the *Khedive* at least a week before, still stood on the jetty where they had been unloaded. Why hadn't they been hauled up to the fort, where they'd be of some use? Why weren't they at least being sandbagged in emplacements down around the station now? Jephson scanned the chaotic throngs, trying to spot Nelson or Emin among them, but it was late in the day, and approaching from the Nile's east bank, the sun was in his eyes.

"You there, grab hold."

The dory came alongside the jetty on the upstream side, the side opposite that against which the *Khedive* was moored; and as the askaris shipped their oars, Jephson tossed the boat's painter to a soldier standing there. The fellow, a regular from the Wadelai garrison–most of the people on the jetty, Jephson realized, were Shukri Aga's soldiers–caught the painter, more out of instinct or surprise than by design, and Jephson hopped up on the jetty. The askaris scrambled out after him.

"Where's Captain Nelson?"

The soldier didn't respond. He didn't have a chance to respond. Almost as soon as Jephson was on the jetty a commotion broke out. Apparently no one had noticed the dory while it was making its way crossriver; but now that it was here, it became the center of attention and there was a mad rush for it. Jephson was pushed aside. One of the askaris was knocked into the river. This could have had dire consequences, as there were crocodiles in the river. Moreover, the chap got himself trapped between the dory and the jetty; but except for his own mates, who pulled him out, no one paid the slightest heed to his shouts. All the soldiers cared about was the boat.

Jephson's first thought was of the crowd on the landing stage at Duffile, their pathetic yearning for a boat in which to flee. But that couldn't be what so exercised these soldiers. They didn't need this boat in order to flee. There were plenty of boats here. The *Khedive* itself was here. Besides, flee where? There was nowhere to flee from here. This was the last station. This was where they would have to make their last stand. After this there was only wilderness. And then it dawned on him that of course it wasn't the boat they were after. It was what was in the boat: the Maxim, the terrible killing machine, the famous killing machine, the magical killing machine that had held off the dervishes in Duffile. Its reputation had gone before it.

"Hold on. Now you just hold on there. Leave that gun where it is."

Jephson tried to get back to the boat. But the crowd was too thick. He was shoved out of the way. Soldiers were jumping into the boat, hauling at the Maxim, heaving its boxes of ammunition out onto the jetty. It wasn't random behavior. An officer was in charge, an Egyptian barking orders. Jephson recognized him. He was from the Wadelai garrison, Shukri Aga's second-in-command. What was his name?

"You, lieutenant. Tell those men to leave that gun alone. That's not their gun. That's Bula Matari's gun."

"Let them have it, Arthur."

Jephson spun around. Nelson was hurrying out on the jetty.

"Robbie, for Christ sake, man, what's going on here? Have these chaps gone crazy?"

"Yes, they've gone crazy. They've gone completely crazy. They've arrested Dr. Emin."

"What?"

"Come away from there. Come on, on the double. You, askaris, fall in." Nelson grabbed hold of Jephson's arm; and with the askaris following, carrying whatever of their kit they had managed to get out of the boat before the soldiers had swarmed in, he walked Jephson rapidly off the jetty into the station.

"What do you mean they arrested Dr. Emin?"

"Just that. They arrested him. They've got him confined to his quarters up in the fort."

"But he's their mudir."

"Not any more. They've stripped him of the office and title."

"But why?"

"I don't know. And what's more, they don't either. They don't have the slightest idea what they're doing. It's what you said. They've gone crazy. They've just gone plain crazy."

They passed quickly through the station, heading for the path that led up the hillside to the fort, a mob scene all around them. Refugees streaming in from Duffile and the other northern stations clogged the streets with their cattle and carts and wagons and donkeys and mountains of baggage. Makeshift shelters—tents, mud huts, lean-tos, thrown up any which way—cluttered the marketplaces. The din was terrific—the lowing of oxen, the cries of children, the yapping of dogs—and the smell was awful, the smell of garbage and ordure and panic.

"When did it happen?"

"As soon as we got here. They were waiting on the jetty. They grabbed us as soon as we came off the steamer. Faratch Ajoke's the ringleader."

"Faratch Ajoke?"

"Shukri Aga's second-in-command."

"The Egyptian back there? The one who's seized the Maxim?"

"Yes. He's the ringleader, at least of one of the factions. He had me arrested too. But he seems to have forgotten about it. There's nothing organized about any of this. The whole thing's a mess. So far, anyway, they let me come and go as I please."

"But what about Shukri Aga? What does he have to say about it?"

"Nothing much. He's lying low. They got this harebrained idea into their heads that they can buy off the dervishes with Emin. They've talked themselves into believing that that's what the dervishes really want, the Pasha, and that once they've got him they'll call off the invasion and take him back to the Khalifa in Khartoum."

"Oh, Jesus."

"But they don't know how to do it. Actually what it is, they don't have the nerve to do it. No one is willing to go to the dervishes and make them the proposition, offer them the exchange. They know what happened to that delegation from Rejaf. So all they do is run around here like madmen, arguing with each other. Every day it's something else. Every day someone has a new scheme. The other day it was silver bullets."

"Silver bullets?"

"Yes. Some bright bastard, I think it was the apothecary, Vita Hassan, announced that the dervishes were helpless against silver bullets, that a delegation armed with silver bullets would have nothing to fear; and so everyone went chasing around looking for silver to cast into bullets. Now it's the Maxim. They're telling each other that a delegation would be safe with the Maxim, that the dervishes are terrified of the Maxim. Tomorrow it'll be something else."

They crossed the plank bridge over the moat on the east side of the fort and entered by the east gate. The gate stood wide open. No sentries were posted on the earthwork rampart above it. No one challenged them when they entered. It was a shade less hectic inside. To the left, on the upriver side of the parade ground where the garrison's barracks were located, a number of the wives and children and concubines of the soldiers were scurrying around at God only knew what pointless tasks, and several of the station's officers and officials were gathered in the *barazan* at the center of the parade ground, carrying on some kind of noisy meeting. But on the right, downriver, the Pasha's compound, secluded in fruit orchards and flower gardens, was quiet.

"That damn Italian, Casati," Nelson went on, steering Jephson toward Emin's compound, "he's the one who set the whole blasted thing off. The damn fool couldn't keep his mouth shut. When he passed through here on his way back to us in Duffile from Nsabe, he let everyone know there was no sign of Mr. Stanley or the rear column. And that did it. Things were touchy enough as it was. These buggers have been on the edge of mutiny ever since that peacock dervish with his tongue cut out showed up here, but they still might have been willing to dig in and put up a fight if they thought relief was on the way. But thanks to Casati, the way he talked—you know, you heard him at Duffile—they've given up all hope of that. They're convinced it was all a ruse, a pack of lies, that there never was a relief column or, if there was, it came to grief in the Ituri."

"Where is he? Is he under arrest too?"

"Yes, like me. They've forgotten about him too. He could come and go if he liked. But he's chosen to stay in his quarters. He's in one of his sulks. He says he's making himself ready for death."

"That's a great help."

"Yes." Nelson turned around to the askaris who had been following them up from the river. "*Nendeni kule, warafiki.*" He pointed to a *boma* of mud-plastered bamboo huts located just outside the row of lime and lemon trees that marked off one side of Emin's compound. The askaris and Wanyamwezis who had returned to Wadelai aboard the *Khedive* with Emin and Nelson were billeted there. Jephson's askaris, in a state of confusion, went over and were met by the subdued greetings of their equally confused mates.

"Let's go to Dr. Emin, Arthur. He's been asking about you every day. I don't think they'll stop us from seeing him."

Jephson followed Nelson into the compound. No one did stop them. No one was around to stop them. If Emin was meant to be a prisoner, the guard, like everything else going on in Wadelai, was a thoroughly disorganized affair. It seemed to Jephson that Emin could walk out of the place whenever he wanted to. But evidently he didn't want to. He too wasn't around. Jephson and Nelson went up on the veranda and looked into his house.

The interior was dim. The last rays of the sun streamed in through the shutters of the windows at the back but no longer reached across the front room to the table in the corner where Emin was seated. There was a lantern on the table; and Emin, the wandering Jew from Silesia dressed in fez and caftan and looking the very picture of an Arabian astrologer, was writing in a notebook by its light. He looked up and squinted nearsightedly through the thick lenses of his spectacles at the two figures who had appeared on his veranda.

"Who's there?"

At the sound of his anxious query, his daughter, Faridah, the beautiful, dusky Faridah, the mysterious daughter by an Abyssinian princess, stepped quickly into the parlor from another room. Her expression, as Jephson remembered it always to be, was somber, serious, so out of keeping with her radiant youth. Although they hadn't seen each other in more than four months, she looked at Jephson with no change in that expression, with no particular sign of pleased recognition, he was sorry to see.

"It is Jephson effendi, father," she said quite matter-of-factly. "And Captain Nelson."

"Jephson effendi? Arthur? Arthur, my boy." Emin jumped up and came around the table to grasp both of Jephson's hands. "My boy, my boy, you are back. You are back safe and sound."

"Yes, Pasha."

"I'm so glad to see you, my boy. So glad. You've been weighing heavily on my mind these last few days. I have often thought how wrong it was of me to allow you to remain alone in such a dangerous place and how grateful I am to you that you did, for the sake of my people. All went well, I take it."

"Sir?"

"The dervishes didn't attack?"

"No, they didn't attack."

"And you saw everyone get safely away?"

Jephson paused a second, and his face flushed. He had expected the question of course. And he had every intention of lying in reply. He had made up his mind during the journey up the Nile that when he was directly questioned about his actions in Duffile he'd point-blank lie about them. He was pretty sure he could get away with it. After all, even though he had behaved as the basest of cowards, even though he had run away, the people he had been left behind to protect almost certainly had gotten safely out of Duffile. The dervishes almost certainly had allowed them to get out. But now that the question actually was put, he discovered he didn't have to lie. In the present circumstances, another answer occurred to him, which wasn't a lie but which as effectively dodged the truth and saved his face.

"Why do you care?"

"Eh?"

"Why do you care whether or not they got safely away? Why should you give a fig whether or not they live or die? Look how they've treated you, Pasha. Look how they've repaid you for caring about them. They've arrested you. They've deposed you as their mudir. They're scheming to sell you to the dervishes—these people you care so much about, these people whose safety and welfare and happiness is so uppermost in your mind. I'm only surprised they haven't already cut off your head and taken it as a peace offering to Omar Saleh."

Emin was still holding Jephson's hands. He released them now and went back around the table and sat down and removed his spectacles and began polishing them distractedly on the hem of his caftan. Faridah went to stand behind him, resting a hand protectively on his shoulder.

"Is there coffee, *Schatze?* Bring us coffee." Emin replaced his spectacles. "Sit down, Arthur. Sit down, Captain."

Nelson pulled a chair up to the table, but Jephson remained standing. Emin closed the notebook on the table and carefully put it aside and, by doing this, avoided for a moment looking into Jephson's eyes.

"It is a terrible thing they have done, Arthur, I know. It is a terrible, disgraceful, ungrateful thing they have done, not only to me but also to you and Captain Nelson and your askaris and Wanyamwezis, who fought so bravely for them at Duffile, and to Bula Matari and Surgeon Parke and Mr. Hoffman and all the officers and men of the expedition, who have come so far and suffered so much in order to help them. I am ashamed of them, my boy. I cannot tell you how profoundly ashamed I am of them, and how angry I am with them." Now he did look at Jephson, and there was a wistful appeal in his expression. "But we must be patient with them, my boy. They will come to their senses. They are children, frightened children. They do not know what they are doing. A few bad apples in the lot, a handful of troublemakers among them, stirred them up to this insanity. But when Bula Matari gets back—"

"When Bula Matari gets back? Pasha, we don't know when Bula Matari will get back. At the very best we can hope that he will get back in a month. And by then it might be too late. By then these buggers might have sold you to the dervishes. By then the dervishes might have attacked. This place is totally undefended, Pasha. There isn't a single soldier on the battlements. Not one of the mountain guns is manned. If the dervishes attack now, the condition this place is in, they'll take it in a minute. And then it won't matter a damn when Bula Matari gets back."

"I know, I know. It is precisely what I keep telling them. At least that. At least defend yourselves. Do with me whatever you like. What you do with me isn't important. Sell me to Omar Saleh if you think that will help. But man the guns. Put the soldiers in the lines. Defend yourselves. For the love of Allah, defend yourselves. But they won't listen. They won't listen to me. They won't listen to Captain Nelson."

"Well then, let's get out of here, Pasha. Then let's just get the hell out of here."

Before Emin could respond to this, Faridah returned with a brass tray bearing a pot of coffee, cups, linen, bread and honey, and a bowl of fruit. She set these down on the table in front of her father, and instinctively, out of his innate courtesy, he began pouring out the coffee for his guests.

"Do you hear what I say, Pasha? Let's just go. Let's go while we still have the chance. If they won't listen to you anyway, if they won't make any effort to defend themselves, if they're such damn fools as to believe that all the dervishes want is your head and once they've got it they'll withdraw to Khartoum and leave Equatoria in peace, what's the point of staying? What could we accomplish by staying? All we'd accomplish is to get ourselves massacred along with all the rest of them."

"Where would we go?" This was Nelson. He had taken a cup of coffee from Emin and turned away from the table to look up at Jephson. Obviously Jephson's idea struck a sympathetic chord.

"Nsabe," Jephson replied. And now he too pulled a chair up to the table. "The way these chaps have the place guarded, we could get to Nsabe without any trouble. We'll just steal out at night and take Casati with us. Maybe we can even get away on the steamer. We can wait for Mr. Stanley there. We can wait for him there just as well as we can here. If he gets back in time, before the dervishes attack, while there's still some hope of saving the station, well and good, we'll return. If not, well, we'll at least have had the good sense of not throwing our lives away for nothing."

"Will you take honey in your coffee, my boy?"

"Pasha! For God's sake, Pasha, listen to me."

"I am listening to you, my boy. And I agree with everything

you say. I fully agree with it. I think you and Captain Nelson and Captain Casati and your askaris and Wanyamwezis should go to Nsabe. I am sure you are right. You won't have any difficulty. No one will try to stop you. And there is nothing further you can do here. You have done everything you can. You have done far more than anyone could have required of you. You have risked your lives. You have fought like lions. And I will forever be grateful to you for it. But as for me . . ." Emin again removed his spectacles and rubbed his eyes. "As for me, I will stay. This is my home. These are my people. I will not leave it. I will not abandon them. It is my place to share their fate."

"And Faridah?"

Emin lowered his hand from his eyes.

"Is it her place to share their fate as well? Is it her place to be massacred along with them? Or worse yet, to be dragged off to the Khalifa's harem?"

Emin looked around at the young girl standing behind him.

"It is my place to share my father's fate," she said.

"Oh, Jesus." Jephson stood up and stalked out of the house.

Evening now was fast approaching. The great crimson ball of the sun had sunk low on the horizon, casting long blue shadows through the compound from the base of the fruit trees; and the moon had risen over the river, bringing a chill to the air. To the north, beyond the orchards and flower gardens but still within the compound, was the pretty gazebo in which Jephson had stayed when he had first come to Wadelai. How long ago that seemed. How pleasant those days had been. He could see its peaked thatch roof above the branches of the fig and pomegranate trees that enclosed it, and he thought how much he'd like to go there now and get out of his filthy uniform and have a bath and put on his caftan—Did it still hang in the wardrobe?—and lie down on the *angarep* and go to sleep and forget about all of this. But then Nelson came out of the house.

"Well?"

"He won't go."

"And what about us?"

Nelson shrugged.

"I've got a very bad feeling about all this, Robbie. I think something terrible has gone wrong. I don't know what. Maybe with the rear column. Maybe they got lost or something and Mr. Stanley can't find them and the dervishes know about it and that's why they're taking their own sweet time about finishing us off.

They don't press any of their attacks. They let us get out of Duffile without any trouble. Doesn't that strike you as queer?"

Nelson nodded.

"I think we should get out of here, Robbie."

"And leave him?"

"You said he won't go. What are we supposed to do? Take him with us by force?"

"No."

"So?"

"So we'll stay."

Jephson turned away.

"We can't leave him, Arthur. You know that. We can't just rat out on him."

· FOUR ·

EXCEPT THAT it could be the death of them all, the mutiny at Wadelai was a farce. It had no leader, no plan of action; it was all anarchy and confusion. As Jephson came to see in the following days, the scheme to sell Emin to the dervishes, while supported by the most fanatical of the mutineers, was actually only one of a number of schemes and plots roiling the place, none any more sensible or likely to save their skins. All discipline had broken down. No one obeyed anyone's orders. Everyone came and went as they pleased. There was a great deal of drinking of palm wine and *m'tama* beer and in the wake of the drinking a great deal of drunken brawling and shooting off of guns and terrorizing civilians. The local Loor and Shuli tribes, taking advantage of the disorder, also revolted, some going over to the dervishes, others turning to freebooting and raiding the station's cattle and fields. Trade with them ceased, and the price of goods in the bazaars doubled. Hoarding became endemic. With refugees still streaming in from the north, there were riots over living space, battles for food, looting and burglaries, the threat of cholera. And through it all the fort's battlements remained unmanned and the station undefended.

In the face of this chaos, even Emin's optimism gave way. Although his imprisonment was anything but close—the soldiers assigned to guard him were as undisciplined as the rest—he spent his days in his compound with Faridah, writing in his notebooks, working on his scientific experiments, cataloguing his collections of stuffed birds and pinned butterflies and dried flowers, shut off from the turmoil outside. This angered Jephson, as virtually everything going on now angered him. He felt that in this vacuum of leadership Emin, if he insisted on staying here, should at least try to assert *his* leadership, should go out among his beloved people and command them in no uncertain terms what to do. But this wasn't Emin's style. He had never commanded. This gentle professorial man had neither the temperament nor the talent for command. All these years he had governed by reason, persuasion, compromise, not by orders and commands. But in this situation, reason and persuasion and compromise were of no damn use. This situation demanded not a fatherly figure, not a benign schoolmaster, not a sweetly logical man but a tyrant, a Caesar, a Stanley, who would seize the reins of this runaway beast and by brute force bring it to heel. And this Emin was not and knew himself that he was not.

But there was something else as well. The mutiny had come as a terrible shock. He had never imagined that his people would turn against him in this perfidious fashion; and the betrayal of the trust and affection between them of so many years' standing had dealt him a shattering blow, had inflicted a wound to his pride and confidence far deeper than he was willing to admit. And so, as much as anything else, he remained in the seclusion of his quiet compound in order to save himself the humiliation of confronting his people and experiencing their contemptible ingratitude at first-hand.

Jephson and Nelson, who had reclaimed Jephson's gazebo in the compound for their billet, took their meals with him. These were dreary affairs. As Emin's cookboy and houseboy and other servants—all of the Loor tribe—had deserted, the fetching and hauling and cleaning and cooking around the place fell to Faridah. More somber and withdrawn than ever, worn weary by worry and work, she came and went like a wraith, watching her father with pain in her eyes. He ate little. He pushed his food around his plate. He suffered from headaches. And his conversation, once so lively and bright with anecdotes and observations, circled monotonously, broodingly around and around the same pathetic irritating themes, the need for patience, the belief that the people would eventually come to their senses and restore him to power.

From time to time Casati joined them. His presence certainly did nothing to enliven things. Deep in his funk, he had little to say, which in itself was a blessing. Convinced that he was soon to die, he daily grew more filthy in his personal habits. He didn't bathe. His clothing stank. He picked at his nose. His fingernails were long and black. It was disgusting to have to eat at the same table with him. As soon as they decently could, Jephson and Nelson fled these gloom-filled occasions and returned to their vigil, either up on the battlement looking north for a sign of Omar Saleh and his army, or down on the waterfront looking south for a sign of Stanley and the rear column. It had all come down to that. Which would get there first? Unfortunately, Jephson did not believe it would be Stanley.

"What are we going to do, Robbie? We've got to do something."

They were crossing the parade ground on their way back to their billet from the waterfront. It was midmorning, hot and bright and dusty; and yet another of those noisy, pointless, interminable meetings was taking place on the steps and veranda of the *barazan* at the center of the parade ground. Shukri Aga was participating in this one. So were Faratch Ajoke; Vita Hassan, the station's apothecary; Signor Marco, a stranded Greek trader from Khartoum; a few of the station's principal merchants; the garrison commanders from Muggi and Chor Ayu; and several clerks from the old provincial government. Almost all were drunk.

"Look at those stupid bastards. For God's sake, will you just look at them. We're going to go down with them, Robbie. We're going to wind up having our throats cut with all of them if we don't do something."

"Hey, where are you going?"

Jephson, his anger once again on the boil, had started toward the *barazan*.

"Hold on, Arthur. You're not going to do any good there. You know that. You can't talk any sense to those people when they're full of pombe like that."

But Jephson kept going, and with a shrug Nelson went after him. Shukri Aga was the first to notice their approach. To call what was going on at the *barazan* a meeting was to dignify it out of all proportion. What it was actually was a shouting match, with everyone shouting at the same time and no one listening to what was being shouted. So when Shukri Aga, on seeing the two Englishmen coming over, broke off *his* shouting, the others didn't particularly miss his contribution to the general din. It took a few minutes before they too realized that Jephson and Nelson had joined them; and one by one they fell into a suspicious silence. Most were seated, either in the wicker chairs on the *barazan*'s veranda or on upturned crates or on the veranda's plank floor. Some now stood up. Most, however, were too drunk to stand up. Faratch Ajoke, who had been sitting in the largest chair on the veranda, was one of those who stood up, although unsteadily, a gourd of pombe in his hand.

"Well, what have you decided?" Jephson asked. "After all your talk, have you decided anything?"

No one replied. Shukri Aga, who might not have been drunk at all, or at least not as drunk as the others, looked away in obvious embarrassment.

"You still haven't decided anything? An army of ten thousand dervishes is thundering down on you. They will be upon you in a week, a fortnight at the latest. And you still haven't decided what to do? You sit around here day in and day out, drinking and quarreling and scheming and plotting, and you still haven't decided on a plan to save yourselves? What are you? Women, children, or men? No, men you are not. That is plain to see."

"Hold your tongue, effendi," Faratch Ajoke said.

Jephson turned to him. "Or what? Hold my tongue or what, Faratch Ajoke? What if I do not choose to hold my tongue?"

"Arthur."

"No, I'm not afraid of his threats. Why should I be afraid of threats from this . . . woman? He warns me to hold my tongue? I laugh at his warning. I spit in the mouth of his warning." Jephson suddenly started up the steps to the veranda. "So, Faratch Ajoke? So? You see I do not choose to hold my tongue."

This startled the tipsy Egyptian, and he instinctively took a step back, stumbling against his chair. The others also stepped back. Only Shukri Aga had the wits to come forward and interpose himself between the two.

"Stand out of my way, Vakeel."

"Jephson effendi, please."

"Stand out of my way, I say. I do not speak to you. I speak to this woman hiding behind you. I speak to this coward who would sell the Pasha to the dervishes."

"For God's sake, Arthur, come down from there."

Jephson wasn't armed. Faratch Ajoke, on the other hand, was wearing both a pistol and a saber and, doubtless, if it came to it, wouldn't hesitate to use them. But Jephson didn't care. He wanted a fight. In his frustration with the state of affairs in Wadelai, in his anger and fear at being trapped in the place by his sense of loyalty to Emin, the satisfaction of a fight, with anyone, about anything, would be a relief.

"No, Faratch Ajoke, I do not choose to hold my tongue. I call you a woman. I call you a coward. You who would sell the Pasha to the dervishes. You with the brilliant plan to exchange the Pasha's head for your life. Well, why don't you do it? What prevents you? You have the Maxim. You have your silver bullets. Why don't you take the Pasha to Duffile? The dervishes are in

Duffile. Take the Pasha there. Take him aboard the *Khedive* and go to Duffile and sell him to Omar Saleh. You believe it will save your life. You believe it will turn the dervishes away from Wadelai. Well, do it then. Why don't you do it? I will tell you why you don't. Because you are a woman, Faratch Ajoke. Because you are a coward. You do not have the courage to do it. You would have someone do it for you. Would you have me do it for you?"

"Come on, Arthur. That's enough of this." Nelson had come up on the veranda. He took Jephson's arm. "Let's get out of here."

But Jephson pulled away. "No. I want this woman to answer me. Answer me, Faratch Ajoke. Would you have me do it for you? Would you have me take the Pasha to Duffile? I will do it if you wish. I have the courage to do it. I am not a woman. I have no need of silver bullets. Just give me the Maxim, Faratch Ajoke, and I will take the Pasha to Duffile and sell him to Omar Saleh for you."

"How you provoke me, effendi. How unreasonably you provoke me. Be wise and do what Captain Nelson asks of you. Go with him and provoke me no further." Faratch Ajoke sat back down in the big wicker chair and with a flourish, as a gesture of dismissal and disdain, drank off the last of the beer in his pombe gourd.

"Oh, what a coward you are, Faratch Ajoke. And what a stupid coward into the bargain. After all your talk, this was the one plan you managed to devise for saving yourself, the one scheme you hit upon to turn back the dervishes. And you do not have the courage to do it. But not only that, you do not have the sense or wit to seize this opportunity when I offer to do it for you."

"Why do you speak this way, Jephson effendi?" This was Shukri Aga. A big fat man, he turned Jephson away from Faratch Ajoke and with his great bulk nudged him a step or two down from the veranda. "What is the point in speaking such nonsense to us? We know you are not serious in saying you would take the Pasha to Duffile."

"Give me the Maxim, Vakeel, and discover for yourself how serious I am."

"Why do you waste your time with him, Vakeel?" Faratch Ajoke called out. "All he means with his talk is to cause trouble among us. Send him away. Send him back to the Pasha's compound. He is under arrest in any case and has no business wandering around here causing trouble."

Shukri Aga ignored this. He continued moving Jephson off the veranda and away from the *barazan*. "I do not believe you,

Jephson effendi," he said. "I know what feelings you have for the Pasha. You would never do such a thing. You would never take him to his death."

"Then what should I do? Should I sit here dumbly like the rest of you and wait for the dervishes to come and slit my throat? No, Vakeel, I am not so anxious to die as all that."

"You no longer believe Bula Matari will return?"

"Oh, I believe he will return. I am sure he will return. But what good will it do if Wadelai has already fallen? And it will fall. I am also sure of that. Look around you, Vakeel. The battlements are unmanned. The guns we brought from Duffile still stand on the waterfront. Your soldiers won't obey you. You cannot even get them to stand watch to warn us when the dervishes come."

"That is true, but if what concerns you, Jephson effendi, is saving your life, why don't you just go away from here? Why don't you and Captain Nelson just go away. You could go away whenever you wished."

"I thought we were prisoners."

Shukri Aga shrugged. "You see what kind of prisoners you are. You come and go as you like. You could go away from here whenever you like. Who is there to stop you?"

Jephson glanced at Nelson.

"No, if saving your life was what concerned you, effendi, I am certain that both you and Captain Nelson would have gone away from here long before this. But saving your lives is not what concerns you. You are Englishmen. You are bound by your duty, by your code of honor, by loyalty to your friends. You have not gone away long before this because the Pasha would not go away with you. And you would not leave him behind. Your honor, your duty, your sense of loyalty would not permit this. So you have stayed. Despite the peril to your lives, you have stayed with the Pasha. So how can you expect me to believe that you would now sell him to the dervishes? How can you expect me to believe that you would so fly in the face of your honor? No, Jephson effendi, do not expect me to believe that. I do not. I understand what trick you have up your sleeve."

"Then you are quicker than I am, Vakeel," Nelson said. "I haven't the first idea what trick he has up his sleeve."

"I have no trick up my sleeve. I offer to take the Pasha to Duffile because no one else here has the courage to do so. I offer to sell him to the dervishes because I am willing to try anything that might hold off the dervishes until Bula Matari returns."

Shukri Aga shook his head. Then he closed his eyes and sighed. "Very well," he said. "If this is what you would have us believe, I shall see if I can persuade my friends to believe it. I shall see if I can persuade them to accept your offer, your most brave and generous offer to take the Pasha to Duffile and by that save us all from the dervishes." And having said this, he went back to the *barazan*.

"I'm not following this, Arthur. Not any of it. Will you tell me what the devil's going on?"

"I'm not sure myself. But round up our people and find the Maxim. I'm pretty sure it's still down on the jetty. I don't think they ever got around to bringing it up here. Go down there with our boys and keep an eye on it. Don't try to take it away from anyone. Just keep an eye on it so we know where it is."

"Arthur, I've got to know what this is all about. I'm not going to let you do anything to harm Dr. Emin."

"Go on, man. Just go on. There's no time to talk about it. It probably won't work anyway."

Nelson hesitated, studying Jephson quizzically. But when Jephson didn't say anything further, he headed for the *boma* outside Emin's compound where the askaris and *pagazis* were billeted. For his part, Jephson went back to the *barazan*. He didn't go all the way back. He stopped a few yards from the steps. The shouting match had resumed on the veranda. It was in Arabic, so he didn't understand much of it but could make a fair guess what it was about. His plan was full of holes. Shukri Aga had shown him just how full of holes it was. The big fat Nubian turned and looked down at him from the veranda. There was no telling what he really thought or believed about Jephson's offer. Faratch Ajoke came to the veranda's top step and also looked down at Jephson.

"You are a cunning man, effendi. You have managed to convince Shukri Aga that your offer has merit. I do not know how you have done this but you have."

"I do not understand why you do not see the merit in it as well, Faratch Ajoke."

"For a very simple reason, effendi. Because I am not so stupid as to believe that you would actually do it."

"Well then, come with me, Faratch Ajoke. Come with me to Duffile so that you can see for yourself whether or not I actually do it."

This took the Egyptian aback. Whether Jepson was bluffing or not, it in any case put him on the spot. And Shukri Aga was quick to seize the opportunity it offered.

"That seems fair," he said. "Does it not seem fair? What could be fairer?" He turned to the others and put the proposition to them in Arabic and by that set off yet another outburst of noisy argument.

"Well, Faratch Ajoke, will you come with me? Do you have the courage to come with me? Or at least the good sense to let me go alone and do the work for you?"

The Egyptian came down from the veranda. He obviously had consumed a great deal of the *m'tama* beer. He walked unsteadily and was bleary-eyed; but the rage in him, his sense of being taunted and humiliated, was cold sober. "Yes, as I say, effendi, as I say, you are a cunning man. A most cunning man."

"And you, Faratch Ajoke, what are you?"

The Egyptian came to within a single step of Jephson so they stood virtually nose to nose. Jephson steeled himself to stand his ground. Faratch Ajoke's breath was foul. His left hand gripped the pommel of his saber, his right the stock of his pistol. His whole body tilted forward at a precarious angle. Seeing the menace in the situation, Shukri Aga broke off his arguing and hurried down from the veranda.

"This was your idea, Faratch Ajoke," he said. "From the very first, it was you who said we must sell the Pasha to the dervishes. It was you who said the dervishes had come only to capture the Pasha and would return to Khartoum and leave us in peace once they had him. Was this not what you said? Was this not what you argued from the very first? Well, let us see if you are right. Let us stop arguing about it and do it. Either take the Pasha to Duffile yourself, Faratch Ajoke, or let Jephson effendi take him for us. But for the love of Allah, let us stop arguing about it and do it before it is too late."

"Shukri Aga is right. It is time to stop all this argument. We must do something while there still is time," the apothecary said, also coming down from the veranda.

And now so did the others, shouting, gesturing, clamoring to have their opinions heard.

"Come, Faratch Ajoke," Jephson said. "Let us go for the Pasha. Let us go together so that you can see I mean what I say."

The Egyptian hadn't moved. He had held his position rigidly within inches of Jephson's face. But he had begun to sweat, and his sweat stank as badly as his breath. He was on the spot all right and he knew it.

"Come," Jephson said again. "There is nothing to fear. We will have the Maxim with us, and as you know, it is a magical machine." He took firm hold of Faratch Ajoke's upper arm and started him off in the direction of Emin's compound.

Shukri Aga and the others fell in behind them, still disputing noisily among themselves; and seeing this, people from all parts of the fort broke off what they were doing and joined the procession to find out what was going on. So it was a crowd that entered the garden of Emin's compound a few minutes later and disturbed its quiet.

"Pasha."

Alerted as much by the unusual commotion outside as by Faratch Ajoke's command, Faridah stepped out on the veranda of Emin's house. Her expression immediately registered the fright she felt at the sight of the unruly crowd.

"Have the Pasha present himself, girl."

She looked at Jephson.

"Do what he says, Faridah."

She hesitated.

"At once, girl," Faratch Ajoke snapped. "Or I shall come in and fetch him myself."

"What do you want of him? He is resting."

"I haven't come here to discuss that with you, girl. Have him present himself at once."

Again the girl looked at Jephson, looked at him hard. He knew she was looking at him for some sign of reassurance. But he didn't dare betray any. The situation was ticklish enough as it was.

"Go on, Faridah. Fetch him."

But she didn't have to fetch him. Emin, hearing the noise, came out of the house on his own. He was wearing his fez and caftan and house slippers.

"Get into your clothes, Pasha," Faratch Ajoke commanded.

"Get into my clothes? What clothes? I am in my clothes."

"Your suit. Your boots. You are going for a journey."

"A journey?" Now Emin looked at Jephson in much the same searching manner as had Faridah. "What is this, my boy?"

Jephson started toward him with a sudden pang of sympathy for his befuddlement, thinking to get into a position where no one other than Emin would be able to see his face. But Faratch Ajoke was too quick for that.

"Stay where you are, effendi. Stay exactly where you are.

There will be no private conversation between you and the Pasha."

Jephson shrugged. "As you wish, Faratch Ajoke. I have no need of a private conversation with the Pasha."

"I don't understand this, Arthur."

"What is there to understand? The time has come, as you surely knew it would someday. You chose to remain here rather than abandon your people. You chose to remain here even though those people had turned against you. You chose to remain here knowing that by doing so you were risking your life. Well, now you are to be repaid for choosing to remain here. We are taking you to Duffile."

"No." Faridah flung herself against her father.

He put his arms around her but continued looking at Jephson over the top of her head. "We, my boy? You say, we? By that do you mean to include yourself?"

Jephson hardened his expression and didn't reply.

"*You* are taking me to the dervishes, Arthur?"

"You want to help your people, don't you, Pasha? Isn't that what you want? Isn't that all you care about, not yourself, not your own life, only helping your beloved people? Isn't that why you wouldn't leave here? Well, maybe this is a way you can help them. You are certainly no help to them hiding here in your compound."

"I can't believe you are saying this, my boy. How can you say this? You know better than this. You know taking me to the dervishes won't be of any help. They will kill me. Yes, of course, they will kill me. That's all right. I'm not afraid to die. But after they've killed me, they will come here and kill all of you anyway. My death will be for nothing."

"Are you getting into your clothes, Pasha, or aren't you?"

"No, Faratch Ajoke, I am not getting into my clothes."

"Very well. Then you will meet the dervishes as you are." Faratch Ajoke started up to the veranda.

"No. Keep away from me. This is insanity." Emin pulled back, pulling Faridah back with him.

"Don't make trouble, Pasha. Don't make a fuss. We will take you by force if necessary."

"I say, keep away from me. This isn't going to do any good. This isn't going to help matters. I am not going. I am not going anywhere. I am staying here. This is my home. These are my people. Stay away from me." Emin, pulling his daughter with him, tried to get back into his house.

"Lend me a hand."

The garrison commanders from Muggi and Chor Ayu went up on the veranda. Jephson turned his back. He couldn't bear to watch. He heard the scuffling, Emin's protests, Faridah's cries; and he wished he could stop his ears.

"Arthur, Arthur, my boy. Don't let them do this. It won't be of any help. You know that."

Jephson walked out of the compound, not looking back. He could tell by the ugly sickening sounds that they had pulled Emin down from the veranda and were dragging him out to the parade ground, that Faridah was desperately trying to cling to him and was being pushed away. He kept walking toward the fort's east gate and the path down the hillside to the waterfront. Shukri Aga fell into step beside him. He didn't say anything; he simply walked alongside Jephson, also looking straight ahead.

More and more people followed them. By the time they passed through the east gate and were halfway down the hill, there were hundreds. By the time they were making their way through the winding streets of the station, there were thousands. They knew what was going on now. The word had spread like wildfire. And it was to their credit that not everyone approved. The years of Emin's care of and affection for them had, after all, made some mark; and many, especially women, rushed forward in consternation, wailing pitifully, grasping at the skirts of his caftan, clutching for his hands. Jephson caught sight of Casati in the mob, following along at a distance as if debating the wisdom of letting himself get involved. Jephson didn't signal to him. He could only hope the damn fool had sense enough to come down to the jetty.

Nelson and the askaris and the Wanyamwezis were on the jetty. And as Jephson had suspected, so was the Maxim. After the mad scramble to haul it out of the dory that day when Jephson returned from Duffile, Faratch Ajoke had made the annoying discovery that neither he nor any of his soldiers knew how to operate the terrible machine and so had abandoned it where it was to dash off on some other idiotic scheme. The askaris were now paraded around it. The Wanyamwezis sat beside it on the crates and sacks and bundles of their loads. Nelson, wearing his revolver, stood with them, studying Jephson's face as he approached with an expression of uneasy puzzlement.

On reaching him, giving no sign, Jephson turned around abruptly to watch the rest of the procession come out on the jetty. So did Shukri Aga. Faratch Ajoke was a few steps behind them, then came Emin between the commanders from Muggi and Chor Ayu. He was no longer struggling. Although he was still held by each arm, he walked with a semblance of dignity in his caftan and slippers and fez. His spectacles had slipped far down his nose; and as his hands were not free to adjust them, he probably couldn't see very much. But he probably wasn't particularly keen on seeing very much. He seemed resigned to his fate. Faridah had followed him faithfully. She was halfway back in the mob on the jetty but was anxiously shoving her way forward to get to her father's side. At the very end of the jetty was Casati.

"Well, Faratch Ajoke?"

"Well, effendi?"

"I suggest we take him on the steamer. It will be quicker and safer on the steamer."

The Egyptian didn't immediately reply to this. He looked around at the excited crowd pressing in on all sides.

"However, if you prefer to go in the dory or one of the other small boats, it is all the same to me," Jephson went on matter-of-factly, even though his heart had now begun to race. "It will take days longer in a small boat of course and there will be more trouble making the best use of the Maxim. But it is for you to decide. I am willing to do this in whichever way will most assure you of my good faith."

"The steamer, of course, Faratch Ajoke," Shukri Aga put in. "Naturally, the steamer. If there are difficulties, if Omar Saleh does not respond as you imagine, there will be a far better chance of getting away in the steamer."

"Yes, all right, the steamer."

"Captain Casati, will you come up here please?"

The Italian, in no great hurry, started up the jetty. Faridah had reached her father by now and stood close to him, an arm entwined in his, her chin resting on his shoulder, her eyes wet with tears. Jephson couldn't bring himself to look at her.

"Is the *Khedive* wooded, Captain?"

"Yes. Why?"

"There is enough fuel aboard for a journey to Duffile?"

"To Duffile? Who is going to Duffile? Duffile has fallen to the dervishes."

"Just answer my question, Captain. Is there enough fuel aboard her for the journey?"

Casati nodded.

"Good. Go on board and fire up her furnace."

"What? Are you mad? I am not going to Duffile. You must be mad to think I would go to Duffile with the dervishes there."

"Faratch Ajoke."

"Do what you are told, Captain."

"Oh, no, effendi. You may be mad but I am not mad. I am not going to the dervishes. I am content to wait for them to come to me." Casati turned away and began walking off the jetty.

"Captain!"

Casati looked back—and flinched. Faratch Ajoke had pulled out his pistol and had it leveled at the Italian's gut.

"Go on board at once, Captain. I want to see smoke coming from the stack within five minutes."

Casati looked from Faratch Ajoke to Jephson to Nelson, from Nelson to Shukri Aga and then to Emin. While he was hesitating in this way, Faratch Ajoke slowly, very deliberately pulled back the hammer of his pistol.

"You are mad. All of you are mad," Casati said, but he went up the gangway onto the *Khedive*.

"Captain Nelson, board the Maxim."

Now it was Nelson's turn to consider the situation. He obviously still had no idea what—if any—trick Jephson had up his sleeve.

"Go on, Robbie." Jephson would have liked to give him some sign of reassurance; but the Egyptian, tense with mistrust and suspicion, was watching too closely. "Go on, man. I know what I'm doing."

Finally Nelson nodded, then he and the askaris began hauling the Maxim up the gangway after Casati. The Wanyamwezis picked up the gun's ammunition boxes and their other loads and followed them. This immediately caused trouble.

"Where are those men going?" Faratch Ajoke snapped. "No one gave them permission to go."

"*Warafiki. Simameni.*"

On Jephson's command, Nelson, the askaris, and the Wanyamwezis stopped abruptly halfway up the gangway and looked back.

"Who is to go, Faratch Ajoke? Tell me. If not these men, who? It should be exactly as you wish."

The Egyptian still had his pistol out. Now he let the hand holding it fall absently to his side. He was confused. Obviously, he had never really thought the matter through. When he had first hit on the scheme of selling Emin to the dervishes, the problem had been to find men willing to undertake the dangerous task. Since Jephson had volunteered to do it, he hadn't had the chance to figure out how actually it should be done.

"We must have men with us, Faratch Ajoke. Surely you agree with that. We cannot go alone, just you and I and the Pasha. We must at the very least have men to operate the Maxim. After all, it is the Maxim which the dervishes fear. It is the Maxim which will keep us safe."

"Yes, all right. The men who operate the Maxim can go."

"That is Captain Nelson and the three askaris of the gun crew. Four men and ourselves. Will that be sufficient, do you think?"

The Egyptian didn't reply.

"There are perhaps eight thousand dervishes in Duffile, Faratch Ajoke. I would suggest we make a slightly better show of force than just those four and ourselves. My men are willing to go. The askaris and Wanyamwezis will obey my orders. That would give us a force of nearly forty. In my opinion, that would be sufficient. With forty, we could put up a reasonable fight, enough of one anyway to cover our retreat in the steamer in the event the greeting from Omar Saleh is not what we hope. Yes, I would say forty would be sufficient. I would feel easy enough with forty good fighters and the Maxim. But it need not be these forty, Faratch Ajoke. It need not be my forty. Let it be your forty, Faratch Ajoke. Let it be forty of your men. It is all the same to me."

"I see now. Yes, effendi, I see now how very cunning you are. I see now the trick you mean to play."

"Trick, Faratch Ajoke? You still think I mean to play a trick? Very well. Captain Nelson, you and the gun crew take the Maxim aboard and position it in the stern, on the fantail deck. The rest of you come down from there."

"No, wait."

"Wait? Yes, I'll wait, Faratch Ajoke. I'll wait for you to muster your soldiers. Muster forty of them. There must be at least forty of them, brave and good fighters all, or I will not go. I am not so stupid as to go to the dervishes with any less."

The Egyptian said nothing.

And so Shukri Aga spoke up. "For the love of Allah, Faratch Ajoke, you know you cannot muster forty soldiers. There aren't forty soldiers in all of Wadelai who would be willing to go to Duffile. That has been the trouble all along. Wouldn't we have done this long before now if we had been able to find forty soldiers willing to go to Duffile? But we haven't been able to find even ten soldiers willing to go. If Jephson effendi's soldiers are willing to go, if they will obey his order to go, then, for the love of Allah, let them go."

Still the Egyptian said nothing.

"Board your men, Jephson effendi," Shukri Aga said. "Board them and take them to Duffile."

Jephson shot the fat Nubian a quick glance. He was helping him. There couldn't be any question of it. "Very well. Go on board, *warafiki.* The askaris to Captain Nelson on the fantail. The *pagazis* to the forward deck."

As the askaris and Wanyamwezis trooped aboard, the first puff of smoke appeared from the *Khedive*'s stack. Casati had got the furnace going.

"All right. Now the Pasha. Take the Pasha aboard."

The commanders from Muggi and Chor Ayu gave Emin a rough shove forward. Immediately, Faridah grabbed hold of his freed arm and clung to him.

"What is this, effendis?" Jephson asked of the two commanders. "Are you not coming with us? You do not wish to make this journey with us?"

Both looked away.

Jephson smiled with contempt. "Very well. Faratch Ajoke, bring the Pasha aboard." Jephson turned around and started up the *Khedive*'s gangway.

And stopped. No one was following him. He looked back. Emin, held in his daughter's desperate embrace, peered at him over the tops of his spectacles with what was as close to hatred as Jephson had ever seen the gentle little man express. Faratch Ajoke stood behind him, the pistol in his hand hanging loosely at his side.

"You too, Faratch Ajoke? You too have no wish to make this journey? You have decided to let me make it alone?"

"But that is out of the question," Shukri Aga said excitedly. "What can you be thinking, Faratch Ajoke? You would allow him to go alone? He cannot be allowed to go alone. Someone must go with him."

"Then you go, Vakeel. You go with him."

"Me? Why me? This was never my idea. This was your idea. This was your idea from the first."

"What difference does it make whose idea it was from the first?" the apothecary, in sudden exasperation, said. "It is now all our idea. We have all agreed upon it. In the name of Allah, are we going to start arguing about it all over again?"

And yes, they did start arguing about it all over again, Faratch Ajoke, Shukri Aga, the apothecary, the merchants and clerks, the stranded Greek trader, the commanders from the northern forts. They argued as they had been arguing from the very first days, noisily, angrily, pointlessly, not one listening to what another said. Jephson made a quick decision to take advantage of the ruckus. He came back down quickly from the gangway and grabbed Emin's arm.

"Come, Pasha."

"No," Faridah shrieked and clung to her father tighter than ever.

But Jephson had no difficulty dragging the little man up the gangway—he weighed hardly more than a child and didn't particularly resist—and as she stuck to him like glue, dragging Faridah along as well. This caught Faratch Ajoke's attention.

"What are you doing? Where are you taking the girl? Leave her. She is not to go."

"And why not? Why shouldn't she go? Do you think Omar Saleh would not be pleased to have her in his harem? Do you think he would be any less pleased to have her than to have her father's head?" And reaching the top of the gangway, Jephson shoved Emin and the girl into the steamer's forward deck with such force that they both sprawled on their faces. "Cast us off, Faratch Ajoke. Make yourself of some use. Cast us off. All of you, cast off the lines."

Jephson couldn't believe it. It really might work. All were aboard—Emin, Faridah, Nelson, the askaris, and the Wanyamwezis. With his heart thudding with excitement and anxiety, Jephson dashed across the *Khedive*'s deck to the engine room. A good fire was blazing in the furnace, and Casati was fiddling with the dials of the boiler, building up a head of steam.

"You are mad, signor. This is madness. I don't even have a crew."

"The Wanyamwezis will serve as your crew. Just tell them what to do. Robbie, get some of the boys over here to work as firemen. You go up to the wheelhouse, Casati, and make for the other side of the river."

"You do not have to instruct me how to go to Duffile, signor."

"Just listen to me, will you. For God's sake, just listen to me and do exactly what I tell you. Make for the other side of the river. Make way slowly, at half speed. And then when you get to the island over there, sail around it and put on all the steam you've got."

"There is no need to sail around that island on the way to Duffile. One follows the channel on the other side of that island only when going upriver, into the lake."

"And that's where we are going, Casati. We're going upriver, into the lake. You really didn't think we were going to Duffile, did you? We're going to Nsabe, you damn fool. We're going to Nsabe, not Duffile."

Casati looked at Jephson. It took him only an instant to understand, and he went scampering up the ladder to the wheelhouse. Jephson ran back to the fantail deck. The steamer was beginning to edge away from the jetty. Faratch Ajoke was watching, doing nothing; but Shukri Aga had managed to get the others to cast off the steamer's mooring lines, and the Wanyamwezis on the forward deck were hauling them in. Emin and Faridah were also on the forward deck where Jephson had shoved them. They sat huddled together against the bulwark, talking softly to each other, consoling each other, not paying any attention to what was going on.

"Is the Maxim ready to fire, Robbie?"

"What?" Nelson looked back as Jephson dashed to the stern.

"Is there a cartridge belt in the gun? Run a cartridge belt into the gun."

"What for?"

"I don't know what these buggers might do. Probably nothing." Jephson went to the fantail rail and looked down at the crowd on the jetty. They were now some twenty yards away as Casati angled the steamer out into the river. "No, there's probably nothing they can do. But just in case."

"Just in case what?"

Jephson turned around to face Nelson. "We're going to Nsabe, Robbie. We're not going to Duffile. I already told Casati."

Nelson began to smile, his toothless old man's smile. "Yes," he said, "I figured that might be what you had up your sleeve."

"It was the only way to get Dr. Emin out of here. We'd never have got him out any other way. He'd never have come on his own."

"You're right, you know, you're right."

"It came to me in a flash," Jephson went on, now smiling delightedly himself, pleased as punch with himself. "Just like that, in a flash, when I was arguing with Faratch Ajoke. But I didn't really believe it would work. We've got Shukri Aga to thank for that."

"Yes, he caught on a hell of a lot sooner than I did."

"He's a good chap. I don't think he was ever really against Dr. Emin. In his own way, as best as he could, he stayed loyal to him." Jephson turned around again to look back down at the people on the jetty.

They were now more than fifty yards away and still, of course, had no suspicion as to what was actually happening. From their vantage point, the *Khedive* was simply making way into midriver in search of a navigable channel. It wouldn't be until she reached the island more than halfway across and sailed around it that they would realize she wasn't going to Duffile. And by then they'd be too far away to see the expression on their faces. And in his elation over the success of his ruse, Jephson wanted to see the expression on their faces.

So he shouted, "Faratch Ajoke, can you hear me? We are not going to Duffile, you dumb son of a bitch. We are going to Nsabe. Do you hear me? We are going to Nsabe." And having shouted that, he burst into wild schoolboy laughter.

Emin was outraged. It didn't altogether surprise Jephson, but he figured he'd get over it in time. He didn't. He had been tricked and betrayed, tricked into leaving his home, betrayed into abandoning his people, and no amount of explaining that it had been for his own and Faridah's good, that in any case it was only temporary, that he would return to his home and people and return in triumph once Stanley got back, lessened his bitterness. He seemed totally to have forgotten how viciously the very people he worried so much about abandoning had in fact abandoned him, how unconscionably eager they had been to sell him to the dervishes in order to save their skins, how great the danger he and Faridah had been in in that place he regarded as his home, both from his own people and the advancing dervish army, which his people had made no effort to defend themselves against. No, now that he had been plucked to safety, it was Jephson, not his people, he perceived as his betrayer. In his muddled, peevish thinking, it was Jephson who had pushed forward (although, admittedly, for a different purpose) the scheme to take him to Omar Saleh in Duffile, not his people. For all their talk, he was sure they would never actually have done it, that they could never have brought themselves to do it, that eventually, for all their initial panic, they would have come to their senses and turned to him, their mudir, their protector and benefactor of so many years, for leadership and guidance. And now he wasn't there for them to turn to. Now he wasn't there to guide and advise them. Now he wasn't there to share their fate. Against his will, against all his best intentions, he had been tricked into leaving them in the lurch.

The foolishness of this sort of talk, the complete lack of a grasp on the ugly reality of the situation, irritated Jephson almost beyond endurance. But he didn't let it dampen his high spirits. He was just too pleased with himself. He was just too thrilled with what he had done. He was positively euphoric. He couldn't quite get over his own wit and daring in spiriting them all out of a hopeless predicament and could barely restrain himself from parading around congratulating himself. Thanks to him, they were all well out of harm's way, and all they had to do now was wait for Stanley. And, certainly, compared with the chaos and the daily prospect of disaster and death in Wadelai, the waiting in Nsabe was easy.

The advance column or, at least the remnant of it that had made it through the Ituri—Tom Parke, Will Hoffman, Sudi, ninety-two *pagazis*, thirty-three askaris (at the moment minus Uledi and the fifty picked men who had gone back through the Ituri with Stanley)—had by then been in Nsabe for more than five months and had in that time made for themselves a thoroughly comfortable camp there. Also, they had cut a stepped path up the rocky face of the 2,500-foot-high cliff that plunged down to the lakeshore from the grasslands of the Watusi above, where a second village had been built for lookouts who were kept posted day and night there to watch for Stanley and the rear column's return.

Hoffman was no longer on crutches. He had a wooden leg. The infection from the skewer wound that he had sustained to his foot at the outset of the march through the forest had finally spread so alarmingly that he had let Parke amputate just below the knee and had carved a replacement from the branch of an acacia thorn. But apart from that, everyone was in splendid shape—fat, sleek, and happy. And why not? There was nothing to do but fish and hunt. The climate was near perfect, the landscape of magnificent beauty. And the tribesmen of the local fishing villages couldn't have been friendlier, bringing charcoal and salt to trade, joining in the dancing and singing and games around the campfire at night, cheerfully letting their girls and women be taken as concubines.

Parke had taken one. He had also gone native in his dress, exchanging his tattered uniform for a tribesman's brightly patterned *kanga* and a necklace of crocodile teeth. Bare-chested but wearing his sun helmet and boots (he was afraid of stepping on something), his long greasy hair and beard now plaited in braids, he looked like a slightly lunatic castaway and was always on the hunt for someone with whom to play skat. He found him in Casati. The Italian couldn't believe his luck at having escaped the deathtrap of Wadelai and had emerged from his sullen gloom with a Latin exuberance that was almost as difficult to bear. With Uledi gone, Sudi, Jephson's good right arm through most of the journey, had emerged as Uledi's surrogate, paramount chief of the Wanyamwezis, and ruled them with a quiet natural authority, conducting shauris to settle disputes, overseeing the distribution of rations, generally running the camp like a peaceful village back home in Zanzibar. Oh, yes, it was an easy time, the weeks of waiting in Nsabe. Emin was the only one who didn't enjoy it.

On arriving in Nsabe, he had been offered Stanley's big command tent (with its cot and field desk and sling-back canvas chairs) for his quarters; but he wouldn't take it and chose instead one of the meanest huts in the camp, one without any amenities, where he had to sleep on the ground. And there he remained in a seclusion even more severe than he had practiced in Wadelai. What he did there, apart from brood, was a mystery. He didn't have books to read. He didn't have his collections or experiments to work on. He didn't have his notebook to write in. All he had was Faridah. She attended him as faithfully as ever, bringing him his meals, keeping him company, trying to anticipate his wishes and needs.

But if Jephson had any qualms about what he had done, he had only to look at Faridah to know that he had done right. She didn't say anything, nor was the change in her dramatic in any way; but there was no question that away from the tensions and terrors of Wadelai, here in this idyllic village on the shore of the lake, her mood lightened, her somberness eased. She took to running about a bit, collecting flowers and unusual plants, catching butterflies and strange bugs, at first to bring to her father in order to give him something with which to occupy himself, then just for her own amusement. And even on occasion Jephson saw her smile, the smile of a young pretty girl from whose shoulders a terrible burden had been lifted. And when he saw her smile, his pride in himself, his euphoria, his sense of having accomplished something monumentally clever and good, soared.

· FIVE ·

"Sah."

Jephson was asleep on Stanley's cot in the command tent. Sudi's urgent whisper woke him immediately and his first thought was of Emin.

His thoughts nowadays were almost always on Emin. In the three weeks since being brought to Nsabe, the little man had grown progressively more remote, reclusive, depressed. And then, to make matters worse, just three days before, the dory in which Jephson had fled from Duffile had appeared on the lake in front of Nsabe with a delegation from Wadelai. It included the apothecary, the stranded Greek trader, a few merchants and clerks, and commanders from the northern forts—indeed many of the same mutineers Jephson had tricked in getting Emin out of Wadelai, except Faratch Ajoke and Shukri Aga. Jephson wouldn't let them beach. He had the Maxim positioned at the water's edge for just such a contingency and warned the dory to stand off or it would be fired upon. So they had to shout back and forth across a hundred yards of open water. The dervishes had come and laid siege to Wadelai. Faratach Ajoke had been killed in the first exchange of gunfire. Shukri Aga had taken command of the fort and was desperately trying to organize its defense. And they had been sent to beg the Pasha's forgiveness for their disloyalty and to implore him to return and tell them what to do. Emin, of course, was ecstatic by this turn of events—it was precisely what he had predicted would happen all along—and was more than eager to go. But Jephson wouldn't hear of it.

In the first place, he didn't trust them; they might want Emin back only to try their nasty scheme of buying off the dervishes with his head. But even if that wasn't the case, the situation in Wadelai was now far too dangerous. There was no telling how long, without the relief supplies being brought by the rear column,

Shukri Aga's soldiers could hold off the dervishes; and he'd be damned if he'd let Emin go back only to get himself killed. No, Emin would return to Wadelai when Stanley returned with the rear column, no sooner, and he drove the dory away with a threatening burst of Maxim gunfire.

Emin's reaction to this had been frightening. After throwing what could only be described as a lunatic tantrum, in which he physically attacked Jephson and had to be pulled off by Nelson and a few others, he had sunk into a profound melancholia that bordered on the suicidal. At any moment Jephson expected to hear that he had done himself harm.

So now, jumping up from the cot and hurriedly dressing, he asked, "What is it, Sudi? Is it the Pasha?"

"The Pasha, sah?"

"Has something happened to the Pasha?"

"No, sah, I know of nothing that has happened to the Pasha."

"What then?"

"Bula Matari, sah."

Jephson was sitting on the edge of the cot, pulling on his boots. He looked up at Sudi standing in the tent's entry. Sudi was smiling.

"A caravan comes across the grassland above, sah," the young Wanyamwezi went on. "The lookouts up there have sent word down. They believe it is Bula Matari's caravan."

"Bula Matari's caravan?" Jephson stood up. "Bula Matari's caravan, you say?"

"Yes, sah, Bula Matari's caravan," Sudi replied and grinned even more broadly.

Jephson stared at him like a dummy for a moment. And then he just let it explode. "Hallelujah! Halle-goddamn-lujah, Sudi! Bula Matari's caravan. Bula Matari's caravan at last." And he went bounding out of the tent.

It was first light of the first of June, a day that promised to be the brightest, most glorious day of them all. Faridah was up. She was standing by her father's hut wearing a tunic Jephson had given her over her long hooded aba to ward off the dawn's chill. Her concern for and attendance of Emin had grown more intense with his worrisome descent into morbid despondency, but Jephson didn't think she blamed him for Emin's condition. In fact, he fancied that she was secretly rather pleased that he had prevented Emin from returning to the terrible uncertainties and perils of Wadelai. In any case, she watched him now with an amiable enough expression as he and Sudi hurried over to where Hoffman had got a cooking fire going. A couple of native women from the nearby village had a kettle on for tea and were frying plantains in honey and rice. Two Wanyamwezi trackers from the lookout post atop the cliff, the ones who had brought Sudi the news, were also there.

"Mr. Stanley's on his way back, Will. They've spotted his caravan on the savanna."

"So I heard," Hoffman replied and kicked at the fire with his wooden foot.

Jephson had to smile. Nothing, not even such wonderful news as this, ever seemed to affect the sullen stolidness of this huge, hairless and now peg-legged monster of a man.

"I'm going up to meet him. I don't suppose we'll get back until well after noon, so there's no need to roust everybody out yet. But when they do get up, let them know, will you? And get them started making ready for the journey to Wadelai. Especially Casati. See that the *Khedive* is well wooded. I'm sure Mr. Stanley will want to board the relief supplies and get under way as soon as possible."

Hoffman nodded. One of the women handed Jephson a cup of tea and a plate of the rice and fried plantains. He waved the plate aside and took the tea. Sudi and the two trackers, however, took plates as well as tea and sat down by the fire to eat. With his teacup, Jephson went over to Faridah.

"Bula Matari has come, Faridah. He's come at last."

She too had heard and merely nodded. Like Hoffman, the news brought her no particular joy; but in her case, it was more understandable. After the peaceful sojourn in Nsabe, she could be in no great hurry to return to Wadelai and the fighting against the dervishes that would now ensue with the arrival of the relief.

"Have you told your father?"

"No. I will wait until he awakens. He has slept very little this night, and now that he sleeps at last, I do not wish to disturb him."

"I'm going up to the top of the cliff to meet Bula Matari. Would you like to come with me?"

The offer surprised the girl, and pleased her. Her eyes widened. She smiled shyly.

"Oh, yes, come with me, Faridah. You've never been, have you? It's very beautiful up there. The climb is easy and from up there you can see everything, the whole of the lake and all of the world around."

"How long would it take?"

"A few hours. We should be back early in the afternoon."

"Oh, so long? That would be too long. By then my father will be awake and I must be here. He will wonder what has become of me."

"Captain Nelson will tell him. I'll tell Captain Nelson to tell him that you've come with me to meet Bula Matari."

She shook her head.

"Oh, come, Faridah, come. It's so beautiful. It will be so much fun."

"Another time, Jephson effendi. We will go together another time."

Sudi and the trackers came over from the cooking fire. They had finished their breakfast and waited respectfully a few steps away. Jephson glanced at them, then back at Faridah. Another time? What other time? In the hurly-burly of the rear column's arrival and the preparations for the return to Wadelai, there wasn't likely to be another time.

Even so he said, "You promise, Faridah? You promise you will come with me some other time?"

"Yes, Jephson effendi, I promise you."

"All right, Faridah. I'm going to hold you to that promise."

He went back to the command tent to fetch his sun helmet and binoculars—the only time he carried a weapon these days was when he went hunting—and with the trackers in the lead and Sudi behind him, began the climb up the cliff face to the grasslands of the Watusi above.

As he had told Faridah, it was an easy climb. The path had been well made, stepped in some of the steepest places, zigzagging around the biggest of the black granite boulders that jutted in precarious ledges and slabs from the cliff face, with plenty of handholds provided by the shrubs and dwarf trees that sprouted from the cracks and crevices. But it was also a long climb; 2,500 feet—and with the zigs and zags probably more than 3,000—was a long way to go and every so often he and Sudi and the trackers would stop for a rest and look back, look down, look out. It was beautiful, every bit as beautiful as he had told Faridah it would be, a panorama of Africa of breathtaking beauty: lake and sky, cliff and shore, and the rising sun casting a roseate light on it all. His heart sang. What a long time they had been traveling. What a great distance they had come. How much they had seen and experienced and suffered. But now it seemed worth it. Now it seemed to have been the grand adventure it had promised to be at the start, a heroic adventure to be crowned by the glory of success at last.

It was nine o'clock when they reached the top of the cliff. There was another camp up here, a cluster of huts around a nine-foot-high watchtower. Jephson and Sudi made straight for the tower. Two askaris and three Wanyamwezis were there and with big grins they moved out of the way to let Jephson and Sudi see, pointing westward across the vast expanse of the rolling grassland at what they should see.

Yes, a caravan was coming. Although it was still a few miles away, perhaps still a good hour's march away, although all they could see of it were specks in the high yellow grass, disappearing and reappearing in the hills and dales of the rolling savanna, under the brilliant blue African sky, it was clearly a large caravan. There were surely several hundred people in it, maybe as many as a thousand. And that was as it should be. Counting the 600 Manyema porters Tippoo-Tib was to provide from Singatini plus the original members of the rear column, those left behind with Barttelot and Troup at Yambuya and those who came up later from Equator Station with Ward and Bonny, the caravan should number at least a thousand.

"Greet them, *warafiki*," Jephson shouted down to the men milling excitedly around the base of the watchtower. "Greet Bula Matari and his people. Fire your rifles in greeting."

And as the rifles cracked in jubilant, almost dangerously enthusiastic volleys and some of the men let go with high-pitched exuberant ululations, Jephson raised his field glasses to his eyes. They didn't help much. The distance was still too great, but he fancied that he could make out Stanley at the head of the caravan or, in any case, a lone figure far ahead of the others, striding forward with that relentless driving pace that so characterized Stanley on the march. It brought a smile to Jephson's lips, a thrilling tug of nostalgia for all the months and miles he had followed that man's unstoppable pace. There was, however, no rifle fire in reply to the lookouts' greeting. This was mildly puzzling. The caravan seemed close enough to have heard it or anyway to have seen its puffs of white smoke. But maybe not; maybe a wind was blowing in the wrong direction and the rising sun was in their eyes.

But after several more minutes Jephson noticed something else: Many of the people in the caravan seemed to be wearing the magnificent headdresses of ostrich feathers and eagle and quail plumage that the Watusi warriors wore. They could be seen bobbing and swaying like graceful birds above the high grass even when the heads of others had disappeared beneath it. Were they Watusi? When the advance column had crossed the savanna, it had been accompanied by hundreds of Watusi warriors. It was certainly likely that the Watusi had provided a similar escort for the rear column. But if they were Watusi—and of course they were; at their great height, many over seven feet tall, only *their* heads would be seen when all others had disappeared in the high grass—then the caravan wasn't anywhere nearly as large as it had first appeared. Then there weren't anywhere near a thousand in the caravan. Subtracting those with headdresses, those who likely were Watusi warriors, there probably were no more than a few hundred in the caravan, if that.

"What do you see, Sudi?" Jephson asked, handing the field glasses to the young Wanyamwezi. "Do you see many Watusi warriors in the caravan?"

Sudi adjusted the focus of the eyepieces as he peered through the glasses out onto the sun-bright yellow grassland. After a minute or two, he nodded.

"Are not most of the people you see in the caravan Watusi warriors?"

Again Sudi nodded.

"And how many of our people do you see?"

Sudi didn't answer right away. Then he said, "Two hundred perhaps."

"And Manyema? How many of Tippoo-Tib's Manyema do you see?"

"I do not see any Manyema. There are no Manyema." Sudi lowered the glasses. "It may be that the caravan marches in two sections, sah. Because I also only see one other white man in the caravan besides Bula Matari. The Sergeant Major Bonny. He marches behind my father, Uledi."

Jephson took back the field glasses. "You don't see Major Barttelot or Jack Troup or Bertie Ward?"

"No, sah."

Jephson brought the glasses to his eyes again. Sudi's sight was far keener than his. He not only didn't see Barttelot or Troup or Ward, he also didn't see Bonny or Uledi and was still only assuming that the figure he saw at the head of the column was Stanley. "Do you see any sign of a second section of the caravan?" he asked, handing the glasses back to Sudi.

"No." Sudi said this without bothering to look through the glasses again. "If there is a second section to the caravan, it is still too far away to see."

Jephson looked at Sudi, then back out across the savanna, and his heart sank. What Sudi was suggesting didn't make any sense. And Sudi knew that it didn't make any sense. What reason would Stanley have for marching the caravan in two sections and marching one section so far behind the other that it couldn't be seen? There was no reason. And Sudi knew there was no reason. He knew there was no second section to the caravan.

The men beneath the watchtower had stopped firing their rifles, had ceased their joyous shouting and ululations. A few had started forward to meet the caravan halfway, but they also had stopped. Jephson didn't take back his glasses. He wasn't anxious to see what they would reveal. It would be soon enough to see what there was to see when the caravan was close enough to see with his naked eyes.

And then he saw Stanley and Bonny. And he did not see Barttelot or Troup or Ward. Stanley was marching at the head of the column. Bonny was marching behind Uledi. Uledi was leading him, like a dog, on a rope.

"I'm sorry, Pasha," Stanley said.

Emin made no reply. He merely watched dumbstruck as the last of the rear column struggled down the face of the cliff. They were a horrifying sight—not 200, probably not even 150 altogether—men and women, askaris and *pagazis* almost indistinguishable one from another in their emaciated condition. They were skeletons clad in rags, covered with sores, shivering from fever, emitting sounds that scarcely were human, and bringing not the tons of long-awaited guns and ammunition and other relief supplies but the paltriest, meanest, most worthless collections of sacks and bundles of junk with which they had eked out their lives crossing the terrible Ituri.

Everyone in the Nsabe camp watched them with the same expression of horrified disbelief as Emin. No one went near them. Despite the fact that these were friends and kin, no one helped them with their loads or offered them food or even so much as greeted them, so repulsive and inhuman did they seem. The greatest horror was Bonny. He stood rigidly at attention. Apparently, he could be made to move only by pulling the rope around his neck. When he wasn't pulled, he came rigidly to attention, Barttelot's riding crop tucked under his arm.

"What happened?" Nelson asked in a whisper, as if at a funeral.

Stanley didn't hear him and went on making his apologies to Emin.

But then Nelson's voice suddenly turned shrill. "I ask you, Mr. Stanley, what happened? I want to know what happened. I have the right to know what happened."

Stanley turned to him. "I don't know what happened, Captain Nelson. I don't have the first idea what happened. By the time I found these poor devils, there was no one to tell me what happened. Jack Troup was out of his head with fever. He died in my arms a short while later. Major Barttelot was already dead. Mr. Ward had vanished. As best as I can make out, he went back downriver to Equator Station. He may have deserted. The only officer alive was Sergeant Bonny, and you can see for yourself how much can be learned from him. As for the rest of them, poor devils, all they could tell me is that Tippoo-Tib's people refused to help them and, once on the march, attacked them and made off with the most precious of their loads—the guns and ammunition. I can only surmise that in one way or other Major Barttelot or Jack Troup or Mr. Ward or all of them together did something to antagonize Tippoo-Tib and the Manyema and so brought this dreadful calamity down on their heads."

"Excuse me, sir. Excuse me." This was Jephson, not Nelson, but his voice was suddenly as shrill, as close to breaking with emotion as Nelson's had been. "*They* brought this calamity down on their heads? You say *they* brought this calamity down on their heads? You are blaming *them* for this calamity?"

"I'm not blaming anyone, Arthur. As I say, I don't know what happened. I don't know who to blame."

"How about yourself, Mr. Stanley? How about blaming yourself?"

Stanley's face went white at this. He stared at Jephson for a long moment with blazing eyes, the muscles in his jaw working furiously. But when he spoke, he spoke calmly enough. "I suppose you're right, Arthur. Yes, I must blame myself. As leader of this expedition, I must ultimately take the blame on myself."

"No, not ultimately, Mr. Stanley. Not ultimately. Specifically. You chose this route, Mr. Stanley. Not Jack Troup. Not Major

Barttelot. Not Bertie Ward. You made the arrangements with King Leopold for the Congo steamers. You made the arrangements with Tippoo-Tib for the porters. Everyone was against it. Everyone told you it wouldn't work. Doctor Dick—you remember Dr. Dick Leslie, Mr. Stanley? He said it wouldn't work. He quit the expedition because he knew it wouldn't work. But you didn't care. You wouldn't listen to anyone. No, you insisted on it. You were going through the Ituri or you weren't going at all. That's what you told Sir William and the others. You were going to be the first white man through the Ituri. You were going to add that feather to your cap. And this is what's come of it. Jack Troup is dead—"

Jephson broke off, the words choking in his throat. Jack Troup dead, the good, kind, loyal Jack Troup. And Major Barttelot. He had never much cared for Major Barttelot, but now he was also dead. And poor Bertie Ward had vanished somewhere in the forest, somewhere on the river, and was also probably dead. And look at Bonny. And at the wreck of a man Nelson had become. And look at Hoffman with his wooden leg. And at the ridiculous Parke in his native dress and braided hair.

"Yes, this is what's come of it, Mr. Stanley. This!" Jephson swept a hand over the ghouls of the rear column coming down the cliff and over the survivors of the advance column awaiting them on the lakeshore with horror in their eyes. "We set out with more than eight hundred people, and not a third of them are left. Not a third. More than five hundred have either died or disappeared. Like Jack Troup. Like Bertie Ward. And for what? For what, I'd like to know. I'll tell you for what. For nothing. Because what we set out to do, we've failed to do."

"That's enough, Arthur."

"No, don't tell me it's enough. Just listen to me. We didn't set out on this expedition so you could be the first white man through the Ituri. We set out to bring relief to Emin Pasha. We set out to save him and the people of Equatoria from the dervishes. And at that we have failed, Mr. Stanley."

Emin hadn't been listening until now; but the mention of his name and of Equatoria roused him from his dumbstruck trance, and he looked at Jephson in surprise.

"Had we taken any other route," Jephson went on in fury. "Had we taken the route Colonel Grant and Colonel de Winton suggested, up from the Indian Ocean coast—"

"I said that's enough, Arthur. That's quite enough. This isn't the time or place to discuss such matters." Stanley turned back to Emin.

But it wasn't enough for Jephson. It still wasn't enough. He stepped between Stanley and Emin. "We've failed, I tell you. We've utterly failed. Jack Troup and all the others are dead for nothing. Because Equatoria is lost, Mr. Stanley. All the forts and stations have fallen except Wadelai. And it's under siege. The troops there won't be able to hold out for more than a week. They are in a state of rebellion. They don't have enough ammunition. They're waiting for us to bring them the ammunition. And we haven't any ammunition to bring them. Had we taken the route up from the Indian Ocean coast—"

"Mr. Jephson, stand aside, sir. I've listened to all I'm going to listen to from you, sir. If you have charges to bring against my conduct of this expedition, the time to do so is when we return to England. Until then, sir, I remain in command, and you will obey my orders. So stand aside, sir. Stand aside, I say."

Stanley's hands were on his hips, his face was drained of all color, his countenance was terrible to see. He was in pretty dreadful physical condition himself. He had crossed the Ituri three times. Everyone else had died or almost died crossing it once, and he had crossed it *three* times. It was an incredible feat, a feat of the most extraordinary will, of the expenditure of almost superhuman energy, a feat probably no other human being could have performed, and it showed. His hair and beard were completely white. His cheeks were sunken and scarred with bruises and cuts. His eyes were bloodshot and glittered with fever. His uniform hung from his half-starved frame in rags. But the brute determination in the man—the stubborn, unyielding, unbreakable resolve to let no one and nothing stand in his way—was still there to see in the ferociousness of his stance, in the burning blaze of his gray-green eyes. He would brook no insubordination. He would tolerate no mutiny. He would fight. At the end of his resources, drained of all his strength, mortally wounded in his ambition, in a place where other men would give way to despair, he was ready to fight to preserve his authority, to have his way. Jephson saw this. So did Nelson, and he took hold of Jephson's arm in order to avoid a confrontation. But before Jephson could pull away from Nelson, before he could make up his mind if he also was ready to fight, before he could do anything at all, Emin spoke up.

"There are no charges to be brought against you, Bula

Matari," he said, and it was immediately apparent that in his muddled mind he hadn't grasped what was going on. "How could you imagine I would bring charges against you, sir? I would not dream of such a thing."

Stanley turned to him, startled not only by what he said but by the strange, vaguely disconnected tone in which he said it. It was the first time he had heard Emin speak since getting back.

"I have only praise for you, Bula Matari, and gratitude for all you have done on my behalf and behalf of my people. I know Africa, sir. I know what sufferings you have endured, what perils you have faced. I know at what cost, with what courage, against what odds you have done what you have done. And if you have not succeeded as you would have wished, I know the fault lies not with you but in this terrible Africa. No, of course there are no charges to be brought against you. I have not the slightest doubt you have done everything humanly possible to save me and my people from our fate. And for this, I will be eternally grateful to you."

"Thank you, Pasha."

"But I have one last favor I must ask of you, one final effort I beg you to make on my behalf. And then you are quit of all responsibility toward me."

"What is that, Pasha?"

"Allow me to return to my people. Allow me to go home."

"To Wadelai?"

"Yes, to Wadelai. I was taken from there against my will. I have been held prisoner here by this young man."

"Dr. Emin!"

"Please, Bula Matari," Emin went on, ignoring Jephson. "I beg this of you. Free me. Let me go."

"But what nonsense is this, Pasha? It is not for me to free you. You are not my prisoner. You are free to come and go wherever you want. But to Wadelai? From what I understood Mr. Jephson to say, Wadelai will soon fall to the dervishes as have all the other stations. Or did I misunderstand Mr. Jephson?"

"You didn't misunderstand me. That's why I got him out of there in the first place. And why I've kept him here ever since."

"I did not wish to be got out of there, Bula Matari. That is my home. Those are my people. It is my place to be with them and share their fate."

"I understand your feelings, Pasha," Stanley said, but with an unmistakable trace of irritation. "And I admire them. They are noble feelings. But you know what will happen. You know what happened to Gordon Pasha in Khartoum and to Slatin Pasha in Darfur and to Lupton Pasha in Bahr al-Ghazal."

"I know."

"So what is the sense in it then? What is the need for another such useless sacrifice? Why should it also happen to Emin Pasha of Equatoria when the means are at hand to avoid it?"

"So you will not let me go? So I am, in fact, your prisoner?"

"Pasha, be reasonable. The expedition can at least accomplish that much. If we've failed in every other respect, we can at least save you from going the way of Gordon and Slatin and Lupton. No expedition came in time to save them. But we have come in time to save you. Let us snatch you from the dervishes' clutches and take you with us to Europe."

"I have no wish to go to Europe. There is nothing for me in Europe."

"But there is, Pasha. I don't think you understand. You are a great man in Europe, a great hero, a second Gordon. Much will be made of you in Europe, I promise you. You will be feted and honored. A brilliant career awaits you in Europe."

"Do not speak to me of such things. I have no interest in such things. I despise such things. I despise Europe."

"But how can you despise what you don't know?"

"I know Europe. I know Africa. I know this terrible Africa, but I also know Europe. I am from Europe. This surprises you. But, yes, I am from Europe, Mr. Stanley. I am a Jew from Silesia, Eduard Schnitzer by name. But that was long ago. I left Europe long ago with no wish ever to return there. I left to find a better place. And I have found that better place here on these lakes and rivers, in these mountains and deserts, in this terrible Africa. And here I wish to remain. And here, if that is Allah's will, I wish to die."

"And Faridah?"

Emin turned to Jephson sharply. "You asked that once before, Mr. Jephson. The answer is the same as before."

"She is to remain faithfully at your side and die with you? Or, worse yet, after you die, live out her days in the harem of Omar Saleh?"

"That is no concern of yours. She is my daughter. There is as little for her in Europe—a nigger, a half-caste—as there is for me, a Jew from Silesia."

"Is that how you feel, Faridah?"

The girl stood beside her father, her arm linked through his. On being addressed, she tightened her grip. What ease and joy had come into her pretty young face during the weeks in Nsabe were gone. All the somberness, which had so characterized her mood and demeanor during the months before that, was back.

"Yes," she replied.

Jephson shook his head. He really hadn't expected her to answer in any other way. It what other way could she answer? She didn't want to return to Wadelai, that was clear, but she was a faithful child. Emin had welded her to his side.

"Allow us to go, Bula Matari. Please, I beg this last favor of you. And then you will be quit of all responsibility toward us. Then you can return to Europe with a light heart, knowing that you have done all that was humanly possible for us."

Stanley sighed. "I'm tired, Pasha. I've come a long way. I must rest. I must see to my people. We will talk about this tomorrow."

"What is there to talk about? There is nothing to talk about. Just let me have your steel boat. I ask for nothing else, not for provisions or weapons or any sort of escort. I do not ask to be taken back to Wadelai on the *Khedive*. I give you the *Khedive*. I will trade you the *Khedive* for your steel boat. She will be of use to you. Captain Casati will take you to the southern end of the lake on her and go on with you from there to Europe. I know he has no wish to return to Wadelai. Wadelai isn't his home. Europe is his home. Just let me have your steel boat so that my daughter and I can return to ours. Is that so much to ask?"

"No, Pasha it is not so much to ask. And yet it is a great deal to ask. Tomorrow, Pasha. We will talk about it tomorrow and make what arrangements we can." Stanley turned away. "Will, get these people something to eat and find them billets. Surgeon Parke, what are you standing around for grinning like an idiot? Don't you see these people are sick and hurt? Look after them."

Stanley's roughly barked commands jolted the camp out of its stupor. The days of easy living were over. There was work to do. A long hard journey, the journey southeast out of the heart of Africa down to the Indian Ocean coast, still lay ahead. As Stanley strode away, stirring a bustle of frenetic activity in his wake, Emin, with Faridah clinging to his arm, stared after him, unsure whether he had in fact agreed to let them have the *Lady Dorothy*.

Jephson, lingering for a moment, tried to imagine the two of them alone in the *Lady Dorothy*, without provisions, without weapons, pulling away from Nsabe, pulling out across the lake, making for the outlet to the Nile, vanishing down its current toward Wadelai. He couldn't imagine it. The small man and the young girl wouldn't be able to manage the boat on their own. The boat ordinarily required ten strong oarsmen and a coxswain at the tiller. He and Sudi and some of their boys would have to go with them. That was what it probably would come down to; that was what the final chapter of this ill-fated enterprise would be: He and Sudi and some of the boys would go back with them to Wadelai—and run the risk of getting killed or captured along with them.

Stanley slept away the rest of that day in the command tent. He reclaimed it from Jephson, and Jephson moved his kit into Nelson's hut. Casati, who shared the surgery tent with Parke, passed the afternoon watching Parke doctor the worst of the ill and injured. Hoffman, taking charge of Bonny and totally misunderstanding the purpose of the rope around his neck, tied him up in a hut next to his own. Bonny stood at attention in there until he was brought food, then dutifully sat down and ate.

The rest of the ruined creatures of the rear column were herded into the square at the center of the camp by Sudi and also given food. Huddling on the ground, they fell on the food with the avidness of the starved animals to which they had been reduced. Watching them, touched by their pitiful desperation and remembering their own after their passage through the forest, their friends and relatives in the advance column overcame their initial revulsion and gathered around them and began quietly talking to them, questioning them about their ordeal. Jephson and Nelson also came over and began asking questions of their own. Jephson particularly wanted to hear what had happened to Troup.

No one could tell him. Munichandi, the chief of the rear column's *pagazis*, started on a rambling account of Troup's going to Stanley Falls and getting killed there in a fight with Tippoo-Tib and being brought back to Yambuya sewn in his blankets but was immediately contradicted by several others. It wasn't Troup who had been killed at the Falls by Tippoo-Tib; it was Barttelot. Troup had been killed later, after the column was already on the march, in the first fight with the Manyema. But this version also provoked a dispute. It was Ward who had been killed in the first fight with the Manyema. Troup had been killed in the first fight with the Washenzi when the column was portaging the great cascades on the Aruwimi. No, no, a chorus of voices broke in. How could Ward have been killed in the fight with the Manyema when he was no longer with the column by then? Didn't they remember? He had deserted before the column ever left Yambuya. And furthermore, the fight at the cascades had occurred only after Bula Matari had come back, and by that time Troup was already dead. He had died of starvation. And then someone brought up the woman, Tippoo-Tib's woman, the witch and poisoner. She was the cause of the entire calamity. She hated the white men and poisoned both Troup and Barttelot and so bewitched Ward that he ran away.

And so it went, distorted, confused, exaggerated fragments of accounts continually interrupted by and interwoven with other equally garbled accounts that made so little sense that after a while Jephson stopped paying attention to them. They told him nothing that he wanted to know. Perhaps no one could tell him what he wanted to know. Perhaps no one would ever know what really had happened to Jack Troup and Major Barttelot and Bertie Ward and the rear column, but perhaps it didn't really matter what happened. The dead were dead, the relief supplies were gone, and the expedition had failed. In a day or two Emin and his daughter would start back for Wadelai to die at the hands of the dervishes; and in a few days after that Stanley and his survivors would start their long trek home, and that would be that.

With dusk falling, Sudi lit the bonfire in the middle of the square. And the talk went on, talk of terrible sufferings and dreadful events, of desertions and floggings, of cannibals and slavers, of ambushes and battles, of starvation and dying. But in a few days, Jephson was sure, these ghosts of the rear column would begin to recover their health and strength, just as the survivors of the advance column had. They were amazingly resilient people, full of courage and good humor and had a tenacious hold on life. They were little inclined to dwell on their misfortunes, too generous to blame anyone for ill-using them, and in a few days, he knew, this talk of suffering would begin to take on a glow of pride. These accounts of dreadful events would be elaborated into wondrous tales, these memories of battles fought and won would evolve into the stuff of legend. How they had gone through the dreaded Ituri, how they faced and overcome the perils of that unknown forest. By the time they had told these tales often enough, certainly by the time they at last reached Zanzibar and Aden, these tales would have become tales of a great and extraordinary adventure undertaken by great and extraordinary heroes; and it would be as heroes indeed that they would be greeted by the time they at last returned home. But how would he and Stanley and Nelson and Parke and Hoffman and Bonny be greeted when they at last returned to England, with Emin dead and Equatoria lost and the expedition a shambles? With pity? With sympathy? Or with contempt? But, in any cases, not as heroes. No, surely not as heroes.

Stanley awakened and came out of the command tent when Sudi lit the bonfire. He had washed and shaved and changed his uniform, and looked the worse for it. Without the concealment of his beard, his head was skull-like; his clean clothes revealed the shocking amount of weight he had lost. But he too had amazing recuperative powers, and Jephson had no doubt that in a day or two he would be strenuously engaged in organizing the column for the march home. He sat down now on an upturned packing case in front of the tent, and one of the native women in the camp brought him supper. Uledi and Hoffman were with him. With Troup and Ward gone, they were his oldest companions in travel. Uledi sat down next to him, also with a plate of food. Hoffman remained standing. It was still daylight on the savanna above, but with the sun now far to the west, the lakeshore camp lay in the dusky blue shadow cast by the cliff. Stanley ate leaning forward with his elbows on his knees, talking between mouthfuls. Doubtless he already was making plans for the march home. Overhead, in the still bright blue sky, a flight of cranes arrowed southeast down the lakeshore, the direction the expedition would take.

"You know, Robbie," Jephson said, "this is the first time he's failed."

"Mr. Stanley?"

"Yes. Every other time he got his trophy. He set out to find Livingstone and he found him. He set out to prove that the White Nile emerged from Lake Victoria and he proved it. He set out to map the course of the Congo and he mapped it. But this time . . ."

Nelson turned away from the bonfire to have a look at Stanley. "It doesn't seem much to bother him though, does it?"

"No, but it must. It must, Robbie. It must bother the hell out of him."

"I don't know. Maybe it's what you said before, Arthur. Maybe all he wanted to do really was get through the Ituri, be the first white man ever to get through the Ituri."

"He won't win kudos for that. Who gives a damn whether he got through the Ituri or not? All anyone is going to give a damn about is whether or not he saved Emin from the dervishes."

Nelson shrugged. "Maybe kudos don't matter to him, Arthur.

Who can say with a man like that? Maybe all that mattered to him was doing this, proving to himself that he could do it, go somewhere no one had ever gone before, where everyone said no one could ever go."

"Oh, I doubt that, Robbie. Kudos matter to him all right. I don't think anything matters to him more. He's built his whole life on kudos."

As if realizing they were talking about him, Stanley looked up from his plate. "Mr. Jephson."

"Sir?"

"Would you and Captain Nelson come over here please?"

"Yes, sir."

Stanley resumed eating while Jephson and Nelson went over. Not looking up from his plate, he said, "Tell me something, Mr. Jephson. Are you making love to the girl?"

"Sir?"

"The girl, Faridah. Are you making love to her?"

Jephson flushed. The question infuriated him. Stanley infuriated him. "No, sir," he replied sharply.

"You're not?" Stanley stopped eating and looked up. "Why not?"

"How can you ask such a question? She's a child, for God's sake. She's Dr. Emin's daughter. What sort of scoundrel do you take me for?"

"All right, all right. Don't get excited. So you're not making love to her. I thought you were. In fact, I rather hoped you were. It would have made the situation a bit easier. Still, I suspect she has special feelings for you."

"I have no idea what her feelings are for me, sir. But I doubt very much that they are special in the way you are suggesting."

"Don't underestimate your charms, Mr. Jephson. You're quite an attractive young man, especially in the eyes of a little half-caste girl like this stuck away here in the middle of nowhere. Oh, yes, I'd say you must seem quite an attractive and dashing and romantic figure to her. But let's not argue about it. Whether you are or not, I am making her your responsibility."

"My responsibility?"

"Yes, I'm putting her in your charge," Stanley said and returned to his food, forking out the last few chunks of venison from the rice *posho*.

Jephson watched him for a moment, expecting him to say something further. When he didn't, Jephson, "I suppose you mean by that I'm the one who's to take her and Dr. Emin back to Wadelai in the *Lady Dorothy*."

"Back to Wadelai? Don't be an ass, Mr. Jephson." Stanley set his plate aside and wiped his mouth with the back of his hand. "You don't for a moment think I'm going to let Emin go back to Wadelai, do you? You don't for a moment think I've come all this way to stand by and let him slip out of my grasp like that? You don't for a moment think I would go back to England without him?"

Jephson didn't say anything. He glanced at Nelson. Nelson pulled a face.

Stanley stood up. "I'm not Wolseley, sir. This will not be a reprise of Wolseley's expedition to Gordon in Khartoum. I assure you, I have no intention of returning to England in defeat as he did. I have no intention of returning to England empty-handed, the prize I sought left dead in the wilderness behind me, as he did. No, sir. I set out on this expedition to rescue Emin Pasha. And by God, rescue him I will. I intend to return to England with Emin Pasha or not return at all."

Epilogue

For very nearly two years the outside world had had no news of the Emin Pasha relief expedition.

There had been news when the expedition called at Alexandria on its outbound voyage, when it picked up its escort of askaris at Aden, when it boarded the *pagazis* and the hundreds of tons of supplies at Zanzibar, when it rounded the Cape of Good Hope at Simon's Bay, and when it disembarked at Banana Point at the mouth of the Congo. And there had been news from Boma and Matadi during the journey up the Congo's estuary and news again, scandalous news, after the expedition had marched around Livingstone Falls and reached Leopoldville and Stanley had seized the *Peace* from the London Mission Society to add to his flotilla of steamers and barges that carried his men and loads the thousand miles up the Congo to Yambuya. And then there was the news Shagerstrom brought back from Yambuya that Stanley and an advance column had set off into the Ituri and was soon to be followed by the rear column with the bulk of the relief under Major Barttelot's command. That was in September 1887, eight months after Stanley had departed England, and it was the last news. After that, to all intents and purposes, the expedition vanished into the forbidding wilderness of the heart of Africa.

Although there were other excitements on the world scene at the time—the dispute over home rule for Ireland, the discovery of gold in South Africa, the succession of the young Kaiser Wilhelm II to the German throne, a particularly gruesome axe murder in Paris—curiosity and concern about the expedition remained very much in the forefront of the public mind; and long after there was anything solid on which to base them, speculation and wild imaginings about its progress and fate circulated widely and passionately. Hardly a day went by that one newspaper or another didn't print some sort of rumor or fragmentary tale, from a rubber trader on the Congo, a missionary in Buganda, a fugitive from the dervishes at Wadi Halfa, an Arab slaver recently returned to Zanzibar. Stanley was dead. Stanley was alive. His followers had been massacred. They had got through triumphant. Emin's garrisons had fallen. They had rallied, thanks to the arrival of relief, and were driving the dervishes back to Khartoum.

The matter was raised during the question periods of both houses of Parliament. The Prince of Wales repeatedly expressed his personal interest. Again and again the Queen sent to her First Minister for information. Sir William Mackinnon and the members of the relief committee met regularly to sort through whatever scraps of intelligence were to be had and issue bulletins as to what they thought might be happening. But it wasn't until the summer of 1889 that the world finally learned what had happened. For it wasn't until then, more than a year after departing Nsabe on the Albert lakeshore, that the expedition finally emerged from the depths of the African continent and arrived at Bagamoyo on the Indian Ocean coast.

Bagamoyo, directly across the narrow strait that separates Zanzibar from the mainland, had for a hundred years been the principal staging depot for the caravans of the Zanzibari Arabs on their slaving and ivory-hunting forays into the African interior. It was a considerable town of mosques and villas and winding streets and teeming bazaars, nestled around the sparkling beach of a natural deep-water harbor where hundreds of dhows and boats and ships of all descriptions and many nations could be found lying at anchor under a brilliant azure sky.

In addition—and this mainly during the years the expedition had been under way—it had acquired a rather sizable white community, a reflection of Europe's rapidly growing political and commercial interest in Africa that would ultimately set off a scramble for colonies and trading concessions of the sort Sir William Mackinnon and his colleagues had in mind with their scheme for an Imperial British East Africa Company. Indeed, at the time, besides two French Catholic missions and an American Baptist mission, an English vice consulate and Italian and Austrian consulates, a Portuguese factory and a Dutch supply house and dry goods store, besides a polyglot of settlers and planters, geologists and mapmakers, traders and big-game hunters and adventurers of every stripe, there already was an Imperial *German* East Africa Company in Bagamoyo, backed up by a garrison of German and native soldiers under the command of a certain Major Hermann von Wissmann. And it was this Major von Wissmann who was the first to greet the expedition on its return.

He was seated that summer day on the second-story veranda of his garrison's officers' mess, just having finished lunch, his boots up on the railing and in the process of lighting a pipe, when an orderly brought word of the approach of a caravan from the north. Now there was nothing unusual in this; caravans of one sort or another were continually departing from and returning to Bagamoyo in those days, but something about this one tickled the German major's fancy and he decided to have a look for himself. In the humid coastal heat of early afternoon, most of the town's inhabitants were indoors enjoying a siesta, and the streets and bazaars were deserted; but two young officers of the garrison, seeing their commandant pass by and wondering where he was off to at that unusual hour, hurried out of their barracks to join him on his postprandial stroll to the Kingani River on the outskirts of the town.

The caravan had come more than 7,000 miles in a great sweeping arc from coast to coast across the entire breadth of the continent, the last 2,000 southeastward from Lake Albert down the valley of the Semliki, along the western flank of the Mountains of the Moon, into the country of the Nkole and Karagwe, around the southern end of Lake Victoria, and then along the well-beaten trails of the Arab slavers and ivory hunters through Unyamwezi and Ugogo to Bagamoyo. There were 493 people in the caravan. Of these, 232 were the survivors of the original expedition, returning home. The rest were Emin's people, fleeing their homes.

Actually, before Stanley had started on this last leg of the journey, in the weeks before Wadelai finally fell to the dervishes, nearly a thousand people had managed to get to Nsabe from Wadelai and join the caravan on its flight to the sea. But many of these were women and children or the old and infirm and couldn't keep up and either died or were abandoned along the way or turned back in despair.

Stanley marched at the head of those who remained, preceded by his faithful *kirangozi*, Uledi, and the spear-armed trackers, followed by Nelson in command of the askari front guard and the Maxim, and then by Hoffman leading the ragtag company of *pagazis* bearing the last of the expedition's loads and also leading Bonny on his rope. Parke and Casati marched with them, amused by Bonny's pathetic condition and often playing stupid tricks on him to heighten their amusement. In their van came Emin's people with their carts and mules and hodgepodge of baggage, and Emin himself riding a mule with Faridah walking beside him. Jephson brought up the rear guard of askaris with Sudi (the *Lady Dorothy* had been scuttled at the southern end of Lake Albert along with the *Khedive*), but more usually he left the askaris in Sudi's charge and walked with Faridah and Emin.

Emin was mute. He was also half blind, having lost his only pair of spectacles somewhere along the way; and he didn't seem to hear either. He certainly didn't seem to hear when Jephson spoke to him. Day after day, from sunrise to sunset, he sat his mule, staring straight ahead, allowing Faridah to lead the animal, being carried out of the heart of Africa like a piece of baggage, not hearing or speaking or seeing. Stanley had given up on him. His silence was impenetrable, his dejection repellent. Having seized him by force, having by that struck the blow that finally crushed his spirit and reduced him to this state of deaf-dumb-blindness, Stanley no longer wanted to have anything to do with him. For him Emin *was* a piece of baggage or, perhaps more accurately, the trophy he had gone out to Africa to bag and, having bagged, was now grimly, determinedly bringing home.

"Who are you, sir?" von Wissmann called across the river.

"Henry Stanley."

"Henry Stanley? *Mein Gott!*"

"Henry Stanley, I say. Do you hear me, sir? Henry Stanley, commanding the Emin Pasha relief expedition. I have the Pasha with me."

"Yes, yes, I hear you, Mr. Stanley. My God, this is extraordinary. Please, sir, be patient a moment. I will bring the ferry across to fetch you." And then turning to one of his young officers, von Wissmann said, "Get the word to the cable office in Zanzibar, Lieutenant. *Macht schnell.* Tell them Henry Stanley has returned. Tell them he has rescued the Pasha of Equatoria from the dervishes."

The world went wild. The news wiped every other off the front pages. Within twenty-four hours, cables of congratulations were flooding into the telegraph office in Zanzibar—from Queen Victoria, from the German Kaiser, from King Leopold, from the Khedive of Egypt and the President of the United States, from the Royal Geographical Society and the geographical societies of a dozen other nations, from the mayors of cities and the chairmen of boards, from newspapers and magazines and publishers and private clubs, from old friends and old explorers and people no one had ever heard about. And the mood of hysterical jubilation soared to even greater heights when Stanley and his officers actually got back to Europe. Later, questions would be raised about the expedition, about what exactly had happened to the rear column, about the wisdom of the route Stanley had chosen, about the stupendous loss of lives, about the fact that Equatoria had fallen to the dervishes for all of that. Later, Mackinnon and Hutton and de Winton and Grant would realize that, in what they had sought to accomplish and laid out hard cash for, the establishment of a royal charter company in the territories Emin had governed, the expedition in fact had been a thoroughgoing failure. But that would be later. Stanley had judged right. He knew his public. In the flush of his triumph, before anyone was interested in examining details, while the thrilling phrase of the headlines—"Emin Rescued"—was on everyone's lips, all that mattered to the great cheering public was that Stanley had done it again as only Stanley could do it. The Pasha of Equatoria had not been allowed to go the way of Gordon; England's honor had been redeemed, thanks to the bravery and audacity of Stanley and his men. They were national heroes. There were parades and banquets for them. There were audiences with the Queen. They appeared before the houses of Parliament to standing ovations. Silver medallions were struck in their honor. They were granted the freedom of cities. They were besieged by reporters and invited on lecture tours. And Stanley himself, the bastard workhouse boy, was knighted and awarded the Grand Cross of the Bath. When he married Dolly Tennant, the ceremony was performed in Westminster Abbey in what was the most glittering social affair of the season.

In time, of course, as with all such spectacular events, the public's interest turned to other things and the excitement subsided and the heroes of the Emin Pasha relief expedition eventually slipped quietly out of the news and back into a semblance of normal life. Stanley undertook a worldwide lecture tour, then settled down with Dolly in her home in Richmond Terrace. He was elected a member of Parliament for the North Lambeth constituency. He returned to Africa only once in subsequent years and then but for a brief comfortable tour of South Africa just before the outbreak of the Boer War. He had no need to endure any further suffering and hardship in that continent; he had nothing further to prove. He had accomplished and proved everything a mortal man could accomplish and prove on that continent, and he had gained everything a mortal man could hope to gain by doing so. Sir Henry, the Breaker of Rocks.

Jephson never returned to Africa. The expedition had made a profound mark on him, had transformed the young man into a figure of undoubted character and strength; but somehow he never put it to any use. It was not for the lack of opportunity. The British government wanted him to take the post of district commissioner in Nigeria. King Leopold invited him to lead an expedition to Katanga in the Congo Free State. Sir William Mackinnon, still dreaming of salvaging his scheme for an Imperial British East Africa Company, similarly asked him to take command of an expedition to Buganda. And the Royal Geographical Society offered him the chance to travel in the footsteps of Mungo Park through Liberia and write a series of descriptive articles on the country and people. But he turned them all down and returned to the easy, indolent London life of the English aristocracy that he had lived before he left, serving variously and frivolously as Queen's Messenger and Usher at Court. No one ever really understood why.

Nelson, on the other hand, did return to Africa. Because of his badly damaged physical condition, he was obliged to resign his commission in the cavalry; but his fascination with Africa, which had brought him to the expedition in the first place, was undiminished by all he had gone through, and he secured the position of commissioner of a Kikuyu district in Kenya. But he had overestimated the state of his health and died there six months later. Hoffman also died in Africa, at least as far as anyone knew. He went back to the Congo as a rubber trader in King Leopold's employ and was never heard from again. Parke resumed his service in the Army Medical Department and was posted to Netley Hospital in Hampshire, where he spent his days regaling his colleagues and patients with tales from those few brief years of his glory. Bonny was institutionalized in another Army hospital, where he died a few years later of consumption.

And Emin, the object of all these men's travails?

On the evening of the day after the expedition arrived in Bagamoyo, Major van Wissmann arranged an appropriately lavish banquet to honor the extraordinary achievement. It was held in the second-story dining hall of the officer's mess. By then the news of Emin's rescue and Stanley's return was known in Zanzibar; and so, besides the leading figures of Bagamoyo's European community, a clutch of dignitaries had hurried over from Zanzibar to be in attendance as well. It was an exuberant, festive occasion. The food was excellent. There was iced champagne. Toasts were drunk. The telegrams from Queen Victoria and Kaiser Wilhelm had already arrived and were read out. A German warship, the *Schwalbe*, happened to be in harbor at the time, and her band was disembarked to add to the entertainment. And outside in the streets and bazaars below the Wanyamwezis and askaris carried on their own happy, raucous affair, singing and dancing and feasting in celebration of their return home.

In all the noise and excitement, von Wissmann and the other outsiders didn't particularly notice the oddities and tensions among the men of the expedition itself: that, for example, Hoffman and Bonny weren't there; that Parke instantly got drunk and made a spectacle of himself; that Casati carried on in an extravagant fashion; that Nelson, lacking teeth, devoted himself to cutting up his food into pieces small enough to swallow without chewing; that Jephson and Stanley spoke to each other only in the most formal terms; that Emin didn't speak at all.

Emin at first had in fact refused to be present, but Stanley insisted. He recognized that Emin's absence would provoke the kinds of questions and speculations that he was anxious to avoid at this stage of the game; and so, just as he had forced Emin to leave Equatoria, he forced him to attend the banquet. But once in attendance, seated in the place of honor, Emin was stone. Stanley more than made up for it. He was constantly on his feet, responding to toasts, making his own toasts in return, relating the adventures of the expedition, turning the horrors of the march into tales of grand heroics, unstinting in his praise of his officers and men, lauding Emin as a second Gordon, a Gordon who had done what even Gordon couldn't do. Indeed, Stanley so dominated the party and so completely fulfilled his role as Bula Matari, the indominatable smasher of rocks, that, as everyone grew drunker and happier and noisier and more full of a sense of being present at a historic occasion, no one noticed when Emin left.

Jephson probably was the first to notice, but he didn't make much of it at the time. He was well enough aware of the reasons for Emin's crushing despair and simply assumed that he could no longer abide Stanley's self-serving bombast and had fled to the quiet and comfort of Faridah's company. A half-hour later, this assumption was proved tragically wrong.

The door to the dining hall flew open. The band stopped playing. The hubbub of conversation and bursts of laughter abruptly ceased. Uledi stood in the doorway. Stanley jumped to his feet.

"What is it, *rafiki?*"

"The Pasha, Bwana."

"The Pasha?"

Now everyone began looking around the hall and realized that Emin wasn't there.

"What about the Pasha?"

"He has suffered a fall, Bwana, a very bad fall."

Emin had fallen from the second-story veranda of the mess and cracked his skull open in the street below. It was immediately taken to be an accident, and there were any number of explanations to account for it. Unused to champagne, the poor fellow had got drunk; without his spectacles, he couldn't see where he was going; not having been in a building taller than a single story in more than fifteen years, he had forgotten where he was and simply stepped off the veranda, thinking to get a breath of fresh air in the street outside. But Jephson knew better; in his heart of hearts, he knew Emin had flung himself off the veranda. He had been expecting the little man to do something of the sort ever since he had tricked him away from Wadelai.

By the time everyone got downstairs, Emin, unconscious, bleeding from his ears and nose, his eyes fast swelling shut, had been taken to the hospital of the German garrison. And there he remained, hovering between life and death, for the next several weeks. No one, apart from Faridah and the hospital staff, saw him during this time. At first, this was for medical reasons (the base of his skull had been fractured), but even after he regained consciousness and was out of imminent danger, he refused to allow anyone to visit him. Jephson made repeated attempts but each time was turned away at the door by Faridah, looking at him with all her old joyless severity, as if he were a total stranger. He was sure she no more blamed him for this than she had blamed him for what had gone before; it was just that whatever hope he may have awakened in her of some other life than the one she had always known had now completely died.

At the end of the first week of Emin's hospitalization, Stanley transported the remnants of his expedition across the strait to Zanzibar, but he himself immediately returned. He was in a state. He simply couldn't believe that this stupid "accident" was going to cheat him of the glory of returning to Europe with Emin in tow, and he tried to have the man transferred to a hospital on Zanzibar, reasoning that, whatever else might happen, it could then at least be said that he had brought him to the safety of, if not Europe itself, what could be considered an outpost of Europe. But this was rejected on medical grounds. Emin could not be moved; he certainly could not be permitted to undertake a trip of that sort. In consternation and disgust, Stanley went back over to Zanzibar. He had much to do there: notes to compile, accounts to settle, reports to write, dispatches to send, telegrams to answer, a round of banquets to attend. He had to pay off Uledi and Sudi and the other surviving Wanyamwezis with proper ceremony in their villages for their faithful service. He had to visit the widows and orphans and families of those who had not returned and distribute pensions to them. He had to secure passage for the askaris aboard a British vessel bound for Aden and Suez. Parke, Casati, Hoffman, and Bonny went over with him. Jephson remained in Bagamoyo with Nelson for company. But less than a fortnight later, with barely half his tasks done, Stanley was back and again tried to get in and talk to Emin. But it was futile. Emin wouldn't see him; he wouldn't see anyone; he had drawn a curtain around himself and was simply waiting to die.

And then the simple truth dawned on Stanley: It didn't really matter, in fact it might be the best thing. As far as the world was concerned, he had accomplished what he had set out to accomplish: He had saved Emin from the dervishes. The triumph was real. It was an established fact in the public's mind. All that remained was to greet the hero himself in the flesh. To bring Emin home with him actually wasn't necessary. It would merely be icing on the cake. It would prove nothing that hadn't already been proved. Indeed, given Emin's behavior, it might even be an embarrassment. So let it be. Let Emin be. If this was what the man preferred, why should Stanley quarrel with it? It did not diminish his achievement. It in no way tarnished his accomplishment. And there was nothing to be done about it anyway. So once again, and for the last time, Stanley returned to Zanzibar to complete his tasks and make arrangements for a British warship, HMS *Somali*, to take him and his surviving officers home to England.

Jephson lingered a few days longer in Bagamoyo while these arrangements were being made. His hope, however, of having a parting word with Emin was in vain. On the day before the *Somali* was scheduled to sail, Sudi came over to fetch him. He went to the hospital to say goodbye to Faridah. She met him in the corridor outside Emin's room and, very formally, with no show of emotion, shook his hand. The door to Emin's room was open and Jephson looked in. Emin, his head swathed in bandages, his hands lying upturned on his lap, was sitting up in his bed, staring at the wall. After a moment, realizing someone was in the doorway, he turned to Jephson. Without his spectacles, he almost surely couldn't see who he was. Even so, he turned away and resumed staring blankly at the wall. Jephson left.

Despite his intentions, Emin didn't die. He recovered. It was a long, arduous recovery, which he did nothing to assist and which left him half deaf as he was half blind. Finally, in the first weeks of 1890, he was deemed fit enough to leave the hospital and was installed in a comfortable little villa overlooking the sea, where, in Faridah's care, he continued his slow, silent convalescence through the winter.

The people who had come out of Equatoria with him scattered. Some made their way over to Zanzibar, others moved farther up the coast, still others blended into the busy bustle of Bagamoyo, setting up as traders or hiring out as guides or askaris in the increasing number of European caravans now heading upcountry on empire-building missions. Faridah employed a few of the familiar faces as servants in Emin's household. But as he continued to refuse to allow visitors or have anything to do with the outside world, interest in him, not surprisingly, waned. The excitement was over. Stanley was home. The expedition was done. Winter passed into spring.

And then one day in late April of 1890, sometime in the early morning hours, the former, the forgotten Pasha of Equatoria vanished from Bagamoyo.

Faridah, of course, must have immediately discovered his absence and probably also knew where and why he had gone; but if so, she never said and went on living quietly behind the high walls of the villa by the sea. It wasn't until some years later, when the British under Kitchener reconquered the Sudan from the dervishes, that the world learned what had happened to him. He had returned home. It took him more than three years but, with a strength and tenacity that are unimaginable, half deaf and half blind, he managed to make his way halfway across the continent back to the headwaters of the Nile, back to those rivers and lakes, mountains and deserts from where Stanley and his men had at such great cost extricated him. And there he was captured by the dervishes. We know what happened next from an account by a certain Ismaili, a lieutenant of Omar Saleh's, given in the form of a confession on the night before he was hanged for the crime.

"The Pasha was thrown flat on his back," Ismaili tells us.

"One man held each leg and I held his head. He showed no sign of fear. He made no effort of resistance. I drew his head back until the skin across the throat was tight and then, with one swift movement of a knife, a fourth of our number cut off his head. The blood spurted over us and the Pasha was dead."

So he did go the way of Gordon after all.